HURRY SUNDOWN

HURRY SUNDOWN

By

K. B. GILDEN

Hurry sundown
See what tomorrow bring . . .
—*From the songs that Rose Scott used to sing*

VOLUME TWO

Garden City, New York
DOUBLEDAY & COMPANY, INC.

CONTENTS

VOLUME ONE

BOOK ONE

BOOK TWO

BOOK THREE

VOLUME TWO

BOOK FOUR

III

THE BRIERS AFIRE

[*Saturday, May 3–Thursday, May 8*]

1

Henry's timing of the eviction notice, allowing Chalmer Coombs to deliver it to the Scott farm before Rose's funeral instead of after, seriously affected the outcome of his plans from the start. Of course it shocked the family and their friends. "Why he didn't even wait till she was in the ground. *Before she was cold in her grave.*" But the shock alone would not have been fatal. A similar shock might have been produced had it been delivered after the funeral. "After the way they all showed up at Zion to pay their respects to her—this! This *thing.*" The impact would have been just as great, but not as widespread. For the timing of the notice was crucial in an even more important respect than its shock-effect. It gave the family *time.*

Between Saturday night when Rose's body was laid out and Wednesday noon when the last rites were read over it, the family came together.

Vergilia was the first to appear, driving down from Nashville right after she received Reeve's wire and arriving just in time to attend church Sunday morning, where she created a sensation with her black-swathed white hat and the ten-dollar bill she waved in the air when Father Hall called for the Silver Offering.

By driving from Chicago twenty-five hours straight without stopping even for a Pepsi the last half of the trip, Ben and his boys were "home" before dawn on Monday.

For the second time in six weeks Sister Mae took the coach down from Newark, riding all night sitting bolt upright, this time bringing her husband and the son Rose had raised till he was more Grandma's boy than his mother's.

Janet, Mae's daughter by her first marriage, also for the second time took the train South with her baby; but this time she traveled in style,

treating herself to a roomette. She dismounted at Bay City so full of the
ruckus she'd had with the conductor over switching to the Jim Crow car
—she refused to—that she had no emotion left for the purpose of her
journey.

Lila-Lee, Rose's youngest—the pretty one in the family as Mae was
the sweet one and Vergilia the vixen—created another sensation by flying all the way from Seattle. Could she afford the fare? No. But Mamma
would have expected her, it was the last thing she could do for Mamma,
and so she borrowed from a loan shark, scooped her rent money up from
under a floorboard and took off, caught the first plane out. She was the
lone colored passenger through changes at Denver, St. Louis, and Atlanta. When she staggered down the steps at the final landing in the Bay
City airport, her face was rigid with grief held in check over the space of
a continent. Her eyes were stony with tears unshed. Her innards were
heaving with nausea contained. And her mother's lifelong admonition
was still reeling through her head. "Be a lady. Never make a holy show
of yourself." Ahead of her, on the concrete apron, a double row of white
folks was lined up, giving her the double-eye. She walked between them
—for the first time, no separate exit in her own home ground—toward
her brother Reeve who was waiting for her, and instead of collapsing
into his arms she most composedly shook hands with him. The money
the flight cost her and the physical misery were worth that one triumphal
march, to be told and retold over the space of a lifetime.

Because of the size of the family and the distance they had to travel,
the funeral at first scheduled for Tuesday was early postponed until
Wednesday. Even so, by Tuesday noon Fred, always the incalculable,
had not yet arrived. And no word had been received from him. Before
Ben left Chicago, he had tried twice to call Fred in Detroit, thinking he
might pick him up in his car somewhere along the route; but the only
number he had for Fred belonged to a rooming-house pay phone, and
the shouts in the hall on the other end brought no answer from Fred's
room. So with the exception of Fred they were all together again now,
and not one of them would admit to any outsider how close they were
coming to giving Fred up. "*Only two ways I'll ever go there again,
Mamma,*" Fred had once written with the rashness for which he was in-
famous. "*I'm dead and they send me down for you to bury me. Or you're
dead and they send for me to come and bury you.*"

Grimly they waited for Fred to fulfill his word, and even more grimly
for him to fail in it.

All day Tuesday visitors from all over the county and from as far away
as Waycross and Valdosta and Fernandina were debouching by the carload, as they had been since Sunday, in the clearing in front of the

cabin. The women ran to the sisters and rocked with them, weeping. The men clasped the shoulders of the brothers with a squeeze that conveyed compassion, comfort, and the community of all flesh. Then came the inevitable comment.

"Well, I see you all here. Where's Fred?"

"Oh he'll be here," Vergilia interjected sharply, seconded by the family. "We're expecting him every minute."

The visitors trooped up the path to the house of death to sit with the family, to commiserate with them through long reminiscences of the dead woman's past, to review with them the curiosity of the tree felled by lightning the night before she was carried off, the ring lost, her last words, and such is the irrepressibility of the life-force—to learn the circumstance in which each of her children was enmeshed when the news reached them, to exchange with them similar experiences and thence to socialize.

After lunch Augusta Varney arrived with a covey of callers from the St. Augustine's parish. She settled on the porch bench, fanning at deerflies with her handkerchief. "You ever see my niece in Chicago?" she inquired of Ben following the usual amenities. "Yessir, they say Chicago is a fine city for colored folks." Out of the corner of her eye she glimpsed Lulabelle McDowell mounting up the steps to the door, bearing over her rounded belly a covered pie from her house down the track. "A fine city for white folks too," Augusta added graciously out of regard for Lulabelle, a concession that provoked gales of giggling long after Lulabelle had vanished back down the track. "Well, you look my niece up, Ben, just as soon as you fall back there, hear? Got a daughter just about the right age for your big boy." With this she gave her daughter Frederica a nudge toward the door inside where Reeve, numbed by the incessant flow of people and food, was rendering his attention to Lulabelle's berry pie, slicing it till the warm juice oozed red over his hand.

His grief dulled by now to an aching emptiness, vaguely angry—why don't they all go away and leave us alone!—Reeve served up or rather spooned up a wedge of pie for Frederica. "You should have waited till it cooled before you cut it." He had once last winter before the advent of Vivian made love to Frederica, and he could never meet the quizzical expectancy of her eyes without a twinge of guilt, as if he had defaulted on a debt. I never promised her anything! Evading Frederica he spooned up another slab of pie for his niece Janet and took it out on the porch to her; but was left foolishly holding the plate while Janet recited to the company for the umpteenth time, while she burped her baby over her diapered shoulder, the adventure of her train trip down.

"And when that conductor poked his head into my roomette and told me to get out of there, it was five-thirty in the morning and I wasn't dressed yet and I was salty, I'm telling you. But I said to him just as polite as I could, 'Sir, I paid for this place on my ticket,' and right then, what do you think? Johnny woke up and let out a howl that roused the whole corridor up and down, wasn't that clever of him? Izzums oozums was clever," Janet nuzzled at the baby's cheek, "wasn't oo? Wanted his nini and didn't care who knew about it."

The company all clustered up about Janet and the baby, crowding back Reeve and his plate of pie. "Mm-mmh! Look at him, look at them bigbig eyes, look at them little fat hands, look at that little square bottom. Oh, I could bite it off!"

He was Rose's first great-grandchild and she had lived to see him before she closed her eyes. The wonder of it drew the women together, the continuity of the lifestream lodged within their bodies. Oh yes, Johnny was clever, the cleverest thing that ever drew breath. A positive genius. Not three months old and already whipping the peckerwoods down!

"Then everybody started hollering at the conductor," Janet finished grandly. "'Be quiet there, hush up, close the door!' And that's what I did and that was the end of it. That time anyway."

"Gimme that baby!" Thrusting the dish of pie at Janet, Reeve took Johnny from her and sitting down on the porch bench laid him belly down over his knee and with his hand over the broad small of his back began jigging. Instantly a gob of coagulated cream flew out of Johnny's mouth and Reeve heeled it out on the floor. "That's how Mamma always bubbed 'em," Reeve said with a measure of relief, passing him on to Augusta. Were they here to moan Mamma or to make over a baby! But the burst of laughter that greeted his remedy, at Janet's expense— she, the R.N.!—sent him angrily back into the house.

This period of waiting was hard on him, the interlude of suspension between death and burial. He resented the continuous intrusions of life, inappropriate to the occasion, that would not allow his grief to find itself; and at the same time he was impatient for the day when the business of life could properly be taken up again. As he sat scowling over the pie on the table, finishing it off, Frederica slid into the bench beside him. "Don't look now but you gotten fat." "Fat where?" "Fat in the head." He moved away from the warmth she emanated, a warmth as temptingly tart as strawberry pie. Frederica did not offer love on the lofty plane on which he desired it. If this were Vivian now next to him . . . Was this a time to be distracted by girls!

Even the pie he was so hungrily wolfing down on top of a late lunch offended him. Lulabelle had brought it, he thought, as a peace offering. From her anyway. Rad had been after him about dynamiting the ditches, blowing hot and cold over it, and now after they had spent yesterday staking their course and this morning making their purchases, he still didn't know whether Rad would go through with it Thursday as they had planned or not. They had parted this noon in a mutual huff. He's afraid of it, Reeve felt now, that's why. He's still afraid. But why I should be pestered with his hot head and his cold feet at a time like this—!

The extra day before the funeral also weighed heavily upon him. On account of Fred who for all they knew might never have received the telegram. To be put through these interminably dragging hours . . . Out on the porch Augusta was actively promoting, if not actually selling tickets for, the school dedication party.

"Cut it out!" Reeve shouted though the kitchen at his nephews playing jacks on the backstep. "Ain't you got no respect?"

As he had waited for the inevitability of death, the waiting was in him now, intolerably attenuated, for an event that must like the clap of doom take place, and had not.

Uncle Lee sitting at the head of Rose's bed beckoned him over and, glancing about, slipped out from under his vest a pint of Johnny Walker that he had brought from Valdosta. "Take a nip of this, boy. You look like you could use it."

Before leaving Augusta paused with her contingent on the top porch step just as every other visitor that day had done.

"Well I think it's wonderful, simply wonderful, how you all come," she murmured in admiration of the family's devotion to their mother and the magnitude of their mother that she should command such devotion from them. "You all made the effort, the sacrifice, and no part of it was easy." In her position as deaconess of St. Augustine's, Augusta always felt it incumbent upon her to express the public sentiment. She wet her lips, delicately. "Will Fred . . . you think Fred—?"

The family winced in anticipation even before she said it. Praise sought out the chink in their armor, picked at the flaw among them, the missing element. Vergilia looked at Mae and Mae looked at Ben and Ben at Lila-Lee, and all of them at Reeve. Reeve stood in the doorway, filling it, the flat of his hand up against the upper doorpost. He was mainstay of this house now, ridgepole and rooftree, keeper of the bond that held them together.

Where the hell is Fred!

"He'll be here," Reeve said and turned his head away. Not one of them would admit that with Fred you could never tell.

The first afternoon wave of company rolled off after Augusta to the funeral parlor. In the brief lull that followed the brothers and sisters sank down around the long black table inside in attitudes of fatigue.

They were exhausted by an emotion that wouldn't come, that had not yet been permitted to cohere, to accumulate, to break into that bursting agony of the soul that affords the first balm. The elevated sentiment in which they were supposed to hold their mother at this time had an artificiality to it incompatible with their true feelings; feelings so vastly amorphous, so incomprehensible they could not yet give vent to them.

On the table an assortment of dishes was scattered, still sticky with runnels of pie filling. One was heaped with cigarette butts smoldering in a cemetery of ashes. On another a fly perched, daintily picking its legs up out of the syrup. Those dishes in their desert dreariness contained all there was to know, it seemed at the moment, of the nature of man's destiny.

Brothers and sisters, precipitated out of their separate paths into union once more, they sat about the family table and fretted over Fred.

"After all she did for him," Vergilia railed. "Getting Old Man Colfax to get him out of the lockup that time he was arrested for sassing back. Traveling all the way up to the hospital in Detroit when he needed her and carrying him here. Nursing him to health—"

"Maybe the message is still laying there on the floor of his room," Sister Mae defended Fred, giving him the benefit of the doubt. "Maybe he's sick again. Maybe he's broke—"

"Fred broke!" Ben snorted. Ben, the policeman, was the success of the family, as Fred was the rebel and Reeve was the rock. "Fred's never broke. Why that chick he's got now made sixty bucks a week all through the war as a blackjack dealer in Las Vegas."

"Now Ben," Mae defended Fred's wife, "you don't know that for a fact. You always had it in for Roxy, Roxy's all right—"

"She a cold-hearted bitch," Vergilia said, "and what Fred is I'd just as soon not say. Where is he, that's all . . ."

"Hush, will you hush?" Lila-Lee begged. "Mamma's still here. She's all around us. She hears you!"

The dead live on for a while afterward in their familiar places. Rose's presence was powerful among them. In every corner they caught glimpses of her, fleeting expressions, an angle of her cheek as she eased the comb up through her hair, the frosted sheen of her knuckles as she tatted an edging, her lips puffed out in a continuous muttering as with wetted forefinger she read through her Norfolk *Journal & Guide*.

They looked around the room out of which they had sprung as from a common womb. Desultorily Mae began scraping out the dishes. "Our daddy's been carried off," she sighed. "And now Mamma. Ain't no one left to run to."

"We don't cry for the dead," Ben declared somberly. His ponderous face, firm once with a ruddy glow under the brown, sagged in contemplation, raked with lines, yellow-tinged; the face of a cop who has seen too much of compromise, corruption, and cruelty. "We cry for ourselves."

"Ain't no more father and mother," Reeve said to them. "We our own father and mother now."

They could not wholly face it yet. They could not face the central fact, the reason for which they were here. They could not face the unutterable range of emotions it stirred up. It was easier to preoccupy themselves with superficial matters such as the price of "the box" in which she lay in state at the funeral parlor, rather than to express their fundamental conviction that the cost of the funeral was a waste, a shame, and a racket. It was easier to scold the youngsters running about and to laugh at Vergilia's cracks and Ben's police-force anecdotes, rather than to plumb the emptiness in which they now moved, exposed to the winds of chance, the older generation from which one of them—which one?—would next be plucked. It was easier, far easier, to indulge in a fit of anxiety over Fred's delinquencies than to plunge painfully down down into the weed-tangled mystery of themselves and of her who conceived and birthed and reared them; into the sources of their disaffection from her as well as their attachment to her; into what they were because of her, less and more than she was, different from each other and from their forebears and yet marked by the imprint her life left upon them as surely as by the genes and chromosomes passed down to them through the chain of the generations. They could not face it. Not yet.

"That dog! Probably laying up drunk somewhere." Vengefully Vergilia scrubbed the crumbs off the table into her hand and went to the door, a black and reedy figure, rigid with spite, to throw them down over the porch edge into the cedars. Then she screamed. From inside the house they heard her high heels clatter down the steps.

"Fred, Fred, Lord God, it's Fred! I knew you'd come! I knew it! Didn't I tell everybody—"

Shouting and crying they all rushed out to embrace him. Their favorite brother, the reckless one, the restless, the most ambitious of them all. Fred came slowly up the path toward them, but a Fred so changed they faltered in their tracks. His clothing was rumpled from two nights on a bus and he was covered with dust from the walk down the River Road. The line of mustache that limned his upper lip, giving his soft sensitive mouth a look of supreme scorn, shaded off murkily into two days' growth of beard, and his hair, usually cropped close with a side parting, bushed up from his head like a floor brush. He was limping slightly as he plodded up the path, dragging a sore heel. This was Fred, the man-about-town, always in a hurry, going somewhere important. Pinched now, compressed like a plant in which a borer has sucked out the pith. But not so far gone he couldn't grin at them, jauntily, revealing a missing front tooth.

He set his canvas bag, not the smooth calf leather of years ago, down on the bottom step and surveyed the house up to the weathered roof under the cedar boughs.

"All my life," Fred said, "I been running away from her. And she was the only solid thing I ever had."

They walked into the house holding one another up, in one of those rare moods that occur during the solemn passages of life, in which old jealousies and criticisms are quenched by an all-engulfing comprehension. While Mae plied Fred with cold buttermilk and chicken sandwiches, the others plied him with questions. "Why didn't you let us know?"

"Didn't they deliver my telegram?" Fred always had an answer for everything even if it was only another question.

"Why didn't you catch a ride from the highway?"

"Looking like this?"

And Fred had come with his own queries, turning with them to Reeve just as his brothers had done from the moment of their arrival.

"Did she—" *Did she go easy?*

Reeve spread his hands. *Don't ask.*

"Did she—say—anything?"

Some word Fred sought of him, just as Ben and the girls had, that would be his own. Some one final word for *me*, Mamma, for *me*.

Reeve shook his head. "'What happen to me? What done become of me?' That was the last she ever said."

"Nothing more? You sure there wasn't something?"

That she hadn't said anything—the soreness still rankled with Reeve. She should have said something, left them with something of herself, some word of love or forgiveness or instruction. Not one word to them. From around the table, now complete with Fred, they looked at him, expecting something of him that he did not have to give. All of them begging from him with their eyes what their mother had withheld even from him. Some word. Some sign. Some lasting message.

He had never felt as close to his brothers and sisters as he did at this moment. Ben, the law enforcer, who was being pulled apart by departmental politics and the perversities of the law he was enforcing. Fred who had had so many great ideas and made so many false starts in life till now he was back at the bottom, starting all over again. Sister Mae, so kind of heart that everyone took advantage of her, her floor boss in the dress factory and the business agent of her union, her husband who cheated on her even though he depended on her and her children who hardly knew her; and yet she could never stop being what she was because if she had to be hard, how could she be happy? And Vergilia just the opposite, selfish, self-willed, putting no one on earth ahead of herself and her girls; and yet to this day she still had her admirers and followers and hosts of friends, people who would do anything for her. And Lila-Lee, the prettiest one, the baby. All of them so mixed in their strength and weakness, engaged in such monumental struggles from day to day . . .

"She was dying," Reeve explained lamely to Fred, "and calling for her sassafras tea."

Fred choked on his buttermilk and Mae pounded his back and in a moment they were all shouting with it as if Reeve had brought her walking into the room. Oh that sassafras tea! Your blood gets thick in the wintertime, she used to say, remember, and in the spring you have to thin it. And she'd boil the roots twice over and strain it and on a lazy logy spring day when you were half asleep on your feet, she'd make you drink it down and man! you were jumping . . . And jimson weed, the remedies she'd make up out of jimson weed, remember? Remember how Old Man Colfax got boils on his legs and all the stuff Doc Willingham prescribed for him didn't help any and she made up a salve of jimson weed and spread it with Vaseline and sure enough that helped him. And those yellow flowers, jessamine, for fever . . .

Mm-mmh! Oh yes.

And the things she'd say. Stand straight in the world, child, stand straight up to it. Never forget that. Yah, and Fred said to her once: How can I stand straight when I'm crawling sidewise like a crab all the time? . . . Did I say that? Mm-hm. You said it . . .

So engrossed were they with one another that they did not hear the car drive up to the clearing outside nor the repeated sound of its horn. Until Vergilia piped up in a mock-plaintive tone, chiding her brother: "Can't you never go anywhere, Fred, without bringing the law on your tail?"

Chalmer Coombs, the sheriff, was holding the heel of his hand down on his horn, summoning them to him. Chalmer was not the sheriff who had arrested Fred years ago for wearing a college suit of clothes in town and getting into a scrap over it, nor the one who had taken umbrage at Ben as a fellow officer, but a successor who in tune with the times prided himself on his ability to get along with colored and handle them just right. The three brothers wandered out onto the porch and studied him a while.

"Say there, boys," Chalmer called out cheerfully, letting them know that it was nothing serious. "Come on down here a minute."

Led by Reeve, they ambled casually down the path to Chalmer's car. "How you, Sheriff? Anything we can do for you?"

Chalmer thrust a long envelope at Reeve and a receipt book to be signed. "Got nothing to do with me," he explained hastily to Ben, addressing him man to man. "I don't know what-all's in there. Ain't you Fred?" He reared his head back, casting a sharp glance at Fred. "I like to keep account of who's in town round here." And deeming this sufficient warning, covering all possible varieties of difficulty, he revved up his engine and backed around, throwing overboard to them in his circuit his heartfelt condolences.

"Sure was sorry to hear 'bout your mammy. She was a good old soul. Never had no trouble from her. You live like she did, you'll do fine."

Jerkily Reeve ripped open the envelope. Staggered by the influx of visitors, stunned by the long weeks in which his mother had held at bay the onslaught of death, sunk in the aftermath of a battle irremediably lost, he had lived through the vacuum of the past few days with a sense of waiting that never deserted him, as if the end itself were not yet over. He was still fighting an invisible foe, still being hurtled in a direction over which he had no control. Against the disbelief of his family he had maintained that this was coming, and now it had come like the clap of doom. Reading the paper, he was galvanized out of his trance, reintegrated into his living self once more.

"I told you, I told you it was coming!" He shook the eviction order under Ben's nose and at his sisters who had come hurrying down around them. "I told you Julie drove Mamma to her death over it. They after this place—"

"But they can't!" Ben said as if it were still open to argument. "They can't take and throw us off what's ours."

"Ha!" Vergilia, previously inclined to support Ben, dismissed him and his legal niceties with an annihilating yawp.

"What is this, what is— Let me see." Fred who had once taken a business course at night and had once organized his department at Ford into the auto union and once spent six months trying to write a book snatched the order from Reeve and perused it word for word.

"They couldn't wait," Mae wailed while Fred examined the terms down to the fine print. "Couldn't they wait to do their dirt?"

"Ha!"

"Before she's even in the ground," Lila-Lee summed up with stupefaction what was to be the universal first reaction. "Don't they have the common ordinary decency—?"

"Not worth the paper it's written on." Fred tossed it back at Reeve. "Dated as if it was drawn up today, and witnessed yesterday. Take a look at the notary's seal. Will never stand up in court."

"Ha!"

"Court? You mean we have to go to *court?*"

"For God sake, Mae, of course we got to go to court! It gives us this week to show cause. Are you so willing to keel over at the first breath? When your own husband was murdered—"

"Fred!"

"I mean it. Your own first husband shot to death by those bootleggers he was running with, and you knew who it was and wouldn't fight it—"

"Fred!"

"All right. All right I won't say anything. Herb Loren was my friend. He was my friend too. We buried him and nobody ever said anything, no one ever mentions him—"

"Fred—" Ben laid his hand on Fred's shoulder, a shoulder thin to the bone, pitched with the tension of a long-forgotten passion, shaking with an ague of such passions repeatedly denied their consummation.

"He bled to death," Fred hissed through his missing front tooth at Ben. "Right in there on the kitchen floor, in front of his own child. And Mamma washed the blood out. And Mae packed her bag—"

"But Mamma always said, she always said it can't be sold out the family! It's written in the deed—"

"Ha!"

"We're not selling it, they're taking it—"

"Shut *up!* Will you shut up?" Reeve shouted above the clamor. "You already talkin' like they already got it. Just because it's written here"—he punched his forefinger down upon it, eyeing their agitated faces all around—"does that make it so?"

He was almost glad to have it at last here in his hand. It released forces pent up in him since before his mother's last illness, since long before that. He was almost looking forward to what it presaged. When the enemy shows himself. When you see the whites of their eyes . . .

"Ben, go fetch Aunt Tee here," he said. "Right on."

It was the only sensible thing to do, the necessary next step. Although Tee had nursed Rose for so many weeks, there had been some hard feeling between her and the family ever since last Saturday afternoon. Tee had been going about dramatically hinting, and thus focusing attention upon herself, that if Reeve had not forced her out of the house that afternoon "nothing like this would ever have happen. I should never have quit her side." Vergilia who had been staying with her girls overnights at Tee's caught wind of the slight to her brother and that was enough to spark off a few words. Now Tee was going about hinting that nothing you ever give up for others, not your service nor your sleepless nights nor your best bedsheets, is ever appreciated. Her complaints were all the bolder because of a power she held over the family for the time being in a matter about which everybody was curious but nobody would be crass enough to refer to until after the funeral. Rose had entrusted to Aunt Tee the key to the tin box on the marble-topped dresser by her bed.

In sending for Aunt Tee, Reeve dispensed both with circumspection toward the box and any grudge that might obtain between himself and her. Ill feeling was wiped out by the turn of events. Vergilia threw herself into the Buick with Ben, unabashedly eager for the expedition, and they tore off.

After Fred's tirade against her, Mae had drifted away, down to the line of peach trees that tossed their leaves like dancers in the sun. Reeve followed her now. Her plump shoulders humped, her head drooping, she plucked along the branches for the furry green, russet-cheeked nodules of fruit, fondling them over with her fingers.

"Isn't it funny?" She straightened up at Reeve's touch on her elbow, her large eyes splendid in the creamy shapelessness of her face. "When Daddy was carried off I walked down this selfsame path with Mamma and she kept talking up how much she cared for him. Reckon she wanted for me to say something to her. But I didn't. Now I never can. I wouldn't say what wasn't true and couldn't say what was. Because the truth can hurt too much. Now Fred has said it to me. Let me look at that paper there. Let me look at it too."

Reeve unfolded the paper once more.

"And Julie-Ann signed this—this *thing*?" Mae traced over the pillared architecture of the signature. "With her own hand. If Mamma were alive, it'd kill her all over again. Isn't it funny?" Mae smiled, a writhing half-smile, tasting, swallowing an intolerable medicine. "I always thought if you were nice to folks, they'd be nice to you. And if they weren't, that was their affair. I thought it was the Christian in me. It's not. It's cowardice. I'm afraid to inflict pain. Afraid to hit back."

Fred joined them among the trees. Harassedly he mowed back his hair, raked down over his eyes and cheeks. "I got to get some rest. Got to get cleaned up. Got to get a haircut. Got to go see her." It was his apology to Mae.

When Ben and Vergilia returned with Aunt Tee, Mae had Fred's bag unpacked and was ironing up shirt and slacks for him, and Fred, wrapped in her husband's bathrobe after a bath out of the bucket, was lying on Reeve's maroon daveno couch, his head being tenderly massaged by Lila-Lee. Aunt Tee bustled in importantly with the key in hand. Reeve placed the tin box on the table, the black metal box worn grey at the corners in which his mother kept the secret of her private affairs. "If I tell you a secret," she would say, "and ask you to keep it, then I'm asking you to do more than I'm able to." What she had in that box was not to be bruited about. Even Tee and her son, Carter Scott, who had arranged the means for most of it were never told what it was.

Before opening up, Aunt Tee smoothed her black hair back and jabbed a pin through an imaginary wisp in the tidy bun at the nape of her neck. She dabbed with her handkerchief at her plum cheeks and tapped down the starched collar of her dress, making herself proper for a task that like every other act of her present life became transformed by her into a refutation of the scandal of her past. She inserted the key, the box could easily have been broken into but no one had thought of that. She lifted the lid, "No, not all at once!" And herself opened the envelope that lay on top.

The box was crammed with similar envelopes, the contents of which when unfolded were similarly drawn up, signed and duly attested to. Not only the original deed, of which they all had copies. But more. Much more. Rose Scott had worked for Brandon Colfax in that back parlor of his year on year, dusted his desk and his books for him, carried in his whiskey when he had business there. She knew precisely what had to be done to preserve what was hers, and over the years she did it.

This was her last word to them. This was their legacy and their heritage.

"Mamma!" they cried. "Mamma!" With tears not of mourning but of pride. "Why that old devil! Mamma, you a devil with two horns!"

"Glory be! She's still standing 'em off! From six feet under she'll stand 'em off!"

Suddenly the room was full of people. Mae's husband had come back from the funeral parlor where he had gone with Uncle Lee to sit a spell. Augusta Varney reappeared with another contingent; she had heard somewhere that Fred was back and she'd come to see for herself. Augusta had always had a weakness for Fred. Sanderlee and his wife, Bessie, had observed Ben driving by with Aunt Tee, and interpreting the significance of it aright had hurried here to confirm their judgment. Everybody as they took in what was happening began talking at once, giving contrary advice. Take it to court. Don't take it to court. Take it to Lars Finchley, he's a good lawyer. But it's Lars that's working for Henry! And Judge Purcell, if he's in it too: look at how he snatched Sunset Point that time for Old Man Colfax, look how he did that veteran's family out of their twenty thousand dollars, look what he's doing to that Marquis' land north of town . . .

"But this, this time it's different!" Reeve sitting up on the corner of the table waved a fistful of papers. "This time we got all the stuff to *prove—*"

"I can swear to you right now," Sanderlee tempestuously with hand upraised in oath shook back at him, "and may God strike me dead if I'm wrong about it, the Judge is hand-in-glove with Julie and Henry Warren. He's advising them every step of the way. If you so much as dare to contest this—"

Meanwhile Aunt Tee sat in Rose's wicker chair in the fireplace corner, her hands prissily placed over one another in her lap, her mouth tucked in at the corners, her black eyes glinting with lights, waiting for the proper moment to propose the next move, the prelude to the superdrama of her life, her vengeance on Arcady.

Outside in the clearing a horn once more sounded repeatedly an official summons. Chalmer Coombs had driven up on a second delivery stint. "You folks keepin' me busy these days." He handed to Reeve another long envelope, stamped in the upper left corner: *Superior Court, City of Arcady, County of Colfax, Georgia.* Reeve ripped open the envelope and puzzledly displayed an order as different from the first as day from night. It was a courteously phrased communication from Judge Purcell himself, informing the family that for their convenience he would waive the usual preliminaries and hold a court hearing this Friday to appoint an administrator for the estate.

"It's a cinch they're not working together," Uncle Lee very reasonably pointed out to Sanderlee. "They're crossin' each other up—"

"But it's not legal," Ben declared. "They have to run probate ads in the paper for three weeks running—"

"But what does it *mean?* Do they take the estate for ours or not ours? They can't have it both ways—"

"Ha!"

"Let me see that." Fred snapped the letter away from Reeve and perused it. "Well! It's perfectly plain. Don't you all see? Can't you understand? They're out for us to make a deal."

"What kinda deal? What you talkin' 'bout?"

"And Friday," Ben said. "I never aimed to stay here to Friday." He had been planning to leave tomorrow directly after the funeral, as soon as the tin box was opened and whatever small business it included resolved.

"Me neither." Vergilia had two jobs and roomers to attend to, and besides her girls had to get back to school.

"For goodness sake," Sister Mae chimed in with Fred's anguished, "For crying out loud—" "Can't we once, just *once* in our lives, stick together?"

Reeve rescinded the letter and reread it for the motives between the lines. The fight was now out in the open as he had always longed for it to be, no longer subsurface as it had been in his mother's time. In the flashing vision of his mind, in the agate-hard clarity of his sight, in the tension of his muscles he was ready for a fight to the finish. But whose finish? And with what? A handful of papers in a box, a shotgun in the corner and a pistol buried in the sand of the fire pail behind the porch door? And if he should lose, whose turn would it serve? Another defeat. Another death.

Again advice flew thick and fast around him, and from the agitation that underlay the confusion of views he began to discern an inkling of his answer.

"Administrator, he'll administrator you like he done everybody else. Stay away from that administrator line—"

"It's your only chance, don't you see. If y'all wait on them to put you off, then you have to sue to get back on."

"What we need is our own colored lawyer in these parts."

"Lawyers—colored, white, they're all alike—it all ends up with them—"

"There you go, killin' 'em off before we gets 'em. It's folks like you that hold the race—"

"Out in Tulsa, Oklahoma—back in the First World War—just as soon as that downtown real estate got to be worth anything, they burned the colored out of it, burned 'em out—"

"Step into that courthouse, they'll chain-gang you so fast, declare you bughouse—"

"Quiet!" Reeve shouted. "Will you be quiet? Aunt Tee? You got something on your mind, Aunt Tee?"

Aunt Tee rustled out of the doorway to the top step of the porch where she stood above the din with complacently folded hands. "You," she said to Ben, "drive down to the docks and just as soon as Carter's boat pulls in, bring him here."

"Oh!" Like wavelets the sound, expelled from one mouth and another, lapped up about her feet, a sound of abrupt and total enlightenment. Oh . . . She's sending for Cart . . . From eye to eye leaped a wild surmise. You don't think he'll—? You don't suppose he's going to get—? You believe he can persuade *him* to take on—?

Reeve mounted up the steps and took his place beside her. What did he have to fight with? She passed it like a loaded musket to him from her bygone years. They lifted it up to him like a burning torch out of all the defeats smoldering across the years—the blood of Herb Loren, the pension money accrued by the dying stump of a veteran, a cinder blown on the winds from Tulsa. Every one of them in every one of their lives had something.

"No colored person," Reeve stated flatly, "has ever won such a case in Judge Purcell's court. But as sure as I'm standing here and may God strike me dead, Sanderlee, if I'm wrong about it—we have a chance to win this one. And it's up to us to see we do."

2

At the family council that afternoon around the black table, it was decided that Reeve would drive with Carter Scott tomorrow afternoon, the earliest time at which an appointment could be arranged to consult with Carter's half-brother, a man Aunt Tee still referred to as "m' son, Mayor Carter Sillens of Bay City. When the family dispersed for supper at the various houses at which they were being put up, the decision—or a suspicion of it—had preceded them, creating a rage of speculation from porch to porch, yard to yard and out car windows. Was it possible that Carter Sillens could be persuaded to accept the case? Would he actually show up here at the Colfax County courthouse to represent a member of the colored branch of his family? And how would the white folks around here take it? An outsider from outside the county, coming in to mess in their affairs, show them up . . . It was inconceivable. And yet . . .

"Spread this," Reeve had said when he spoke from the top of his steps. "Spread it just as far and as fast as you can. Anybody want to talk about it, we'll be at the funeral parlor tonight."

It spread of itself. After supper there was a general convergence on the funeral parlor in Fruit Street where Reeve, following his evening farm chores, joined his family for the nightwatch. Rose's body lay in the closed pine box surmounted by flickering tapers and decked with floral tributes, beginning now to wilt and exuding a sultriness as thick as ether. Around it an informal meeting broke out, overcoming the mandatory hush of the atmosphere, spilled out into the street and into barbershop and poolroom next door. The crowd about the box became so unwieldy at times that the candles, tilting dangerously, dropped hot wax upon it and had to be straightened out.

In the lowered voices, plying the same questions over and over, rang the incredulity of outrage:

"Is it true they sent it while she's—*she's still here?*"

And a depth of admiration akin to awe:

"Is it true she left a—a *last will and testament?*"

And a titillation of novelty akin to cuteness:

"Is it true that Carter's going to—*Carter?*"

The questions were met less with explicit answers than with an eloquent look from under the brow. *They ain't holdin' all the cards.*

John Lomax, the funeral director, who owned the block of store fronts and was buying lots out on the Fallona Road adjoining those of whites with the idea that the city was bound to expand in that direction became quite heatedly involved. "If that claim don't stand, there isn't one of us has a patch of dirt in this county can call it his own!"

Professor Thurlow arrived and after a few words with Lomax and Reeve the meeting adjourned to the courthouse where by custom and tradition and with the consent of the white authorities who paid no attention whatsoever to it, in the courtroom before Judge Purcell's bench the local chapter of the NAACP was holding on this, the first Tuesday of May, its regular monthly session. It was also the last session of the current season and thus more than usually well attended. Even so, the number present tonight exceeded that of times of peak activity. The chapter was composed largely of teachers and ministers, churchworkers, a few merchants and housewives, and those farmers and fishermen who also happened to be deep readers, strong talkers or good listeners. The meetings were largely devoted to membership drives, fund drives, celebration of Emancipation Day every January and promotion of voter registration before every election. Moral and monetary support was rendered to areas—at a safe distance from here—where injustice prevailed. In the matter of injustices closer to home, resolutions were passed sometimes and committees were formed and approaches were made to the appropriate white person—Martin Walters, the school principal, to D. C. Lacey, the school superintendent; Carter Scott, the political contact, to Chalmer Coombs, the sheriff. And so on. After long patience, endless maneuvers and the expenditure of the most elaborate anticipatory anxieties, some modicum of result might be obtained. More often it was not. The more explosive issues always, if they were undertaken at all, died somewhere en route. But at least an outlet for discussion was provided by these meetings even if it never went outside; or a word or two was dropped around where it might count even if only as casually as a sidelong hint from a fisherman to his boss; or an effort was made even if it never took ultimate effect.

Reeve had the impatience of many of his generation for the roundabout methods of the organization. After having fought for his country on strange strands halfway around the world, why now that he was home again must he shillyshally and pussyfoot whenever he and his were threatened? But this particular meeting, coinciding as it did with the immediacy of his eviction order and the imminence of its execution, with a moment when feelings were running high and were still on the ascendancy, came as a windfall to him. Tonight he was glad of the meeting, not so much for himself as because it polarized something that had been lurking about in the shadows. Because it had an excitement to it. It was hot.

The fire-escape entrance to the courtroom reserved for Negroes, although they paid their taxes and transacted other business through the front door of the courthouse every day, was jammed with late arrivals. "There he is. That's him. Say Reeve!" They made a path through for him, clapping his shoulder in passing and uniting with the escort that accompanied him. All the lights were ablaze inside. The seats arranged as in an amphitheater, semicircularly, descended in tiers to the welled enclosure of counsel tables, jury panel and witness box presided over by the Judge's bench. The tiered seats were divided into two segments by the white entrance from the main corridor of the building, a balustraded platform with a short flight of stairs down both sides to the outer aisles. The white half of the semicircle was empty now except for a couple of children who had cut loose from their parents clambering among the seats. The colored half was filled to capacity with standees ranged against the tall windows. As always in a crisis the non-members had poured forth, swamping the membership three to one. Reeve recognized a farmer from Fallona, others from the Crest and similar out-of-the-way localities.

"Say Reeve, over here!" Several of the veterans from his class in Army and Legion caps hailed him over. He lifted his hand in response and threaded his way downward to the one person he was looking for, to the one person he'd hoped most to reach when he said, "Spread it," to the one he most wished to arouse on his behalf, seated now in the nethermost ring, the front row at the rim of the rail, Vivian. An old gentleman next to her yielded his place insisting, "You'll need it, they'll be callin' on you," and he eased himself down beside her, leaning his elbow over the back of the chair, facing her.

The spring sun had deepened her hazel-brown, and in her flower-sprinkled white dress her darkness leaped up at him with a flaming brilliance. Her eyes lifted to him with the same spark of compassion she had shown when visiting him after his mother's death. "I just now heard . . ." The same words. "I'm sorry . . ." The same white-gloved pressure on his wrist. "I loved that place too," as she had said, "I loved her too." And, "You've no idea how much."

It was a compassion he craved as a thirsty man might crave a drop of water, and it did not satisfy him anymore than a drop of water would. It was so much less than the intimacy of last Saturday afternoon at her house with her records and paintings, but more than the airy impersonality with which she had left him afterward. He kept looking at her with all the excitement, anticipation, and dread of his plight thumping through him, his heart lurching painfully as if it must burst from its moorings.

"Lord, you're beautiful!" He squeezed his eyes tight and shook his head with it. "Lord, you're beautiful! All gonna die someday. Lemme love you, pretty mamma, before it pass away."

"You!" With upraised handbag she struck out at him. "You can jive at a time like this?"

"You got no business walking the streets like that. Somebody'll steal you."

"Oh go 'way! Seems like you're always in trouble and it's your trouble that drives us together. Trouble has a positive attraction for me—"

"If that's all that attracts you—"

"Sh—sh—shuh—"

At the table below the bench Professor Thurlow was with the Judge's gavel pounding the meeting to order.

Reeve and Vivian settled back in mutual disaffection, heads raised attentively, arms crossed over their chests, elbows grazing. But out of the corner of his eye he caught a smile twitching at the corners of her mouth. A dimple doweled into her cheek.

"If Shakespeare could say it in his sonnets, I suppose you have a right to." She turned to him, her eyes lighting with a query that went beyond mere distress for him. Absently she pulled off her glove and laid her hand with soft urgency over his wrist.

"What are you going to do?"

"What you think I ought to do?"

"What can you do?"

He gestured with his head toward the counselor's table inside the railed enclosure where Miss Lenore Mills had begun to singsong in her tinkling lady-voice through the minutes of the last meeting. To be followed by the annual treasurer's report over which Mrs. Hall and Harold Sanderlee were now poring, making last-minute annotations.

"This?" The tensile warmth of her fingers withdrew from his wristbone. Her eyes flitted back over the murmurous throng, as thick as the leaves of autumn.

"And what," he bridled defensively, over his own doubts, "is the matter with this?"

"You're not expecting anything out of this, are you? If you're count-ing on this to accomplish anything— Oh I know, I know, there'll be a lot of irate speeches and impassioned calls for action—"

"Sh, shshsh down there, hush!"

She was right about the speeches. Wrongs ignored or gone-by-the-board for half a century, relevant and irrelevant to the present instance, were disinterred this night.

"All these years we been going back," Professor Thurlow declared, "in-stead of forward. This the last piece of farmland left to us with access to the river. It's time to call a halt!"

"If this claim don't stand," John Lomax warned, "there's not one of us with a patch of dirt in this county can call it his own. The rest of you out on the River Road—you all out on the Marquis' land north of town —if they get away with this one, make no mistake about it, you're next!"

"You can say it's Reeve they doing this to." One of the veterans known as High Power, a guide and a gambler and hard as they come, knocked in his intensity at the shield of breastbone under the open col-lar of his shirt. "And I say unto you, it's me!"

Now and then Vivian peeped around at Reeve. He lounged back against his chair, his arm dangling overside. Or hunched forward, his black head jutting out of his starched white shirt, his shoulders glim-mering through the cloth as if all the starched-whiteness of the world could not contain him, his muscled hands loosely knotted between his knees. He was listening intently, culling every phrase as if he could hoard it like buried treasure inside his chest. His trustfulness embarrassed her. It also shamed her. To be able to trust like that . . . For all his ease of attitude and concentration of attention, there was impatience in him too, a latent spring in the posture of his haunches; a runner awaiting the signal shot. But when he was called upon to come forward, he shook his head. "Not now. After you all."

"We"—they were all somehow implicated whether they owned a piece of land or not. The common emotion surged to an apogee and halted as it did so often with them, at a loss for the action that should have consummated it. A lawyer? What about a lawyer? Is it true that Car-ter's getting the lawyer? There's a white fellow up in Macon who some-times takes NAACP cases, if you can get to him. There's a colored fellow up in Atlanta, if he's available on such short notice.

A minor interruption occurred as Sam Waldron, the nightwatchman of the building, who had taken his stance on the balustraded platform, leaning against one of the partially opened double doors leading out into the corridor, stiffened up, touched his cap and half-bowed in the direction of approaching footsteps. "How you, Mr. Arthur? Forget something, Mr. Arthur? Can I help you any?" The tax commissioner hurried by with barely a glance at the door. The voices inside immediately subsided to a hassle between Father Hall and Bessie Sanderlee over a point in the bylaws. Did the present situation fall under the province of the organization? After all, no law yet's been violated.

"Do we have to wait for that!"

Shouts. Cries for recognition from the chair. Uproar.

"Do we have to wait till we're hung by the neck!"

Up on the platform of the white entrance, leaning back against the doorpost, Sam loudly whistled *Dixie*. Everyone caught himself in midair, mouths, gestures, bodies half-risen petrified in suspension. "Good night, Mr. Arthur," Sam bobbed his head out the door. "Have a nice evening, Mr. Arthur." Until the footsteps on the black-and-white tile of the corridor died away. Sam was twin brother to Sheldon, the barbershop shoeshine boy who pranced so nimbly on his haunches at the feet of customers while the business of the white community passed overhead, filtering in osmosis through him to the colored.

Sheldon Waldron who was never called anything but Boy in the barbershop unless it was Snowball or Sunshine by travelers stopping for a cut—in fact, it was doubted even by Ed Stowe whether he had a name at all—Sheldon Waldron now demanded the floor. "I'm not namin' no names but there are some people in high places"—from his small cramped figure a fist shook out in a direction that might have been interpreted as the bench high on its dais or one of the white-globed standards at the corner of it—"before whom we got no more right than a dog. That's right, I been pat on the head by 'em and kicked in the shin and spat upon. Never would admit it, I had too much self-respect— But it's the living truth. Lawyer, this'll take more'n a lawyer. It'll take a Daniel, a Daniel come to judgment!"

Vivian closed her eyes, the hot light beating red through her eyelids. In the end they'll pass a motion to call the Savannah chapter head to send down an observer on Friday, maybe Macon and Atlanta, and maybe one of them will come.

"What happens," she intoned under her breath, "to anger unredeemed? Does it build up like a head of steam? Or turn the bloodstream into acid? Or simply disappear?"

The chair beside her squeaked as Reeve heaved himself up out of it. He brushed by her knees into the center aisle, swung through the gate into the center enclosure, planted himself before the Judge's bench, his back to it, with the air of a man who has taken up the cudgels, the confidence that commands confidence. He lifted his arms over Thurlow's repeated pounding of the mallet, gradually bringing the hubbub down to silence. Poseur, Vivian thought. Toreador. He was good at it. Where does he get that jazz?

Actually Reeve had never before faced such a crowd, or thought to. His shirt had collapsed into a thousand creases, clinging to his back. He wiped his forehead with the back of his arm, then stuck his thumbs through the belt loops of his pants, stilling the tremor of his thighs beneath. The Judge's bench stood directly opposite the balustraded platform and he had to turn on his heel to address the full-packed ranks of seats on the colored side. Their faces swam together in his eyes, dissolved into a magnification of those below his porch steps this afternoon, only now instead of looking down upon them he had to look up.

"What you want us to do about it?" Sanderlee hollered from the back. "What can we do?"

They had worked themselves up to a pitch, and unless he captured the moment, held it fast between his hands, it would falter, fall apart and be forever lost. He caught Vivian making a monkey face at him, teasing, her mouth puckered with the poignancy of a skepticism that questions and answers everything before it has happened.

"Now we been woofing and beating up our gums long enough," another one of the veterans, known as the Baron, boomed through his cupped hands. "Give us the high sign!"

A chorus of titters flitted upward to the fans that Sam had shortly before turned on. Against the coffered ceiling the blades chased one another faster and faster, wings whirring to a speed that blurred their outline to invisibility. Nothing will come of it. In the end, nothing . . .

"When I said this afternoon," Reeve began conversationally, leaning his elbow up on the edge of the Judge's bench, "to my folks, 'Spread it,' looks like they didn't waste no time."

Laughter. "Yah. That's right." "You tell 'em."

"And somebody asked me then, 'ain't you afraid? Ain't you afraid that someone'll run to the white folks with it? Anything that colored get going about, first thing someone always runs to his white folks with it.'"

A quiver of common recognition out of the core of inhibition and intimidation, the twinge of a nerve exposed, the twang of a sword blade flexed.

"And I said, 'If there's anybody low enough to do that, let 'em. I can't stop it.' It took a lot of courage to say some of the things said here tonight, knowing that. It is a fear and will be but we can't worry on it, because there's too much else to worry on that we can do something about.

"Now there's been a lot of talk about a lawyer. The lawyer's the key thing. Who will be the lawyer? I won't answer that now because I can't say what I don't yet know. We trying to get a lawyer.

"But the lawyer's not the key thing. A lawyer can play footsie with the other side, sell me out behind my back, dump me so fast— Unless he feels there's something more to this than just a routine case."

He was speaking with a sureness he would never have guessed he possessed. The words tapped out of him like a ballpeen hammer on a row of nailheads, and every one of them struck home. He could feel that. Clean. Clear. Bang bang bang.

"It's not the lawyer that's the key thing, but what's behind him. Which is to say, what's behind me.

"You all.

"You you you," he pointed in a sweeping arc. "You all.

"What can you do? Come this Friday, ten o'clock in the morning, be here. That's all. Like you are right now. Every one of you and as many more as you can bring. Be here."

He swung out of the gate and was immediately surrounded. He had asked of them only the possible, but a possibility that would demand an invincible determination. Vivian caught up with him later in the midst of the departing crowd at the foot of the fire escape. "You enjoyed that," she poked an accusing finger at him, "didn't you?"

"Enjoyed?" He was taken aback by her attack. Then rubbing at the back of his neck, puzzled, had to admit: "Yes, I enjoyed it. If it wasn't for what's in jeopardy— But then if it wasn't for that," he had to admit further, with rueful perplexity, "I'd never have spoken, would I?"

"I'll be here." In front of everybody milling around on the dark dew-drenched, palmetto-planted side lawn of the courthouse, under the roseate beam shed by the fire-escape bulb against the brick wall of the building, she stretched tiptoe and lightly kissed his cheek. "Come Friday, I'll be here, for whatever that's worth. I'll be."

"Hey—"

She was gone and he was left amidst whoops of laughter foolishly holding to his cheek. He had, he felt, grown larger in her sight because of this. Almost as large as he felt in himself. His shadow leaped higher and higher on the gravel path before him as he took his way back past the jail in the rear of the courthouse to Fruit Street.

He spent the remainder of the evening with his family in the funeral parlor. But the room was too small to contain his restlessness. His mind raced with stratagems, fitting the pieces together. He could see so clear what had to be done, when and how. To hold it, move it ahead, against nibblings from the outside, a failure of nerve from within. He kept knocking his fist in the palm of his hand, on his knee, on the pine box.

"Reeve, will you stop that whacking?"

"Who's whacking?" He stared down at his clenched fist. "Was I whacking?"

There was no mourning in him even now. Only a superb elation, closer to cheers than to tears. This was the moment, he knew even more certainly than he had in the afternoon, what he had been building up to from the past months, from his years in the war, from the day he was born. He had it in his grasp. He was at grips with the force that opposed him, knee to knee, hands on throat—he was battling it, he could beat it, and he was not alone. Out of the red-rimmed flame points of the tapers, casting light in the darkness, out of the lushly wilting fragrance of cape jasmine, a spiciness too sweet and a sweetness too spicy, the fragments of his mother's face gathered. They ain't got it all their way. Never had.

"Reeve, will you sit down?" Sister Mae pleaded. "Will you please please please—"

In the narrowness of the room, their knees pressed from their folding chairs against the bier that bore the box. "I wonder," Reeve mused aloud, "if she knew she'd have a wake like this one here."

"Ahhh . . ." Did she know . . .

He was sustained through the next day by the energy of his conviction, by that infusion of adrenalin with which nature supplies body and spirit in periods of stress. Even through the outpouring of white people at his mother's funeral he was neither disconcerted nor disrupted from his purpose. When Julie stepped with Henry into the church vestibule, a vibration rippled through the crowd clear to the family in the front pew. "What's the matter with them?" Fred whispered fiercely. "Have they no shame?" "They don't realize," Reeve said, "what they doing. They haven't got the slightest little bit of a notion."

The presence of the whites imposed a strain upon the colored, who were constrained by habit to receive them with friendliness and to preserve before them in the expression of their bereavement the formality of good taste and nice manners. At the same time it split their unity of feeling half a dozen ways. Last night in absentia the whites had hardened into the image of a menace, the enemy against whom one girded one's loins and braced one's bones. But here they were, big as life and twice as pleasant. Where was the menace? Where the enemy? They were shocked in part beyond any previous shock by the brazen effrontery of their appearance, and in part they were undermined by it. It was assumed that they all knew of the eviction order and being here must therefore approve of it and approving it must believe that they had the right of it. And if they're right, where are we? If they could come here and sit up so high and mighty and sure of themselves . . .

And it was impressive. Three whole rows with chairs for the overflow. Heads turning cautiously ticked them off. Miss Ada. Mr. Telfer and Mrs. . . . If Rose could see this wouldn't she be pleased, wouldn't she be proud . . .

Then Aunt Tee began to rock and moan. And Lila-Lee who had held herself in check all the thousands of miles from the northwest coast to the southeast shrieked out. For the first time at long last, all mundane considerations forgotten, all trivialities banished, the brothers and sisters gave themselves over purely to the anguish of their loss. The tree was struck down. The sheltering boughs had vanished forever from their landscape.

From then on it was all feeling. They stumbled out of the church with tear-blotched eyes into a daze of light. Waiting in the churchyard for the funeral director's limousine to take them to the graveyard on the Fallona Road, they stood tightly linked as if through the support of hand and arm, the touch of shoulder and flank, the tenderness they shared would flow from one to the other. As they stood, Julie-Ann came directly toward them, her face under the sweeping brim of her black hat soft with grief, luminous with the eulogy she had just rendered to Rose. She reached for Vergilia. In purity of feeling, impulsively, the women embraced, kissed, wept together, their cheeks wet with one another's tears.

But an hour afterward, on their way home from the burial ground in the limousine, immersed in the bleakness that follows the scraping of the shovel, the heaping-on of dirt—it's all over now, that hiatus in which the dead dwell between this life and the hereafter is passed, the earth has covered over the last vestige and sun and rain, night and day, she will lie there underground until she rots—in this mood, Vergilia gave voice not so much to the effect as the aftereffect of the morning behind them.

"It was a beautiful funeral," she began tentatively through her swollen lips. "Wasn't it a beautiful funeral? Naming the school for Mamma."

She was greeted by a frigid silence.

"What I mean is—" she began again, "they must have something on their side, or they wouldn't—"

"Vergilia!"

"Now wait a minute, listen to me. Will you listen? There's two sides to everything."

"Sure," Fred turned on her explosively, "there's two sides. Theirs and ours. Which one you on?"

"What I mean is, there's so much back-history to this—"

"You bet there is. They got their history. And we got ours! Our fore-fathers worked that land and they bought it with their blood-money—"

"Will you hear me? Will you hear me out? You said yourself, they're out for a deal. Didn't you say that? And if they name that school for her, praise her up and honor her that much, they're not just going to out-and-out—"

"Vergilia." Heavily, Ben wheeled around on her from the jump seat. "You saw yourself Eula Purcell was sitting with them. They're in this together up to their ears. It's a squeeze play."

"That's what I mean. They got it all stacked, they forcing us— If they was to make an offer . . . What I mean, we all have our own lives to live. We all of us could use the money—"

"Vergie! She isn't cold in the grave and you already—"

"Why you dirty double-crossing little viper—"

They were all screaming at her, about to bring the roof down. Vergilia was always the weak link, the selfish one, so self-centered . . . "Let her say it," Reeve yelled, "let her spit it out!"

"Will you let me finish, just let me finish? Even if they was to offer us five thousand dollars, say, and that's more than they'll ever offer—there's six of us—it wouldn't go far enough to do us any good. That's all I had to say. Naming the school for Mamma. Falling all over us and kissing—"

Vigorously Vergilia rubbed her mouth over with the back of her hand and with pursed lips blew pooh! out the car window.

It cleared the atmosphere. Vergilia had spoken a thought that must have lurked in back of all their minds but Reeve's, too shameful and too treacherous in its very concealment to be acknowledged. Unitedly they now all fell upon Julie, ravening on her.

"I always admired her," Sister Mae reflected. "I always thought she was the world's own wonder. But now—"

"That was no admiration," Vergilia corrected her. "It was jealousy. I used to watch Mamma iron up those blouses of hers and think about the house she lived in and her looks and her position—and oh my! When I went to bed nights I'd ask God in my prayers: Why should she have so much and me so little? That's right, I'd ask that. And even now when I see some girl driving down the street in one of those white roadsters, you know, with red leather seats, I'm still asking that. Why can't my girls—? And I get mad all over."

"First time I ever come around," Lila-Lee recalled, "now don't look cross-eyed at me, Reeve—how we all could grow up on a farm and be told so little and live so prissy— It doesn't seem possible but when I come around for the first time, it was something I never suspected. I didn't know what it was. Even when Mamma said that every woman had it, I didn't believe her. I asked her did my schoolteacher, and she said yes. And did the preacher's wife, yes. And this one and that one till finally I asked did Miss Julie—she's my same age, you know—and Mamma said: Her too. Then I was sure she was lying. How could Miss Julie-Ann have anything so funky and sticky and nasty to her? Oh no. Not her. It couldn't be. I thought it was because we were poor and colored and didn't know any better."

"I thought it was because I was black and ugly," Vergilia said.

"Whoever told you you were ugly? Vergie, you're not ugly."

"Yeah. But it's taken me a lifetime to find out."

"And those toys," Ben said, "those baskets of beat-up toys. Giving with one hand so she could take with the other."

"The great benefactor. Champion of the colored race. God save us from our friends!"

John Lomax discharged them at the house from his seven-passenger Reo—never made a better car, where'll you find a car nowadays, these so-called streamline models, with a chassis high enough to clear some of the places I got to go? But jouncing over the cattle barrier, bumping down the track to the clearing, he winced at every jolt up through the floor. Mainspring, an axle . . . the limousine was getting old. They shouldn't have brought him all the way out here. Ben needn't have loaned his Buick to his boys to drive Aunt Tee in the cortege—just for the showing it would make. Lomax had maintained a discreet professional silence through the family squabble and female reminiscence, but now in a state of peevishness for reasons he couldn't identify—his view of the larger interest which embraced his at war with his usual narrow self-interest, the sting of some childhood wound of his own expanding unbearably against the constraints of his normal cautiousness—he got out of his car uninvited and purposefully accompanied the family up the path to the house.

"Thurlow called Savannah this morning for an observer," Lomax asserted with argumentative loudness. "But I don't know, I don't know—A strange Negro showing up in the middle of a thing like this, in a spot as small as this—"

The family tightened up, interpreting the drift of his tone. "Thurlow will be with him, won't he?" Ben said. "We'll see he's never left alone for a minute."

"Or maybe," Vergilia snapped back meaningfully over her shoulder, "they'd better send a her."

Nevertheless Lomax persisted in following at their heels to the house, the purport of which they also interpreted. "Reeve, you gettin' that law-yer, aren't you?"

"We got everything on our side," Reeve answered him with an effort at mildness. "If we just stick together—"

"Better get him too."

The family in an access of hostility quickened their step, drawing away from Lomax. Fred however stopped at the bottom step to address a squirrel friskily hanging from the porch roof. "Why is it the hound that bays the loudest is always the one that scares shitless?"

"Fred," Mae demanded, "You apologize! Using that kind of language in front of your sisters."

"I apologize," Fred said, looking full around at John Lomax, the only one of them who dared do so, "to my sisters."

High Power and the Baron, also known as The Long and The Short of It, the one lean and rakish, the other solid-pack, were waiting up on the porch settee for them. It had been decided last night that the house was not to be left unwatched as long as the present crisis lasted. "All quiet," they reported. "Not a stir. Just that cracker-boy from down the track, he was just now moseying round."

"Oh he was, was he?" Reeve said. "Then that takes cares of that. See you tomorrow, huh?"

"You're not," John Lomax admonished from behind, "going through with that ditch-blowing tomorrow, are you? Of all times, this is no time—"

"This is the time," Reeve answered him with more self-control than he would have believed he could muster, "of all time. When it's ripe. Later can be too late."

They proceeded into the house but still did not shake off Lomax. Ben went straight to the tin box on the dresser and took from it the pol-icy of the Sons & Daughters of Arcady, his mother's burial lodge, and threw it down on the table in front of Lomax. "This what you looking for?"

But Lomax, mollified by the sight of it or shamed, or appeased some-how by Reeve's oblique admission of the chanciness inherent in their cause, waved it off. "Not now, not now, in a few days will be time enough. What burnt me up," he wrathfully burst out, "was not how they come—some of them must have meant well enough—but the way they took over! Anywhere they walk in, they take over! Did you notice how Henry knocked against the casket—"

"Yah. I thought he was about to fall in."

"You'd have thought—" Lomax's shoulders started to heave, his neck wrinkled up in back, the solicitude of demeanor in which he was schooled crumbled. "That she—that she—hyeh hyeh hyeh—jumped up and—k-k-k—whopped him one."

Their laughter beat up against the roof in an anguish of abandon. They pounded on the table. Stomped the floor.

"My people," Fred said and wiped his eyes.

"A thing like this," Lila-Lee blew thinly into her handkerchief, "coming one on top the other, it puts you through the wringer. Takes so much out of you, nobody knows—nobody knows."

Reeve rubbed his cheek as if to touch a talisman, as if to hold the kiss that had been so lightly given last night in permanent tenure. Or does it simply disappear? The seed had been sown. It was. It had to be.

John Lomax left without the burial insurance. He would be telling that one on Henry all afternoon. He was a man who carried quite a bit of influence up and down Fruit Street.

Reeve however could not forget the climax of tension first with Vergilia and then with Lomax. They were all tense, all being drawn fine. The first phase was over, the second thoughts had set in. But after the wavering they were for their various reasons reconsolidating, stronger than ever, perhaps because of the very thing that had shaken them: the face of the opposition. More factors than he had any way of calculating would enter into his support or the vitiation of it between now and the Friday hearing, but at this point one was critical. The lawyer. More so than he would acknowledge in the event that Carter Sillens was otherwise busy or for any number of reasons unwilling. *Did you get the lawyer?* To get him now was every bit as decisive as to have him later in court.

Carter Scott had not been able to arrange the appointment with Sillens for earlier than four in the afternoon. Reeve rounded up his nephews and put in an hour with them staking the tomatoes in his vegetable patch. "There's a time when you know you must plant," he said to the boys, "or take like peas when the season gets on, they won't come up. And so much fertilizer and not too close or take like corn it'll die on you. And as soon as the seedlings shoot up, plenty of water but not too much or you'll be sure to lose them. Now these tomatoes I already let them go too long—careful with that stake there! Don't drive through the roots." He crouched among the tomato stalks, drooping of their own weight, and secured them, giving to the vines a contour and direction. "Everything has to be nurtured. Aside from the forces out of your control, there's a lot you can do to cultivate a good crop. It's hard work, the hardest kind of work, but"—he rubbed his cheek for the evanescent kiss —"if only you could cultivate your life as easy!"

With his mother's tin box in his hands he rode off with Carter Scott to Bay City. Professor Thurlow accompanied them in order to lend weight to their plea. Carter Sillens himself received them at his back door and showed them through the kitchen—up-to-date, spic-and-span and empty as one felt the house was empty both of family and servants —to his study.

Like everyone else in Colfax County, Reeve was curious about the relationship between the two brothers: Carter the fisherman and Carter the political boss. The Mayor was a tough, tenacious bulldog, his snowy hair rumpled and his shirt collar unruly, his face healthily tanned but creased with the scowl of the ulcerous, at once aggressive and suspicious. He was so noncommittal that even when he greeted Carter Scott with the query, "How's Mamma? How she been keeping herself?" he left the impression that he hadn't spoken at all. He bore himself down the hall ahead of them in the manner of one whose path has been hewn with a broadax.

In the Mayor's study Carter Scott made himself thoroughly at home. He ruffled the long ears of the two basset hounds sleepily nestling before the fireplace, helped himself to pipe tobacco from the copper canister on the desk, drew up a chair for the Professor and invited Reeve to sit down. Then borrowing a book from the shelves, he withdrew to the fireplace and leafed through it, interjecting a remark only now and then. If he was at all aware of the portrait he presented, tall and tobacco-brown, grey-haired and black-browed, black-mustached, pipe in mouth, morocco-bound book in hand, hounds at his feet, he didn't show it. Possibly he had developed the pose as a means of self-assertion, pitting his personality against the Mayor's superiority in worldly goods. Or possibly it was natural to him.

The Mayor showed no awareness of it either. Reeve transferred the will from his tin box to the desk but was deterred by him from disgorging the additional documents. "I have copies," the Mayor said and clamped his mouth upon the words as if he had said nothing. Thurlow who functioned as an unofficial lawyer for colored and poor whites in Arcady, preparing official papers as well as notarizing them, giving quasi-legal advice at a minimal fee, undertook to furnish the background of the case. Sillens listened to him without comment, his pale bloodshot eyes fixed on him without a flicker of response. He took no notes.

"You see, the land all around has been bought up by this outside company. There's only this one tract left, this here fellow on the road and a white fellow down on the river."

Reeve moved uneasily. Was Thurlow telling too much? The whole geography and history and the interests behind it. The man looked as if this immensity, in which he himself was so intimately implicated, was as remote to him as a speck on the other side of the room.

"She's most awfully concerned about this," Carter Scott remarked from his book, "or I wouldn't be here."

Carter Sillens levered forward in his chair, his snowy head slowly swiveling about toward Carter Scott. He knew that.

"Folks are all up in arms over it." Reeve leaned urgently across the front of the desk. "Feelings are running that high, it's spread all over the county—" Was he saying the right thing? Or scaring him off? "It's more than a piece of property. It's all these memories that go way back . . ."

The Mayor slumped back in his chair, his blank eyes blinking at the chintz-draped windows. Then seeing something before him that none of them saw, some aspect of personal advantage or poetic justice or simply an answer to his brother's audacious pose, he said matter-of-factly: "Well, I drew up the instrument. No reason why I shouldn't file it."

Glory be! Victo-ree! They came out of Carter Sillens' house with his promise to file the will for probate in the Colfax County courthouse this Friday at ten. Reeve was jubilant. "If you'd asked me," he reiterated all the way home, "what I was going to do if he'd turned us down, I wouldn't have known what to tell you. Now we got this much behind us. Drive down Fruit Street, man, past the bar. I want to stick my head out the window and throw my hat in the air."

And that's what he did, though he wasn't wearing any hat. We did it! We got it! We made it! He sprawled back in the car seat, satisfied. Peculiarities of circumstance, unforeseen and yet foreordained, were amassing with a cumulative power that impelled him onward even as he attempted to compel it. Only one thing more he had to do. Only one thing left now that he could do. Tomorrow when he was dynamiting the ditches with Rad, he would have to inform him of the eviction order. It was not, even in his mood of triumph, a task that he looked forward to with any relish.

3

When Rad McDowell made up his mind to do a thing, he could never rest until it was done with. Therefore from the moment he proposed to Reeve that they proceed at once with dynamiting the ditches, and learned in the same moment of Rose's death, he had been chafing over the delay. The lower side of his cornfield, submerged by last Friday night's storm, still held three days later standing pools of water between the rows.

He did persuade Reeve on Monday to go over with him the course
they would follow below the cornfield to drain it off and keep it drained.
They plotted the transverse line from the Sunset fence through thickets
of swamp to the old rice canal, which itself would have to be blown
from the trunk on the riverside up to the road. They marked two large
trees that would have to be cut down before beginning with the actual
ditching on Thursday. They also cleared a shed some fifty feet back of
Rad's house for temporary storage of the dynamite, Reeve cautioning
against firing a gun or lighting a cigarette, spilling water or trash, driving
a nail or allowing a child anywhere nearby once they had the explosives
inside.

"This'll do for now. But before we do anymore of it, we gonna have to
build us a magazine away off from everything."

"What for?" Rad demanded. They had just finished cleaning all the
rusty broken parts of old farm equipment out of the shed and hanging
on a door so it could be padlocked.

"Well dynamite's a tricky thing. You never can tell how it will act.
Can just lay there building up a spark, and boom."

Reluctantly under pressure from Rad, Reeve agreed to go into town
with him next day to make the necessary purchases. But it would require
two trips, not one. "You can't cart powder and caps in one and the same
trip."

"Why not?" Rad demanded. He had already wasted the best part of
today and tomorrow would take all morning.

"You askin'," Reeve demanded back, "or you tellin' me?"

Rad could hardly blame the man. He had just lost his mother, he was
grieving for her, you had to respect that. He was doing more than anyone had a right to expect of him under such conditions. Yet Rad was
impatient, impatient with the fact that under such conditions he was
forced to coax Reeve, convince and coerce him into action when it was
Reeve who had broached the plan to him in the first place. The pressure
should be operating the other way. It wasn't right. He didn't feel right
with it. Reeve should be parking on his doorstep, courting *him*.

He was also irked by another fact, much more oppressive than that of
Reeve's period of mourning. This implicit fact had, without being de-
fined by him, aroused his initial resistance to blasting the ditches,
despite the obvious advantage in it for him. He had suspected the dynamite as a trick and a trap. Had rejected it. Evaded it. Indirectly sounded
out the county agent about it and more directly questioned Marcus
Hadley, the contractor, concerning it. Had taken their opinion under
advisement, turned it over in his mind every whichway till suddenly he
was living with the idea, ready for it, jumping at the first chance to reap-

proach Reeve, get going on it with him. But still the stinger of the original fact behind it had not been pulled. It was Reeve who had thought up the plan and Reeve who would have to carry it out and Reeve he would have to rely on. He was dependent in this on Reeve, on Reeve's competence and Reeve's disposition and his pleasure.

Now already Reeve was riding over him. "You askin' or tellin' me?" With that morbid preoccupation with inferences of inferiority that was part of his nature, more acute now than ever because of its suspension during the war, Rad brooded over the fancied slight. Not another white man in this county Reeve would dare snap back at like that. He was bringing him to his knees, rubbing it into him.

Rad worried himself up into quite a state over the one retort. "I'm gonna have trouble with that boy," he said darkly to Lulabelle late Monday evening. "You wait and see, he's gonna give me trouble."

"What's the matter now?"

"That is the damnedest nigger in this county! I know Reeve like I know myself, and I'm telling you he's the peskiest, touchiest, contrariest—I apologized to him, didn't I, for throwing him out of this house? I give him the gun we bought. What more does he want?"

Lulabelle was ironing up the week's wash. Linens and clothing, sprinkled with handfuls of water, were heaped up on the table, all but burying her alive. She changed flatirons at the woodstove, and the sizzle of hot spit as she tested the bottom with wetted finger popped through the room like a comment and sent a smell through it like that of summer rain before it falls.

The smell, dusty, ferny, expectant, penetrated Rad with the pang of a reproach. He squirmed around on the bench, bracing himself against the area of her activity, insulating himself against it but too proud to move out of it. He could never feel comfortable while she was working and he was sitting no matter how hard a day he'd put in.

"And all that about explosives," he continued his complaint, a querulousness in his tone that he didn't himself like to listen to. "How dangerous it is and how careful you have to handle it, building himself up, what an expert he is, *whuff whuff whuff*. He's a regular old woman. Lulabelle, you ain't heard a word—"

"When the REA comes in," Lulabelle said dreamily, "first thing I do after we wire up this house is buy me an electric iron."

It had been announced recently that the REA was to run an electric line through the River Road this year. Lulabelle could think of nothing else. She had her mind so full of how she would change her house and her work around, she couldn't wait for it to happen. She was impatient too. Her iron hissed swiftly over the dampened starched garments, shaping shoulders, creasing sleeves, weaving through button rows. As soon as she had finished with one she flung it on top of the heap, wrinkling up what she had wrought even before she started on the next.

"Rad, you ain't doin' nothin'. Get up out of there and put these away."

Disgruntled, he got up from his bench by the table and marched out through the parlor where the children were sleeping to the porch in front. Doggone. A woman will never rest until she has a man down under, doing her will for her. Then she'll laugh and despise him for it. On the porch he stumbled through the pots she had set out, boxes, pails, buckets and tubs—anything a plant would grow in. Lulabelle had a passion for growing things, and all about the edge of the porch and down the steps and along the path she had her flowers: blazing star, monkey-face, sultana, chicken gizzard, shrimp plant, butterfly lily, white-leafed reeds for background and air potatoes sprouting little brown balls among the rose climbers. And verbena . . . Rad kicked a pail back in place, but not hard enough to turn it over. He had found some wild azalea in the woods today where he was plotting the ditch with Reeve and brought a sprig home to her and right away she had to root it.

The night swarmed with fireflies, thick as stars. He walked around the house to the back and down the path a piece past Wyatt's henhouses and his rabbits. He had bought an old bicycle for Wyatt a while back and Charles had pieced it together: anything that would run Charles was right in there, he'd even fixed the truck once, listening to the motor, tinkering with it, "That's your feedline, Daddy." And after Charles had the bike going good, the wheels straightened, a new chain in, all greased up and the fenders painted and the handlebars adjusted, damn, if Wyatt didn't turn right around and trade the bike for two rabbits. Now he had six of them nested away and a box of pigeons and in a special place, mounded up in the sun, some alligator eggs he had found in a mudhill down the river and carried home in his hat. Cracked eggs. Broken-shelled. Wyatt was hatching, he claimed, little baby 'gators out of the embryos still alive in the yolk.

Rad left the path and struck out for the shed where the dynamite was to be stored. He waded waist-high through plumes of dog fennel frothing marine-green under the small bright eye of the new moon, covering fields once long ago plowed, sown, harvested. In the shed he had left a broken harness this afternoon, meaning to bring it home later and mend it. He unlatched the door now and groped in the thick darkness along the raspy board wall for the snag over which it was looped, found it, took it down and with his fingers searched over the smoky sweated-through

supple surface of the leather for the hame-strap that had worn down to
a final shred. He unbuckled the strap and stepped outside to inspect the
break under the light of the moon. That harness was older than the
horse his father had left him, older than he was. All around him, invisible
in the night, crickets zinged, buzz-sawing at his breastbone, filling him
with a gnawing sensation, larger than loneliness, keener than longing of
the flesh—a loneliness and longing that might momentarily be assuaged
by the flesh, lulled to sleep by love-making, but never fully satisfied
by it.

The shadow of the harness in his hand dangled like a noose on the
wall of the shed. A short distance away, in the grass-grown outline of an
abandoned track lay the skeleton of a singletree that had not yet been
removed. On a night like this, through country like this—even now he
still measured terrain with the eye of a soldier—he once led a platoon of
tanks that had lost its lieutenant; had piloted them through the sleeping
grasses of just such a field till the bazooka shells burst upon them like
floating moons; and he had brought them safe into the cover of an or-
chard. Where was that Rad McDowell? Where had he disappeared to?
You were supposed to forget all that. Put it behind you. All gone. His
wife with her pregnancy, his kids with their noisy absorptions, his farm
and his crop of winter cabbage washed out by too much rain, his wartime savings in the bank leaching off day after day at a rate he didn't
dare think on, the electric line and the electric iron and all that had to
be bought—this consumed him now, this *was* himself and he could no
more jump out of it than he could jump out of his skin. But there was
more to it than that. There was the loneliness, the longing for something bigger, some infinitude of self beyond the compass of his particular identity at this particular moment.

"All right," he said aloud and slapped the slack of his harness against
the shed that for so long had contained nothing but a tangle of rusty
parts. "Tomorrow'll be different."

Things stand still so long and then comes a time they have to change.
They have to change and you can't wait for it.

"All right." He dragged the singletree off into the dog fennel away
from the building. "All right, he's just as smart about this as I am." It
was said. He'd said the words. "Maybe a hell of a lot smarter."

With the harness over his arm he took the abandoned track back,
heading for the smokehouse where, he remembered, there were strands
of old beargrass hanging over the rafters that might do at least temporarily for binding up the broken strap. The smokehouse, an upright out-
building of rough-hewn logs, loomed up in the bare spot between the
raggedy black silhouette of wild plum trees and the trio of giant per-

simmons that shielded the well. Late last fall after his return from the service, just before Thanksgiving, he had butchered a couple of porkers, salted down the hindquarters in the curing trough till just past Christmas and then smoked them over a hickory fire for two and a half days running. When he stepped into the smokehouse now, a ham still hanging on beargrass from its rafter, ripening to full flavor in the warm weather and frosted with mold like a ghost of the departed porkers, set astir by the opening door, bumped against his forehead.

Rad stood tiptoe on the rim of the trough, hewn by Lachlan McDowell out of a poplar log three-quarters of a century ago, and reached along the crossbeam for the shaggy clump of strands that had been soaked in boiling water till they were limber enough for use and dried in the air till they were tough as whit-leather. The musky-dusky odor of aging meats permeated him. The smoke of long-dead fires seared up his nostrils, bringing tears to his eyes. He unwound several lengths of the grass but as he reared back, taking it down, the ham socked him again with the thud of a muffled blackjack. He wheeled around and socked it back. Going and coming! Get me go-ing and com-ing! He left it swaying to and fro in the darkness behind him.

He emerged from the reek of the smokehouse into the moisture-soft green-sweet scent of field and wood. The sweetness was so all-pervasive that within it the fetid odors of livestock close by, chickens and a litter of pigs and the bull-calf born of lightning last Friday, possessed a pleasant familiarity, warm as residual sunlight. A breeze ruffled from the river, indicating a fair day tomorrow. Whipping at the dew-drenched legs of his jeans, he started back toward the yellow beam of the lamp in his kitchen window, his spark in the night, his star.

Carefully he scraped the soles of his shoes on the slatted back steps, avoiding the patience plants—always something underfoot! No more than twenty minutes had elapsed from the time he walked out the front door until he came in the back, but though his jean cap was pulled down over his eyes and his cheeks were tight under the dark unshaven prickle of beard, and his thin curly mouth worked truculently, Lulabelle recognized that his mood had lightened. He set aside his harness, whisked his hands off with yellow-bar soap in the bucket, wiped them on the roller towel and held them out, catch. She flung out toward him the end of the rough-dry sheet she was fixing to put away unironed. They joined in the folding of the sheets, stepping back for lengthwise and forward to each other for sidewise, meeting with the corners. She smiled at him, but never directly, always as she was turning her head aside, a smile shyly sassy, enticing, and independent as all getout.

"Well, I ain't takin' no two trips in that truck tomorrow!" he grunted out defiantly between foldings. "One's enough!"

He did not reveal to her the real reason for his grudge against Reeve, nor his conciliation with it. Lulabelle did not seek it out nor give voice to her own suspicion. She had her own private interpretation of Rad. Rad had a vision of himself, she thought, as the All-Father, All-Provider, Protector and Guiding Light, at least in relation to his own particular bailiwick. And when he failed to fulfill that vision in any particular, he took umbrage at everybody. Anything you could say to him then was an insult. So she smiled sidewise at the blue eyes blazing from the shadow of the peaked cap, at the taut cheeks glimmering through the swarthy fuzz that softened his expression whether he would or no, and drew her own conclusions. He's talked Reeve into going in to Ozzie Higginson's tomorrow to buy that stuff with him and now—she guessed, not too wide of the mark at that—he's a-wishing he could back off from it.

They met up against each other with the last sheet. "I'm go'n to bed," she said. "You comin'?"

But obdurately Rad refused to go with her, rejecting what comfort she could offer. He settled down at the table and began working on his harness, substituting beargrass for the broken hame-strap and threading it through the buckles. Tested it by pulling between his hands with whitened knuckles, strained biceps, spread groin and gritted teeth. It would hold. Beargrass is pretty strong.

Even then he did not go in at once to the ease of his wife and bed. He stopped in the parlor where the three boys were sleeping in the big white iron bedstead and Ruby on a cot at the foot of it. Ruby was snoring, a mouth-breather, asserting herself even asleep. Rad straightened the thin cotton blanket over her. On the bed Charles, growing full-boned this past spring, solider, sure of himself, was stretched out on his back, spilling over the edge. Rad lifted his trailing arm up and nudged him inward. On the other side Wyatt, the thin-boned dark intense one, hugged up to the wall, and in the middle Timmy, the five-year-old lay on his stomach, spread-eagled, taking all the space he never had awake.

"Rad, that you out there?" Lulabelle called slumbrously from their bedroom. "It's late."

Still he didn't go in to her. A man aches for something beyond himself. Sometimes he looks for it in a woman or in more than one woman, sometimes in drink and brawling and drifting around. But he only debases his need by taking the edge off it. A man has to feel he's more than an animal set upon this earth, that after he's gone leaves no more trace than an animal does. He has aspiration, the drive to accomplish something with his life that wasn't before. To leave his mark.

He pulled the frayed shade down in the curtainless window by the children's bed to the sash. Let them sleep a little after sunup . . . Then he did a strange thing. On the doorpost generations of children had, over scoldings and spankings carved their initials until now it was a regular totem pole. His was up near the top: he had climbed up on a chair, he remembered, to put his way up ahead of everyone else's. He reached up, feeling for it with his fingertips. It was there all right. But as he traced with blind fingers the varnished-over indentation of R and M, he remembered something else. It stole up on him, hit him from behind like the ham, struck him with a thud that resounded thunderously through his head. On a night like this, just this same time of year, as the war was ending in Europe, he drove with a company of tanks into a concentration camp. Initials scratched by fingernails all over an inside wall, scraped, gouged out . . .

He had only one question that May night and he had it now as he went into his bedroom, undressed and lay down beside his wife without disturbing her from sleep. Why? *Why?* WHY?

Howcome?

In the morning Rad conveniently disappeared at just about the time Reeve was expecting him to show up for their journey in to town. He busied himself with his sweet potato draws digging them up out of the holes in which he had deposited them and replanting them in rows. It was about ten-thirty when he reappeared in his kitchen and helped himself to a cup of coffee.

"Reeve's been down here lookin' for you," Lulabelle told him while he sipped at his coffee, taking his own good time about it.

"Uh-huh?"

He took his time washing up, too.

"Ain't you go'n change your shirt?" Lulabelle asked him. "And here, here's a clean pair of suntans, all pressed up for you. Change into these."

"What for? Ain't no call to get slicked up."

In his dirt-smeared field clothes he proceeded at a leisurely pace to his truck. But when he had climbed up into the cab and was starting the motor, Lulabelle came running out after him with Timmy and Ruby at her heels. "Wait, wait up a minute."

She was toting in her arms one of her knocked-together wooden plant boxes, filled with soil and the leaflets of cuttings. "I promised some of these here to Mrs. Hawley over to the church." She boosted the children up ahead of her into the cab. "Besides, I'm clean out of meal. We're goin' in with you."

"Now Lu—" He was jarred out of the evasive tactics with which he was easing into his venture with Reeve. "This no trip for a woman, and in your condition. Let alone these kids."

"That's why we goin' with you." She packed her plants in under the truck window, plumped down on the sprung leather seat, flounced her starched pink-checkered smock out over her abdomen and took Ruby in her lap. "Drive easy."

Reeve was waiting for them at the bobwire fence or rather he was so deeply involved with his pole beans there that Rad had to toot three times before he heard. The truck was on the move when Reeve came running and hoisted up inside. Lulabelle slid over against her husband to make room for him and chattered cheerfully at them both all through the ride into town. Reeve didn't say anything about Rad's tardiness. Rad didn't say anything either. The plant box kept threatening to tip down the back of their necks, the young ones were climbing all over and Rad was furious at the whole truckload, animal, vegetable, and mineral, for misconstruing what he was sure had been his good intentions from the start. Couldn't they understand that having made up his mind to this he was going to go through with it, come what may?

"First stop," Reeve said to Lulabelle as they swung from the River Road into the highway leading into the center of town, "is the fire marshal's office. Have to get a permit."

Rad drove straight past the hose house of the volunteer fire department where the marshal was generally to be found.

"Stop," Lulabelle jerked at Rad's elbow. "Mr. Finchley's right out front there now, I seen him—"

"Don't need no permit," Rad said to her. "I got a right to ditch my own land any way I durn well please."

"Best get a permit," Reeve said, addressing Lulabelle's dusty reflection in the windshield.

"Rad McDowell, you turn right around—"

"I wanna drinka water." Both children started bouncing up a chant. Any excuse to go trooping into the firehouse. "Daddy, I wanna drink—"

"Rad, you only going to have to turn around and go right back there after you get to the Hardward & Feed."

"You could maybe do without a permit," Reeve said, addressing the air over Lulabelle's head. But didn't add the obvious: Only it ain't you doing it.

"I'se thirsty—"

"Daddy, I wantsa drink—"

Barely slowing down for it Rad wheeled over in the middle of the road and taking a U turn headed back to the hose house.

Mr. Finchley was sitting out front, his chair tilted back, his straw hat pulled down over his eyes and a stogie in his mouth. His seersucker shirt was open half down his protruding chest over a white athletic undershirt, and his fat legs, tightly encased in black pants, stretched out before him. At their approach he pushed his hat back, revealing a large face sculptured with finesse about the tiny mouth, the flanges of the jutting nose and the ringed deep-set eyes. James Finchley was a retired real estate operator who had had a lot of tragedy in his life, which was outbalanced only by the number of tragedies he had seen befall to others. His only surviving relative was his nephew Lars, the lawyer, for whom he had the profoundest respect and affection. He shone with a jocular serenity that had survived, made peace with or become immune to loss.

"Go right on in, kids," Finchley patted their little bottoms. "Water cooler's out back."

But for all Finchley's manner, Rad's interview with him was fraught with minute obstacles, augmented to mountains in his mind. He met and surmounted each one as it arose however with a nimbleness that afforded him considerable self-gratification.

"Oh," Finchley nodded sagely at Rad's request. "Blowin' ditches. Whatever put that in your head?"

Rad was annoyed by the question. If it was Pulp & Timber or Sunset Hill or Hadley Contractors coming in here for a permit, if they ever bothered with it, no such interrogation would take place.

"County agent says it's a good idea," Rad replied reasonably enough. "I already talked with him about it. Told me himself that's what he's recommending to farmers around here."

"OK then." Finchley braced himself out of his armed canvas chair. "I suppose you know what you up to." He trotted in to his headquarters, a scarred desk wedged into a front corner of the hose house. With a single deft motion he swept together paper and carbons, rolled them into his typewriter. Pudgy fingers danced over the keys. Name. Place. Purpose. Date. He was almost down to the signature line when he remarked casually over his typing: "Of course you've handled dynamite before?"

"Well no," Rad was obliged to admit, honestly, as Finchley zipped the paper out and passed the top sheet to him to sign. With a jerk of his head he indicated Reeve standing passively the requisite three paces behind him. "He has."

"Oh." Resting his fist on his thigh Finchley arched himself up and around to regard Reeve as if he hadn't noticed him at all before. "You lettin' him," he asked Rad, "work dynamite for you?"

Again Rad was nettled. If it was Henry Warren or Marcus Hadley or Old Man Colfax in his time having a colored man do for them, whether they bothered to mention it or not, nobody would take the least exception.

"Get off them ladders." He stepped away from the desk and yelled into the cool dark recess of the hose house. "Lulabelle, get that child off the end of that ladder! This here fella," he explained very patiently to Finchley, "is an expert dynamiteer."

"Yeah? Where'd he learn?"

"Best school in the world." Rad grinned at him, with a taste inside his mouth as delicious as peach melba sundae. "Uncle Sam. He has a certificate from the U. S. Army Engineers. Built airfields all up and down the Southwest Pacific."

"Is that right? Well, what do you know? Matter of fact," Finchley poked his head past Rad, speaking to Reeve, "we have lots of fine colored boys in our volunteer fire brigade. Colored and white, they work together, just alike. Many a time they've rushed into a burning house at the risk of their life— You can sign here for him, Rad."

"He can sign for himself," Rad said. "Writes just as good as I do."

He didn't know why he said it. He didn't know where it came from. It just popped out of his mouth. And it piqued him so as soon as he said it, he could have swallowed his tongue. Whatever in the world made him go say a thing like that to James Finchley?

"Funny thing though," Finchley continued on to Reeve, covering the corner of the paper with his hand and withholding it from him, "we never let a colored boy drive the fire engine. Wonder why that is."

Rad seized the paper, signed it and insisted on paying the full fee out of his own pocket. All the while burning at the shadow that hovered behind him. Son of a gun, he's using me, he's driving me.

"Well, we got it," Reeve said when they clambered back into the truck. "That's the important thing. All that stuff about the fire engine, I could have told him a thing or two."

"Then why didn't you?" Rad snapped.

"Don't worry, I will. Or somebody will. When the right time comes."

"He's not so bad," Lulabelle defended Finchley. "He's a right nice man. Suffered a lot. Losing those three fine younguns one year after another."

"Sure he is," Reeve agreed with her. "All nice people."

4

At the Hardware & Feed, Rad sent Lulabelle on in the truck with the children to deliver her plants and do her shopping. He was feeling self-

conscious enough in the company of Reeve without trailing into the
store with a couple of kids on his tail and his wife on his neck. "Come
on," he said testily to Reeve as they crossed the pavement. "Come on,
you don't have to put on with me. You can walk alongside."

Nevertheless apprehension yawned within him like a door opening
on unused hinges. The Hardware & Feed had always been in a desultory fashion, as he well knew, a center of race-baiting. Here from time
to time in a spirit of idle fun dogs were sicced on tots, girls were lured
out back and youths were taunted until they fought or ran. At present
the white frame store was being renovated. Under scaffolding a façade
of stainless steel and plate glass was being installed. The usual hangers-
on had no room to loaf while construction was going on, but even on
the completed side where the scaffolding had been removed from the
display window they were absent as if like insects they found the new
materials inhospitable to them.

Rad entered simultaneously with Reeve through the double alumi-
num doors that replaced the old black wood-and-wire. Inside, nothing
was changed. The resinous atmosphere of paints and turpentines, creosote and cedar struck Rad as if he'd walked head-on into a wall. He was
a kid again come into town with Reeve Scott to buy a secondhand shotgun, reaping the first bitter fruit of their association.

The crowd of hangers-on was lounging about the counter and Ozzie
was presiding over it, pink-cheeked and perky as ever. Ozzie still enjoyed in the form of sly nudges the reputation he had earned in his
younger years as a cocksman and Klansman, a male who never hesitated
to throw his weight around. Nowadays however the exploits of his past
had been superseded by a prurient morality and the prudence of a pros-
perous merchant who must watch his step.

"Well Ozzie," Rad leaned one haunch familiarly up on the edge of
the counter, took his cob pipe out of his breast pocket, lit it, drew on it
and waved out his match, "I see you getting a face-lifting. Looks good
out there." He was not after all a kid in his first long pants. He was a man
who had seen a lot more of the world than Ozzie Higginson ever would.

"You think so? You like it?" Ozzie fairly twinkled at him. "It's my
son's idea. I told him it'd scare folks off, but you know how these boys
are. Want every improvement. What do you think of this?"

From the shelf behind, beside his cash register, Ozzie took out a cylinder of paper and unrolled it on the counter. An architect's elevation of
the present building extended sleekly around the corner of the block
with O. HIGGINSON & SON in neonized block letters around the
top, HOME FARM MARINE & BUILDING SUPPLIES.

"Isn't that something? We'll be handling lawn furniture, bath fixtures, tractors—you name it, we have it. Yessir." Ozzie rerolled the drawing and returned it to its pigeonhole. "It's about time Colfax County made a little progress. Things is opening up all around. Hear your cousin Henry is starting up his freezer plant at Sunset this week. Marc Hadley is talking about putting up a real modern deluxe motel on that property he has up the highway. And if the county blacktops some of these country roads . . . And look here, boy, looka what I got in this morning's mail." Ozzie turned to a long envelope resting over the keys of his cash register and jiggled the letter out. His eyes slid zestfully back and forth on guard against eavesdroppers, and his voice slurped confidentially down out of the corner of his mouth. "You know Dan Garner, he keeps me in touch. What do you think of that?"

The letter from the congressman was a reply to a complaint of Ozzie's concerning his last income tax rebate. In the course of assuring Ozzie that he would investigate the matter, Garner had the pleasure of informing him of the appropriation he had just had passed for surveying the Ocachee Basin. Rad returned the letter to Ozzie, duly impressed.

"Yessir," Ozzie said, "everything's improving, everything's developing. What do you think that farm of yours is worth now?"

"Well," Rad pursed his mouth, figuring, "I turned down an offer"—he hesitated, the figure was so much higher than the going price—"of fifty dollars an acre."

"*Pvvvff,*" Ozzie sprayed out a raspberry. "Hold onto it, boy, you hold onto it. Ten years from now you'll be turning down six hundred an acre. There's a future ahead of us. We're boomin'. What can I do you for?"

"Well sir," Rad said expansively, "tell you the truth, we're improvin' too. Me and Reeve here's got a little problem we'd like your assistance on. You know his place adjoins mine between the road and the river and the two of us have a common condition we're out to lick. Go ahead, Reeve. You explain it to him."

Reeve explained. Ozzie listened. "Black powder or cartridges?" Ozzie directed his question to Rad.

"Black powder or cartridges?" Rad threw the question back at Reeve.

"Regular farm-use eight-inch cartridges," Reeve said to Ozzie.

"We-ell," Ozzie pulled thoughtfully at his chin, "seems to me we're all out of forty percent. Will fifty do you all right?" he asked Rad.

It was a perfectly natural question. Ozzie was perfectly straight-faced. But the game had begun, and in some obscure way that Rad couldn't fathom he was being drawn into it against the side he meant to be on. The audience—hangers-on, a clerk across the store, a woman customer—pricked up to a signal as subtle as a drift of air. Ozzie had a knack for ferreting out and extracting the maximum humor from such situations. People were always returning from the Hardware & Feed with stories of what had happened there. It was as good as a stage show.

"Will fifty percent do?" Rad shuttled the question over to Reeve.

A snicker broke out. What is this, the Gold Dust Twins? The loungers rallied about and encircled them. The woman customer crossed the floor, taking the opportunity of paying at the cash register to peep in over their shoulders. Rad was boiling. The details of the purchase should have been worked out on the way here, but every time Reeve had made the slightest attempt to coach him he'd been too proud to listen. But he was less embarrassed by his ignorance now than he was by quite another aspect of his entrapment. If it was Cousin Henry in here now or Marcus Hadley or Benson Reece from down the bank boasting up what a smart nigger they had and showing him off, nobody would make anything of it. That would be all right. But since it was he, Rad McDowell, and Reeve wasn't his nigger-boy . . . In Rad's imagination they all guessed what was going on between the two of them, recognized and condemned it. Thin-skinned as he was and incapable of duplicity, he felt himself transparent as glass before them, all his fine-skeined nerves and blood vessels, his convoluted tubes and organs exposed to their derisive eyes.

Only now he was not a child to be tossed about on the laughter of adults. They were all his friends and equals here. He was acquainted with every one of them.

"Say Richard-Gene." Shifting his cap back, he craned around to one of the circle. "I didn't see you before. How's the fishing been up your way lately? Catch anything 'sides pure branch water?"

He slipped his haunch from the counter and taking Richard-Gene by the arm hauled him off to the other end of the counter, the others following with an anticipatory chuckle. Richard-Gene as one of The Terrible Jeems Brothers brewed a pretty fair catch of branch water. "Go ahead," Rad shouted back to Reeve, "tell the man. You the one's got it all figured out."

"Why yes, Mr. Higginson," Reeve said to Ozzie. "Fifty percent straight will be just fine."

But Ozzie was not to be so easily outfoxed. He moved up the counter after Rad, the zestful gleam of his eye waxing joyous. Reaching across the counter he tapped Rad's chest with a flirtatious intimacy. "You ain't said yet how much?"

"Why don't you ask him?"

"Ya-ah yuk yuk yuk . . ." It was one of those reasonless inexplicable donkey-brays of laughter with which the store had so often resounded. Only this time it was on Ozzie instead of by him.

Ozzie's cheeks were not after all the solid pink of youth, but mottled with red patches. His ashen hand was visibly trembling as it withdrew from Rad. He turned his attention to counting out the change from his cash register for the woman customer. "Go ahead," she laughed in Ozzie's face. "You heard the man. Ask him."

"Ken-nee!"

Crisply Ozzie summoned his clerk and dispatched him with Reeve to the storage house out back to fetch his goods. Graciously he invited Rad down beyond the foot of the counter to an archway freshly carpentered through the side wall to the new annex of the store. It was being readied under the supervision of his son for a Grand Opening on Saturday. "Take a look in there. Get a preview."

Rad looked about, nodded and whistled. It was all so light, so clean, so resplendent. Pine paneling and green tile flooring waxed till they shimmered under the palely shining fluorescent tubes. Enamel, chrome, formica. Display of siding and roofing being arranged by a couple of salesmen against a background of white cottage anchored like a ship upon waves of summer farmland.

"Maybe you'd like to order something?" Ozzie suggested smoothly. "Fix your house up?"

"Well, not right now," Rad answered what he considered to be a dig with a dig of his own. "But might could be after my electric line comes through next fall or so, who knows? I'm thinking about a water pump."

"That's right." Ozzie was suddenly all business again. "You a veteran, aren't you? You could get a home improvement loan. If you'd like to go through my catalogue . . ."

"Say Ozzie—" Kenny, the clerk, back in the store, frantically beckoned to him. "That is the craziest nigger, won't take what I give him."

Reeve was in trouble again. Rad accompanied Ozzie out the back door through the yard to the storage building standing isolated in a vacant lot. The hangers-on, Ozzie's son, and a salesman flocked after them. In the tall weeds outside the cinderblock building Reeve was examining a carton.

"This here's a couple years old," he said to Rad, "and it's been soaked through once, you can see by the cardboard."

"You can take it," Ozzie said. "Or leave it. That's it."

Rad's throat tightened up. A weight descended on the back of his neck. Trouble. Nothing but trouble. You mess with a nigger, you take on their trouble. Glancing neither to right nor left he marched into the storage house.

Ozzie followed him in. "That stuff's so well packed no water can get at it. I wouldn't let no rain water—"

"Reeve, which ones you want?"

Reeve came in, chose three fifty-pound cartons from the wall opposite the window. "If you'd just tie this up, please?" Rad said to Kenny. Kenny tied and Reeve took it.

"And caps," Rad said. "We'll be needing caps."

Reeve paused down the yard. "Not this trip," he hollered back to Rad, reminding him. "We'll be back for them."

It was the last straw for Rad. He had protected the man, talked up for him, saved him from being run out of here or worse. Now Reeve was issuing the orders.

"We takin' one trip in that truck," he said with slow emphasis, making sure that everyone present heard and understood whatever it was that had to be understood. "And that's all. I ain't takin' no two trips. Now how 'bout them caps?"

They all returned to the store in a body. Electric caps, wiring and a blasting box were delivered to the counter by the colored sweeper. With maddening deliberation Reeve unpacked and went over each item. Rad watched him in a frenzy of impatience, every nerve screaming: For God sake, let's get outa here! They were all hanging over Reeve, studying his every move. He turned back a defective cap. Asked to have the batteries tested.

At last he was finished. In haste Rad began helping him assemble their purchases. "Let him carry it," Ozzie sharply admonished Rad. Reeve was loading up with the cartridges. Rad took the blasting box.

"I said"—Ozzie, crimson-faced with near hysteria, shrieked at Rad—"let him carry it!"

Rad continued with the blasting box as far as the door and passed it out to Reeve. Then he returned to the counter and ordered from Ozzie a bag of four–twelve–four that he didn't even need. Ozzie totted up the not inconsiderable amount owed him. His reddened ears faded gradually back to normal.

"You investin' quite a bit in this place," Rad observed with solicitude as he unzipped his wallet and counted out the bills.

"Costing me a mint. But I don't mind telling you," Ozzie, restored to good humor by the cheerful jangle of his cash register, confided, "I did pretty well during the war. Course it's not all my money."

"But you expect to get it back?"

"Well that all depends. All depends on young fellas like you. When you get ready for that water pump now, don't forget—"

"Would you believe it," Rad said and zipped his wallet back all the way around, "but that nigger out there owns just as much acreage as I do? And has just as much cash to his name right now as I have? And maybe more, a hell of a lot more?"

It was perhaps a form of self-justification. He never intended to say it. He never intended to place Reeve in so favorable a light. But the temptation was too irresistible. The expression on Ozzie's face, and on Ozzie's son even more than Ozzie . . .

Rad shouldered his bag of fertilizer and waved his cap at Richard-Gene. "See y' fellas." And smiling walked out to the sidewalk where Reeve with the packages stacked up by him was waiting for Lulabelle to arrive with the truck. He was feeling ebulliently warm and generous toward Reeve. "Well, we handled that right smart," he was about to say.

Only Reeve was not alone. He was chatting with the sweeper from the store and another Negro and, if Rad was not mistaken, they were making fun of Ozzie, mimicking his self-importance. That old fag white man . . . They fell back immediately at sight of Rad. He was the outsider, the intruder.

"What's my share?" Reeve inquired of him with a spark of what Rad conceived to be unmitigated arrogance.

"What do you mean," he hedged, "your share?"

"My share of the ante. Didn't we agree we'd share—"

"That's all right, it's all right," Rad said, "forget it. After all, you contributing the labor."

Reeve took his wallet out, a replica of Rad's, one of those whip-stitched calf jobs sold in PXs across the country, and unzipped it. Right there in the street he insisted on giving him fifteen dollars as his equity in the equipment. "Keep it, keep it," Rad attempted to shut him off, "you don't have to right now—" But the thought of his outlay in the store must have outweighed his defensiveness, for he didn't quite manage to prevent Reeve from pushing the money into his breast pocket.

"Just so," Reeve said, "there won't be no misunderstanding."

Eyes as dark as well water met lightning-blue with the impact of an exchange of blows.

The money did something. Rad puzzled over it for weeks afterward. The money made a difference. There's something about money between people . . . Later, much later Reeve was to tell him, confessing to a similar puzzlement: "I don't know what made me do it. Felt I was being a damn fool for a gesture. Always figured anything you get freeby from the white folks is only back interest on an unpaid debt. But you and me—we grew up, share and share alike. There's something about money . . ." That money was an active ingredient.

At the moment however Rad was unhappy and sick with disgust over it. He saw himself degraded by it. In the eyes of his own self-pride. In the glint in Reeve's eyes. In the laughing eyes of the sweeper. Eyes in the store back of him. In Oglethorpe Square all around him . . . *I ought to take and shove it between his teeth!* Reeve had manipulated and maneuvered him up to this point. He was putting him through the meat chopper.

They teetered on the curb between two glossy palms planted in foot-square plots in the pavement, Rad sullen and Reeve resentful, waiting for Lulabelle. "You think it was any picnic for me in there," Rad growled, "frontin' for you?"

"You think I enjoyed it," Reeve grunted back, "any more'n you did?"

"You talk so fly to me, why don't you talk like that to Ozzie and all of them?"

"Look Rad, I have to accommodate enough around here. Do I have to accommodate to you too?"

"Where in creation is that woman! Gabbing away somewhere . . ."

The longer he stood with Reeve and their load on the edge of the pavement, the more exposed he felt in the public eye. Everybody was staring at them. Everybody knew. Normally he would have crossed the street to the green in the middle of Oglethorpe Square and settled down on a park bench to chew the fat with the other benchwarmers until his wife's return. But this refuge was denied him now. He couldn't go sit and leave Reeve standing. He just couldn't do it and be comfortable about it.

Side-glancing he noticed the sheen of sweat on Reeve's face. His own face was stinging with sweat. It occurred to him only then that Reeve had undergone in the store a stress that matched or outmatched his own. That he had manifested a nerve equal to or exceeding his own. Changing the cartons in the powderhouse, then taking all that time over the batteries . . . Why couldn't they have gone into Ozzie's for the stuff and bought it like any two people would? Why did they have to go through all that rigmarole? Why were they standing here so estranged, he under his palm tree and Reeve under his?

Rad plucked at the boots of the palm trunk, bruising his fingers on the armored sheath. Feeling the bruise to his soul, like his dog Boysie with a spur thorn in his paw looking up at him with wounded eyes, black-jelled, begging, *take it out!* In the center of the Square the Oglethorpe-Tomochichi monument towered up into the noonday blaze, the bronze stained by a fusion of color, green of trees below and blue of sky above. They had climbed that monument before the eyes of the whole town. *Come on, you kids, come on down outa there!* But still they kept climbing. Till they reached the tiptop and scratched their initials in the verdigris bonnets, Scottish general's and Indian chief's. Making their mark, that they'd been there. Initials gouged out in blood on the walls of a Bavarian concentration camp on the road to extermination. How did a thing like that ever happen? Howcome? Why did it have to be?

Why can't we just be human? Why?

"Now look, Rad," Reeve said to him in a softened voice, "this is the stupidest thing in the world. They give you a hard time in there and you took it and dished it back and I appreciate that. But I'm not going to let you carry these explosives all together in one and the same trip, with your wife in the truck and those little children and you in the mood you're in."

"I ain't comin' back here!" Even while he said it Rad knew he was in the wrong, and because he was in the wrong he had to say it.

"All right then. I'm taking these caps down to Fruit Street, find one of my buddies there to ride me back."

"Well go then, go! Nobody's holding you."

Reeve gathered up the smaller boxes and strode off across the Square, leaving Rad with the cartons of cartridges and his bag of fertilizer. If Reeve had acted humble or pathetic, Rad would have felt more kindly toward him. But he would have liked him a lot less.

He was sorry as soon as Reeve left him. He stood fidgeting by himself, all prickled up with himself like the palm tree, feeling increasingly conspicuous in his dirt-streaked field clothes. He kept stepping off the curb to look for Lulabelle. Where in thunder is that woman? Soon as she gets together with another woman . . . Under the heat of the sun a urinous reek was beginning to issue from the fertilizer. His hair needed cutting. If he was to attend Rose's burial tomorrow . . . The old men basking on the park benches in the green all had witnessed his parting with Reeve. If he was to go over there now, he'd have to joke with them about it . . . He rubbed at the peak of hair growing deep into the sweat-soaked sunburnt hotness of the back of his neck. How, how, how could he have spoken so low-down mean to a person who'd just lost his mother?

Hauling sack and cartons, Rad went into Ed's barbershop and so walked into a bit of badinage that he believed was being staged for the sole purpose of raking him over the coals. The barbershop was filled with town dignitaries who inched away from him in distaste. And he hadn't sat two minutes when they all started in on the nigger problem. The word about him and Reeve must have traveled from Ozzie's to Ed's, because all the time he was in the barbershop they didn't let the subject go, needling him with it. He took as much of it as he could without answering back. They were on the nigger vote when he climbed into the chair, and out of some chemistry seething up inside him, at the peak of the argument he had to blow off. Had to say something he never thought of before or would have said if he had thought of it.

"That's Hitler talk!"

Had to say it out of an extreme of self-defense for his own conduct to, of all people, none other than Judge Purcell for whom he had voted every election he ever voted in ever since he was old enough to vote.

When he came out of the barbershop, Lulabelle was waiting with the kids outside the truck in front of the Hardware & Feed. "Where you been?" she wanted to know. "We been out here in the hot sun . . ."

"Where the hell were you?"

She had transplanted some of the cuttings for Mrs. Hawley and you know her when she gets talking, and Timmy had fallen on a rusty rake —Timmy displayed his bandaged arm like a badge of honor—and she had to shop for her groceries and the kids got hungry—their mouths were rimmed with soda pop and cookie crumbs—and she had sold the market an order for ten guinea hens to be delivered on Saturday. She was overheated, overtired and flushed the same scalding pink as her smock.

"Didn't take me long a-tall," she said. "Where's Reeve?"

"Get in the truck."

"But where's Reeve? You had a fight! You been spoiling for a fight ever since yesterday! What is the matter with you, Rad McDowell? The minute I turn my back—"

As always he reacted badly to criticism, especially when it seemed to him undeserved. Almost, before the illuminated new display window of the hardware store, in the public square, he had a row with her that might have rung the police down on them. Because of Reeve. Still Reeve. Nothing but Reeve.

"Get up in that truck!"

"Don't you yell at me—"

"Get on up there!"

He himself took the driver's seat. The back of it was crowded with plants again. Mrs. Hawley's donation. Disdaining his helping hand, Lulabelle hauled herself up into the cab after the children, plunked herself down beside him. In a steam of bodily heat she untied the pink ribbon from around her head, shook her hair loose and retied it severely in a bunch in back. Her mouth clamped upward in a bitter arch.

"But that's not the way home," she was forced to cry out as he circled

Oglethorpe Square, heading north on the highway. "Where you going now?"

Rad plunged down on the gas until he passed the Zion Church and took a left turn on the Fallona Road. He had made a damn fool of himself today all over town, driving in with Reeve right up front with his family, getting into a fuss with the fire marshal and his friends at Ozzie's. With the Judge in the barbershop . . .

"There's a couple of farms up the road here a piece," he said to Lulabelle, "I'd like to take a look at. Been for sale a long time."

"But why, why just now—"

"It's a bottomless swamp. You get started with a nigger, it's a bottomless swamp. Now I like Reeve. I can't think of anyone in this world outside my own family that I think more of than I do Reeve. But he's in a different position from me. His problems are his'n. And mine are mine. I got enough on me as 'tis. Some ways he's better off'n I am. Do you know he gets sixty-five bucks a month every month he goes to that GI school of his and that goes on for four years, year round? While we . . .

"Sometimes, Lu, I don't know what the hell I'm doing. I don't know which way to turn."

She said no more.

The first farm they stopped at the land was high and dry enough, situated on one of several ridges that striated the county. But the soil was sandy and the blades of corn almost as desiccated as the plaintive old man who showed them. Rad scooped up a handful of dirt, sifted it through his fingers, and fled. The second farm was off on a side road deep in the woods, behind a stand of slash pine being bucketed for turpentine. The fields which had lain fallow for many a season would be fine if one had life enough and back enough to clear them. Lulabelle refused even to get out of the truck to look at the house here. The REA would not be through to this district till Lord knows when, and she couldn't wait that long. She consented begrudgingly to drive on to one more place. Fortunately the house attracted her at once, at least from the exterior: small but painted yellow and white, with a tidy peaked porch in front. While Rad tramped around to the rear, she spent her time inside with the housewife. They returned to the truck together without comment, and Rad wheeled around in the direction of home.

He was defeated. With a pregnant wife and a couple of wildly active kids and a load of dynamite in the van, he had driven all over in a crazy hegira. That was the measure of his desperation. And had accomplished nothing thereby. He was snared in a cocoon spun of his own living days. If there were anything better for him outside it, he would fly there. But there wasn't.

When he steered down the familiar track once more, he was sure of it. The chinaberry tree spread its umbrellaed boughs over his roof—his mother used to pierce the shiny seeds out of the pods, late autumn, and string beads of them. In back, over the well, stood the three giant persimmons.

"Why that last place didn't have a good-size tree around it," he said. "I never could stay in a house without a tree nearby it, no matter how painted up she is."

"Why that little old house," Lulabelle said, "with all the siding on it, it ain't half as good as the one we got. Leaks like a sieve every time it rains. There's a hole chopped in the kitchen floor just to let the water out."

"This as good a piece of land as there is in this county. Ten years from now, Ozzie Higginson says, it'll be worth six hundred an acre."

"Yeah? How much he offer you?" But smiling, she accepted it as a vindication of what she'd always claimed. You're not going to find anything better than this.

"Soon as the REA comes through I'll get an electric pump down at Ozzie's, run a pipe from the well into the kitchen—"

Hungry, thirsty, exhausted with exasperations, they all spilled out of the truck. "Someday, someday, Lu, we'll build us a brick house here."

After they had eaten, Lulabelle baked up a batch of wild strawberry pies and carried one up to Reeve's for his folks who were visiting. Rad went back to work on the land he knew so well he could find his way anywhere around it blindfold at midnight.

5

That day and the next Rad tried several times to see Reeve in order to ease the harshness of their parting. But when he strolled up to the cabin Tuesday before supper, there was so much company there all talking at once that he didn't even attempt to make his presence known. Later, after supper, the cars were gone from the clearing and the house was dark. He comforted himself with the thought that he would catch up with Reeve and speak to him before the funeral in the morning. At his first break then in his hoeing next morning, he took the path from their cornfields through the woodlot to Reeve's. On the way he was diverted by something that distressed him so much he never completed his journey.

He was walking through the misty green stillness of the woods, as still at this hour as if all the birds were napping after the activity of their dawn chorale and their search for breakfast. Some distance ahead of him a crackling broke out that sounded startlingly like a tussle. He continued on past the back of Reeve's house to investigate. Nearby the roadside he came on his two older boys, Charles and Wyatt, who should have left on the school bus long before. They were rolling on the ground, locked together in a vise of blood-thudding ferocity, panting with wordless fury, bashing each other's head down into the dirt.

He yanked them up, wrenched them apart and held them. Blotched with crimson rage and clods of dirt, they strained at his grasp, battering out with fists and feet, a couple of marionettes wound up to a pitch that would be satisfied with nothing less than mutual annihilation.

"Now what is this? What's this all about? Why ain't you in school now?"

Charles rarely fought with the younger children. He scolded them, bossed them, assumed sometimes too much authority, along with his responsibility, toward them, but it was beneath the dignity of his paternal role to engage in combat with them. He would sometimes hold Wyatt off, stiff-armed, laughing at him, while Wyatt whipped himself up into a passion, but he wouldn't get into a fist fight with him. Wyatt, for his part, was more likely to scrap with Timmy or Ruby than with Charles. Wyatt was too unaggressive, too reticent, too inarticulate even, except with his animals, to put up any serious opposition to Charles' lead. Besides, because of their very isolation on the farm they were especially close companions.

Yet here they were about to claw, gouge, strangle, bang, destroy one another with a blow. It took Rad some time to get to the bottom of it.

"He started it!" Charles, glowering at Wyatt, finally gained sufficient control over himself to assert.

"His fault," Wyatt, shaking with the dying shudders of repressed sobs, managed to mutter back from under a wrist trailing a mixture of tears, snot, and grime across his mouth.

Rad had to step between to keep them from flying at each other hammer and tongs all over again. "Why didn't you take the bus?" he demanded. "Look at you, look at your shirts, and your mamma feeling so low this morning. Shame on you, Charles. I'm surprised and disgusted—"

It was the wrong language to use toward Charles. In the months since his return Rad had discovered to his chagrin that the boy had played the daddy too long during his absence to be relegated back to childhood. He could not rebuke Charles directly. He could not issue a direct order to him. Only when he sat down and talked with him as if he were another adult would Charles respond; and respond then with an openness, an eagerness, a sparkle so clean and clear as to make a father's heart soar. But he could not rebuke him, the boy would only turn on his heel and walk off. As he did now.

"Charles, you come back here!" Rad roared after him. "Charles, when I speak to you—"

He had to charge down the road after him and bodily haul him back. It was the wrong way to accomplish anything with Charles. Force never brought forth the desired result. Rather, the contrary.

"Now tell me!"

Charles stood obdurate, his fair face working, his bright eyes fixed on Wyatt in warning. Wyatt dodged back as if about to be jumped again. But neither of them would answer.

"Were you late again? Did you miss the bus? One of you, tell me!"

No, they didn't miss it. Little by little, from one inadvertent hint to the next, Rad elicited the story. They had been waiting for Cousin Henry. In the past few weeks every other day or so Henry had been passing by here in his jeep just before the school bus was due to arrive and picking the boys up for the ride in to town. This morning when Henry failed to appear, Charles had persuaded Wyatt to hide from the bus and let it depart without them. When Henry still failed to appear, as the minutes slid on and on Wyatt became more and more apprehensive over their predicament. As nearly as Rad could reconstruct the incident—kids are so intricate—Charles then tried to induce Wyatt to hike up to Sunset with him and maybe catch a ride there. But Wyatt had had enough of providing Charles with company in dubious pursuits. He refused to budge. And Charles couldn't leave him alone there by the roadside. Growing panic-stricken himself, he resorted to appeals, blandishments, threats—nothing would move Wyatt. Then quite suddenly Wyatt had grabbed up a branch from the ground and switched it with all his might at Charles. And the fight was on.

"Henry lets him drive—" Wyatt pointed at Charles from behind Rad. "That's why—"

"And what's wrong with that?" Charles dived after Wyatt.

"Now wait a minute! Wait . . . a . . . minute," Rad shook Charles back. "If there's nothing wrong with it, son," he said to him more in sorrow than in anger, "why you been keeping it from me? You pass up your bus, you miss school, you in a fight with your brother like to kill each other over it, you offend me—"

With a sniff and a shrug, Charles pulled away from him. Rad was bewildered by the boy's behavior. Although he had never expressly for-

bidden him to have anything to do with Henry, his instinct should
have told him. He should have understood. It went back to that afternoon when he drove off with Henry to Sunset and, Rad remembered,
he had slammed the car door on him, shouted at him to go and expected him not to. Then Henry had taken him home with him first,
bathed him up and bought him an outfit of clothing. And when
Charles came back to his own home again, the clothes were tied up in
a bundle to be sent back, no thank you Cousin Henry. From that time
alone when he was told never to accept anything from anybody without
his parents' consent, Charles should have perceived. To go riding now
with Henry after all that, it was an act of disloyalty to his own.

"Promise me you won't do it again."

Silently, biting his lip, Charles brushed himself off. He went over to
Wyatt and brushed the bits of twigs and leafmold off him, took out
his pocket comb and whisked it through Wyatt's dark hair, scrupulously dividing the side part.

"Promise me this'll never happen."

In spite of himself, Rad's severity was tempered by a touch of sympathy for the boy. He stooped helpfully to gather up their books: if
they hurried now, he could ride them into town in time. Both boys
plunged at once to prevent him, and holding them back, under the
books Rad uncovered a new, barely smudged baseball mitt. He had
never actually held anything like it in his hand before. Puffed reddish-
brown leather richly pillowing the palm, fingers laced with leather
thongs. It was a boy's dream. A father's dream of what he gives his son.

The puffy leather glove took his heart in its hand and squeezed,
squeezed the blood out with the infinite pain of betrayal. More than
once he had seen men jump out of a tank with their legs sheared off.
This was how he felt now, viewer and victim coalescing.

Six months ago he was a hero to his sons. Now he was nothing nothing nothing.

"Which of yous is this thing?"

Wyatt nudged over into the shelter of Charles. No hints or cues
dropped from them now, both in league together against their father.

"Which of you'd he give this to? You were specifically told and you
were warned: don't take nothin' from Henry."

Their lips were buttoned. Gingery-fair and gypsy-dark, shoulder to
shoulder, neither of them yielded the slightest indication of his own or
the other's guilt.

"What's going on here anyhow? What kind of business is this building up behind my back?"

Only their eyes stirred, glowing upon him with the relentless hostility of fear. In icy calm Rad took the field knife from his belt and slit through the leather bindings between the fingers. He was cutting through his own heartstrings, through the ties that bind . . .

"Daddy!"

Charles threw his weight upon him, hanging to him with a howl of agony that cried out of his own heart. "That cost fifteen dollars, Daddy, don't! Don't don't!"

He flung Charles back off his arm more savagely than he meant to. It was an awful, terrible and brutal thing to do, but he slipped his knife inside the proud-puffed palm and slashed, and it wasn't easy to slash through, slashed through the suèded reverse calf and ruddily gleaming grained surface. Slashed and slashed.

They'd never forget this and maybe never forgive him. But they got to learn he told himself, slashing. They got to learn, they got to learn.

He pitched the glove, a piece of trash, out into the brush.

"Now come back with me to the house and change into clean clothes, I'll ride you to school just as soon's I can."

He marched the boys back to the house and entered with them, all palely stricken and a-tremble. Lulabelle who had overexerted herself yesterday was lying belly down athwart the boys' tumbled bed, where she had sunk to rest before she could begin to make it up. "What is it? You ain't sick, is you?" She sprang up, not so tired she couldn't plumb out of them what the trouble was.

"What's happen . . . look at you . . . you went outa here peaceable . . ."

She wrung the broken tale out of Wyatt. "You took and tore up fifteen dollars?" she said incredulously to Rad. "You took and done that to something didn't even belong to you? Belong to him—" She tried to put her arm around Charles but averting his face he twisted away from her. "You done that?"

"He wouldn't promise!" Rad railed back at her, the more violently because he was beginning himself to wonder how he had come to do it, how he could survive it or ever straighten himself out with the boy. "He refused to promise he wouldn't . . . What's Henry up to anyhow? Ask yourself that. Sneaking around here, playing up to my kid, luring and enticing him, making a nothing outa me! What else is going on that I don't know about? Come on, Charles, what else you holding out from me?"

"You, both of you! Charles, tell him you won't . . . Rad, tell him you sorry."

Charles turned his back, his shoulder blades braced to points of resistance through the thin white of his polo shirt. He's stronger than I am, Rad thought with amazement. Swear to God I ought to break his back, I ought to . . .

He suffered a passing suspicion that if he were very gently to touch that back now, it would cave in. Or would it shake away from him again? He didn't dare chance it.

Still filled with anger and a regret too large for him to cope with, Rad took his Sunday suit out of the curtained cupboard in his bedroom while the boys changed into clean shirts and jeans. The wire hanger had imprinted a crinkled crease across his grey twill pants which he vainly tried to smooth out. He had had it in mind to attend Rose's funeral this morning if he possibly could; he'd had his haircut in the barbershop yesterday for that purpose. Now that he had no time left in which to see Reeve before the funeral and had to drive the boys in to school anyhow, he decided that he might as well stop at the Zion Church before coming back.

Lulabelle didn't feel up to going with him. In fact, she couldn't see the necessity for his going either. She had baked that pie up for the Scotts yesterday and carried it over there and now her ankles were swelled on account of it. Last Saturday evening Rad had ridden into town to notify Reeve's folks for him. That was as much as they could be expected to do. "We done paid our respects."

"But she was good to me, Lu. When I was a youngun' and had just lost my ma, you don't know—"

"She was good to me too. Ain't no reason for you to be traipsin' off aways somewhere any longer'n you have to when I'm a-feelin' so peaked."

Half-decided, half-dissuaded, Rad drove the boys to the consolidated school in Arcady. They balked against entering the school so late and he had to deliver them to their classroom doors. Wyatt's teacher accepted the father's glib excuse, but in Charles' teacher a new humiliation waited.

"You stay here a minute," she said to Rad while protectively drawing Charles on inside the room. "Go on up to the blackboard, Charles. That last problem up there, I'd like you to try it."

Rad watched Charles drag slowly to the blackboard, all hunched up in himself, then take the chalk from the grooved molding and, after standing still scanning the lines, relax, open up, reach with the chalk.

"That's the trouble with you country folks," the teacher said beside him, loud enough for the whole class to hear and Charles too. "Always holding them out of school. They miss days at a time in the winter. In spring it's the hoeing and in fall it's the crop. You take them out before they ever reach high school—"

She would have none of his explanations about the bus and the last of January flood and the shoes sprouting holes.

"Now there's a right bright youngster," she went on upbraiding him, brandishing her chalk under his nose. "Do you realize that with the right opportunity Charles could be anything? Anything he wants to be? But will he?"

"Abe Lincoln," Rad retorted with a flash of asperity, "was born in a log cabin. And he was a plowboy too."

And burning with insult, scorched to the soul, his soul skinned raw, quivering to the faintest current of the air, he stalked out of the school and drove on in his truck to the church. There, where he thought he'd be the only white person present, he found almost all the leading citizens of the town, or at least their ladies, stepping out of their cars and trooping to the door. Among them of course, Miss Julie; he should have realized that Julie would most certainly attend. Accompanied out of Judge Purcell's black Lincoln by a covey of ladies of a type that never failed to raise the hackles up his spine. And escorted by Cousin Henry through the crowd that parted like the Red Sea before him.

Rad was so incensed at Henry that he could not bring himself to dismount from the truck and join in an occasion of which Henry was part. He drove past the church, turned around and drove past it again. With all those people flocking in, what need was there of him? He drove on down the road. At the Hardware & Feed he stopped for a purchase that took every dollar he had in his wallet, and from there he headed straight home.

Reeve did not appear that afternoon to help cut down the two large trees that stood in the way of their ditch line. Rad kept popping back from his fields to his house. "Is he here yet, Lu? You sure you ain't seen him nowhere around?" He grew peevish with himself over it. "It's my fault. After I near-bit his head off yesterday. And then this morning didn't show up to the burial. Neighbors all these years."

"You're right," Lulabelle agreed, trying to soothe him. "You right. I don't know what got into me. Just didn't feel I could—"

"Oh, I'm not blaming you. It's me. I'm the one. If you really intend to be somewhere, you there. Must be so mad at me by now . . ."

Late in the afternoon he forced himself to track back to Reeve's place in order to offer whatever poor explanation he had. But up on the porch Reeve's brothers and sisters could give him no information as to Reeve's whereabouts. "But he was suppose to come work with me," he said. "Cut a couple of trees down. He must be around here somewhere." Blankly they shook their heads. It was only after a round of conversation that he was able to gather that Reeve would be absent the remainder of the afternoon. "But you must be expecting him back sometime. When you expectin' him?" They weren't sure, couldn't tell, had no idea.

"Why he isn't even there," Rad stormed back into his house. "Took off on some business of his own. I should have known better than to depend on a nigger. What do you bet he don't show tomorrow? After I've gone and bought the stuff, spent all this time getting ready for it—"

"But he paid his share," Lulabelle reminded him. "He's got his own money in it."

The money, the fact of the money, that was the faith that sustained him. He took his ax from the bracket and a coil of rope and went down into the wet ground below the foot of his cornfield. A brush-grown depression in the land, a vestige of the old ditching dug by slaves, marked the main direction of their course. The tupelo he was to cut down shot up from the undergrowth straight as a mast, soaring into the sunlight.

He climbed high up into the branches and lashed the trunk tight. Down on the ground again he fastened the rope around two jackpines, between which the tupelo was to fall. Then he swung his ax into the cross-grained timber of the tupelo, bit a notch into it, hacked through the notch. He never liked to cut down a tree. A tree is a living thing. But he hacked into the tough resistant fiber as he had hacked through the butter-soft glove this morning. What made me do it? How could I take and cut it up like that? The stern arm of his father, Douglas McDowell, hacking down with a strap. Take that and that and that. Because he'd planted a plot of beans for the 4-H where his old man wanted sugar and tobacco. Always after a whipping he ran away from home. Out into the woods. Over to Reeve's. Anywhere. Praying for someone to come looking for him who never did. Swore he'd never never do like that to a son of his. Now he was the daddy.

Sunlight blew like a wind through the topmost branches. The warning creak from below mounted to the groan and crack of splintering bones and to the toppling crash downward. He went on to the next tree and when he was through with the hewing he began hacking at the branches, prone upon the ground and alive with thick-lipped oval leaves. Trimming down the trunks, maybe the sawmill would give him something for them. Tupelo makes good wagon wheels. He hacked himself into insensibility.

When he returned home, supper was on the table, Timmy and Ruby were scrubbed shiny, and the two older boys had attended to all their chores. Wyatt was unusually talkative, all excited over a nest of eggs he'd discovered hidden by his old red hen. But Charles drooped over his food, still subdued. In the end, Rad had to speak to him first, sur-rendering in his weariness—he's stronger than I am.

"Pass the butter-peas, son. You, you make up for lost time this morn-ing?"

"Mm-hm. Missed a test, that's what she was so sore about. You—" Charles peeped out tentatively from under his light eyelashes. "You sure told her off."

"Never mind," Rad said loftily. "Never mind about that. She's a good teacher. Takes an interest in you. You listen to her, you'll be all right."

Through the rest of the meal Charles, kindling up to his animated self again, expatiated on how the tupelo could have been cut much easier. "Hook a bandsaw up to the battery of a tractor engine, or bet-ter still, if you got one, a generator."

Half-pleasuring in his chatter, half-piqued by it, Rad waited until the table was cleared and the dishes were washed before he took down from behind his ancestral Scripture on the shelf the purchase he had stopped for at Ozzie's. A glove laced through the fingers, pouched and puffed, ruddy with the health of prosperity.

"Gee, Daddy, gee." Pinkness mantled Charles' skin clean up behind his ears. "You didn't have to—"

"Of course it's not as good as the other. There was only one of them—"

"It sure is. I like it better." Charles punched into the palm. "Not near as stiff, I just didn't know how to say no to him after he went and ordered—"

"Then stay away from him. I want you to promise me that. Stay away from Henry. And from Sunset . . . oh yes, I know you been hanging out there every chance you get."

The guess hit home. Charles shrank as if stung, and seeing it Rad felt with a pang as deep as the ax-bit in the trunk of the tree—all this, all this growing up on me, that I have no idea of.

He never did extract the promise from the boy. Lulabelle who had been feeling unwell again after supper walked in from the yard just then and when she spotted the glove on Charles' hand she let out a shriek. "You went and spent our good money for a thing like that! You out of your mind, Rad McDowell?" For a moment he thought she was going to snatch it away and rip it to ribbons as he had done with its predecessor. "Not for him, not for him—" She flourished her fist furi-ously at Charles. "For your own pride and glory!" She thumped her fist down in a tattoo on the table. "Yourself!"

Shaken and pale, Charles stared up at them, from father to mother, mother to father. For a moment Rad thought he was going to burst into tears, throw the glove on the floor and bolt. I don't want the god-dam thing . . .

"Come on outside, son. We'll throw a few fast ones."

But it was no use. There was something about that glove from the start, it had no luck in it. He threw a few balls to Charles, then to Wyatt, then in his fatigue sank down on the steps, leaving the game to them. They tossed a while, smacking their palms, "Come on, play ball." But there was no joy in it. They were only performing for his benefit. Charles had closed up again. He was not the fine frank child of a few months before, giving off like ginger ale a fizz of exhilaration. Life had lost its simplicity for him. It had grown complex, confusing.

Rad had planned to go up to Reeve's after supper to let him know that the trees were cut down and that he was all primed for tomorrow. But he was so tired he went to bed instead, only to writhe about in a state of self-imposed and quite unnecessary uncertainty. Suppose Reeve was mad at him for acting so ornery. Suppose Reeve wouldn't be back in the morning from wherever he went today. Suppose Reeve thought that he, Rad, was mad at *him* for not helping this afternoon and there-fore stayed away. Suppose . . . He hacked at himself, hacking at branches that sprang back full-leafed as soon as he had hacked them off. Yet who can say what is necessary and what is superfluous in the gyration of emotions that magnified in the present become submicro-scopic when passed? That which costs such agitation in the chemistry of the brain, the transitory and subsequently infinitesimal impasse, who can tell how much it may contribute to the substance, development, and ultimate shape of events?

Rad's anxiety for the morrow, a desired end toward which he has-tened but which he had failed to insure through taking the most ele-mentary precaution, a few words with Reeve, intensified the importance to him of what they had planned and was the measure not only of his disappointment if it should fail to materialize but of how much he had at stake in it and how much he would eventually be willing to stake for it.

"You ain't go'n get in no kind of ruckus account of this?"

Under the naked bulb Lulabelle was undressing. Removing her blouse with her back toward him and bulkily slipping into her nightie, an old shirttail of his, before wriggling out of her jeans beneath.

"Ruckus?" he asked, knowing exactly what she meant and rallying up against it. "What kinda ruckus? First you push me into going ahead with this, and now all of a sudden you talking about a ruckus."

"Well, the way you been carryin' on today . . . Punishin' that child and rewardin' him just to get even with Henry. Runnin' off to burials and comin' back without goin' there. Workin' like a crazy man, worryin' and tormentin' yourself . . . This blowup tomorrow, won't nobody raise no ruckus over it, will they?"

"Of all the damfool notions! All I'm worried about, is it gonna be? And you already lookin' for—"

"Well, I just asked."

"Now you ask me! Now we almost on top of it, now you want to know—"

"Well I didn't think—"

"Of course you didn't think! You never think till you about to jump."

Their voices rose in a bickering that shattered through the walls into the children's room. "Woman, hold your tongue! There's a time to shut up!" "Don't you shut me . . ."

Yet Rad knew full well—he understood more than he wished to—that by throwing everything together in the same pot and sniffing at it, she might have guessed better than he the source of his trepidations, just as she might have guessed, without graphically imagining it, what would transpire at the funeral scene and so had eschewed it. As with the dichotomy of love and hate, there was the dichotomy of need and fear that drove him ever closer to Reeve and kept him from him.

Yet they whirled closer, closer . . .

First thing in the morning when birdsongs spill like rain from the dark leaves of night, when cock-crows split the air like pealing bells, in the crystalline blue transparence that precedes sunup, Rad walked out on the porch and found Reeve there sitting on the top step, leaning over his knees with folded arms as if he'd been fixed there for hours. After a cup of coffee they proceeded without explanation or recrimination down to the shed where the dynamite was stored. By seven o'clock Reeve had drilled Rad sufficiently in the technique of propagation blasting for them to work together with confidence.

Only one thing about Rad bothered Reeve. He could not impress upon him very deeply the danger of the materials he was handling. "You can lose a finger or your foot just like that. Or the head off your shoulders." But with an almost boastful negligence Rad persisted in holding the eight-inch cartridge, over an inch thick, a half pound in weight, filled with a highly sensitive nitroglycerin, between his fingers like an oversized cigar.

And one thing bothered Rad about Reeve. Both on their way down to the ditching area and later he made a number of friendly overtures to him. But Reeve remained aloof from him, reserved and self-contained, holding himself to himself as if he were holding back something.

6

A wet soil, so the farmer's adage goes, is a cold soil. It cannot be sown as early in the season. In it the seed germinates more slowly. Roots spread too close to the saturated surface; under the spring rains they drown out and in the drought of late summer when the water table falls they burn out. But a drained soil, so the adage goes, breathes. Sun dries it soon after rain. The warmed air soaks through the porous earth, quickening the bacteria that convert organic matter to the use of plants. Roots sink deep into the subsurface, safe from the exposure of storm and drought. To plow, to plant, to cultivate is less laborious and less costly and can be done all at once. The yield is larger and more even at harvest.

Paradoxically, it is precisely those fertile bottomlands which, drained, would produce the most abundant crops that so often grow nothing but tribulation.

Reeve had mapped out the low ground many months ago, using the old-time drainage system as his guide. On Monday he had with Rad staked out the course they were to follow today from the Sunset boundary, past the foot of Rad's cornfield, through a stretch of brush and swamp to the rice-canal outlet, calculating the level to which the ditch was to be blown in order to drain off the adjacent acreage, the fall of the slopes, the maintenance of uniform direction and bottom. They had driven the center-line stakes, sighting them by eye, checking on each other, as straight they hoped as a surveyor's level would make it. Now on Thursday they skirted Rad's cornfield, still splotched here and there with sky-tinted puddles in which green-pennanted stalks had foundered like sinking ships, through the willow-choked silt-filled groove below it to the proximity of the Sunset fence. Here Reeve fired off a few test shots. The spacing, size, and depth of the load were determined. Rad bored the holes in the ground one after another with an old crowbar. Reeve loaded the holes with cartridges and tamped them down with the detached wooden handle of an old shovel. They retreated the length of a half acre away with the old-type blasting machine they had bought at a bargain. After Reeve had attached the lead wires, Rad placed it firmly between his legs, raised the rack bar as far as it would go and with all the strength of both arms plunged down, stiffening his stroke against the buildup of current in the box till he hit bottom. Instantaneously the spark traveled through the connecting wires into the red-lacquered electric blasting cap planted in the center of the row of charges and instantaneously the wave of detonation passed through the charges rooted a foot and a half apart and as much as that deep in the moist earth.

The first explosion jarred through Rad with the pure joy of release. His mind leaped up tearing from the earth in the reflex of a dive that would never leave him, but the war was over now. A trajectory initiated by a seventy-six millimeter gun trained on a flourishing farm in the Rhineland ended here in a ditch with the removal of a hundred feet of scrub, stumps, and muck in one fell swoop. The concussion, much louder than he expected, louder than anything ever heard hereabout before, rang through the marrow of his being, dissolving in its waves of sound the rigidities that had accrued within him during his months of isolation. He caught a glimpse of parallel field ditches emptying into the collection ditches and these into the channel of the rice canal and the canal into the river. Of his fields extended, row on row of bumper crop rippling like a lake in the summer breeze. The nature of this landscape, unchanged for decades, was being metamorphosed by the work of his hands multiplied a thousandfold.

He side-glanced at Reeve and good-humoredly stepped away from the machine. "All right, all right I was outa turn. Who drives the fire engine, huh?"

All along the bobwire fence back of the cornfield, Reeve's kin and a couple of his classmates had assembled, lined up like a protective cover watching over them. Lulabelle joined in later with the children. When Rad rushed up to warn the two older boys that the school bus was due, she insisted, "I told them they could stay home today. Let them watch their daddy." "Then for God sake keep them back, don't loose a one of them." But he was pleased just the same. And even more pleased when all the personnel of Sunset, field crews and after them the office staff, tumbled down to the paddock fencing. "What is it? What's going on here?" And when Cousin Henry himself appeared just as he was finishing up the loading for a blastoff and tried unsuccessfully to halt the operation, Rad's exultation knew no bounds.

"Did you see him," he kept chuckling at Reeve after Henry had vanished back over the fence. "Did you get a load of his face when I told him—"

"Yeah," Reeve said, "I seen him." He had tried several times during the morning to inform Rad of the eviction order that, wadded up, rested uneasily in his back pocket. But each time the opening had slipped away. Not yet. Later. When the right moment came. The longer he postponed it, the harder it became of course, and now in his alarm over Henry's antics and the renewal of his rancor over what was being done to him he couldn't trust himself to explain.

"Hot dog! Did he skedaddle! And when he skinned over the fence, and up atop the truck, shooting into his own help . . . Did you see that?"

"Yessir," Reeve said, measuring off by foot a modification in the distance between charges, "I most certainly did. Next time—" He licked his lips, halted. "Next time we buy a core punch for making these holes. Save a lot of trouble."

Rad gazed after Reeve's back, sun-blackened and soot-coated, with a touch of chagrin. When Reeve spoke to him so boldly in the Square the other day, speaking straight what was on his mind, it wasn't sass. It had been a compliment.

The cornfield was now far behind them. They plunged through pools of feathery dog fennel so thick they had to stop and get their bearings before they could locate their range-stakes; ducked through curtains of large-leafed kudzu, honeysuckle, and grapevines. Rad produced a ball of string from his pocket and drawing it taut, knotting it at intervals, he marked off a series of hole sites, then punching and twirling worked his crowbar down to the notch scratched in its side. His high spirits could not be stilled. "Wild muscadine," he whipped the tangled strands out of his path. "Bitter-tasting. But cooks up a fine jelly. Wisteria. Better not take that home to my old lady or she'll want to grow it. Beargrass." He threaded through a clump sprouting out sharp as Spanish bayonet. "Made me a pretty good pair of hame-strings t'other night out of beargrass. Remember, Reeve, remember the beargrass with all them big white flowers on it in the Spanish cemetery? And when the wind blows at night and the old folks used to pass it, *whoo-ooh*, so superstitious. Ha!" He jerked back from a swarm of bees and plucked one from his neck. "Bee stings are good for you, my daddy used to say. Cures headache, rheumatiz. Always did like bees."

With a sudden warm vision of his father, that contradictory man, Rad turned and squinted at the bees that hovered shimmering over blossoms of sparkleberry, blueberry, huckleberry, dewberry. "I kept bees once. My daddy was after me to grow sugar and tobacco and I was that dead-set on growing a plot of beans . . . Hided the hell outa me and I wouldn't do it for him. Run off from home so I wouldn't have to do it. And when I fell back he promised he'd give me some bees to keep if I'd only do it and I didn't even then. And he give me the bees anyhow. Sure did enjoy them, used to take the honey off in jars and sell it."

Reeve squatting on his haunches rammed cartridges into holes that had filled with water as soon as Rad withdrew his crowbar. "Getting pretty wet around here. Maybe we better each of us load our own." Rad stuck a cylinder from the carton precariously behind his ear. "And don't drop that stuff," Reeve advised sharply. "Or use your crowbar to put it down. Just one spark—" But Rad was less occupied with the threat of a spark than he was with the stirring under a sodden log off to his right. Could be cottonmouth. Rattler . . .

"You know where this is, Reeve? You know where we are? That little creek yonder: we came down through here with Henry one time late summer, dry season, all the creeks were low and the water had gone brackish. And Henry was so thirsty when he hit that creek. And we told him: Don't drink from there. But you know Henry, he was always so much smarter than we were. He scooped up a hatful of water and tasted it and sure enough it was brackish. But never mind that, he had to drink it to the last drop. Right after he was finished he caught sight of an old dead alligator laying up on a log there half outa the creek, and *whoops!* All that water come up . . ."

"You sure that's all the way down?" Reeve craned over with his measuring handle, inspecting. "Too deep'll scatter too much loose dirt about. Too shallow we'll lose the full force. Here, use this stick to go by."

Silenced again for a while, Rad crawled after him. For a short stretch of swamp the foliage was so inextricably matted they flattened out on their bellies and slithered underneath through masses of creeper and twisting roots. Rad was suddenly conscious of the cartridges packed into his pants pocket: he had assured Reeve that he had no matches on him, but wasn't there one, just one down in the seam? The crowbar hooked in his belt dragged along under him. His belt buckle scraped. Dynamite is a gas that on release rapidly expands until it meets some form of resistance. Soil moisture carries the concussion from one stick of powder to the next. He was a human detonator, digging in, pushing down and pulling forward again into the stillness of a subterranean jungle that locked away the sky, the surrounding world and all human contact but the sole of Reeve's boot toeing in just ahead.

The land dipped into black slime. A stalk switched across his eyes. Thorns tore gashes down his torso. Something, a creature akin to himself, whisked by his arm. An odor of decaying flesh grew and grew upon him as he inched forward until like the swamp it overpowered and shut out all experience but itself alone. Ahead of him the boot soles came to a dead-stop.

"Something wrong?" Rad wriggled up alongside Reeve. Between the serpentine knees of cypress the carcass of an enormous white sow sprawled sidewise, blocking their way. The buzzards had not discovered it yet beneath the density of the greenery, but the ants and the flies had. One pink-jellied eye quivered out as if from somewhere deep inside the bloated body the heart still sent out a pulse.

Rad made a move toward it but a reluctance—the glaring eye or his own distaste?—prevented him just the sliver of a second too long from touching it. Without a flicker of expression but expressively, Reeve seized the animal by the forelegs and flung her over into the swamp. There was that in his manner that struck off between them a burning flash of interaction: the edge of scorn, concealed, to an edge of shame, equally concealed, a click of joints to the grit of teeth. Why that piss-proud bastard, Rad thought defensively, bristling at himself for his own defensiveness and bristling at Reeve the more for being the cause of it. That so slight an action, so natural and so spontaneous, should be so charged with centuries of meaning that every good feeling, every accomplishment . . .

"Now look, Reeve," he began angrily and cleared his impacted throat with a resounding rasp. All morning, all morning he'd tried so hard to reach the guy and all he got for it was a wary turn of the head, eyelids stiffened in appraisal.

"Now look, Reeve, I didn't mean for you to—" This was going to have to be thrashed out between them, faced up to and cleared out once and for all. No more of it. No more. "What I mean—" His words stumbled through a wilderness, unmarked, unchartered. "I know you a man as good as any. If all the niggers—Nigras—in this county was like you . . ."

"Right now," Reeve said, "you looking at the maddest Negro in this county."

Fused-up, flinty, they completed the series in the tall grasses of the rice canal. And working together quickly, efficiently, interdependently they primed the last charge, Reeve inserting the cap laterally through the middle of the cartridge and axially into the end, drawing tight the wire in its train; Rad splicing the leg wire from the cap with the lead wire to the blasting machine, scraping the waxed cotton insulation down to the copper filaments, intertwining them with a hard twist that could not be pulled apart nor broken. They sunk the primed charge in the center of the series in preparation for the blasting, and dragging the lead wire after them they clambered with the box up a mossy gold-sparked bank of camomile to the top of the riverside dike. But just as they were up there, Rad turned and thrashed back through sawgrass, cordgrass, rice reed, juncus to the patch of swamp. Squirming on his belly past wires and stakes he reached the ant-carpeted carcass. He took hold of the sow's hind legs and with a haul and a shove gave her another heave over. On the return trip he plucked a sprig of myrtle in passing and sniffed at it all the way back, driving the rankness out of his system. On the bright dike top Reeve was squatting before the box, about to affix the lead wire to the binding posts.

"Smell of this." Rad waved the waxy green myrtle under Reeve's nostrils and ostentatiously under his own nose again, inhaling it. "Ain't nothing prettier in this world then the smell of sweet myrtle."

Deaf and dumb, biting at his lower lip, Reeve concentrated on peeling back the waterproofed coating of his wire another inch.

"Here, use my knife, it's sharper." Rad passed his knife down to him. "Look, Reeve—"

Looking down into Reeve's upraised eyes, not sheathed now, wide open, flaming-red like his own with the smart of fumes, he made one more attempt. "I didn't make things the way they are. I'm not responsible for it. Why you blame me? I ain't like these other folks—"

"You mean you"—Reeve let out a short sharp snort—"you different, huh?"

"Well not exactly. What I mean— Yes. And no."

"So you told Henry off." Swaying back on his haunches, Reeve uttered a wry dry laugh. "You think that's the end of it. Well now, look, you look for a change—" He wiped his hands on the camomile and took from his back pocket a paper smudged and folded over many times. "Look." He spun the paper wrathfully over to Rad's feet. "Look what your cousin done me! What do you think of that?"

Rad stooped down for the paper and smoothed it out. Reeve wound the wire about his posts, completing the circuit, and standing up, plunged. Back over the trail they had traveled and the wire they had knit together, brush, swamp mud, chips of wood erupted in a cloud of darkness that rose two hundred feet into the air.

Before the sound had died away or the debris had settled, Rad with the paper doubled up in his fist was screaming, "He ain't doing this to you! It's me, it's me he's out for!"

"You?"

"Me—me!"

With a bitterness as salty in his mouth as sweat and tears, Rad pounded at the eviction paper. He was blackened and blistered and lacerated, seared to the eyeballs and scorched to the gullet. The landscape where in a brief hour of glory he had glimpsed fields rippling with blades of corn like a lake in a summer breeze narrowed down now before him to a smoldering crevasse.

"Now he's got you, he's got me, don't you see? Just like he said he would! I'm next! All my life he's been after what I had. He's that kind, whatever's mine he has to have it too. Even my kids—do you know he's been riding my boy around, buying him presents, turning him against me? Behind my back, squeezing me out—"

"Well, not yet," Reeve said. Strangely calm, he crouched back down on his heels, pulled up a daisy-head of camomile. "Squat," he patted at the spot beside him.

Rad was too shaken to sit. The ground pitched and rolled up through the shaking of his legs. "Why didn't you tell me before? Why did we have to go through all this? Buying up this stuff, blasting, tearing everything up so? At risk of life and limb—"

"Because I didn't know before we bought it. And when I did know, I wasn't sure of how you'd take it."

"I chased him off, and laughed about it, while all the time . . . Oh Jesus Christ—we went through all this, all this—"

"Camomile," Reeve said. He twirled the juicy stem, the ferny fronds whirling in a carousel swirl of spiciness. "Used to have this growing all around our chicken yard. You know Miz Hemmings down to the courthouse? You know her husband Ray when he was alive? They come down here one time to my daddy for some chickens. And she saw all this camomile. 'Mmmmm,' she takes a deep breath, 'don't that smell good! I tell you what, Hadley,' she says, 'you pick this when it's time and dry it up and I'll pay you two dollars a pound for it.' And my daddy says to her, 'I tell you what, ma'am, you come down here and pick it and dry it out and you can have it for nothing.' Her husband Ray was listening and he intervened. 'Why Hadley,' he said, 'two dollars'll buy you a bottle of whiskey, you can drink it up.' So my daddy told him, 'Mr. Hemmings, you pick it and you can drink it up.'"

"You saying?"

"My life is as precious to me as yours is to you. My home and my family mean just as much to me as yours do to you. I'm not lettin' 'em have it."

"How you gonna stop it?"

Reeve lay back in the spicy-green bed and crossed his arms up under his head. "Ever see how a turtle," he inquired of the sky, "lays her eggs? Way up over the waterline and deep in the sand?"

"Yeah?"

"My mamma saw from way back in Old Man Colfax' day what was coming up now. And she got ready for it."

Slowly Rad lowered himself down on his haunches beside Reeve, and skeptically, voraciously pieced together the bits and scraps of information Reeve fed out to him. Rose Scott had left a will and with it quitclaims bought from cousins twice removed to assure the inheritance to her children. Rad himself had no will from his father. His two brothers had died in childhood and his older sisters had married off and the half-sisters that followed him laid no claim to the farm and so logically it had descended to him. He never needed any papers to prove ownership.

He had his white skin. Not so white right now. Not white at all. He had to punch his finger down through the grime on the back of his hand for a glimmer of lightness.

"And what makes you think," he asked Reeve, "your papers'll stand up in, uh, court?" The very word intimidated him, bespeaking a sphere outside the control of ordinary logic and custom.

Reeve pulled up a wild oat and chewed reflectively on the stem. He chewed a good while before he answered. "Ever see when the little baby turtles hatch out how they all head up out of the sand and straight for the sea?"

"Uh-huh?"

"My people, they all wrought up over this. They all with me."

Rad listened incredulously and this time abhorrently. All the colored freeholders for miles around were going to converge on tomorrow's probate hearing and impress upon Judge Purcell by their numbers that though he may have pulled a lot of fast ones in the past, the saturation point had now been reached. He was being subjected to public scrutiny.

"You mean you all in some kind of—organization?" The very word shocked him as he pronounced it. It reverberated of dark and secret movements creeping up from hidden corners, exercising on every household the frenzy of massive retaliation. "You mean you all been holding—meetings—about this?"

"That's right," Reeve said. "Right out in the open like we always do." He eyed Rad hardily, measuring like a gambler the amount of faith he could safely place in him. "This last Tuesday night. In the courthouse."

"In the courthouse? Just now, this week, you held a meeting in the courthouse?"

"Biggest we had in years."

"Well—" It came out of Rad with some difficulty. "Well, I wouldn't go runnin' my mouth about it to no other white man if I was you. What I mean—" He pinched at the back of his hand till the grained texture showed. I'm me, Rad McDowell, no one else, born the near-house from here, not the yonder one. He had wanted more than a working relationship with Reeve. A neighbor. Companionship. Something personal, with its own special quality to it, you and me. Reeve himself. Not the whole gang of them.

"What I mean, I wouldn't take no walks in the woods alone if I was you."

"Sure enough?" Reeve eyed him hard again but without reservation now; amused. "Who'd walk with me?"

"Looks like I'll have to."

"Man, you worried!"

"Ain't you?"

Once more Rad shook out the eviction order. He'd known from the start that he was dealing with a black man and a black man's a target, he can be beat out, burned out, bamboozled and bombarded. The Gothic lettering danced and the typed letters paraded, all down in print, implacably accomplished. There was still some time left in which he could come to terms with Henry. This afternoon? This evening? Crawling?

He rolled the paper up and with utmost gravity biffed Reeve in the arm with it. "About them little baby turtles, let me tell you something else. When they start hittin' for the sea—"

"Uh-huh?"

"If the crabs don't get 'em, the gulls usually do. What I mean, why you so cocksure that just because you got your folks behind you, you'll win?"

"I ain't sure of nothin'. Just thought you ought to know about it, that's all. Come on." Reeve got up from the ground. "We better check them shots."

Together they retraced the ground they had covered, cautiously inspecting the spoil-piles for signs of misfire. Rad prodded through the morasses with a long-handled pole, freezing when it encountered an object—what are we doing, all on a dream?—and once Reeve reached down the length of his arm and extracted an unexploded cartridge. *What are we doing?* Better keep the kids and the calf out of here next few days . . . They went on past the cornfield. Lulabelle and the children had long ago left the bobwire fence, but Reeve's folks were still hanging on and new arrivals were joining them. Their presence no longer afforded Rad any sense of protection; they were a source, rather, of possible embarrassment to him because of the attention they might attract. A burden to him and a jeopardy. He bumped against Reeve, a glancing blow of the shoulder noticed by neither of them. Once you get started, there's no end to it. Once you're in with one of them you're in with all of them and in so deep you're committed over your head.

"I don't know," Rad said aloud.

"What don't you know?"

"I just don't know."

Back on the riverside dike, they walked along the flat-topped barrow nodding with the blue corollas of passion flowers, and from it surveyed the results of their morning's work. The first leg of their project was there all right, translated from lines plotted on the back of an envelope to a great jagged trench, faired for over five hundred feet but encrusted with masses of rubble.

"My Lord," Rad said, "we can't leave it like that. It's all banked up. I'll still have standing water in my cornfield."

"You'd have the same thing with a bulldozer. What we really need is a tractor with a dragline, that'd leave space between for run-offs. We'll have to dig them ourselves. And lay in willows to keep the sides from buckling. And put in some kind of cover crop to hold off erosion."

"But I thought we'd finished."

"No," Reeve said, "we've only just begun."

They'd have to clean it up and level it off, deepen here and widen there and fill in the other place. The parallel ditch through Reeve's land had yet to be blown and the rice canal opened up from the sluice gate to the road, and the sluice gate itself . . . Rad pointed to the rotted timbers sinking into the mud, the chains rusting away. "All that'll have to be repaired and reinforced." It was a colossal task, requiring feats of labor and ingenuity, reserves of patience and persistence that they could not even imagine at the moment.

Below them the river lapped, fluid and mysterious, striated with sunlight. At the foot of a rickety slip extending into the water, their two bateaux, squared at both ends and flat-bottomed, bobbed alongside each other. It was a long time since they had gone fishing together. Reeve twitched up a passion flower, the buds of his lips rounding in response to the pistil sticking impudently stiff-tongued out of the blue-fringed blossom. "Maypops. My mamma used to make a kind of jam out of the berries we brought her."

"Yours too?"

"Come out green. Didn't taste like nothing a-tall."

"Sure didn't. No kinda taste a-tall."

They were both kicking off their shoes as they spoke and starting down to the slip. With their pants still on, standing barefoot on the edge of the sun-hot splintery greyboard, they lifted, surged. Soared outward, dived into the water but not deep enough to stir the mud up from the bottom. Came up spluttering. And treading water, scrubbed with a sliver of lava soap from Rad's boat, passing it back and forth.

"Something else," Reeve said, "I ought to tell you."

"What?"

Panting, dogpaddling, face-washing. "We got a lawyer."

"Say! Who?" Hopefully.

"I ain't told no one, wouldn't want this to get out—"

"For God sake, what do I have to do? Don't you know yet I wouldn't—"

Reeve hesitated, reckoning the effect of disclosure against the enclosure of safety. Playing the longshot. "Can I trust you? All the way?"

"That's up to you."

"When a person delivers himself to another one's hand—"

"We already done that. When we blew the dynamite."

"Still—"

Their chests wavered in the water: curly-haired tan; brown-smooth except for a single brusque line down the cleavage and the wisp-puckered nipples. Reeve breast-stroked back.

"Carter Sillens."

"The Mayor?" In his amazement Rad stopped kicking, went down, came up coughing and gasping, wiping at his streaming eyes. "But him?" In dismay it caught up with him. "Why him? They say he's a rough one. Folks round here won't like—"

"Which folks?"

Clean-cool-skinned they swam over to the sluice gate in a crawl, faces underwater, bubbling. Their fingertips met gelatinous wood.

"Six hundred an acre, Ozzie said."

"I heard him."

"Of course it was just talk. Don't mean nothin'. But—" It had entered their veins like a vaccine, permanently injected.

They were hanging onto the sluice-gate timbers, counting the number of four-by-eights that would be needed to restore the trunk to working order when Carter Scott came running over the dike and peered down on them through the reeds.

"Reeve? Reeve, where you been? Chalmer Coombs is on his way here. Waldron sent word from the barbershop. He's been rounding up deputies—"

Crystal-dropped, their draggled pants dripping, they hiked up out of the water, scuffled into their boots.

"Take the boat, hit for the marshland—"

But Reeve ran toward his house and the crowd from the fence with him and Rad. It was coming, Rad had known all along it had to come. They had tried too hard, built too large, attempted what was not supposed to be. It was coming like Judgment Day. But still he kept running with Reeve. The thought that he could drop back never once entered his mind.

IV

TRIAL AND TESTIMONY

[*Thursday, May 8–Saturday, May 10*]

1

Chalmer Coombs was not a man to become easily excited. He was in his office adjoining the cellblock back of the courthouse, adjudicating a case in the absence of Judge Purcell, when Henry Warren telephoned from Sunset ordering him to get off his fat ass and get the hell out the River Road to arrest a nigger on charges ranging from trespass and destruction of property to riot and intention of assault to commit murder.

Chalmer knew at once what had happened, just as he knew when he went hunting by a system of rapid calculation that amounted to instinct —by the feeding habits, lay of the land, direction of the wind, margin of error in the sighting of his gun, velocity of his bullet—which way the quail would fly from the ground laurel even before the quail knew and where the deer he was tracking would head even before the deer got there. So he knew from Henry's temper exactly what Reeve Scott was up to. Oh the goddam fool, he thought, not unsympathetically, as he replaced the receiver. What'd he have to go and do a thing like that for? It was plain to him that as a result of the eviction order Reeve must have blown his top in an encounter with Henry—that is, one thing leading to another, he'd gone berserk, was running amuck and throwing dynamite around. A not unpredictable development, given all the circumstances involved. "The poor dumb bugger."

When a leading citizen of the county, the manager of a leading enterprise, surpassing shrimp and coming up behind pulp, cracked the whip, Chalmer normally would have jumped. But if he accepted literally what he heard from Henry, he would have had to call out the militia. The picture he himself conjured up was alarming enough: a nigger who doesn't cringe when threatened but chooses instead to fight back offers a problem comparable to that of a mad dog. You have to go in and get him, subdue him and possibly in the process do away with him. But even a mad dog may be somebody's favorite pup.

He was acquainted with Reeve as a hard boy to talk to but otherwise steady, well-liked and belonging to a family of standing in the colored community. Chalmer prided himself on his capacity for maintaining law and order among the colored as he did among the white by exercising on-the-spot judgments, in which the nature of the offense and of the party committing it and the details surrounding it were balanced with such nicety that no sizable portion of the population could be antagonized by his ultimate decision to arrest or exonerate. He maintained for this purpose lines of communication in both groups, sources of information and agents of influence, with one difference: his relationship with the whites was open and aboveboard, and with the colored distinctly sub rosa. True, when old Mr. Hemmings got riproaring drunk he was safely delivered to his daughter's door, and when old Uncle Steven got equally drunk he was deposited in the cooler. But the existence of double standards notwithstanding, Chalmer felt that by his willingness to treat with both groups separately he achieved a fine equilibrium of peace and quiet for which the whole county ought to be grateful to him. "Them is them and us is us," was a favorite saying of his, "and never the twain shall mix."

The incidence of crime committed by members of either race was extraordinarily low during his years of office, if one overlooked as he generally did a trickle of traffic in illicit liquor, gambling, prostitution, and occasional affrays exploding in fisticuffs or shootings in which for many reasons justice could best be served by being hushed up. When a colored fisherman shot to death another colored fisherman for the theft of his wife's affections, Chalmer called Carter Scott in for consultation; and upon Chalmer's later review of the facts before a closed session of the Grand Jury, the indictment was dismissed. When a young white woman of ill repute was bludgeoned into insensibility by her current boy friend and left to drown in a storm, Chalmer didn't bother to follow up the autopsy with an investigation, seeing no sense in subjecting the woman's family to any further shame than they'd already suffered and the man's family to the loss of their sole support. He was not always so lenient, but so long as violations of the law were conducted all-white or all-colored, he could deal with them at his discretion. The white citizenry didn't object to his methods so long as he kept the colored citizenry under control, and the colored citizenry knew very well that he was the fairest officer they could hope to have. Consequently Chalmer Coombs, though still in his early forties, counted on being the only sheriff in the history of the county to be returned to office long enough to receive a pension.

In the meantime, what he most dreaded and avoided was a situation in which members of the two groups collided. Despite the seriousness of Henry's complaint over the telephone, an emergency summons if ever there was one, despite his own monitory interpretation of it, despite the coordination of his mind and body and the swiftness of his reflexes, Chalmer did not move at once. He remained fast in his chair behind the worn table that served him as desk, bench, and pulpit. Chewing on a toothpick, giving himself time for more thorough reflection, he proceeded to dispose of the case before him. An itinerant septic tank cleaner from Iowa had been arrested several days before for "insurrection." Chalmer now reduced the charge to "disorderly conduct," imposing a fifty-dollar fine and pocketing half of it, the other half being destined for Purcell's pocket. He released the culprit with a lecture and a warning to quit the area before the hour was out.

He then telephoned for a city policeman to come from the city hall and take charge of the jail's two inmates: a colored vagrant awaiting transfer to Bryant County as a suspect in a filling station break there two months ago; and an eighteen-year-old white youth en route to Florida, now awaiting a wire of bail money from his parents. The white youth had been caught on the edge of town in the speedtrap operated by Chalmer in cooperation with Mayor Dakin, and he had compounded his guilt by trying to lie out of it. Chalmer could forgive an honest admission, but not an attempt to deceive him. That lie would cost the kid plenty. Nobody ever fooled Chalmer, not even a bobwhite quail, without paying for it.

By the time he had finished loading his gun and buckling on his holster he had a pretty good idea of what was required of him by Henry and how he would handle it. "Goddam fool," he muttered in irritation over Reeve, "why's he have to go and put me in a spot like this?" And again: "Just when I have everything running so fine, you'd think they'd appreciate it. What's he have to go and upset everything for?" His regular deputy was out somewhere on the road around the county, and he had to call him in. During the intervening half hour he sent the policeman who had arrived from the city hall over to the barbershop and around to scrounge up whomever he could find to be deputized. If the worst should come to the worst, Chalmer calculated, at least he wouldn't have to bear the responsibility alone. The blame would be dispersed. It wasn't that he cared about the reaction of the colored in this instance one way or another. It was just that an election was coming up this fall and he liked having their goodwill at such times, and there were certain other more nebulous considerations—and well, things are never as simple as they seem. It's not as simple as some people may think to go gunning for a nigger, even in the line of duty.

"What's up?" The policeman was curious to know before he left.

"You know Reeve Scott? Has his place out the River Road?"

"Auntie Rose's boy, ain't he?"

"That's right."

"He's no good."

"Why you say that?"

"He's smart enough. Too smart. Was in Ozzie Higginson's day before yesterday and everybody's talkin' . . . What's he done?"

"Never mind that. You just bring my boys in as fast as ever you can, that's all."

That was the public impression of him then, a nigger who doesn't know enough to keep his place. The scrap of information was seized upon by Chalmer, weighed for its implications and amalgamated with the totality of evidence. Nevertheless when the policeman finally brought two men in to be deputized and the regular deputy breathlessly bustled in after, Chalmer enlightened them on the reason for their mission with remarkable restraint.

"Now don't nobody get excited and hot under the collar," he instructed them, "I don't want the whole town on our tail. It's no secret Henry Warren's been out to get hold of that farm down there. Well, this boy just went off his rocker over it. Threatened Henry with a stick of dynamite."

The effect of this speech being what he had unerringly anticipated it would be, he was now ready to start.

A small crowd who had caught wind of something afoot was gathering on the back stoop of the jailhouse when Chalmer strode out with his men, tight-lipped. They rode off down Shrimp Alley, throttles wide open. When the driver swung the car into the River Road, Chalmer sitting beside him showed his first sign of perturbation. Here, keeneared, he detected a soft, peculiarly resonant thud in the distance that sounded to him like blasting. "My Lord, he's on a regular rampage. With all those folks working out there." A few moments later he glimpsed in passing the driver of a car traveling full speed in the opposite direction. "Jesus God, it's Doc Harrington! Must be somebody hurt he's carryin' in." He stopped outside the upper section of Sunset long enough to ascertain from a trucker that whatever dynamiting was going on, it was on the other side of the fence. "They blowin' them some ditches out there," the trucker explained. "Yah yah yah, we know all that," Chalmer cut him short, too much in a hurry and too convinced of his own conclusions by now to amend them. Before reaching the twin mailboxes he had Bobby, his driver, run the car into a thicket off the roadside, and from there dispatched him through the woods to reconnoiter the field. He remained in the car with the others, keeping his own counsel while they fretted aloud over the meaning of the silence that engulfed them. "Damn crickets. Singin' so loud, I can't hear a thing. You hear anything, Sheriff?" A carload of curiosity-seekers that had trailed them from town bumped to a halt behind them, followed by a second.

At last Bobby was back from his scouting expedition. He crashed out of the woods, eloquently gesturing, empty-handed.

"Ain't nothin' back there but corn. Ground's tore up something awful though, I'm tellin' you it's terrible. No hide nor hair of him anywhere. Quiet as all getout. Give me the creeps. Cracker-gal down the other place yonder claims last she saw he was skinnin' up the track—"

"You didn't tell her nothin'?"

"Oh, no. She sure enough asked, but I didn't tell her."

Must be holed up his house, Chalmer decided, if he hasn't flown the coop already.

He led his men to the mailboxes and staked them out in three directions. "Now he's armed with high explosives," he warned them, "and he's dangerous. But I don't want no fast and loose play with firearms, you understand? I'm going down to that house now, and I'm going to try to talk him into giving himself up. Of course if he don't—first sign of attack—remember, you coverin' me. And you all," he addressed the newcomers, "get back to your cars and stay there. Out of the line of fire."

All by himself Chalmer began walking down the grass-grown rutted track. Contrary to Henry's imputation he was not the least bit fat in the backside; in fact, Chalmer had not an ounce of excess weight on him. His was a spare frame, trimly clad in white shirt and black pants, his black felt hat aggressively tilted over his forehead being the only outward symbol of his authority. He bore himself, however, with the weightiness of a marshal of the Old West or a metropolitan ward boss traversing his precinct, elastic of gait and solid on his feet. His arms swung freely by his sides, thick-muscled under the short sleeves of his shirt, hirsute, elbows outthrust, the arms of a hustler accustomed to throwing together hastily whatever materials he has on hand. He was keyed up now with the excitement of his lone foray. In every blade and twig lurked the possibility of danger. His bulging blue eyes, ordinarily affable, popped about, sharp as a pointer's, at the jump of a squirrel. If Reeve had come bursting out of the brush at him brandishing an arsenal, he would half have welcomed it. He almost regretted that it was not to be so. Instead, he harbored a vivid image of Reeve stalking from window to window, the hunted prey, primed with the recklessness of pure terror. Chalmer was completely confident that he himself would come out of whatever ensured with a whole skin. Only it would tax all the skill he possessed to flush the quarry.

He was somewhat disconcerted therefore upon arriving at the clearing in the cedar grove before Reeve's house to find a number of cars parked there, including a couple of out-of-staters. He had not counted on having any outside witnesses to the struggle. Jesus God, he wondered, recalling the funeral, ain't they gone yet! How long do they keep this up? Resolutely he took the path through the cedars, deciding on a bold approach as the best one, barging in as he would into any colored house, taking for granted that his presence was sufficient to quell any act of hostility. A couple of children were perched on the porch steps, shelling a pot of peas between them. Up on the benches several men were seated, wearing black armbands.

"Why Mr. Coombs," one of them hurried down toward him, "it's good to see you. You looking fine and hearty. Come on in."

Chalmer halted halfway up the path. The man hurrying so welcomingly toward him, grey-haired and black-mustached, having the air of distinction that somehow even over faded tans and fisherman's jackboots suggested a British earl, was the last person Chalmer would have wished to meet at this moment. "Carter, what you doing here? Why ain't you out fishing?"

"Just now come in from the sound. You know how it is this time of year, Mr. Coombs. Didn't net enough shrimp to pay for the gas."

Carter Scott was an influence among the fishermen and Chalmer made a habit of calling him in for consultation on certain matters affecting the waterfront. Along about election time Chalmer always managed to drop down to the boat Carter operated with Johnny Herrera and talk about the renewal of fishing licenses, even though it was well known that he had nothing whatsoever to do with the issuance of licenses. Moreover, as Chalmer was only too well aware, Carter was half-brother to Carter Sillens of Bay City, and though Sillens' machine had not yet spread its tentacles into Colfax County—you never can tell. As tenuous as was the relationship between himself and Carter Scott, Chalmer held onto it as a tentative line to Carter Sillens, a man he would never care to have as a political enemy.

Changing his tactics, Chalmer swerved from the path, away from the periphery of the house, and beckoned Carter Scott confidentially after him. "Tell me something, Cart. Is Reeve in there?"

"Let me see." Carter reflectively drew out his pipe, rapped it against a

tree to shake the leavings out, repacked it with tobacco, tamped it down
and accepted the match Chalmer held out to him. "I believe he is. We
got so much company . . . Nothing wrong, is there, Sheriff?"

"You known damn well there is! Now you send Reeve out here to me.
Tell him I want to talk to him. Alone. And if he tries any funny business—"

"Reeve!" Carter lifted his voice from where he stood and hollered.
"Say, Reeve—Vergie, tell him there's someone out here wants to talk—"

"Why Chalmer Coombs!"

Vergilia who had appeared on the porch tripped down through the
yard and flung her arms about Chalmer's arms. She shook him with delight. "They told me you were here the other day, I was sorry to miss
you. What's the matter, whyfor you wearing all that crape on your nose?
Pick up your lip, man . . . Oh I know how you used to like to fall in
here and pass the time of day with Mamma. But she's gone . . . Come
on in, I want you to meet my daughters."

Over Chalmer's protestations, smothering the few words he was able
to get in edgewise in a shower of sociability, one instant grinning like a
dervish and the next glittering with tears for her mother and the next
reviving convivially back to her duties, Vergilia surrounded him, a whirl-
wind swooping him up, magnetizing him in her orbit. "It's Reeve you
lookin' for? You can talk to Reeve inside as well as out here. You know
how hard he took Mamma's passing, he was with her all the time right
up to the end. Now don't be so backward, no need to be shy—" Hospi-
tably she carried him in with her through the screendoor. "We got a
spread on the table . . . Look everybody, look who's here. Chalmer
Coombs!"

Vergilia had been a great flirt and a tease in her younger days, the
devil's own imp, but no one, as Chalmer recalled it, could ever catch up
with her. There was nothing in her manner now to indicate to him that
only a short while before she had been throwing herself about the yard
like a madwoman, in a fit of hysteria. Reeve was to take her car and ride
out of here to Nashville! He was to dash back to the river and row across
and run from there! He was to cut down into the swamp and hide
overnight . . . Anything, anything but stay here and be caught. "Once
they got you in the lockup, that's the end, it's the end of you!"

There had been a few moments back then of pandemonium, everyone crying and shouting and arguing at the top of their lungs in a frenzy
of feeling. To add to the confusion, Professor Thurlow rambled up
from the bobwire fence with a young white preacher in a cream serge
suit and presented him all around. "This Mr. DeLavery. Come down to
see how my class students are doing." Without any preliminaries, Mr.

DeLavery at once zeroed in on Rad and Reeve. "That's a mighty interesting thing you fellows are up to. You planning on sowing the slopes with lespedeza or kudzu? Or one of the fescues? Or millet"—he snapped his fingers—"that's the thing! Never could understand why they don't grow millet as a breakfast-food cereal in this country."

"Professor," Reeve said, "why don't you show the preacher round? And come back here to the house later, hear?"

Reeve had then ended the controversy in the yard by retiring into the house, drawing a chair up by his mother's bed and sitting down there. He wasn't going to be a fugitive from justice, tracked and traced for nothing from one state to another. Only way anyone would ever take him out of here was on his back. Then suddenly he pounded on his knee and hooted, shaking convulsively with private laughter.

"Ben, give me Mamma's Bible. Now don't ask me nothing, just give it here to me. Sis Mae, you got them chittlins cooked up on the stove yet?"

In another moment, they had all fallen in, bustling with activities. "Children, you shell these peas. Reeve, don't sit there without a shirt on, here's a clean one. Rad, you too. Fred, you get down to the Professor and tip him off." Carter and Vergilia assumed the role of official greeters.

Grudgingly—but what after all did he have to lose?—Chalmer allowed himself to be ushered by Vergilia into the house. From the doorway he glared suspiciously about the chiaroscuro of the interior. It was spotted like a leopard slinking through the jungle with sun and shade, face and form, trick and trap. Chalmer felt vaguely that the wool was being pulled over his eyes, that a snow job was being done on him, that he was being taken in—but how? They couldn't have guessed that he was about to descend on them. And even if they had, knowing that Reeve's assault on Henry, whatever form it had taken, must be followed by its logical penalty, they could not conceivably have been so crafty as to stage a scene like this.

The house was indeed full of company, more people all told in Chalmer's prompt reckoning than he had brought along with him, counting the two carloads that had trailed him from town. Above their heads, compelling his attention above all, was the deerhead over the fireplace, arching proudly out into the room, a trophy such as he had never had for display in his own front parlor. It had not been here when he visited last, a summer ago. Where'd they bag it, a twelve-point buck like that, he at once tried to guess, envious of the chase. Its throat swelled in patches of dun and white, its antlers flared back, sheathed in dull velvet and tipped with horn, and in its amber glass eyes a sunbeam glimmered. Wherever on earth, Chalmer tried simultaneously to guess, did they manage to have done for them a first-class taxidermy job like that? The deer reigned over the house, a crown imperiously assertive, affronting Chalmer with the very admiration it foisted upon him. What the hell right did they have to put up a thing like that, who give them the *right* . . .

Below the deer, leaning rakishly up against the mantel like a walking stick, was the scapegrace of Colfax County, a veteran of barroom brawls from Keesler Field to Sacramento, Hagan Power, otherwise known as High Power. His eyes, oblique as the deer's above, flicked over Chalmer, stripping him to the bone. High Power ran a few tables in the back kitchen of his farm Saturday nights, at which considerable folding-money changed hands. Chalmer not infrequently sat in on a game. On his longer hunting jaunts he always had High Power along as guide, cook, and boon companion.

"Hey Chalmer," High Power saluted him with casual familiarity, and turning back to the two older Scott brothers resumed his conversation with them. Of the two brothers, Fred the troublemaker and Ben the policeman, it was Ben who disturbed Chalmer more than he could possibly afford to admit; and it was against Ben's capability of disturbing him that he most especially steeled himself. Chalmer had often heard from his predecessor the story of how he took that nigger policeman from Chicago down a peg by informing him that he was no policeman around here. Only Chalmer was never so narrow-minded as to exclude from his estimations a fact that might in some unexpected way affect him. He was chief law-enforcement officer in these parts, and as honest, he was sure, as any in any other part of the country; as honest, certainly, as was consonant with humanity, good sense and local conditions. Yet his conduct of his office, as the presence of Ben made him most acutely aware, could not stand too close an inspection. Through Ben's eyes the national spotlight was focused upon him.

Clustered around the fireplace and the daveno couch, identities detached themselves from the common brown blur in which they dwelt in Chalmer's mind. Old Willie Bean who grew beefsteak tomatoes as big as your head and peddled them door to door, a favorite of every housewife in town. Colfax Loren, church deacon, chicken farmer, and Saturday handyman. Harold Sanderlee who regularly repaired his car for him as a courtesy, for which he billed the county. Grif Ryals, mainstay for the last twenty years of the seafood plant owned by Miss Jessie, Eustis Telfer's wife. Interspersed so they seemed all over, three–four more war veterans in odd pieces of uniform . . . And as if his calculations weren't sufficiently upset already, Chalmer discovered to his shocked astonishment that there were whites among them. Rad McDowell, the cracker-boy from down the track, draped over the radio cabinet, chewing on a drumstick. And hovering behind Carter Scott by the doorway like a vision heaved up out of the ocean-deep, greenish slouch hat and clothing of a color as dank as seaweed, wind-flayed red of face and storm-grey of eye, jut-nosed and gap-toothed, was the famous Johnny Herrera, Carter's neighbor and shrimping partner, Isabel Colfax's son and only true heir, it was sometimes hinted, to Sunset Hill, the Colfax house and all the privileges and appurtenances that pertained thereto.

In addition, altogether too many women were swarming around for the convenience of Chalmer's purpose here. In the male sphere which he inhabited, women had little place and less importance, falling according to his scale of values somewhere below a good gun, a good bottle, and a good fighting cock. Vergilia's handsome daughters eddied from man to man, flaunting their sex with flash of eye and dimple, shoulder and hip, superb in the conviction which they shared with their mother that the root of all the trouble in the South was the white woman; for if things were any different those women wouldn't stand a chance, not a chance, would they? Their skirts flounced by Chalmer, twirled at the soldier-boys. But it was not the girls that aroused in Chalmer now an importunate and most irrelevant craving. Sister Mae toted in on her fingertips a steaming platter and lowered it to the table. Many a time passing by this way and finding an excuse to stop for a chat with Auntie Rose, Chalmer had sat down to quite a repast at that table. He was hungry now.

All this Chalmer absorbed upon his entry into the house with the trigger-swiftness of impression for which he was noted. He glared about, catching them all with the whiplash of his eye in a stinging instant of suspended motion.

"What's going on here? What all these people doin' middle of the day—"

"Well, you know," Carter, ever courteous, murmured in his ear, "this lady just passed on and we all gathered together. This here's the Graves Dues Committee from the Sons & Daughters of Arcady Lodge of the Liveoak Chapter of the Golden Isles Burial—"

Ignoring him, Chalmer started across the room toward Reeve in the bed-alcove. "Then what's all this firin', shootin', explodin', and mayhem?"

"Oh, that," Carter, keeping up with him, murmured, "that's just a little land-improvement these boys are onto. And this here's a few of the young fellas from the GI farm-training course at the high school, down to observe—"

Over Chalmer's uneasy suspicion that they were all dissembling, another suspicion was growing, expanding sickeningly in waves of hungry nausea from his stomach. That the original situation had been so grossly misrepresented to him by Henry that even with all the caution he had exercised toward the charges, he was still in error. That falsification or not to begin with, he was now forced to go through the motions anyhow and to carry them to their appointed conclusion. There were his deputies outside surrounding the house waiting for him to appear with the prisoner. There were the two carloads of indignant citizens. There was Henry to be answered to. He himself was captive and victim, being catapulted forward.

But this whole line of thinking was so repugnant, Chalmer dismissed it. Except for a necessary readjustment or two in his sighting, nothing was essentially changed. He had made no mistake. Everything was turning out as he had foreseen. He was going to have to take the boy into custody. And the boy being the kind of boy he was might very likely—as Chalmer believed and most devoutly hoped not—put up resistance or make a break for it somewhere between here and the jailhouse. Only one detail, the matter of making the arrest, would be a little harder to handle than he had bargained for.

Chalmer's progress across the room was impeded. The company who should have been struck dumb and shot through with a tingle of fear flowed along with him like a body of water. Something was always getting between him and his object. High Power interposed himself with a cocky reminder: "Where you been lately, Sheriff? We missed you down to the place." The girls stumbled over his feet with hasty excuse-mes; Harold Sanderlee created a diversion around the deerhead, recalling the shoot on Campion Hummock; the radio bleated out a catchy country blues and the girls bumped back over him again, snapping their fingers and tapping their toes to a running argument with their aunts over the propriety of the music; a richly heaped dish was wafted under his nose.

Unabashedly they played up to an aspect of Chalmer's nature of which he himself was not conscious, to a trait he shared with many white people, even the most rabid racists. Chalmer liked Negroes. Not the childish monkey-jumping eye-rolling yassuh-nosuh Mandy-Rastus kind of Negro he often joked about, whose clowning he incited by the indulgence with which he regarded it. And not the humble knee-bending hymn-singing hat-in-hand ever-so-respectful and respectable colored gentleman he often extolled, and never read into. Chalmer's feeling ran much deeper than that. He liked to *be* with Negroes. It was a need and a longing with him, to be sucked into the brown blur that dwelt in his mind; to abandon himself to the speech sounds, the flesh tones, the smooth and angular movements, the kinetic harmonies, the joshing and jiving and scolding, the tales and the habits, the taste of snoot and foot, jowl and ear, the intimate texture of their living. He had to be around it, with it and into it until he rolled in it like a boy in the grass, making himself one with the earthiness of earth, until it was his. He was always straying into their bars and juke joints. He now and then pleasured himself with a girl, and none of these little yalla gals either. Blacker the berry, sweeter the juice. Mainly however he preferred to attach himself to men. Whenever he came upon a bunch of colored fishermen squatting around a fire on the riverbank on a rain-misted fall evening, roasting oysters, Chalmer always had to squat right down with them, attracted to them, having a mystic affinity with them, needing to be accepted as one of their circle, taken in.

He brusquely refused the dish Sister Mae proffered him. But the tangy scent of chitterlings traveled with him across the floor. His wife had left him early in the morning before breakfast on the pretext of going to visit her sick sister in Bay City, but actually, as Chalmer knew from the tilt of her hat and the surreptitious touch of rouge on her cheeks, to take a look-see at that wedding she hadn't been invited to. Not that she gave a damn for the Judge or the Judge's daughter or anyone else but Chalmer, of whom she was scared to death. It was the fanfare that drew her. She had to be in the swim. Chalmer could have called her bluff and stopped her departure, but then he would have been deprived of the opportunity of catching her later in a skein of prevarications. She left a skillet of fried grits on the stove for him and their three young ones, which were cold by the time they ate them. His eight-year-old daughter tried to allay the storm she sensed brewing in her father by heating up a can of beans for him. It didn't seem possible for anybody to burn canned beans but the girl succeeded in it, and the beans scorched-black, dried-out, thickened to a lump, burned in Chalmer's esophagus now. He was voraciously hungry. I'll have her head, he cussed his wife out as he blundered past endlessly intervening individuals to Reeve, I'll tear her tongue out . . .

The boy was reading his Bible. He had it open on the yellow chenille spread over his dead mother's bed and was nodding over it, oblivious to the noise around him, his lips moving with the words. Pray boy, Chalmer thought, you better pray, the fix you're in.

Nevertheless he took Reeve's shoulder and spoke more mildly to him than he otherwise might have. "Now boy, it's no use trying to hide and conceal what's happened. I've a very serious complaint against you from Mr. Warren over to Sunset. You going to have to come along with me."

"But he had nothing to do with Henry. He was never even near—"

"Now Rad," Chalmer turned slowly about and fixed Rad with a stare, "you stay out of this."

The crowd had all arrived on the spot, pushing and shoving about the bed, Carter with Johnny Herrera glowering pugnaciously over his shoulder, the girls, the brothers and High Power.

"Now stand back," Chalmer snapped at them, "and clear this space before I have to clear the house. Now go on, stand back."

They wavered back, only to surge forward the more closely as soon as he started in again on Reeve. Reeve's shoulder under Chalmer's hand—Chalmer could feel its warmth radiating through the thin T-shirt, a rock fleshed with life, smooth-hard, indestructible—had not stiffened aggressively as he expected at his touch, but went slack, sagging so that it almost slipped out of his grasp.

"Well, this book ain't go'n tell me," Reeve closed the Bible and looked up inquiringly at Chalmer, "so I reckon you'll have to. If you don't mind, Mr. Coombs, what am I suppose to have done?"

"You know good and well what you did. Now come on, because if you don't I'm going to have to make you. And I got a half-dozen men outside to help me."

"Well, Sheriff—" It was Carter Scott, and in Carter's elegantly amused eyes Chalmer read the figures of the last county primary election. Five hundred and thirty-one whites for his opponent; no colored. Two hundred and fifty-nine white for himself; and over five hundred colored.

"Some of these folks, I don't mean from around here, from out of town," Carter explained, "mightn't understand you the kind of man that always likes to do things right and proper. If you'd just state the charge—"

"All right, Carter," Chalmer after due pondering conceded generously, "there's no reason why you shouldn't know as long as you all don't give me no trouble over it. I grant you this boy may have had his provocation. But he took and shook a stick of dynamite at Mr. Henry—"

"Why, he was never even near to Henry, he never even talked—"

"Now Rad, I told you, you stay out of this. If you got anything to say on this boy's behalf, you can say it on the witness stand. An accusation has been made, I have to take him in and lock him up. If there's extenuating circumstance on his side, it'll come out at the hearing. It's not up to me."

"Why, that's all right, Sheriff." It was Ben, the fellow officer from Chicago, offering him the sympathy of his professional insight. "It's hard sometimes for folks to understand that we can't act outside our province. You got a warrant?"

Chalmer was beginning to feel pent-in. It was not a quail hunt after all. It was a fox hunt, hound dogs baying, hunters closing in. Only who was the hunter, who the fox? He didn't have a warrant. Of course he didn't have a warrant. Where would he have got a warrant? Henry had never presented himself to swear one out. And even if he had, there was no magistrate around to sign it—they were all off at that goddam wedding. Whoever bothered with a warrant?

"I don't know how you handle these things in Chicago, fella," Chalmer said to Ben, "but from what I hear it's a criminal paradise. If I was to wait on a warrant every time a law is broke—" Here his voice rose, losing its composure. "What the hell do I need with a warrant in a case like this? Here this boy goes throwing dynamite around, endangering life and property, jeopardizing all those hands over to Sunset, attacking a man with intent of assault—" He tripped over the words and readjusted them. "Assault with intent to commit murder. If that's not enough—"

He was shouting over the hubbub of protestations. "All right, you asked for it! That's what he done. Now I don't want no fracas, but if another one of you obstructs me . . . Clear the way, clear outa my way!"

In the course of his shouting at the crowd he had let go of Reeve's shoulder and instead of standing where he thought he was, by Reeve at the bedside, he was back at the table, separated from his object once more by a press of persons. In one hand he was holding a plate which he had no memory of receiving, loaded with fried chicken, a grey mound of chitterlings, coleslaw, beaten biscuit, rice, and gravy. In his other hand High Power nonchalantly placed a chipped china teacup and tipped over it a bottle from the table, his hard thin reckless face conveying to Chalmer a message of peculiar significance. High Power was his key, his touchstone, his open sesame to a privy chamber carved out of Saturday night stud poker, October campfires under the pine-tall stars, and rainbow-streamered piccolos spinning records in the musky-dusky congeniality of jumping joints.

Hey little mamma, say gal, don't you hear me huh call-allin' you-ou?

The radio at Chalmer's back was still bleating its country blues. A woman reached across in the breathless panic of the moment, "Excuse me," to switch it off, and the girls scurried across, "Excuse me," to intercept her, forcing Chalmer to retreat further. As in a comic ballet, the more he attempted to recoup his territory the more he was buffeted about. Back toward the door.

Chalmer got rid of the splashing cup in his hand by quaffing it and stepped to the door to summon the two deputies he had assigned to the foot of the clearing. Nearby the door he noticed for the first time Professor Thurlow, the leading Negro elder of the community, and with him, formally garbed in cream serge clerical suit and collared black shirt, the pastor of the leading white church in the county.

"You here too?"

Inadvertently in his extremity, Chalmer took a bite out of the chicken in his plate, sinking his teeth through the crusty skin into the juicy meat, seeking in it consolation for the emptiness that yawned at the pit of his stomach.

"Now look, Professor, I have a warrant for this boy's arrest. It's being prepared now. But meantime I got to take him in for questioning. If it looks like he can clear himself, we'll release him on bail in the morning. Now that's fair and square, ain't it?" He forked up a spaghetti-swirl of chitterlings and sucked them in, savoring in his mouth a redolence of blood and guts, piss and vinegar, the salt and savor of man's essential animality. "Now you know I've always given you folks the best part of a break. Treated you better'n a daddy would."

"Why certainly," the Professor said. The thick-pillowed puffs over-hanging his eyelids drooped somnolently behind the gold-rimmed twinkle of his lenses. "This here boy's one of my students. Been doing some real fine work under me. Come on up, I'm sure he'll cooperate right on with any questions you ask of him. Reeve, son? Sheriff here'd like to question you."

Accompanied by DeLavery, Thurlow piloted the sheriff back to Reeve with no disruptions en route. A chair was shuffled up for Chalmer and he sat down with Reeve, knee to knee, face to face, and cross-examined him forthwith.

"Now I know," he informed Reeve, "exactly what happened. Because I delivered the notice here myself. Henry's evicting you from this place you all have farmed so long. And when you saw him this morning, you jumped salty over it. You blew your stack. I understand it and I don't altogether blame you for it, it's only natural you'd defend your home. That's the way it was, wasn't it?"

"Well, no sir, not—"

"You contradicting me?"

By the end of the questioning however, Chalmer was left with nothing but the categorical imperative imposed upon him by Henry's call. There had been no encounter between Reeve and Henry in the field. The boy hadn't touched him, spoken to him or even so much as given him a cross-eyed look.

"It was me that argued with him," Rad kept insisting. "You want to arrest me for it, here I am."

"Now Rad, I've warned you before and I warn you again, you got nothing to do with this. Let him answer for himself. But you made up your mind, didn't you, Reeve, that before you'd let Mr. Warren get hold of this land you'd destroy it. That was your intention, wasn't it?"

"Well, no sir, I never—"

"You denying what's out there for everyone to see? Why it's the sorriest spitefulest thing I ever heard of, destroying a man's land before he can lay hands on it. And roping his own blood-kin in to help you—"

"Well, no sir, I wouldn't destroy my own land, why should I? When it's all going to be settled in court tomorrow anyhow. You deliver that notice to me too, if you remember. As I'm sure you do."

Chalmer remembered. It was a fact which he had not—no!—not allowed to escape him, but one which he had discounted. He had delivered the communication from the Judge concerning the probate hearing shortly after the eviction order and collected his fee for it; and had relegated it to the back of his mind when he summarized his case before setting out here. Now he had to reorganize his perspective around it.

"Are you that sure," he inquired, probing for further facts that might prove useful to him later, "the disposition of this property'll run your way?"

"I don't know why not. When all the evidence is put before the Judge, I'm sure he'll do what's legal and lawful. I trust in that, don't you?"

"Then what in creation were you up to? You done something! You must of done something! The whole town's up in arms over it."

He was only blasting a ditch. To drain the cornfield now, save the crop from blanching, and later in the dry spell bring the water in from the river, save the crop from parching. A ditch. That's all.

Chalmer could elicit no admission from him beyond this quite unspectacular objective, easily verifiable and concurred in by too many witnesses present to be disputed. It didn't seem possible to him, however, it was not to be believed that there was nothing more to it than that. There had to be more. Confounding the matter further, one of those absurd anomalies typical of Colfax County events intruded as a minor footnote. It wasn't even his land that Reeve had blown the ditch through this morning. It was Rad's. They weren't ditching Reeve's land until this afternoon.

For once in his life Chalmer was stumped. Plainly he couldn't make an arrest for a homicide, attempted or intended, that hadn't occurred. Or for damage that hadn't been committed. He scrutinized Reeve's face for small signs of duplicity, seeing in the sheen on the nose that spread up through the furrow between his brows and over the dark luminosity of his pupils the sweat of stress. Sweating all over, even his eyes were sweating. And fresh, fresh as they come. But when a nigger's that fresh under the pressure of being sweated out, Chalmer figured, at least it connotes he's frank. Much as he doubted the truth of what he'd heard, the more awful doubt which he had previously repressed now took possession of him. Henry had lied to him. Had played him for a fool. Had used him as a man uses a dog. Go in there and get 'em . . .

They tell you to go in and get 'em, but nobody tells you how. Under the conditions that prevailed inside the house, he couldn't just handcuff the boy and haul him off. And under the conditions attendant upon him outside the house, he couldn't step out of here without the boy, empty-handed. Chalmer shook the folded handkerchief out of his breast pocket and wiped his face over from the sweatband under his hat to the corded ligaments under his chin. When one of his deputies cautiously approached the porch to find out what was going on all this time, he sent a child out with a message: "You all hold your horses till I call you in."

He got up from his chair and paced heavily up and down, his service revolver bumping in its holster against his hip. Sister Mae plied him with food and High Power replenished his drink. Finally he hitched up in front of DeLavery who had been following developments with taut intentness, and tried one last gambit.

"Reverend, I'm going to have to ask you to help me. I don't know what this boy is guilty or not guilty of, that's not my function. But you look out the door, there's a crowd of men out there armed to the teeth. They're all fired up over this."

He trotted Clem to the door, and Clem looked out upon colored spilling down over the steps and a ring of whites at the edge of the yard staring perplexedly at them. He had driven here with Thurlow to view what Thurlow blandly described to him as an experiment. He had viewed it from the bobwire fence with a thrill that drove back at least a little the appalling omnipresence of Augusta Varney kneeling on her kitchen floor; with a thrill that went back to his summers with the croppers on his uncle's plantations, to the old irrepressible dream with Joe Hata. While he was deep in discourse with the Professor over the future management of the ditching, the crowd around them had started running. He did not understand then what was brewing. Later, while the Professor wheeled him about the grounds, he had been haunted by an uneasy sense that they were acting as lookouts. He had tried more than once to break away: whatever was up, he couldn't afford to be caught in the middle of it. Not now. Not for his mother's sake nor Nancy's nor his own. Nor the church itself.

But whenever he met Thurlow's eyes, the deft excuses had refused to pass his lips. From their vantage point in the woods, they had seen the cars drive up from the road, the deputy scouting the terrain, the march of the sheriff down the track. "Maybe you'd better leave," Thurlow had suggested then. "Well, maybe . . ." he had said indecisively, and frightened by what he sensed had lingered.

The sheriff gripped his arm now and pointed out the door. "You see that, Reverend? I don't know what brought you here, but it must have been God's own mercy that guided you. Only one thing we can do."

Clem had a fantastic vision of himself standing on the porch spread-eagled against an advancing mob. The sky was blue through the green embroidery of the cedars. Jays squawked like clothesline on a pulley. He had looked down into a ditch, and the consequences, the train of consequences . . .

"Ride him into town," the sheriff whispered hoarsely at him, "and place him in custody for his own safety and protection. If you'll just persuade him—"

Yells were rising from the yard. "Chal-muh! You all right in there, Chalmer?" "You need any help?" "Come on out." The voices joined in a chant. "Come on out. Come on out."

"We can hustle him out through the kitchen shed," the sheriff prodded at Clem, "and make a beeline for my car. If you'll just lead the way?"

"Of course," Clem heard himself say without hesitation. "If it's the only way."

Come on out. Come on out. Come on out. Come on out.

Clem passed by the table to the bed-alcove and laid his hand on Reeve's shoulder, the warm living flesh, electric with vitality through the T-shirt. "You'd better come," he said peering down with God's own mercy into the man's eyes. "We'll get you into town where the sheriff can put you under protection."

"Protection?" Reeve said, eying Clem and with the slightest of gestures lifted his hands outward. All the protection he needed was right here in this room.

Cmon cmon cmon cmon cmon cmon . . .

"Maybe," Clem suggested to Chalmer, "if I went out and spoke to them, appealed to their sense—"

Throwing him a disgusted look, Chalmer roared, "Quiet out there!" Gun in belt, badge on hat, forces at his beck and call, he barely refrained from grabbing Reeve up by the scruff of the neck and jerking him to his feet. Come on, boy, you comin' with me . . .

Come on outa there! Come on, Chalmer, you comin' out?

"You go out and tell them," Chalmer jerked his head at Vergilia,

"I'm busy conducting an investigation. And when I'm through with it, I'll come out. Not before."

"Oh sure." Vergilia stretching on tiptoe peeped out the window. "That's Floyd Bird out there. I know him." And gathering her daughters about her, with an insouciant smile she sallied forth.

Chalmer resumed his pacing about the table. High Power shook a few last drops out of the bottle into his teacup. Lila-Lee heaped his plate. In varying degrees they all knew, despite the danger still obvious on the surface, that the initiative had passed from Chalmer to themselves. If only because it is very difficult for a man to be much of a menace with his mouth full of Bessie Sanderlee's whipped-cream lady-cake. The main problem now was to provide him with a means of graceful egress.

Thurlow buttonholed Chalmer in a corner with a meandering account of an incident back in 1906 when he, Thurlow, was publishing a newspaper, the only newspaper in the county then, and he printed a story in it that someone didn't like—"If I told you his name, you'd recognize it right away"—and one day the man followed him to the railroad station where he was about to take a train with his wife to a convention. "He pulled a gun on me and if my wife hadn't restrained me, I was so mad I had my pistol out, I would have shot back at him right then and there. Afterward I had him arrested for carrying concealed weapons."

Evidently to Chalmer it was a white man the Professor was speaking of, and evidently he was implying that the law he was able to call to his side in those days was not at his disposal now. "Sometimes"—the Professor waved his panama hat, fanning up a breeze between them—"I think we goin' backward. Yes sir," he pronounced, driving home his favorite theme, "sometimes when I hear about all the progress we made in the last eighty years I think about it. We progressing backward."

In sheer self-defense Chalmer was compelled to parry the thrust with an account of his own. He cited the case of the septic tank cleaner whom he had freed this morning. The cleaner, a Yankee from Iowa or Idaho somewhere, big tall redheaded Swede, had been going all over the county making slurring references to race segregation. A few nights ago he had stood up in the middle of a tent movie out Fallona way and pulled down the rope that separated the sections and hailed all the Negroes to scramble down out of their places and show these clodhoppers a thing or two. "The lights went on and the niggers around here being smart niggers," Chalmer confided with a fond pat on Thurlow's shoulder, "they all dove for under the tent flaps and off they went. The whites jumped the man and roughed him up a little and some of them, the Jeems brothers in particular, were all for dumping him. But cooler heads won out. They dragged him to the law. Had him charged with breach of peace, incitement to riot, insurrection, and I don't know what all.

"But you know me. I'm not one to get excited. This morning I reduced the charge to drunk and disorderly in a public place, and let him go with a good talking-to. I hope he's learned his lesson now. Ain't no one from the outside going to come in and make trouble for our Nigras in the South. Because they know that so long as they keep their place, they got nothing to worry about. Them is them, I told him—" Chalmer crammed down the last crumbs of cake and lusciously tongued his mouth, "and us is us, and never the twain shall mix. Ain't that so, Professor?"

With their tales they had crossed swords, each getting under the other's skin with the unkindest cut in his repertoire of innuendoes. Now these preliminaries being over, they launched into the bargaining, a veritable comic ballet of bargaining, a dancing back and forth of nimble pas de deux and entrechats, a ritual of negotiation prescribed for such occasions but not contrived, spontaneous, weaving implicit motion by motion, allusive gesture by gesture toward resolution.

"I'm from north Georgia," the sheriff asserted, reminding them as he often did of his ancestral non-slaveholding origins, a reference he never made before his white constituents. "I'm all for you folks. I'm on your side."

"Nobody hoodwinks you," High Power sagely nodded.

"You said it."

"Anybody tries to mislead you, you rightaway smell a rat."

"You bet. Hasn't nobody crossed me up ever got away with it."

The compromise eventually improvised by Carter Scott out of their counterpoint was accepted by the sheriff as satisfactory to all parties concerned: himself, them, Henry. He had begun to fear, looking ahead to next week when he must execute the eviction, that he would be confronted by a situation even more unthinkable than the present one: an armed barricade of the property, with the united support of the colored population behind it. Such a thing had happened once or twice before in local history. Back in the 1920s, when Ozzie Higginson was Kleagle of the Klan, a crowd of colored men showed up in Arcady one Saturday shopping day, carrying their squirrel guns. And back in the 1900s, there had been some flareup . . . Chalmer didn't mind dealing with a single opponent, quietly, behind closed doors; but when it came to the whole lot of them or even a small part of them, he concluded as sensible people around here always had: You can't shoot them all. He did not above all want to be faced with the alternative: fight or surrender to them, do or back down. His job, his strategy, and his intrinsic character, all, were dedicated to the avoidance of just such a confrontation.

"Why don't we leave it up to the court tomorrow?" Carter proposed to him reasonably. "Then if it turns out anybody has done anything illegal on land don't belong to him, you can take him in then."

The formulation, vague as it was, full of loopholes and ambiguities, furnished the perfect out. It was a victory for the colored: they had won a stay of judgment for Reeve, albeit a temporary one. And it was a victory for himself, Chalmer believed, having no doubt at all as to how Purcell would assign the ownership. Without passion or prejudice, relying on his knowledge of Negroes, he had accomplished even more than he hoped for. He had their avowed consent to the ultimate action he would have to take against Reeve on behalf of Henry. He had his game cornered, his gun aimed and his finger on the trigger.

Chalmer's departure was most cordial. He shook hands with the three white men and familiarly squeezed the shoulders of the colored. He walked out of the house with a plump paper bag under his arm. A little brown bantam, not yet plucked, but still warm and leaking from its decapitated neck a few drops of blood through the bottom. For his wife to cook up for supper.

By a strange dichotomy what appeared sane and rational inside the door became inexplicable outside it.

"Where is he, Chalmer?" the deputies demanded, running up to him.

"Ain't you go'n take him in, Chalmer?" the aroused citizens encircled the deputies. "Ain't you gonna book him?"

"There's a meeting," Chalmer broke through them, "going on in there of the Cornpone Burial Society. You want one of 'em, you have to take 'em all. But don't you worry." Turning about, walking backward from them, he waved his dripping paper bag under their collective noses. "I got him. I got him where I want him. Right in the palm of my hand."

They gave him a hard time over it just the same. He had failed them in an obscure manner that produced both disappointment and relief.

"No tickee no laundlee," one quipped to the other as he reentered his car for the drive back to town.

2

It was not the least of Henry's torments on that catastrophic day to be chewed out by Chalmer Coombs, not once but twice. After rushing his son home from Sunset in Dr. Harrington's car and summoning Miss Bird, the only nurse available, to attend him, he went downstairs to the telephone to call Julie back from the wedding. When he picked up the leaden black instrument however, he decided instead to call Chalmer first. Once Chalmer had Reeve under arrest, it would be easier to explain to her. It was he who did this awful thing. He's in the lockup now for it. Punishment cannot eradicate an evil deed, but surely in the balance of human nature it provides the one drop of alleviation that makes suffering bearable. Justice is being meted out.

The city policeman at the jailhouse answered. No, Chalmer wasn't back yet. No, he had no information. He'd let Henry know just as soon as he had any. Henry hung up, the receiver cold leaden dead in his hand. Nothing. In a fever of impatience, burning for action, decision, something concrete to report to her as a means of mitigating the blow, he called Chalmer's office back every five minutes until he reached him.

"Chalmer, you catch that nigger right on?"

"You hoodwinked me," Chalmer shot back at him. "You tried to pull a fast one. Now I don't mind you foxing him, that's your business. But when a man tries to outfox me—"

"What the hell," Henry asked, "you raving about? I begged and I pleaded with him not to blast, my kid was back there—"

"I don't know nothin' about no kid. All I know," Chalmer said vindictively, "I went all out for you. The whole hog. Laid my job on the line and my neck on the block. Whose land was he standing on when he's suppose to have threatened you? His or McDowell's?"

"How should I know? What difference does that make!"

"Tomorrow after court," Chalmer said, "when you've proved your wife's possession of that land, you can have him. For malicious mischief."

"Tomorrow? What good does that do me? Tomorrow!"

"Oh?" Chalmer said. "You wanted him jailed before the court decision, is that it? Then why didn't you lay your cards on the table and tell me straight out? Instead of sending me off on a cock-and-bull chase."

Henry slammed the receiver down on him. He had been attacked, he was the injured party, the victim. And no one was to pay for it? No one? My God, he thought, Purcell is right. The niggers run the county!

When a law officer can't arrest a nigger, a nigger that's blowing everything you got to smithereens . . .

His eyes closed over blank blackness out of which a bonfire geysered, he put in a person-to-person call to Julie at the wedding reception in the Lanier Hotel ballroom. Better come home now. Coley wants—needs?—is crying for?—you.

"Julie, honey?"

"Wow," over the wire the husky surface of her voice exploded in pinpoint bubbles of mirth, "the champagne is flowing out of the buckets. Come on in."

A Viennese waltz filtered through, wafting with it the swish of skirts, the whiff of fragrances, the glint of mirrored walls, the lilt of flirtations behind potted palms. He couldn't tell her about Colfax, what was to be gained by it? It would only be two of them instead of one agonizing through the interminable hours until his awakening, sinking in quagmires of fear, grasping at straws . . .

"You just go on having yourself a time," he told her. "Coley's asleep now—yeah yeah yeah—plumb wore himself out. I'll stick around the house with him, keep in touch with the plant from here. Yes, it went off all right, they're freezing 'em up like sixty."

He had no more than walked away from the telephone when she rang him back. "Henry? Maybe I'd better come home now? You sure he's all right? He didn't miss me?"

"Julie for crying out loud, can't you once, just once in your life, enjoy yourself?"

Maybe, maybe by the time she came back something would turn up, turn everything back to where it was before. Then the peril over, the tiger claws extracted and the scars healed, she could shudder in safety, commiserate with what he must have endured and never having known the worst put it all behind her. Oh my Lord, he prayed as he ascended the stairs once more to the boy's room, turn it back, back to where it was before . . .

The yellow blinds were drawn nearly to the sill, vines shadowed in patterns against them. Miss Bird's starched white figure rocked in the corner between the windows, her crepe-soled white oxfords plopping gently with the movement. She shook her head to Henry's question, "Any change?" "He won't be out of the sedative before tonight. You sent for Julie yet?" The rockers tipped upward in expectation, demanding reply.

"I'd like to spare her all I can," Henry said. He crossed the room, not daring to look toward the sleeping child on the bed, and switched on the grinning goblin nightlamp on top of the chest. "Better have this on, if he should come to for a minute . . . When I think it was that nigger, that son of Auntie Rose's, would cause a thing like this . . ."

A man has a right to protect his wife from a knowledge so cruel she could not bear up under it. A man has a right to protect his marriage from a revelation that would shatter it. A man has to protect his mind against realities it cannot admit. Things become blurred. He was proceeding down the road with Colfax so nice when boom! out of the blue . . . Someone was to blame for that child on the bed. Someone had done it to him. And was getting away with it. Scot free.

With eyes closed again over a geysering bonfire, Henry approached the bed. He groped along the boy's spine. The rigidity, that awful rigidity arched in a bow—the bow of the back arched as if frozen into rigor mortis, you'd have to break it to straighten it—the rigidity had relaxed, had collapsed into a blob of resistless softness.

"It would, it would have hit any kid," he said pointedly to Miss Bird, "to have an explosion like that go up before his face." Turning back with closed eyes, he pulled the sheet up, up with the sightless tactility in which materials take on a life of their own, up to the cool silken shell of the ear. "You think when he wakes up, he'll snap out of it?"

"I can't rightly say." Miss Bird brushed past him, bustling him out of her way, her pink curls bobbing under her cap as she retucked the bed. "I never was on a case like this before."

To Henry Miss Bird's presence was a most unwelcome intrusion. Now she knew too. It was one of the disasters of the day that she should be seated now in the innermost privacy of his house, able to contradict its pretenses, to spread whatever she learned here all over town. Similarly his secretary had managed to catch a glimpse of the child in Dr. Harrington's arms as he was bundled out. She saw. And the porter he smuggled into his office to clean the place up under lock and key . . .

Restlessly he maintained contact with Sunset throughout the afternoon. "Cracking," Rosen crisply reported. She had been a WAC officer in London for a brief period during the war, and the vocabulary of it served her well on occasion. "Everything's AOK now. Sir? Will do. Roger." They might have to scrap the morning's batch. The blasting had begun again. Otherwise, good deal, piece of cake! He had his car brought in, and in midafternoon, not able to stand his thoughts another minute, everything in suspension, nothing settled, he informed Miss Bird that he must attend to a few matters of business downtown. "If you're sure he won't wake."

He drove at once to Chalmer's office. Chalmer, picking at the dirt in his fingernails with his penknife, his feet cocked up on his table, was observing his afternoon devotional. The radio on the shelf back of him tuned up full blast on a bush league game, the Bearcats vs. the Graybars. As usual Chalmer had a two-spot on the Cats. Score tied in the ninth inning. Bases loaded. And Regan, the star hitter, up at bat. The Grays had a new pitcher in the box, Lefty Lopez, who was proving nothing short of phenomenal.

"One and one." The office vibrated with the monotonous blare.

"Chalmer," Henry stormed in upon him, "I'm not satisfied with what you done today. Not one bit. Now get up off your fat ass before I have to kick it—"

"Two and one."

"And get crackin'. My bean-crop ruined, my land tore up, my boy driven half out his mind—"

"Two and two."

"I got ten reliable witnesses," Chalmer regarded a dirt-scraping from his fingernail poised on the tip of his knife, "including some of your own help."

"You been tampering with my help? You went and interfered—"

"Three balls." The breathlessness of the distant duel issued from the loudspeaker into the office and through the barred door to the bated breath of the cellblock.

Chalmer half-started up out of his chair, twisting toward the box on his shelf with a savage intentness that nothing short of a bank robbery could have disrupted, if that. Henry stalked up to the radio and switched it off, setting off a clangor of banging bars. "Turn it on! What the hell—"

Ferociously Chalmer switched it back on, knocking at the box to hasten the dimmed voice. A dinning cheer from the stands, prolonged . . . Walked him? A fly ball? A homer? He wouldn't have missed that for . . . Tears were forming in his eyes.

"And—out!"

Blinking watery blue eyes, Chalmer sank back. Another inning or two or three.

"You placed me in a position of public embarrassment today, Henry. I crawled way out on a limb for you and got it chopped off. But still, even so, I got this nigger-boy tied up and bound and ready to deliver for you. Now if that ain't good enough, you go down there and provoke him like anybody else would and when the Grand Jury meets you can plead justifiable homicide. That is, if you want to make yourself and this town the cynosure of all the headlines in the country—OK— But don't ask me to."

"You made a deal with them!" Henry charged. "You sold out to the niggers! They own you lock, stock, and barrel!"

"Get outa here," Chalmer said, thereby making the mistake of his lifetime, out of principle he would later claim but, as likely, out of a vanity that still smarted from his morning's errors. "No man says a thing like that to my face or behind my back." True, realizing, he tried to temper it. "Tomorrow after you've beat him out in court—"

But Henry left, raving. The niggers run the county!

He raced down the corridor to the front section of the building and boiling with rage—niggers, niggers, all sold out to the niggers!—checked through some details for tomorrow's hearing. After stopping at the post office for the mail—maybe something there, maybe, and miraculously there was—he sped home with his palpitant heart in his hands.

No, Julie hadn't arrived during his absence. The boy hadn't awakened. All quiet. He laid out the mail on the telephone table. On top the airmail envelope with its bright bordering of diagonals, no name or return address but distinctly Elwell, the stamp smudged out in a series of overlapping cancellations. Henry experienced a certain nervous stimulation rather than jealousy over these intermittent communications from Elwell; they piqued his curiosity, tickled his ego, quickened his desire for his wife and his sense of dependency on her, making her the more tantalizing by placing her one remove outside his sole domain and the more gratifying because she was his. The letter now was a boon. For such small reprieves . . . Marcus Hadley's revised estimates for the remodeling due to begin a week from Monday: Marcus hadn't lost any time on that one. Along with a catalogue of bathroom fixtures, all chrome and color. He almost jumped out of his skin when the telephone rang at his elbow. It always rang much longer with out-of-town calls. He stared at its mouth, uptilted to him, too paralyzed for a moment to release its arm.

Miss Bird thudded softly a few stairs downward. "Oh, you there, I bet that's Julie now." She viewed his failure to call Julie home with disapprobation. It was none of her business, her attitude plainly stated, but she always believed that you should let the mother know.

Henry lifted the receiver numbly to his ear. It was Judge Purcell. "You don't mind, do you, if we steal Julie from you for just a little longer?" A small party of them was driving down to The Cloister together for dinner and they simply had to have her. "How'd it go?" Henry asked. "Splendidly. Splendidly." It isn't every day that a small-time judge of no background to speak of, who has made his way by riding the back of a buckboard into sump and hogwaller, damning the Yankees and the big-city slickers, marries his child off in a blaze of political glory, comprising half the state senate, the district congressman, two Federal judges, an ex-Governor, and a raft of New Jersey Republicans. "It went off like a house afire," the Judge gloated gleefully to Henry, "and I must say we owe a lot to Julie. She swept them all off their feet. She stole the show." "Tell her not to worry," Henry said. "Everything's under control. AOK."

Henry hung up with the acrid conviction that Julie was having her own private wonderful ball. Making fun of herself and them as a means of expressing her residue of rebellion against having been dragooned in, and carrying off her buffoonery so well they all fell for it, swallowing her bait and smacking their lips over it. His conviction was confirmed when a short while later Cousin Tibby and her retinue arrived, ready to pick up the bags they had packed in the morning and take leave.

"Isn't Julie here yet? Whoo! Did she whoop it up—" "When somebody started in about how she looked just like something out of *Gone with the Wind* and she said, 'Why shouldn't I? My path is strewn with cracked skulls'—" "And when she stood up on the chair in the middle of the toasts and hailed the Judge as an unreconstructed Southerner, a true-blue Bourbon and a gentleman of the Old School—" "Why he went around afterward handing out five-dollar tips to the colored flunkeys—" "You notice how she took the best man off Annamary? And the commander of the Coast Guard station off his fiancée? Then quit all the young squirts for the Judge. He squired her around all over, introducing her to everybody, left poor Eula dumped in a corner—" "And that uncle from Trenton sticking to her like white on rice . . . Henry, it's a good thing you weren't there."

He managed to outface their anticipation of being fed some refreshment before departure, steered them out of their insistence on kissing Coley goodbye, which in truth they were relieved to forgo, saw them out to their cars and waved them off. The sun had vanished and the fringed foliage borne on the great arms of the trees was dripping indigo against a claret sky when the Judge's Lincoln rolled up the gravel driveway, ringing with the strains of *Carry Me Back to Old Virginny*.

The car was tiered to the roof with riders. Julie unfolded herself from a lap and in a final froth of hugs and hilarity parted from them. "Thank you," the Judge gallantly bowed her to the porch, "I want you to know how much we thank you." Trailing laughter, her veiled headdress all ablow about her hair, her rumpled skirt winking with sequins, the shiny bits and tatters of the day clinging to her, in an aura of crushed flowers and stale tobacco she waltzed up to Henry at the door.

"Kiss me, sugar." From stilt-heeled yellow satin pumps she tipped toward him. "I'm standing up three dates."

Whisking past him into the hall, she unpinned her veiling and tossed the headband off on the table. "Oh what a wedding—darling, we should have been married like that. Instead of running off—it's the drama of the thing, the spectacle, the fairytale of it. When the organ peals out with that march and the procession starts and we all take up our stations and the bride, in that lace veil and the court train all spangled with bugle beads . . . I'm telling you I wept. Why is it women always cry at weddings and men always mop their brows?"

She was brimming over with the people she hadn't seen in years, the lavishness of food and drink, the floral decorations. "Everyone was doing mental arithmetic: How many at how much per head? And the Judge kept making such a point, he didn't have to worry about Sukey anymore, she was taken care of and since she was his only daughter and this was the last thing he could do for his little girl and she wanted it so . . . But I know, it was to put the in-laws on the griddle. He put out, now let them! My, it's quiet in here, are they all gone bag and baggage? Thank God. Is Coley, I thought he'd come running— Oh."

She had discovered Elwell's letter and was tearing it open, too grateful for the respite it allowed her to inquire further at the moment. "How perfectly lovely." Shedding her flippant pose, she dropped down on the tufted green velvet chair by the table. Reading, her eyes moving swiftly over the sheer white paper, she fingered her cheek, her throat, her pearls, suffused with a dewiness of delight. "How very sweet, no"— she snatched the letter out of Henry's view—"don't look at it, you'd never understand. And guess what," she read on, "he's coming back! He'll be here this summer! He even hints—perhaps—I can fly over to Heron's Nest."

"Just you?"

"Now Henry, don't start putting interpretations, you're worse than Cousin Tibby. I'm sure he didn't mean . . . Where's Coley?"

"In bed."

"Already? You sure must have hit it off. If he's that relaxed— Henry—" She was suddenly alarmed, reacting to the resounding hush of the house, to a quietness in him. "Henry, where is he?"

"Now Julie," he tried to force her back down into the chair, "there's nothing you could have done if you'd been here. We were driving along the road, getting along so well, you'd hardly believe, when that boy of Auntie Rose's—he was dynamiting—and . . ."

She sprang out of his hands and flew upstairs. Her satin heels slashed through a rip torn by some dancer in the hem of her organza skirt. "But Julie," he climbed up after her as he had so many times before, "Julie, he's not hurt. There's hardly a scratch. It's just—"

She threw herself past the orange beam of the goblin-lamp and Miss Bird's deterring hand to the bed. "Honey, it's Mummy. It's me."

Despite his hopes of cushioning the blow by delaying it, it was as shattering when it came as a car collision with its clash of metal, crash of glass.

She stripped the sheet off the boy and opening his pajamas examined him head to foot. She lifted his hand. The hand lay limp as death in her hand. "Honey, it's Mummy, I'm back, I'm with you." She brushed his hair back from his forehead, covered his face and arms with kisses. She picked him up to her breast and rocked him. His head flopped back. His eyes quivering open rolled listlessly.

"What have you done?" she said to Henry. "*What have you done to him?*"

He attempted with Miss Bird to detach the child from her, but she was like a wild animal with a wounded cub, fighting them off. "It wasn't me," Henry explained over and over. "It was that damn nigger, Reeve—I begged and I pleaded with him . . ."

"It was that colored boy," Miss Bird mercifully supplemented him. "He was the one."

"But why? Why would he? When I've been so good—"

"Because," Henry said harshly, "people always take what you give them and turn it against you!"

She smoothed the sheet back over the boy and standing up, with a vehement gesture took the fluffy yellow collar of her dress between her hands and tore it down the front, tore the gauze down even through the hard cutting seams, the bindings and tuckings, all the way down, kicked out of the bedraggled mass at her feet and stamped on it.

"I trusted him to you. *I trusted you!*"

"Julie, Julie, you got to pull yourself together—"

"I never wanted to go, I never wanted any part of it, it was you, you, always you—"

"Julie, dear, this isn't doing him any good. Here, dear, here's a pill—"

She knocked the pill out of Miss Bird's hand. She wouldn't be dulled, she wouldn't be doped, she had to live this through. The tearing of her dress however had taken some of the impetus out of her attack on Henry. Shaking and sobbing, clutching her hair to the roots, she sank down in the rocker in the corner and rejecting everything they had to say demanded more.

Henry never did describe to her fully what happened that morning. There had been an explosion set off by Reeve and—the details were hazy—it affected the boy, he went into shock over it.

"But you had him with you? You didn't leave him alone?"

"No, of course not," Henry said, and this was his only deliberate falsehood. "He was right with me. Believe me, if it would have helped any for me to kill myself over it, I'd do it. I'd have died right there."

Her questions darted about, barely satisfied with one answer before they were off on another tack, leaving the course of events unclarified. As important as what had happened was what would happen next. Henry had only half-averted the blame from himself when he was caught up in the cross fire concerning the doctor's diagnosis. "Nobody could have given him better care than Harrington did. He's been here twice and he'll be back this evening—"

"Harrington?" Julie cried up at him in horror. "You called Harrington in? Instead of Tom Willingham?"

"Willingham was at the wedding with you—"

"Tom was not at the wedding. And neither was Grace." Her voice throbbed with disbelief. "You didn't call Tom because you were afraid for him to see, you knew he'd tell me—"

In a fresh accumulation of suspicion she rushed downstairs to call Willingham. He could hear her at the telephone, shrill with her burden of trouble. "Tom? Oh Violet. Is Tom there? Oh-h-h." Her voice dwindled, disappeared, her trouble displaced by a tremolo of sympathetic murmurs. "Oh how terrible, how dreadful, oh Violet, I'm sorry."

When she retraced her way upstairs to Henry, she had wilted. "I'm terribly sorry," she said to him. "Birdie, please overlook . . . I didn't know it. I just didn't realize. Tom hasn't been home since last night. He found out about Grace's lump and without a word to anyone, not even Violet, flew her up to Hopkins right away. Violet's at their house now with the children and she's just about out of her mind over it. You know Grace was always the goddess of perfection to Violet. And Tom too, especially Tom. There doesn't seem to be much doubt, it's spread, she's in surgery—"

She was winking with tears over Grace Willingham, a woman ten years her senior, with whom she had never been at all intimate. Not out of altruism so much as because it blunted her own pain to divide it. "I've always felt that to lose a tooth is to be disfigured for life. But when I had a toothache once, I wanted to tear it out by the roots. Anything to get rid of the thing that was hurting me! And to think, she's been going on like this for months. Because she didn't want to hurt him."

She asked Henry no more questions but sat contrite by the boy's bed, wrapped in her housecoat and sipping black coffee until it was cold, waiting for Dr. Harrington's arrival. "I shouldn't have hopped on you the way I did. You've been through enough . . . Only you should have told me right away, you should never have let me go on dancing, clowning it up." She slowly drained her coffee down, black and bitter, refusing to let them fetch her a hot cup. "He always hated me," she reflected. "I never understood it before. I never would accept it. He always has."

"Who?"

"Reeve. Even when I was a child bringing a basket of toys for them Christmas, I always had this feeling, he'd scoot out the door . . ."

"I hollered on him to stop," Henry said, recollecting it with unfeigned violence at the outrage. "I hollered, and still he plunged down on that box . . ."

"And that last afternoon I visited with Auntie Rose and told her she could stay for as long as she lived, he came in drunk, I could smell the liquor off him—drunk as a coot in the middle of the afternoon. He all but bodily threw me out of the house."

"For God sake, why in the name of God didn't you tell me—"

"Because I was afraid you'd make a fuss over it. Isn't that hilarious? I was afraid you'd raise a fuss, do something to him that'd only make things so much worse . . . Though I can see now how sometimes, they provoke you so—"

Under the fortuitous influence of the Willinghams, overanxious now to compensate for her previous accusations, she flung herself into the arms of the very logic she had always so passionately repudiated. *Folks take what you give them and turn it against you.* Of course. How true. She surrendered to its bitter embrace like a flagellant to the lash. "He was doing it to me. To *me*. He was getting back at me! When he saw Colfax with you, Coley looks like me when I was little . . ."

She saw it all so clearly, father and son, Henry showing the boy around the place as her father had shown her, perhaps pointing over the fence, this all belonged to your forebears, that's where the mansion-house stood. And out of the bush the brute black face watching in all its viciousness. There have always been bad niggers, that revert like hunt dogs gone feral . . .

"I suppose he just didn't give a damn, it was a golden opportunity, to shoot it off in the child's face—ha ha—"

"And the hell of it is," Henry said heavily, "there's nothing we can do about it. I sent Chalmer Coombs down to arrest him, and what did he do? Jawed around with him. Had a regular chin session. So long as I ain't proved yet it's your land he was standing on . . . When I think it's decent citizens like you and me and our friend Benson Reece that allow a situation to develop where a thing like this can go on without any recourse to reprisal . . . The niggers run this county! They run us—"

She jumped up, not listening, and began methodically pulling the drawn shades down below the sills, as if something outside in the darkness, something warm and friendly and safe in the atmosphere, something she always believed was there, respect, gratitude, lovingkindness, a part of the air that surrounded and sustained her with every breath, wasn't there anymore. Had never been there. The spring night was poisoned. She went from room to room pulling down shades and returning knelt by the boy's bed, nuzzling at his unresponsive face.

Miss Bird brought in some cereal she had prepared for the boy while having her supper downstairs. Placing her arm behind his back, she raised him to sitting position. Julie attempted to insert the spoon between his lips. "He seems to be conscious now, but—" The milk dribbled from the lank mouth. Julie lowered the slopping spoon. "Where is that Dr. Harrington? Where is he?"

"He said nine o'clock, not before nine. He has his office full of patients."

"Damn his patients! He knows we need him . . ."

When Dr. Harrington arrived however, Julie received him with marked reserve. It was more of an adjustment than she could make to regard the physician who had extracted her cook's gallstones, ovaries, and other sundries as a person of sufficient competence to serve a member of her family. Harrington's black tousled head and broad white back moved over the slight figure on the bed, taking possession of it as he went through the usual routine of heart, knee, fingertips, thumb-lifted eyelid.

"I think you ought to know, Dr. Harrington," Julie stated, "that I'm taking him to Atlanta for treatment just as soon as he can go. There's a Dr. Wolf who's attached to the Children's Clinic—"

"By all means." Harrington's brooding face, vised in the stethoscope, lifted briefly. "Why haven't you done it before?"

"Because—" Her eyes met Henry's; back over the path they had come together lay another one of the truths she had spurned like brittle breaking sticks under her feet. It was Henry who had always urged her to place the child in expert care. And it was she who had always resisted it because she thought he wanted to get rid of him. Anything, she felt now in a flash of compassion for Henry, anything to get rid of the thing that most hurts you!

"Because," she said to Harrington, "I was too afraid of what they'd tell me. Tom Willingham has as much as said it, and in Savannah it was the same thing . . . That he's hopelessly feeble-minded. And he's not. He's not. I know he's not."

"I don't think so either." Harrington removed the rubber tips of the stethoscope from his ears. "It's one of the possibilities, but I've seen too many other cases like this diagnosed as feeble-mindedness when the patient is as intelligent as you or I and perhaps more so."

"You don't think, Dr. Harrington—" She cried out as any mother would over a sick child at a hint of joyous news, humble with it, pleading. But still she held back, mistrustful of him, eyeing him dubiously. "What do you think his problem is then? In your opinion?"

"You admit now at last at the height of a crisis that there is a problem. That's one step. And you recognize that you must do something about it. That's the second step. If you ever actually take the third step and go through with it—"

"Dr. Harrington, I asked you . . ."

"There is no indication, Mrs. Warren, that you place the slightest confidence in my capacity to render a professional opinion."

"Dr. Harrington, please, I want to know. You think he's mentally normal?"

"I didn't say that. He may be of subnormal intelligence, and schizophrenic. He may be of normal intelligence, and schizophrenic. Or a genius, and schizophrenic. But schizophrenic he most certainly is. That means he lives in a world of his own, with its own closed system of logic—as many people, particularly in this vicinity, do. They are the captives of their own subjective impressions, like Childe Roland who to the dark tower came. Completely incapable of viewing objective reality and forming their judgments on the basis of it. They may sit on a volcano, proclaiming that all is sweetness and light. Or they may rot in the slough of their own fears and fantasies—"

"Please," she interrupted him, "please, I'm not interested in being lectured on your theories about people around here. I don't care about that. Just tell us what's wrong with him now! What can we do for him?"

"He's had a catatonic seizure, a syndrome of the disease that can be almost impossible to overcome. He's still totally withdrawn, but the muscular rigidity has passed. Has he ever had an episode like this before?"

Again Julie's eyes met Henry's. Now it was his turn to walk barefoot over the brittle breaking sticks. Henry bowed his head in his hands.

"Miss Bird," Dr. Harrington suggested, "will you please leave the room?"

"All right," Henry croaked after a long pause. "All right. Frank, there's not another living soul but Julie that knows this. I've always claimed to myself that it began when he was born. But I'm the one. It began with me. I did it. When he was just a little tyke—"

"Never mind." Julie laid her hand over his. "Never mind the rest of it for now. We'll go into all that if we have to in Atlanta. Dr. Harrington, when can we take him?"

Dr. Harrington, being no practitioner of procrastination, obtained her permission to handle the arrangements and without any further ado tramped downstairs and called long distance. In a very few minutes the appointment was made.

"Monday afternoon at two," he reported. "Dr. Wolf will be expecting you at the clinic. If Colfax hasn't improved by then, they may hospitalize him. If he has, they'll start putting him through a series of physical and psychological tests that will take a month or longer. I might as well warn you now that it will be very expensive. And when they get through, they'll tell you they don't know. They don't know a thing about infantile autism. They don't even know whether childhood schizophrenia is the same disease as that in adults. They may recommend drugs, shock treatment, play analysis if he's accessible to it. All of it also expensive enough to pauperize you. In the end they'll throw up their hands, they have no idea what to do for him. Then you'll come back to me."

He snapped his bag closed. "Meantime," Francis X. Harrington's drawling self-sneer curled out of the corner of his mouth, "I'm at your disposal."

"Why, he's crazy," Julie said after his departure. "Stark raving mad. But—" She was tremulous with hopefulness, almost gay with the prospect of movement, as if everything were already in the process of being solved. "He said Coley's as intelligent as anyone, you heard him, he said . . . Oh darling, darling—"

Her fingers laced convulsively through Henry's, she pulled herself up to her feet. Nothing could shake her faith in him now. "You meant to tell— You took it on yourself. The hardest thing anyone ever had to say."

Marriages are not made in heaven but in the hell of such experiences as these, out of the searing flames in which two persons are indissolubly forged into one. "What would I ever do without you?" She hid her face against her husband's chest, her arms tightening around him as his tightened about her.

They sent Miss Bird home and spelled each other by the boy's bed throughout the night. Henry was up at six for an early drive to Sunset since he would have to be back in town for the court hearing at ten.

His office had been restored to a semblance of order though its former pleasantness was reduced by the glaring absence of Venetian blinds and draperies, the potted ferns and other touches of refinement. The freezer plant was operating smoothly under Rosen's supervision though half of yesterday's run of beans, it was now confirmed, would have to be dumped. In the fields the pickers were toting their baskets to the trucks. In the packing house the loaded conveyors were sliding past the flying hands of the produce dressers. Soon down the corridor from his door the clacking of typewriters began, punctuated by cheerful tinkles at the end of each line and the slam of the carriage.

Henry reassembled his plans for the freezer plant opening next week. He'd have to get Eula to pinch-hit for Julie—it was a shame—at least behind the scenes, and Annamary to act as hostess—what a mess—but it was the best he could do. Then he took out his file in preparation for the hearing and reviewed it. Yesterday's scene of terror had virtually evaporated into thin air, but Henry had not altogether recovered from it and fragments of the debacle, those footsteps up the wall, would continue to haunt him. Life, however, seldom has the finality of tragedy. Or the singularity, the thread of pure feeling is only too rapidly consumed in the multiplicity of overlapping threads. Nothing had come to a dead halt. Everything was in action here, on into the next phase, carrying him with it. Still he remained in the grip of a kind of awesome astonishment. Out of yesterday's confluence of accidents and coincidences, out of the teeth of the gale he had attained an end for which he had been striving and might have striven yet for weeks, months, years. The stalemate over his son was broken.

His lawyer, Lars Finchley, telephoned, full of cautions and anxieties over the procedure this morning. He was extremely insistent that Henry allow the Judge to appoint an administrator for the Scott estate rather than press Julie's claim. "You still worried about that?" Henry demanded. "Purcell will press the administrator, I'll press the claim and between us we'll press the son of a bitch out of there. Look Lars, look, listen to me. The truth is what I say it is. You hear that? *The truth is what I say it is.* How's Grace? Yeah, Julie talked with Violet last night. She was all cut up over it."

He had no more than finished with Lars and his worries when Judge Purcell called up in a fit of excitement over his own set of panics. "Henry, you hear me, Henry? I just had word—the niggers are all riled up over this. They're coming in to the courthouse by buggy, wagon, and truckload. I'll call a postponement."

That was the Judge. For petty crimes he snapped out ready-made sentences according to who the miscreant was. But in any clash that involved more than a minor insurance suit or a family feud, the first move he made was to play for time. If he protracted long enough, the Judge felt, things always seemed to come around as he saw fit. It was only when time was too short for latitude that he folded.

"Now, wait a minute, Judge," Henry said. "They got you on the run too?"

"If you mean to imply that I'm being influenced—"

"Judge, I wouldn't imply that for anything in the world."

"My best advice to you, Henry, is to postpone until feelings have died down. Inside a month—"

"Postpone, my eye! This couldn't happen at a better time if we tried in a million years. You wait till you hear some of the things that have been goin' on. Just as soon as this is done with, I'm coming over to discuss with you ways and means of throwing all these nigger-lovers around here out of office. Now you just stick to the letter of the law, Judge, leave the rest to me."

He returned home shortly after nine to check on the boy's condition. Miss Bird was back, rocking in the corner between the organdie-ruffled windows. The slight form ridged under the sheet did not stir. No change. Dr. Harrington had been here and left with a promise of obtaining some pharmaceutical preparation in Savannah incorporating a new synthetic that was being used experimentally for treatment of hypertension. "Oh he keeps up with all the latest, all right." Driving up there himself for it. He'd be in with it tonight.

Julie was soaking in the bathtub. Henry, having been out of the house and away from all this, his attention engaged in affairs of less significance and more immediacy, was glad to avoid her. He was in the middle of putting a solid breakfast under his belt in the dining room, when she appeared, all dressed up in her black-and-white silk print. Purple stains trailed downward from her reddened eyes into the porcelain whiteness of her cheeks.

"Julie, you look awful. Why don't you get yourself some rest?"

"All night, all I been able to think of is how it must have looked to Coley—the whole earth blowing up before his eyes—"

"Julie, don't! It don't do no good to go over and over, I been through it, it don't . . . Where you going?"

She was pinning on her black cartwheel straw hat. "With you. I'm going down to that hearing with you and look that boy in the face and let him know. It's my land he's lived on all these years. It's my generosity that's fed and supported him. I just want to look in his face and let him know how I feel. That's all."

"But you can't leave now, you want to be here—"

"Kissie's here. Coley'll sleep to noon anyhow. Even if I stay, I can't help. That's what I can't stand another minute, sitting by helplessly . . . I'm going to go down there and look in that boy's face. Henry, I've got to do it! Don't stop me!"

It was the best thing she could possibly do insofar as he was concerned. Without any effort on his part, with none of the usual pushing and shoving and shouting, she accompanied him out of the door, her eyes blazing in the sunlight, her mouth garish against her pallor, her large black patent-leather bag swinging from her arm, her white-gloved hand tucked under his elbow, holding to him.

3

Rad almost failed to attend the probate hearing although he fully intended to the evening before. For the details of living can overtake and undermine the solidest resolution, logically and inevitably arrived at, until, being unable to follow through, you drop it. Then something else may come along, or nothing at all, and you're swept up again . . .

He spent the hours after the sheriff's departure with Reeve, blowing the ditch above Reeve's cornfield; opening up the main channel; speeding into town to replenish supplies and speeding back to continue on. In a headlong race that left no time for prudence they were driven to cover as much territory as possible before an excuse could be found to stop them.

It was long after dark when, heads aching with fumes, ears dinning with concussion after concussion, they returned to Reeve's house to chew over between bites of cold side meat and gulps of hot coffee the situation in which they were both entrapped. The discussion, prolonged by their fatigue, consisted mainly of amazed self-discovering mumbles of mutual congratulation.

"You all right. You know you all right?"

Thus they were pledged. United we stand, divided we fall. Together we beat 'em.

On the tide of this mood Rad was moved to offer to stay up with the men who were guarding the house for the night. It didn't seem important to him right then, in the midst of Reeve's family and friends, that should Chalmer's cohorts or anyone else, put up to it by Henry or under their own steam, drunk or sober, show up here, an attack would find him on the wrong side of the fence. But his offer was waved off. "You dead on your feet. Best go rest up, you'll need your strength for tomorrow." He left High Power, the Baron, Sanderlee, Ben, and Fred lounging over the porchside, shooting irons propped up beside them, dogs prowling about the yard.

"Good night!" "Good night for possum!"

If he had really all-out wanted to stay, Rad couldn't help feeling in prickly self-consciousness as he hurried away, he'd have stayed despite the out they gave him and they knew it. Keyed up with the exhilaration of the day's accomplishment; plagued by a sense that far from being the burden on him that he had anticipated with such dread, these colored were instead providing for his protection; jittery with the uncertainties that loomed ahead, he lurched through the darkness down the track. To his right the cane growing thick and tall, sucking almost audibly at the ground for moisture, brushed his cheek with a silken urgency. What will tomorrow bring?

He hastened into the kitchen without noticing the floor his wife was mopping, wet as a sheet of ice. He made straight past the table for the high corner shelf where the family Scripture was lodged. Lifting it down he blew dust from the time-blackened cover. It was as large and heavy as one of his wife's plant boxes and so old it was seldom used anymore except to enter births and deaths. So old it went back to his grandfather's grandfather and back before that to the first Oglethorpe Scot settlers.

"Now look what you done tracked in!" Lulabelle, flushed up fever-red with exertion and the discomforts of her pregnancy, vigorously shuttled her mop after him. "Where you been all this time? Had me so worried up, I waited supper and waited—"

Intent on his purpose, her complaint no more than an irritable humming in the back of his head, he laid the volume on the table, turned the loose back cover to the family records and began searching through pages so yellowed and sear a breath of wind might have crumbled them to dust. Douglas McDowell, Maryalice, Rena, Ellamae—only a generation back, his father wore three wifes out and buried them before their time. Mattie, December 1, 1887 to June 6, 1888, Phoebe, Buster, Gentry —only two generations back and his grandmother birthed baby after baby and buried them before they'd barely started to live. Lachlan McDowell . . . And there it was! Right where it should have been, sealed inside the uneven-edged pages so deep it didn't leave so much as a dent between them.

"And the sheriff, what was he doing there? And all them deputies? I sent Charles up to find out and they wouldn't let him go near." Bulkily Lulabelle stooped low, ramming her mop under bench and table and in and around his feet until he was compelled to lift them up out of her way. "Then when I went up there after, there wasn't no one could tell me—"

Rad unfolded a sheet of accounting paper, legal size, double-ruled in red across the top and down the left margin, blue-lined across. The original whiteness of the paper had become tan with age and the ink grape-brown; its creases were dingily worn through to cracks that would have to be mended over with cellophane tape. ". . . *Now this Indenture witnesseth that the said Superintendent of Taxation of the City of Arcady, County of Colfax . . . hath given, guaranteed, conveyed and exchanged to Lachlan McDowell, To have and to hold the said parcel designated by the letters S.T and U, and bounded southerly by . . . And to his assignees to this sale and only use, benefit and behoof forever . . . Hath hereunto set his hand and caused the corporate seal of the City of Arcady to be affixed . . . I hereby certify the above conveyance to be a true copy from Folio A, Book C, pages 17 and 18 . . ."*

Rad quickly skimmed through the facsimile of the deed of sale, leaving what was illegible of its clauses and signatures for later perusal. There it was all right, all of it, the letters crawling like beetles across the paper. How much cotton Lachlan McDowell must have chopped and baled right along with the freedmen in order to acquire this entitlement Rad could not imagine. They wouldn't grow cotton, that was the story his father had told him. Old Jonas B. Scott and Lachlan McDowell agreed between them not to grow cotton and got everyone else around to agree the same and that way they were never at the mercy of the cotton market or the brokers or the creditors and speculators or any element outside of pests and the weather. That was how they kept hold of their land.

"And every time them younguns run out of here this afternoon, I was so scairt sick every step they took they'd blow themselves up. And all that noise today. I never thought there'd be that much noise to it—"

"Look!" Excitedly Rad thrust the paper up at her. "Look what I got here! I was so scairt sick I wouldn't find it—"

"Look! Now look what you done!"

He had inadvertently knocked against the pail she dragged after her, splashing black suds water out onto the floor. Wrenching with her hands she wrung her upended raggedy mophead out over the pail, then raking it to and fro sopped up the puddle. "Why don't you look what you doin'!" With the scrub brush from her pail she threw herself bodily down on hands and knees to scrape at a hardened food stain between the trestle legs.

Her checkered shirt clove to her bowed back and spilled out over jeanpants unfastened for comfort and rolled up to her thighs. Her buttocks rocked back and forth over calves streaked with dried runnels of water. The wet soiled soles of her feet obtruded, terrible in their nakedness. When Rad looked down at her, his heart and his very flesh contracted. Guilt? Pity? Repugnance? Love? She was like Reeve with the flyblown sow, a living reproach he couldn't bear up under. Only now he was too exhausted to do anything about it even if she'd let him. Neither could he go to bed as he must and leave her as she was. He could only shrink into himself, making himself smaller in his own containment while he continued turning back through the back pages as if in incompletion he were still searching for something, some answer, some solution, some sureness that would soothe him. Back and back through the mustiness of unrecognizable names. Was delivered of a man-child. Was united in wedlock. Departed this life.

The brown-ink beetle tracks all but faded into the brittle brown-splotched paper, the writing so queer he could scarcely decipher it, all the *s*'s like *f*'s and the *th*'s like *y*'s. Interleaved between the pages, sealed in like his copy of the deed so tight and so long it took no space at all, was another document, only this one of a paper as soft as a piece of cloth that would crumple in your hand. He had seen it once before as a child or heard talk about it though he couldn't recall what the occasion was. A resolution against the introduction of slavery into the colony passed by the first council of the first settlement of Arcady back in 1741, of which Radford McDowell, the first Rad in this country, was a member.

He drew the kerosene lamp over close and turned the wick up high. *By the Will of Providence and the Grace of God, we herein signatory* . . . Word by word he spelled it out just as the hand before his had written it down, moving in a blur of its own shadow over these very lines. Prohibiting forever within the bourne of this territory the purchase, sale and maintenance in involuntary servitude of such captives as have been delivered from the Afric continent or of their offspring or their descendants. *For they too must love freedom, therefore what chaos and bloodshed it must bring about.* . . .

"Why they knew!" Rad said aloud in awed surprise. "Way back then, over two hundred years ago, they knew! If those folks aren't given their born-rights as good as you and me, if they're tramped on and beat out—Lu, listen to this. Just listen. Therefore what chaos and bloodshed—*it*—slavery—"

"Bloodshed?" Blindly she struggled to her feet. "What you up to, Rad McDowell! What you fixin' . . ."

"Lu, I got to go in to court tomorrow. Reeve's having a court fight over that land of his and if he don't win it . . ."

"Court? They haulin' you off to court? I knowed it, I knowed it. That sheriff, and them polices . . . You in trouble with the law!"

In vain he tried to explain to her. Sullenly beet-red, obdurate, she leaned on her mop handle, refusing to absorb the import of his words. "I knowed it, I felt it, I seen it! Here I been workin' and worryin' and

wonderin' all these hours, should I go over there and get you out of
whatever you in . . . I never thought it would go all this far!"

Hefting up her pail she took it outside to swish down over the back
steps. Rad slammed off to the bedroom. Peeling off the grime and sweat
of his clothes, he could hear even through two doors her every movement in the kitchen. They were right back in the middle of last night's
bickering. He hadn't wanted to start this with Reeve, because from the
start he suspected what it might lead to. And she who had urged him
into it from the start was now shying off . . .

Did they always have to be like this? Barking and biting at each other
out of sheer stress and strain? Was this harshness the material out of
which their life together was woven, unable ever to break out of itself?
Knowing he ought to go back out there to her, he couldn't. Too proud
or too peeved to cross her path again, he washed up in the little tepid
water that had stood in the pitcher on the dresser since morning. Picking with an expert pinch of his fingernails through his armpits and
crotch for wood ticks, shiny-backed and crawly legged, that crablike had
fastened upon him.

He crawled across the lumpy bed into the farthest corner and
stretched himself out against the tongue-and-groove wall, hearing with
his whole body the swabbing of her rinse water over the kitchen floor.
When the floor dried she would walk barefoot over it to feel through
the soles of her feet how clean, how smooth, how free of grit it was.

Tired as he was, the harder he reached for sleep the more tautly awake
he grew, reaching for the crack of her step on the threshold. But as soon
as she entered the hushed confinement of the room—all brown tongue-
and-groove, vertical on walls, horizontal on the ceiling—antagonism expanded from her into every last joint and corner. She climbed into bed
beside him, her breath hissing sharp out of pinched nostrils, and lashed
about from back to side and back again, unable to make herself comfortable. Hugging the wall, he felt her every twist and turn and twinge
behind him. Like it was all on him, all his doing, all his sin come home
to roost, the devil riding his back with a pitchfork after him. Pretending
sleep, he had to pretend he believed her asleep too. But she wasn't sleeping. Everything bothered her these nights. Leg cramp that caught her in
the back of the leg sometimes so bad she'd wake up shrieking. Backache
so mean she couldn't straighten out. Heartburn, gas pains, bowels
stopped up, piles puffed out, kidneys that kept her on the run for a drop
or two. And swollen ankles, a danger sign. The other children had come
to them without his turning a hair. He'd never minded anything like this
before. Never even noticed. But this time, this baby . . .

The bed sagged as she heaved herself up from it. She groped across the room to the commode, flung up the lid and flung herself down with a long-caught breath and, grunting, with every resource of her strength pressed internally downward. And nothing. Again. And again. Nothing. "O Lord O Lord a-mercy—"

He sat up. "Lu?"

"O Lord God . . ."

"Lu? You all right, Lu?"

Her answered issued forth at last, reluctantly. "Well I ain't pickin' no daisies."

Restlessly unrelieved she returned to bed and with her back to him punched at her pillow, emanating sparks of resentment like a spitting cat. "Goin' up there to Reeve and talkin' all hours instead of comin' home where you belong." She always tended to be suspicious if not downright jealous of anything that took him outside the immediate purlieu of home and family. And now that she was so closely bound to it herself, there was no escape for her, she resisted and opposed his flights more than ever.

"Why if Mr. Coombs or some of those men of his had come back there tonight, there'd have been a fuss and a fight, and you in the middle . . . And court! Now you goin' on about goin' to court. You'll end up in the lockup!"

Rad, with his back to her, plastered himself against the narrow boards of the wall. It was the kind of night when every least little sound catches at you like a gill net so that snared like a fish by the gill slits you can't retreat. Clink of bedsprings in the children's room. Rooting of varmints under the floor. Tappings on the roof. Termites in the wood. It was the time of night when you can hear all creation nibbling away at your efforts, and nothing you can do to stop it.

Later, he didn't know how long later, he awoke to find that she was gone from the bed beside him and from the room. Then he became aware of a thumping like the thrum of insects against the screened window that fronted on the porch. "Rad?" Lulabelle was calling to him. "Rad? Come on out here a minute."

Swaying with sleep he stumbled through the parlor to the porch door. "Over here," she called to him, and barking his ankles against the tubs that contained her plants he made his way to the far end of the porch.

"Look," she whispered, and in her tone there was something of the same awed surprise he had experienced when searching through the old records, "look what I have here."

She held out to him by the handle a battered and blistered agate stewpot.

"What is it?" Morosely he shook himself awake. "I don't see nothin'."

"The night-blooming cereus. It blooms just once a year. For just one night."

She wheeled about under his fingers the long leathery oblate leaves that curled in upon themselves and sprouted so strangely from out of themselves their new leaf-growth until he discerned, hung upon the speared stalk, palely shining, the blossoming.

"Don't it look," she whispered softly, "just like little Jesus in his manger with the star up above?"

"My old lady." With a smile that curled out of him like the capricious turn of the leaf, he took the plant from her and set it down. "Anything you put a hand to, sweetheart, will grow for you."

They stood for a while on the edge of the porch, arms around each other's waists. "See all them stars up there?" Rad pointed skyward. "As many, they say, as there are sands in the sea. Billions and trillions of 'em. They say there's other suns up there and worlds spinning around them and maybe people— Makes you wonder sometimes. Don't it make you wonder?"

"So far," she sighed. "Trillions of miles. Years, Charles says. So far, he says, that the one we lookin' on right now may have burnt itself out before our world began."

"We come. We go. We bloom overnight. Wherefrom? Whereto? Whyfor? *Whfffft* . . . If I thought that's all there was to it I'd take and cut my throat right now."

"Rad!" In her present state even the stars in their courses were a threat to her, a peril she must snatch him back from. "Don't I mean nothin' to you? Don't your younguns?"

"There has to be a reason behind it all," he said. "There has to be a purpose to it."

Legs astride he stood on his porch as that first Rad McDowell might have stood on decks awash with the high seas, a man in movement because he had to move or be crushed, staring into the limitless expanse of the skies, his familiar shores far behind and the coast of a new untried land yet to be reached.

"Trillions of miles, years, that what Charles told you?" He laughed. "Howcome him to know so much more about it'n we do?"

"Rad—" She reached over for his free hand and placed it over the old shirt of his she wore for a nightgown, over the huge taut-skinned radiant mound of her belly. "You feel that?"

Under his fingers a movement as light as the burst of a bubble. Her flesh, drum-tight, rippled and rolled.

"I'm your wife. This your baby."

Flip. Flipflop.

"Rad, I'm afeared!"

"Now Lu-honey, don't let nothin' I said—"

"I'm afeared. Ever since all that dynamite went off today, seemed like every explosion hit right through me. It's gonna be born stone-deaf. It's gonna throw fits . . . gonna bark like a dog . . . It—I ain't go-n come through this."

"Now Lu, nothing's going to . . ."

"All this day long I been feelin'—I can't see what's ahead! I steppin' off into . . . nowhere! My heart's been a-poundin' and a-shakin' so . . . Rad, I want you to swear on the head of this unborn baby of ours you ain't gettin' mixed up in nothin' that'll hurt it."

"Lu, you shiverin'. Let us go in now."

She gripped his hand, holding it fast over the globular chamber within which was cushioned beneath layer upon layer of tissue and fluid the living and as yet unimaginable being.

"Swear it now! Swear you won't do nothin' that'll bring harm on this family."

He swore. He took his solemn oath. But couldn't refrain from chucking at a bulge that jutted from the rotund wall. "That his little head or his hiney I'm pledgin' on?"

By morning he had convinced himself that it was after all unnecessary for him to attend the hearing. It would make no difference whether he was there or not. It was only a matter of filing a will. Reeve had it all in hand. He was glad to be able to plunge back into the work he'd let go through the past week, the sweet potato draws to be transplanted, the weeds romping through the peppers . . .

Between the peppers and the potatoes he wandered down to inspect the ditches they had blown yesterday. It was one of those days when the sky is brilliant one minute, no sign of a shower, and the next minute clouds heap up; the air is full of warm and cool spots by turn, humid and breezy, serene and stormy, squalls of rain and sunshine chasing one another. The sunken areas held the sultry heat and were so thick with deerflies Rad had to keep sweeping them with his arms away from his face. But when he reached his ditch, sure enough a trickle of yellow water was flowing through it.

The birds frightened off by yesterday's blasting were back. Shrike flew overhead like bullets on the wing. A cuckoo winged through the trees in snakelike flight. Red-winged blackbirds teetered on the slenderest of twigs, balancing on their long tails. They lifted their black wings at his approach, the red glowing out of the black like epaulets, and in a flutter and flurry beat him off from the proximity of their nests. Underfoot the meadow resounded with chuck-chuckings from the ground nests.

Marsh hen, king rail, dove: good game birds, good eating. You could grow brown-top millet along the ditchsides, the preacher at Reeve's house yesterday had suggested. Attract duck. He hopped a creek on the way back to his field, and the brown water was a-swim with bream. Redbreast around the sunken logs. Wamout around the stumps. The boys would be down with their poles before supper tonight. He caught a glimpse of a scarlet milk snake, white-bisected black stripes between red, orange, and yellow; red-nosed in contrast to the black of the equally dazzling but venomous coral. Wyatt would have gone chasing after it in a flash. And caught it, too.

Through drenching rain and burning sunshine he dug his sweets up out of the common holes in which the slips had rooted and replanted them in rows. Along about nine he went back to the house for his coffee. Ruby and Timmy came running out of the yard toward him, screaming with excitement. "The 'gators! The 'gators has hatched!"

Between them they dragged him out back of the sty to the mound Wyatt had built up out of dirt and humus, almost five feet high, in imitation of a mamma alligator, and in the summit of which he had deposited the big snow-white broken eggs he had found, the seemingly lifeless embryos attached inside to the yellow yolk sacs. For over a month he had like an alligator carried mud and water and rotting vegetation to the top of the mound, keeping it saturated, heating in the sun, fermenting. And now unbelievably the babies were wriggling out, horny, brown-and-white stippled, like seashells on the move.

Rad quaffed his hot coffee in the kitchen and under his wife's disapproving eyes poured a steaming kettle of water into the enamel basin, washed himself up and shaved. Against her heavy silence—she wouldn't lift a finger to help him—he went into the bedroom and searched through the dresser drawers and cupboard for a clean outfit. In stiff-starched khaki shirt, blue pants, and brown socks that didn't quite match, he came back to the kitchen. She was standing over a skillet rendering lard, starting back at each spatter of the hot fat.

"I got to go, Lu. There's something about this, I just got to go there."

"You promised! You promised to stay out of it!"

"Ain't nothin' going to happen. It's all cut-and-dried. He's got his papers and his lawyer and everything on his side. Everything'll be all right."

"You believe that? You can stand there and say to me you believe that? When you know they'll never give in to him. Never! Never in this world—"

"Then where does that leave us?"

"I don't know! I don't know anymore! God knows I don't. All I know

right on is to close my eyes, shut my ears, and sit tight. Rad, don't. What
for? What good will it do?"

"I got to," he said from the doorway and left her shaking the skillet,
the spitting grease stinging at her cheeks, and tears—she never cried,
only got angry—tears spilling from her eyes. He took the truck, leaving
her with the children to chase after and the guinea hens ordered by the
market for tomorow to be caught and killed and dressed, and herself
without any help should her time prematurely come on her. But if he
stayed, where would her respect for him be? And his for himself?

It'll be all right, he argued with her all the way, mainly because he
was in his mind unable to conceive of any other workable outcome.
Reeve had his proof, dead-to-rights, in black-and-white, and proof no
court could get around. I won't do a thing, he vowed to her as he took
the long curve from the River Road into the highway, won't even open
my mouth. Just sit there, one friendly white person from his own back-
yard.

But when he entered the courtroom through the double doors from
the corridor among the white onlookers who were beginning to drift in,
attracted from their offices in the building and from the Square by por-
tents that something unusual was up, when he paused briefly on the
balustraded platform that marked the division of the races and surveyed
the scene below, he knew that he had been living in a fool's paradise.
This arena with its tall fretted windows in the wings and lofty coffered
ceiling overhead bore no resemblance whatsoever to the homeground of
a backwoods shack in which a tilt with the sheriff had been won.

Directly opposite the entry platform the Judge's bench, as yet un-
occupied, presided, majestic on its dais, over the railed enclosure in
which the battle was to be conducted. Twin cast-iron stanchions surmounted by white-globed lamps elevated the bench still further in effect, and twin pilasters framing the door to the Judge's chamber in the
rear heightened still further the dignity of the chair he was soon to assume. Behind the leather chair and to its right the flag soared, a slash of
red-and-white falling in folds from the blue field under the gold-eagled
standard. Over the entablature of the door, on which the state shield
was affixed, and over the dado that, in alignment with the cornice, separated the polished paneling below from the strip of crinkly parchment-
painted wall above, hung the gilt-framed photographs of three early
judges, saved from the fire that had ravaged the entire Square at the
turn of the century. Two burnsided gentlemen flanked one, full-bearded
and beetle-browed, as formidable of demeanor, as inscrutable and inaccessible as Zeus wrapped in the clouds of Olympus.

Directly below the balustrade of the platform, a broad center aisle inclined to the gate of the inner sanctum, splitting asunder here and bringing closest the white and colored segments of the semicircular seat arrangement. At the foot of the aisle, in the first seat of the first row on the colored side, Rad sighted Reeve hunched intently forward over his knees. Reeve turned as if sensitized to the identity of each new arrival and for an instant Rad thought that he was about to raise his hand in welcoming recognition or that he himself was about to raise his hand; but whether it was discretion that stayed them or a residue of mutual doubt or something more dubious he would never know. In the same instant Benson Reece of the bank came tap-tapping in on his cane and greeted Mr. Arthur, the tax collector, both of them immaculate in white glossed shirt and black bowtie.

"Come to view the slaughter?" Benson inquired with a geniality that included all the loungers on the platform.

Laughing they all trooped after Benson as, helped by Mr. Arthur, he descended the three–four steps on the left end of the platform; then clambered up the aisle on the wall side of the white section, looking for the most advantageous spot from which to watch proceedings and hail their friends over. Rad followed them, his hand shoved deep in his pocket over the copy of his deed that he had brought with him, seeking in its worn-dry reality for reassurance. Just as he had quailed before Rose's funeral in the anticipation that he would be the only white person present or one of only very few, and thus painfully conspicuous, and then had arrived at the churchyard to discover, worse still, a crowd that dwarfed him, he suffered now a hundred qualms. There was no point to his being here. What was the use of it? But this time he didn't turn and go home.

He took his place high up and far back, growing tighter and tighter with the buzz of expectation that focused on the recessed doorway behind the bench through which Judge Vernon Clay Purcell would shortly appear.

4

In a test where irrefutable proof is pitted against implacable power, it is the intangibles that shape the course, if not the upshot, of the encounter. Before the Judge's appearance, the atmosphere of the courtroom was already charged with currents set to rippling by the most irrelevant of conditions and incidents. The whites who were "just passing by" and "happened in" to "see what's going on" were not animated by any special partisanship. Their attitude was fluid rather than fixed.

They dispersed among the roan-highlighted ranks of chairs as in a theater, settling down with the high good humor and the zest one brings to a classic drama of which the end is already well-known but which nevertheless never fails to arouse the fiery tingle of suspense in its unfolding. Almost no one had made up his mind beforehand as to which party had the right or wrong of it; almost all of them if polled just then would, while astutely refusing to commit themselves, have taken in the privacy of their own thoughts an educated guess that "the nigger is about to be jacked." But as to how, ah, that was the case in point! They had come with the appreciation of connoisseurs, and with a grim amusement not unmixed with a pang of compunction, to follow the performance by which Judge Purcell would pull his unimpeachable legal decision out of the hat.

As the colored filed in from the outside fire escape which constituted their entrance, across the length of the courtroom, and filled their banks of seats from the highest row to the lowest, facing them vis-à-vis, the whites reacted with a quiver not so much of hostility as of annoyance. Farmers in overalls as if they had just quit their plows in the fields for the occasion, others more formally attired in gingham shirts and seedy black pants, mothers with babes in arm and tots in tow, youths arraying themselves against the wall. They kept coming and coming. More still! "Whatever's got into them?" a covey of women in front of Rad, driven in from the streets by a sudden gust of rain in the uncertain temper of this day's weather, asked of each other. The air about him fairly crackled with coughs of peevish risibility. Why this case? Why now?

The quiver stiffened when at the first solemn bong of ten from the clock on the courthouse cupola Henry Warren escorted his wife in through the double door to the platform, and to the accompaniment of repeated bongs down the short flight of steps on the white side and at a word from her around to the fore and down the center aisle to the gate. There with the gravest solicitude for her comfort he seated her in the first chair of the first row on the white side, apparently at her request, in a position exactly counterparting that of her opponent, Reeve Scott.

The entire white section craned forward to catch a glimpse of the pale profile under the black circumference of the hatbrim. That she should choose to appear here personally in this matter in which she was a quasi-principal came as a startling surprise. Such a thing was never done. Being who she was and what she was she would have exerted a potent influence here by her very absence. But the ineluctable physical sight of her, turning deliberately in her chair to stare at Reeve who, hunched over hands folded between his knees, stared straight ahead, did after all carry more weight than her poltergeist would have. Moreover, some rumor of her little boy's derangement as a result of yesterday's blasting had been bruited about over several breakfast tables and now circulated from row to row. "They say he was most scared out of his wits." "Well nobody knows exactly how it happened, but . . ." Thus Rad learned for the first time that, like the flock of butterflies dancing over the sparkleberries in the path of the cartridges, like many a nestling on the bush and snake in its burrow, the child had been an inadvertent victim of his ditching.

"She looks all done in," the woman in front of him breathed on the wave of sympathy that rolled downward toward Julie. "Don't she look all done in? Poor thing . . ."

With no more ado than if he had been passing through his own front door, Henry swung open the gate to the welled enclosure and joined his attorney who had already deposited himself at his counsel table and was unbuckling his briefcase. Henry with one hand on the back of Lars Finchley's chair and the other on the tabletop consulted with him, raising his brows and gesturing with his head toward the packed rows. It was this picture of Henry with Lars half-pivoted toward him in the splayed fork of his arms, Henry so shrewdly alert and Lars sunburnt to the color of Georgia clay, jut-nosed over his flattened-out heart of a mouth, craggy with that lean clean homeliness that always betokens an intelligence of unshakable integrity—it was this picture of the two men engaged in their off-the-cuff conference, a quality it possessed of authority utterly at ease with itself, that caused Rad's heart to sink altogether. Why we got no more chance against them than a couple of bugs under a stick of hot powder. We don't mean anymore to them than a word did yesterday to us. He was caught in a pattern of nature, in one of those mazes in which a line continuously turns corners around itself, the larger perimeter always girding the smaller. And again the sole reality on which he could grasp was the paper folded in his pocket.

The entrance of the Judge was somewhat delayed due to the splashing spurt of a cloudburst that had sent shoppers scurrying from the street to the courthouse portico for refuge and thence inside to the courtroom. On alighting from his car at a propitious interval in the downpour Purcell had stepped into a pothole that, he felt justly, Harold Wylly who was chauffeuring him should have averted him from or at least warned him of. In his chambers he was met by Ada Hemmings who, ostensibly rearranging in order the buckram-bound law tomes that lined the shelves behind his Spanish-style desk, was awaiting him all agog. "Judge, they're all here! Have you seen them? Why it's a regular fish fry!" Noiselessly opening the door into the courtroom the merest fraction, the Judge received an impression of numbers that more than confirmed the call he had earlier made to Henry in an effort to secure a postponement. How a hearing that he had conceived of as a little family tête-à-tête, confined to the parties involved with himself as arbiter, conducted so quietly and quickly as to escape the notice even of passersby in the courthouse corridor, over almost before it began, had become transformed into a public affair he could not by any stretch of reason adduce.

"It's after ten," Ada reminded him. "They're all waiting for you out there on pins and needles and tenterhooks. Well, you're not going to allow them to remain, are you? There's Chalmer Coombs," she herself peeped out the door, reporting with a positively enjoyable kissing of her lips. "And D. C. Lacey. Come hotfooting over to see which way the wind'll blow, I suppose, so they'll know which way to jump. And all these other white folks—you can't turn them out?"

The Judge retired to the comfortable round-backed mahogany chair, snapped up like the desk at an auction, on which the Harvard seal was inscribed with its circled motto *Veritas*, and unlaced his wet shoe. "Here, Ada, will you put this under the fan for a minute or two?" Then thoughtfully swinging his foot in its clocked black silk sock, he relaxed back until it should dry off a little. They'd all come here without his invitation. Let them cool their heels while he composed himself.

Actually, despite the disconcerting crowd and the dampness of his foot, Vernon Purcell was in excellent spirits. He was exhausted of course almost to the nadir of stupor by his daughter's wedding yesterday and exalted almost to the zenith of mental energy—both at once as in a state of intoxication—by the fact that he had pulled the whole coup off, everything about it exceeding even his fondest expectations. During the wedding breakfast, on the heels of Julie's toast to him which because of the very flipness of its satire perhaps achieved a sophisticated credence that was most gratifying, in the middle of the stuffed squab Bob Burnson had cautiously but of his own volition offered to put up the risk-money for the Marquis' land when it should become available. During the dancing, when he stepped off the floor after yielding Julie to a cut-in in the midst of a nostalgic tango, Dan Garner had grabbed him into a corner and confided to him in strictest secrecy that the old Senator's health was failing and that he would indubitably resign along about next November, with three years left to his term.

Without Dan saying so in so many words, this intimated that he was moving heaven and earth to advance his prospects for the unexpired term, that his succession to it depended largely on who the next governor-elect was to be, and that this in turn depended on how the rural counties voted. It also intimated that Dan, expanding his view from that of his congressional district to statewide, was, if certain assurances were to be forthcoming, prepared to shift his allegiance to the woolhat column, the Judge's faction; and that if the Judge could swing the county for the gubernatorial candidate of his and Dan's choice, there would surely be in it for him the desideratum of his professional career, an appointment to the Federal bench.

While he was conversing with Garner, subtly feeling out his hints, who should amble up but Benson Reece with Julie on his arm and a most interesting bit of news. To crown success with success, DeLavery had knuckled under! "We paid a little call on Lady Augusta this morning. Know what I mean? Poor old soul, admits herself she must have been off her rocker." "Isn't it wonderful?" Julie had cried. "I just hate this infighting. Welcome back to the fold!"

What the Judge needed now was a period of leisure in which to pursue, exploit, and consolidate his gains. He should be on his way right now with Dan Garner speeding up to Ol' Cal Hubbard's plantation midstate for a picnic get-together on the lawn. On the other hand he had to prove himself able to deliver, and much of what he had to deliver lay right outside here in the courtroom. At this stage of the game, four months before the September primary and two months before the campaign would draw the lines hard and fast, one makes it one's business not to attack but to attract. Antagonize nobody. Woo 'em.

His problem then was not such a difficult one. In fact, the Judge concluded, as he stamped his foot back into his shoe, there was no problem at all. He was familiar with the details of the estate in hand, he had the administrator he was to appoint well in mind—Eustis Telfer who belonged by habit to Benson Reece's political camp, an inspired choice if ever there was one—and he was willing if it should prove necessary to add the name of a colored preacher out Fallona way as co-administrator. He had only to maintain himself as he always did on the bench without bias and above criticism. To adhere scrupulously to the dictates of his conscience and the letter of the law. Come what may.

"What do you intend to do?" Ada in a pink flurry, gathering up her sharpened pencils and stenographer's notebook, asked him.

"Why I haven't made up my mind yet, Ada," the Judge benignly answered her. Eschewing his robes, leaving them hanging on the hat rack, he passed on to the door in his shirt sleeves, black-tied and black-gallused, trimly informal. "What's there to intend? No one can ever claim, I'm proud and pleased to say, that this court is not above all else open and aboveboard. We have nothing to hide from anyone."

The tentative twitchings of the door from the Judge's chamber had not been lost upon the onlookers. As when a theater curtain makes several false starts, croaking on its rings, or when reel-numbers are flashed upon a darkened movie screen, murmurs broke out, scrapings and even stampings. Cellophane crackled as fresh cigarette packs were opened. Gum wrappings, balled up, shot past serried heads toward sand-filled cuspidors which they invariably missed. The rain that had caused windows to be banged shut and had thereupon rattled down the panes like hoses played upon them ceased abruptly. Bands of sunlight streamed freshly downward. With grunts and grimaces of effort the windows were balkily forced up again. The sultry heat that had accumulated in the closed interior remained.

All restlessness subsided as the bailiff appeared on his side of the bench and Ada on hers and took their places.

Oyez oyez oyez . . .

From his august portals the Judge issued forth. All rose to their feet until he should be seated, something of the pageantry of ritual holding them each in sway. Purcell, impassive as priest and king, immune to the human faculties of sight and sound, lifted his gavel. The court was now in session.

"If you please, Your Honor?"

The voice broke out of the sacrosanct hush, interrupting the descent of the gavel. Faces wheeled about in shocked perplexity. Rad's heart dropped like a stone. Down in the first seat of the first row on the colored side, Reeve Scott was standing up, leaning his hands on the rail before him.

"Your Honor, if you could just wait a few minutes longer? Our lawyer, I think, must have been held up by the rain."

"His what?" "What's he say?"

The Judge reared forward. He had during his brief and apparently unswerving passage to the bench managed to scan a pretty fair portion of the room, particularly as he rounded his chair the colored half. To his dismay he had at once remarked a group who looked, if he was not mistaken, like the long-term occupants of the Marquis' land. He now, austerely adjusting his pince-nez, recognized—and he could not be mistaken for his memory of it was too fresh—the sister of the dead veteran who had tried to make trouble over the disposition of his pension money. And Thurlow who had had that farm down on Sunset Point that Brandon Colfax took over . . . What dismayed and angered him more than the conspicuous presence of these individuals was that Wylly, on whom he depended for information, had failed to forewarn him that all this was building up. And a lawyer on the way! How the Scotts could

have obtained a lawyer without the news of it being leaked to him by
the whites and without a single word of it from the colored, not from
any of them, not even Wylly . . .

What the Judge did not know about the Wyllys, father and son, was
that they lived in relative isolation from the colored community and
except for Harold's recently acquired wardenship at St. Augustine's held
themselves clannishly aloof from it, neither seeking nor receiving its
favor. Nobody ever told anything to the Wyllys. The fourthhand gossip
they traded on in their service to the Judge they themselves regarded
as more or less worthless. In addition, they were both this week in a
temper due to a misunderstanding over who was to pay them for the
hours they had put in at Julie's party last Saturday night. The Judge
had studiously ignored Harold's complaints and the Warrens when
called upon somehow never caught the idea that they were, ever so circumspectly, being dunned. In any event the pipeline the Judge relied
on as his loyal and faithful ear to the colored was plugged.

With all due deliberation the Judge removed his glasses, wiped and
replaced them. Wasn't that the old woman over there who had drunk
from his chalice? Or over there? Or there? Why didn't I hear about this!

"Come here," he motioned over his bench to Reeve.

"A lawyer?" "A lawyer did he say?" "What lawyer?" Among the scattered but rapidly increasing whites speculation was running rife, on a
wave of titters. Which of the three remaining lawyers in the county,
active or retired, could have been prevailed upon at what price to lend
himself . . .

"That's right." The Judge motioned Reeve through the gate. "Right
up here to the bench. Don't be afraid, there's nothing to be afraid of.
What is it now? Speak up so we all can hear you."

"Our lawyer, sir," Reeve was forced to repeat in a tone that rasped
out unnaturally loud. "We're expecting him any minute."

"Shuh now," the Judge gently chided him. "Shame you had to go
throwing your money away on anything like that. This court is here to
guard and protect your interest, I want you all to remember that. That
is our chief concern in the conservation of any estate, no matter how
small or how simple. It is our purpose today to aid the family of the deceased to the best of our ability in the resolution of her affairs under the
provisions of the law. That clear to you, son? And if you or anyone related to you has any question, if our language confuses you or our
references elude you, please don't hesitate to ask. The court is willing
to receive any reasonable query. We are your instrument. You may
stand down."

The Judge's earnestness was softened by a smile of disarming candor, which followed Reeve in his retreat to his seat. His mind was aseptically purged of all influence but the consideration before him as it developed. "And since this lawyer-fellow"—he raised his head, sweeping the room from wall to wall with a frown of reprimand—"whoever he is, hasn't shown up yet . . . And furthermore," he added severely, returning to the interrupted business of lifting his gavel, "I don't see what all this crowd here has to do . . ."

On the final stroke of the gavel, as if he had been lingering outside in the corridor for the cue, a stocky figure impeccably garbed in a white linen suit walked briskly in on the entry platform. Snowy haired, healthily tanned but with the dourly distasteful expression of the ulcerous on his face, he paused there if not like Juliet upon her balcony, at least like a generalissimo overlooking the hoi polloi assembled below. He withdrew his gaze to closer quarters, studying in disdainful perplexity the short flights of stairs on either end of the platform and then, deciding on the correct one, jogged down the white side and circled around to the forefront. His head truculently cocked, he advanced down the broad center aisle with the measured tread of a wedding march. With his briefcase he prodded open the gate. As always with Mayor Carter Sillens of Bay City one could almost catch the crackle of breaking bones beneath his footsteps.

In the compass of his journey every eye on the white side of the room had flown from the Mayor to Carter Scott sitting in the front row, half-around the quarter-circle of the rail, and from Carter Scott back to a small plum-cheeked woman seated unobtrusively behind Reeve, crocheting on one of the interminable antimacassars from which she earned a few pennies. Instantaneously the connection was made, as no stranger from the outside could ever have guessed, between the present moment and an ancient scar, presumably long forgotten—a lesion suppurating in the darkness of time since long before most of them were born. That woman in her prim white-collared black dress and taupe satin turban of archaic vintage, pinned forward over her glasses, must have been counting time for more than fifty years to accomplish this scene. To throw it up before all their faces. Her day in court.

"Why I didn't know," Ada Hemmings, aghast, formed with her lips in the direction of Lars Finchley, "that she was still alive!"

The story of Aunt Tee, Septima Scott, had, in all its dark whorls of a lifetime, never quite died away. At the age of ten she had been sent out one late fall evening that was turning frosty to pick up some firewood in the woods to last the stove till morning. She was surprised by a wandering party of white boys, about a dozen of them between the ages of fifteen and nineteen, who had gotten tipsy on a case of whiskey they had found. They surrounded the girl and started to have a little fun with her, chasing her back and forth between them, spurting liquor at her and then hilariously unwilling to waste so much of it on her outside they had pinned her down upon the ground and forced it down her throat. In the end, having excited themselves to such a pitch, they completed their experiment in manhood upon her. But they didn't abandon her to the cold night. They bore her home from the party, passed-out, summoned her father to the door, "Here's your daughter." And ran.

Her father had harnessed up his wagon and driven with her to the doctor, whom he aroused from bed. She was badly ruptured and the doctor in the heat of his outrage was ready to summon the sheriff as soon as she became coherent enough to name her attackers. She was able soon enough to name them: sons of almost every civic leader in Arcady, including the doctor. The doctor waxed even more incensed than before, but he did not send for the sheriff. "I'll talk to the boy myself first."

Her father brought her home and sat up awake with her until almost dawn. Then he took his shotgun down from the wall. A few hours later he returned with his gun still loaded, and with a misery of self-loathing that superseded his ire, wept, stormed at and cursed his lot. He had broken into the manse of the Presbyterian minister with his gun and had been talked out of using it. "Your tragedy," the minister had pleaded, "is less than mine. To discover that one's own flesh and blood should be capable of such brutality is a blow no parent can recover from. But—" The longest word in the English language to a colored man is *but*. "But what good will be achieved if you add one crime to another? Let the onus be on his soul." The boy would be dealt with, punished, horsewhipped if necessary.

Her father did not give up. Within a few days he determined to bring the matter to court for justice. But when he visited the county attorney to discuss the charges he wished to press, several practical obstacles were presented. All of the boys had already been dispatched from home in disgrace, either to private schools in which the strictest discipline was practiced or to jobs of rigorous physical labor in sawmills and shipping companies owned by relatives. Besides, how did it happen that he had sent his young daughter out alone in the woods at that time of night? Wasn't this a pretty irresponsible thing to do? Why didn't he go himself? And how could he be so sure that the girl, well developed for her age and robust, had not herself played some part in inciting the assault. She had been brought to the doctor, had she not, stinking to high heaven of rotgut whiskey.

And still, though he was warned against it, her father persisted. He went to the sheriff to swear out a complaint. The sheriff agreed to undertake a thorough investigation of the circumstances in order to determine who enticed who. "But if you breathe another word about this to anyone, the investigation will be dropped. Understand?" Not another word was breathed. A few months later her father left home one morning and never came back. Gone off, some people said, because he couldn't stand it anymore. Bought off, other people said. Or was run off. Within a year the doctor and the minister had moved away from Arcady, though the story by now had taken a new turn. The girl was crazy. She had imagined the whole thing from start to finish. Her family was told that if they ever so much as mentioned her again, she would be shut up in the asylum where she belonged.

Her mother conceived a repugnance for her and the women of her family manifested an aversion toward her as though she were tainted and men, colored as well as white, behaved in her vicinity with too close an interest. She must have gone a little mad with it all for, over a period of several years, she rambled about the woods at the mercy of anyone kind enough to feed her or debased enough to abuse her. There was at this time living out in the pines, in a substantial but down-at-the-heels dwelling, a fellow named Carter who had once seen better days but now contented himself with his hunting and his dogs and a schoolmarm wife that he had unaccountably married. Late one night Carter and his wife were awakened by a storm banging at shutters and doors. While they went about making things fast they caught a glimpse through a window of a half-wild creature staring in. Carter ran out and caught her, shivering and wretched, cowering with fear, and deposited her like a drenched puppy dog before his wife. Mary Carter tamed the girl, trained her, taught her, discovering in the process a satisfaction that overcame the isolation in which she lived. Some years later when Mary Carter lay dying after giving birth to her first living child, she entrusted her baby, Sillens, to Septima Scott and Septima to her husband, Evan Carter.

Not long afterward, people became accustomed to seeing Carter drive his wagon into town for supplies with Septima beside him where his wife used to be, with the baby in her arms. Carter would hand her down from the wagon with the same courtesy he had once shown his wife and he addressed her as *ma'am*. Well, they were both a little queer. It was no surprise when presently Septima rode the wagon with two children, the boy Sillens between herself and his father, and Scott in her arms. It was scandalous of course, particularly when the elder Carter took to referring to her as Mrs. Carter, but somehow no one dared interfere. In time both boys were sent to the school nearest their home in the woods, which happened to be a colored school, attended in part, it so happened, by the children of a colony of Japanese who had leased a tract of land nearby and converted it with much diligence to produce farming.

Thus Sillens Carter, bearing the family name of the first wife, and Scott Carter, bearing the family name of the second wife, grew up together. When Sillens was ten and Scott eight their father died. Tee continued on raising the boys, collecting rents from woodlots leased out and driving in to town once a month for supplies. Then quite suddenly the Sillens family showed up from the next county and took possession of the house, the older boy and the timberlands Evan Carter had owned. "Mrs. Carter" and her son were turned out.

The scandal so long confined to a wink and whisper now erupted full force. Not over the illicit relationship but over the woman's claim to a legitimate marriage and inheritance. She had in her possession a marriage certificate signed by a white justice of the peace in Fallona, her husband having apparently posed as colored for the purpose of the ceremony. She not only had documentary evidence of her rights but, with the brazen persistence of her father before her, she intended to sue in court for the restoration of her stepson and her property. This was the scandal.

The Sillens family—an uncle and cousin of Mary Sillens Carter—nipped the second wife's intentions in the bud. They at once assumed guardianship of the boy and instituted steps for his adoption, renaming him Carter Sillens. Simultaneously Tee was served with a court order demanding that she and her offspring cease *instanter* from use of the surname Carter. The sheriff who delivered the order to her at her brother's house, where she had taken shelter, took it upon himself to remind her of the old assault in the woods and the moral stigma attached to it. And of her ramblings afterward. "Didn't younguns used to taunt after you, *Tee Tee, crazy Tee?*" He also repeated some talk that was going around. The demise of her benefactors had occurred, had it not, with suspicious advantage to her. "And if those bodies are exhumed and any trace of toxic substance is discovered . . ."

The same day after the sheriff's conversation with her, when she was leaving the yard with her nine-year-old son, she found herself surrounded by a mocking circle of white youths. *Tee Tee, crazy Tee.* And the little children began to take it up, dancing after the coterie who escorted her down the road. *Tee Tee, crazy Tee.* And her son looked up at her, "Mamma? Mamma, why?" That night as they all lay asleep a rock smashed through the side window. "Get out of this town before tomorrow sun go down." *Tee Tee, crazy Tee.* They were going to shut her up in the asylum where she belonged.

The next morning she went to see the Sillens family in the old Carter dwelling place in the woods. And that afternoon she left the state. Gone off, some people said, because she couldn't stand it anymore. Bought off, other people said. Scared off. But she didn't, like her father, stay away forever. She came back the following year and settled down quietly in her father's old house with her son, now renamed, in some final flash of intransigence, Carter Scott. The Sillens had sold out and moved back with their boy to Bay City. Nobody bothered her so long as she bothered no one. Let sleeping dogs lie.

With the encouragement of some white ladies who felt sorry for her— and a number did feel now belatedly that in some ways she had been wronged—she began taking in fancywork. In those days there was a steady market in handmade linens, lingerie, and christening gowns, counterpanes and altar cloths. Though the pay was poor she managed to eke out an existence and even to send Carter away to a colored college where he received the equivalent of a high school education. She never made mention of the past but devoted her efforts exclusively to reinstating herself with her kin and church as a pillar of the deadliest respectability. Only she always did love to create a dramatic effect, in which she commanded the center of attention.

Now after all these years, Carter Sillens, who had battered his way up to the mayoralty of Bay City with the backing of gambling and vice interests and who had been elected ten times over with the aid of stuffed ballot boxes, brass knuckles, and a baseball bat, was barging down the center aisle of the Colfax County courthouse like Caesar on horseback at the behest of—who else?—Septima Scott!

"Who did you say?" "Which? Oh, *that* one. I thought she was dead." The storm of associative memories was such that it palpably palpitated through the courtroom. The young assailants she had named of such-and-such family, but of course she'd made it all up. And the marriage, but of course she'd put it over on a gone-to-seed recluse. And sending a white child to a colored school, though it was half-Jap . . . But even this, the memory of the Japanese who had worked so hard to make a go of it here and protested so vociferously against being Jim Crowed and had in the end, despite their tenacity, given up their fields and vanished overnight, unable to come to terms with the conditions of life in this county, even this stirred up a hornets' nest of hapless associations.

And always bracketed with Aunt Tee was another memory that most objectionably and irresistibly now sprang to mind, another notorious case of miscegenation of about the same period, this time a white girl who claimed to have been married to the colored man she was living with back in the swamps. The liaison had been going on for four–five years when someone lodged a complaint against it. An attempt was made to arrest the man but he escaped: smuggled by the other colored out of the county and shipped up North. The girl was arrested on a charge of lascivious carriage and was produced before the Grand Jury to testify against her paramour so that an indictment could be brought down and a warrant issued for him as a fugitive. She was to swear that she had been subjected to all his indignities under duress. The children of the union were delivered into court as evidence of the crime visited upon her. She stood up in the witness box and testified: "He was as good a man as I have ever known and as good a father to our children as any man could be and if I cohabited with a Nigra, which of you"— she pointed an accusing finger at the jurors—"has not done the same thing?" With this she gathered her brood together and walked out of the courtroom, scot-free—nobody tried to stop her.

All this and more remembered, fraught with explosive issues that had no pertinence whatsoever to the present matter, flooded through the courtroom in a storm of stridently vivid images, voices. Now everyone on the white side spotted the occupants of the Marquis' land, the dead veteran's sister, a family that had once owned a farm down Sunset Point.

Rad felt those about him flinch as if sleeping dogs had lunged up snapping in their faces. As if the finger of accusation were being shaken at each one of them by the dark mass across the room, charging them individually and collectively with all the crimes of their white racehood against the other, against a black child, a black man fleeing through the swamps, a black soldier's grave, a black piece of soil, all the crimes that had never come to justice, of rapine and robbery, spontaneous and systematic, over the generations—crimes never committed nor admitted, not I, not I . . . They reacted with a bridling of common denial, a rallying to the common defense. Even those previously inclined to give Reeve the benefit of the doubt lost whatever sneaking sympathy they might have harbored for him. Whooping up such a to-do over this! And bringing in someone from the outside! Carter Sillens!

As Carter Sillens approached the bench and entered into a low-voiced colloquy with Purcell and Finchley, D. C. Lacey, the school superintendent, leaned back in his chair and whispered up at Chalmer Coombs who was standing behind him.

"Too bad he isn't as smart as a one of his brothers."

Julie's old gibe, awarding to a lowly shrimper the edge in intelligence over the Mayor, passed choicely from mouth to mouth. By which no one meant that Carter Sillens was exactly stupid. Only that he was crooked as a snake. Of course during his long tenure he had also wheedled or bribed two new high schools, two recreation parks and three housing projects out of the Federal government. And of course the poor, of whom there are so many, regularly supported him at the polls. "Carter Sillens is so slick," they always exonerated him, "he's done so much for Bay City and saved it so much money that nobody'll ever miss the half million he's stole." Carter Sillens was a force to be reckoned with. But no gentleman. A crook. Watch him.

"Representing the estate of Rose Scott." The Mayor's self-proclaimed role grated forth like gravel.

For the colored people, their own familiar colored folks, to have invited such a person here today to meddle in a purely local affair was, Aunt Tee and her past notwithstanding, an affront to the entire white community, as bewildering as it was unforgivable. It constituted a deceit and a treachery too colossal to be believed. The Negroes themselves alone could never have thought of it. He must be here for his own nefarious purposes.

"And before we go any further"—the snowy-ruffed head tilted sidewise, pugnaciously, before the ascetically aloof Judge—"I wish to state most emphatically my objection to the irregularity of this proceeding. It was illegally called. It is being illegally convened. It has no legal status . . ."

Over the ensuing hubbub and the hammering of the Judge's gavel, Benson Reece's comment could plainly be heard. "Well," he said, beaming about, moon-faced, "that blows the cork off. Here we go."

All along the row on either side of Rad the stubborn butts scrunched back; the hardened spines surged forward; the expectant grins broke forth in the direction of the home team captain, the champion of their cause, their rooster in the pit, Vernon Purcell, cheering him on.

5

The Superior Court of Colfax County had been charged with irregularity on a few previous occasions, notably by Lars Finchley a decade ago during his defense of a cracker on a manslaughter count. Lars had been made to pay dearly for his temerity at the time, and he had been paying ever since as an attorney known to be out of favor with the Judge. And once, more recently, the State Supreme Court had sent back an accident case to be retried due to the unusual composition of the list from which the original jury had been impaneled. The plaintiff, a South Carolina merchant of some consequence, won his case the second time around but with an award so puny and at costs so exorbitant that it would have paid him better, far better, never to have sued at all.

As Mayor Sillens began to challenge the jurisdiction of his court over the estate of Rose Scott and his right to sit in probate on it, Judge Purcell judiciously arched his brows and pursed his lips. True, his thin-skinned ears were tingling; and especially his hard-of-hearing ear forti-fied itself, helix and anti-helix, tragus and anti-tragus, concha and canal, tympanum, and cochlea, the tender labyrinthine chambers of outer and inner shell ossifying, become obdurate as a stone wall against the fusil-lade of syllables directed to it. Under the bench, in the humid encase-ment of his puddle-drenched shoe, within his dank sock, through the webbed seams of his underfoot and the curled caverns of his toes, inside this soggy blackness, a latent susceptibility to athlete's foot revived, and the prickle of the fungus feverishly crawled about, cracking the skin, crusting up.

"Hutsat hutsat?" He motioned the Mayor up closer to the bench, leaning forward as if to catch the dry unemphatic tones with which he was so audaciously being attacked. Then smiling silkily, peaking his fingers, he leaned back to the solid comfort of his high-backed black leather chair.

"I am very much afraid, Mr. Sillens, that you are laboring under a mis-apprehension. Firstly, if you had taken the trouble to familiarize your-self with local affairs, you would have discovered that our Ordinary, who generally handles probate, has been absent in Bay City the past several months, taking care of her sick brother. We would wish for the gentleman a speedy recovery, but in the meantime we do feel that ex-tended delays in the settlement of estates, particularly those that would eventually wind up under the purview of this court anyhow, should be avoided if at all possible. Secondly, if you had taken the trouble to pe-ruse carefully the communication which I addressed to your clients, you would have noted that it was merely an offer, and a most public-spirited offer if I may say so, undertaken at considerable personal inconvenience, disadvantage and even hardship, to make myself and my good offices available to them for consultation at this date. That they hastened to seize upon the opportunity of my offer I may presume since they are here present. And thirdly, if you had taken the trouble to arrive here punctually, you would have heard me instruct the family of the decedent to engage most freely in any areas of discussion or difficulty they wish to raise with me.

"This so-called proceeding, Mr. Sillens, to borrow your term, is no more nor less than a simple informal parley between myself and the parties concerned for the purpose of thrashing out details that might otherwise, after the family's dispersal, call for expenditures in money, time, and, yes, emotion, that are entirely unnecessary. I don't know how you process these matters in your county, Mr. Sillens, but in this county, where we are intimate with all our citizenry, we don't hesitate to cut red tape for their benefit."

"A simple informal parley did you say?"

"A simple informal parley." The Judge good-humoredly stretched his shirt-sleeved arms out—see, no robes?—and withdrawing them allowed himself a cool glance up and down the ranked rows of colored. "Your clients, I am sorry to observe, chose to bring a crowd with them. And as you know, a crowd always attracts a crowd. We have nothing to conceal from anyone but if you prefer we can clear the court or withdraw to chambers."

The Mayor also regarded the crowd, with a weighty scowl to the right and to the left. "I never mind company. No one need bestir himself on my account. This being such a simple informal little parley, what may I ask"—without turning his head he lifted his shoulder toward Lars Finchley sitting innocently at the table of opposing counsel—"is he doing here?"

Lars sprang up. "If Your Honor will permit, I am here on behalf of an interested party in the disposition, as I shall soon make evident . . ."

There followed among the three of them one of those preliminary skirmishes of protocol conducted in the desultory drone customary to gatherings where the fate of nations or individuals hangs in the balance.

"What's he saying?" "What are they arguing about?" "What's that got to do with, is he trying to *oust*—" "Hey, what's the big idea?"

To Henry and Julie's consternation Lars was summarily dismissed by the Judge until such time as his participation would be required. He was forced to repack his briefcase and retire from his position inside the gate. "Don't worry," Lars grinned down, only a trifle grim-jawed, as he pushed past Julie who insisted on retaining her outside seat and Henry to an empty place beside them. "This is doing us a lot more good than harm." And from the heads thrust forward to him in eager alliance and the murmurs of indignation that ascended rearward, unreproved by the Judge, indeed it seemed so.

The Judge assembled his notes before him. "Now if counsel is quite finished with the objections and obstacles he seems determined to place in our path—and may I warn you, Mr. Sillens, that any further interruptions or resort to intemperate language will not be tolerated by me— then we may get on with our business. For your information, Mr. Sillens, I would like to enlighten you concerning a most unfortunate condition prevalent in these parts. The deplorable fact is, and at meetings of the bar association in this section of the state I have time and again called attention to it, the large part of the population hereabouts is highly re-miss in its attitude toward documents of all sorts. Therefore this court is constantly compelled to deal with complications arising from the ab-sence of birth, death, and marriage certificates as well as other papers, and from property and inheritance claims whose intrinsic value is ex-ceeded beyond all bounds by the problems involved. You would not believe the costly lengths to which we have sometimes had to go to con-tact distant lawyers, place advertisements in distant newspapers, trace distant heirs. Small wonder that the job of disentanglement some-times reduces whatever assets there may be to naught, and less than naught, indebtedness.

"The present instance is a case in point. Rose Scott died intestate, leaving six children, living mainly in various parts of the country. The court believes that in order to safeguard the share of each member and of any other rightful claimant who may come forward and in order to supervise the payment of taxes and other fees and to provide for a legal, fair, and just distribution of the property or the proceeds thereof, a com-petent administrator should be appointed. One who though this affair may seem to be of negligible importance will give unstintingly of his time, mind, and energy to bring it to a proper conclusion.

"Now if you wish at this time, Mr. Mayor," he nodded courteously at Sillens patiently standing below, "to inject any remarks with regard to my statement of the issue and my recommendations for its solution, you may do so."

"Well yes, Your Honor." The Mayor browsed among the papers he held in his hand and extracted a blue-bound sheet folded in an elon-gated oblong. "If that is all, I think we can reach a proper conclusion in a very few minutes. Without obstacle or obstruction. Simply and infor-mally. Short and sweet. To save you all the expenditure of any further time and energy, which I am sure could be devoted to more profitable purposes, let me inform you—as you will no doubt be delighted to learn —that I am here for the sole object of filing the last will and testament of Mrs. Rose Scott, relict of Hadley B. Scott and née Scott."

Reversing benchward, faceside-to, his slim blue folder, linear-bordered and blocked off, with its title typed in the space allotted for it above and the signature of his law firm printed in its appropriate space below, Sil-lens handed it upward, unopened, to the Judge. The Judge demurred, changing his pince-nez for reading glasses which he could not at once locate on his person. In that long moment until he received the sheet, unfolded it, shook the white bond paper down to full length from the blue cover to which it was stapled, every last rustle in the courtroom faded away. Ada Hemmings' pencil, lifted from her notebook, remained poised aloft, pointed as a comment.

While Judge Purcell studied the will, holding it fastidiously or far-sightedly off a distance, Reeve hunched forward in his chair, hands clasped between his knees, only his eyes roving hither and yon. He had spent a restless night upon a restless week, unsure whether the preparations he had so intensively built up toward today would cohere or collapse. In spite of the confident prognostications he had made to Rad yesterday when informing him of the hearing, he had in his heart of hearts been certain of nothing: not of his people, not of his lawyer, not of the capacity of the papers in his possession to overcome the opposition. You never know, you can't know till it happens. All he could do was try to hold everything together in his hands.

His sister Vergilia—she had changed off with Lila-Lee who stayed the night with Aunt Tee—had kept popping up at all hours, drinking coffee and dragging about in a dither of anxiety. "You wait and see. Nobody'll show up in court tomorrow. The worst of it is, your own people don't support you. Isn't that right, Fred, you ought to know? They don't support you."

"That's right," Fred had agreed with her, "we don't stick together," and launched into a recount of how he had helped organize the body department at Ford and been fired for it and no one, no one, came to his aid. "And when I was supposed to land a paid job with the union, the ofays couldn't tell the difference between me and some hustler who had climbed up my back and was dropping a hype on them. My own people cut me out. Nobody knew me."

"But they all saved me today," Reeve reminded them. "They all saved me from Chalmer, I'll never forget that."

"And that's as much as it will come to," Mae said, more in resignation than in cynicism. "That's as much as anyone can expect. All we can do now is pray."

Fred at the door struck himself in the chest and trumpeted out into the night:

> *"Jesus loves me, that I know*
> *Because the Bible tells me so."*

And Ben taking up the mock heroics threw his arms wide and hollered: "*Give me Jesus, you can have the rest!*" And appended, his voice dropping an octave: "Cause the white folks ain't left us nothin' else."

That broke them up in laughter. Except for Sister Mae. "Say what you will, say what you will!" she cried. "Times like this you have to feel there's something larger than yourself out there. You have to have something to turn to."

"Buy a candle," Fred ironically advised.

They all went back to bed. But they were up again. None of them slept much.

Reeve had had a hard time getting them started in the morning to round up what folks they could in the time left them. Vergilia couldn't drag herself up off the couch she was feeling so poorly. And Fred was bending over double with stomach cramps. "You know what the old folks say." Reeve had sought to goad them on with a faith he didn't feel. "When the bandwagon starts, nobody looks to see if the horse is blind, they all jump on."

If he could only hold it all together in his hands . . .

The bandwagon had turned out. People did come from miles around, aroused to a new pitch by news of Chalmer's attempted arrest and the repulse of it. The identity of each new arrival grunted through the colored section of the courtroom as if to be chalked up on an invisible scoreboard, each identification reaching Reeve with a prick of consciousness. "There's Tyco Jones, why I thought he'd up and left this part of the country. And Leroy. And Guy Scanlon." The old defeats had piled up and piled up until now the ranks were closing. You bide your time. You choose your ground. And when you fight, you fight to win.

"And McDowell, there's Rad McDowell."

Reeve had lifted himself up and about to scan the balustraded platform almost before he heard the name. "Good for him."

But when bracing his hands on the flecked golden oak rail before him he had raised himself up to request a delay from Judge Purcell for the arrival of his attorney, he hadn't known even then for sure that Carter Sillens would put in an appearance. He was only trying to hold it all together in his hands . . .

Now amidst the browns and tans and parchment hues of the courtroom, the hour anticipated with such trepidation was in progress. It was passing like a fantasy before him, a nightmare in which he sat excluded from the operating theater in which his flesh and his vitals, his earth and his air, his life and his future were being wrangled over in dull and all but drowsy phrases, accompanied by puttering and all but indifferent movements. The private sparring between the Judge and the Mayor bore no reference to his person. The quick-change artistry with which the Judge at one turn alluded to "the family of the decedent," placing himself on their side against the Mayor, and then again alluded to "your clients," placing himself on the side of the Mayor against the family, did not escape him. A wedge was being driven between them and their spokesman, driving them apart. Under appearances didn't those two, the Mayor and the Judge, belong to the same club? Wouldn't they meet sometime somewhere afterward and over a shot of bourbon joke about this?

The Judge crackled down over the page of his mother's will. Around himself and toward himself as a pivotal point, Reeve felt breathed forth, poured into his consciousness, the sentiment that had brought his people here today and bound them in all their range of diversity, if only for this hour, into one expanded selfhood. *Child, if that title don't stand, ain't one of us worth a blackeye pea* . . .

He was holding it all agonizingly between his hands . . .

Across the aisle from Reeve, Julie, pale under the stiffly sweeping disk of her black straw hat, tautly fragile in her drape-bosomed, black-and-white silk print, turned from time to time and looked at him. Her eyes burned with the aridity of tears she couldn't shed, her throat burned with words she couldn't utter, every bone in her body burned with a violence she couldn't inflict. She had come here not as the prostrate victim the ladies avidly watching her supposed, but as an avenging fury. *To look at him and let him know how I feel!*

The stolid brown profile across the aisle did not by so much as a flicker of expression respond to her pressure. Quite at ease with himself in his summer grey suit, having taken her kindness, her softheaded idealism and turned it into a weapon against her. Without a care, without a hoot in hell. She could have stood up and slapped him. Shaken him. Pounded him to a pulp. *You walking over your mother's grave!*

Upon the presentation of Rose's will, her hands and her feet went icy. As the Judge scrutinized it, a tremor—not a projection of her feelings but physically rooted and uncontrollable—passed through her chill hands. "Why it can't be, she wouldn't—" she whispered to Henry over the pall of silence in the room. "She distinctly understood—"

But Henry was fastening upon the Judge and then around upon Lars a stare of baleful triumph. He had never put any stock in the Judge's advice: to work through the administrator he would appoint for the estate. He had never relied on that! Never!

"Why it's a fraud," Julie said hoarsely, half-aloud. "Don't you see," she turned venomously back toward Reeve, "it's nothing but a fraud!"

The interminable pause broke like a comber hurling itself up against rock-ridged shores. Reeve started up from his chair to meet eyes blazing at him with a savagery for all the world like that of a woman jilted, cast-off, infamously betrayed; and was jerked back down from behind by Aunt Tee. Against the protesting rumble on the colored side, the white side burst out in a babble of excitement.

"She says it's a put-up job!" "They cooked it up!"

Within seconds the impression was speeding up and down the rows surrounding Rad: Carter Sillens had invented the whole thing! And gotten Reeve to go along with him! The court action and the will with it were nothing more nor less than a plot concocted by Sillens to use the niggers—and the niggers were letting him—for the purpose of bringing his political machine into Colfax County and taking it over! That gangster . . .

The Judge, still holding the will off a safe distance from himself, hammered imperiously for order. "Any further demonstration on the part of the spectators . . . What's that?"

At the height of the uproar, from the fire-escape entrance on the colored side a line of boys and girls filed in, shepherded by a crisply dressed young woman. "Who are you?"

"This is my senior class in American history and government, Your Honor," the young woman replied in a thin clear treble. "I telephoned Mr. Lacey, the school superintendent, last night to ask if we could attend? And he said he thought it would be all right."

D. C. Lacey shoved himself back in his chair, startled. "Who, me?" And remembering, muttered with embarrassment: "Oh yes, I didn't see where—" He'd been snared into it.

"And Mr. Maclay," the voice sweetly continued, "I called him too. I thought it would be a fine opportunity for my students to observe the operation of our judicial system, and he agreed."

"Why yes," Mr. Maclay, the recorder, seconded her from his seat with a twinkle of mischief recalled: he always seized upon any pretext to twit the Judge. But now he felt bound to add, with plaintive defensiveness, "Didn't seem to me like it could hurt anything." He'd been bamboozled into it.

The dozen boys and girls lined up against the windows and Vivian slipped into a seat offered her. She kept patting with her string-gloved fingers at her throat. Her throat ached as if the explanation just given had been squeezed out of it with a pair of pliers. She hated herself for that strangulating constriction of her throat, for the craven crumbling in her bosom, as if after an heroic effort of danger passed she were falling away. To be reduced to such blithering idiocy by fear. Fear of nothing. I can't stand it. Her eyes flitted about the courtroom in whose very architecture, formality, and forms the verdict was already written. I can't take this godforsaken place . . . I can't live here . . .

"If you wish to read aloud this, uh, instrument"—the Judge gingerly by one corner passed the will back to the Mayor, detaching himself from association with it—"please do so. Should there be any exceptions to its contents, it would be best, don't you think, to hear them now."

"Absolutely."

Humored by the diversion of the students, part and parcel of that homey, homely maladroitism with which colored never fail to leaven the dignity of any event, and convinced by now that what they were about to hear was a forgery, soon to be exposed in all its absurdity, the whites folded their arms and crossed their knees, exchanging with each other glances of sagacious significance.

"But he's not actually going to, how can he—" Julie turned with a shocked whisper to Henry. "She knew, I told her . . . It can't stand—"

"Don't worry," Henry patted her hand and slapped Lars on the knee, "this is doing them more harm than good, huh, Lars? They're playing right into our hands."

"*BE IT REMEMBERED that I, Rose Scott, of Arcady, County of Colfax, State of Georgia, being of sound and disposing mind and memory, but mindful of the uncertainty of this life, do make, publish and declare this my Last Will and Testament.*"

The old time-worn dusty words, hastened over in a liturgical incantation by the Mayor, nevertheless swelled forth sonorously, sanctified by usage, falling upon every ear with the incontrovertible ring of validity.

"*I direct my executor, hereinafter named, to pay all my just debts, funeral charges and expenses of administration . . .*"

She bequeathed the farm to Reeve to hold in trust for the remainder of her children and to be maintained by him as a homestead for them and to be passed on upon his decease to that grandchild of hers who in the concerted judgment of the family was best equipped by bent, ability, choice, and convenience to assume his place.

The old entailment written into the original deed was reiterated. The aforesaid property was not to be sold, given or appropriated to any other use or benefit behoof but that of the descendants of Jonas B. and Maria Scott, in perpetuity.

"*SIGNED, SEALED, PUBLISHED AND DECLARED by the above named Rose Scott as and for her last Will and Testament in the presence of us, who, at her request, in her presence and in the presence of one another, hereby subscribe our name as witnesses thereto . . .*"

Who would have dreamed that an old nigger woman would pull a trick like that? The surmise that Carter Sillens had cozened the colored into acting as pawns of his, much as it antagonized the whites, had provided them with a species of solace. The reading of the will, impervious clause after clause, duly witnessed and attested to, signed and sealed, dated over a year ago, stripped away this solace, this clothing against the elements, this second skin, leaving them bare once more, more intolerably so than ever, with the knowledge that their Negroes, their own familiar Negroes, had themselves engendered and engineered the—well, hoax, scheme, intrigue, conspiracy, call it what you will. And Sillens was *their* willing tool.

"Now you know," Henry said to Julie. "You know what they're like. All of them. Now go on." He bodily heaved Lars Finchley up by the arm from the chair beside him. "Get in there and enter that eviction order."

So Lars, who had disowned the eviction order even while he was filling it out, who had opposed its initiation, its delivery, its employment as strategic threat or weapon in any way, shape, or fashion, now dredged his copy of it up from the manila file in his briefcase and tendered it to the bench.

"You intend to contest the will?" the Judge inquired.

"No, Your Honor. It is my contention that it should not be admitted to probate because of the existence of a prior claim to the property of which the decedent and her son, named as trustee, were informed some weeks ago by my client, Mrs. Julie-Ann Colfax Warren. An eviction order was issued against Reeve Scott *et al.*, in the interest of this claim only a few days ago. Therefore the alleged 'will of Rose Scott' is being petitioned here not in good faith but with the full cognizance that it is in all probability null and void. Moreover—"

"If you would like," the Judge graciously inclined toward the Mayor, "to request a deferment at this time? That the argument introduced by Mr. Finchley may be considered as a separate action?"

"Not at all," the Mayor averred. "Go on. I'm just as anxious to see this through here and now as anyone else is."

"Moreover," Lars plunged on, almost too quickly, "we question the legality of the instrument not only from our own point of view but from that of the psuedo-heirs. A cursory survey of the descendants of Jonas B. and Maria Scott over the past few generations will reveal that their various shares in the property would by now be so fragmented that no one individual has the right to dispose of the whole. However—"

Almost too hurriedly he spilled the contents of his briefcase out upon the counsel table and riffled through his envelopes. "Having in view this circumstance and without prejudice to my client's investiture as sole proprietor, I have been empowered by her to make a gift of moneys equivalent to the would-be shares of such living descendants as I have so far been able to trace. Naturally this gift is being extended on the understanding that it will be promptly and appreciatively accepted. Otherwise it will be as promptly withdrawn. The choice is clear then: protracted litigation that may well mount into the thousands of dollars or an immediate gift of what I am sure must be much-needed funds.

"Now if the court please, I am prepared to announce the names of the recipients forthwith. If those who are here today will come forward and make themselves known a check will be given to them at once in an amount that accords with a fair and just division of the current value of the property, in return for their signature to a quit-claim."

"Well now—" "That's something like—"

A sigh of relief exhaled from the heart of the white section, sloughing off the perplexities and passions into which hostility with the colored always threw them. Nobody likes race conflict. "Now that's the smartest thing I've heard yet today." "That's what I call fair. Fair and square." "Isn't that just like Julie? After the way they've treated her . . ."

In the colored section, however, on the opposite side of the semi-circle, as Lars began to read off names with the authority of a summons, the tautness of tension—this one struck through the heart as if fired upon and that one about to be—leaped from person to person, row after row.

"Lee Scott, whose address is 22 Sago Street, Valdosta, Georgia.

"Wilda-Mae Scott, a non-resident of Georgia, whose address is unknown.

"Colfax Scott, Nags Head, Alabama.

"Gaylord Scott . . ."

"Now just a minute, just a minute—" Sillens at last succeeded in silencing Lars. He too was spilling envelopes from his briefcase.

"Honestly!" "Now what!" "Of all the stupid, disgusting—"

Elaborately Ada Hemmings, suspending her shorthand notes, poured herself a glass of ice water from the pitcher on her high-placed desk and drank it with an air of disapproval that spoke for all on her side of the courtroom.

"Am I to understand," the Judge demanded, "that you are advising your clients to reject the liquidation—"

"Hardly," Carter Sillens said.

"Are you questioning the figures that have been arrived at?"

"No sir, I am not. If opposing counsel will please read through his list—"

"Lee Scott," Lars began again from the back of an envelope.

"Lee Scott," the Mayor echoed him, from the back of an envelope he drew forth from his pile.

"Wilda-Mae Scott, a non-resident of Georgia, whose address is unknown—"

"Wilda-Mae Scott, a non-resident of Georgia, 1932 Hoxie Street, Houston, Texas."

"Colfax Scott, Nags Head—"

"Colfax Scott, Nags Head . . ."

Lars went on doggedly a few minutes more, his clay-red skin heating to blood-red. For every face card he laid down, the Mayor topped him. He glowered at the short stocky figure, stupefied. Even if they were dead-to-rights, why did they have to pick such a scoundrel? At least, Lars justified himself, if they'd had someone decent, mannerly . . . In Lars' veins still ran something of the old dictum that you don't gamble or duel with anyone but an equal.

"Raymond Scott, 794 St. Nicholas Avenue . . . As you can see," the Mayor imperturbably fanned out his envelopes, "I already have the quit-claims of next-of-kin. All of them. Bought and paid for by Rose Scott over the last fifteen years."

"But she never registered them!"

"Since there was no question of her ownership during her lifetime, there was no need to register. Since the question is being raised upon her demise, we will, if His Honor has no objection, register them now."

With a bow to Lars, he slipped an elastic band over his envelopes and slapped them up on the bench.

"Mr. Maclay, I believe Mr. Maclay is in court?" The Judge with a back-flick of his fingers swept the envelopes away from himself. "Mr. Maclay, will you please examine this material and correlate it with Mr. Finchley's?"

"Now wait there, hold on!"

Henry Warren left his chair, trampled over his wife's feet and rushed through the gate. "Your Honor—" He muscled Lars aside—why must he always be surrounded by incompetents?—and addressed himself directly to the bench. "Those papers aren't worth a hog's tit, anymore than the will is! That's my wife's land out there. They got no proof it ever was theirs!"

"It was apportioned out," Lars recovered himself, "by the original owner, Gilbert Colfax, to Jonas B. Scott for cultivation during the latter years of the War between the States, with the verbal agreement that it was to be returned at any time upon demand. This verbal contract has continued between the Colfax and Scott families up to the present day, the occupant paying taxes on it in return for its use.

"Since, if I follow Mr. Sillens correctly, the magnanimity of my client who now wishes to have her property restored to her is being declined, then we have no choice but to insist upon the execution of the warrant of eviction that we have obtained. And if that is opposed, we hereby apply also for an injunction restraining Reeve Scott *et al.*, from habitation and use of the property until a final determination of ownership is made."

"Is that all?" the Mayor asked. "Since you apparently have nothing to support your assertion of a verbal contract but your client's word—"

"You calling my wife a liar?"

"Order, order! Mr. Warren, take heed!"

"I have here," the Mayor said, "a photostat of a certified copy of a deed of sale issued by this county to Jonas B. Scott on October 16, 1866."

Henry saw before him the splotch on the plate-glass window wall of his office where his son had smashed the ink bottle yesterday. And in the washed surface this morning, in the early light, the threadlike flicker that no one might ever notice except those privy to it and for them it would always be there. The fine crack in self-esteem, the flaw of self-discovery upon every soul who had been tested by the blasting yesterday, tested, weighed, and found wanting—himself, Spenser, Rosen, Lightfoot, Mason—that might never quite be made whole again. Only by seeing it as he did now, and by seeing consciously surmount it, could one heal the wound and regain one's being. And more, more! By overcoming it, be enlarged by it.

He'd built this case up piece by piece and it wasn't going to crack. He'd seen to that . . .

"What deed! Where?" He grabbed for the photostat from the Mayor.

"Gentlemen! Gentlemen, you're all jumping the gun! Mr. Warren, Mr. Finchley, Mr. Sillens, will you kindly step forward? Remember I'm in charge here."

Henry and the two lawyers united with the Judge in a huddle over the photostat. In the interlude Eustis Telfer wandered up and down the aisles on the white side, heaping coals on the fire. And not without reason. There was a story about Eustis that his mother had bought him off from a court-martial after World War I, in which he was to be tried as an officer who had deserted his men on the battlefield. The story for whatever truth it contained, known only to himself, had ruined his life; he never got over it. He married a girl who later inherited a shrimp factory, but he had no knack for managing it and in the end stayed away from it altogether. He fathered with Jessie four rough-and-tumble sons, whom he could scarcely recognize as being of his own blood and breed, and the two eldest now ran the factory. Eustis had been looking forward to his appointment as administrator of the Scott estate ever since the Judge had questioned him as to his availability. It promised him one more busybody means for filling his idle hours. Now deprived of the self-importance he might have assumed, seething with a disappointment he couldn't communicate, he wandered about pouring incitements into the ears of anyone who would listen.

"Did you see that? Did you see how that Sillens had Lars expelled from in there? Coming into our courthouse and ordering us around, who does he think he is?"

"Wait," he was assured, "wait, you'll see. The Judge'll fix him. The Judge'll pin his ears back."

"And that nigger! Did you see the way he jumped when Julie spoke? I thought he was about to clobber her."

"Is that right? You see that?"

"Yessir I did. And if you hadn't been so busy looking elsewhere you'd have seen it too."

"Hmmm. Purcell won't let 'em get away with this. They ain't putting anything over on him. You wait."

At the first mention of the deed of sale Rad had groped about in his pocket for the copy of his own deed, reaffirming his grip on its brittle reality.

"Look at her." The two women in front of him were craning their heads, searching out Julie. "Subjected to all this embarrassment . . . wouldn't go through what she's going through now in a million years. Have you heard about Grace Willingham? Isn't it awful? Stricken just like that. You know I've had this pain, I've never told anyone about it, but it comes and goes—right here . . ."

Sympathy for Julie and Grace was compounded one with the other and with themselves.

"And Lars, poor Lars, in the middle of all this. I feel so sorry for him. With Violet trying to run two households—I tried that once . . ."

"Look—the Judge."

. . . For their part the colored were looking not at the Judge but at the gilt-framed photograph above him on the wall over the paneling, probably placed in the center because it was the largest of three: the bearded Zeus. He was one of the early justices of the court, but to their knowledge he was not a white man. A colored man who had owned vast tracts of forest, handed down from an Indian grandfather and acquired by purchase, along the railroad right-of-way. Educated in the best schools of the time, both in law and medicine, he was taken over by the whites who dealt with him. He married a white woman or a mighty fair one and they adopted a white child or a mighty fair one and branches of the descendants were intermarried with leading families all over the state.

In this central portrait commanding the bench from its high position over the entablature of the door to chambers, resided the one drop of colored blood, and more than blood the tinge of humor deriving from their private knowledge of it, that sustained them against the regnant face of Judge Purcell below. And against the thick hot air—another shower was brewing outside—that pressed so heavily about them.

Purcell himself, having no illusion whatsoever as to the goal toward which he must necessarily gravitate, was confronted by a predicament that as it taxed his skill troubled, tantalized, and titillated him. Sillens was politically an unknown quantity, whose espousal of a candidacy invariably went to the highest bidder. Dan Garner would no doubt like to count on Sillens insofar as the race for the governorship and his senatorial appointment were concerned. And therefore within the boundary of this morning's dispute, his own hopes of a Federal judgeship were at stake.

On the other hand, Purcell was irresistibly moved to administer a public spanking to the Mayor for the aspersion he had cast on the court and for the manner in which he confounded every counterattack. Also, more crucially, Purcell could not afford to let down Henry and Julie or the collective expectation of that audience situated, like the flag, to his right. Above all, between the will of a giant corporation that had come into the county to develop an enterprise and the whim of a little ragtag colored family, there could be no choice for a man in his position but the rational one.

A method of adjudication then that would satisfy the conflicting elements of interest and inclination could not be easily arrived at. It offered a nice problem in synthesis. In the Judge's right shoe his ordinarily dry and well-powered toes sweltered piercingly, invisibly insisting that he strip his foot and rub it against the other foot as a means of relief. In his mouth an old tendency to cankers had erupted—too many spiced seafood canapés yesterday—and the two lumps forming in the stringy tissues of the hyoid pit hankered after the intervention of his tongue tip, as if by being explored the welts could be exorcised.

"I'm very sorry, Mr. Sillens." The Judge amicably smiling, over his rash of petty plagues, returned the photostat to him. "But as Mr. Finchley and Mr. Warren have so aptly pointed out, this is merely a reproduction of a putative deed of sale. And a rather blurred one at that. I don't wish to sound skeptical but I should hate to have you or anyone else taken in by it. It cannot be accepted in evidence as a true copy."

"As you wish. If I may have a moment?" The Mayor retreated across the floor to Reeve and whispered with him over the rail. Reluctantly Reeve removed his wallet from the inside pocket of his jacket and as reluctantly took from it a paper as worn as an old dollar bill. Retaining his hold on it as if unwilling to yield it up to anyone else's keeping he circled through the gate and joined the Mayor in his return to the bench.

"This, Your Honor," the Mayor introduced it, "is a firsthand certified true copy made on the date of purchase, October 16, 1866."

Reeve handed it up to the bench, retaining his hold on the upper edge of the paper as if between one white hand and the other it might vanish in thin air.

"What's the matter, boy?" the Judge, arching his brows, chaffed him. "Don't you trust your attorney to handle it?"

"Come now, Reeve," the Mayor likewise arching his brows chided him. "I'm sure Mr. Warren and these other gentlemen won't swallow it."

Chafing under the use of his first name in contrast to the last name of the others as if it were a kind of sellout, Reeve unwillingly allowed the paper to be slid away from him by his lawyer and over to the Judge. But still his fingers, dancing like hounds on the leash, crept under the paper as the Judge glanced through it, itching for it.

"Hmph." Judge Purcell looked up. "This does have the look of an authentic copy. Unfortunately so many of our original records were destroyed by the fire that took the old courthouse back in 1901, it cannot readily be verified. You understand I will need some time to dig into sources, if any such are extant."

And without further ado he impounded the paper. "You trust *me* with it, don't you?" Smiling at his witticism to Reeve in passing, he turned his full attention back to the Mayor. "Now if your calendar and mine can be adjusted, Mr. Mayor? I have a two-week vacation coming up now, and then my circuit takes me into Freeland County. That puts us over into the July term . . ."

"Now look," the Mayor, taken aback, threw his arms in the air, "if you people here in Colfax County think you can bulldoze me—"

"But—" Reeve, obdurately rooted to the spot, cried.

"The July term. I shall overlook your outburst, Mr. Sillens, as I can well understand the burden this imposes on your valuable time . . . Twenty-first or second—"

"Sir? Your Honor?"

From the upper reaches of the audience to the left of the Judge a high thin treble mounted momentarily to a squeak. Vivian rising to her feet caught at the piping in her throat with her fingers, holding it down. Her voice, steadied, went on, while under her, her thighs melted away. I can't stand it, I can't stand to be like this, it's not me . . . What was she so afraid of? To get up out of a crowd and speak? Of *them*? The place? The place was rampant with fear. Fear you could cut like cheese, that you could smell as if it were being stuffed up your nose, that you could taste as if it were being crammed down your throat . . .

"I believe I can help you out," her voice flowed on without let. "You very kindly gave me your permission the other day to look into the back records and Mrs. Hemmings was gracious enough to show me where they were. And Mr. Maclay, he was there too. I think we can all be very proud that at the time of the fire some of our citizens had the courage to save a good part—"

"Hutsat hutsat?" The Judge was so astonished, as was everyone else, that he had not thought to intercept her.

"That deed of sale is up in the library, Your Honor. Folio A, Book C, page ten."

"Now listen here, girl—"

But Ada Hemmings, rising to her feet and tacking up the backhair that had escaped from her bun in the stress of the hearing, was answering the girl for herself. It was never a good policy to interrupt Ada.

"You say I showed you?"

"Well, yes ma'am, you surely did. I know you were very busy, Mrs. Hemmings, but—" Vivian's voice locked in her throat and she caught at it in self-despisal: I can't live here like this, I won't do it, they'll have to hang me . . . "You pointed out the alcove in back and, and took down my name, if you recall."

Afterward and for long afterward the clash between Ada and Vivian would be related as one of the high peaks of a morning in which peaks soared ever higher. Never in the history of the court before had a colored woman attempted to contradict a white woman, and in the King's English too. More than one woman, with her eyes on Ada, sucked back her breath as if a trayful of china were about to come crashing down. Ada was being provoked to the point where, give or take a few degrees of high blood pressure, the stream of invective, so charitably characterized as "Ada's nervous breakdowns," was about to break forth from her lips, here, in front of everybody.

Ada, jabbing pins into her hair, drew herself up sinuously to the fullness of her handsome height. "That's right," she said with a dangerous sparkle. "I remember now. I gave you a dustcloth to clean up back there. You told me you were looking up something for your history class, didn't you?"

"And while I was looking, Mrs. Hemmings, I happened—"

"I don't know what you did or how you did it, and for you to infer or insinuate that I showed you anything of any kind is unethical, immoral, and—" Her tongue darted over the crimson bulge of her underlip. Now, now, the topmost teacup and all the saucers . . . "And a prevarication," Ada said evenly, with truly superb control. "I don't know what-all you looked at, Vivian."

She sat down in a pink shimmer, her aplomb preserved. Only the colored girl didn't sit down.

"But Mr. Maclay, I had the books out on the table, and he was right next to me—"

"Yes I was," Mr. Maclay unexpectedly seconded her from his chair. "And since my name has been brought into this—"

"Mr. Maclay," the Judge rapped out with the touch of acid he always reserved for the prankish recorder, "if you have anything to add to this, will you please rise and do so in a proper manner?"

Mr. Maclay not only rose but betook himself inside the gate and up into the witness box.

"Did you expect to be sworn in, Mr. Maclay?"

"Yes sir, I do."

"Bailiff?"

Mr. Maclay on being sworn in testified that he certainly had observed the books being opened on the table and later returned to the shelf.

"Did this girl examine the contents?"

"Yes sir, she did."

"And you were sitting close enough to her to be sure of this?"

"Well—" A nervous twitch tugged the corners of his mouth upward in a self-conscious smile, over a surge of snickers roundabout. "It was of interest to me in my office."

"And you were interested enough to follow after her to the back shelves where she placed the volume back in?"

"Yes. She got a tick in her hand while she was scootching down to the bottom shelf with it."

"A tick?"

"You know, one of those little hairy wood ticks that burrow in."

A tick? How would a tick find its way into the court library? No one would make up a thing like that. It had the unmistakable ring of veracity. For the first time the possibility that what the girl had said was so and that she might have seen such a paper and that it did exist was taken seriously.

With an intensity of hope, on the verge of vindication, Reeve rested his hands on the rail before him, absorbing through palms as hardened as a layer of shell every last grain in the golden oak beneath. Down the row from him Fred leaned his brow in his hand—was *he* praying?—and Vergilia yearned forward with mouth rounded in wonder, as naïve as a child's. Up in the back rows Vivian at last sank down into her seat.

"But did you with your own eyes see this deed of sale, with the specific name and date—"

"Well, when she noticed me watching, she started turning pages—"

"Did you with your own eyes read—"

"I never said that. I said I saw *her* read. But then again she could have misread."

"That is all, Mr. Maclay."

"I just wanted to clear my name—"

"Stand down, Mr. Maclay."

Evading the Mayor who stood by, head cocked to one side, egging him on with a bumptious half-smile, the Judge beckoned to Lars. "Mr. Finchley." If there was going to be any scapegoat in this situation, it would not be himself. "Mr. Finchley, as counsel for Mrs. Warren in a property claim of some complexity, didn't it occur to you that it would be a good idea to search the title?"

"Of course."

"And did you search it?"

Lars hesitating threw over his shoulder to Henry the look of a drowning man who has been pushed in. Henry who had withdrawn to the counsel table was parked up on the edge of it like a fence-sitter at a rodeo, impersonally viewing from his vantage point, *hors de combat*, the struggle of heaving horse and panting rider, the bloodied spur, the steaming flanks, the frothing dust, the primal freedom of nature in collision with the ability of man to master it.

"Yes, Your Honor, I searched it."

"All the way back as far as it could be traced?"

"Yes."

"And did you or did you not come upon a deed issued to one Jonas B. Scott in the year 1866, month of October, on the sixteenth day."

For ten years Lars Finchley had been waiting for the one right opening to catch the Judge out in the handling of a court case, and now it was the Judge who was catching him. Only a half hour ago he had taken the offensive with the eviction, a tactic not of his making and against his advice, in order to save a deteriorating front, and he had met every difficulty as it arose, he felt, with all the proficiency anyone could muster on the spur of the moment. The whole case he now saw with the clarity of hindsight had been constructed on a series of false premises—Purcell's, Henry's, his own: that there would be no testament, that there would be no copy of the deed in the family's possession, that there would be no awareness of an existing record, that in short what they had to deal with was the average condition of ignorance combined with negligence. And none of it, now that they were actually engaged with it, no part of it had evolved the way they preconceived it.

"Before you answer," the Judge interposed with the weight of poured concrete behind every word, "may I indicate to you, Mr. Finchley, that if you drew up a writ of eviction to be served by this court with the knowledge that the premises to be vacated might—even just might, mind you—be the presumptive property of the evictee, it would constitute a most serious breach of professional conduct. And I would imagine that your colleagues will call it to the attention of the state bar association for action. Now think this over carefully—"

"There's nothing to think over."

He had admitted to searching the title all the way back because he could not by denying it, simply could not bear to, publicly traduce his own professional competence. And now it was his profession itself up on the execution block . . . Somewhere along the line, Lars recognized, he had irrevocably committed himself. And not once. But again and again and again. On that convivial evening in his office, in that moment of weakness when, nudged into it by Henry, he had thumped two-fingered over his type keys. On that shining vision of himself at the helm of the glossy cruiser in his desk drawer, in the eyes of his wife, as opposed to the repressed humiliation of her hives. On the ordeal of the last forty hours, from the deposit on the boat so blithely made in anticipation of the Sunset account; through the frantic discovery of Grace's illness when in the space of a moment—or is it ever only a moment?—the cohesion of a happy family was shattered; to the ceaseless hovering over the telephone—incision into the thoracic cavity, O my God they're carving her up! and the chaos of the children . . .

He was committed and he couldn't, not now, not humanly, fail Violet. He had to come home the skipper of the vessel, rugged enough to weather any gale. The conquering hero ruthless enough to slaughter any adversary, no matter how his stomach might revolt in horror . . .

"I can tell you without the slightest hesitation, sir. I saw no such record."

"And I may rely on that? I did not intend, counselor," the Judge said in a kindlier and yet still urgent tone, "to cast any reflection upon your legal repute or your personal honor, but when these become involved—"

And the alabaster goddess, that abstraction to which he clung, that one who governed the interrelationships of men and on whom depended the orderly operation of society? The Law? What about her, Lars wondered, where does she fit in? Defiled, violated, broken on the ground like the illustration of a piece of antique statuary in some old-fashioned book that no one ever opens anymore.

"With your indulgence, sir, to make quite sure, perhaps I have a notation covering the period in question."

He retired to his table, pausing beside Henry who offered him a whipflick of a glance—contempt, command?—for God sake, grow up! And separating his file folders scrupulously leafed through each as if looking for some scrap of information that might accidentally have become misplaced.

He had committed himself to a course from which there was no drawing back, in which there was no recourse but to stay with it and stick it out, enmeshing himself deeper and deeper. But precisely how he had gotten into this, where he had gone wrong, whether in that moment of weakness last Saturday evening under Henry's contemptuous glare, or from some unsuspected strain in himself of complicity, knowing that Henry would carry out his device once it was prepared for him and yet dissociating himself from responsibility for it by warning against it, harboring within himself at the same time the wishful thought that it might prove useful to him later as leverage in bargaining for a retainer? Was it collusion from the beginning then? And not from a moment of weakness but from a weakness of his own nature? And from long before this ever began?

"You doing fine." He caught the mutter out of Henry's unmoving mouth. "Just keep it up." And the whipflick of a glance contained neither contempt nor command. It was from under the short straight black eyelashes a warm browneyed gleam of encouragement.

To Lars, who was standing with his back to the bench as he sifted through his papers, the courtroom when he curiously lifted his eyes up to it resembled nothing so much as a wedge of apple, cut in half, out of which the core—tabernacle, stage, arena—had been scooped. On each sector of the apple the auditors so interpenetrated in their daily contact sat divided, overlords versus underlings, sundered from one another with a visible distinction that weighted the decision in the core space below of every issue between them. Up on the balustraded entry platform Chalmer Coombs lounged against the doorway, holster on hip, a law unto himself in the field, on-the-spot judge, jury, and executioner; a cruder counterpart of the man who ruled, absolute master within these walls, over bench and court. Lars had long since grown to accept the old homily: There's one law for the white and another for the colored. And its corollary: A nigger has no rights that a white man is bound by. This day had begun—and his plight now—with that acceptance. So long as The Law did not apply equally to all, there was in this county no law for anyone.

The Law was no alabaster goddess here. She was the child Septima Scott wandering wild in the woods, at the mercy of anyone . . .

He suffered an adolescent impulse to shout out: Fellow citizens! Good people all! We are on trial here today. But the apostrophes and declaratives of a more naïve era had irremediably vanished. "Don't lose your nerve," the mumble trickled from the corner of Henry's mouth. "Now don't flub the dub."

Lars removed a sheaf of typewritten pages from his last folder, took the time to respread the legs of one of the four brass-headed clips that fastened through the side, and turned back to the Judge who held him patiently pinched between thumb and forefinger like a bug, either to squash or set free.

They know, Lars thought, as with head high, haughtily, he made the transit back to the bench, they know what they're doing when they cut the balls off a nigger, when they flog the fear into you, when they let you feel with a word the pinch of their power. They know what they're doing.

"Your Honor, let me assure you after the most thorough investigation of every resource pertaining to this property, the transaction of which a purported copy has been offered here was never recorded and to the best of my knowledge never took place."

"You're positive of that?"

"Positive. I would like to offer instead at this time—" With his own brand of retaliation for the position he had been placed in, Lars now produced, deliberately evoking popular sentiment on his behalf, the brief he had prepared for Julie, a description of the Colfax holdings circa 1825–1850, compiled with a scholarly zest in unearthing recondite detail, from old diaries and memoirs. "If you will accept this in evidence . . ."

"Your Honor, Your Honor!" the Mayor rudely forestalled Lars. "May I respectfully submit—"

"Yes yes?" Peevishly the Judge awaited the request that he had long foreseen, led up to and was now prepared for. "What is it?"

"May I submit that this whole question of the record can be immediately resolved by a visit to the court library? If you would call a short recess—"

"I was just about," the Judge observed, "to suggest the same thing. Mrs. Hemmings, Mr. Finchley, Mr. Sillens, if you will accompany me? The court will now adjourn for fifteen minutes."

If the atmosphere of the courtroom had at times been as dense as cheese and at other times as frangible as tea china, it was during the past interval like a sheet of rubber being endlessly attenuated. The phalanx led by Purcell passed through the gate, Lars with it, his face as ribbed with corrugations as a painted mask on a totem pole. Julie caught at Henry as he followed after. "But why? What are they up to now? Don't they take Lars' word for it? He staked his integrity. They're lying! Turning everything over on its head."

She had been growing sicker by the minute from the time she arrived here and began viewing in its embodiment what she had from a notion in her mind precipitated. She had noticed Aunt Tee across the aisle and up a row, crocheting, her black eyes glinting now and then through her steel-framed glasses, needle-sharp. Don't I have baby dresses still in a chest somwhere that she embroidered, and the Madeira cloth? Then the girl leading her class in from the fire escape, so well-dressed and sure-spoken. Isn't that she, isn't that Vivian, the little pigtailed pickaninny who went up East to college instead of me? And stumbling over her legs to take Henry's empty seat a fisherman in slouch hat, battered tans and jackboots, reeking of the waterfront, who turned on her a grizzled gap-toothed grin. Johnny Herrera! Isabel Colfax's bastard son, like a ghost risen up.

So sick she could barely stagger to her feet now and, hanging to Henry's arm, trail after the whites who shot out into the corridor in the wake of the Judge and his company.

"They're right, they're right when they say you should never take anything to court. No matter how right you are, they tear it all apart. They take what you know to be true and muddle it up so no one can ever tell for sure."

"Julie," Henry said distractedly, "Julie, I've got to get to Lars. Just give her a little air," he said to the crowd who with attentive solicitude at once accorded her a path. "Let her through."

"I'll be all right, I'll . . . Just go! I don't need anyone! Let me alone!"

She fled over the black-and-white tessellations of the corridor to the ill-lighted staircase in the rear that led down to the lavatories. In the dim dank square of hall below she dazedly pushed through the first of the surrounding doors and was inside before she recognized that she had turned not into the sanctuary she sought, the cleanly reposeful white porcelain-and-tile ladies room but into the dingy brown untended one, paint scaling from the walls, plumbing clogged.

The heavy fumed oak door had swung closed behind her. It was too late to turn back. All the smells of the cell, of stale urine and feces, of blood-soaked cotton pads that, once bloated, had dried out like decayed fish and now spilled from a rusty grey pail on the floor: all of it converged on her and came heaving up out of the pit of her bowels. In a swimming blackness she groped for the toilet stall. Spasm after spasm, like a convulsion of the earth's crust over uncontainable pressure, retched shudderingly upward and poured splattering down into the maw of the stained toilet bowl. Yesterday's champagne as vile as lye, the rank pulp of rich foods, Coley's blank face and Reeve's as blank, Aunt Tee's flashing needle and Vivian's thin treble, the briny penumbra of Johnny Herrera and Lars—Lars walking through the gate like an automaton, his cheeks scarified as in one of those tribal ceremonies where they slash the skin and keep rubbing dirt into the bleeding incisions to keep them from healing until the ridges formed become permanent decoration. . . .

Where is truth? Where is love?

The retching reacted like an expellant on her tear-ducts and nasal membranes, her bladder and intestinal passages as if from every orifice of her body the fluids must come spouting forth. There was no seat on the toilet to sit down upon. No paper on the wall to wipe with. No door on the stall to be shut. One stood like an animal, exposed.

The hall door slowly opened and Julie watched it, immobilized, unable to conceal herself. A broad brown woman in a polka-dot dress and tattered straw hat stood transfixed opposite her. Her eyes, large with frightened concern, fell on Julie's desperately shaky extraction of tissues from her handbag, pursued her in her blundering escape from the toilet stall, her blind searching about under the scimitar of sunlight that fell suddenly from the lowering clouds through the foully dusty ground-level window.

"Ain't no basin in here, ma'am," the woman said and held open the hall door for her. "Can I help you any?"

"No, no thank you."

The stairs came flying up at her. Her foot caught on the top step and everyone came flying to her with handkerchiefs dipped in cold water, snifters of brandy and sniffs of aromatic vinegar.

"No, I'm all right! I just tripped, I stubbed my toe . . ."

She wouldn't hear of Henry seeing her home or anyone else either.

"I can drive myself, I'm perfectly able. I've got to get back to Colfax. Now I'm going, so let me go!"

Outside in the car she laid her head down on the ivory steering wheel and cried. She cried as if all the tears of a lifetime could not relieve by a single drop the bursting of her heart.

6

The throng milled about the courthouse corridor all during the recess in a welter of comment and speculation that had proliferated beyond any recognizable relationship to the merits of the case being heard. D. C. Lacey ardently defended his school system against all insinuations implied or imagined: "I never had any one of my teachers, colored or white, go messing about the court library before. Never! If she wasn't the Professor's granddaughter and if it wasn't so near the end of the school year . . ." Chalmer Coombs buttonholed Mr. Arthur: "Now I'll lay you dollars to doughnuts Sillens has got himself in with these niggers just to raise the ante when he's bought off from them. That's right. Why in no time at all he'll be dictator over every job, elective and appointive, in this part of Georgia. And where does that leave you and me, huh?" "And I know just how he'll do it too," Mr. Arthur shook his finger under Chalmer's nose. "He'll have them all running bolita for him." Eustis Telfer strayed up and down, proclaiming: "Now I got nothing against the Nigra. I'm all for them having their rights. But when they come into where I belong like they done today and try to overrun me . . ."

Ada Hemmings' two brothers, the tubercular veteran of World War I and the thriving father of five, materialized in a unit, paired together as a bulwark of silent menace, geared to protect their sister from any further onslaughts. And Edna Telfer appeared belatedly from her newspaper office, not that any hint of today's conflict would ever be published in her columns, and demanded in distress from one person to another: "But what's happened? Whatever caused this? I just can't understand. We're the most advanced county in the state for colored, in the whole South perhaps for that matter. Why are they acting up so? What are they after?"

While Benson Reece standing in midstream over his cane sententiously declared: "The two-toed sloth spends his life climbing through trees by night upside down and in reverse though capable of walking upright."

Only Rad stood apart, jostled and scuffed as he lurked in the embrasure of an office doorway, rereading with a concentration he had not given it the night before his copy of his deed. When Johnny Herrera shouldered through to him, he passed it on to Johnny, pointing to a line: "You see what I see? Does that read to you like it does to me? And that name there, what does that name look like to you?"

Johnny held the paper up to the light and shook his head. "Used to read. But not much anymore. Can't make out a thing without glasses and I got no money for that. I been without back teeth"—he spread his mouth—"for nigh two years. My old woman, she got them though. Falls in one night and shows me: Look hon, falsies."

It was the most that Rad had ever heard Johnny Herrera say. He was quite loquacious. "How's this going, do you think, Johnny?"

For answer Johnny lowered his sea-green slouch hat down over gold-flecked blue slits of eyes. "Treason from within. Invasion from without. Patriotism, Rad. Where's your all-fired patriotism?"

In a rush the crowd stampeded past them to the basement stairs. "She fell! She lost her balance! She fainted! She's collapsed!" And rushed back to the marble staircase that descended from the court library above.

"They're coming! Aren't they coming?" It was Henry hurrying down to his wife's aid.

Callously with a fat smack of his two fingers Johnny wafted a kiss down toward the foot of the corridor. "You can wrap this one up in Christmas ribbon if you haven't already. Might's well shut up shop and go home right now. Colfax always runs away with the show."

"But what about Reeve? Didn't the sheriff say that if it turns out in court the land ain't his . . . Didn't they agree . . ."

"Too bad. It's a shame. He hasn't got a Chinaman's chance. I wouldn't like to be in his boots, would you?"

"I am," Rad said. "That's the hell of it. I am."

The colored had remained seated in the courtroom. Among themselves the young people clowned out the Judge's gingerly handling of the will, as if it might contaminate him. And the older people chortled over the quit-claims. "How she ever got her cousin Des up Charleston to sign away anything, no matter how much folding-money—" "That's easy. All she had to do was send him his share of the tax bill." "And me," Uncle Lee said, "when that Finchley called me up, do you know I all but went? Huk huk huk . . ."

Vivian left her seat, circled around the back windows, along the wall down to the dividing platform and down the center aisle. From behind she laid her hand on Reeve's shoulder, stooping over to whisper to him. Reeve reached up and laid his hand over hers.

"Hello, love," he spoke to her before she could speak to him.

"Hello you."

"You made it, huh? You stood up to them."

"I died a thousand deaths."

Their hands remained one over the other, hard over soft, tough over tender, in a passage as warm and natural as sunlight.

"How's it going, Reeve, for true? You really really think it can come out?"

"I think it's a miracle," he said soberly. "That we're all here together over this, it's a miracle. And my family—" He looked back down the row. "We could all be scratching each other's eyes out over that piece of land, and instead . . . I'm proud to be one of you."

"Wait," Vergilia scoffed. "So long as they're all on us, we're together. But wait till we've won. Plenty of time then to start scratching."

In spite of the confident hilarity around him—Fred and Lila-Lee were doing a take-off on Ada, little finger curled, shoulders fanning— Reeve was very much on edge. He had stepped up from his place in an attempt to join the group heading for the court library, but Ada had slowed down to deter him. "Judge Purcell is dealing with your attorney now, Reeve. He don't need you." Up on the platform Purcell and Sillens had walked out side by side, hobnobbing together, for all the world the best of friends.

"If only the Judge hadn't taken that copy away from me."

"Now Reeve, it was plain in the sight of everybody," Mae said. "He can't do anything to it."

"But if only he hadn't."

Up to now he had been holding it all together in his two hands, and now somehow it was all getting away from him. There was something about that Judge. He was too willing to go look.

"Will it really really come out, Viv? You tell me."

Thurlow too was looking troubled, his grey eyes blinking in their leather pouches behind his glasses, his spatulate fingers drumming on his spread knees. "It's not in the bag yet. I've seen too many bags all tied up on top with a hole cut out of the bottom."

And the word about Julie's "fainting-spell" when it filtered through caused momentary consternation. "But how does *that* affect *this*? What I mean—" "Oh I can just hear them. Can't you just hear them? 'After all she did for those folks, naming the school after their mamma and all—no wonder . . .'" "Do we have to think for them too? Do we have to knock ourselves out with what's on their mind!"

"She gave me such a look," Reeve recalled. "I never saw such a look.

They say if looks could kill—but why? What have I ever done to her that she should look at me so?"

Their frets were dispelled by the youngsters whispering around a scurrilous and probably unfounded tale, in circulation among their elders for years—that Harold Wylly, the Judge's butler, had been seen washing Eula's back for her because she was too fat to reach around it.

"Here they come! They're coming back."

The whites returned to their places with the air of an army solidified, shoulder to shoulder, shield to shield, swords grimly fixed. It must be they're losing, the certainty flashed through the colored with an ebullient and fearful thrill. On the entrance of the Judge everyone rose in a movement that had become as rhythmic as the tide, and fell back. While the lawyers resumed their stance inside the gate, Reeve suddenly struck himself in the forehead. Ben reached over and gripped his arm, and Fred with a grimace of anguish, eyes and jaws locked tight, turned his head away. The same thought had seized all three at once. Of course! It's not there. It's gone.

While Ada was debating with Vivian over the record and the Judge and the lawyers were palavering over it, some flunkey had stolen upstairs and removed it. If it was still there, even then . . .

"In the absence of any record prior to the year 1868," Lars, reopening the argument, began in the clear ringing voice of one unjustly accused, now absolved, "and in view of the fact that all records previous to the War were destroyed when, as you know, a detachment of Sherman's troops razed this town—"

"Mmmm." A responsive murmur rumbled from the white side.

"May I again offer, as I was about to do when I was so abruptly interrupted, in evidence—" He strode back to his table, lifted the brief from his file folder with an appropriately solemn gesture and bore it forward. "The only existing account, taken from valid sources, familiar to many of the people here today, among them our most respected citizens—"

"Hmmmm."

"Covering the Colfax proprietorship of Sunset Hill as it was in the old days. Now I freely admit that certain sections of Sunset Hill may have changed hands many times since then, but that's all water under the bridge. Insofar as the area we are disputing here is concerned, this is—"

"Yesss."

Lars clapped his hand down over it. "This, I repeat, is the record. The sole record. And the true one."

There was an outbreak of applause. None of them, not one, would ever again sigh over Lars Finchley: "Trouble with that fella, he's too honest."

The Judge frowned around. The flutter ceased. He inspected a few pages of the brief. The cankers at the root of his tongue and the swellings between his toes still chafed, but he was in much improved humor, having paid off a few scores and without risk to his own skin.

"I will reserve this for further study, Mr. Finchley, as I have the copy submitted by opposing counsel. In the meantime the court will hold the estate in escrow. It is my opinion that the premises should be vacated as a means of safeguarding them until a decision is rendered. I will entertain such a motion—"

"Your Honor?"

"Yes, Mr. Sillens?" He peered down over his bridged fingers with a perspicacity that was altogether beguiling. "Before you say anything further, Mr. Sillens, let me state that in my experience the truth usually lies somewhere between two extremes. It is my hope that in this instance we shall arrive at it there."

"With all due respect, Your Honor," the Mayor said, "I beg to differ. In my experience, the truth may be found at either extreme as well as in the middle or somewhere else altogether. I was about to remind you, sir, that I have not been given an opportunity to complete my argument. May I continue?"

"By all means. If you still feel bound to."

Carter Sillens was angry as only a man of elephantine hide and calm, coupled with bulldog stubbornness, can be angry when at last thoroughly aroused. He was acquainted from the past reception accorded him at political wingdings here with the attitude of the local inhabitants toward him. Their sly dig, "Too bad Carter Sillens isn't as smart as a one of his brothers," had even once or twice reached his ears. But if they considered him a corrupt politician that no decent person would touch with a ten-foot pole, he for his part had his own attitude toward them, of a piece with that wry shrug, that moue of humorous despair which the populace of Bay City never failed to display in reference to their more rural neighbors. "Those people over in Colfax County, well, I don't know . . ." A bunch of yokels and yahoos. An insular breed who being in the main poor as pease pods, having no high degree of education or culture and possessing no distinguishing genius, still managed to think of themselves as the cream of creation. He might receive under-the-counter campaign contributions from a syndicate of slot-machine operators, but leave it to Colfax County to license the slot machines, illegal under state law, and collect a good part of its revenue from them!

Sillens could not have extrapolated the mixture of motives and emotions that had brought him here to do minor battle in a locale he had left so far behind. But it was not to be defeated in a grubby small-time courtroom under the thumb of a tinhorn judge. And it was not to be made a poltroon of before the colored half-brother who occasionally came begging—or was it commanding?—a favor of him and before the foster-mother whom he only rarely saw but whom he still remembered with a fondness he harbored toward no other human being. He was not overly shocked by the disappearance of Folio A, being no stranger to purloined records. He had his own theory about its present where-abouts: either in Henry Warren's desk or Lars Finchley's office or the Judge's chambers, if not resting at this moment, most likely, under the mattress of the redoubtable Mrs. Hemmings. But that they should be-lieve that they could pull such hanky-panky on him, that they should underestimate him so far—this was unendurable.

"If you will bear with me a little longer?"

"As long as you like," the Judge said generously, "so long as you understand that I must under the circumstances deny your petition for admission of the will."

"To cut the Gordian knot, sir, needn't take very long. While I have not had the pleasure of reviewing the brief composed by my gifted colleague, may I venture to point out that though it may have some value as literature and some virtue as analecta, in legal terms it is com-pletely worthless. This is not a deposition but a diversion—"

"Grrr." As if caught off guard by a below-the-belt blow the white side let out a chorus of grunts, which swelled at once into a threatening growl.

"However, so long as history has been introduced as an active factor in this, uh, informal parlay, and since the name of General William Tecumseh Sherman has been summoned up from the grave—"

"Sss, boo-ooo . . ."

"Hush," the Judge admonished. "Go on, sir."

The Mayor in the extremity of his provocation was either trying a final desperate gambit or tying a lynch rope around his own neck. For after lifting a tome from among his folders in a parody of Lars' earlier gesture, he began to read aloud Sherman's celebrated Field Order 15, issued on January 16, 1865, reserving the islands from Charleston south, the abandoned rice fields along the rivers for thirty miles back from the sea to the country bordering the St. John's River, Florida, for settle-ment of Negroes made free by the acts of war and the proclamation of the President.

"But that was rescinded!" "It was nullified!" "We got it all back!"

Ignoring the outcries, the Mayor persisted in reading through to the end of his paragraph. "Yes, Your Honor," he snapped his book closed, "this circular was later nullified. Except in those few places and during that brief period where the land had already been auctioned off for nonpayment of taxes by its prewar owners under the Tax Commissioner appointed by the Federal government for that purpose. Over half the plantation land in Colfax County was so sold and according to state records all the land on the River Road from the highway to the Point, including every acre of Sunset Hill.

"That this land may subsequently have been surrendered, abandoned or lost by reason of debts and liens, or that the occupants thereof may have been frightened off or driven off or hornswoggled off by such shenanigans as I have here witnessed today is immaterial. That land belonged to the colored and the crackers, sir, who bought it."

If Carter Sillens had intended to smite the gentry of Colfax County hip and thigh, he could not have succeeded better. As though he had called into question the tenure of every property holder of any status memories raced back, checking over the origin of every transaction from recent to far past. Many of the whites were so staggered by the intimation, later discounted, that what was indubitably theirs might not be, even the instinctive retort, "Throw him out!" was reduced to a mere gasp in their throats.

"In view of the absence—by reason of the passage of time, the fire which took place at the turn of the century or whatever agent or cause —of the original deed of sale and of Folio A, Book C, in which it was entered, the true copy produced by my client supersedes Mr. Finchley's memorabilia both chronologically and substantively. As signed by the superintendent of taxation, certified by the town clerk and notarized, under the law it must stand. I'm sure, Your Honor, that I don't have to cite chapter and verse?"

"Your point is well made," the Judge smoothly acknowledged, "and the court will take it under advisement. However it will still require some little time. This superintendent of taxes you allude to, for example, appointed by the Yankees for so brief a period, wrote, you must admit, a pretty illegible hand. His signature will have to be identified."

"The signature—may I see that?"

"Unfortunately, as you will agree, the paper at that particular point is quite worn through and, in fact, the signature comes close to being indecipherable."

Somehow in the process of exchange between Judge and Mayor, the paper ripped along one of its creases, slightly but audibly enough to act like the scratch of a match on exacerbated tempers. From the sixth row of the white section Ozzie Higginson shot up and in a voice shaking with passion delivered the delayed counterblow to the Mayor.

"Sherman's troops burned most this town of Arcady! And they burned the Baptist church over there"—he pointed dramatically to the tall fretted windows on the colored side, rippling now once again with sheets of rain—"down to the ground! And that was the most dastardly deed committed in the whole War—in that or any war before or since! December 12, 1864, it was. On the centennial of that day, if I'm still alive as with God's help I hope to be, on that day I am going to lock up my store and walk around Oglethorpe Square in my white suit and think about it. Just think about it. Whether anybody else knows what for or not!"

"But that was a long time ago," the Mayor said politely in an effort to placate him. And to quell the smoldering-grey quavers of the air that ascended to the fan-bladed clusters of yellow light nested in the tan coffers of the ceiling, quaverings of the air that even he sensed might prove his nemesis.

"My father, O. Z. Higginson," Ozzie replied to him, "was born the day after the War ended. And he's eighty-two years old now. When you think about it like that, it's not so long ago. Is it? Not so long ago a-tall!"

Ozzie's shrill tremolo tingled through the room like the yelping of a dog run over by a car in the street. The Mayor had by a leap of inference committed the ultimate outrage: disparagement of the most sacred of all Colfax County institutions: its octogenarians.

"I move," the Mayor plowed on, regardless, "that the claim of Mrs. Julie-Ann Colfax Warren to the property named and hereinafter referred to as 'the old Scott place' be set aside."

"Motion denied."

"I move that the claim of Reeve Scott *et al.*, to the property bequeathed them in fee tail—"

"Motion denied."

"I move that the certified true copy of the deed of sale issued to Jonas B. Scott by a party to be specified as 'Superintendent or Commissioner of Taxes for the year 1866' be recognized—"

"Denied."

"On what grounds, sir?"

"On the grounds previously stated. The court is obligated to substantiate the copy, if such it be, especially in the light of an unascertained signator."

"It all hinges on that one moot point?"

"You may call it moot, but I do not. When so much hinges on it, no labor should be spared . . ."

To the whites, as well as to the colored, it was a transparent dodge. The Judge had lit upon his last-ditch loophole and he obstinately clung to it, let the Mayor haul in precedent or howl to high heaven as he would. "Now you don't honestly expect this court, do you, to accept a contract from which the name of a principal is lacking?"

Meanwhile Rad in the upper reaches of the white section sat throughout on the answer in his pocket. Though he felt with all his heart and knew with all his head that his own fate was being decided in the fight down there he couldn't, wouldn't, and didn't move. He was never able afterward to explain his inertia to Reeve. "But it was your own farm as much as mine . . ." "I'd have let it go . . ." It was as if he were chained and manacled by the crowd around him: the women in summer dresses leaning intently forward, exchanging veiled glances, giggling; the men in shirt sleeves as if they'd rushed here from the middle of a job or officiously neat in their light suits, their sleek heads wagging in appraisal of the joust below, eyes sliding. All appreciating, neighbor to neighbor, the secret gist of every phrase and gesture, lunge, parry, and riposte—as if the outer appearance, rousing though it was, concealed a realer reality apprehensible to each of them in the inmost recess of his soul.

At Rad's right sat a girl of delicate Elizabethan features: petaline eyelids and posy mouth, fine-drawn flower-face under a basket of a bonnet; sweet-scented, cleanly of person, cleanliness emanating almost tactually from her bud-sprigged cotton dress and from the parting of her collar where it dipped down to her breast. She jigged a blanket-swathed infant in her arms, into whose mouth she thrust a nippled bottle. Under her breath she soothingly shushed a child nestled up beside her, into whose mouth she stuck a lollipop. All the while her eyes never wavered from the protagonists more than fifteen rows down.

On Rad's left sat a state trooper who had dashed in from the rain, a small-boned fox of a man, tawny hair brushed back from a tiny crest over his forehead, little tiptilt eyes pleasantly crinkled, keen nose snubbed, thin mouth a curl, lobeless ears hugging his head close. He dug his elbows into knees, fists into cheeks, seemingly unaware of the white-circled arm patch on his grey shirt, the .38 jutting from the hip pocket of his green trousers.

Beyond the trooper, next to him in the same row sat another man: heavy-set, pudgy-framed, gimlet-eyed. And beyond him sat still another, all sharpness but with large dark eyes that moved eloquently. In a fracas, Rad felt, these men would be quicker to shoot than speak.

In front of him the two middle-aged women no longer talked. The plump hand of one continuously strayed to the specks of black hair sprouting out of the back of her short neck. Her companion, stringy-tall, grey-haired, hollow-eyed, continuously stroked at the reticulations of her throat. They were both rapt with absorption. Enthralled.

He was held down by a pressure he couldn't buck. He was penned in with his own kind, wedged in among them, impacted. Incarcerated on the side of the courtroom that by law, tradition and habit was his. He had thought that for Reeve he would represent one familiar friendly white face. Now he looked for the friendly white face from which he could borrow strength.

Johnny Herrera with his sardonic toothless grin? He was too far off, down in the front row next to Henry. Tolerated and indulged as a character whose peculiarities must for some reason be overlooked. The village crackpot. All he could see of Johnny was the back of his head, with the disreputable hat slung rakishly over one ear. It was not enough.

Rad looked down at the sun-bleached khaki shirt he had donned in such a hurry at home and the faded blue chinos, too short at the ankles, from before the war, and the socks that didn't quite match, one chocolate brown and ribbed, the other plain caramel. He couldn't lift hand or foot.

He couldn't bring himself to act even after Chalmer Coombs slid into the row behind, following Ozzie Higginson's oration, and bending over the girl's sprigged cotton shoulder spoke into his ear.

"You know, Rad," Chalmer informed him conversationally, "I'm going to have to jail him? You know that was agreed on?"

"But why?" Rad hissed back, although he had anticipated it, dreaded it, tried to convince himself that it was not to be so. "It's still his land. Nothing's settled yet."

"It's as good as settled, ain't it? Who says it ain't settled?"

Rad gazed across the room to the opposite sector. The crowd, even thicker than it was here, mounted row on row, every single one of them with his own eyes, ears, mouth, manner of holding his arms . . . "*Therefore what chaos and bloodshed it must bring about,*" he had read aloud last night to his wife from the old town council resolution against slavery. And had added, "If they don't get their born-rights, if they can't enjoy what's theirs by right as good as you and me . . ."

"You know, Rad," Chalmer said, "that I warned him yesterday to cut out the mischief and after I left he went right on blasting. Did you help him? Or can I call you as a witness?"

Rad's neck hardened as if with the stir of Chalmer's breath upon it the white fang of a rattler had sunk in. His throat closed. His spinal column shrank. "Swear to me," his wife had said to him last night, "on

the head of our unborn baby that you'll bring no trouble on this house."
And he had sworn.

"You know, Rad," Chalmer continued, "I could arrest you right along
with him and then tell you this. But I thought I'd tip you off first. One
good turn deserves another, hey?"

With a playful slap at his shoulder Chalmer slid away again. Mending his fences, bent on reestablishing himself however tardily in Henry's
good graces, Chalmer tramped down the aisle and preempting a seat
behind Henry posted himself in an advantageous position to stop Reeve
when he should start up to leave.

Rad stared at the minute black flecks of hair on the dough-plump
neck of the woman in front of him. He could make a break for the door
now, slip out without anyone noticing, take off in his truck, disappear
for a couple of weeks. Until it was all over. All over. All of it. The
woman's neck twisted about, ribboning in a swirl sideward from her
cheek. "That Sillens! Why don't he give up?" she confided to all and
sundry in an exasperated mutter. "Don't they know when they're
licked?" He knew the woman. A nice-enough person. Husband wasn't
doing well. Had three boys to raise. He picked at a loose thread from
his buttonhole, unraveling it in a thin spiral. Knotted it. Snapped it
off. "Sleeping," the girl next to him formed sweetly at him with her
mouth as she jigged the round-cheeked infant in the crook of her arm.
Moving back to allow her more room he struck sharply with his bare
elbow the gun butt in the trooper's back pocket. He jerked away from
it with a start. The trooper, unaware, grinned on.

Rad took the copy of his deed out of his pocket, smoothed it out over
his knees and traced through once again the key lines. It was all there.
He had it all. Between his two hands. He thought of the colored-girl
who a short while ago had stood up in court for what she knew. He
thought of the swamp-girl who almost a half century ago had stood up
against the whole court for what was hers . . . And still he couldn't
move.

When he looked up again he saw tall among the standees at the
nearby window the preacher who had been in Reeve's cabin yesterday,
just arrived out of the rain, glistening with the storm, his black slicker
shimmering, although out the window the sky was clearing, bright
blue, the sun out, slashing through the palm fronds.

Rad would have liked to believe that when he did move it was of his
own volition. But he felt bound ever afterward to confess, to his
shame: "It was coercion. When Chalmer threatened to throw me in the
pokey if I didn't testify to a lie . . . After all that hard work I went and
did right along with Reeve, oh man! Even so I come awful mighty near

not to . . ." Though it wasn't only coercion that moved him. It was a lot of other things he could never quite put his finger on, let alone give tongue to.

He got up then and tapping Clem's elbow signaled him to his seat. "Now you take it, I'm leaving it." And with the frayed paper in his hand he left behind all those who for all their participation still retained some last slim margin of detachment. He didn't know what he was afraid of or what could happen to him, but that walk along the side wall and down the declivity of the center aisle to the gate and through it was long as a walk to the gallows.

The Judge finishing up with Sillens, "Now you can be sure, Mayor, I'll send to the Capitol for whatever they got as soon as ever I may," lifted his smile expansively beyond the snowy head to the lone figure approaching him, bony and awkward in its ill-assorted clothing, half-shy, half-bold. "Anything on your mind, son?"

"Well, sir," Rad said, "I can save you the price of stamps to Atlanta, if validation's all you need." With an effort, straining upward from his toes, he placed his paper on the bench. The two lawyers, Finchley and Sillens, were instantly there beside him, hanging over his shoulders, peering at it.

"Right there, my title confirms his. You can see for yourself: bounded southerly by the Ocachee River and northerly by land of Jonas B. Scott, purchased this day . . . with mutual right-of-way from the road to the river through both properties. And the signature's there . . ."

The proof was plain, nothing more was necessary. He was in enough hot water already. Still, some demon in his chest prompted him on. "Don't the name of that superintendent of taxation appointed by the Yankees look to you, Judge"—he traced it out with the tip of his fingernail—"if you read it real close, like 'Vernon C. Purcell?'"

From somewhere in the background someone blew his nose, too loudly. A breath released too rapidly through closed lips puffed forth with the vibrant flatulence of a Bronx cheer. There was a gurgle. And a splutter. A yawp. A whoop. Laughter rocked from wall to wall, eye-wringing, throat-splitting, belly-whopping, knee-whacking, heel-stomping laughter. The mystery of the Purcell ancestry, so long suppressed, was out. Scalawags!

Even then the Judge did not deign to demean himself to the ignominy of a public surrender. He had Ada telephone the Ordinary at her house, five minutes away, where she generally spent Fridays, and had her come over. While he retired from the scene, she accepted the filing of the will for probate with the efficiency of a thoroughly mastered routine.

Out in the corridor and again out on the portico Rad was halted at least a dozen times over. "Now I remember," Mr. Arthur, taking hold of his arm, held forth to the ring around them. "There was always something about Vern's grandpappy. And his daddy, Ol' Vern—had a little country grocery store out Fallona way—was a single-taxer and a Populist, got his start with Tom Watson. All for the poor white and the colored man. Now his son is the worst nigger-hater there is . . ."

Lonnie Truelove, a friend from the Legion post, who farmed a good piece of bottomland with his daddy on the other side of Arcady, pulled Rad away and pumped his hand. "Boy, did that take guts and don't I know it! I was settin' all the way through with my tongue atween my teeth. You know the place we got was acquired in just that way?"

A man Rad hadn't seen in years, so beat-up and beat-out he wouldn't have recognized him, a bench-warmer from out in the green, shuffled up. "You recollect me? Collins? Used to be down the road a piece from you all? And back in 1938 when the county sent out a whole raft of tax fi fas, we lost all we had account of sixteen dollars in delinquent taxes? You remember that? And next thing we knew Old Man Colfax had snapped it up?"

And Edna Telfer, the newspaper editor, cornered him: "I've been making a collection of old family papers that have shown up in Bibles hereabout. If you could loan that to me sometime to have it filmed? Imagine—" She reached out and drew over Eustis, her husband's stepbrother, and said to him with a significance that would eventually cost Ada her secretaryship of the Historical Society, "Such carelessness in the handling of those folios up there. Our priceless archives, not even catalogued . . ."

And the stringy-tall grey woman who had sat in front of him pulling at her throat gleamed at him flirtatiously in passing: "My mother's great gram on her father's side was a rootin'-tootin' Abolitionist all her life long and I don't care who knows it! You did fine, Mr. McDowell. You did just right. Don't let anybody ever tell you different."

He was quite suddenly someone. A person. If there was any villain in the piece now, it was Brandon Colfax. "You know he had a regular monomania about Sunset, drove that poor wife of his clean out of her mind. You can't blame Julie, she must have got it from him. I reckon she—"

Interestedly eyes followed Lars hurtling down the granite steps toward his car in the Square and Henry after him, expostulating. Lars slammed the car door shut in Henry's face, but Henry pulled it open again and got inside and they drove off together.

"I reckon she's not married to any bed of roses either."

Rad caught a glimpse of Clem and tried to get to him, and Clem tried to get to Rad. But there were just too many people intervening, some of them choosing to converge on Clem as if *he* had won something. They streamed out of the front door of the courthouse light with release, buoyant as if an oppressive burden had been removed from their shoulders, and flowed together with the Negroes spilling down from the fire escape on the side, pausing to exchange amenities with them. In all their voices danced a liberated freshness, a merriment that twinkled like the raindrops, shot through with sunlight, dripping from leaves and eaves.

7

The victory of the court hearing bore other consequences too, a by-product that, though intrinsically unrelated, developed as an unexpected bonus, of importance to Rad and not only to him.

All the next morning, Saturday, market day, farmers from around the county kept drifting down the River Road to take a look at the ditching, inquire about its costs and debate its usefulness. Both Rad and Reeve were working with pick and shovel at cleaning it up, flattening bottom, sides and spoil piles, a task that would not be finished in a day, a week or a month of their spare time. But it was a start. Some of Reeve's classmates came down and after kidding around a while went to work with whatever tools, branches, and boards lay handy. "Now you know what the Geechee mean, *be' d' groun.*" About a half hour later Lonnie Truelove showed up with Carl Maynard and Richard-Gene Jeems from Rad's Legion post. "What you got here?" Carl asked. "The Suez Canal or the Panama?"

"Jump in," Rad invited. "Get your free mudbath. I understand it's good for the complexion."

As often happens, those who had come to razz remained to sustain. In no time at all they were all beating with branch and board, and it wasn't just the ground. The laugh was on Purcell. On Henry. On Ozzie Higginson who held the mortgage on Carl Maynard's farm. On Chalmer who collected rakeoffs from High Power for the gaming in his kitchen and from Richard-Gene for the still in his woods. Back to back, in mire up to their calves, they slapped the slopes into shape.

"Howcome," Richard-Gene wondered, "I'm a-workin' so hard?"

"VIP," Reeve answered him enigmatically. "And VIP means 'Bam. And 'Bam means *down there.*"

Wham . . .

Everyone has some VIP down 'Bam he's got to wham.

In another half hour Clement DeLavery was there. "Well I see your cornfield's drained after all those showers we had yesterday." He stood a while looking from Maynard's gold-fuzzed bronze back to the Baron's stocky blackness, from High Power's lanky laconic scythe-like sweep to Rad driving like a piston. Then he rolled up his black shirt and pulled it off over his head. Though he folded it carefully, when he laid it on the ground it soon crumpled like an old skin shed for new. Bare to the waist, the matted hair stirring pleasurably on his chest, he rolled up his dungarees.

"Say Rev!" "Hey Preach!"

He caught the shovel someone tossed him and jumped down into the ditch with them.

"Keep an eye out for sidewinders." "Never turn your back on a cotton-mouth."

He had come here to explain, as if an explanation were expected of him, why he had not turned up at yesterday's hearing until it was almost over after having promised the day before that he would attend. The explanations now seemed superfluous and extraordinarily remote. His mother's despair: "Stay away from there! You're no sooner out of one scrape than you're looking for another . . ." And Hazel Allenby's desperate call: "Clem, I need you! Something's happened to Ronnie—I've just had a cable from Greece . . ." And his headlong drive to her doll house, praying: "Oh God, don't let it be that, not to her—" Only to learn that the dreadful thing that had happened to Ronnie was not death from a guerrilla's rifle-shot but marriage to a Greek girl. He had spent all morning arranging with the Red Cross over long-distance to advance Hazel's sailing date and assuring Hazel—but he had assured her —that her new daughter-in-law far from being "a greasy foreigner who'll never fit in here!" must be a veritable caryatid.

At noon they all sprawled around Rad's porch, slopping up the coffee Rad's wife had sent out from jars and cans, anything that would serve as a mug; licking up slabs of hot spoonbread that crumbled in their hands as they ate. "But what happened yesterday?" Clem wanted to know. "I've heard nine different versions." Among them, with hoots and howls, they filled him in. "And you think that's all there is to it?" Clem asked. "They'll let this pass?"

"Well, I didn't sleep home last night," Reeve admitted.

Lonnie screwed up his thin face, incredulously. "Aw g'wan, they ain't go'n do nothin'."

"No," Reeve said, "they won't do anything now. Not with everyone onto it the way they are. But later—"

TRIAL AND TESTIMONY 711

"Aw g'wan. You got 'em on the run, they runnin' like a whiptail cur. You ever been through anything like this before?"

Reeve looked at High Power and High Power looked back at him, warily. "N-n-no. Can't say as I have."

"Then how do you know?"

"I know."

The colored, feeling their oats with the battle won, still saw it as only a reprieve, a stay of execution, a stage in some much larger panorama. The recognition of this, their long view, estranged the whites. After the spontaneous camaraderie of only a moment before they all brooded uncomfortably over their coffee, swirling it around to stir up the sugar from the bottom. Clem was all of a sudden acutely conscious that if any of his St. Paul parishioners were to see him now in the state he was in, in the company he was with, in so controversial and critical a spot . . .

Richard-Gene lumbered upward from his haunches. "Well, I better be goin'."

"Now, wait a minute." Rad hauled him back down. "You're not through here yet. Say Preach, hey Rev, now we got you on the spot, how about teaching that GI course for us?"

Clem was besieged from all sides. "What you doin' this summer? You ain't doin' nothin'. You can do it." "These fellas here is gettin' sixty-five a month and more for dependents, ain't you guys? All for picking up a little know-how." "Would you believe it—I went in it for the checks and that's no lie—but this the first year I ever had beans free from mosaic?"

"Well." Clem looked up at the circle of faces, so warm, so urgent, so free of those shadows that ordinarily separated them from each other, and from him. It was a sight he would remember for a long time and one that would not easily be achieved again. "You have to remember, my first responsibility is to my church."

"Granted. But what about your second responsibility?"

Clem promised to think about it. But as a matter of fact he had already been thinking about it, far more seriously and for many more weeks than he knew.

Back in town at midafternoon he knocked at the brass-plated door of Benson's bank, closed since twelve. Benson unlocked the door from inside and welcomed him in to his front desk behind the taupe half-drawn curtains across the window. "Some people get drunk on booze, and some on books. This is my form of alcoholism."

"What do you do here every Saturday afternoon?"

"Just set. And mull."

Clem sat and mulled too for a few minutes. "You know anything about Henry's reaction to that hearing yesterday?"

"He's too busy to have a reaction. Taking Julie up to Atlanta tomorrow with the boy."

"I know." He had stopped twice at the house in concern to offer whatever aid or comfort he could. But his messages had been returned at the door by Kissie. Julie was refusing to see anyone.

"And driving straight back here Monday . . . he has that freezer plant opening next week. He's all tied up. Everything at once."

"Oh."

"The two-toed sloth," Benson said apropos of nothing at all, "is the slowest and stupidest creature there is. With the greatest capacity for survival. It's been known to live with its brain removed for as long as thirty hours. And the heart removed from its body has gone on beating for as long as thirty minutes."

"What about the three-toed sloth?"

"I didn't specify him because he's just a smidgeon smarter. I told you I get potted in here."

"Benson, I'm here for advice. Though I know you'll say no."

But Benson didn't listen to him more than halfway through before he was on the telephone, oiling the wheels. "There are about twenty of these boys, I understand, already processed through the VA. All the paperwork's been done on it. Will bring at least two thousand a month into the county, not including what the school gets. Best thing in the world for him—syphon off some of that excess energy of his, not to speak of that excess of zeal . . ."

Within an hour Benson had located the state superintendent of vocational education and scheduled Clem for a two-week refresher course up in Athens, which was luckily due to begin week after next. Within a month he would be instructing the farm-training course at the Arcady high school for white veterans of World War II in cooperation with Professor Thurlow who instructed the course at the colored school.

"Remind me," Clem said on parting from Benson, "to come in and mull again some Saturday afternoon. Only one thing, I want to be sure of the full approval of my parish."

"To hell with the parish. With what we pay you, you need another income. All right, all right, I'll put it up to 'em. We'll conduct a poll. Let Eustis handle it."

When Clem enthusiastically announced his new plan at home however, Nancy was not as delighted with it as he had thought she would be. "But that means we'll be staying here all summer." "What's wrong with that?" "Nothing." She tipped back in her chair, viewing the greyed dining-room ceiling. "I just have to catch up with the idea, that's all."

His mother too evinced some hesitation. "It's just that I hate to see anyone plunge into anything, ever, in such a rush."

"Is that your only objection?"

"Well, I don't believe people want their preacher to be a teacher. They don't want that."

"But that's up to the parish. Benson's having Eustis run a poll."

Later when she was washing the dishes and he was wiping, Laura said, "Clem, I've been doing a lot of thinking about you and me. I've wondered whether you see me or whether I am one of those interfering meddlesome mothers who out of a mistaken love attempt to swallow up the lives of their sons."

"Now Mother—"

"Let me go on." Meticulously she rinsed a dish under the hot water faucet that was never hot enough and shook the drops off before passing it to him. "But I've come to the conclusion that that's too facile an interpretation. All my adult life, you must understand, I have had to project whatever ability I'm endowed with through the medium of a man, your father. Whatever experience I've accumulated, whatever wisdom I've earned, it was all poured into him. And it worked out very well. He failed me only once."

"And when was that?"

"He died."

She switched off the faucet with a twist of that steel-corded wrist through which must flow such enormous will power—that had so willed her husband to live it must have been like a physical force holding him up through the depredations of hunger, tropic heat and disease and the torments of captivity—and with all that will, had failed.

"Clem, I had hoped that I might have something to give you as well. That I could function, with all that I have in me to give, through you."

"And I always fail you."

"You thwart me. But not nearly as much as you will be thwarted."

He bent awkwardly to kiss her cheek, but she turned away too soon. "Dear, I do wish you'd fix this faucet. It's so hard to turn. And it's forever dripping . . ."

He got out his wrench and a Prince Albert tobacco tin in which assorted washers, rubber bands, and paper clips had collected, and whistling repaired while he prepared in his head his sermon for tomorrow.

That Sunday at St. Paul's the congregation, except for the understandable absence of the Warrens, was all together again for the first time since Augusta Varney partook of the cup. Peace and harmony reigned supreme. With the news of Clem's visit to Augusta, the spirit of the more rational elements who had never participated in the hysteria over her now reasserted itself. As for the rest, along with their triumph a certain contriteness for the lengths to which they had been willing to go was now manifest. A chastened Judge Purcell, a subdued Ada, a Eustis at cross-purposes with himself were not only eager to forgive and forget the past but to dissociate themselves from it by praising to the skies whatever Clem chose to say or do. He was now once more the perfect pastor.

The news of his class had preceded him to church and opinion in support of it could not have been stronger. Eustis showed around the poll he had drawn up, exquisitely aligned in margin and indentation—it read more like a petition than a poll—with an American flag, sketched a-flutter, in each of the four corners. It was not to be signed now, it was carefully to be pondered over first. Nevertheless it created an effect, and very sincerely so, of piety united with patriotism.

His text for the day Clem took from Micah. Not of course that provocative prophecy which cries woe on the beds of those who covet the land of others. But that most familiar, and appropriate, passage: "And they shall beat their swords into plowshares, and their spears into pruning-hooks: nation shall not lift up a sword against nation, neither shall they learn war anymore."

Only he did not stop here. He read on, with a monitory stress, to the next verse. "But they shall sit every man under his vine and under his fig tree; and none shall make them afraid."

They flocked to him afterward. "I think it's wonderful, just wonderful, what you'll be doing for those boys. I think our country owes it to them, and so do we . . ."

"The sacred mushroom hasn't a patch," Benson Reece commented, "on the smell of money when it comes to producing mass intoxication."

Laura stood aside with Nancy at the foot of the church steps, watching Clem. If she had any further reservations, she could not voice them now. The sun touched to soft fawn his shorn head, and he was alive, alive again, with that scintillation which she so craved always to see in him and the source of which she always so mistrusted. He's running away, she thought. He's running away again.

BOOK FOUR

BOOK FOUR

I

THE CLASS

[June–July]

1

There never was such a summer for growth, never a summer for such a sense of expansion. The bottled-up needs of twelve years of depression, four years of war and another of material shortages burst out all at once in all directions, and were satisfied only sufficiently to whet the need for more.

Mid-May the two new high schools, Arcady Academy and Colfax-Scott, were officially opened and dedicated, though still incomplete, in time for commencement exercises. Early June the five-man Board of County Commissioners, operating on a cash basis for the first time in almost two decades and showing a cash balance of almost ten thousand dollars at the end of the past fiscal year, launched its long-planned road-improvement program with the delivery to the contractor of new heavy equipment, on order for months. The highway through Arcady, a pock-marked stretch soundly cussed out by every tourist, was to be resurfaced; and miles of country road, deserts of sand drift in dry weather and sloughs of muck in wet, obstacle courses rather than arteries for pupil-to-school, farm-to-market and inter-town travel, were to be cleared and grubbed, ditched and shouldered, back-filled and underdrained, compacted and test-rolled, graded and black-topped.

In addition, the county board projected an ambitious four-year schedule of proposals for further road construction and consolidation of schools; installation of drainage and sewerage systems; the assignment of property in the public domain for future use as an airport, to be furnished with sod landing strips; and, as a direct result of "Miss Bird's success in obtaining the cooperation of Dr. Willingham in administering D.P.T. shots," an allocation of budget toward the erection of a health center. At the same time Mayor Dakin of Arcady and his four-man council—the city also being solvent to the extent of a thousand dollar surplus —voted to replace the inadequate firehouse, expand recreation facilities, pave streets. To finance the estimated costs of these various items, a gradual increase in local tax revenue was anticipated; plus that sine qua non, that magic formula parenthesized after each entry, that possibility without which none of it would ever have been considered: 50% *Federal and State Aid.*

During May and June also, Benson Reece was stumping the state up- and downriver, addressing civic leaders and businessmen, organizing them into a pressure group called "The Ocachee Development Associ- ation." Its purpose: to get after Washington to send a team in forthwith from the U. S. Army Corps of Engineers for the preliminary survey of the river just approved by Congress; and once the survey had determined the feasibility of damming, dredging, and flood control, to get after Washington again for the "planning money" to be appropriated next year and the "starting money" year after that and the "doing money" from then on until the appointed task was accomplished. From Renalee, high in the hills, where a spring spurted over into a trickle that could hardly be called a jet of spit and thus became one of the many sources of the Ocachee, down the desiccated towns that crowned the eroded red banks of the river midstate, to Colfax County, deposit and outlet of the river's many mouths, Benson urged: "Look at TVA. Look what it's do- ing for those folks up there. Same thing can be done for us. We can be so transformed, ten years from now you won't recognize yourself."

That Benson, the eternal skeptic, should bestir himself so over a vista so far ahead in time and so remote of realization served to convince the dourest of his bank patrons, the most mundane of his political support- ers. To look to the future of their region with confidence seemed at this date as practical as it was visionary. For close by, this passing day and every day, transformations were taking place under their very eyes. In the Fallona and Willow Road sections, work gangs were drilling post holes for the Rural Electrification Administration under the supervision of one of the Bird brothers while the contractor, Marcus Hadley, at- tended to his booming building business around town. The new annex of Ozzie Higginson's Hardware & Feed held its grand opening with door prizes for the ladies, balloons for the kids and a display of plumbing fixtures that only a year ago would have been beyond the dreams as well as the means of nine out of ten of the county's inhabitants.

"Yessir," Ozzie greeted his customers, looker and buyer, colored and white alike, "things are on the upswing. We're going places. We're on the move."

Over at Sunset Hill the new freezer plant was formally initiated with ribbon-cutting ceremonies, speeches and news photos that made the feature section of Sunday papers all over the state and the trade press nationally. A cocktail party that followed in the Warren house, presided over by Annamary in the absence of Julie, went on and on into the small hours like the Ocachee tide which rose, memorably, ten feet that night under a gale-wind from offshore. Whatever problems may have confronted Henry consequent upon his failure to take possession of the Scott land the week before, they were apparently smoothed over in the hoopla, at least for the moment. For as soon as the district management and guests were at last off and gone, Henry had Marcus begin on the house.

While Julie stayed in Atlanta with Colfax for his pre-diagnostic tests, the sagging dining-room floor was jacked up, the rotting sills underneath were removed and creosoted timbers, mildew-and-termite proofed, were inserted, putting the foundation on solid footing. The black hip roof was overlaid with green asbestos tile shingles. Clapboard by clapboard the old paint was burned off in preparation for primer, and shutters of fresh-sawn wood were hung on the front bedroom window and the third-floor side dormer.

"My, it's good to see that place shaping up again," people told Henry. "Why I remember when that shutter was blown off in a northeaster, must be all of twenty years ago."

They wandered curiously in and out of the house throughout the month that Julie was gone, attracted to it as symbol and example. Every floor up and down was scraped and sanded. Ceilings were calcimined and walls stripped to the plaster. The pantry was converted to a laundry area, the back-bedroom el over the kitchen to a playroom. The odor of polite decay that always greeted the entrant, a whiff like that of moldering hay, disappeared under the piercing-clean onslaught of lime and turpentine. Hollowed out, inhabited only by the shrouded furniture, all the basic renovations completed, the house awaited Julie's return for the selection of color, wallpapers, tile, style of bathroom and light fixtures, the surface refurbishing. But on the outside at month's end the walls glistened with two coats of white as if permanently wet from the brush. Green-roofed, green-shuttered and green-doored.

Henry never stopped these days. Weekends he was driving the two hundred miles up to Atlanta to visit with Julie and the boy and to confer with Vail; dropping in en route, either going or coming, at Ol' Cal Hubbard's plantation where Judge Purcell, after a trip to Washington, was spending his vacation politicking. At Sunset, the freezer plant was operating beyond capacity, as he had predicted, and plans were being drawn up for additional installations. The Extension Service was locating an experimental substation on the grounds. And the runabout he had taken off Lars Finchley's hands after a vicious argument with him over the missing deed book was in drydock, being overhauled under his direction and reupholstered, a fine pleasure craft for family excursions when Julie would bring Coley home.

The *County Courier* of June 16 featured a studio portrait of Henry Warren, thick-browed, firm-mouthed, clean-cut and incisive, over the news that he was announcing his candidacy for County Commission in the September primary. When a man of his position chose to run for such an office he could virtually count on being elected; and when elected he could virtually count on being chosen by the board of commissioners as chairman.

It was not the lead story in the *Courier* that week however. A banner headline and double columns on the right hailed the formation of the GI farm-training course now beginning classes at the Arcady Academy under the instruction of Rev. Clement DeLavery. Its advisory board was composed of eminent citizens, representing a cross section of public opinion: Benson Reece, Ozzie Higginson, Marcus Hadley, Lloyd Bird, Horace Truelove, and the county agent, Earl Goodfellow. Under a subhead the progress of the colored class, whose existence had previously gone unnoted, was praised, its advisory board also listed and special tribute paid to its leader, "the widely recognized authority on coastal soils, Professor G. T. Thurlow."

The two classes together would bring sixty thousand dollars of income into the county this year and every year for the next four years, including teaching salaries and fees for use of the schools. The classes had the backing of the State Departments of Agriculture and Education, the Veterans Administration, and the United States Government. Whether individual members happened to be heroes or heels, serious students or spongers, as a body they enjoyed a prestige which few in Colfax County would have dared to slight.

In the office of the principal of the Colfax-Scott school, Carter Scott and John Lomax met to plan an intensive drive through the summer months for increased registration of colored voters. Last year the Supreme Court had outlawed the white primary. This year Ol' Cal Hubbard was running for the governorship on a platform of nullification of the court's decision by passage of state laws that would circumvent it. Meanwhile Ol' Cal's campaign "to keep the nigger out of our election" inspired hooded conclaves at Atlanta, Gainesville, Columbia. Crosses were burned, violence was called for, arms were distributed. In Colfax County where the colored vote was nothing new but had continued over the years despite the overwhelming futility of trying to change things from below on a minimal scale when the maximum conditions were imposed from above, Lomax the businessman and Scott the fisherman, Thurlow and Martin Walters of the school, Father Hall and other church leaders, a committee of the younger men from the Colonel Young Post, the NAACP and so forth, were out to give Ol' Cal Hubbard and his local lieutenant, Ol' Vern Purcell, neither of whom had ever yet won this county, the trouncing of their lives. Ol' Cal's incitements invited a supreme demonstration of their numerical strength.

Reeve's courtroom victory encouraged all of them on all fronts as a sign of the times. Things are moving. Say what you will, we're on the move. Many a person was moved to cast off timidities as cramping to the soul as those bindings which used to be worn on the feet of Chinese women. The porter in Ozzie Higginson's store asked for a dollar raise and got it. The family of a fisherman lost the night of the high wind on one of Hill Caslon's leaky tubs asked for compensation over and above the customary collection. They didn't get it. But they did seek it. One day the pickers at Sunset laid down their baskets in a dispute over a change in the size of their loads, and the change was rescinded. There were some who were more alarmed than emboldened by these manifestations, but the talk among the farmer veterans in front of the school building before and after class was said to be fly, man, fly.

There was even some expectation that the promises so long denied them, the equality of birth embodied in the Declaration of Independence, the equality before the law guaranteed by the Bill of Rights and the 13th, 14th, and 15th Amendments to the Constitution, those promises never delivered by the Revolution, canceled out after the War between the States, postponed after the War to Save Democracy, might now at last after this war, the War against Fascism, be on the way to fulfillment. This in the face of riots against colored soldiers, beatings and jailings of civilians, killings by gun, knife, and blowtorch of men, women, and children, in Georgia, the nation at large and overseas. The expectation was there, accentuated by every gain whether it was in the Supreme Court or the Colfax County courthouse, and enlarged by the magnitude of its every frustration.

"They're afraid of their own law," Professor Thurlow, the principal emeritus, commented to Martin Walters, the impatient new principal.

"We're going to have to stop waiting for the white man to give us anything," Martin passionately declared. "Even our just due. We're going to have to do for ourselves."

"Will it come to that?" Thurlow mused. "Will it come to that?"

But it was not only equality of rights they expected, it was opportunity. All the anticipation of prosperity in the air indicated to the white man that from the bounty of his table he would be able to throw to the colored who waited on it a few crumbs and a bone. To the colored it indicated the necessity of a place at that table.

Ever since anyone could remember, old Uncle Steven had been singing before the white folks a wordless little ditty for which they tossed him a dime. *Reedom, Reedom.* But now he could be heard mumbling aloud from his station on the courthouse steps, if not precisely with clarity, with a devilish twinkle of tongue and eye, *O Reedom O Reedom, Befo I'd be a slave I'd be buried in my grave, I'd go home to my Lord and be free.*

In the green before the courthouse, under the shadow of the Oglethorpe-Tomochichi monument, a century plant, rooted in the ground forty years ago, was blooming. It rose out of a fountain of broad-leafed foliage at its base and stark-spined of stalk climbed upward fourteen feet, bearing aloft like a lampstand at its crown huge globes of chartreuse blossoms. On market day people from miles around crossed the street to the green to look at it.

Sizzle of hot tar on a country road. Wires skeined from pole to pole across the deep-blue heart of a country sky. The sound of running water through inside pipes. A classroom. A path out of the self-perpetuating cycle of poverty, out of the sterile monotony of isolation. The gleam ahead of a power dam, a health clinic, a coat of white paint. The sensation of joining the mainstream, of becoming part of the age in which one lives. It stirred through them all with the intoxication of a flower opening to the bee's sip, to the dusting of pollen upon its petals. Progress is a shibboleth only to those who take it for granted. Not to those for whom it can make the difference between life and death of a human being, the fruition or withering of a human soul.

2

Although Arcady Academy was three times the size of Colfax-Scott and far more imposing, the one of brick and the other of cement block, both were designed in the new open style with interspaced window areas, asphalt tile flooring, pastel-tinted walls, pale-toned furnishings. Something of their clean crisp modernity was imparted to the young back-country men in jeans and ODs attending. The surroundings accorded the students a respect to which they responded with soaring self-respect. They belonged to the light, to the brightness of today's world, its ease and comfort were theirs and its illimitable perspectives.

Twice a week Rad and Reeve drove in to school together on which-

ever one of their old jalopy trucks was working, each of them going out
of the way to drop off and pick up at the other's school according to
whose truck it was. At first on their trips they couldn't stop talking
about the court hearing and how they'd won it and what might happen
next as a result of it.

"Henry's up to something, you can bet on that. He's got some move
up his sleeve. He'll never let this go by."

"And Purcell, he'll never get over that one. He'll be out to get
back . . ."

But one week passed by and a second and a third and nothing happened. The will of Rose Scott was processed by the Court of Ordinary
and admitted to record as prayed. No unaccountable creditors, no missing heirs, no contestants, none of the tricks and dodges that Reeve expected momentarily to drop down out of the heavens, or from much
closer quarters, occurred. During this period he never worked in the
fields beyond earshot or eyesight of Rad. He never went anywhere alone.
At night there was always someone with him in the house. His brother
Fred stayed on for a while, then Ben's boys one after another came
down to spend their usual farm vacation, and friends from nearby were
always stopping in. But he was visited neither by shotgun blast nor fire
of unknown origin nor any of the possible retaliations he was guarding
against.

Only one morning when Rad came up the track to drive to school with
him, he discovered Sport, one of the pack of dogs Reeve kept about
the house nights, stretched out stiff on her side, the flies on her lolling
tongue as dead as she was.

"My God," Rad said as they shoveled her into a shallow grave, "who'd
do a thing as mean as this? Bait a dog with poisoned meat. Who'd do
that?"

He couldn't look Reeve in the eye asking it, on the defensive as if it
were his dog that ought to have been killed instead and full of guilt as if
it were he who had done the killing. "If that was my dog, I'd . . ."

"What would you do, Rad?"

They walked off to Reeve's truck and climbed in. "I'd find out who
did it! I'd go after him!"

"And then?"

"They wouldn't get away with it!"

"No, I don't suppose they would. But then it wasn't your dog."

"Am I supposed to apologize for that?"

"I just said . . . Nobody would've done it to your dog."

"Will you quit needling me!"

They were quiet for a while, jouncing with the movement of the truck.

Then Rad burst out again. "How do you do it? How can you go on like this? I don't understand it. Building up your fields. Adding to your house—"

A few weeks earlier Reeve had started bringing home a load of lumber from the sawmill for every load of roasting ears he sold off to the market. Piling it up back of his house. Going to knock a door through from the alcove, he said, and put up a bedroom there. He had his posts down by now and was laying crossbeams for the floor.

Steering as always with a flick of his fingers on the wheel, Reeve mulled over Rad's question. "They can take my place away from me any day," he said. "And they can take my life any time. But for as long as I live and as long as I have it, I'm going to make that the best damn place I ever can."

His answer impressed Rad. It impressed him a lot. But he was troubled by it too. "A man has a right," he declared, "to be secure in his home and person. He has a right to expect that."

Reeve couldn't remain solemn for long however. For all his apprehensions he had never felt so free in his life before as he did these days and it was the hearing, facing it out, fighting it through, that had freed him. We have met the enemy and they are ours, now devil take the hindmost! He bowed his head to no man nowadays. And hope, he dared hope for all there was to be hoped for. Everything was possible to him. Without a single word to Vivian, he was building the room for her.

He smiled speculatively to himself, driving, the dog already forgotten. Vivian had gone straight home from the hearing and out of sheer contrariness, while her grandfather was suggesting that maybe she'd better take a little trip somewhere for a few weeks or better still take the whole summer off, she had taken her teaching contract out of the fruitbowl on the table where it had been resting so long and signed it. Mailed it at once to the school superintendent.

A few days later D. C. Lacey had stopped the Professor on the street and told him how hard he, Lacey, was working to advance the colored school system and how deeply he was interested in it and how proud he was of what had been accomplished so far. He talked around and around until eventually he made his point. "But whenever any one of you all steps out of line, that makes my task that much the harder. It jeopardizes everything I'm trying to do. It's a real setback. Now there have been some folks pestering me about the kind of American history and government class that girl of yours is teaching. They're after me to have the class dropped. Well, I been telling them she's been away from here so long, just give her a chance to get reaccustomed. Can you guarantee that from now on she'll watch her step?" And a few evenings later Chalmer Coombs had called the Professor into his office. He too talked around and around about how much he'd done for the colored people and how much he thought of them. "Only that girl of yours, have you any idea how near she come to being arrested on a perjury charge when that paper she claimed to have seen in the court library wasn't found? Fortunately for her I pointed out that she wasn't under oath at the time. But there are some folks around, not me, mind you, some folks, who aren't satisfied to let a thing like that go. They don't stand for that kind of thing. From now on you keep her under wraps, hear?"

So of all the potential aftereffects of the hearing, it was Vivian who had received them in the form of warnings and threats of reprisal. She had been planning to go up to Augusta after commencement to spend a week with a girl friend there, but she waited instead for the return of her contract. She just wanted to see if it would come through. It took an inordinately long time, until the end of June, but it did arrive. Then she had planned to join the principal and his wife for their annual jaunt up to Columbia University where, all expenses paid, they were taking credits toward a master's degree. But she didn't go. "I'll wait till next year," she said, "when the state has to foot the bill." She stayed on through the heat of the summer ostensibly to take charge of the clerical work attendant on her grandfather's farm-training course. She stayed and stayed.

Reeve passed his school to take Rad on to the academy. "What are you laughing at?" Rad asked him. "You been laughing ever since we left the dog back there."

"The dog? Oh the dog. She was a good old dog."

"Then what are you laughing at?"

"The high cost of Jim Crow."

He explained to Rad how the colored teachers being barred from the colleges of the state where they could pursue graduate study were furnished with public funds to go up East to much better colleges for their purpose. "And sometimes by staying with relatives or living cheaper than they should, they not only break even, they come out ahead. At the taxpayers' expense. Out of your pocket. You paying for it."

"Is that so?" Rad said, bridling. "Let me ask you this. How much you gettin' for your corn per bushel?"

"Let me see, one forty-five, fifty—"

"Not as much as I am," Rad said with satisfaction. "I'm gettin' one seventy."

"Not as much as you'd get," Reeve said, "if I wasn't gettin' less."

"Well . . ." They stared at each other, sharing a paradox that like the bit of a corkscrew twisted down deeper and deeper. They both began laughing. "That's a hot one."

As they neared the academy they were halted by a bar across the road, hung with lanterns on each end. Beyond the barrier a grader was leveling the sand surface, followed by trucks laying down a bed of gravel. Reeve backed away and took the detour down the next street, Rad watching him out of the tail of his eye. The road to Colfax-Scott wasn't being paved. Reeve didn't say anything. But as nettled as he was by Reeve's silences and as uncomfortable as his own enlarging consciousness sometimes made him, Rad would not have given up their rides together for anything. They were as important to him as the school. They opened up to him a world he had to know, had to explore, even had to identify himself with at no matter what the cost.

A few mornings later he picked up Reeve in his truck for the ride to school. "You know," he announced to Reeve without preliminary, "I'm a fair-minded man."

"Uh-huh."

"I wouldn't say I'm for mixing the races or anything like that. I wouldn't say my children ought to go to school with yours—"

"And I don't know," Reeve said, "if I'd want my children if I had any children to go to school with yours if they're that prejudiced."

"Prejudiced!" Rad said, stung. "Who's prejudiced?" He drove intently, his hands grasping the wheel spokes as if they were levers. "What I mean, now you take like my boy Charles. He's just crazy about anything mechanized. Asked me this morning how a diesel works. Well, I couldn't explain it to him, but supposing the county had just one school system, they could afford a film projector, films, visual aids, all like we used to have in the Army. Teach these younguns in a week what takes six weeks now, whether it's geography or engines or how to store a crop."

"Are you saying," Reeve demanded, "what I think you're saying, or are you saying something else?"

"What I mean," Rad said, "here's you and me paying taxes and here's both these schools unfinished for lack of funds, ours without a gymnasium and yours without gym or a lunchroom for the kids to eat in and the little ones still going to the privies. If it was all combined, we'd have something. But that don't mean," he added sharply, "that I'd want to have a colored man governing over me."

They said nothing more for a while, jouncing along in the truck. "It's losing power," Reeve observed, listening to the motor. "You need a new clutch."

"What I need!"

"We have two senators," Reeve observed in the same tone. "How would it be if one of them was colored?"

"That," Rad considered, "would be fair enough."

"And if we had two governors?"

"Nothing wrong with that."

"And if the General Assembly was equally divided?"

"OK. So long as one race don't run the other, that's what everybody's so afraid of. That's the heart of the matter."

"Now we got that settled, how many of your friends you think would go along with it?"

"That all depends," Rad said judiciously. "All depends on how it's put to them."

Not that he intended to put it to them. Not in just that way. There had to be a time and a place.

Rad knew that Reeve must wonder what he said when he left him, after he hopped off the truck and joined with the boys waiting on the concrete steps of the academy. Whether he said one thing to him in the intimacy of the truck cab and another to them out there. Whether he was what the colored called with their own peculiar intimation "two-faced." Did he use the word "nigger" for instance and "pickaninny" and fall in with the others when they boasted about all the poontang they'd had. Sometimes, indeed, he felt it was a whole new vocabulary he was learning in Reeve's company, a foreign tongue, a code of etiquette, a lore to which everyone else he knew was deaf and blind. They had had a ferocious argument once at the beginning of their rides over language. "What difference does it make?" he'd flamed up over a sudden coldness on the part of Reeve. "A man can say nigger with a lot more of warmth and affection in it than Nigra or Nee-gro. We don't mean no harm by it." "That kind of affection," Reeve had replied, "we can do without." "And pickaninny—all I meant was, them kids are cute—" "It goes back to slavery," Reeve had stubbornly objected, "and we want to forget all that, put it behind us. And Negress—" he said wrathfully. "Once I heard this Yankee refer to my mother as a Negress." "What's so bad about that? He was probably trying to be polite." "Made her sound like some kind of animal."

He had to take care with Reeve not to give offense and he didn't like being careful. At the same time he wanted nothing less than perfect candor in their relationship; he couldn't stand to feel that anything was being withheld from him. And it was he who most often sought Reeve out, resenting the urge that prompted him. Even after supper sometimes he'd find an excuse to run over to Reeve's. To talk over a plague of red mites, a bandsaw they were thinking of buying, what DeLavery had said in class that day about growing pecan trees. And to see what was going on in Reeve's house, who was there, as if it were a secret order to which he wished to be admitted and among whom he asked to be accepted without reserve. They welcomed him. They were pleasant enough to him. "He's all right," Reeve never failed to interject when he introduced him around to strangers, "he's regular." But the stiff manner, the veiled glance, the covert smile, the elusive allusion, that wasn't so easy to penetrate. They must have wondered too whether he, like those white men who frequent Negro taverns and resorts, didn't act one way with them and another with his own. "Whooh," they said when he delivered himself of an opinion that coincided with theirs, "if some folks could hear you now!" "They can kiss my ass," he said, "in downtown Arcady. I say what I want to who I mind to."

He did continue to use the word "nigger" in the presence of the boys at the academy. But it didn't slip out without a thought the way it used to. It filled up his mouth like a rock. It bothered him. After a while without his even noticing when it first happened he began substituting "those folks" and "that fella" every time it popped up in a discussion, and it popped up pretty often whether the subject was crops, baseball, or Ol' Cal Hubbard's campaign for the governorship. The substitution wasn't noticed, or at least it wasn't remarked upon.

"Why if it wasn't for that fella puttin' up the fight he did and if it wasn't for those folks showing up in court the way they did, I'd have lost my place and that's a fact. Inside of a week I'd have been forced off it."

Everybody understood that. His own action in Judge Purcell's court that day had gained him a certain distinction among the whites. By foiling an obvious injustice he had saved the community sense of morality; and that made him stand out. On the other hand he had gone against the community mores; and that set him apart. His conduct was neither approved nor disapproved by his classmates. But it did inaugurate their habit of turning to him for his views. "Here's Rad. Let's see what does he think about this."

As the weeks passed by however and he kept arriving and departing with Reeve, inevitably one day Richard-Gene Jeems started twitting him about it. "You thick as field peas with that nigger. Howcome you always with him?"

"Why ride two tanks of gas," Rad said, "when one'll do?"

Everybody understood that too.

The class that morning concerned "Management and Budgeting of the Family-Size Farm." Or, as Carl Maynard described it in his oral report, "How to Get More Output with Less Outlay." At the end of the first hour the discussion bogged down completely in the one question that haunted them all like a bad conscience. "Is it really possible for a farmer today to make a living hereabouts out of his fifty to hundred fifty acres of land?"

"That's what we're here for, isn't it?" DeLavery said to them. He hitched himself up on the corner of his desk, reached over for one of the glass jars of soil that had been brought in for analysis. "For each one of you to learn all you can about what you have to work with and to figure out how you can get the most out of it. When I see this—" He poured the soil, velvety brown, through his fingers. "With a cash crop, whether it's corn, sweet potatoes or peanuts, truck or fruit or flower bulbs—and some diversification—land like this, even with limited acreage, should yield sufficient income . . ."

"The truth is," Carl Maynard said from his lecture chair, "you can't compete against machines with mules."

"The trouble is," Lonnie Truelove said, "the farmer don't get the price for his product."

"Especially not," Richard-Gene said slyly, nudging Rad next to him, "with these niggers—that is, colored folks—underselling us."

"What we need," Rad said, "is a marketing shed where we all could ship our produce to once at the one price. Corn don't tell who plants or picks it."

They all understood that too.

Deserved or undeserved, Rad was acquiring a reputation as a man who thinks what he says and says what he thinks. If there was any antagonism toward the attitude he expressed, it was not evident at this time.

A few days later, not with antagonism but quite another sentiment, Richard-Gene sidled up to Rad as they were waiting on the steps for class to open and cosily asked to be fixed up with a date.

"A date?" Rad said blankly. "What kinda date?"

"Aw, you know, come on, Rad, you can tell me. She's slippin' you some."

"Who for cryin' out loud? What are you talkin' about?"

"You know. If you can't have chicken, you'll take steak? Dark meat, mister. That little old schoolteacher one?"

Rad was flabbergasted. The few times he had met the schoolteacher he had been so much in awe of her superior education and so confused by the teasing curiosity with which she regarded him he didn't quite know how to speak to her. Miss Thurlow, too formal. Vivian, too presumptuous. He had settled on "ma'am" as a mode of address.

"Now look, Richard-Gene," he said mildly, "I'm a family man. And so are you."

"So?" Richard-Gene heaved himself about with a movement that drew the gathering crowd in around him closer. "Now come on, Rad, spill it. That's why you onto this boy, she's slippin' you some."

"She's his friend."

"So?" Richard-Gene had the kind of face over which the flesh fits like a layer of thick rubber. His florid skin drew together now about his puckered mouth as if pulled on a drawstring, his tongue sticking out mischievously from between his lips. His small lively eyes, shiny as water beetles, danced about from side to side, inviting participation. "A slice off another man's loaf taste better. Don't it, fellas? A slice off another man's loaf—"

Rad turned on his heel and headed for the school door.

Richard-Gene followed him across the terrace with the pack at his heels. "I killed a nigger once," he said roughly and spun Rad about. "You hear that? I killed a nigger once."

"Why?"

"Why?" Richard-Gene, his powerful shoulders braced and his arms raised, poised for attack, sank back. "Why?"

"Why? You must have had a reason."

"Sure I had a reason. A good reason. I was with a bunch of fellas—oh I was no more'n fifteen–sixteen at the time—you know Talbot's store on the crossroads before you get to my place? Well, we were all hanging out there one Saturday night and this little old jig goes in to buy him some meal. 'Jig,' we says to him when he falls outside again, 'dance us a jig. We'll give you a dollar for it.' And we started in shooting dimes at his feet."

Rad looked at Richard-Gene's face, amiable now, the fair beard prickling from his florid cheeks—funny how he had that light beard with his dark hair—and a sheen of sweat over the stubble and his eyes—likable eyes—leering with the humor of his story.

"But he wouldn't dance. So we cocked our guns and moved in on him, just to scare him a little? And he starts to walk off. We give him two minutes, we even extended it fifty seconds—and still he wouldn't. We had to," he said suddenly, loud with helplessness, turning from Rad to the fringe of faces about his shoulders. "Wasn't anything else we could do. He just wouldn't dance."

Rad opened the door into the long light-green corridor gleaming with lockers. The others melting away from Richard-Gene crowded ahead of him into the classroom. All morning long Richard-Gene squirmed about in the lecture chair next to him, shifting as if there were something incongruously alien between the polished blond wood and his thick haunches, the course of his life and the dead-level voice of the lecture, the vision of his eyes and the notations on the green chalkboard.

"What else could I do?" he finally whispered over at Rad belligerently. "We couldn't back down."

He followed Rad out of school that noon plucking at his sleeve, pleading, "We couldn't back down."

It never once crossed Rad's mind that Reeve was undergoing a similar experience at the hands of his classmates. At first the badgering was slight. "What's that cracker always hanging around you for?" they wanted to know. "He sticks to you like white on rice."

"Now you know and I know," Reeve said, "if it wasn't for him standing up in court for me the way he did, I'd have lost my place for a fact."

Everybody understood that. But as his rides with Rad continued and Rad's night visits to his house, suspicions were aroused. "What's he want? What's he after? He must be getting something."

"Getting educated," Reeve said.

They understood that too. For a while. But they couldn't leave it alone. Rad had to have a racket. He had to have an angle. When Reeve bought the bandsaw with him at Ozzie Higginson's, was he sure that Rad hadn't collected a rakeoff afterward from Ozzie?

On the same morning when Richard-Gene laid his line down on Rad —it was a boiling-hot morning in late July—Reeve also suffered something of a crisis under the goading not of any one man but of all his friends.

"Either he's hustling on you or you hustling him. Come on, Reeve, you can tell us. He's giving some little banter the double-eye." The intimation was that Reeve must be providing house-room for the assignations. "Come on, Reeve, who is it? Give us the lowdown."

"He's a nice guy," Reeve insisted, "that's all. Nothing else to it."

"Now you know damn well," Harold Sanderlee said out of his years of part-time work in Mayor Dakin's gas station, "that when a white man shakes a black man's hand, ain't nothing go'n be left in that black hand."

"Not if it's my hand," the Baron said out of his years of part-time butlering in Benson Reece's house. "I always take the best lamb chop. When you cotton up to an ofay at least let it be someone can do something for you. Not some square who's just as beat as you are."

"If he's not chasing pussy," High Power said decisively out of his years of gambling joints and hunting jaunts, "then he must be fagging. If it ain't one end, it's the other. They all diggin' their graves with their pricks."

"Great God!" Reeve almost came to blows with them. "What's the matter with you guys? Are things so far-gone between one race and the other there can't be a simple man-to-man relationship without sex has to enter into it? Either he's a fag or I'm pimping! All right, am I a pimp?"

"OK, OK, you straight with me, see. Now don't jump salty . . ."

Nobody wanted to fight him over it. They all went in to school to-

gether to engage in the problem of the day. A man and a mule can produce only a third as much per acre as a man and a machine at half the
expenditure of time and labor.

All that morning the razzing with all its connotations rankled in both
men, the need imperative in each of them to rush to the other with a
revelation of what had passed and the conviction as imperative in each
of them that such a revelation could not be made without irreparable
injury to the frail and tender thing, whatever it was, like the union of a
marriage, the mutuality which they had so far achieved. When Rad
drove up to Colfax-Scott that noon and Reeve climbed into the truck
they were so constrained and awkward they could scarcely look at each
other.

Rad leaned across Reeve's lap to give the truck door an extra bang.
Reeve jerked back, furious with himself for the instantaneous reflex.

The truck cab was like a blast furnace inside, having heated up even
under the shade of a tree until its dull black metal burned to the touch.
Even in movement with the windows down, the heat consumed them,
beating through their blood, blazing in their cheeks, exacerbating rather
than ennervating their sensitivities.

3

For the first few miles they maintained silence, their experience of
the morning drubbing at their lips and burrowing in their bellies. Heat
shimmered whitely on the dulled black hood of the radiator and struck
with blinding white force through the dust-splotched windshield. A
bluebottle fly hit the outer glass and too stunned or too languid to detach itself stuck there, simmering in its own juices. In surprisingly short
order it shriveled, atrophied, and slid downward, leaving a smear in its
train.

Under the thin clinging stuff of their faded tans their flesh sweltered
with self-consciousness, their nerve ends tingled with irritability, their
hearts pounded with a stifling urgency like that of stage fright. Apprehension swelled through their blood, a fever of apprehension such as
that which precedes some chaotic upheaval that precipitated by no apparent cause has been in the making for a long time. The excitement
that gripped them exceeded by far the import of the incidents that had
aroused it, and being unable to grasp its proportions, sensing peril in it,
they could only husband their self-knowledge, half-formulated, groping,
evanescent, in the safety of non-communication.

Rad had acquired enough of an instinct by now to realize that he could not burst out: Richard-Gene, my friend, my blood-brother, skin of my skin, killed a Negro once in front of Talbot's store. He thinks I'm running with your girl, your love, the one you hold the highest. It's the only way he can understand you and me, the only thing that enables him to accept . . . Too often in the recent past, in Reeve's house, before Reeve's company he had sympathetically cited all the humiliations and degradations practiced against colored, how terrible it was, how sorry he felt. And during his recital of some abuse, even while they nodded agreement, he could feel them shrinking away from him, their spreading coldness, their glances over and around him. Until one night Reeve interrupted him. "We don't need anyone to come telling us how low-down bad off we are. Anybody says to me I live in a shack I'd throw him out the door. I got too much pride for that. We may be stomped upon, but we're not stomped."

Once he had brought in to them a handbill he had found in his mailbox, flame-yellow, imprinted in maroon: CRACKERS OF COLFAX COUNTY, AWAKE! It reprinted excerpts from an address made on the floor of the U. S. Senate by the honorable senator from Mississippi, charging that five thousand German women had been raped by French Senegalese soldiers in the Stuttgart subway station. "Nobody falls for this kind of stuff anymore," he had said as he showed it around. "It's all politics. Everybody knows that." But they'd all looked at him as if to ask: Whatfor you shoving this shit in our face? And Reeve had said, "Every time I hear about one of these senators or congressmen ranting against all the niggers in Dixie, I just know that back home he's basking in the sunshine of some black woman's arms."

Only five days ago up in Taylor County one of the few Negroes on the voter registration list had been dragged out of his house by four white men, pistol-whipped and shot to death. He had gone to Reeve's house that night in great personal embarrassment, and had added his voice to the denunciations. But he couldn't help feeling that they were all looking at him as if they expected something more of him, bright-eyed and gleeful, he thought, with malice: What are *you* going to *do* about it? He couldn't do anything. It was too remote. "Everybody recognizes," he had appealed to them, rationalizing it, "that it's because Ol' Cal's out to keep the colored away from the polls this election. It's because someone has something to gain of it. No other reason." And Reeve had reassured him with a reassurance that yielded him less than a full measure of comfort, "It's nothing to do with you and us. We all individuals here."

They didn't want his pity. He was learning when to keep his mouth shut. To listen. That there was a skill at which he had to earn his stripes:

how to be around colored people. A sensory tact, keen as a safecracker's fingertips, which came only with repeated familiarity, which they sensed in you, which opened the door. And sometimes now he believed he almost had it. Before him as if he weren't there, as if he were one of them or as if their color having become invisible to him his at last was becoming invisible to them, they opened up, the floodgates loosed. And rather than pity what he felt was admiration. They're bigger than we are. Live two lives for our every one. They have to comprehend two worlds. With what wit and charm, wisdom and tolerance.

He no longer mentioned race. Yet no matter what they talked about, weather or crops, religion or politics, baseball or Hill Caslon's boats, strangely enough as with his classmates it always came back to that. They robbin' us blind! How the man put one over on me and how I paid him out for it. Blaming themselves sometimes too much, he thought, for abstract conditions that shaped their personal existence. "I get so tired, I get so fed up with all this talk about the poo-ah Nee-gro. It's up to us . . ." They were all individuals, but sooner or later race crept into the picture, tinged its hues, multiplied its facets, changed its aspect.

Now in the truck with Reeve, Rad slipped dark glasses over his eyes against the relentless glare of the July sun. The glasses cloaking him in invisibility as if he could watch without being seen, he glanced about at Reeve only to catch Reeve swerving toward him. The strongly marked brows were creased, the cleavage between them repeated in the barest touch of an indentation in the broad tip of his nose, in the ripeness of his underlip, in the jut of his chin. Reeve glanced quickly away, and so did he. *She's slippin' you some . . . Jig, dance us a jig. . . .* Difficult as it was for one of his hasty impulsive nature, with his compulsive demand for absolute honesty between people, disturbed though he was, he could feel with all the relentless pressure of the heat that smote him how it would be for Reeve to hear a thing like that from him. Yet he couldn't live with it by himself. He had to say something.

Being unable to tell Reeve this much about Richard-Gene he couldn't soften it by telling him how Carl Maynard had caught up with him at the truck later and drawing him aside had informed him: "This thing has got to change. It can't go on like this. Some of these days they going to change all this." But how it would change, when—Carl wanted no part of that. And after Carl, Lonnie Truelove had traipsed up into the truck with him and conspiratorially confided: "These folks are going to get their rights. Of course I wouldn't say this to anyone else but you and I wouldn't want anyone to know I said it but . . . These folks are going to get their rights. Why there was a boy I met in the Navy I'd rather bunk with than a lot of whites I know . . ." If he could have

counted the people, Rad thought, who in the past several weeks had
made such statements to him, making sure that no one else overheard
and being sure that they were alone in making them, it would have
added up to quite a number.

But he hesitated to tell Reeve even that.

As unaccustomed as Rad was to curbing his tongue, especially under
the uneasiness of a mood fraught with the unsayable, Reeve was habituated to controlling his in the same circumstance. He was swirling now
in a whirlpool of contradictory emotions. *Zekiel saw the wheel of time.
Wheel in the middle of a wheel . . .*

The insinuations of his classmates this morning, the public impression of himself and Rad, the public image, could not forever be concealed from Rad. But the mere verbalization of it could inject an
element in their consciousness of one another—as it already had in his,
when he jerked back from the graze of Rad's arm across his chest—an
element that didn't belong there, that might nevertheless spread like
slow poison, infecting root and branch the bond that had developed
between them. And this bond that was so solidly founded, that had
been sown out of their necessity and had grown with such hardship step
by step, that had withstood stress after stress up to now—what was it?
What was it, of such delicacy that a shadow of doubt, a misplaced word,
a slip of the tongue could like the indiscernible egg of a moth destroy
it? What was it?

He was perplexed by it himself. He had not wanted anything from
Rad from the beginning but a working accord, a recognition of their
interdependence and a willingness to cooperate in solving the problems
that plagued them both. But in addition to that, they were neighbors,
a source to each other of help and advice. And beyond that they were
two persons of like mind and background, sharing a common soil and
common memory, with so much to say to each other. It was here within
the realm of the intimate and the internal that the whole thing got
away from him. While Rad's feelings toward him were simple and direct
insofar as he could interpret them, his own feeling toward Rad contained contradictions, involutions of contradiction that spun like whirli-
gigs in crisscrossing orbits. Contradiction upon contradiction. Wheels
within wheels.

It was Rad who assiduously sought him out; not he Rad. It was Rad
who with a drive and a need that would not be denied attached himself to him, entered his sphere; while his own needs, drives and attachments remained essentially with his own. His people. His kin. The girl he
was building a marriage chamber for on a basis no more substantial than
a glimmer of hope. That Rad must be aware of how often he was the

one to do the pursuing and must therefore resent it, Reeve knew and sometimes felt a twinge of guilt because of it. A guilt that he at once brusquely shrugged off. After all he's knocking on my door, not me on his! At the same time he was inordinately gratified by Rad's knock; it contributed to the sensation of freedom and facility that was his these days. So that when he introduced Rad around it was always with a peculiarly meaningful intonation, intimating by its rhythm a chiaroscuro of depths, mellow as a cello: "This is a friend of mine that I want for you to meet."

Perhaps he was showing him off a little. Perhaps he was exulting in his own position. Exhibiting him as a trophy. And every colored man who saw him with Rad scented it out: those subsurface feelings and motivations. Easier to do without such a friendship, to eschew it altogether, than to subject oneself to an invasion of petty spites and pleasures, too deviously shameful to be acknowledged; than to expose oneself to the scrutiny of those only too swift to perceive the slightest sign of human weakness, themselves motivated by Lord alone knows what.

And there were also other contradictions. Wheels on wheels. *Wheel in the middle of the air. . . .*

Was Rad more willing to extend himself beyond the boundary of his people than he from his? Was he more willing to risk their criticism? And if it should come to more than criticism, how far would Rad be willing to go? Far enough to become estranged from the other whites? And if Rad were to become so estranged from his own people, Reeve asked himself, how much would we think of him for it? More? Or less? Both?

And if Rad should turn out to be one of those characters who, being rejects of their own race, seek a place for themselves among the other, what then? If that turned out to be the motivating force in Rad, unconscious though it might be, would he hold Rad in the same respect as he did now? Or in contempt? The same man.

Wheels within wheels. *Zekiel saw the wheel of time. Wheel in the middle of a wheel. And every spoke was humankind . . .*

There was also the other side of it.

Last Sunday Lulabelle had had a big spread at her house for her family who drove down from Bay City with aunts, cousins, and kids to pay her a visit. Reeve had had no desire to go over there. He didn't care about it. If he were invited, he probably wouldn't have gone. That is, depending on the degree of hospitality he gauged in Rad's voice— whether Rad meant it or was only going through the motions because he thought he ought to—and depending on whether something more interesting didn't chance to come along. If he were invited, it might have posed a dilemma for him, thrown him into the throes of indecision over something he didn't consider it especially appropriate for him to be at. But he hadn't been invited. And the omission stayed with him, and with Rad too. The apologies came later. "I was afraid they'd do something or say something, you wouldn't be comfortable." "You don't owe me no explanation, just because you have your folks down don't mean—" "They're good people, they just don't know any better." "No matter to me, don't make no difference." "If I'd thought for a minute—" "Skip it, will you please!" Still it stayed with him, resting on his stomach like a lump of undigested food.

Wheel O wheel . . . Big wheel run by faith, little wheel run by the grace of God . . .

Would they have made him uncomfortable—he being the best judge of his own comfort—at their feast board? Or would he have made *them* uncomfortable? Or—?

Wheel in the middle of the air . . .

His cousin Carter Scott and Johnny Herrera had buddied up over the years and no one took exception to it. Not now anyhow if they ever had. But Carter and Johnny were by parentage special cases. While he and Rad—they could be anybody.

O wheel . . .

In the blistering heat of the truck cab Reeve glanced from time to time at Rad, at the profile tautly lifted under the jaunty angle of the jean cap, the sunglasses casting a greenish-brown luminosity over the eye-sockets. When Rad caught him watching, the glasses which only a moment before had given Reeve a sense of being protected from view piqued him. He hated to have anyone looking at him whose eyes he couldn't see. Behind his glasses, with a clear view of his surroundings, it was Rad who was shielded from sight, impenetrable and unfathomable. Reeve pulled his fatigue cap down low over his brow, slouched down on his spine and crossed his legs, thigh over thigh.

"Jesus, this a scorcher," Rad said at last.

"Yeah."

Rad chewed over his mouth. Dissatisfied with the inadequacy of his comment, floating so frivolously on the surface of his disquiet as to be a mockery and profanation of it, he blurted out now, to his own astonishment, not with the events of the morning but of another time altogether.

"It's all a matter of the prevailing condition. Now you take like when I was in Europe, in the Bavarian mountains near Munich toward the end of the war. We hit this concentration camp one night—I'll never forget that, never! How could a nation of people allow a thing like that? What got into 'em?

"Now I always thought that folks were more or less alike, none of us perfect, neither good nor evil. And what's good, what's evil? No one when he looks into it can say for sure. But I think different now. There is good. And there is evil. You believe that?"

"Well yes," Reeve said, straightening up. "Your radiator's blowing up a storm."

Rad stopped the truck at the bend in the river and reached back for the bucket. Steam was hissing up from under the radiator cap. The water tank not filled when it should have been? Or the water jacket a-leak again? Or evaporation? He swung open the door and without getting out, too intent in his pursuit of the queries that haunted him, turned back toward Reeve.

"And afterward, after that place—Dachau, that was it—we were quartered in this castle, not far from the city. The war was already over or just about. And the things that went on there . . . Our CO was so busy feathering his own nest he didn't care and our officers were so busy dating up fräuleins and buying up cameras—most the rest of us were drinking pretty heavy . . .

"Well, there was a lot of china in this castle and all these little figures out of porcelain. The men were all having a ball with it, throwing it at each other, using it for target practice, smashing everything up. And there was this tapestry, before anybody could steal it it was tore up for bootrags. And this furniture, nobody thought twice of putting out their cigarettes on it. Most beautiful carved chests you'd ever hope to see and they—they were crapping in the drawers.

"Now I don't think I could ever do like that, but I was there, I saw it, I never even thought to try to stop it. It was all going that way. What were they trying to prove? What iron men they were? What big dicks they had? Or was it purely disgust? With the Germans? With ourselves? With the way it was winding up after all we'd been through? What caused it? What was it?"

They clambered out of the truck into the dusty heat of the roadside. Rad loosened the sizzling radiator cap and stepped hastily back from the steam that geysered whoosh up into his face. Wiping the back of his arm over his glasses he started mistily after Reeve, who had taken the bucket, through the thicket of wateroak and willow. It never occurred to either of them anymore to think which of them was toting and which of them was tarrying. At the riverside he took the bucket from Reeve and dipped it through the surface of the water as if skimming gravy, separating insofar as possible what was clean and clear from the silty suspension.

"Howcome a thing like that, Reeve? Why did I look the other way? Was it something in us? Or was it, was it something in the air? Something that permitted and encouraged, that once it got started—? What I mean, the prevailing condition?"

Reeve filtered leaves and insects out of the bucket with his fingers, too full of his own self-queries and misgivings to reply. The river was wide here, smooth as glass, returning to them their faces, the overhanging boughs, gold-green spray of willow and darker plumes of cypress, the burning-blue sky overhead. With such fidelity that what belonged up and what down became interchangeable. They were not alone. Farther down the bend, in the middle of the river, a dredge-rigged boat somnolently rested at anchor like a hippopotamus becalmed. From beyond the bend of the riverbank voices sounded, a couple of men in conversation, an intermittent murmur not quite identifiable, too curt-edged for fishermen but not disputatious.

"Now you take like Richard-Gene," Rad persisted after a pause in which he received no answer. "Richard-Gene don't care which way the wind blows, from the north or from the south. I could go down there and tell him I was Jesus Christ and he would follow me. And somebody else could go down there and tell him something else again and that would be it. So much, so much depends on what the leadership is."

"Well, what kind of leadership you giving him?"

"Me?" Rad said. "It's not up to me."

"The other day," Reeve said, not looking at him, scooping the water up in his hand and slapping it down over the back of his neck, letting it trickle down his collar, "when I come by the school to pick you up, he wanted you to stay and have a beer with him, he'd ride you back later. But you came with me."

"Well, sure—"

"Why?"

"Because I prefer your company to his! OK?" Rad was suddenly angry. "I thought you'd take it amiss if I didn't come. What makes you so high and mighty? What gives you the right, why am I always the one on the spot?"

"You come to me," Reeve said, wrathful himself, slapping water over each shoulder, letting it soak down his shirt, "asking me all these questions. What's good? What's bad? What's right and wrong? Why me? Am I any different from anybody else? Any wiser or nobler? Well, let me tell you this. I don't want to be raised to the skies! And I don't want to be throwed to the ground! I don't want to be taken for anything but what I am. Me. Myself. I."

"Are we talking," Rad asked, bewildered, "about the same thing?"

"My strength may be as the strength of ten because my cause is just. But injustice don't necessarily make angels out of people. More like the other thing. We got all the same weakness everybody else has, and with the same right to have it. We have our villains and vandals, our profiteers and parasites, our leeches and larcenists, boasters and beggars, seducers and sodomists, all kinds of phonies and nuts by the dozen. Take off your glasses."

"What for? I can see just as good."

"But I can't see you!"

Rad's eyes when he removed his glasses looked so like innocence betrayed that Reeve couldn't help but feel sorry for him and not only sorry but enjoyably so. He had enjoyed belaboring him, and relishing his enjoyment he was ashamed of it, and being pierced with shame was borne on the wings of an exhilarating satisfaction.

"Here we are two men, friends, huh? That should be the beginning and the end of it. But it's not. There are people, Rad, and some of them my people too"—he felt it out carefully, was this the truth of it or was there more and more?—"that would tear apart and undermine anything they can't have and don't believe possible."

"All right. What happened?"

Reeve told him, watching and waiting for him to blow up. Not all of it. But enough. " 'It ain't natural. It ain't normal.' There has to be some kind of underhand motive—"

Rad stared incredulously. "They think that *I* must be looking for some kind of—*advantage?*"

"Or me from you. That would be the more honorable course. Better I should play you for a sucker than you me because it's the sucker that's always the fool in the case."

"Of all the—why that's the damnedest, screwiest . . ."

"Is it? You mustn't forget that to most of us there's nothing lower than a colored man who runs to the first white he can attach himself to and runs his mouth off against his own, making an exception of himself. And if that"—Reeve lifted his two hands full of water out of the river in an abrupt agony and clapped it over his head, "is what I'm doing now! You see how screwed-up it gets?"

Rad was hurt and horrified. Humiliated. Affronted as if he were under attack. In the quiet water as through a glass darkly giant waterbugs, hairy-pincered, threatened his dabbling fingers. Those things can bite and when they bite it swells. At the snap of his fingers whirligig bugs, black as watermelon seeds, dived into their own ripples, carrying a bubble of air on their undersides. Downriver two men waded around the bend, sun-helmeted, hip-booted, their light tans dappled with leaf shadow. In muted voices they communicated with the boat in the channel through walkie-talkies hung around their necks. They were also equipped with camera, binoculars, the folded tripod of a surveyor's level.

"And not only your people," Rad said at length to his own image and Reeve's wavering on the surface of the water. He had a need almost vengeful to set the record straight, turn reality rightside up. It's not me, it's you at the bottom of the barrel. It's my goodwill, my sacrifice, I'm the one . . .

"OK," Reeve said. "Spill it."

Rad told him, sparing him only the names and details. "Well, one of the fellas thinks I been shackin' up—"

"Natch."

"And he wanted for me to fix him up, I won't say with who. And then when I ignored it, he started in bragging up how he—"

He glanced sidewise at Reeve, moved by a desire almost vindictive to give it to him, drive it home. *Jig, dance me a jig.* And closed his eyes. *He knows. He knows I'm going to hit back. And with what.*

"Go ahead," Reeve said harshly, braced for it. "He killed a nigger once."

Rad took the bucket and they tramped back from the cool of the river to the broiling truck. The disgruntlement hung between them of having fished in troubled waters and come up with no answers, of having delved in subtleties that touched too close on the delicate and dangerous springs of the inner man. Was Rad deriving the pleasure of a secret martyrdom from their association? A self-heroism that set him apart from his fellows and distinguished him from them in his own eyes? But as a sojourner among the outcast, a dweller in their wilderness, always reserving at last resort, under pressure, the privilege of pulling rank on them? Pulling his white skin . . . And did Reeve seize upon Rad's white-guilt, now that he obviously felt such guilt, and exploit it for his own secret delight, giving it every now and then a fiendish twist . . . ?

The water gurgled into the rusty radiator of the truck.

"Maybe," Rad ruminated, "the fellas I know would take it easier if there *was* nooky in it. That'd make it all right. They don't have to think about it then."

"And maybe if you did have a motive, my folks would understand it more. Though they'd never forgive you for it."

Ruefully facing each other over the radiator cap, they rubbed their caps back down over their heads. That's a hot one . . .

They had hardly remounted the truck and started down the road again when Rad abruptly braked up and backed swiftly in reverse gear to the spot they'd just left. "Just a sec." He hopped off and disappeared through the thicket of willows on the riverside and was gone several minutes. When he came back he was sparkling with elation.

"You know who that is down there?" he settled himself back down behind the wheel. "You know what's goin' on down there?"

They'd come! They were here! The U. S. Army Corps of Engineers had sent a team down for preliminary survey of the river basin.

From the river bend past the upper section of Sunset and all the way home Rad was full of it. Only a few weeks ago Benson Reece had delivered a lecture on the proposed project to his class. Reece had mounted maps on which he tapped out with a pointer the possible sites upriver for a series of multiple-purpose dams, reservoirs, artificial lakes, and reforestation preserves. He had shown slides of monumental concrete emplacements bestriding the water channels, serrated with flanges like flying buttresses through which the spillways flowed. On the green chalkboard he drew a rough table representing the shifting course of the Ocachee in the Arcady region for the past quarter century. From fifty miles inland through Arcady and down to the sound the river would be dredged. Deep enough to bring navigation back to the somnolent waterfront, reactivate the foundering warehouses, the shipping of naval stores, timber, deer-tongue. And deep enough to contain the flooding that periodically poured down from midstate over the level plains of the delta.

"You know how the Ocachee spreads when she floods," Rad said to Reeve. He had been reluctant to mention Benson Reece's lecture to Reeve before, as he always was to mention any event that took place in his classroom and not in the other. But now in his enthusiasm he couldn't hold back. "Why I remember one time—you remember?—the river here spread out all of seven miles wide. And the water was red as rouge. Bet I could still if I looked for it find the high-water marks in your house and mine. We lost our chicks, and my daddy had got him some gilts, fattening up right smart too. Put money in 'em he didn't put in our mouths. And it all went. And our fields, that was a dead loss . . . Oh yes. Yes. And just a while back—you remember that high wind in May when the tidewater rose up so? A couple of old folks crossing a little old creek bridge in their car that night, a flash flood swooped up over it just like that, washed them clean off, car and all. Drowned to death. Swept them away downstream. Callaway Creek—"

He was stricken with the wonder of it, his throat constricting. Flash flood. Out of the night. Out of nowhere. Just like that. And *poohm!* You were gone . . .

"And when Reece got through talking all about it and we all had our say, he wound up with a pitch for some dough for this River Development Association he started? And we all kicked in, even Richard-Gene coughed up a nickel. Of course I had to poke him some. And then"— Rad's eyes slid sidewise, mischievously, for this too he had withheld from Reeve out of an obscure compunction—"DeLavery dropped a hype right back on Reece. He—" He laughed aloud, slyly savoring it. "Why that old bastard wouldn't lend us the time of day. And DeLavery puts the bee on him to donate a hundred bucks for fertilizer. Here he's been teaching us all about what kind of fertilizer to use and how much of it and when, when most of us ain't got the cash to buy navy beans with, let alone nitrogen and potash. And what do you know? We each of us got a fifty-pound bag. How do you like that?"

Reeve was less enthusiastic than Rad, more cautious of expectation. Dams, lectures, fertilizer donations, it was all like most public benefits in these parts, only too apt to pass him by.

"How much you say this river-thing is about to cost?"

"Oh hundred, two hundred million . . . Reeve, I'm telling you we can't miss! It's all ahead of us! We gonna make it, it's there. And let me tell you something else."

He turned his wheel hard over and bumping over the cattle barrier jounced into the familiar track. "Ain't nothin' go'n stop us. Can't Henry, nobody, do nothin' to harm us. And you know why? There's somethin' that's a-work against it. Somethin' in the air now—in the atmosphere here—you can fairly smell it. What I mean, the prevailing condition."

They drove past Reeve's clearing and halted by the summer corn, sprung up like a bannered army, leafblades tossing in the sun. Here the same thought, voiced or unvoiced, always struck them both. It was not enough. They had intensified their planting by plowing up fallow fields on either side of the bobwire fence, sowing the new crop with high-yield seed and improving their cultivation practices. And it was not enough, the harvest would not pay enough to carry them. They were planning to expand their acreage by clearing more land in the area they'd drained. And still it would not be enough. Not all the work they could do with hand and hoe, not all the hours they put in, not all their strength nor all their mind could ever catch them up enough. Not in this age. Not without power equipment. Not without motor-drawn bottom plow, tandem disc, drag harrow, planter, spreader, cultivator, weeder.

To ride as they rode the truck, from high up, on a seat, behind the wheel.

They jumped down from the truck and strode to the ditch in the field. "This the place I was telling you about," Reeve pointed. "Silting up." The spoil pile had never been completely leveled off and behind a weedy tangle the muddy water backing up was forming a shallow mosquito-infested pool. "Drainage what ain't kept up," Reeve moodily kicked at the knotted weeds, "is worse than none at all."

"What we need is a bulldozer."

"And a dragline."

"If we had that, if we had the moon . . . My God, I left Charles with all the weeding, and here we are shootin' the breeze."

Rad turned back to the truck, hastening over the awkward moment of parting. At this point Reeve usually said to him, "Be by tonight?" or he to Reeve, "I'll be by." But after their words by the riverside, which thrummed back of his mind like the echo of a distant quarrel, the spontaneity was gone. It was as if climbing a mountain they had left all the known landmarks behind, and ascending into strange territory they had to learn from scratch plant life, rocks, the signs on which their security depended, the method of ascent, the nature of the air. Rad wasn't sure now that he could count on being welcomed.

"Say Rad—" Reeve called after him as he reached the truck.

"Yeah?" He waited for Reeve to come up.

"You ain't goin' away mad?"

"Well I am, some. Though I'm not one bit sorry that we had it all out. If a man can't live with the truth . . ."

Reeve was not so sure of that. He was unhappy over their talk as if he had betrayed someone by it, himself, his friends, his people. The truth, though not all of the truth. And better none of the truth than only part of it. But who can deliver all of the truth? The more you chase it, the faster it flees. The harder you grasp it, the more it changes. And it's off again, leaving you with only its cloak in your hand. Better to have said nothing at all to Rad. To leave him with his illusions. It's all good. It's all wonderful. You and me, that's it.

"You see," Rad said, "every day—every day I'm finding out things I never knew before. I hear things all new to me—I think about them— I talk. I'm stretching out. Sometimes," he stretched out his arms, straining from the bulge of his biceps to his fingertips, "I'm stretching out so hard it hurts me."

"Rad—" Reeve shook his head at him. Impossible to resist the man, impossible not to be tempted into further betrayals, revealing too much. Not that there was any secret to what he was about to say. Not that there was any reason why he shouldn't say it. His reluctance was too complex, too contradictory for reasoning. The part of him that as a person gladly flung open the door to Rad. And the part of him that belonged to racial reserves that went back for centuries, reserves of suspicion, skepticism, hard-headed realism.

"We're buying a tractor," Reeve said.

It came out in response to the radiant outwardness of the man, to his sincerity as if sincerity must needs call forth some token of proof in return. It came out as a gift freely given, as an act of faith. And yet not without a pang of remorse, not without the flagellation of self-reproach —it was none of Rad's business, it had nothing to do with Rad.

"A tractor? Who?"

"My class. We been studying it for a long time. I'm going down to St. George this afternoon to look at one selling out there." Running my mouth and drowning in it. "Some of the fellas'll be at my place tonight to talk about it. You be over?"

"Sure, well sure."

Rad drove his truck through the ruts toward home, whistling. Every day, every day something new. Every day something different. Everything is opening up. Everything is on the move.

"Say, sweetheart," he called toward the house as he leaped from his truck.

He skipped over a broken slat in the back steps, shouldered through the stacked baskets of okra, picked yesterday evening and waiting for the produce jobber's truck from Bay City, and bore it in with him like a gift in his hands.

"Say Lu, where are you? Where the kids?"

4

The kitchen too was crowded with baskets and the table was heaped with vegetables, furry pods of okra, crimson-globed tomatoes, spotted or squashed or otherwise too marred to be marketable. In the cooking cubicle off the kitchen Lulabelle stood swathed in steam over a simmering kettle of okra and tomatoes.

"Say honey," Rad called to her, "guess what, you'll never guess . . . They're here!"

"Don't you take less than dollar a basket!"

"Oh—Towle's. Ain't they been here yet?" He glanced back at the baskets on the porch, of course not. "The engineers! The engineers on the river survey."

"Great," she responded to his spiel, "great," with a touch in her of the tomato acid that dripped livid red from her ladle. "Where's m' gaskets?"

"What gaskets?"

"I asked you just before you left to bring me four dozen gaskets for these here jars. You mean you forgot? You were right there, in town . . . Where's your head? You worse than the young ones."

"What are you, crazy? Canning on a day like this."

"Now what'll I do? I ain't got rings enough left . . . Your dinner plate's over there behind the quart jars. Now don't knock up against 'em! And don't touch, they're all boiled up . . ."

Rad took his plate of cold meat and collards from behind the galaxy of jars on one end and ate standing, too wound up and too cheerful with his news to be discouraged. "You know what this means, Lu? You realize what this means for us? Inside of ten years this land'll be worth—remember Ozzie Higginson said it—six hundred an acre. And that's not half of it—"

"Sure," Lulabelle said, leaning the bulk of her underbelly against the top of the oven door to take the weight off her feet. "Great. Fine. All my old rings, they done lost their spring."

Against Rad's prattle she mentally estimated the number of kettles it would take to put up the amount of vegetables left on the table. She didn't have to can today. Only the tomatoes were running away with her, going softer by the minute, and she always did like to have tomatoes stewed through okra. And the baby was due according to her reckoning in a week or so now, and she had to race, race, to get in as much as she could before it was too late. There'd be near a week in the hospital as she calculated it, and afterward near a month before she'd be fully back on her feet. And with the impending arrival of the baby her fears of the spring were back full force, hanging imminently over her. That something was about to happen, something that would interfere with the normal course of events, that would descend on them like a twister, seize up all common routines and hurl them into chaos. In the face of such fears and such a time, she stirred the bubbling cauldron.

"And guess what, something else," Rad said, coming over to take the pot of reheated coffee from the back of the stove. "You'll never guess in a million years."

She looked up at him out of a torrid red haze, through a red mist of moisture. He was always arriving home these days with some shining nugget of information, gleaned from his ride with Reeve or the morning's lecture or his exchange of experience with the other boys at class or an argument he'd won or lost or fought to a draw. And whatever it was he had to tell, she rendered it only a jaundiced eye, a tin ear, a stony back. She begrudged it with all her might. She resisted it with all her soul. She put no stock in it. But why, that was what bewildered her. She had nothing against his attending school. It was bringing in a regular income. His first check, delayed by a snarl of red tape, would be delivered, he assured her, at the end of this month. It was helping him with his crops. He was full of plans for improvements that would increase his yield at the end of this season or surely next, and he was easier to get along with. He was no longer a man thrashing about in the dark, turning in upon himself, self-gnawing, biting at his knuckles, flailing out so that every now and then she had to cry: "Sometimes, Rad McDowell, you an awful hard man to live with!" He was now like a man who has come up from underground into the light, who sees the world unfolding before him, who has found a direction and a future. And it was this that she misdoubted. What is the future? When is it? Where?

The future is not as close to hand as a kettleful of slippery green fish swimming a sea of boiling blood through suspensions of yellow seed and shoals of pulp. Nor as clear-cut as an array of sterilized jars that will, within the hour, be filled to the brims. Next month, next season, next ten years can be never.

It was his air of certainty that she could place no faith in. This and his obsessive drive—I got to go, I got to know!—repelled her. Always blowing into the house and blowing out again, in too much of a hurry to stay put. Detaching himself from his family. His responsibility vested not in her and the children but in what he had to do. The center of his existence lay elsewhere. I got to go, I got to know! I got to be, I got to see . . . She had never really forgiven him for going to Reeve's court hearing that day back in May when she begged him not to. Even though she understood now that he had to be there, that if he hadn't stood up and spoken out as he did Reeve would have been forced off his farm and they off theirs. Even though she took pride in him for his part in the battle, she couldn't forget how he'd gone off and left her. And before that—even though he was drafted into the Army, even though it was not of his doing, she still couldn't forget how he'd ridden off in the troop truck leaving her with three small children and a fourth on the way . . . And now even though she had agreed to his enrollment in the class, even though she was as convinced as he was that it was the best thing for him, even though she derived from it a species of relief for the outlet it provided that restlessness in him which she could never cope with, even though she accepted it with all her reason, she was in her elemental animal state, in her long and brooding hours, opposed.

With an opposition as rigid as a steel wall inside her. Every third day off like that, leaving her as she was. Every other night over to Reeve's, every other blessed night. I got to!

He's finding his satisfaction outside, she thought bitterly as she looked over the cloudy pot into the brilliant blue glimmer of his eyes. Baching it!

And yet, and yet, his male self-assurance, the masculine confidence which impressed her as ill-founded and excessive, moved the woman in her and the womb. So that at this moment, the hollows of her eyes smarting with pools of sweat; her shirt drenched down her back; the heavy mounds of her breasts dangling unbound because of the weather, surrounded with streamlets that poured down the declivity between them and under the creases; her loins sodden under her too-tight white shorts; in this moment, in this welter of melting flesh, she yearned toward him, carried on the wave of an orgasmic spasm as thin and fine and all-compelling as a sneeze.

"Reeve's class is buying them a tractor. How do you like that?"

"Oh boy." For a long instant she contemplated flinging the ladle of scalding liquid into his face. "What's that to me? What in Lord God's good does that do me!"

"Lu." Rad touched her wrist timidly, as if afraid. "You hadn't ought to, you look skinned alive."

"Get away, get away from me! Git!"

He retired hastily, gulping his coffee. It was too hot and too black, rank with the flavor of overused grounds; but he wouldn't deign to reach past her for the milk in the icebox. In his eyes she had always been pregnant. Before he went into the Army and a month after he was home she was carrying, it was all one long endless carrying. At first when he started class he hated to leave her alone with no one but the children around; but then he began to take it for granted, trusting she'd have some warning sign beforehand. When she needed, he'd be there.

"Why don't you set?" she said to him and exasperatedly, interrupting her cooking, passed him the milk from the icebox.

"Ain't got the time."

"Then what took you so long gettin' here? We all et, waitin' on you. Why you so late?"

He hesitated, warily watching her from his distance. She skimmed the foam from the surface of her preserves and began spooning out into the first jar. How late he was coming home, that was what set her off. More than the missing gaskets. The gaskets merely furnished the springboard. Last time it was the store bread—he had contributed to

Benson Reece's development association the quarter in his pocket intended for store bread.

"Water tank boiled up," he answered her. "It's sprung a leak."

"Again? I thought you had it fixed, and that step out there, you don't hammer it down them kids'll sure as shootin' break their necks."

He began sliding out along the length of the table, carrying his coffee cup toward the dish pail, heaped with dishes, standing on an upended box by the door. "Later. Maybe tonight."

"It's always later."

"I better get to them boys. They'll need a hand."

"You bet you better. Better an hour ago."

That was another sore point between them. In her opinion he was imposing too much of a burden on the two older boys, leaving too much of the field work to them. Though he couldn't help it. He had to. There was no other way for it to get done.

"I notice you always have plenty of time to chew the fat with Reeve," she threw over her shoulder at him. "Always plenty of time to go chasing after him."

"You too?" he said with a vehemence that startled her.

His arm drew back as if about to smash the coffee cup into her face. Then he set it down among the dishes gently enough, but with a tremor that rattled through the pail.

"You too, Lulabelle?"

The screendoor squealed closed behind him. His footsteps creaked down the steps, the broken slat rasping.

Grimly appeased—she had succeeded in getting through to him, had brought his head down out of the clouds, had hacked him down to size —Lulabelle filled the jars and fitted her remaining rubbers over the rims and when she ran out of rubbers took Mason jars down from the top shelf of the cupboard, standing precariously tiptoe on a chair, and prepared to boil them up. Punishing him for his negligence.

And punishing herself, for under her sense of appeasement she was defensive as if somehow he had robbed her of her victory or she had robbed herself of it by her final volley. She had not intended to attack him through Reeve, the most sensitive of all issues between them. She had always been well-disposed toward Reeve. Only something about the way Rad was going all-out for him, the curiosity and zest with which he pursued him, offended her. In some obscure fashion she was in competition with Reeve for Rad's favor and thus instinctively she found herself hostile to Reeve as she would have been hostile to any competition, male or female, that she wasn't sure she could oust. But refusing to define her jealousy, feeling something ludicrous in it, she could not give any valid reason for her hostility and therefore constantly denied it. And denied it especially because Rad would at once interpret it as race prejudice. And race had nothing to do with it! "My mamma were the most wonderfulest woman," she was constantly proclaiming before the children. "She was a true Christian. She taught us to love everybody regardless of race, creed, or color. Why, I grew up with colored folks, in rent-shacks back to back with theirs ones . . ." And it was so. When she looked into Reeve's face she saw, clearer she believed than Rad did, wholly the person there.

But it was race—race—that always intruded. It had spoiled for her last Sunday's gathering of her family here. Rad fidgeting around all through until she had to haul him aside: "Go, go on and get him here." And of course he wouldn't, it wasn't fitting. Still it was with them all that afternoon, with them every minute like a ghost at the banquet table. And even now, now in the middle of a spat with her husband, there it was again, rearing its ugly head. Race! When she didn't mean that at all. Not that.

And yet, and yet, race was there in her meaning too, in its very core the vein of fear. Running with that boy, taking up for him everywhere, acting hand in glove with him. What's it going to lead to? Where is he taking us?

She screwed the grey metal lids down on the Mason jars, leaving them loose at the last thread to be tightened later. Rows of shining jars covered half her table. An ugly burn streaked redly up her forearm, raising a blister. When you've hacked your husband down to size because of what you most care for in him, when you've reduced him to chop-fodder, what do you have?

What is now? When is now? Where is it?

Rad spent most of the afternoon in blind turmoil tearing weeds up out of the sweet potato ridges. It was a job not for one man but for two; not for a one-horse plow but for a paired team under experienced hands. When he first approached the field from the house, however, he spied one lone figure, a solitary boy, ineptly and, at sight of him, frantically hand-hoeing. Wyatt who had the touch for handling livestock had neither the strength nor the patience for crops. And Charles who had the strength, if not the patience, was nowhere to be seen. Had deserted his younger brother. Disappeared again.

"Look out what you doing," Rad hastened toward Wyatt, yelling. "You breaking up the vines! Where's Charles?" As if he didn't know the minute he observed Charles' absence.

Wyatt flushed darkly, ducking his head aside, guilty though he was the innocent one. His narrow shoulders squirmed off a shrug.

"Well, where is he?" He grabbed the hoe from Wyatt. "Like this, and like this, and this. Alongside the ridge and throw the soil back up. Where's the plow? I thought you were going to use it."

He gathered from Wyatt's muttering that the spring-tooth had rusted off. And that Charles after an hour of doing his damnedest to attach the implement, getting nowhere fast, and after two hours of hand-hoeing, had suddenly upped and decided to see what he could do about soldering it. And off he'd gone with the spring-tooth, no doubt, Rad imagined, as if the devil were after him, as if drawn by a magnet . . .

Wyatt's dark hair drooped lankly over his forehead, his shoulders sagged, he plodded. Rad could tolerate it only so long. "Go on, go on home to your chickens! Go on, go, I don't need you. I'm better off without."

Rad himself went back to the plowshed and harnessed Ida up and tried cultivating the ridges with the rotary hoe. It wasn't suitable for the purpose. You need a spring-tooth to tear the weeds out both sides of the ridge, and later a sweep to work the soil back up. Or better still, less time-consuming, a two-horse riding cultivator that straddles the row, equipped with multiple shovels; angle and level regulated by your feet. Or better than that, a high-wheel tractor, discs cutting away at the ridges and throwing the weeds out of the middle; the sweeps following immediately after, restoring the soil to the ridges and weeding upside all at one and the same time.

Months ago, on the first hot day of early spring he had put down in the mother beds—plowed weeks before, fertilized, weeded, sun-warmed —thirty bushels of seed roots. With his hands he had patted each one of the bulbous coppery-tan tubers firmly down, a half inch apart all around, allowing fifteen square feet to the bushel. He had covered the plants with a fresh clean layer of light sand, never used for growing sweets before, and sprinkled it over with water to settle about the roots. If among the gonadal stock he had blanketed in earth, one disease bruise, one strain of internal rot had escaped his attention while sorting out, the entire bed would be infected.

When the first sprouts appeared, he had covered them with another inch of sand. In the late spring he prepared the land that had lain fallow during his war years for transplanting, plowing up the coarse wild brush and working it over, harrowing. Marking off the furrows with the plow, spreading fertilizer by hand and then mixing it through the soil by running the plow over the furrow again. It was while he was dragging a pole along to form the narrow flat-topped ridges that Charles called his attention to a tractor over the fence at Sunset that dropped fertilizer uniformly, mixed it with the soil and built a precise ridge, all in a single operation.

When the leaves on the oak trees are full-blown, then it is time to transplant sweet potatoes. Budded from the seed roots in the mother beds, thirty thousand draws, their shoots over six inches aboveground, were ready for the first pulling; and fifteen thousand more for the second and third pullings. With a yard-long stick, forked at the end, Rad set each plant into the ridge, Charles following in his footsteps pushed it down into the soil with his fingers and firmed it about with his foot, and Wyatt watered it from a barrel hauled into the field. The plants, placed fifteen inches apart in the row on ridges three and a half feet apart, extended over more than four and a half acres. It was during this period that Charles began vanishing regularly over the fence into Sunset to watch the three-man crews with the machine planters. Sweet potatoes are among the least mechanized of all crops, but with a machine those men were setting as many as four thousand plants per hour. It took him and his boys, Rad figured, ten times that long.

The transplants for the most part took hold promptly, their half-open leaves pointing skyward, their fibrous roots sinking downward, making in their new abode a vigorous start on their next phase of development, toward the eventual production of their own progeny: thick-clustered, robust, orange-fleshed. Those that failed to take hold lagged through the season: fruitful only of scanty, stunted, and misshapen tubers or barren altogether.

Rad now had as of today, solidly established, about forty-five thousand plants, from which he hoped to harvest in the fall a minimum of three hundred bushels. All about him the vines crawled in large-leafed layers over the ridges, their dusky greenness threaded with purple veins. But the same fecund weather that fostered their growth also fostered the weeds and pests. It was getting almost too late to weed, the vines were becoming so heavy. With his walking plow and the ineffectual rotary hoe attached to it he was doing more harm than good.

Looking back at the end of a row he saw that he had pulled up and broken off the swelling nodules of a good dozen plants. And in the next row he encountered a yellowing of leaves that sent a hump, a thump, and a bump through his heart.

Kneeling he scratched down through the earth and placing his hands under the hairy bunch lifted. Sure enough, weevil grubs had been tunneling through potatoes and vine. He located an insect by splitting the debilitated stem. It wriggled in his palm, legless, white, tan of head, almost twice as long as it would be in blue-black crimson-belted adulthood. He crushed it with his thumb, flicked it off, examined neighboring vines. He looked back over his shoulder at the row he himself had damaged.

He didn't have the wherewithal. That was the plain fact of the matter. For harvest he had only his father's old middle-buster, rusted too, that was wont too often to injure the roots as it dug them up or to bury them under beyond finding. What he needed was a tractor plow with a shield coulter. The class which had expanded his knowledge of the possibilities within the reach of his hand, just beyond his fingertips, had also sharpened like a knife in his gut his awareness of what he lacked. The promise was so large. And the present was so meager.

He led Ida over to the Sunset fence and tied her there—not that she had spunk enough to run off if he let her loose—and climbed over the white-painted spars in pursuit of his son and his spring-tooth harrow.

He had not set foot on Sunset since the morning after his arrival home last fall, and crossing the fields he felt dwarfed by them. And when he halted in the enormous doorway of the equipment shed, he felt more than dwarfed, pulverized.

Time and again he had forbidden the boy to hang around here, and the boy would comply for a week, a few days. Then he'd slip off again, tagging after the men, tinkering with their tools. There was no good reason he could give Charles why he should stay away, but the boy, he felt, should have understood without being told. A disloyalty to himself was implied in this action, a criticism of him, an insinuation of inadequacy. Charles should have understood that. And maybe he did understand it, he did have an inkling, and still he went, went as if he couldn't help himself, compulsively, in spite of and because of the implicit prohibition. He had never actually forbidden Charles to have anything to do with Henry, not even after the incident of the baseball mitt nor after Reeve's hearing, but this too, he felt, and this much more, the boy should have understood. Charles should have understood that the man was a threat to his father, a foe and the worst kind of foe. Not stranger, motivated out of the impersonal necessities of the stranger. But kin, motivated out of a range of promptings that went back to family inheritance, boyhood memories, the lifelong quiverings of the raw ego.

The equipment shed was almost as huge as a hangar. Light filtered bluely down from tall windows into grey interior. Under the vaulted ceiling, colonnaded on each side in stalls shone the strong yellows, oranges, and reds of a wilderness of equipment, gas-fueled, diesel-engined, caterpillar-tracked, wheeled with corrugated tires heavy enough to flatten a man out and grind him to pulp. The jointed boom, beams, and connecting rods of a fourteen-foot backhoe clawed up at the blue sky plastered like a piece of paper against the window. Over the hood of the same vehicle, facing into the aisle, the bucket of a heavy loader, capable of lifting a ton, reared at half-elevation. In the next section the skeletal iron of a rear-hitch hookup gripped in its head a slotted blade, reversible, tiltable, and adjustable to any angle. The attending mechanic dismounted it at a touch from the tractor to which it had been attached and rolled into its place a shielded cutter wide enough to tooth through a seven-foot swathe. For every machine, Rad glimpsed along the back and side walls a multitude of accessories, intricately engineered organisms on their own account—of interlocking drawbars, belts, gears; designed for baling, combining, field-chopping, grain-drilling, hauling, mowing, raking, discing, stalk-cutting, dusting and spraying, wood-sawing, picking, feed-grinding. Single-purpose, multi-purpose, hydraulically operated from the driver's seat by the man at the controls —regulating with wheel, lever, push-button, pedal; gauging speed to workload in accordance with the indication of the meters on the glassed-in instrument panel.

In the doorway, bursting with the heat of the day, with the exertion of his row-hopping hike across the fields, with the frustration of his weeding and the lash of his wife's reproaches, Rad laboriously breathed in the fused fumes, condensed within the building, of scorched rubber, metal, gasoline, oil, and grease. In the free center space between the colonnades an engine had been dismantled part by part, anatomized like a corpse on the dissecting table. While two of the maintenance crew hovered on the outskirts murmuring suggestions, Henry supervised its reassembly by the boy.

Charles was kneeling on the concrete floor, ginger head bent, engrossed in pistons, piston pins and piston rings, valves, guides and bearings. With paternal possessiveness Henry's hand rested on the back of the boy's neck.

"And what's that?" he asked Charles, indicating an enclosed mounting on the crankshaft. "That's right. The governor. And what's its function and how does it work? That's right. That's m' boy."

His quick brown eyes lifting, Henry saw Rad before Charles did. Without removing his hand from the nape of Charles' neck he went on smoothly, "You see, Charles, it just naturally don't pay any of these little here dirt farms to buy and maintain this motorized stuff. For the acreage they have to till, they wouldn't get enough use out of it to earn back the initial investment. Ah Rad." He flipped his hand up with offhand cordiality. "Your spring-tooth's back in the repair shop. My man'll have it ready for you in about fifteen minutes. Retooled and shined up. Good as new, huh, Charles?"

The boy had stiffened, afraid to lift his head. Henry's fondling hand scratched up through the back of his hair, tweaked at his reddened ear. He stood protectively over the child at his feet, his power-packed frame clad in bow-tied white shirt and grey sharkskin pants, cool and crisply managerial amidst the shop surroundings. Charles, hunching with fright and defiance, huddled in closer to him.

"Git up outa there!"

"Now Rad, keep your shirt on. You know this kid, why he has this whole thing figured out into cooling system, lubricating system, fuel system, electrical—"

"Git up outa there!"

Ignoring Henry, Rad stood astride the threshold, as unwilling to cross it as he would have been to enter Henry's house. The vastness of the chamber swallowed his voice. The conglomeration of paraphernalia, the sheer technological proportions of it swamped him, as if within the space of a quarter hour he had wandered out of a past era to which he no longer belonged into a future era that, like the sign posted on the door, warned him: STRICTLY NO ADMISSION PRIVATE PROPERTY KEEP OUT!

But what was his was still his.

Within the frame of the doorway he waxed taller and taller. "Charles, you come! If I have to go in there and get you . . ."

"Now Rad, don't be a jerk! He ain't done nothin' but what I put him up to."

As Rad advanced toward him, the boy, flaming with a mortification that mirrored his own, dodged away on his haunches, scuttling like a crab in his panic. He could never give Charles a direct order. He never could exact of him the respect that most fathers did of their sons: yessir, nosir. Not the manners. Nor the obedience. He could ask him but he couldn't tell him. He could give him a task, but he couldn't make him . . .

Before the shamefaced twitching grins of the work gang, he had to chase after Charles, jerk him to his feet and in an odd agony of almost-pride, almost-sympathy, push him, resisting every step of the way, past Henry's attempts to interfere, boot him from behind with his knee over the threshold, the white-hot pavement, the sun-softened blacktop, out of there. Somehow he got the boy, panting and sobbing, twisting and wrenching, over the obstacle course of the fields. The struggle incited in himself a savage ardor, the brute-will of subdual. He's got to obey me! He's got to learn to obey! And with the shaking, clutching, kicking forced march, a sorrowful sense: I'm losing him, I've lost him.

"Git, git back—" He slammed Charles from behind. "Git back to your own side of the fence!"

The grease-streaked swollen cheeks, the puffed lips spewed forth a choked stream of invective. "You bum, you bum—"

Rad yanked his belt off from around his waist and lifted it like his father Douglas McDowell, not meaning to, never meaning to, not to his boy, not this.

"Nigger-lover! Goddam nigger-lover!"

The scream ripped out of the strawberry mouth, the honeyed cheeks sprinkled with fine freckles fanning from the bridge of the nose, the fine fair eyelashes. Like a scar of disfigurement.

The belt descended, each of them hurling at the other the weapon that would wound the most.

"Nigger-lover! Dirty rotten nigger-lover!"

"No son of mine—no son of mine—"

The belt licked out across the blue-checkered shirt, the too-small shirt straining at the seams over the shoulders. Out across the jean-rolled legs.

At the fence Rad tried to hoist him over, tugging painfully upward from under his armpits. The boy slumped, slack as a sack of potatoes. He's broadening out, Rad felt with that odd surge of pride even as suns burst behind his eyeballs. Grown really heavy.

"Rotten stinkin' nigger-lovin'—"

He gyved, heaved, flung him over the fence. To subdue, beat into submission all that so obdurately thwarted and negated him: leers and jeers, earth and dearth, the patiently waiting horse and plow. Once over the fence, Charles ran from him. Ran like the wind.

"Niggah—niggah—niggah—luvah . . ."

On a wail that whistled like the wind in the windless air. And died away.

Gone. What had started out of nothing more than using on him the wrong tone of voice.

Ennervated, eviscerated, shaking with a soul-shriveling misery, Rad took up Ida's reins again. What got into me? Where'd the boy get it from? Out of this chaos, out of this ferment, the peak of his rage and the depth of his discouragement, resolution was born.

An idea that must have been floating vaguely about inside him all afternoon coalesced, crystallized. He knew precisely what he had to do now. Irrationally, perhaps, but as irrevocably as if the law were being laid down on him. He jogged back to his sweet potato field and worked, with a spark of cheer that took fire from his illumination, until supper-time.

By the time he reached home his idea had matured with the rapidity of fantasy into the semblance of full-fledged reality, embracing the color and specific detail, the anticipated obstacles and the methods of overcoming them that pertain to reality. First he would sit down with Charles on the edge of the well, under the shade of the persimmon trees. Explain to him. "Henry's got his way. We got ours. And our way can work for us, not as good as his does for him maybe but good enough. If we know who our friends are. You have to know who your friends are." Consult with the boy. Put it to him as a question. "Now what do you think of this? Reeve and his class are buying them a tractor . . ."

But Charles was not at the sty with Wyatt feeding the spotted sow that was to farrow in September. Nor with Ruby and Timmy on the broken porch step, shelling beans. Nor in the house helping his mother lay the table.

As Rad arrived through the door, Lulabelle in a much better frame of mind than when he'd left her slipped a voucher from her breast pocket and waved it at him: twenty dollars wrangled out of the produce buyer, her price for the okra within a few pennies.

"Charles?" she answered his query, "I thought he was with you." And quick to suspicion, her smile fading. "You didn't have a fight with him? Wyatt—" She seized on Wyatt who had come sidling in seeking to snitch a pre-supper snack. "Where's Charles? Oh . . ." Listening to Wyatt's recital of their woes with the spring-tooth. "He went over there to get it fixed and *you*," she said incredulously to Rad, "you didn't *hit* him, did you?"

He sent Wyatt searching down by the river, Ruby and Timmy calling through the fields. He himself took the wood and swamp, trying every refuge where after a whipping he used to flee from his father, swearing eternal quits. And hoping, praying for someone to come looking for him. Only no one ever did. Behind every tree he thought he saw Charles skittering away: he'd have to sprint after him, coax him out of it, argue him back with a self-abnegation that made him angry all over again just to contemplate it. Only Charles was not there, not behind the next pine nor over the next creek.

"If he's hiding," Lulabelle said when Rad came back, sure he'd find him already home ahead of him, "wherever he is, he's not coming out now. We might's well eat."

Supper was a stiffly silent meal, the overboiled greens and hamhocks lubricous in their mouths. Lulabelle's lips were outthrust in their bitterest pout as she fished up the hamhocks, showing him, Rad imagined, how few there were for so large a family. Wyatt gnawed every pink shred of meat from the bone and licked where he'd gnawed, still moody, Rad suspected, over his sharpness to him in the field. Timmy and Ruby were uncustomarily subdued, using forks instead of fingers without being spoken to, sweet as angels; afraid of incurring their father's wrath or currying favor with him or, Rad was convinced, glorying in the secret glee of children when one of their number falls into disgrace.

Charles' place was empty. The source of all the liveliness. The origin of discourses that provoked laughter, controversy or sometimes just plain bedazzlement. In the rickety green chair with the spindle missing in back, Charles would spontaneously spin out a philosophy, if it was a philosophy, that consorted ill with his technical interests. "Human beings are too complicated. They always go about things the hard way. Then they have to figure out easy ways of doing it. Like eating and sleeping. All you have to do is eat and sleep. A possum knows that. But human beings have to go out and work their fool heads off to earn a living. All that jazz. It's stupid. Curiosity killed the cat. And it'll kill man too."

Or once in a spirited defense of Wyatt's latest horde of kittens, a monologue that positively jingled:

"*What would happen if all the cats were killed off?*
There'd be too many mice and too many birds.
The birds would eat up all the insects.
Then all the birds would starve out.
And the moles would die out.
Without moles and insects, for instance bees,
All the plants would die out.

"*Then all the animals would die out.*
Everything would die out except microscopic animals and plants
And plenty of them would die out because they're dependent on
  larger plants.
In the end the only thing left would be plankton
And the things at the bottom of the food-chain.

"*We'd have to start all over again. Bye-bye.*"

"What," he had asked Charles, "is plankton?"

"Bye-bye." And off with Wyatt out the door . . .

And another time, expatiating on a book his teacher had loaned him over the summer. ("Charles, eat up, your food is growing cold! Charles, you taking too much time up talking!") "The trouble," Charles said, "is we live in a time where we can understand as a mind what we can't understand as people. This causes our instincts to cry out, 'Fight! Fight!' But our mind says, 'We can't fight, it'll cause a war that will destroy everything.' This brings about a mental short circuit. What I mean, thinking you can't get out of it. Like, 'You wait and see there's gonna be a war and everyone'll be killed.'

"These old instincts are old-fashioned in this day and age with all our means of mass destruction. We got to shuck these old instincts."

"Is that," he had asked Charles, "all in that book you reading?"

"Well, no."

"Is that what kids think about nowadays?"

"Sure. Why not?"

He had not had the time or mind to pay much attention to Charles' discourses lately. The green chair with the missing spindle was empty of the lively young body, the eager glow, the blithe surprise. What connection was there between that boy and the sullen rebellious creature who had turned on him this afternoon with the disfiguring scream upon his face . . .

Lulabelle caught his glance from chair to window and door and back to chair. And relenting, she offered an escape hatch for his torment. "He'll be getting hungry now. It'll be getting dark soon. He'll scoot home then."

He had to win Charles back. The means to accomplish it lay within his grasp. Like the paper in his pocket during the court hearing . . . If he had the guts to take it up.

The children cleared the table without being prodded to it. Rad leaned across the table to his wife, taking his steaming mug of coffee from her. "When you going somewhere, Lu, even if you don't know where to, if you feel it's right, only thing you can do is keep going the way you going to the end of it."

"You going," she said with a wry twist of smile over her coffee. "I'm not."

He hadn't even taken a good look at her in the past few months. As her body enlarged her face had grown thin, her cheeks honed down to the bone. She had given up the calcium tablets Dr. Harrington had prescribed for her, four dollars a bottle, and given up Harrington after her first visit, ten dollars a month every month until the baby was paid for before it arrived. Twice this week she had dreamed of waking up in a pool of blood, and twice again he had promised her, "I'm taking you to Bay City Hospital." "You sure of that now? You sure of it?" She didn't really believe it.

Taking their coffee, they went out on the porch together to catch the evening breeze from the river. They leaned against the twin posts over the steps, scanning the fields for a sign of Charles. An airplane glittered and swooped over the marshland across the river, capturing the gold of the sun in a silver flash.

"Must be one of those government planes spraying mosquitoes."

"Mm-hm. Can't stand the smell of it."

"Everything's changing, Lulabelle."

"You changing." She wiped her sweat-coarsened hair back. "Not me."

"Why, not so long ago folks were dying off by the hundreds because of them mosquitoes. My mamma died of the swamp fever." He didn't add what they both knew, that it was while she was in her last month carrying she was taken.

He drained off the last of his coffee in a gulp. "Lu, I got to go over to Reeve's for a while."

She was already geared for it, expecting it. Every other night. Every other night.

"If it's all right with you?"

She helped him, giving him the excuse. "I suppose Charles won't show till he's sure you're out of here." And she opened the gate wider, "Soon as you're out of sight he'll be here like a shot."

He set his cup carefully down inside the door, speaking over his shoulder. "You feelin' all right? You don't feel nothin'? If you need, you'll send for me right on?"

"What about this here step? You promise to fix—"

He was already down the steps, skipping the rotted slat. Knowing with every step he took away how wrong he was. Neglecting his home. Mistreating his children. Deserting his wife. When he reached the track he looked back. She was sagging in unutterable weariness against the doorpost, her empty coffee cup in her hand.

Still he went. Tired? He was never tired anymore. There was something driving him. There was something he had to get to. He had to.

5

Charles did not appear as soon as his father vanished. Wyatt performed his job for him, lugging in the water for the dishes, and was proceeding with his own job, washing up the dishes, when Lulabelle came in from the porch and took the rag from him. "I'll do that. You go look for your brother." Wyatt hovered in uncertainty a moment. "Let me, I'll finish . . . Mamma"—trying to assume Charles' authoritative tone—"you better rest a while." With her sudsy hand she flipped up the shaggy lock that was forever hanging over his right eye. In Wyatt's gypsy-dark face she suddenly saw her mother, a bruise from a guinea-hen peck on his cheek accentuating the same smallness of feature, the just-ness of the tiny triangle of a nose, the velvetiness of mouth, the shyness. Her mother's face as she rarely remembered it, back at the beginning of time, her hair tied back with a butterfly-winged white bow ribbon.

"You go find Charles now and bring him home. Tell him I need him."

Wyatt stood another moment fitfully: *I'm* here, *I'll* help you. But like his father she had to have the older and sturdier one. He slouched off, scuffling.

"Skip," she hollered after him. "Pick up your feet. Scat."

Timmy, the funny little in-between one, always running after his older brothers and always outrun by his younger sister, was hopping up and down. "Can I go too? Can I go too?"

"Go on," Lulabelle said. "Not you." She plucked Ruby back by the seat of her britches. "Young lady." While Timmy trotted off after Wyatt, Ruby for once was spanked on into the house to do the job she generally managed to shift onto Timmy.

All my kids, Lulabelle reflected complacently, are crackerjacks. But that was the one ameliorating drop of complacency that was to be hers all evening.

Ruby stood on the rickety green chair taking the dishes her mother passed her out of the rinse pail, and with a whip of her towel and a flip of her hand sent them flying into the cupboard.

"You break that dish," Lulabelle warned her, "I'll break your bottom."

"What you worried about, Mamma?" Ruby peeped out from under her yellow bangs. "I ain't broke one yet."

The pert mouth, Lulabelle recognized with a start, was her own. The bold red cheeks. The roguish eyes. Herself. And the brisk whip of the towel? The fine careless tip of the hand? Ruby had never known what worry was. That was the difference.

"What you thinkin' 'bout, Mamma?"

"I ain't. It's too hot to think."

After the supper dishes she lay down for a while on her bed, listening for Ruby to shoo the chicks around the house, waiting for the boys to be back with Charles. Sinking slowly slowly into a lump of passivity. In her present condition she always felt that she was running a tempera-ture, and all through the oppressive blaze of this day she felt the heat of her blood, surely a degree or two above normal, combining with the heat of the outside atmosphere until at times she was swimming like the okra she'd put up in a boiling tomato bath. With one of her prodi-gious bursts of energy she had tried to beat the heat, but now she suc-cumbed to it, flopped out on the gritty unbleached muslin sheet under the red glow of the sun through the tattered window shade. Too done in even to push the grimy T-shirt Rad had dropped on the bed away from her face and off onto the floor. "You don't understand," Rad said to her, "you don't understand what I'm going through now. You don't understand what's happening to me." "I understand," she told him, "I understand everything. Everything." She was her body. An incubator oven from which she could not escape. And he—she could no more tie him to her side than she could to the sty of the spotted sow back of the plowshed. "We can make it pay," he said to her. "We'll have everything we need. Not so much as some folks maybe, but enough. Inside plumbing. Washing machine. Paint on the house. Georgia Tech for Charles. Old Abe Baldwin for Wyatt, or Berry. We'll have the things we want." "Sure enough?" she said. "Sure enough?" While he ran off to Reeve . . .

She lay, a mass of molten jelly floating through the dusk. Lay on her back supporting her abdomen from beneath with her hands. On her side with knees updrawn. On all fours, bottom up, elbows and knees undertucked. On her back again with a pillow propping her calves. Recalling how she used to climb out on the spars of a Liberty ship with her welding torch, high up over the ways, as freewheeling as the gulls skimming over the harbor. And lounging with the other girls on deck over lunch pails, squealing like the gulls over some piece of foolishness. She'd brought home steaks and chops for the kids, even with meat rationing. Bought shoes for them. No child of mine is going to school barefoot. Not as long as I'm alive.

Not as long as I'm alive . . .

Anxiety had been in her from the day she was born. One of a twin, her weaker brother being given what nourishment there was until he died anyhow in the middle of their second year after the next baby arrived. She was the oldest of ten children in a house where there was never enough to go around. And no sooner was one child out of the cradle than her mother swelled up with another as if it were a chronic disease. So before she was five, Lulabelle remembered, she cried out, "Oh no, not again!" and was licked for it. Before she was Ruby's age she was rocking babies and wringing their diapers out. And after her father was put off the land he sharecropped, it was worse. They moved into Bay City then, in a little old room with never enough wood for the stove winters and no furniture, just a bed and pallets they made up on the floor, never enough covers to go over them. That was when she stopped blaming her mother for the babies that kept coming and started blaming her father. How could he do that to her in the night and look her in the face next day? How could he bring so much misery on them all and never turn a hair?

Cardboard in her shoes. Newspapers buttoned up inside her blouse. Scavenging through ashcans for clinkers. In her raggedy red sweater, wiping her nose with her sleeve, shuffling up the windy block-long line with her father to city hall to beg a sack of meal. Those were the bad years, the depression years when every week she would see down their row of houses someone or other, old folks or babies, being carried out, dead of pneumonia or heart failure, anything but starvation. When every month someone she knew would disappear from their row: soon as a boy was old enough there was nothing for him to do but leave home, hop the first freight . . . So when the job in the shirt factory opened up, she grabbed it. Quit fifth grade. And her dreams of herself, grown up, a secretary behind a desk, a schoolteacher, Miss Louisa-Belle Wyatt in white-tie blouse and black crepe skirt. And other dreams too: a tap dancer though she'd never owned a pair of taps. Oh she'd loved to dance. Or a florist: her mother always had camellias in the windows and she was always taking cuttings from her mother's plants and potting them for neighbors. She was sure for a time she'd be a florist. She'd help her family. She'd save them all. She made three dollars a week in the shirt factory. The factory swallowed her up and spit her out, swallowed her up and spit her out, in season and out of season for four years running. And it was never enough. Never. Six of the ten children her mother bore didn't survive their childhood.

When you grow up in a house of hunger you never get over it. No matter how much you may store up later, the fear stays in you like a rat in the grain bin. Never enough. And here she was now like her own mother, Rad's mother, bringing another mouth into the world. Douglas McDowell buried three wives, used them up, shucked them off. And forgot them all. And her father—her brother Bose had told her about it at the family spread she'd thrown last Sunday and she was still all afire over it—her father was living in some room in Bay City with some young girl, boozing it up.

A woman is an incubating oven. "You'll be all right," Rad promised. "I'll take you in to Bay City Hospital and if you start hemorrhaging they'll have everything there. You'll be all right." "Sure enough?" she said to him. "Sure enough?" While he ran off . . .

She must have dozed off in the dusk, no more than a few minutes though it seemed hours, because when she woke with her face pressed up against the rank male scent of Rad's T-shirt, it was no darker in the room than it was before. A shriek or the echo of one, like tearing cloth, was throbbing through her head. It split the air again, tearing from a high note of pure terror or pain down to fragmented bits. She jumped blindly up on her feet, running, and shrieked back into the shocked suspension of sound, into the reiterated shriek. "I'm coming, I'm coming, Mamma's coming!"

The broken slat had at last given way, and Ruby was trapped like a small animal in the splintered board, too terrified by the gush of blood on her leg to extricate herself. Lulabelle tried to ease her out without injuring the tender-skinned inner thigh any further. "Look honey I have to," she shouted at her, "I just have to," and kneeling twisted and jiggled at the leg while Ruby screamed to high heaven. She freed the leg at last, blood streaming over hands. "Nothing's broken, it's not broken." With shaking fingers she pulled a stiletto of wood out of the bleeding thigh, then little pins and prickles of slivers. And with the incessant screams ringing in her ears she ran for a basin of water. Washed down the skin, "See it's nothing, just a big old scratch. Open up your eyes! Look at it!" But the blood kept welling up as if it would never stop and Ruby kept screaming and she kept washing till the water was red.

Wyatt materialized out of nowhere with Timmy behind him. Running up terrified, screaming, the bruise on his cheek jumping. "Mamma! Mamma, you ain't—" As if the baby were about to be born out of her.

"Where's Charles?"

"Nowhere. I done looked and looked."

"You mean you come back here without him? You go right back out there," she pointed with shaking arm, "and don't you dass show your face again till you get him. And don't forget to look," she shouted after him with a sudden premonitory clutch of her heart, a new terror, "all along the ditching. Timmy," she ordered, "you stay here with Ruby."

She bandaged Ruby's leg with clean strips of gauze from an old curtain, took the claw hammer down from the bracket and a jar of nails from the shelf and set them on the edge of the porch. "Now don't you either one of you dass to move till I get back," she admonished the two young ones, and leaving them sucking on sticks of sugar cane she wiped off her hands on her pants and started out for the track to fetch Rad home. He was going to patch that step tonight if he had to do it in the pitch-dark.

She hoped to find Charles somewhere along the way. She kept hollering his name till her throat felt as scratched as Ruby's leg. But long before she reached Reeve's clearing she subsided. In the summer evening, still strong with light, the cedars that surrounded Reeve's house were stark black, devoid of brightness. Through the fretted branches the windows twinkled with the amber beam of a kerosene lamp, as cosy and beckoning as firelight in winter. A guitar twanged, weaving an insidious blue note over and under mingled male voices. *Duh* duh *duh* duh *duh*duhduh. Coaxing, caressing, a husky song bawled out:

> "Baby bay-ayby beh-bee
> What d' matter with you
> Baby bay-ay-by behbee . . ."

Lulabelle slowed down by the two cars parked in the clearing as laughter pealed from the house. "Play it! Sing it! Pick that box!"

Hesitantly she started up the path through the cedars, hitching at her shorts which slid, unbuttoned, sloppily about her waist. Her shirt, she noticed suddenly, was blood-smeared all over the front.

> "Oh my name is James, the last one never been told
> My name is James, the last one never been told
> I been loving pret-ty wim-men
> Since I was twel years old
> I been loving pret-ty wim-men
> Since I was twel years old . . .
>
> "Yes yes yes my love
> Yes yes yes yes yes . . ."

It called to her out of the rows of dusty shacks where she'd been a child, plucked at her out of the back alleys on those lonesome nights when she'd driven her truck back from the swing shift in the shipyard. Play it! Fall on in and join the fun! Amuse yourself. All those lures and enticements against which she must seal her ears. She stopped in the path now, transfixed by an incomprehensible longing. Up by the porch a dog barked and she slipped quickly back out of sight behind a tree. So Rad had to see Reeve, talk with him. All so high-and-mighty great and important. "Lu, I got to go over there." Sure he had to go. Because he couldn't stay away.

> "Oh I left my mamma standin' in d' back do' cryin'
> I say I left my mamma standin' in d' back do' cryin' . . ."

She had to go up to that house now in front of all those colored men and get him out of there. Someone spoke from the doorway quieting the dog. She dodged back farther among the trees. There was a rip in the armhole of her shirt and she pinched it together by holding her arm against her side. Trying to gather the courage to call out loud enough over their babble to bring Rad running.

> *"She says, You got a home dad-dee*
> *So long as I got mine*
> *Says you got a home dad-dee*
> *So long as I got mine . . .*

> *"Yes yes yes my love*
> *Yes yes yes yes yes . . ."*

"Ra-ad?"

It issued out of her throat in a gasp almost too faint for her to hear. She knew of men like that. Hill Caslon. Chalmer Coombs. Leaving their families in the background, treating their wives as merely a necessary adjunct while they conducted their lives, the life that was important to them, their *real* life, among their male companions, sporting and drinking and carrying on. Their wives had nothing to say about it, not what they worked at nor where they went. Shuddup. You keep outa this.

"Ra-ad!"

It was no more than a squeak, drowned under a jangle of chords.

She lingered so long trying to force herself forward that when a third car parked in the clearing she was still behind her tree, frozen against its trunk. The driver did not immediately leave the car, and Lulabelle began to retreat obliquely back toward the track, scratching her legs in the juniper bushes. A light inside the car switched on and she flattened herself against a tree again, shrinking into the shadow.

The driver was a female, colored, young—Lulabelle had a clear view of her flipping open the flap of her handbag, studying herself in the inside mirror, combing up her hair till every curl stood in place. She touched her lips with lipstick, studied herself this way and that in the mirror, rubbed a powder puff over her cheeks. Snapped her compact closed, dropped it into her handbag, knocked a cigarette out of a pack, stuck it in her mouth, struck a match from her thumbnail to it, the flame spurting. She slid from under the wheel and opening the door dipped a long shapely leg out, then emerged in toto. Brushing down her flowered skirt. Fluffing up the ruffle of her white blouse, the ruffle starched crisp, fluted, whitest of white, framing the dark column of her neck as the aureole of her hair framed her head. She reached back into the car for what looked to Lulabelle like a little black suitcase. But more than lipstick, dress, cigarette, suitcase, it was the way she walked that struck through Lulabelle like a sledgehammer, with a blow that exploded in fractured phantasms as contorted as the branches through which she peeped. The walk of a woman full of the pride of life, a woman who owes nothing to anyone but herself, a woman who

looks the world in the eyes and laughs it in the face and tells it: go roll
your hoop . . .

"Say, sugar."

"Hey, Viv."

"Fall in, girl, the joint is jumpin'."

> *"Oh I loved a lot of women*
> *In this lo-one-some town*
> *I loved a lot of women in this lo-one-some ta-own*
> *Wouldn't none take any money*
> *Wouldn't none turn no man da-own*

"*Yes yes yes my love . . .*"

Lulabelle crept away. Dragged back down the track. A mess. A mess.
How'll I ever get out of this mess I'm in?

When still another car entered the track she stopped and looked back
toward the headlights, peering through the blue gloom. Who else now?
How many more? The car slowed almost to a stop at the clearing but
didn't turn in. The headlights were bearing blindingly down on her and,
frightened, she darted across the track, trying too late to hide herself.

"Lu? Lulabelle? It's me." Henry Warren's tan convertible drew up
alongside her and Henry big, breezy, and comfortable in open-collared
sports shirt and slacks held open the door. "Get in."

She hung back in the scrub against which she was pinned by the car.
As many steps as she'd taken from Reeve's clearing it was only a few
yards behind her. Music still tinkled in her ears. Ahead of her the walk
home stretched interminably.

"Come on in. I'll ride you home."

"You better go long."

Henry stepped out of the car and, placing his arm around her with a
strong yet gentle lift, steered her inside.

"Why, you shakin' like a leaf."

He slid under the wheel but before starting the car looked back over
his shoulder to the light twinkling through the cedar grove. Then he
looked about at Lulabelle with a concern and consternation which, accepting with all the craving of her heart, she refused to respond to. She
turned her head away to conceal from him the uncontrollable writhing
of her mouth.

He shifted and they rode on in silence, not needing to say anything
of what communicated itself so eloquently between them. Henry didn't
speak until he had passsd through the opening between the up-and-
down bobwire fence.

"Parties every night, huh?"

From Henry's tone she couldn't tell whether he was being sympathetic or by his sympathy trying to incite her. She pressed her lips together, gritted her teeth, drew in her shoulders. *He's my own true husband! He's not that kind. He wouldn't. But he'd walked in foreign cities. He'd gone with foreign women . . .*

"It's a shame!" Henry burst out. "A shame and a scandal." He was in dead earnest. "I declare the war must have done something to that boy's head. Making a regular fool of himself over them damn spooks. When I was working in the tropics we used to see things like that. A man'd quit his job and his home, shed all his ties and his loyalties to move into shantytown with some wench and her folks. Gone native we called it."

"If you've come here," Lulabelle said coldly, "to talk to him again about this here piece of land, you might's well turn around right now and go back out."

"That," Henry said. "I'm not worried about that. It's not me he's bucking, Lulabelle. It's not Sunset. It's the times. You know that."

She knew it.

"Now I've always liked Rad. I've always wanted to do my best for him. But no matter how high I climb, he's always wanted to reserve the privilege unto himself of thumbing his nose at me. He'll sacrifice anything for that, and that's the God's truth. And you know it."

She knew that too.

"Well, we'll see who has the last laugh. He can't win. It's not in the cards. Only thing I can't understand is why *he* don't understand."

"Stop behind the truck there," she said. "You can let me off."

"Just a minute—" He bumped to a halt behind the truck, a decrepit phantom in the glare of the headlights. "It's not Rad I come here about, Lu. It's you. I'm glad I found you alone. I want to talk to you about you . . . how old you, honey?"

She bit her underlip, wanting to cry it out to him, to anyone that would listen, yet holding back as if to divulge the information to him, any information, would constitute a betrayal of herself, of her pride and of her dignity and of the integrity of her marriage. The door handle as she pressed down on it was slippery in her palm—like, she thought wildly, when you make love and can't get a grip on it—and for some reason the door wouldn't dislodge.

"Twenty-six," she said. "Seven come December."

"You had Charles before you were sixteen. And three more since, with the war between. And now. Before you forty—"

"Yeah." Begrudgingly. "Seems like."

"Hmm. There you are. Them that wants can't," he repeated the old saw with the grimness of a groan, "and them that don't do. Now wait a minute." He put his hand over hers on the handle, staying her. "I haven't told you yet. This important to me. To you too. Just hear me out. Hear me."

What followed she couldn't quite make head or tail of for several minutes. At the sound of the car Ruby and Timmy had come pelting from the darkness of the porch to the safety of company, and now were climbing all over the car so that throughout Henry's plea she was scolding them. "Git down, git off there . . ."

His wife, Henry said, had been in Atlanta with their boy all last month and now was back with him. "We haven't had a diagnosis yet or any course of treatment recommended, we're waiting on that, but from all I can make out there's not much we can hope on."

This she understood. This she could nod understandingly to, understanding what difficulty every word of this disburdening must cost him. A child that's sickly, a child that's afflicted, marked or crippled, touched.

"And the damnedest thing is, the thing that triggered this—it was the blast Rad set off with that nigger-boy."

This she understood too. The blast had frightened her too, frightened her so that now, listening to Henry, she laid her hand over the drum-tight vellum of her abdomen. She was startled by a distinct and formidable thump from within, like a knock at the door. "Oh-h-hhh . . ."

"One thing, you got healthy younguns," Henry said as Ruby dangled over the windshield, hurt leg or no. "If they wasn't so neglected. Of course you do your best for them. But realistically, what's your best . . ."

It was here she lost Henry entirely. He had grasped her free hand in his earnestness and she was returning his pressure as if it were she who must sustain him. But what he was hinting at? That she should bear a child for them by him? That he was seeking the parentage of the child that even now was thumping so peremptorily to be admitted into this world?

"There are some children," Henry said, "that are born blessed just as others are born cursed. There's a blessing on them. You can see it on them. They have all the attributes: the disposition, the energy, the alertness. Smart as a whip. And independent as a hog on ice. Staying power. Everything. Why they could grow up and discover something that would change the course of history. It's in them. If there's only someone there to give them what they need. And the lucky ones, Lu, the lucky ones have an instinct for what they need. They lookin' for it. They fall into it—"

She finally understood that it was Charles he was talking about. Who else but Charles?

"I picked him up crying in the road and I took him home with me. He didn't want to come but I made him. Reckon he was headed for Mexico or some such . . . He was all broke up. Just went to pieces."

"Charles is at your house?"

"Mm-hm. I told him I'd come talk to you all and he even went frantic over that. Nothing nothing nothing could ever ever ever . . . Lu, I saw that whack on his back. It was still red."

He was asking to keep Charles. To provide him with clothing, books, schooling, camps, travel, opportunities to become whatever he had it in him to become. He was asking to take her firstborn and give him his name, make him his own.

"He can go to Annapolis, West Point. I know Dan Garner, he'll be senator one of these days, he'll see my boy gets an appointment. Or MIT, Cal Tech, anywhere. Why I talked to his teacher just a while back—"

What right did he have to talk to Charles' teacher!

"And she told me that in the last twenty years she's had four–five like him. Start off like a house afire. But without direction they never come to anything. One of them's an electrician's apprentice over to Bay City now. But with backing and encouragement all the way up—"

Lulabelle disengaged her hand from his clasp and lifted both her hands, palms inward, high in the air above her. "My mother had ten fingers and ten children. And every time she lost a one of them, it was like the first time. She died all over again."

"I'm not talking about losing, Lulabelle. I'm talking about *saving* . . . Where's Rad now? Where's he at at a time like this? You yourself must realize . . . Where's his responsibility?"

"Some men," she said deliberately, vindictively, violating a sacred bond, desecrating herself as much as Rad, revealing him naked before the eyes of his enemy, besmirching and befouling what was theirs, but unable out of the harshness of her heart and the nimbleness of her tongue to stop herself, "are like dogs. They got no responsibility. They just put 'em there."

With the handle depressed, she kicked open the sticking door. "You send Charles home right on!"

"He's in bed now, asleep."

"First thing tomorrow."

"Lu, if it'd make any difference to you, I'd like to help you out—"

"Git out! Outa here!"

"Lu, you out of temper now. You think about it. Think—"

"Out!"

Instead of remaining in the car as good sense would have dictated and requesting him to drive her now, immediately, to Bay City to the hospital, she sent him off. Desperately telling herself: it's not time, it's not time yet, it's another week off. And stumbling back toward the house, weeping with rage: What kind of people are we! You have a child you can't build up into anything, and you've no right to him. You have a piece of land you can't make the most of, and you've no right to it. You have a family Scripture up on the shelf and a lady editor from the newspaper comes down to look at it and offers you fifty dollars, you have no right to that either. Because it'll just fall apart there anyhow.

She reached the broken slat of the step and snatched the claw hammer up from the porch side. With great wrenches of the hammer she began tearing the slat up from the joints.

"Mamma," the children clamored at her as she wrenched at the yielding, cracking wood. "Mamma, stop that!"

Timmy who was afraid of the dark ran off yelling for Wyatt and brought him home from somewhere back of the plowshed.

"Mamma," Wyatt cried, "you'll hurt yourself. Mamma don't, don't! Give me the hammer!"

"Git away! All of you! Off my neck!" The rusty nails splitting from the wood jerked up with an ominous whine. "Go on, go on to bed!" She shook the hammer at the children. "Go on. Wash up. To bed. Do I have to stand over you!"

Fumbling through the jumble of implements in the plowshed she found the clean slat of wood that Rad had sawn up weeks ago for the repair job he never got to. In the thick hot moon-silvered night she laid the slat across the riser and began hammering it down. Down on the nailhead. Smash. Smash. Rad Rad Rad Rad Rad.

Afterward, squatting on the commode in her room she tentatively inserted a square of toilet paper between her bulging thighs. Drawing it out, she leaned toward the oil lamp and inspected it. A penny-sized tinge of rust, mucus-rimmed. The sign of blood. But it wasn't time! The time so long impending couldn't be here. As she was about to raise herself up, she fell back gripped with surprise and horror. A bursting fountaining gush spurting downward. Water bag . . .

In a pellucid vacuity, without pain but on waves of increasing urgency, she dumped half the bucket of well water Wyatt had brought in into the basin on her washstand, peeled off her clothes and scrubbed herself down as if she had to rid herself of something filthy that clung and clung. She washed her hair from the pitcher, scraping at her scalp as if to tear it from the bone, rubbed her hair dry with the towel hard enough to tear it from the roots. Hurrying in a frenzy of impatience she dressed in the clean outfit she'd had ready since the first of the month. Tying the drawstring of her skirt in a knot and retying it. Buttoning her pink blouse up the wrong buttonholes and rebuttoning. Then shaking her hair out over her face she combed it down; bounced it back over her shoulders and bound it tight with a red ribbon, from which it fluffed out soft brown and full over the nape of her neck. Searching through her white leatherette handbag she fished out lipstick and leaning toward the brown-splotched mirror on her wall, cheeks high-colored, eyes sparkling, she drew over her mouth a coat of flaunting scarlet.

In the parlor she whispered at the head of the bedstead, "Wyatt?" The children had covered themselves against her hammering with the sheet over their heads and fallen asleep that way. "Wyatt?" she tugged at the sheet.

"Ma'am?"

"I got to go now, honey. You take care."

"Huh?"

"You ain't scairt or nothin', is you?"

"N-n-no." Sitting up. "Where's daddy?"

"He'll be here. He'll be here when he gets back."

Seated under the steering wheel of the truck cab, she pumped her foot on the starter. The motor rasped over slowly, dryly, the gas tank low or the water tank. She pumped and choked it and pumped again till the motor coughed, spluttered, caught. She loosed the brake and got it rolling on the incline. "I'll take you to Bay City Hospital," he had said, not once but many times. "There's nothing for you to be 'fraid of." She mashed down hard on the gas, picking up momentum. Over all the brave promises, all the unfulfillable vows, all the inability of a man to live up to the obligations of his manhood.

This baby was going to be born in Bay City Hospital and that's where she was headed for. Still in her state of pellucid emptiness as if suspended in space, without pain or the first spasm of labor but with the inexorable urgency on her, she forced the truck, gasping, lurching, faltering, into the parallel ruts of the track.

6

Reeve brought back from St. George a manual on the tractor model he had inspected that afternoon, loaned him by the family who were selling out their father's place. And an excitement he could hardly restrain. He was not one to fancy every passing attraction. When he saw what he wanted, that was it. It required a major feat of diplomacy to persuade the family to part with the manual, he practically had to promise them the tractor was as good as sold already to the class. Now all he had to do was sell it.

He had the manual out on the table, pointing out its diagrams and illustrations to some of the boys who had come early, when Rad knocked his knock, two taps and three, on the porch post. High Power lifted a sardonic brow and a sharp shoulder in the direction of the door. Sanderlee who was draped over the divan jangled a few chords on the guitar that lay like a woman he was making love to athwart his crotch. The Baron leafing through the manual growled out gruffly a bearlike grunt.

"Who dat?"

"Dat me."

The exchange a form of humorous password they all used, now borrowed by Rad.

There's your cracker.

Reeve unhooked the screen and hauled Rad in to the manual. "Wait till you see this!" Rad's presence in his house tonight served no purpose insofar as he was concerned. He had invited Rad on the tide of an impulse, in response to a sincerity he couldn't doubt. As a gesture of reassurance—my place is always open to you—which contained its own built-in barb. Now their moment in the field was gone and Rad was here and why'd he come.

And he was glad to have him. If Rad hadn't come he'd have been disappointed, would have felt badly let down. He flicked through the pages of machine parts. "Fella let me take it for a few days to make up our minds on. See here, here it is all together, this model. Medium heavy outfit. Hardly a scratch on it." He looked to Rad not for approval —the white man's nod, then do as you please—but for an honest opinion, for moral support, for backing of sufficient weight to help influence the others. He also looked on Rad with the fond protectiveness one might have for an infant loose among a den of wolves.

"And it's got everything. Bulldozer, cultivators, grain drill, every kind of attachment you can name and some you can't. It can till, plant, weed, harvest, spread fertilizer, spray and dust, pick corn, bale hay, pull up stumps and haul logs. You could even hook it up to a milker in a pinch and milk your cows, if you had a milker."

"Man, you gone." High Power leaned languidly up on his elbow and winked at Rad. "High as a kite, mellow as a cello and tall as a Georgia pine. That a heap you talkin' 'bout, gate, or a hunka ass?"

"All in top condition. Somebody really sold the old man—now he's dead and the family's scattin' . . . Well that's another story. With what we got and our work animals and a thing like this, why we can double our tillable land inside a year. Look at this."

Reeve turned through half a dozen illustrations for Rad and the Baron. "There's a tiller rake you hang onto the back of the cultivator that grades, levels, and scarifies, all to once. A flail mower. And a rotary cutter that'll clear the thickest growth, with a wheel gauge that adjusts to height."

Sanderlee strummed out a mocking blues, bawling the refrain, a bleat of pure agony over a series of notes that shook like rice in a can.

High Power drew a deck of cards from his pocket, zipped his thumbnail down the edge and flexing his fingers with a gambler's dexterity went through the motions of shuffling.

The Baron—called the Baron because of a Prussian officer act he liked to pull—screwed an imaginary monocle into his eyesocket and scrutinized the specifications which he couldn't interpret with haughty condescension.

"All right, you convinced us. What's the catch?"

"Sounds almost too good," Rad ventured his opinion at last, slowly, with a glow of enthusiasm and the natural caution that tempers such enthusiasm, "to be true?"

"It's true enough," Reeve glanced back at Rad, grateful at least for the enthusiasm. "The minute I laid eyes on it, I knew. This is it. I'm telling you we'll never have another chance—"

"What's the catch?" Sanderlee strummed. "How much?"

"It's wonderful," Reeve raved on. "It's marvelous. It's just what the doctor ordered."

"But?"

"We can't have it. Must have come to about eight–ten thousand dollars new. And we can get it for about twenty-five hundred."

The guitar solo wound up abruptly in a clang of dissonance.

High Power threw his deck on the table, disgusted, tossing in the towel.

The Baron clapped his hand over his imaginary monocle.

"We started out in class talking about a little old secondhand rig we could pick up for five hundred dollars if we could hit the right one. And now you talkin' up—"

"Couldn't we just buy this tractor by itself and add on implements later?"

Reeve shook his head. It was all of one piece in his mind and it was this or nothing at all. "I talked to them about that. They won't break it up and they'd be fools to. And I talked to Thurlow about it on my way home. He'll be here in just a little while. This meeting can come to order then."

With that he left them to the manual and themselves, awaiting Thurlow's arrival. Stopping only to pick up his tool kit from beside the couch, he went out back through the kitchen shed to work outside on his annex. Rad followed him from the table a few steps into the kitchen wanting, Reeve sensed, to talk to him privately, pursue the subject further. Without turning his head he let the screendoor slam behind him on Rad, taking surreptitious satisfaction in the act of rejection and ashamed of it. He liked Rad as much as he did anyone in that room and more than some, and he hated these feelings that swarmed up in himself unsolicited, like those horrid anticipations last spring of his mother's death. He couldn't accept such feelings as part of himself. They were imposed on him from the outside, from some external source. Descending on him like a swarm of chiggers . . .

Under the framework of the room he was building against the side wall of the alcove, the objectionable feelings, Rad himself, the intrusion of experience upon what he hoped was his innate decency, were all soon forgotten. The skeleton of the structure was up, posts, crossbeams, uprights, the enclosure of windows, the rafters low-pitched from the house roof. A cage of timbers made up out of lumber he had culled from a building Marcus Hadley was dismantling and from sawmill rejects he had cut to size just this side of the splits and knotholes. From his keg of nails—even some of his nails were secondhand, gleaned from around the schoolhouse and the rust oiled off them—he took a handful, knocked a few straight with his hammer. In the last daylight, straddling a beam, he laid down his first floorboards.

Inside, among the company around the table Rad was thoroughly enjoying himself. He had wanted to speak to Reeve about the tractor and about the idea that had taken hold of him this afternoon out in the sweet potato patch and that now, with the manual open before him, was burgeoning into a necessity he couldn't miss. Something of what he had seen in Henry's equipment shed was condensed here in this single contraption, which could be his, his too. The jean-capped farmer on the glossy page under his hand, riding high with his hands on the wheel spokes, resembled himself. "Look at this, Charles?" He could understand how Reeve felt. When you see what you want, nothing else will measure up. Nothing less will do.

But he couldn't follow Reeve outside to his carpentry anymore than anyone else around the table could. They all knew what Reeve was building the room for. Or rather, for whom. And nobody could watch

him at it, nobody could mention it to him. Anything at all, a twitch of
the eyelid, Reeve would take for teasing and this was one thing he was
so touchy about . . . Exchanging wry grins, they listened till they heard
his tapping on the other side of the alcove wall. Then they looked toward the yellow pine dresser in the niche beyond the fireplace. It was
standing at an angle, half pulled out of place. The outline of the door
to be cut through was chalked up on the wall behind it.

"And with a bathroom yet," the Baron said.

"Who says?"

"You know that old house they tearing down on Fourth Street? I
saw him there one night looking at pipe."

"And he ain't asked her yet?"

"Nope. Because if he ask, she might turn him down. So long as he
ain't, he can keep on dreaming, can't he?"

"And she don't guess?"

"If she do, she don't let on."

Sanderlee struck up another one of his lo-O-one-some blues.

"Hmmm." They all shook their heads in comic despair over the pre-
posterousness of human folly. Rad nodded with them, keeping to the
background, holding his peace.

"Still"—High Power leaned back from his bench, pushing the overseas cap he habitually wore down over his brow and rasping his nails
up through the back of his finespun hair—"how do you know?"

He tilted his head all the way back till he was looking up into the
oblique eyes of the deerhead over the fireplace. "Reeve set out to cop
that veterans' hunting permit freeby, and he got it. He set out to blow
him some drainage through his fields, and he got that, didn't he, Rad?"

"Sure did."

"And to save this farm, and it was saved. Now"—Power reached for
the manual with a long claw and drew it out from under Rad's hand—
"he's hot on this tractor jag." He spun the manual away again with a
snap of his slender fingers. "Always biting off more than he can chew.
Some of these days he's gonna choke on it."

High Power scooped up his cards and dealt himself a hand. Sanderlee cried the blues. The Baron brought some bottles of ginger beer he
had cooling out in the icebox onto the table. A couple more fellows
arrived, one with a bottle of redeye from which they all, including Rad,
took a shot. Rad didn't know the man whose redeye he was drinking,
and High Power introduced them.

"John Newgate. And this"—Power leaned over and slapped Rad on
the knee, instilling in his voice that particular inflection Rad knew from
similar moments with Reeve, an emphasis that was code and password

—"this is one of the"—with a little rough break in his voice—"one of the swellest people I have ever known."

Rad thrust his hand out to John Newgate. "Put it there." They shook. He was all right. He was in there.

Rad saw no sign of the suspiciousness Reeve had reported to him at noon. Perhaps his consciousness now—knowing that they wanted no more to be idealized by him than to be degraded, knowing that he was no saint to them and they were no saints either—wrought a subtle change of attitudes, wiped out the walls of Jericho. The mood was right tonight. There was a rapport and an attunement, a camaraderie and a sense of fusion. The feeling. The music. The stories. He was one of them. They took him in. It was one of the good evenings. The best.

He was especially moved by High Power's display of fervor. Power was a hard thin rakish and reckless character, a little older than the rest of them though still youthful, who had left home at the age of thirteen and wandered all over the country, graduating high school, he said, in Des Moines, and working as a floorman, he said, in a casino on the coast. He had come back here and married the Baron's sister, a widow with three children who had her own farm, and with this as a base he had branched out in several directions. He farmed about twenty acres —he really did like to farm—but mainly he ran games in his kitchen, sold illegal liquor, and acted as a liaison in providing rendezvous for couples engaged in illicit love affairs. He also ran with white men, hunted and fished with them, acted as guide, cook, teller of tales, counselor and friend, scrounged up bottles for them and girls when that was required or any other form of entertainment. And despised them all.

The mood was right and the climate was right but the moment was not yet ripe, Rad decided, to broach his proposal concerning the purchase of the tractor, his willingness to align himself with them, to tie his fate in with theirs. He would have to wait for them to develop their plan with Professor Thurlow first and then, when the propitious opening occurred, make his declaration. Meanwhile he relaxed amidst the conviviality, biding his time. The wick licked under the glass chimney of the lamp in the center of the table, embracing them all in its golden ambience. Sanderlee's haunting heartbreaking plaint, with its burden of love and loss and longing, sang tingling through their veins. And High Power held forth.

He removed himself to the bench opposite Rad, scrunched pleasurably down on his spine, his collar slouched up about his neck as if perpetually a storm were blowing, agreeably, against his back. His knife-scarred nose tip crinkled. A slit in his cheek deepened to a dimple.

Deft-fingered he demonstrated the mechanic's grip with which he manipulated cards and which won him all too many a poker pot.

"My daddy was a gambler. When I was seven years old he taught me how to palm a card. Laying up on his deathbed he taught me that. When I was thirteen years old my mother one day called me in and told me she was going to marry again and asked me would I have this man for father. Well I'd worshiped my own father so and—well I didn't have anything against this man, I just couldn't see having anyone else around the house. And being the oldest of three children I thought I was head-man and kid-like I'd expected her to put all her dependence on me. It meant there was another boss.

"I was on my way to school that morning, walking along, swinging my bookstrap, down by the railroad track—there was still a one-a-day running out of here then. Must have been feeling, you know? It all hit me all of a sudden. Not just that, everything. A freight was pulling out of the yard, I had no idea where, but I threw my books down on the ground, right there where I stood, and hopped a boxcar as it was sliding past me."

He laughed with affection and indulgence, not untinged with amazement, for the kid he'd been.

"I knew already I couldn't take it down here. I'd seen enough to know I couldn't live here. So I did something about it. I ran away.

"Well I was a smart kid and good-looking, I came up against all kinds of propositions. By the time I was sixteen I was the most callous cat you ever saw."

Power's thick eyelashes blinked delightedly and a little incredulously.

"I'd graduated from high school, I'd studied hard, I liked it. Made top grades. Got a nice little diploma all tied up with a pretty ribbon and a shiny gold medal to go with it. Well, one graduate was sent down to a broker's office and another one down to a department store, jobs with some future to them. But you know what they offered me? Elevator operator. *Ell-evator.* You know what I told the man? Kiss my ass. Hell, they had men of forty working those cages who'd graduated high school just like I did. I couldn't accept that for myself. No to all that. N-n-no. I mean no!"

His eyes glowed about defiantly. His body, released like a guitar string twanged, flexed down its length. "No!" He sank back reflectively, with a shiver that traveled all the way down his spine.

"So I took a job in a joint. What I mean a j-j-joint. I thought nothing, absolutely nothing, when I saw a man drinking and having himself a time, of slipping a few knockout drops in his drink and rolling him.

Dragging him down to the creek, laying his head on a rock and his coat over his head and leaving him there.

"I'd do that like you'd drink a glass of water."

High Power was pleased with his punch line. He liked to shock everybody with how wicked he'd been. Oh he was so bad, he was such a scamp, he had a hundred stories to prove that there was no worse villain anywhere on the face of the earth than he was.

"Then why'd you come back here?" Rad asked him.

"Yah, that's the sixty-four dollar question!"

"Answer that one!"

"Ohhh," High Power sighed modestly, "I got me a nice little racket here . . ."

First time he ever ran into trouble with the cops was in Oklahoma. He sold some whiskey to an Indian.

"They arrested the chap and first thing they asked him of course was, where did you get it? So the cops came down to my place, I'd had this panel fitted on my wall"—he chuckled in the telling, tickled with the ingenuity of his cache—"and they searched and they searched and they couldn't find it. So the chief tells me, 'Look, we know you selling the stuff. We had a couple of complaints on you before. Best thing for you to do is leave this town.'

"Well that didn't bother me any psychologically, as so many other things have done. It was on an equal footing. It was up to him to nail me, and it was up to me to dodge . . . That was the first time I ever got run out of town. That was legitimate. Afterward I learned to make concessions. I paid off the cops."

One thing about High Power though, he always started out right. With the best of intentions. "When I went into the Army I had an idea, a naïve idea, that Jim Crow couldn't touch me there. I was going to be a Good Soldier. I was going to fight this war for democracy—dee-mock-racy—with the accent on the mock.

"First thing they did of course was ship me to Mississippi, Keesler Field, the Leavenworth of the Air Force. And first thing I pulled of course was garbage detail. But that was all right. I was beginning fresh in a new framework and the sky was the limit. I did everything they told me till everyone was saying, 'Leave it to Power. Let Power do it.'"

"Mmmm." They all nodded, recognizingly, including Rad.

"Once I told my lieutenant, Weygand, I'd get the payroll signed in twenty-four hours. I did it too. Woke men up out of their sleep at two in the morning. Looked for them through every hangout. Nabbed them in their girl-friends' parlors. And presented it with every name on it inside of twenty-four hours. Inside of three months I was promoted to corporal. At that time, a Negro corporal meant as much as to be a white lieutenant."

"Mmmm. You can say that again." They all nodded appreciatively, including Rad. Taking High Power's recital with a grain of salt, only half-believing it even if it were true but reveling in it.

"I had those men turned out so smart for parade and drill, tapping to the band . . . They won the colonel's commendation every time. I don't care what you say. I don't know how it is, but there's no one can be on the beam like a company of colored troops, band playing, brass shining, uniforms pressed, shoes polished, spic and span. Besides, I'd promised them all one way or another I'd cop them a blanket three-day pass.

"I was really in my element. Issuing orders. Managing. Directing. Working out ways of getting a thing done twice as fast. I really worked at it and I had them all working with me and liking it too. We took care of our equipment. We took pride in it. On maneuvers I'd match those men against anybody. A couple of Irish sergeants woke us up around three A.M. one night, even hotter than it is tonight. Ordered us out on a thirty-mile march through swampland. For a joke. When we found out what was behind it, we were burning. There were a number of little things like that to destroy morale."

"Mm-mmh!" They all nodded reminiscently, including Rad. "I remember one time . . ."

"But we weren't destroyed," High Power resumed, with an air of surprise, discovering it. "In those days we were a unit. When we got a pass out on the town we did it right. Marched down to a hall, pooled our dough, every one pitching in a deuce or a trey, about two hundred dollars altogether, and hired the place. Music, singer, drinks and all. Inside five minutes, all the chicks we needed were there, dancing. It was fine. When the time came to go back to camp, I knew where they all were, rounded them up, turned them out and lined them up at the Pro Station in the middle of downtown. There were no AWOLs while I was in charge. I had it all worked out. Except for one thing. Being in Mississippi. Dixie."

"Mm-hmmm," they all nodded anticipatingly, including Rad.

"Naturally from day to day it had been dawning on me what I should have realized from the start. Here I was knocking myself out to do a job. While everybody else was knocking themselves out to goof off. That was the Army. Do as little as you can get away with. Pass the buck. I'd had it all worked out. Now I was beginning to figure it out.

"Still, still, everything might have gone along smooth—"

"MmMMmm." Now—*now*— NOW it was coming.

"I was going with a girl who looked white. Nice little blonde with thick glasses, nice education, nice family. Local folks all knew who she was of course, but the town was flooded with outsiders. Whenever I went out with her, a couple of my men would fall in behind. A regular cordon would distribute around. Strategically. Sooner or later some white GI would accost us or a whole gang of them, and what they were doing foraging in the colored section that time of night, off bounds —well . . . But all of a sudden they'd find themselves blocked off from us, me and the girl had disappeared and they were surrounded by colored soldiers. I was doing my best to avoid a scrap.

"Then my lieutenant, Weygand, called me in. 'Corporal Power, I'm on your side, you realize that.' 'Sir?' As soon as they open up that way, I know good and well . . . But he'd always been an okay joe. We'd always acted with each other man to man.

" 'Your private affairs are your private affairs. But they're assuming a public character.' He offered me a cigarette across the desk. 'Smoke? Now we know your men would go to hell and back for you. You're perfectly within your rights. But this is a big field, everybody coming and going, new men arriving all the time. We've had to send extra MPs out on account of you, and they have orders to arrest the fellows breaking regulations. But you know some of these MPs. You know who they'll arrest first. There's bound to be a blowup. Where's it going to end up? You ever think of that?'

"I was so floored by it all, by the sheer unfairness . . . Here was this guy I'd taken for true-blue, that I'd been doing up proud all this time . . . And he was only a cog in their machine. And they'd put him up to making a cog out of me too. For no reason, no *reason*, I hadn't done anything. The long arm of the whole thing was reaching out to grab me by the throat. Damn! Here we both were with the desk between us, looking at the same motion picture. RACE RIOT!

"White men strewn around dead. Colored men strewn around dead. And men out of my company sentenced for years to the Federal pen. All starting over nothing. A nasty word hissed out of a dark street corner.

" 'Do me a favor,' he says to me. 'Stay away from her.'

"So I disobeyed orders. I went out with her again. And again. Oh I had so much trouble over that girl. And I didn't even care for her. I mean we hit it off all right, but there wasn't anything . . . Even her family got scared and wanted to prevent her going around with me, they'd sit up nights for her. But she was learning. Got so salty over it all she was game for anything.

"I got broke down to private. I went over the hill. And I was transferred out of there."

Ten out of his thirty months in the Army, High Power boasted, he'd spent in the guardhouse.

"That Weygand, he sent me just about as far north as I could go and still be in the United States. Dow Field. Bangor, Maine. Well, nobody knew me there, I was just one of thousands. When I was assigned to a detail, I'd whip it off if I felt like it. Or I'd squirm out of it on sick call. Afternoons I'd hole up in a little dive and drink and drink till I was juiced like a dog. Pretty soon I had a new bunch around me. We drank hard, we played hard, we gambled till seven in the morning, we took off without leave. Everybody was down on us. And especially the colored boys who were smart enough or ambitious enough to try to jockey themselves into a higher grade. They hated us.

"I had this colored sergeant over me, Merrick. Real solid type, like Reeve here. Do or die. And when Merrick looked over my record he tried to get me to apply for OCS . . . '142 AGCT. IQ as high as that and you acting like you do? Goddam it, Power, don't you want to be a credit to the race!' And all the time *he's* working his butt off for a colonel, one of these Texas colonels, you know the kind?"

"Mmmm—"

"So par-r-roud of his colored troops, out to make brigadier general on it. Well, I wasn't going to be a cog in their wheel. I wasn't going to put myself or anyone else to their use. I wasn't going to conform. Conform to what?"

Power rose from his bench to a staccato point.

"War! Mass murder! And now they're through with that one, they're building up to the same thing all over again. Well, next one, I'm going to be in B Company. B here when they go. And B here when they come back."

He dwindled down into the bench again, folded his hands austerely under his chin, pensively lowered his eyelids.

"Besides, what Sergeant Merrick didn't know and what I've never told anyone but my wife before is this. When I went into the Army from here, I was under a five-year suspended sentence in L.A. On a manslaughter rap. Fella conked me with a bottle and I went after him with a cue-stick. Turned out he had a weak heart."

. . . That was Power. So long as you played straight with him, he was straight with you. But the instant he had any cause to suspect from your behavior the slightest hint of a deal, look out. Hagan Power was holding the dice cup and he was shaking the dice.

A hundred stories. They all had one, including Rad. COs they'd had run-ins with. Fights they'd been in. Jobs they'd held. Girls they'd made.

The lamp twinkled. Smoke gathered in its chimney from their cigarettes and mounted ceilingward, thickening. Sanderlee shouted the blues. Now and then the dog outside would bark up and somebody would look out there. Nothing. No one. Must be a rabbit. At last the Professor's sedan drew into the clearing. Only it wasn't the Professor coming up the path.

"Vivian!"

The Baron took the portable typewriter she was carrying and set it up on the table. Power took her hand and twirled her till her skirts flew.

"Isn't she lovely? Isn't she charming? Look at her. She's a—w-w-woman." He shaped it out with his mouth as if it were the most beautiful word ever pronounced by man. His fingers traced it out in the air as if it were something too exquisite for articulation.

"You'd say that," Vivian said dryly, "if I was a bowlegged cow. Look at her. She's a woo-ooman."

Reeve with hammer and nails in hand appeared through the kitchenshed and stared about the room. Rad was leaning on his elbows over the table, conversing, happy and content, hitting it off with everybody. For some reason this affected Reeve unpleasantly, sending a faint twinge of chagrin—or could it be jealousy?—stinging ignobly through him. And Vivian, the very timbre of whose voice sent hammer-blows thudding through his heart—Vivian, whom he hadn't expected to see, the very sight of whom sent waves of warmth coursing through him—was the last person on earth he wanted here at this time. She had no business riding around the countryside nights after the warning the sheriff had given her grandfather. She had no business coming to his house like this, it would start all the tongues wagging, all the eyes gleaming, all the little clucks and sighs and surmises popping after her and him both. She had no business sitting here among all these men, jiving with them.

Reeve glowered about like an enraged husband who has arrived home after hard toil and tribulation to find a scene of riotous carousal in full swing.

"What are you doing here?" he demanded of Vivian rudely. "Where's the Professor?"

"Grampa's old and Grampa's tired. He filled me in on what you're up to. I'm taking his place. Aren't you glad?"

Reeve threw his hammer with a clatter up on the mantel. The others led on by High Power exchanged significant glances, rocking with unholy joy over all the nuances of the situation.

"These two people," High Power confided to Rad in a loud whisper, "really love each other. Only they're too proud to admit it."

Sanderlee stroked the belly of his guitar, his ear bent lovingly to the instrument.

> *"I got a coolbrown angel*
> *And I love the way she spr-reads her wi-ings—"*

But at a glare from Reeve, he subsided. Vivian drew forward the tractor manual on the table. Not the way Reeve had planned to show it to her. Leaning over her shoulder to turn the pages. Not that at all. He stood before the fireplace arm up on the mantel, hand helplessly dangling.

"So this is it."

Prettily, her throat arching out of the deep-circled white ruffled collar of her blouse, she riffled through the ungainly silhouettes of machinery.

"The American Dream. The Wonderful Postwar World."

Pressing at the spring lock of her typewriter she opened it and began pulling pamphlets out of the pocket inside the lid. "I understand we're to hold a short business meeting."

With a corrugated ripple of sound she rolled paper into her typewriter: every click, every gesture of hers and every word taking her farther away from Reeve, recessively away to the point of unattainability where she had been at the outset, months ago, as if nothing had happened since between them. From over her adjustment of the paper, she smiled piquantly up into his angry eyes.

"Shall we begin?"

7

It was obvious according to Vivian that they weren't going to get to first base with their tractor unless they drafted a concrete plan of action in sufficient detail to be presented for discussion and development to the class on Monday. "And that's our job here tonight. Not *if* you're going to buy it. But *how*."

"But we haven't decided—"

"You jumpin' the gun—"

"That's right," High Power said. "Do it, baby. Put it down."

Reeve sullenly sulking by the fireplace said nothing. They were all sparked up by her presence, playing up to her sex with a mock-courtship which she played back to, glorying in it. There was an easy quick recognizance between her and High Power that playfully with the duality of a trill of notes, treble and bass, question and answer, male and female, played back and forth, creating its own intimate and intimating sexual aura. Even Rad sitting next to her on the bench was keyed up; his eyes with the tiny reflection of lamp flame in their blueness passing her a look of amused appraisal. All too consciously Rad moved his elbow away from her proximity.

"All right, we'll rough it out now," she said, accompanying herself on the typewriter, tapping out a title, "and I'll shape it up for you over the weekend. As I see it, stop me if I'm wrong, this project falls into three parts. First, *Organization*. You have to form yourselves into an association, or cooperative, or whatever—"

"Yeah, yeah, we already know all that."

Rosy-nailed, she fanned out the pamphlets she had brought. "This is some new material Grampa just got in from Washington. Various types of charters and so forth. I can send for more. What your class will have to do is appoint a standing committee to draw up a constitution and by-laws, outlining your purpose, your rules and regulations, your meeting and voting procedures. And a legal contract with each other— Grampa will advise you on that—specifying your shares of ownership, your fees, your allowance for maintenance, depreciation and bad accounts, and your distribution of profits if any at the end of the year. Of course what you could do with the profits is use them to buy more equipment—"

"Now whoa, wait up a minute—"

They each, including Rad, took a pamphlet and examined it cover to cover. Reeve remained aloof, churning with that anomalous agitation, jealousy, or chagrin. She had taken it all over, his idea, and assimilated it, made it hers. And they had taken her over. And Rad who was always with him, his friend, was with them now. Leaving him isolated. He leaned on the mantel, arms folded over his chest, impelled, itching to throw them all out the door. The hell with it.

"I can read this thing," John Newgate complained, "but I can't understand a word it says."

"I can," the Baron said. Screwing his imaginary monocle in, he held the minuscule print of a model format off from himself by the length of his stout brown arm. "Colfax County Cooperative and Hard Larceny Association, Inc. President, Hagan Power—most popular hipster and biggest slickster in the State of Georgia. Vice-president, Harold Sanderlee—farmer by virtue of his old lady's poultry yard, mechanic by trade and king of G-string by acclaim. Secretary, Miss Vivian Thurlow—" He bowed meticulously in her direction, clicking his heels. "Need I say more? Treasurer—ahhh, there's the rub. What happen to the treasurer? Where's the money?"

"Flew d' coop!"

"D' ducks got it!"

"Now if you jokers would just stop jiving . . ."

While they entered into a serious discussion of organization, what kind of committee the class might best set up and who might function best on it, Reeve flung off in disgust to the alcove. Listening to their chatter, he wrestled out of his soiled T-shirt and pulled a clean one out of the drawer of the yellow pine dresser. On the wall back of the dresser the chalk marks he'd measured out tracked upward, plotting the future door to the room he was constructing. The house itself he regarded as belonging in part to his family, to be kept available for their use from time to time; but behind those chalk marks, through that door, the room was to be his own, his and Vivian's. Plasterboard to be painted the same color as she'd had in that apartment of hers in the city. With her pictures on the wall, her books in the bookcase, a place for her desk and her record player. All of hers that would be his too. Theirs. He'd open up back of the chimney for a fireplace, and on winter nights when they were in bed together the flamelight would leap on the walls. He'd have three double-hung windows in a row facing toward the riverside, and when they awoke summer mornings they'd catch the river breeze . . .

"Ain't he a pretty nigger?"

The teasing taunting lilt of her voice caught him like a shot in the spinal column.

"I'm going to enter him in the Beautiful Torso Contest."

He pulled the clean shirt on over his head, wrinkled it down over his rib cage and letting it hang loose on his hip strode back to the table. Shoved High Power aside on the bench and stepped over with a giant step into his place. Lunging about on the bench, he stared relentlessly into her teasing face. He was aware of the breath hissing out of his flared nostrils, his shoulders heaving, the brown of his skin showing through the white texture of his shirt. She turned her head, evading him. And sidewise arched her brow at Rad as if she expected *him* to be shocked by her brashness.

"Look at them," Sanderlee strummed. "Him with those blueblue eyes. And her with those whitewhite teeth. Lord Lord Lord"—he squeezed his eyes up in an apogee of unbearable anguish—"tell me: What is it all about?"

"Look at him." Vivian wrinkled her nose at Reeve. "All moody and broody. Don't be such a purist," she scolded at him. "You're a Puritan Negro. A contradiction in terms."

"Say that again." High Power leaned over the table, urging her. "P-u-ritan." Under the line of his debonair mustache, his lips suggestively formed it. "P-u-rr-itan. I love to see you say that."

"You want me to be a dicty Negro?" she said to Reeve. Pompously she puffed her cheeks out, stodgily she strutted her shoulders. "Or Lady Julie-Ann Col-fax perhaps?" Sucking her cheeks in with an air of long-suffering nobility. Lifting her eyes languorously heavenward. And collapsed out of her pose, her fingers fanning over the bare collarbone above her ruffled collar. "You can't stand for me to be low-down groovy. Well tonight I'm-a s-so-o low-down groovy—"

"Can't you hear the tom-toms"—High Power helpfully heaped coals on the fire—"beating in her blood?"

She was asking for it. Reeve could only believe that she was asking for him to reach across the table and slug her across the cheek so hard that for days afterward her ear would be ringing. To break them all up with a sweep of his arms. Tear the roof down.

"And that brings us," she said with a grin pixieish enough to pickle vinegar, "to our second point. *Management*." As primly as a little girl about to render a piano piece before her mother's doting guests, she placed her fingers on the typewriter keys. "I think you all better bring in to class a pretty definite idea of how you going to manage this tractor?"

"Management," Reeve said, his voice booming out of his strained throat with a self-command that astonished him. "First off, you have to have housing for it." He reached over the table for one of her pamphlets and a pencil and began laying out a carpenter's sketch on the back. "That's easy enough. Newgate, you got a cousin works out to the saw-mill? He can drum up some scrap for us. And we better locate it centrally. How about your place, Sanderlee? Right by the highway where it'll be accessible from all directions. And for maintenance, that's your department too . . ."

Vivian began tapping as he talked, in concert with him.

"And a trained operator to go with it. Cooper down to the Corners would have most time for it, he's working that place with his older brothers and he's looking for something outside. And some sort of conveyance to carry it for any distance, that'll be a problem. And there'll be taxes, insurance . . . Way I see it, some of these small farmers here-bouts will want to rent it by the day and that'll bring in some extra income. Lowest rental around here for heavy equipment runs ten–twelve dollars an hour. We can halve that. Which means we'll have to have someone to keep accounts, with a head for bookkeeping. That could be you, Power, if you had the dependability for it—"

"What does a man," High Power inquired between Reeve's voice and Vivian's taptapping, "really want of a woman?"

"Beauty?" Newgate offered.

"Glamour?" the Baron seconded him.

"Sex?" High Power speculated in his turn. "Nah." He shook his head aggressively no. N-n-no. I mean no. "That's just pastime. A woman has got to have—" His petal of a mouth, tender as an apple blossom in his hard thin reckless face, quirked upward at the corners. "Brains or money. A woman has got to have," he nodded from Reeve to Vivian, wedding them with his glance, "the thing that it takes to help a man become what he really wants to be. There's always got to be that little bit of Gibraltar."

They liked that. They pounded their knees. They stomped their feet. They hollered. Including Rad, awaiting his opportune opening.

Except the two, Vivian demurely typing out Reeve's verbal notes and avoiding his eyes. Avoiding his eyes just as she avoided the pine dresser obliquely half out of the alcove, the chalk marks on the wall behind it and what lay invisibly, rising from day to day, behind the wall, the aim of which she must understand just as well as everyone else did.

"Do you guys really want this thing?" Reeve thundered over the uproar. "Or are we putting something over on you?"

Oh yes, they wanted it. The Baron had about a hundred acres, mainly in woodland that with thinning, log-cutting and hauling could be turned into a paying piece of property. John Newgate had a farm similar to Reeve's that he hoped to improve without resort to supplementary jobs. "Plenty of colored farmers," Newgate agreed with Reeve, "have in the past made a living off a farm and sent their kids through college on it. And as everybody knows," he solemnly averred, "a colored man can live twice as good off the same amount of cash as a white man can. He not only gets the mostest out of it, he gets more joy of it too."

"That's a myth," the Baron objected.

Myth or truism, they all began to argue over it.

"How about you, Sanderlee," Reeve cut through the moot points of the argument, "you with us on this?"

Sanderlee momentarily humped himself up from his reclining position on the couch. "So long as I can have and enjoy my life," he announced his philosophy, "let the other fella take care of his. They tell me I hadn't ought to feel that way about it but I do."

He fell back on the couch, pulling the bump of a hat he wore down over his face. A lot of people claimed that Harold Sanderlee was lazy because he'd let his place run down so and never showed up anywhere on time and moved with such deliberation that he never seemed busy.

But he worked part-time in the grease pit of Mayor Dakin's service station, part-time in the equipment shed at Sunset, part-time at Hill Caslon's shrimp dock keeping Caslon's boat engines in order, and part-time in a little repair shop he ran for himself back of his house.

"I planted all that henfeed for my old lady," he added from under his hat, "and I'll keep the tractor in repair for you for a consideration—"

"Naturally for a consideration, nobody's expectin' nothing for nothin'."

"But let Bessie drive it."

This called for all the obvious jokes, which again Reeve, burning with impatience, had to cut through. "How about you, Power? You ain't said a word yet."

For once High Power had nothing to say. Actually he had, much as he disliked to mention it, quite a respectable garden patch. And he'd fixed up his wife's house quite a bit too.

"Them peas you growin' out there," Newgate twitted Power, "or tea?"

High Power sprang up from the bench, a rapier-blade ready to run Newgate through. He never could stand to be kidded about that farm.

"Get you a gage? Let your smoke go up," Newgate elaborated, pantomiming, "and your love come down!"

"You shut your damn mouth before I shut it—"

Reeve jerked Power back down by the slack of his shirt. The opinion of Power was very important. It carried a great deal of influence in the class. With the flutter of an eyelash he could undermine the accomplishment of the strongest resolution. But right now he wasn't committing himself.

"Newgate, gimme a cigarette!"

Newgate tossed Power a cigarette which he caught in the air and inserted loosely into the corner of his mouth. "Now light it for me."

"Now, Power—"

"What the hell—"

"Light it for me!"

Newgate struck a match and bracing his hand on Rad's shoulder, leaning across the table, lighted the cigarette. High Power lolled back, sybaritically drawing on it, at ease. "Go ahead. I'm listening. Shoot."

"What'd you come here for tonight?" Reeve demanded furiously. "To start this thing rolling? Or torpedo it?"

"I'm here because I was elected to the purchasing committee. But if you asking me personally, I came out of curiosity. To see if we'd end up with anything but a lot of hot air. I'm a realist."

"That's not realism. It's defeatism."

"Sure I know, I know. So-and-so started a college in the pineywood out of nothing more than a notion like this. And so-and-so meeting over a table in a shack no bigger than this . . . So you all want this old firehorse." He unearthed the manual from under the papers on the table and sensually touched over the forged-steel figure on the cover. "You all need it. You can organize and manage it. How you gonna get it?"

"Point number three," Vivian said in a meek small voice as the tension all but audibly simmered down. "*Fund-raising.*"

They had been discussing the possibility of buying a tractor for weeks. They had been reading up on the legal requirements for such a project and thrashing out the details of usefulness to themselves. But now, tonight, they were for the first time being confronted with their idea concretized in an object. To take it down out of the clouds, slap it into shape, particularize it was no simple process. Yet out of the nebulousness of their dissident temperaments, it was emerging as a distinct individual among them, not just the general concept of a tractor but *the* tractor, the one they were going to buy. This one. This big fat red mamma with the ringed numbers around her identifying her internal parts.

"You see," Reeve explained, "we've hit on a peculiar situation. This family, the Odells, have an option out on their place to a white man down the road from them that he's to close in three months' time. Well, he's just waiting for this equipment to drop into his lap right along with the property, and he's got all the other white folks and colored too so scared of offending him, no one around there's making any offers. So if we can come up with a deposit, they'll hold it—"

"Grampa's willing to put up the deposit," Vivian said. "On one condition. If you all can produce a foolproof plan to pay him back and pay it out."

"So it all hinges on one little word," Reeve said. "*If.*"

"Not *if*," she corrected him. "*How.*"

"So you guys screw your think boxes on," High Power ordered, "and start figuring. And girl, you take everything down but the cuss words."

It was plain from the start that they'd have to go outside the class for the major part of the money. They'd have to go to the churches and get the preachers behind it. They'd have to go to the PTA and the Sunshine Mothers and the Eastern Star and the HD club, get the women behind it. Then if you could get everybody together . . . run a barbecue picnic with some star attraction, some recitalist or dramatic reader or concert singer . . . and along with that the high school chorus, that would bring all the parents and kinfolk in . . . And of course a cake bake and a raffle . . .

First off the bat they'd have to secure the sponsorship of the Charles

Young Post, and from there spread out into community-wide sponsor-ship, and then let the sponsors take it up according to their lights. Fa-ther Hall would no doubt insist on his brother-in-law from up North Carolina for top billing—a fine baritone and a good drawing card, but how much would he ask for his fee and expenses . . . And the program, the program and tickets would have to be printed, you got to have print to give it substance . . .

"It'll take a lot of work."

"And more scraps, not to mention jealousy in the pulpit."

"And after you've raised the money and bought it—" High Power in-dicated the immensity of the effort. "And built it all up into something and you going great guns with it, then some fay'll fall in and take it over—" He punctured the air with his cigarette. "Or bust it up. Burn it down."

No one even glanced toward Rad. It didn't even occur to them.

"How much?" Reeve demanded of Vivian, hunching his shoulder up away from Power, so irked he couldn't endure to look at him. "How much can we raise on it?"

Vivian rolled the sheet out of her typewriter and they all, including Rad, put their heads together over it, estimating. You couldn't charge more than a dollar a family for admission, and from most such customers you couldn't collect until they arrived at the gate.

"Seven–eight hundred dollars," she added it up. "If you bring in the whole county and if you solicit contributions from the crowd . . . That is, if it doesn't rain pitchforks on barbecue day."

"Now you falling back on that if!"

"Too many ifs!"

"And the rest would have to come out of our pockets?"

The Baron pulled his two pants pockets inside out. Holes in them.

"Fifty bucks from every member of the class?" Reeve suggested.

It was manifestly too much. And still far from enough.

"I'd like to come in with you," Rad said quietly from his place at the table, next to Vivian and opposite High Power. "I'd like for you to count me in on this. I'll have my check at the end of this month and I still have a little reserve saved out of the war. You can sign me up right along with the rest of you."

Before he had finished, High Power was spitting over his shoulder into the fireplace.

"Sh-sh-shit!"

With a shiver that shook downward from the back of his cap to the base of his spine Power kicked back from the bench. And strode around to the door, where he leaned one arm up against the post staring harshly out into the night.

"Shi-it!"

Angular and graceful, wearing his clothes with an air, a flair, as if they were grown on him, slicked to him, his collar slouched up, his shirt curving with his back, knuckles of one hand implanted on his cinched-in waist, he spat out once again, far out in the night.

"For once, just once in our lives," his voice broke on a note, not unlike the moans Sanderlee sometimes plucked out of his guitar, "we get something good going. And before it can get started, before it can even *begin* . . ."

They were all too startled by the disruption Rad had created in their closed cohesive circle, too shocked by the vehemence with which Power expressed himself and too confounded by the ambiguity of their own reactions to do more than utter a few resounding rasps.

Reeve doodled over Vivian's column of figures, shading his eyes with his hand against the sight of Rad's eyes. Feeling it incumbent upon himself to speak up in Rad's behalf and too inchoate of feeling to speak.

"I know," Rad said. He sucked back the taste in his mouth, choked down his hasty pride. "You think if I come in on this, I'll ride it. I'll act boss-man. But if you'd just think of me as you do of yourselves, as you have tonight . . ."

With part of himself, Reeve poured his response to Rad into the inchoate figures he doodled around the paper. *This* is a person. This is *really* a *person*. With another part of himself, under the shielding shade of the hand over his eyes, he was cringing in dismay. Now he's done it, he's put his foot into it. Knocked this whole thing into a cocked hat!

And with still another part of himself or the whole of himself, he was being consumed by those horrid chiggers that impinged upon his nature; was being invaded by those shameful impulses that could not possibly belong to the pure and fluid being who was the real Reeve Scott; was being polluted by those cruelties that must originate not with himself but with the person who evoked them. To try the man. Put him through the mill. Find his flaw. His breakingpoint. How much will he stand up to? For me? For us?

Under the table, Vivian's foot reaching over pressed against his, warning him: Don't interfere. With her pixieish, picklish grin she was, Reeve saw from under the shade of his hand, not alarmed but amused and speculative, stimulated by the contention. She quickened to it, reveling in it as if she were the cause; and she withdrew herself from it, above it, observing it with an air of experimental detachment. It was all an experiment to her. It wasn't only Hagan Power who had come here tonight out of sheer curiosity. It was, Reeve suspected with sudden dark despair, Vivian Thurlow. Playing . . . Her head reared back, her eyes mischievously sparkling, she took measure of Rad beside her: a cracker in this neck of the woods, under this roof, professing this attitude—oh no, it cannot be!

The others had found their voices. With a host of rationalities they were trying to amend the effect of Power's outcry, to explain to Rad as gently as possible the reasons, those reasons which eluded explanation, for their lack of receptivity. At least they were trying to tell him, not just take the safe and easy course: yesyesyes and fade away.

"It's not that we think you'd beat us out," they said. Though it was that. "We know you mean well." Though they didn't know it. "If there was any white man in this county we'd turn to if we had to, it'd be you." Though covertly, not in the open. Once or twice, not continuously. "We honored by your offer and we appreciate your intention, but with the best will in the world there are things that'd come up—"

"You expect us," High Power snarled from his stance at the door and spun about, throwing his arms wide, "to shout, 'Welcome, brother! Hallelu!' Well, there's a boobytrap in this and you're caught in it just as much as we are. The white man's belief that he's acting out of altruism, extending himself beyond the call of duty, going out of his way to do right. And the colored man's belief that he's being exploited, that he's being used for some ulterior purpose, that one way or another he's going to come out with the dead end of the stick.

"We all know the white who will buy of the colored only two commodities: service and vice. But we also know his twin brother who comes bearing his gift of help and remains to dominate. The benefactor invariably reaps some benefit of his benefaction. Whether it's prestige or profit or a place for himself at the right hand of God. So don't sit there looking so Christ Almighty shining-bright. You only looking out for Number One. And even if I should blackjack you over the back of the head and rob you of every last cent you have, I'd still believe that."

They all stared at Power, too stupefied by his flow of language, too horrified by his frankness and too profoundly moved by admiration to interrupt. It was the truth. The truth itself. But truth is the most dangerous thing there is. Do mothers tell their children the truth? Do wives tell their husbands? Do preachers tell their people? The truth is dynamite.

Reeve turned his hands over, palms up. There it was at last, out in the open. Let devil take the hindmost.

"If that's all that's bothering you," Rad said mildly, "all right, I admit it. I am looking out for myself. When I spoke up in court that day, it was for my farm just as much as Reeve's. And when I ask now to come in with you, it's because I need it just as much as you do."

With a growl, only partially satisfied, High Power turned back to the door, hands thrust in pockets restlessly drumming.

"If you ever think of going on the stage, Power," Vivian said dryly, now that the intensity had worn off a little, and delicately touched her scalp, it was still on, "let me be your agent?"

Emboldened by Power and by Rad's permissiveness—for he too was according Power his moiety of admiration—the others started in now, laying it on the line. Laying bare the pitfalls.

"All right," the Baron said to Rad, "that's fine and it's good that you understand it. But there's another side to the picture. You feel this way now but suppose later on you should begin to feel that *we're* hogging the show. That we're crowding *you*. That we're the ones taking advantage. What'll you do then? How will you act then?"

"I'd bring it up, that is, I hope I'd bring it up in an orderly fashion."

"You say that now. And that's all right, it might could be. If it was only between you and us—"

"What he mean is—"

A short ugly-faced fellow, snout-jawed and broken-toothed, already grizzled as if with age, who had accompanied Newgate here and who had been sitting without a word all evening on the arm of the sofa, at Sanderlee's foot, hopped up and approached Rad and peered with concerned eyes into his face.

"In here, you and me and him and her can be together and it's all as should be. It's great. As long as I've lived in this county I never hoped to hear things like I heard here tonight. But we all," he pointed with stubby finger to the door, "got to go *out there* again."

It impressed Rad more than anything that had been said to him yet. The stubby finger pointing doorward, the bowed shoulders of the man as he hobbled, broken-footed, back to the sofa, left an indelible impression on him.

"What we mean," Sanderlee took up the refrain, "everything you've done so far none of your folks has taken any serious exception to, has they? But if you should take the one step farther than you have so far, all it will take is one person to start stirring things up. And then— *whoosh!*"

"Wait till they start making cracks behind your back, boycotting you. Wait till they start sideswiping your truck and running you off the road. Wait till you get a shot through your window in the middle of the night. Or you fall back from church to find your house in ashes. Wait till they drag you up out of your bed and take you out in the woods and flog you to a bloody pulp and throw you into the ditch and leave you there. You can sign up with us and we could all agree to it, but what it would lead to—"

"I already thought of all that," Rad said. Months ago, when Reeve first broached the ditching to him he had thought of it. Now he no longer believed it. Nothing but scare-tales made up to intimidate him from walking with Reeve into Ozzie's store.

"And you'd still sign up?"

"Yes."

He enjoyed for a brief moment posing as a hero in their eyes, not believing for a minute that he was running any risk. Nothing was going to happen to him.

He was also becoming somewhat nettled. Everything was going so well, he was getting along so fine, they were all having so much fun. He was luxuriating in a world that had existed previously under his nose, unknown to him, and that now was miraculously revealed to him, and to him alone of his kind. Till his announcement that he had come tonight willing to commit himself totally to it. The door was slammed in his face. The bottom dropped out of it. He was right back where he'd been before. An outsider. Alien. Bending over backward and breaking his back to prove himself worthy of their confidence. Moved by some inner compulsion to prove to them that there was on this globe one white man of incorruptible virtue. While they in turn were under no compulsion to prove anything to him.

He was most hurt, most baffled by Reeve, Reeve who should have come to his support, seconded his proposal, cited the many instances in which he had behaved up to scratch and then some. Reeve, evading his eyes, was frowning down on his fisted hands, beating them softly on the scribbled paper beneath. When it comes to a matter of them and me, Rad thought caustically, it's no more right and wrong, just or unjust. I'm the one thrown to the dogs.

"I know what you thinking," Newgate said. He wore small, rather scholarly looking glasses, steel-rimmed, which he kept adjusting on the bridge of his nose. "I know what's on your mind. If you so willing to take the chance of uniting with us, why ain't we? But what you haven't figured on is this. Once you're in, there are things you'd want to do, things you've done all your life without a second thought. We'd all meet and agree with you on it. Then we'd disperse. And nobody would perform. Nothing would happen. And you'd throw your hands up in disgust—my God, those people! On the other hand, we might all go along with the idea, follow through on it. Till someone on the outside would wake up to it—my God, those niggers are way out! Now you, you can always quit, take a run-out powder. Leaving us out on a limb. To take the punishment. I'm not saying you'd do it—"

"You see, Rad—" Warmly, wisely, the Baron placed a placating hand on Rad's shoulder, a hand at once bluff and agile, joined to his thick arm with a baby crease at the wrist. "You can join our organization, but you can't join the race. No matter how genuine you are, your membership would never be solid. There'd always be some one thing. And how would we know, how would we ever *know*—"

"Somebody has got to make the break," Rad said desperately. He was not going to be excluded, not going to be rejected! "Somebody has got to start sometime—"

"Would you want your daughter to marry a nigger?"

It was High Power again, rasping over his shoulder from the door, shocking them all into silence.

"I said—" He turned from the door and with a measured and menacing tread approached Rad, surveyed his face as it swiveled about, paced around the place he occupied on the bench in a short semicircle. If this cross-examination was to be pursued, it would be conducted from now on by Hagan Power. "Would you want your daughter to marry a nigger?"

"Shuddup Power!"

"Watch yourself—"

"You all trying to plumb to the bottom of this man, aren't you? Well I'm plumbing him. Would you want your daughter—"

"What has that," Rad asked, "got to do with it?" He had succeeded in keeping his voice steady, but his cheeks were beginning to burn. He didn't have to take this kind of needling.

"What has that got to do with it?" Power jeered. "What has that got to do—! That's just it. It has everything to do . . . Every one of us in this room, her too"—he roughly grabbed at Vivian's hair, pulling her head back, and she stuck her tongue up at him—"is being denied and deprived every minute and every day in every year of what's rightfully ours. On the pretext of that question. So tell us now. Would you want your daughter to marry a nigger?"

"My daughter," Rad said, putting away anger for the nonce, honestly grappling with it, thinking of Ruby, Miss Sasspants, "will marry who she has a mind to. And I'd like to see anybody, me or the man she's after, try to stop her."

"Mmmm." The nods circled the table. It was a good answer.

"That's not what I asked you," Power said scornfully from his ramrod height, pacing about him, the prosecuting attorney, the grand inquisitor. "Let me ask you again. Would you want—"

"Why don't you ask me," Vivian snapped, "if I'd want my son to marry a white girl? The answer is no. I'd throw a fit, I'd pitch a bitch—"

"Nobody's asking you. I'm asking him."

"My daughter," Rad said, looking Power straight in the eye, "will marry the man she wants, and if he's a colored man there's just one thing I'd want to do. Tell her, 'I only hope to God, sister, you know what the hell you gettin' into!'"

"Pp-ff-vvv!" It was a better answer.

But High Power would not let it go at that. He placed his foot up on the bench, rested his elbow on his knee and his chin in his hand. "You think she wouldn't want to, don't you? You think this is all theoretical, don't you? My kids can't play in the public park here. I can't take a book from the library. An aunt of mine last winter was pulled off a train and slapped and punched and kicked in the stomach and dragged with her head through the gutter . . . They say it's all economic and that's the reason, but it's not the excuse. Because you white men are so scared shitless of a black man sleeping with your women—

"Well, I'm not going to tell you it won't happen. Because it does happen. Plenty. All the time. All over."

They could all guess what was coming now, and fascinated, titillated, apprehensive, they watched Rad for the least telltale reaction, a dilation of the eye, a twitch of the nostrils, a tremor of the lips, a jerk of the shoulders.

Reeve retired to the fireplace, looking down on the company from a tower of frigid aloofness, refusing to give aid or comfort to either side. Vivian was making no effort to rescue the discussion as she had several times before and steer it back into main channel. His manual with the red splotch of the machine on its cover sprawled among Vivian's typed papers, forgotten. For this. For a wild-goose chase through the swamps of sex. That, now they were on it, no one would abandon. They had to see how far it would go. Where it would lead. Even if to perdition.

8

"When I was out on the West Coast," High Power addressed Rad, almost tenderly, "I was nineteen then and I went to work in a joint. What I mean a dj-jhoi-nt. Wheels, cards, dice, the works. I started waiting table and inside of two months I was floorman. Because I knew how to talk to people and handle them." He thrust his arms out before him with a wriggle of his elbows, wearing boiled shirt. A dashing gallant in tuxedo and black tie. Stepping forward as if about to take wing, his ears pointed out slightly, alertly; the tiny corners of his childlike mouth turned up, his fine nose pointed forward, scenting what's up; his eyelids deep and dreamy, heavy eyelashes screening broad level eyes that never missed a trick; his black hair, crisp and wavy, standing up at the corners. His face, narrow and pointed, dimpling with a waiting and challenging skeptical half-smile. "I could always tell which ones were good for business and which weren't. Parties out slumming: 'Look, you know this place is running outside the law, what you want to come in here for?' Girls: 'Now look, girlie, there's none of that in here, go on out the street, you'll do better.'

"Southern white girls, can you beat it? Babes working in Hollywood and around. There'd always been that attraction there, and this was the first chance they'd had to exercise it. 'Y'all know some-body'd lak a lil fffuh-uhn?' Well, some of them didn't mean that, you know? Nice girls too. Not bums. They were just looking for a little fun, period. And the majority of white girls married to buddies of mine or going with them came from Dixie. How do you like that?"

Rad extracted a length of string from his pocket and lowering his eyes concentrated on weaving it from finger to finger, making a cat's cradle of it. His underlip puckered pushing his mouth up into a bulge, his Adam's apple bobbed; but that was all.

"Personally," High Power confided with his arm around Rad's shoulder, "I could never stand them. Whenever I heard that accent, I'd move two seats away." He shuddered down the length of his body as if listening to the scrape of a fork against a plate. He gritted his teeth as if forced to chew glass. "N-n-no. I mean no. No-o . . . This lilywhite Southern womanhood ought to be damn good and sore at what's been done in their name. It's imprisoned them too. It's crippled them too. It's destroyed what might have been the natural course of living for them too. I felt sorry for them."

Straightening he smiled down on Rad with a fine thin curl of his lips, feeling sorry for him too, transferring to him not only his compassion but the repudiation inherent in it.

The others let out a long sigh of relief. At least Power had not, as they anticipated, boasted and bragged of his conquests, bringing them all with him dangerously close to the brink. Their sigh was not untinged with regret however. That Power had not taken the final plunge, had not put Rad to the ultimate test. At whatever risk to themselves.

But they sighed their relief-regret too soon. They hadn't reckoned on Hagan Power's flair for dramaturgy.

He gazed down on Rad so long through his thick eyelashes, feeling sorry for those Dixie belles and the revulsion they engendered, that Rad fumbled the crisscrossing of strings on his fingers. Out of his summer tan, dulled to ash, the rims of his ears were blazing.

"Of course," Power disclosed to him now, "that doesn't mean I never touched a hh-white hh-whuman. Oh I've had them. All kinds."

There was the little clerk in the PX to whom intercourse didn't mean anymore than eating an apple would to someone else. In fact he caught her once while he was laying her reading a *True Confessions* magazine over his shoulder. Hot damn! He got right up then and there . . . Laughing now over his discomfiture. The great lover.

And there was the glove salesgirl in the department store, whose name was Mary. Mary went with him to the colored rec hall on the base, to parties in colored homes, to his favorite dive. Only one afternoon they'd spent in bed together, she got up out of bed afterward and wandered over to the mirror, one of those full-length mirrors, and preened herself naked in front of it. "Aren't you proud to have me, Power?" "What do you mean?" he asked her, though he damn well knew what she meant. "Aren't you proud to have me?" That finished it for him. When she called him after that to make a date, he insisted that she meet him in front of her department store on Main Street at five thirty-five after work. He made her agree to it. When the time came, he didn't show up. He sent a friend of his down to check at six-fifteen, and his friend reported back, "Yeah, she's still there." He would stand up Mary in the lounge of the colored USO, where she came alone, unescorted. In colored bed-houses at midnight, where she'd rented a room. Everyone, even his colored girl friends, scolded him for how bad he was mistreating Mary.

And there was the schoolteacher who was interested in causes. He took a bet with a fellow that he'd make her. She read poetry to him. Loaned him *Lady Chatterley's Lover.* Invited him to her house when none of her family was there. She made him. Wanted for them to run off together. Love is everything. . . .

Listening to Power, they were all extraordinarily tense, their eyes wavering away from Rad now and focused on him. None of them altogether believed Power. Rather, they thought that this might be a compendium of experiences he had accumulated like a rolling stone, from a number of quarters as well as his own. Yet they believed that what he revealed had to be told. They were terrified by it: if Power should succeed in provoking Rad as indeed he was trying to, if a word of this should leak out among Rad's friends . . . And they were catharsized by it, affirming themselves to Rad as men any woman might love and give herself to if she so desired. If Rad could not conceive of the white woman's hand reaching for them in their strength and their color, if he could not accept the fact of liaisons that were common knowledge in every Negro section in the land, if he had to retain the barrier sacred and intact around his women, then what did he see when he looked at them? Be Kind to Animals Week? And what did they see in him? Just Another Peckerwood?

In the midst of it Reeve left the house. He thought he heard a noise outside and went out on the porch and listened, straining with the tension generated by Power for the sound out there in the darkness that he couldn't quite place. He trotted down the steps and took the dog with him into the woods to investigate. He could not, in truth, have stayed in the room a minute longer. Seeing his tractor disappear deeper and deeper under a welter of irrelevancies. Down the drain. For the sake of an exploration that would take them nowhere. Feeling himself drawn by the same curiosity. Because he expected so much of Rad he was always looking for the flaw that must be there—no man is perfect. And when he saw that Power was getting at Rad, getting under his skin, something in him kindled to it. The flaw in himself. The demon Rad aroused in him. With his own people he could be both individual and race, the dual personality in him relatively integrated and at ease. But in the company of Rad, in which he was above all, as Rad was too, an individual, race was eternally rushing in, swallowing up their relationship like the whale did Jonah. A whale that romped and spouted, whipped his flippers and flipped his tail, and lubricously roiled and moiled in the boiling sea.

Of those in the room Vivian alone was as undisturbed as Power. She was howling with laughter.

"What did you say she loaned you? *Lady Chatterley's Lover?*"

"And *The Sheik.*"

"Oh God." She collapsed over her folded arms on the typewriter, her shoulders shaking, convulsed with laughter.

But Power was not through with Rad yet. "You may say to me," he bent over the mute Rad, breathing down his neck, "that was all up North. Out West. And that—" Whirling about, with a sweep—Don Juan in his cape, Harlequin in domino, Mephistopheles in his mantle—he pointed at the Baron. "That was in Germany. All those Fräuleins."

"Who, me?" The Baron stepped out of range, petrified. He had never looked at any woman other than his wife. But before his hip brother-in-law, before those level eyes that would have held him forever after in contempt, even with the quick up-glance from Rad which he felt like the abrasive touch of a rope on his neck, the Baron was too abashed by his marital fidelity to deny the Fräuleins.

"You may say to me," Power shook his finger under Rad's nose, "that's all elsewhere. But what about the South? What about Georgia? What about right here in Colfax County?"

"For God sake, High Power—"

"Now that's carryin' a joke too far—"

Power bodily threw off their attempts to restrain him. "Right here in Colfax County. There are respectable housewives that slip out, places where they can meet their sweethearts—"

"Cut it out, Power!"

"And the evidence of it is plain to be seen. You know Eula Purcell? The Judge's lady?"

They buried their faces in their hands. Oh no, he was not going to rake up that old canard about Wylly backwashing Eula . . .

"She wasn't always so fat. She had her day. You ever take a good close look at her daughter Sukey? A little on the dark side—my wife is about two shades fairer than she is. And that black curly hair of hers and those big brown eyes and that cute little nose? Well, it's not because Ol' Vern jumped the fence twenty years ago. And that Annamary over there in that house. I took her and the boys out hunting last Christmas and she was all over me. Brushin' up and switchin'—"

Vivian, her eyes streaming with laughter, laid her arms over Rad's shoulder. "Don't take it so hard. Stop looking so disconcerted, disgruntled, and dismayed. It's not that awful."

The pressure of the girl's arms rested lightly on Rad's shoulder, but she too was alarmed. With her warmth of fragrance and laughter trying to soothe down . . .

Rad shook the netted string from his fingers into a shapeless mass. He had been listening to things that no white man he knew of could listen to and still call himself a man. And the only answer he knew of to it, befitting a man, was to put a bullet between those scornful sardonic eyes.

"All right," he said in a stifled voice, "you had 'em." He got up from his bench and stretched his cramped legs, flexed his straitened back and gazed sidewise over the table at High Power. "What good'd it do you? What'd you solve by it? What'd you accomplish?"

"Ahhhh . . ." It was the best answer yet.

"Ah ha!" High Power sprang back. "That's it!" With a snap of his fingers he swung his cape about again, rising on his toes, the prestidigitator. "That's just it! You in bed with the girl. You've passed the last outpost. The last limit is off. The last veil is dropped. And there you are skin to skin. Of course you not thinking about that. You you and she she. But is it equal? After all the mess that's made about it, all the stake that's been placed on it, is it equal? I know her and she knows me and there's no prejudice? None? At last?

"Ha! Baloney! It's the biggest hoax of them all. She can be just as prejudice as anyone else is, and still do that. She takes from you what she can and you take from her what you can and in the last analysis it's all a deal, a deal and that's all there is to it.

"And if she's in love and sincere and sweet and fine and beautiful, and it's we two alone in this world between the sheets, is that equal? Is that anymore equal than the other?"

He threw his cape, his serape about him, and swathed in it, wrapped in gloom, the Spaniard in slanting hat, he stood before the fireplace, suffering the pang of memory.

"No. No. That's not it either.

"You think you can come in here," he advanced toward the table and faced Rad across it, "and it's all love and humanity, hearts and flowers? Well, let me tell you, brother, nothing is changed by it. Not for him or him or her or me, nothing! It's all between the sheets. And it's not enough! Not enough!"

In a paroxysm of passion, all the passion of which his hard drained body was still capable, with a harshness of tears in his voice, all the tears of which he was still capable, he took a ginger-beer bottle by the neck and pounded it down on the ledge of the table.

"Not enough! Not enough!"

Leaving the broken glass, splattered over table and floor, he strode past the frozen men on the sofa, past Rad back to the door and stood there, his back to them.

"Not enough!"

"Not enough?" Rad brushed a splinter of glass off his shoulder. He rubbed fiercely at a prickle in his nostrils, an itching in the corner of his eyes. "Not enough?" All his rides with Reeve, his arguments with the boys at school, his evenings here.

He moved on High Power and pulled him about by the arm. "Not enough? What do you think it takes for a man like me to come here like I do? I whipped my boy today because of a name he called me. I whipped him till he run off I don't know where to. I whipped my own son!"

"You whipped your own kid?"

High Power, his self-possession regained, lifted his arms to the others with an irony that totally escaped Rad. You see? You see? He's been coming here all this time and hasn't even taught his kid, his own kid . . .

"And my wife. I left my wife down there alone in the house with no one but the young ones, and she's expecting. I left her against her wish and will to come here. Here! Because under this roof I'm free. Free! Free as I can't be in my own house. And you say that's nothing? Well, I say it's a lot! It's a hell of a lot!"

"You come against your wife?"

Again High Power expressively lifted his arms to the others. You see? You see? Not even his wife . . .

"I've set here and took everything you threw at me. I *humbled* myself—"

"And now you sore?"

High Power folded his arms, satisfied that whatever point he was out to make tonight he had made it. His case was proved.

"You have just had the privilege of an education that no colored man ever gives to a white even if they've been in the N double-A CP together for the last five hundred years. And you're sore?"

"Yes I'm sore. I'll be as honest with you as you been with me. I've tried, harder than anyone else around here has ever tried. And you hit me with it. And I'm sore."

"Well, you gonna be a lot sorer before you get out of here. Because I'm going to rip the clothes off you and strip you naked as the day you were born. You whipped your kid today till he run off. You left your family alone down there when they wanted for you to stay. You come up here to horn in on this tractor deal and now you sore because of what we said to you. How sore do you think your wife is right now because of what you done to her? Sore enough, say, to tell you when you get back there again that a big black booger has been lookin' in the window at her?"

"My wife wouldn't—"

"It's been done before. She's alone in that house all off by itself down there and she's salty and she don't feel so good and she hears something outside—"

They were all at once aware that Reeve had left them some time ago, too long a time ago. That it was a long time since they had heard him beating about the bushes with the dog. That there was no sound at all out there but the thrumming of crickets, the rustle of a branch, the distant hoot of an owl.

"And while she's laying there on her bed she hears the latch lift on the door and a big burly Negro—"

Sanderlee, who had been lying on the sofa all through with his hat over his face, either dozing or pretending to in order to dissociate himself, sat up and swung his legs out over the floor. "Now that's enough, Power!"

"A big burly Negro falls in and puts his hand over her mouth—"

"Stop it!" Vivian jumped to her feet and hammered at Power's arm. "Stop it! Power, are you crazy?"

He swept her away as if she were a little gnat. "Puts his hand over her mouth and before she can do a thing to protect herself—"

Sanderlee slapped his hand over Power's mouth. Newgate and the Baron fastened on his shoulders.

"And she gets back at you." Struggling, he got it out muffled from under Sanderlee's hand. "She tells it. Raises a hue and cry all over the county. The whole county's up in arms." Shrugging them off as if he were made of steel springs, he got it out from between his teeth. "A pregnant mother in front of her children . . . What'll you do then, Rad McDowell? What'll you say then? Will you deny her word?"

Rad walked out. Never in all his remembrance in this county had a white woman accused a Negro of assaulting her. And yet they had accused him, *him*, of acting the way any other white man would. As he would and must. If. *If.*

In emptiness, like the vacuum in the center of a roaring cyclone, he descended the steps without feeling them underfoot. Seeing it—knowing it wasn't so, it couldn't be—and seeing it: the brown hand on the white mound of her belly, the big brown dick. Himself, with this vision, violated and violator, in silken sensitivity tumescently pressing . . . If it were so—if she said it were so. And if they thought that he would if she said . . . After all that had been. All that had been . . .

Brittle cedar fronds scraped his cheeks as he stumbled down the path. Midway he encountered Reeve and the dog.

"That you, Rad?" Reeve attempted to hold him. "Just a minute, Rad."

"You left me," he spat out through thickened lips. "You let them—" The long fine hairs of his forearm rose up against Reeve's touch. "You didn't stand up—" He wrenched away and hurt, more hurt than he'd ever been in his life before by anything, hurt with the pain of a child bereft of his mother and of a man deserted and betrayed by one he has respected and cherished and depended on, hurt with the outrage of a man of good faith who has been told to his face that no faith can be placed in him, he stumbled on down through the ensnaring darkness to the track.

"Rad," Reeve called after him, "Rad, your wife's back there—"

Rad crashed on down the track.

Reeve tied the dog up by the steps. It was quite a valuable dog, belonging to Carter Scott, part boxer, part Walker hound, with a pugnacious pug of a mouth. He petted the warm wrinkled neck of the dog. "Don't you eat no poison bait now."

Something in him was rejoicing. So they got him. They got his goat. They pushed him beyond the bound, there is a bound . . . The demon in him dancing on a grave. Let him go, let him go! If he couldn't stand up to them . . .

He mounted the steps, seething with anger. Last time I was inside his house, last spring that time we were sittng around his table just as nice, talking, and his wife spoke up to me and he put his gun on my back. And I didn't know from there to here whether he'd shoot or not. Now he's blowing his top. What right has he to blow . . . The hell with him. The hell . . .

He lingered on the porch edge, clasping the post and looking upward at the sky through a space in the cedars. With a sense of aching loss, with a void yawning under his feet. The sky was strewn with stars like the crosses on a battlefield, like the souls of all those who have ever lived.

"What happened?" he asked as soon as he entered the house. He saw the broken bottle, the shattered shards of brown glass amidst the disordered papers and pamphlets. He caught the vacant looks, shame-faced, appalled, frightened by what had been brought about but replete nevertheless with a suppressed and irrepressible cat-satisfaction.

"What'd you *do* to him?"

Wanting to know it. Knowing in himself that little tugging quirk. How far'd he go? Where'd he break? Asking of them what he himself had done to create the condition of his own disappointment. It was he who had invited Rad here tonight: as spectator? participant? Guessing at the possibility of such an outcome and shrugging it off, it'll be all right. Only to drive Rad away, destroy what they had with such delicacy wrought.

Just like, he thought with a despairing self-despisal that despised itself for the thought, *just like a nigger!* Overwhelmed by the inexplicability of human folly. *I done messed up.*

None of them would answer him directly.

"What do you think he'll do now?" Newgate peered nervously out the night-black windows. "There's no telling what a man'll do when he's angry."

"I never cared to have anything to do with white folks," Sanderlee said. With shifts and shoves he was inserting his guitar, preparatory to leaving, into its canvas envelope. "Never want to mix with 'em nohow, don't want 'em mixin' with me. Just so long as they leave me be. That's all I ask for."

"Do?" High Power shrugged the shoulder seams of his shirt back into place. He snapped off a button that had been pulled loose in the scuffle and smiled fondly at it. "I'll tell you what he'll do. Go home and slap his chick on the hiney and turn her over." He went over to the table and disinterred the tractor manual. "It's not sex that's at the bottom of this trouble in the South. It's larceny. Who gets what. He'll go back to his class and blab all this about the tractor out to them and they'll drive down to the Odell place in St. George and buy it up from under us. Bye bye, baby."

"If he does," Vivian said, "it's because you dogged him to it."

"And if he doesn't then we'll know, won't we? We'll really know the stuff he's made of."

"Only he won't be made of it no more!"

"If he can't survive this, he's no good to you." Power tossed the manual over to Reeve. "Put this in your memory book." Throwing the papers on the table helter-skelter, he reassembled his pack of cards from beneath. Clicked them smartly together.

"Now wait a minute." Reeve attempted to arrest the general exodus through the door. "We're not through yet. We're not finished. Lets us go back—"

"It's late."

"I got something hot on the griddle and I got to get to it before it chills."

"See you, Reeve."

High Power paused at the door, his shirt collar slicked up about his neck, his Army cap squashed down over his brow.

"All my life," he said, "I been living on the fringes of a system that's rotten through and through. Picking crumbs off the edges. Heads you win, tails I lose. It can't always be like that. I know it's got to change." His level brows bent, commanding it so. "It's got to be basically and drastically changed. And it will be.

"Meanwhile I play the game. I know what the score is. And I beat the racket every way I can. I'm not closing my eyes and let myself be plucked and pretend everything is glorious, all's right with the world. Nobody's slipping *me* any knock-out drops."

The screen twanged back into the jamb behind him. The voices pattered off down the path. Car engines coughed. Reeve stood in the door, left alone now with Vivian, too depressed by the debacle of the evening to turn around and look at her.

"Goddam Power, he use his brains to walk on!"

"Exit. Curtain. Finale."

"You attracted to him."

"I sure am. Fortunately for me however I am familiar with the type. An airman. Made of light and air. A pilot who never flew a plane. Breeze

. . . He'll end up doing something absolutely spectacular and utterly foolish. Or on the ash heap."

He had the courage then to turn to her. She was collecting her typed pages and clipping them together. "The house that Jack built. Out of toothpicks."

The tractor had evaporated and his friends and Rad and now she was evaporating too.

"I'm sorry, Reeve. I'm afraid it was never more than that. Oh Reeve, Reeve—" Exasperatedly, looking for some missing element among her belongings, she slipped past him. "What am I going to do with you? You're impossible. You want the impossible. And sometimes you want so hard you take some of us along for the ride."

"But it's all here! All the pieces are here. If we make something of it—"

"Everything but the glue."

"We'll get the glue. If we just get into it—"

"Not enough of it. The dough. The do re mi. The wherewithal. You'll never make it. Find yourself another tractor, something smaller, more practical, adequate to your means . . . Here."

She located what she was looking for, a letter, and thrust it at him. "If it'll make you feel any better, I'll mail it out tonight. Just sign at the bottom." She groped through her handbag for her fountain pen, extricated it from lipstick-smudged tissues and handed it to him. "I think I have a stamp for the envelope."

He sat down with her pen before the letter. The lines so neatly tapped out, line by line. She had come here with all her little instruments, all her skills and devices, the knowledgeableness that loomed so enormous to him. "Superintendent of Documents . . . Will you kindly . . . Yours truly." With an order blank attached, listing the titles of publications on agricultural cooperatives.

"I thought you could use more material."

Her fingers pinned down the corner of the letter, fanning out from the flanged tendons, the raised curve of her wrist, the line of her forearm. Elation quickened in the pit of his stomach. His skin palpitated with a maddening tickling that would neither quite start nor stop. Self-consciously, under the enclosure of her arm, he signed the letter in tight slanting schoolboy script. Crossing his final *t*'s with a flourish.

Damn!

The pen skidding on an unevenness of the table beneath spurted out a blot.

"Never mind." Vivian extricated a little blotter from her handbag, pink on one side, calendar on the other. "Don't be so upset. It's not a crime." Leaning on his shoulder, she concentratedly dabbed with a corner of the blotter at the spot.

It would have been very easy for him to put his arm up around her and draw her down to him. It would have been very easy to reach up and touch that deeper darkness in the hollow of her collarbone, the line of her upper lip limned as if sketched out with the barest perceptible shadow, the little gold hoops of earrings that glimmered from under her hair. It would have been as easy as breathing. As easy as breathing in her scent, her aura of violets, commingled now ever so faintly with the acrid aroma of kerosene from the lamp. If it weren't for the effect of the blotter upon him. That little old puny blotter.

"Why'd you come here tonight?"

"You asked me that when I fell in. All right, I'll tell you. When you came to the house this afternoon from St. George with all that enthusiasm on you and when I talked with Grampa about it afterward, I had the feeling, the most marvelous feeling that something tremendous could come of this and I wanted to be part of it. And for a while after I came, I still had that feeling—"

"That the only reason?"

She took her stamp out of the pocket of her handbag, licked it with the tip of her tongue and pasted it down on the envelope with the heel of her hand.

"I came to get you out of my system."

Drawing back from the envelope she switched her head toward him, close to him, flicked the tip of her tongue over his lips and then lightly kissed him on the mouth.

"So I can get out of this damn town and forget it all."

He clasped her elbows, her smooth small-boned elbows that didn't belong on any farm, as soft under the toughness of his hands as a mist melting away.

"You think you can get rid of me that easy?"

"Tonight," she said with a lightness that precluded any real depth of emotion between them, "is the night before. Tomorrow is the morning after. I'll get over it. I did the last time."

"You don't think of him anymore?"

"Hmhhhh." A fluff of laughter. "There were moments I had with him, Reeve, moods, I thought would be with me for as long as I live. And it's gone. All gone. None of it measures up to that moment I stood up in court that day, because of you—"

For a moment he had his arms around her waist and his head burrowing into the soft white stuff of her blouse, into a fiery liquid that flowed

with concavities, declivities, sumptuous swellings. *O barn, barn, put
your arms all around me* . . .

She stroked through his rough hair, over the back of his head, down
the nape of his neck, in under his shirt. Then she was gone again, leaving him empty-armed.

"And this'll pass too. And that's the way I want it. There's no sense
to it, no substance."

"You playing with me," he accused her. "Amusing yourself."

"Mood and impulse! Mood and impulse, that's all." Catching up her
papers she began bundling them into the inside flap of her typewriter
case, fending him off with chatter. "Where were you before? You were
out so long—"

"Look out for the glass, you'll cut yourself—" He brushed the broken
glass back out of her way.

"You're a fine fellow. Instead of sweeping me off my feet, Lady Chatterley's Lover, Sheik of Araby, you sweep the glass out from under my
fingers. Instead of flinging me down on your sable-decked couch—"

She was having trouble fitting her typewriter lid on and he took it
from her and slid the back lugs smoothly into the grooves.

"I'm like Newgate," he said stiffly. "I can read this book but I don't
understand a word it says. I listen to you and I can't—"

"Don't let it worry you. Most of what I say isn't worth—"

"Let's go." He snapped the cover down. "Maybe I could have you, and
maybe you'd enjoy it so—be so taken . . . Maybe. I don't want to play
with you, Viv. I want you on my terms. With your mind and your heart
as well as your body. All of you."

"Reeve—"

Miserably, perversely, doing the opposite of what he most wanted,
driven by the obscure instinct that like fate itself dictated his course of
action, he turned from her glowing eyes and opened the door. "Come
on."

She walked out ahead of him. He turned down the wick of the lamp,
seeing in it liquid fire, the flame licking like a tongue, the smoldering
brown vapor, the glow out of darkness.

On the path she shook away his helping hand, found her own footing,
left him jostling behind with her portable. Twigs snapped and crackled.
Small animals skittered through the underbrush. Somewhere a car was
gunning up to a pitch, rattling into motion, sighing out again, *pffft*.

She had reached the sedan and was opening the door when Reeve
spoke behind her, close, closer than she thought he was. "My Lord—"
He was looking down the track. "You don't suppose she's still there?"

"Who? Who she?"

"Rad's wife. Lulabelle. When I was out before I heard this car way down the track and I went down there to look and it was her. The truck had stalled by the bobwire fence and she was trying to crank up—"

"Rad's *wife?*"

"I asked her if she need any help and she let out such a yell, jumped up into the truck and slam the door in my face—"

"You didn't mention this to Rad, did you?"

"I tried to tell him . . . Hush."

"Reeve, you get right in here with me. Power, that fool Power—"

"Hold on, will you?" He shoved her typewriter into the car and started down the track.

"Reeve! You don't know . . . Reeve, come back!"

He was swallowed up in the darkness, hurrying down the track toward the headlights in the distance that spasmodically blinked on, brightened, dimmed out again. In a turmoil of comedy, a comedy of errors, it had its comic aspects, Vivian turned her car around facing toward the River Road, and with her motor on, in gear, the door open for him if he should come fleeing back, waited. She lighted a cigarette with clumsy fingers. Power! Power and his hhwhite hhwhimmin! The bushes were alive with crouching figures about to spring. Gun butts. Bullwhip. This is how it happens. Out of a mixup. Misinformation. A melodrama of coincidence. . . .

She stepped on the gas and backed the car down the track after Reeve, recklessly letting the door swing, blowing her horn all the way.

"Hey—"

She stopped with a shock that threw her forward on the wheel. Reeve thrust his head in through the open window beside her. "Move over. I better drive. This woman is about to have her baby." He released the door in back. "Get in here, Rad. Lu?"

"You don't mind?" the woman asked timidly. "I hate to bother you folks . . ."

Rad climbed in after her, grunting. Patently he was still too angry with Reeve to speak to him anymore than he had to, and too humiliated at being forced into this recourse. As his wife, it soon appeared, was angry with him and humiliated. She had thought that she could drive in to Bay City Hospital all by herself.

With a presence of mind of which she was later quite proud, having little otherwise to be proud of, Vivian stopped Reeve at the clearing and ran up to the house to turn off the lamp and lock up for him. While inside she grabbed up an armful of cotton blankets from the dresser drawer. She ran back down the path in the wavering light of her flashlight and flopped into the car with her load feeling a little silly. "Drive on, Macduff."

Reeve eased the car carefully over the potholes in the track. "You feeling all right, honey?" Vivian inquired over the back of her seat. Somehow for her with this excursion the evening was beginning all over again, in the spirit of an unexpected and intriguing adventure.

9

At first Lulabelle made no complaint. "I'm sorry to trouble you all like this," she kept saying. "I'm sorry to bother you up so." Then she became more urgent. "Can't you go no faster? You got to go faster." When they reached the highway, Rad suggested that perhaps they'd better head straight on through Oglethorpe Square to Dr. Harrington's office. She turned on him savagely. "All these months you been saying you'd take me to Bay City Hospital. You promise!"

"Will you drive us on to Bay City, Reeve?" Rad requested distantly. "I'll be glad to pay you."

"It's not my car," Reeve said. "It's hers." Under his breath he was laughing.

"It's not mine either," Vivian said, disclaiming payment. "It's the Professor's."

"I wouldn't take a dog to treat," Lulabelle subsided grumbling, "to any of these doctors in Arcady."

Then as they sped over the long arching bridge that interconnected island and mainland, over the somnolent darkly glimmering branches of the river, the sibilant marshes, it began.

"Every time"—Lulabelle rocked to and fro, with the intonation of psalmody—"every time you go down into the valley. Every time you go into the shadow."

"Lu," her husband tried to comfort her. "Darling. Sweetheart."

She pulled away from embraces that attempted to comfort, endearments that attempted to ease, ferociously alone.

"Ain't nothing worth this. Ain't nothing on God's green earth worth this. Nothing."

Mile after mile it ground out of her, tonelessly reiterated, increasing in intensity as if through the release of her voice pain could find its only relief. Vivian shivered, her scalp shriveling with cold, her spine congealing in a block of ice. Numbly her fingers, detached from her, searched through the tobacco crumbs in the bottom of her handbag. For an aspirin to offer her. Something safely circumscribed within the limits of paper clips and cosmetics.

"Leave me alone!" The woman flung her husband back from her with a jar that jolted through the car. "I'm a-gonna die! I'll die! Oh God, let me die!"

The marshland flew by. A clump of tufted pine.

"Stop the car!" With the energy of a madwoman she swept Rad aside and seized on Reeve's shoulder. "You hear me? Stop it!"

Before Reeve could slow to a dead stop she had the door open and was jumping out of the car. She fell to her knees. Rad plunged after her but she was up before he could touch her and running clumsily from him over the shoulder of the road into the field. In another moment they were all running through the stubble of a new-mown field in a wild chase that with its sequence always blurred together afterward in Vivian's mind.

She stood with her arms piled with blankets—when had she taken them?—and the flashlight pointing—when had she taken it?—over the woman who must have fallen again or thrown herself to the ground. Rad went down with her. Straddling her, letting her screams slash through him, immersing himself in the ebb and flow, swell and heave, heave and push, the imperative effort of expulsion. "I'm here, I'm with you, I'm holding you, hold to me. Hold! Hold!" As if through his hands her pain could be released into him. Oblivious of the car lights shooting along the highway, of Reeve's breathing as he worked behind him, caring no more than his wife cared so long as he could hold her, talk to her, stay with her through that final cataclysmic burst of violence, out!

"Over here, Vivian," Reeve said. "I need the light here."

She made herself move back from Rad to him, to where he knelt between the thrashing thighs. The flashlight wasn't working well, or was it her finger on the switch, the light only feebly glowing. Up above the sky swarmed with stars, the configuration of constellations, the vaporous filaments of faroff galaxies. What star were you born under? Leo the strong? Pisces the unstable? At dances boys used to ask her that. "What star were you born under?" Not the right one, they'd move on to the next girl. And Reeve and me? Star-crossed lovers. What star . . . Millions of light-years away stars are being born and stars are dying.

"A blanket."

She dropped the blankets from under her arm. Her finger ached from pressing so hard on the flashlight switch. Between his hands Reeve was drawing forth a blob that glided like a fish into this world, trailing after it its bloody afterbirth. He raised it by the ankles and cracked it across the bottom.

"First thing that happens to you in this life," he said matter-of-factly through the thin bleat. "Will you get out my matches and jackknife for me?"

She dropped the flashlight on the ground and fumbled through his side pocket. In the end he had to get them out himself. He struck the match on his pants. "Here, hold this for me." She almost dropped the match while he was passing his knife blade through the flame. "What'd you do with the flashlight?" She didn't know. She couldn't find it. She held another match while he slit through the cord and knotted the stub. The match burned down to her thumbnail.

"Reeve, she's bleeding something awful!" From back in the shadows Rad was shouting at them. "Reeve, we got to get her away from here—"

"Here—"

Reeve thrust the blanketed bundle at Vivian. "No! No! Don't touch me with it!" She shunted it back at him. "Take it away, take it away, don't touch me—" Leaving him with the baby she ran, ran away from the brute nature of it all, back to the safe warm familiar confines of the car.

She huddled into the front seat, shuddering from head to foot, her teeth rattling in her jaw. I'm no good, no good at all. I'm nothing . . . She saw herself the calm strong earth-mother she should have been, in command of those functions which are hers. And she saw herself the distraught creature that she was, turning the car northward, taking flight, hitting the highway through the Carolinas, Virginia, Maryland, Jersey. From nowhere to nowhere, fragmented, discontinuous, forever cutting off the phases of her existence before they could attain depth and meaning. Or being. For without function there is no being, without direction there is no depth, without coherence there can be no meaning. I'm nothing. I'm no one.

Through the open door of the car Reeve placed the baby in her lap. In back, Rad edged Lulabelle, trussed up in blankets, onto the seat and propped her legs up on the window ledge. Himself, he crawled in on the floor and crouching with his feet tucked under him held his semi-conscious wife on the seat. In such posture, ungainly, unlovely, smeared and smelly, they resumed their ride to Bay City Hospital.

Vivian lifted the child to her shoulder and cupped her hand over the round shape of the head hooded under the blanket. She poked an explorative finger inside. They come with hair and fingernails. Eyelashes. Everything. And that broad flat back. So strong. So *here*.

"What is it," she asked Reeve, "boy or girl?" The first question.

"Girl. Good seven pounds. All there."

Sweet little mamma. Poor little thing.

Now Rad was urging them, "Can't you go no faster?" And pleading with his wife as she drifted in and out of consciousness, "Talk to me, Lu. Talk to me. Cuss me out. Anything." Crying out to heaven, "Oh God, oh my God, don't take her. Take me."

They rounded the curve into the hospital grounds to the floodlit emergency entrance at the side of the building. A nurse came hurrying out of the door as soon as Reeve pulled up on the ramp, bulky on slender legs, her motherly soft cheeks as white as her uniform under the harshness of the light. "We're all full up here," she began before she had even reached them. "You'll have to go on to Jax. We're laying them out in the corridors."

"But this woman," Reeve said to her, "this woman has just had her baby in the field—"

"Now go on," she pushed at the door on Reeve's side as if to push the car into motion again, not so callous as frantic in her efforts. "They got more colored beds down Jax. Go on, you blocking the way."

"For God sake." Rad leaped out the back. "My wife's losing blood by the minute—" He rushed past the nurse and dived through the doors. "What is this, a hospital or a mortuary?"

He returned with two attendants and a stretcher.

Lulabelle was eased out of the seat into the stretcher, white, limp, the freckles sprinkled over the bridge of her nose pale as cream. Her grey lips fluttered. "My baby? Where's my baby?"

"Just like a movie," Vivian muttered disgustedly to Reeve. She was now feeling quite soured about the whole thing. They always want their baby.

She stepped out of the car with the baby and ignoring the officious nurse hurried after the stretcher and laid the baby on her mother's shoulder. "You sure you can hold her?"

Her lips puckering, Lulabelle folded the blanket back from the little wrinkled brow. "Seems like I never feel right, lest I have, a, a baby in my arms."

Turning, Vivian almost bumped into Rad. He had stopped to retrieve the bedraggled crimson ribbon that had fallen from his wife's hair onto the pavement.

"We'll wait," Reeve called after Rad. "We'll be waiting on you out back."

Stretcher, attendants, nurse and Rad after them disappeared through the swinging doors. "What'd you have to tell him that for?" Vivian said crossly as she climbed back into the car. "It's his problem. Let him solve it."

"It's your car," Reeve said. "You can do what you like with it. I'm staying."

She didn't deign to answer. He drove around to the parking area in the rear. The three-story brick building was splitting at the seams with activity even at this time of night. Crumbling under the weight of its patient load from a city that had quadrulped in size during the war years. Reeve went off to fetch a bucket of water from the kitchen annex that, blue with fluorescent light and noisy with the clash of crockery, hung onto the end of the building like an afterthought.

She was left alone in the car contemplating the tiers of windows, open to the hot summer night, every one of them illuminated: white-bright columns of corridors, dull gold of bedlamps, spark of night lights. And throbbing with sound: an incessant murmur of voices and hurrying feet, the muted call of bells and buzzers, the metallic clatter of carts, bedpans, bed cranks, instruments. A boiler factory.

Directly over the sidewalk from her in a ground-level basement room a white-haired technician was examining a slide under her microscope. She spoke around to a white-coated wispy young man and he too took a look. The technician wiped at her eye as if to eradicate from it the gim-leted pressure of the eyepiece. The young man cracked out with some witticism at which she laughed. From the floor above a male groan heaved out with every breath. Ah-ah. Ah-ah.

Reeve returned with a pail of water and stood it on the curb. They both washed out of the pail, splashing water over their faces and arms with their hands, letting it trickle, careless of their clothes.

"I'm so ashamed," Vivian blurted out. "The way I acted back there in the field. Shame on me."

"You never birthed a calf." He was laughing again, warmly, under his breath.

"You don't think she's going to—" She glanced fearfully up at the lighted windows. "Leaving him with five kids— Births, kids, family jams, so long as it happens to someone else, not me! If I ever had to go through a thing like that, I, I'd kill myself first."

"Come to think of it," Reeve said, "I was born like that. In a field by the roadside."

He took the pail back to the kitchen and she watched him go, the damp T-shirt clinging whitely to the cleavage of his back. She stood outside the car a while longer, dabbing at her cheeks with the coarse-grained yellow paper toweling he had brought her.

In every window—every window—someone was being born or dying, sickening or mending, sleeping or lying awake, inserting knife or needle, conversing or having a smoke or just sitting. Away from the hospital, across the street, stretched row on row of war-built housing, brick-faced barracks running block-long, one row behind the other for block after block. And these too were astir with activity as if it were the middle of the day instead of midnight. Radios blaring. Beyond them, strung along the horizon, the windows of the chemical plant shone like sheet lightning. Operating three shifts through. Over all hung the odor, an incessant day-and-night odor permeating the air, of the pulp mills that had moved down here from Pennsylvania, Maine, Wisconsin. The metropolis. Within which, as under the stars, she was reduced to less than a grain of dust.

Hastily she slid back into the shelter of the car.

"I never liked being a woman," she announced to Reeve when he slid back in beside her. "I always thought it was a dirty trick played by nature. Not a very original thought, but it was original with me. And not because I envy men any part of their person, but because of the position it puts in. All my life I been hearing: *A woman is wrong from the day she is born . . . If a woman is weak, it's a good thing she has a strong constitution . . . A woman if she loves a man will take anything that comes.*"

"But you don't love anyone," Reeve said, "do you?"

"Love! All the world is looking for love. So they say. If there is anything in this world I most definitely do not need it is love. My mamma had the right idea. *Love,* she used to say to me, *somebody to rub you— that's love. Don't marry anyone,* she'd say to me, *unless it's someone can do something for you.*"

"And that lets me out," Reeve said. "Doesn't it?"

"Reeve, we can't do a thing for each other. What you need is a help-meet. A calm strong greathearted woman who can run your house and milk your cows and bear your young—"

"And what you need?"

"I don't need no man! What for? It'd just be a burden to me. All right, I love you. If that's what you want to know. With all of my heart and over my head . . . You sit over there!" Firmly she pushed him back as he bent toward her with the laughter under his breath, his direct physical knowing-what-to-do, his ruggedness, his stability, his devotion. Gibraltar. "I'll sit here!" She pulled over to her own door. "And we'll talk this one to death. And if talk doesn't kill it, I don't know what will."

They sat apart like strangers on the opposite ends of the seat, his elbow resting on the steering wheel, hers over the open window, the night air stirring in the cool damp edges of their clothing, about collar and sleeve; touching at the moist coolness that lingered in the hollow of throat, the tender underside of their arms.

"If you think it's something to celebrate," she said testily, "it's not. Love is a form of autointoxication. A state of delusion. A disease that attacks the reason, inflames the nervous system and in its acute stage can cause considerable suffering. But as I said before, there's only one thing to be said for it. It's not deadly. One does survive."

She looked outside at the windows. All the windows. Millions of windows.

"The real problem isn't love anyhow. It's not the craving. That can be taken care of. It's loneliness. And you can have a hundred lovers and marry a dozen times over and still be alone."

"And you're alone now? While we're together?"

He had her there and he knew it. He had the laughter under his breath, behind his voice, which she knew so well, the laughter of a man who is challenged by the fight he has been looking for and who feels that the course of it is now in his hands, to stand or fall, take or lose.

"If it lasts," she admitted, "we're together. If it doesn't, we're alone."

"Then let it last. It's not fair to you, you deserve so much more, but Viv, we have a lifetime ahead of us, there's so much we can do. All of us, we need you so. You have so much to give. I have the drive, you have the spirit—"

"You think all you have to do is want a thing and go after it and keep at it. You think all you have to have is loyalty, integrity, ideals . . . Reeve, I know you. I know your eyebrows and that crease between them when you're stymied by something. I know your mouth and that little line down the middle of your underlip and that sinew in your neck when you turn your head ssso-o. And that muscle below your underarm, such a good muscle—"

"Who else, who else in this world would talk to me like that?"

"Reeve, I can't can a pea!"

"You don't have to."

"Yes I do!"

"You can learn then."

"I don't want to!"

With this impasse, they had nothing more to say. It won't work. It can't work. Her father had married the wrong woman for him and messed up his life and then run off with another woman and messed it up more. One of the teachers at school, Mabel Varney, had married a fisherman without half the education she had and before very long he was always off drinking and carousing. It never works out. Hardly ever.

A drunken stumblebum passed by the car bawling out at the top of his lungs a ditty of his own making.

> *"All women are beautiful*
> *All women are beautiful*
> *They nothing in nature that grow*
> *They nothing on earth that flower*
> *As beautiful as a woman*
> *When she open up . . ."*

The drunk stopped at the head of the car, peered through the windshield, pulleyed himself back alongside and stuck his round brown face in the window with a touch at his battered cap. "How 'bout a dime for some whiskey, mister?"

"Now, get away," Reeve said. "Go on now. Beat it."

Vivian opened her handbag and leaning across Reeve handed out a dime. He doesn't know me at all. Not at all! To him the old man was a drag, a millstone around the neck of the race. To her he was a song.

The old man shuffled off, bellowing.

> *"Woman woman de goddam woman*
> *Ruin ma life, make a slave outa me*
> *Sek sek de goddam sek . . ."*

Love me or leave me or let me be!

"Straighten up." Reeve gripped her arm so hard it pinched. "Don't budge. Don't say a thing."

A policeman's flashlight pointed in her face, blinding her. "What's going on here?"

"You looking for somebody, officer?"

Reeve's tone was neither so smooth as to be ingratiating nor so brisk as to offer offense. Upon being questioned by the policeman he explained the situation in terse detail. They were waiting for a Mr. R. McDowell. They'd carried him and his wife here from Colfax County. "It's a confinement case. You can go into the hospital there and check with them if you'd like."

The light remained on Vivian's face. Reeve produced his driver's license from his wallet, his insurance papers, his VA identification. Vivian passed out the car registration.

"Your health card. Come on now, girl. You heard me."

She felt the warning pressure of Reeve's leg against hers. She turned over her teacher's license.

"Teacher, huh?" The policeman beamed his light down over her smudged blouse, her bare legs. "Bet you could teach me a thing or two. Who'd you say you were waiting on?"

Reeve explained it all again. The policeman strolled around the car and batted at the fenders with his billy. The sedate Dodge having like a good horse acquired some of the character of its master must have convinced him that no suspicion could conceivably be attached to it. "McDowell you say? All right, remember I got my eye on you folks. We don't allow no hoochypap round here."

This she was furious at. This she couldn't endure. This she loathed and was debased by. Reeve's hand pressed down on her thigh.

"We're not getting our heads chopped off for no lousy cracker cop. When the time comes, and it will come—"

"No," she said, "we're going to sit right here and wait for that lousy cracker character to wake up to how his baby was delivered back there in the field. And come out and chop your neck off for it. In no time at all."

"I told Rad I'd wait here for him," Reeve said stubbornly. "We're waiting."

She leaned back against his arm which lay casually over the back of the seat. After a while, as was to be expected, it dropped down about her shoulders. And after another while she lifted her hand in the expected manner to his hand on her shoulder and traced over the long cords that twisted downward from the wrist like the roots of a tree.

"And while I'm giving my all to Colfax County, where will you carry me"—she couldn't refrain from one more drop of acid—"for my confinement case?"

Then swiftly as if she owed him solace interlaced her fingers with his.

When Rad came down the paved walk toward them he was grim with weariness, his shoulders hunched and his hands shoved deep in his pockets, his head indrawn as if all the weight of the hospital, bricks, masonry, structural steel, and glass were tumbling down upon him.

He had had no time to think of Reeve and Vivian while he was in the hospital yet he had been thinking of them all the time. When he was brusquely stopped by the nurse as the stretcher moved away from him. "Can't I stay with her?" "Absolutely not." The institution took possession of what was his and curtly impersonal, crisply indifferent, pushing him aside, wheeled his wife in one direction and his baby in another, down around the corners of its corridors, the interminable turning corridors of time in which door after door swung shut behind them.

And when he was directed, again brusquely, into the cubicle of an office. First his credit card: Didn't he have any kind of a credit card? His Army discharge, his VA identification. He wasn't very apt with that either. "Next. Step aside please. Next."

And when he was shown into the overcrowded reception room, a dingy shoebox of a room higher than it was long, banked with bright plastic and chrome chairs, spotted with bridge lamps and the glossy-lipped covers of magazines. A knot of relatives gathered under the window at one end: car smashup involving two whole families. Sunk in gloom. "Awful. Awful." A vibrant Italian waving to an acquaintance at the door. "No, nothing serious. Just a slight case of fracture. My nephew. Playing night ball." A couple of policemen consulting. "Well, that's their story and they're sticking to it. The lamp broke and she sat down on it." "For crying out loud, seven stitches!" The cops scootched down, questioning a pair of men and a stolid woman who accompanied them. Gentle in their prodding. "And that's how it happened?" Too many people . . . He'd sat stiffly in the cheerful yellow plastic chair, holding the cheerful magazine before him, scuffling at the grubby linoleum underfoot.

And behind it all he was still thinking of them when the doctor appeared. He had sacrificed his wife and child to associate himself with Reeve and Reeve's girl and Reeve's people in Reeve's house. For what? And Reeve and the girl had sped him and his wife here over the roads late at night. Why?

"McDowell?"

The doctor, a sandy-haired youngster, nervously supercilious of manner, had beckoned him out into the corridor. "I don't know what to tell you, boy," the doctor had said. "We've shot her full of penicillin and sutured her. If the sutures'll hold."

"What are you getting at?" he had asked the doctor. "You mean she won't pull through?"

"Well, in these cases of postnatal uterine hemorrhage, well, I don't know what kind of resources you got—"

The doctor had spoken as if holding his voice a little distance off from himself. A hand carrying a mouse out by the tail. . . .

He'd felt himself go blazing-red. He had never felt so small, so dirt-cheap, so ground-down-under. Why that little low-down picayune puny little sawed-off squirt of a sawbones . . . Fiddling with his stethoscope.

"I got my farm all clear," he had said very humbly to the doctor, "and my crop and . . . Christ Almighty, man, do whatever you got to! I'll get the money for it."

The doctor wanted to call in a surgeon if it should become necessary. And he wanted at once a minimum of three pints of blood, type O, the most common type and the one they were short on. Red Cross was all out of it. He was putting in a call for professional donors right away. "Any friends or relatives around?"

The only offer of blood he could make was his own. His brother-in-law in the city had had malaria and the brother-in-law's wife had just had her second baby a few months ago and besides they had no telephone.

The technician had typed him and he'd lain up on the table with a needle stuck into his arm, watching the blood being syphoned off in a bottle. The blood was dark. He had never thought of blood as being that dark. Is that my blood?

And he thought, he must have thought a lifetime of thought as he watched the wine-dark globules gathering, joining, sliding down the tube, mounting in the bottle.

When he approached Reeve's car in the rear of the hospital, he was still feeling cut to the heart by a curtness that he had taken all too personally. Trash, they'd all treated him like trash. And that doctor. Acting like a bitch hound with six pups, if he don't keep each one in line they'll be all over him.

He opened the front door of the car only to catch a glisten—like a fractured star—in Vivian's eyes, a darkling glimmer that he couldn't read upcast at him. She moved over toward Reeve and Rad slid in beside her.

"How is she?" Reeve asked.

"She needs at least three blood transfusions. I just give her one." He rubbed his arm. "They've sent out a radio call for donors. What they call the universal type? I asked the man who was taking mine—he's a refugee fella—and he said anybody could have it."

"Well," Reeve said, "you know if there's anything we can do—"

Rad lifted his hands before him, spread-fingered. They were shaking. "I asked him that too. I know I was presuming on you, but I asked him anyhow. He said there wasn't anything he could do about it. I better go back now. If you want to leave . . ."

"We'll wait," Reeve said. "Just tell the cop down there we're waiting."

"Sure. Sure thing."

When Rad came back for the second time he was laughing.

"I seen her. She's over the hump now and they let me see her. You know what she said to me? 'You got me here. You did get me here.' The things that'll go through a woman's mind . . . Look, I want to take you folks out for a drink somewhere. And a bite to eat."

He was very insistent about it. "I don't know what I would have done without you two. We can at least have a drink to the baby. Or a cup of coffee. Anything."

Reeve drove down Oleander Avenue past the Lanier Hotel where the bar was still open, bathed in cerise and orange lights, featuring a

chanteuse direct from Miami Beach. Adjoining the hotel the windows
of the bus station glared on one side, the white lunchroom busy with a
rush of late travelers; and smoldered feebly on the other side, the colored waiting room closed down, a single bulb hanging over the stools
tipped against the counter. The drugstore at the corner was locking up
for the night. "Just a minute." Rad reached across Vivian and tapped
Reeve's shoulder. Then changed his mind and Reeve drove on. He
couldn't have taken them in there anyhow. He could only bring the
food out.

Trucks were drawn up before the Honeyspot Bar-B-Q in the next
block, being served by young girls, marvelously lissome, long-legged in
brief shorts. Chucky's Grill (Wines & Liquors). The Oleander Bowling
Alley (Hush Puppies, Soft Drinks). Charlie's Steak House (Pilsner
Beer). All going strong, open all night in Carter Sillens' wide-open
town.

At the corner of Sycamore Street, Reeve stopped for the signal and
Vivian kicked him sharply in the ankle. He could have taken a left
turn down Sycamore and followed it down across the tracks to where
the street lights and macadam petered off, and taken another left.
There, between the movie house showing double-feature gangster films
and the tailor shop, there was a rib joint where the neon hummed
around the window and the spareribs sizzled with spices over live coals
and in a haze of rainbow lights the piccolo spun out its siren songs.
Reeve stepped sharply back on Vivian's foot. Don't worry! He was not
allowing any respectable young woman in his company to sashay
through the colored section way late in the early bright with two men
in tow and one of them white. A Puritan Negro.

The red signal winked out. The green surmounted it. He continued
on straight ahead. "Where to?" he said to Rad. "Just tell me where to
stop and I'll do that." They were leaving the business for the residential
section. Relenting, he changed the subject.

"What you going to name that little girl-baby?"

"Ella-Rose. For my mamma. And yours."

That's a switch, Vivian thought sardonically. But still was touched.
"Ella-Rose McDowell. That's a nice name."

"You really think so?"

"I really do."

"What's the sense, Rad?" Reeve said and took an abrupt turn into
the nearest driveway and backed around. "We're not all that hungry.
We appreciate the intention—"

"Don't give me that stuff. Don't say one thing to me and mean another!"

"But I do mean it," Reeve said. He did mean it. "Rad, I'm sorry about what went on in my house tonight. Power gave you one part of it. But only one part. One fifteen-millionth part. Because there are as many parts to it as there are of us and you might's well know that."

"You're not sorry," Rad said. "And neither am I."

Reeve drove back down Oleander Avenue to the hospital. "Keep going," Rad said, "to the yonder side of town. Then follow the sound."

"Look Rad, it's pretty late—"

"Keep going!"

They left the multicelled housing project behind and the Carter Sillens Recreation Park and passed through a dreary section of box factory, pulp mill, menhaden works. The pyramid of menhaden waste emitted a stench that rolled like heavy fog through lines of shacks rotting on their stilts. The prevailing condition.

"Take menhaden," Rad observed. "Who would have dreamed a few years ago that menhaden was worth anything? Now it's a million-dollar industry."

A sea breeze freshened the air as they neared the sound. The small white bungalows of pulpmill workers nestled under a tall grove of live-oak trees, tidy as white-painted garden stones.

"Next left," Rad directed. "Lu's brother, Dubose Wyatt, lives out here." They stopped by a streetlamp under the broad umbrella of a catalpa tree. "This is it," Rad said. "If you'll just wait a minute while I wake them."

"You go in there," Reeve said, "and have your coffee and give them your news. It's all right now. We understand."

"I'll call you," Rad said.

They watched him up the gravel walk to the little peak-roofed porch, screened all around. He tried the screendoor but it was locked, and hopped off the stairs to take the path around to the back.

The catalpa tree was so broad, it canopied porch, front walk, and roadside. The streetlamp under it lit the heart-shaped leaves to an unearthly emerald-green. Vivian lay back in Reeve's arm and hid her cheek in the nook of his shoulder. "You woo me," she said drowsily. "You woo me with crackers and tractors. Was there ever such a wooing?"

"When I get my farm equipped and my place built up," he ventured dreamily, "I'm going to screen my porch around like that. I'm going to paint my house like that and have box plants in all the windows. With this room I'm adding now, I'll add others as we need—

"Eating and sleeping, living and dying all in the one room," he said with sudden vehemence. "That's got to stop! We've had too much of that . . ."

"Is this night ever going to end?" she asked of the brilliant leaves that sheltered them like a tropical hut, the stage set of a tropical hut, against the indigo darkness beyond. "Or will it go on forever?"

The last thing she wanted to do right now was bestir herself to go into that bungalow, into some strange and strained involvement. "Let's go home now, Reeve. They'll ride him back."

"All a man can hope to do in his life," Reeve went on with his reverie, "is make things better for his kids. What else is there?"

"Is there anywhere in this white folks' town," she asked plaintively of the leaves, "where I can go pee?"

Under his arm, nestled against his side, such a good muscle, she must have drifted off to sleep. For the next thing she knew he was shaking her. Up on the porch the light was on and Rad was standing in the doorway beckoning them.

They walked into a small parlor that opened through a wide arch into the dining room. Porcelain lamps on end tables at either side of the slip-covered sofa were lit up, all three lights each under the cellophane-covered silk shades. The console radio was playing melodic night music. The dining table was spread with damask cloth, china, and silver in readiness for company. The aroma of cooking bacon, coffee, and hot butter syrup issued from the kitchen, mellow and melting, coaxing up juices from under the tongue. A pleasant young chap, glasses twinkling, clad in unaccustomed moiré robe over hastily pulled on pants, greeted them with a warm handshake.

"Rad told me what you done for Lu. I'm most awfully glad to meet you."

His wife poked her head out of the kitchen, steamily flushed. "What you been through tonight," she said to Vivian, her eyes wide with distress. "And you not even married!" This broke them down, started them all off laughing. "Now baby," her husband chided her, "you not by any chance matchmaking? Let him chase you till you catch him. That's her rule."

"I would like to use the bathroom," Vivian said aloud amidst the laughter. "If I may."

"Of course." Mrs. Wyatt bustled ahead of her through the kitchen. "Call me Annie." She furnished her with clean towels, apologizing, "If you don't mind the mess in there. My two-year-old . . ."

Vivian plucked at her blouse. "Mind it? I *am* it. I've never felt such a mess."

"Ssssh." Annie detoured her into the darkened bedroom. "My baby's asleep in here. Would you like to see her?" Vivian tiptoed to the bassinet. Bottom up, arms up, nothing to see but the back of her head.

"Here, it'll be a little big on you." From her closet Annie, shorter than she was and a good bit plumper, passed to her on a hanger a fresh white shirtwaist blouse.

They sat down at the table. The radio sang, *This can't be love because I feel so well.* Annie served a stack of wheatcakes with bacon and sausage, apologizing. "On such short notice—now don't move, I'll get the syrup." Reeve shook out his napkin, a damask napkin matching the cloth, and wonderingly smoothed it over his lap. It was the first time he had ever been received in a white man's house like a human being. He wanted to say it, was moved to say it, gratefully. And couldn't. Why shouldn't I be treated like a human being!

They talked. Dubose Wyatt, "Call me Bose," it turned out, had also been in New Guinea. In the Seabees. At Rabaul while he, Reeve, was at Port Moresby. Remember the Aussies. Remember that card game. Two-up. And the fellow that went fishing in the stream with hand grenades. Lost a hand. In your company too? And the dengue . . .

Annie, it turned out, was a soldier of the Salvation Army and she was death on liquor. "But—" She went down on her knees before her buffet and rummaged around inside it. For a bottle of muscadine wine she kept for just such occasions as births and weddings. She dusted off some goblets and poured.

"Well," Rad finished off the first toast and mischievously licked over his mouth. "That takes care of the birth. Now how about the wedding?"

"Don't look at me," Vivian said. "We're not wedding. Not yet anyhow."

And Reeve looked at her sidewise in glad surprise. "What do you mean, *yet?*"

"Oh this is good wine," she said sipping, sparkling at them over the rim of her goblet. "And wheatcakes, the *lightest* wheatcakes. And the *best* hot coffee."

The radio music had been interrupted by a news broadcast to which they were listening, if at all, with less than half an ear. Some senator denouncing elections in Iron Curtain countries. A Washington influence-peddling scandal. And closer to home, a comment by Ol' Cal Hubbard on the shooting early this evening of two Negro couples.

Reeve was just lifting his refilled wineglass. "I'd like to make a toast to that word *yet*. That little word, *yet*—"

His smile faded. He turned his head toward the radio in the parlor with a wariness, a wariness that was with him always in field and wood, at home and on the streets, the wariness of a man moving through the ambuscades of enemy country.

". . . two couples, Roger Malcolm with his wife and George Dorsey with his wife, were stopped as they were walking along a country road by some twenty-odd white men shortly before ten o'clock this evening. It is reported that the women were roughed up some and then all four were lined up against the trees and shot with a sixty-shot broadside from rifles, pistols, and shotguns. Roger's landlord, it is reported, was having some trouble with the boy over his crop. Both boys were veterans of World War II. Coming only five days after a similar shooting . . ."

Reeve placed his goblet down, careful not to spill over on the cloth. "Why do you look at me?" he addressed the stricken white faces. "I don't hold you responsible."

But in his heart of hearts, Rad knew, he was thinking: *Ain't you ashame? Ain't you ashame to belong to a race of people that would do a thing like that!*

And he knew that Reeve knew that he knew.

"It's not enough," he said and put his own wine down, spilling. "It's not enough! All this, we here . . . It's not enough, is it?"

"Ten o'clock?" Vivian asked with a note of shrillness. "Did he say ten o'clock? While we—"

Rad went over to the radio, shut off the jabber of the commercial. The appalled solicitude of Bose and Annie beat in his ears, from far off, far off, over the plains of the white damask table, the abyss of the edge.

"Gee, this is terrible."

"It's awful."

Awful awful awful.

And all the voices around Reeve's table tonight throbbed through him, all the voices of those who had so many times lived through this surge of rage, this flexing of the muscles, this will of the body to hurl itself upon the adversary and extract from him justice—justice. And the fist landing in a vacuum, in nothing. The nothingness of nothing being done. Act by act, year by year the nothingness accruing.

Reeve and Vivian drove Rad back to the hospital where he saw his wife again. She had received her second transfusion and was resting well. The baby was already kicking up a row.

"Nothing in this world," Rad said when he climbed back into the car with them, "is born easy."

II

THE CAMPAIGN

[July–August]

1

During the first few months of teaching his farm-training course, Clem excluded all extraneous issues from the classroom. One initial misstep he did commit in making the transition from pastor to pedagogue, which he never later repeated. He invited Rad McDowell to attend Whitsuntide service at St. Paul's.

He believed that he was mainly motivated by the desire to induce his congregation to face, accept, and assimilate the presence of such a man among them. To canalize some of the respect that had been accorded him for "that fine work you doing with those cracker-boys over to the school" into respect for the subject and object of that work. This is the kind of person we need in the church. This is what Christianity is all about, a religion of the have-nots. As for Rad himself, Clem nurtured perhaps toward him just a spark of proselytizing zeal. Oh nothing so crude as trying to recruit from his class new members for his church, of course not! He was only demonstrating his utter lack of snobbery—he believed, a little snobbishly perhaps—by his willingness to welcome Rad into his own fold.

Rad came without his wife who was too far advanced in pregnancy at that time to feel free in unfamiliar surroundings. He didn't bring his brood with him either, being somewhat confused as to whether the invitation covered Sunday school or not. Laura and Nancy took him in hand, seating him between them and introducing him around after service. The congregation, seeing in Rad a touch of vengeance by Clem for the Augusta Varney affair, extended themselves to be extra nice to him.

But when Clem asked Rad a few days later what he thought of the service, Rad was most evasive. "Do you really want to know?" he parried as he was prodded for a reply. "You sure you want to know?" And then had blurted out:

"I couldn't believe you was the same man!"

In Rad's tone rang all the arraignment of a creed that found in the white robes, the flickering tapers, the fragrance of censers, the ritual of the altar a flirtation with the whore of Babylon; in the liturgy an affront to the realities of daily existence; in the solemn intonations and swishing vestments of the celebrant of the feast a loss of masculinity. None of Clem's efforts at interpretation of meaning, explicated in the most colloquial paraphrasing, made any impression on Rad. It was all arrant nonsense to him, so much so that in Clem's own ears the words began to sound like gibberish, an esoteric distillation so far removed from the substance of life as it is lived by the mass of men as to have no affiliation whatsoever with it.

"And another thing," Rad had added gratuitously, with that sidewise shyness of his that slyly disguised a daring leap out of the enclaves of embarrassment, "when you talk to the fellas in class, don't say *ain't*. None of 'em likes it."

Thereafter Clem compartmentalized his thinking, confining his religion to one sector of his time and mind; his teaching to another. The old dream he had shared with Joe Hata, in which the two elements commingled, died hard.

"*Is Mother with all her submicroscopic anxieties,*" he jotted down in his notebook, the relic of his days at Butler Mills, "*right again? As she so often is. Am I repeating my episode with Tim and Gloria Hodges? Are we destined always to enact our essential pattern on ever more complex levels?*" The last sentence trailed off in scratchings. He dipped his pen in ink, holding the plunger pressed against the inner tube overlong. And pushed on, freshly black: "*Was I seeking to have Rad accepted by my world? Or his accept me?*"

Queries for which he had no pat answer.

He tried after he had closed his notebook to grope it out with Nancy, who followed him no more than Rad did but proffered the attention of her sweetest smile. "The brotherhood of man, as basic as it is to our religion—embracing the political, the economic, and the social—cannot be translated from the realm of principle, from our denial of class and race differences, into the practice of viable personal relationships without difficulties of all sorts. Difficulties which we must live with. Which are indeed the material of living. The eternal striving of imbalance for balance and harmony. The stresses, the flux of any intimacy between people—this is nature in evolution, with its trial and error and retrial. Am I on the right track now?"

"On the wrong track," his mother overhearing interrupted. "Why must you always equate yourself with the lowest instead of the highest?"

"Who's he had a run-in with now?" Nancy wondered to herself.

He made no further forays in mixing church and school.

Lecturing to his class and making his twice weekly tours of consultation in the field, he became that other Clement DeLavery, the one inferred by Rad when he so bluntly spoke out: "I couldn't believe you was the same man!" Sunburned, lithely active, outward. And content. Exuding contentment. The only bridge between the two Clems being his attire, that horrible getup of his mother's worst nightmares: the white-collared black shirt (sleeves rolled up and on the hottest days collar removed) belted into scuffed blue dungarees. With the aid of Earl Goodfellow, the county agent, and under the guidance of Professor Thurlow he devoted himself to his immediate task: having the soils brought in by his students submitted to chemical analysis and making recommendations for soil improvement, management, and conservation. With each student he tackled individual problems, mainly at the moment insect and disease control; and for the future, he assisted in the formulation of plans to turn every plot of land into a paying proposition.

His Sunday preoccupation with the spiritual-made-material through the medium of Communion was displaced now by his weekday preoccupation with the strictly material. Unless it can be said that in his teaching capacity he was witnessing the process in reverse. The material-made-spiritual through the revelation these men were experiencing in their discovery or rediscovery of the earth they tilled, in the illumination of their labor by scientific knowledge. From his mouth, Clem observed the word-become-flesh and the flesh-become-word with a directness, a usefulness, that no chalice had ever evinced for him.

But of this he said nothing to his class. He had little time even to think of it.

If religion had no place in his classroom, neither had politics. True, he had had Benson Reece in to lecture to the class, but that was on Ocachee River development. And true, Benson had made a donation to the class, but that was a half ton of fertilizer. Also, Benson was chairman of the Veterans Advisory Board, a body formed in part from the old Selective Service Board, but its purpose was largely administrative: to pass on applicants for admission to the class, discipline of students, provision of aid from community resources. Nothing political.

Clem was surprised then to be summoned by Benson to the bank late one afternoon, after hours, and to be led to the back desk, itself an indication of the gravity of what was afoot. This desk in the rear section of the bank now served Benson as campaign headquarters. The map on which he had traced for Clem the course of the Ocachee had been moved back toward the window. Taped up now on the wall over Benson's desk was a four-foot-high poster of the candidate he was supporting for governor against Ol' Cal. Middleton Morgan, the moderate— also known as Middlin' Morgan and Milktoast Morgan—lifted a mild smile into the winds of challenge, over his red-lettered slogan: *MOVE AHEAD WITH MORGAN.*

Pivoting his dark glasses left and right as if eavesdroppers might be lurking in the teller's cage or in the ice house behind the rear wall, Benson lowered himself from his cane into his swivel chair. He opened up on Clem obliquely with an attack.

"You knocking yourself out over that class for nothing, boy. A waste of energy. First the pulpit. Now this. Why can't you ever take things as they come? Those boys are all sponging on the government and so are you and so are all of us insofar as we are able. This class will tide 'em over for the next few years and that's all there is to it. That's it."

"And then?" Clem preparing for a longish session took a Coke from the cooler. What Benson was driving at would appear only in due time.

"Then, who knows? They'll have to scat. Or be scrapped. Left behind by history."

"But you've said it yourself, it's here. This fall we're thinking of concentrating on a single cash crop, say winter onions. They'll buy the sets in one lot and sell in one lot—"

"If you can get two of those dirt farmers together over anything but their fool notions, I'll eat my sister's hat with the cherries on it."

"But you donated fertilizer, didn't you, when I asked for it? And they rounded up the trucks, didn't they, to distribute it?"

"That's what I mean, waste of energy. Money down the drain. That fertilizer was sold off those trucks before it ever hit the ground. This one's wife is about to have a baby, and he's got to pay her way. That one's roof was blown off in the big blow last May and he's got to fix that first. And another one's got a little still back yonder in the woods and all he cares about is cash for mash."

Clem had heard this before about the distribution of the fertilizer, and it had pained him considerably when he first heard it. But all his sleuthing to ferret out the sellers had turned up only one culprit, Richard-Gene Jeems. He had been sorely tempted to have Richard-Gene suspended from the course, but then had changed his mind. Richard-Gene was well liked by the other boys, it would cause too much of a disturbance to oust him, he was more of a menace out of the class than in. And only one out of twenty. That wasn't too bad. But he could never convince Benson that it was just one. The expense incurred by the fertilizer was worth it to Benson for the sole pleasure of proving that he'd been gulled.

"And even if they put that fertilizer in the ground," Benson said irascibly, "what'll they grow out of it? Army worm. What'll they clear this year out of their crop? Two hundred dollars? Five hundred?"

"You told me before that as a preacher I'm an anachronism. Now you saying that as a teacher—"

"And more than that, Clem. More than that. The day of the intellectual who must walk hand in hand with the common man, every step in living fear of being rejected by him, that day is passing, Clem. It's passing. You're a prewar product and there's no place for you in the age we're entering upon."

"But I haven't even begun! Don't bury me, Benson, before I've begun!"

"Because it don't work out. Brain won't mix with brawn. It never has."

"Some of these boys are as brainy, brainier—"

"Then too bad for them. You seen this?"

His glasses again pivoting from side to side in search of eavesdroppers, Benson stooped to the bottom drawer of his desk and with some jugglery of his fingers known only to himself unlocked it. That side-to-side glance, Clem thought, how often around the county he had encountered it, over the smiling-lipped confidence, sotto voce. From every white man at some time or other, from the frankest countenance, the preface of that pivotal glance. And now from Benson, the top dog.

"Lo, the common man," Benson said. "There's your cracker."

He delved out from under a clutter of campaign stickers and buttons a flame yellow sheet printed with maroon ink. As if it burned to the touch, he flicked it over the desk to Clem with the blunt edge of his nail.

CRACKERS OF COLFAX COUNTY, UNITE!

A specter is haunting our county, the specter of RED RUSSIAN COMMUNISM in the guise of the BLACK VOTE . . . Black troops in the greatest untold scandal of the war raped thousands of German girls in the bunkers of Berlin!!! And now these BLACK TROOPS are here present among us plotting to SEIZE POWER!!! We call on EVERY REDBLOODED GEORGIAN TO PROTECT HIS OWN!

It is a proven fact that the negro race is inferior in intelligence and habitually criminal. He never produced a civilization of his own.

ONLY UNDER THE DIRECTION AND CONTROL OF THE
WHITE MAN has he made any contribution. The wise negro understands this. ASK HIM!

Get rid of the BLIND AND BUNGLING LEADERSHIP that
would sell our county to the RULE OF NIGGERS for a mess of
votes!

SAVE OUR COUNTY!

GET OUT AND VOTE FOR OL' CAL HUBBARD AND
EVERY LOCAL CANDIDATE WHO SUPPORTS HIM FOR
GOVERNOR!!!

"This junk." Clem scanned it. "Yes, I've seen a couple, more or less of
the same order. No one pays any attention—"

"But that's what they'll vote for. The boys in your class."

"The boys in my class aren't even interested," Clem said with conviction. "Only thing they're interested in is how soon they'll get blacktop on their roads and electricity through."

"But they'll vote for Ol' Cal just like they always have. And Ol' Vern
Purcell with him. Those boys of yours must influence at least three hundred others."

So this was the reason behind Benson's attack on him, his job and his
orientation. And its objective? Clem could guess. Foxily grinning, he
flicked the foolscap back.

"That's the anachronism. That's what's passé. You knocking yourself
out for nothing, Benson. Those boys are more up to date than you are.
They all know that you were the leading force in getting their class
started. They're all behind the drive you're conducting for the river
project—"

"But will they vote to return me to the county chairmanship of the
party? Will they vote for my slate?"

"I can't vouch for them, but . . . Whoever's behind this can't have
much support. If it's Judge Purcell, he didn't permit his name to be attached. There's no signature to it, not even an organization."

Benson sighed and fumblingly returned the handbill to its hiding
place under the clutter in the bottom drawer. Though it was growing
dark here in the back area of the bank, shadowed as it was by the blind
walls of neighboring buildings, he did not switch on his desk lamp. Removing his glasses, he tweaked tiredly at the dents they left on the
bridge of his nose.

"Clem, this may be only a straw in the wind but it's an ill wind, believe me. We've never had this kind of thing circulated in Colfax County before. Not even in the heyday of the Klan. You know that just yesterday up Taylor County a colored fellow was pumped full of lead for being a registered voter? You know what they're calling it? The first shot in Ol' Cal Hubbard's campaign. A declaration of open season on niggers. A warning to every one of them in this state to stay away from the polls. And what we have here in this handbill is an attempt to instigate the same spirit in this county."

"It won't go here," Clem said positively. "I don't know how I know, but I know. The whole atmosphere is against it. Except for up Fallona way."

"I never swung Fallona and Fallona never swung an election."

Benson swung about and contemplated the window, faced across the alley by the white clapboard of the next building. For a moment Clem thought that he was about to get up and roll the window shade down to the sill. The machinery in the ice plant behind the bank ceased abruptly, and when it ceased Benson lowered his voice.

"You ever wonder, Clem, why Henry didn't follow up that probate hearing on the Scott place with some kind of retaliation? It wasn't for want of trying. But Lars wouldn't go along with him on it. The Judge had burned his fingers on it. And public opinion was against it. He couldn't take any form of drastic action, open or concealed, and count on being covered. For the time being he's stuck. Unless the prevailing atmosphere—you're right about that—can be changed. I happen to know," his voice sank to a whisper, "that the paper of that handbill—it's a peculiar kind of color—is used by Sunset for its bills of lading."

"Now that," Clem said, "is just plain cuckoo. Henry wouldn't drop a bomb to catch a gnat. If you know so much about it, why don't you expose it?"

"And heap confusion on confusion? Who'd believe me?"

Plainly, Benson was not about to tangle with Henry Warren or Sunset. He had some other idea in mind.

"You just don't want to face the significance of this," Benson accused him. "You just want to stay inside the safe little island you've carved out for yourself."

"I am just enjoying for once in my life the position of not being the alarmist," Clem said. "All right, what do you want me to do about it?" Though he already knew.

"Stop deluding yourself about the nature of the people you're dealing with! Stop being a jackass—"

"Is that why you called me here? To whale me for them?"

"If you think so highly of them, then persuade them to the path of reason! If they can be switched to our slate—"

"I cannot and will not allow any politicking to enter into my teaching relationship with them, Benson, and you know it! That's out." He was clutching his empty Coke bottle, and it was slimy under his hand with his sweat. "I'm surprised you ask me."

"We have to use every means at our disposal."

"Then why don't you," Clem suggested, "encourage the colored vote in the county? They're having some sort of registration drive, I understand. If they turn out in droves—"

"You want me to commit suicide?"

Clem left the bank adamant but chortling over a juicy item Benson had transmitted to him with a lick of his chops, tastily. "You know where that phrase 'a specter is haunting this county' originated?" He had confessed to wondering about it. "*The Communist Manifesto*," Benson had informed him. "Marx and Engels. And you know who put it there? The Judge in person. He cribbed it. Want to know how I know?" Years ago, it seemed, an old country store having living quarters upstairs had fallen with all its stock and furnishings into the hands of the bank. In a storage space under the eaves a padlocked box was found, and Benson being a young chap then and inquisitive had unscrewed the lock. "It was chock-full of books and pamphlets. You know there was once quite a radical movement hereabouts? When the Populists were going strong. Single-taxers. Socialists." "What'd you do with the stuff?" "Read it. Bellamy, Henry George, Gene Debs, Florence Kelley, Veblen . . . It was quite an education. Eventually, some years later, I sent the box back to the Purcells with the padlock on. I never thought," Benson finished archly, "that Vern would open it too."

Benson had however refused his offer to drive him home, although it was past five and close upon his dinnertime. And that was strange . . .

Within the next few hours Clem dismissed Benson's appeal to him as the product of a moment of panic. The suspicion that the lurid handbills had been concocted by Judge Purcell in collusion with Henry Warren rested on rather too slender evidence: the tint of what must be a fairly common stock of paper and the memory of a dusty old box in a storage attic. More likely they were imported from outside, not very many of them, and they left no aftereffect, very little anyhow. What sort of man is it, he thought with a twinge of annoyance toward Benson that he'd never felt before, who uses his so-called realism to keep himself from doing what his best instincts dictate? What sort of supersensitive instincts does he have that he has to build himself such a wall to hide behind? And ducks at the merest shadow.

And Julie, surely Julie, as mistaken as she could sometimes be, would not be crass enough to allow such shenanigans. He resolved to pay a call on Julie at the earliest opportunity. But not tonight. It was never tonight for Julie. He had an appointment tonight with Professor Thurlow and Earl Goodfellow, the county agent, for their regular planning meeting.

Usually such meetings took place in the bleak loft over a garage that Goodfellow used for an office, occasionally in Thurlow's prim parlor or in Clem's crowded and disheveled study. This evening Clem bounded up the outside staircase to Goodfellow's office with extraordinary eagerness, in anticipation of succor no doubt from the concerns that Benson had sought to foist upon him. Thurlow had arrived before him, but Goodfellow was absent. He had left a note on his desk that he would be detained and that they should proceed without him. And that was strange too. Earl was a stickler for punctuality and a demon for wanting to be in on every last detail.

Thurlow was browsing through the upright steel shelves of paperbound publications along the wall. The office was occupied otherwise only with the desk, a long table for conferences and folding chairs arranged about the table.

"I have a problem," Clem tackled Thurlow directly, "that you may be able to shed some light on. Most of my boys are pretty enthusiastic over the course right now and they're putting a lot of hard work into it. That's understandable at the start, the honeymoon period. But how do you maintain it over the long run? We're teaching them advanced techniques, we're priming them with all the latest developments. The government pays for the books and the paper, but not for the equipment to put what they've learned into operation for them. What happens when they realize this?"

Thurlow leafed through a paperbound booklet, without looking up. "Two basic mistakes you can make. Provide the machinery without the know-how to use it, and that's no good. Or the know-how without the machinery, and that's no good either. I can't say which is worse, unless it's nothing."

One of Thurlow's equivocal answers, and not one to soothe the troubled spirit. Thurlow put his booklet away on the shelf and without looking at him took a chair at the side of the desk opposite him, fitting into it with shuffles, wheezes, and ruminative groans.

"It's an old story. The government gives you the right, but it won't enforce or protect that right. So you're left hanging in midair."

Another one of the innuendoes and double entendres with which Thurlow habitually interspersed his speech, and which Clem impatiently did not care to ponder over now. "But doesn't a process of demoralization set in?" he persisted. "Sooner or later don't they begin to feel it's all a fake? Without a sense of purpose in what you're doing, without attainable goals, isn't there bound to be breakdown?"

Thurlow took a snowy handkerchief out of the back pocket of his seedy black pants and wiped over the dome of his brow with it. "Well, you know we been teaching typing classes over to the school for, let me see, eight years now. Got an old Smith-Corona the other school sent over when they bought new ones. Always graduate one or two speed typists. Don't know anyone of them that ever had much use of it. But still those girls keep taking typing."

"What happens to them?"

"Some of them demoralize, sometimes the best of them. And some of them keep figuring if you crawl, you'll walk."

After a pause Thurlow, concentrating on sharpening a broken pencil over the wastebasket, paring off curls of wood and lead dust, appended a footnote. "You know my boys have been planning on buying a tractor. I located one down St. George and Reeve Scott's been elected to go take a look sometime this week. That's not saying anything will come of it."

It was as straight an answer as he would get out of Thurlow and it did offer something of the solace he was seeking. So much for Benson and his division of brain from brawn.

They went to work then on their crop plan for next season. Earl Goodfellow arrived a short while later, flushed and flustered and full of vague excuses. They filled him in. "Winter onions, huh?" They compared figures for estimated acreage and purchasing orders. The orders made by the two classes would of course not be pooled. No one was suggesting that . . .

Dull work but to Clem exhilarating.

Emotionally he derived his chiefest joy, it occurred to him on his way home, from the company of men, functioning together. Wifely attachment, family ties: these were secondary. The meetings always yielded him enormous gratification. Due to his inexperience he had sought help at the start from the two men separately. Then Goodfellow had proposed the meetings as a time-saver and now the three of them by coordinating their information were accomplishing three times as much as they would have alone. No one in the community objected to their getting together. So long as race didn't enter into it. So long as the issue of race was never brought to the fore. Among the three of them they adhered consistently to their subject, staying within the bounds they must observe without ever so much as mentioning them.

Or did they? Clem remembered Thurlow's reference tonight to "rights" granted by the government but not implemented. He was not, was he, alluding to an incident alleged to have taken place in Fallona a few days ago? An incident that was perhaps no more than one of the campaign jokes that seemed to be popping up here and there. An old colored gentleman, it was said, had gone down to the town hall to register to vote. "Well, you know, uncle," the registrar was said to have told him, "you have to answer some questions first. To prove if you qualify." "Yes sir." "The first question is, Do you like pine or oak?" The registrar had then, so the tale went, shut down his window and hung up a sign, Closed Till Further Notice.

Was this, Clem speculated as he drove past Julie's house—the lights were out—what Thurlow intended to convey to him? Was there some truth to the jest? Or did he have in mind those purges of what few colored names there were on registration lists now being executed in other parts of the state? Or that man who was shot to death up Taylor County yesterday? The echo of distant gunfire, the reflection of distant cross-burnings, the reports of beatings, bombings . . .

Parking his car in this rattletrap garage, Clem recalled Thurlow's face, leather-weathered, dewlapped, inured. The right guaranteed that you cannot exercise. The dream instilled that you cannot fulfill. Which is worse unless it's nothing at all. If you crawl, you'll walk . . .

His mother was waiting for him in the kitchen. "Nice meeting, dear?" She was worried about those meetings. Even when they took place here in the house she worried. "How about a nice glass of iced tea?"

The lemon-sweet liquid slipped gratefully down his parched throat.

Nancy was waiting up for him in bed, reading. "How'd it go?"

"What go? You'd think it was something, heaven knows what!"

"Well don't fly off the handle. It's just it took so long."

"Earl was late."

He slipped into bed and kicked the sheet off. Too hot. What had Earl been in such a fuss about? As if he'd had a dressing-down from someone. Henry Warren, at whose personal beck and call he had been up to now? And he had shied off when Thurlow offered his house for next meeting. "I'll let you know." Earl was never that indefinite.

All his pleasure in the meeting was dissipated by an uneasiness that welled up in him with the grueling ache of a hungry void, with the clawing insistence of an unsatisfied passion.

"Thurlow's students," he said challengingly to Nancy, "are thinking of buying a tractor. Mine aren't ready for anything like that. You think maybe in another six months—?"

She stretched herself out on her back with a restless little wriggle.

Their two bodies were forming separate valleys in the mattress with the saddleback of a mountain range between.

"You're not going around, are you," she said, with a breathlessness that took the edge off any offense that might reside in her query, "making comparisons?"

"Nancy, you must know as well as I do"—he turned on the pillow toward her with his raging passion of dissatisfaction—"that this class is as clean as a test tube! There is no place in it for my personal inclinations. Religious. Political. Or racial. It's job enough as it is!"

"Well, don't bite my head off . . ."

2

The uneasiness that stirred in Clem that night flared up soon thereafter in a conflagration that all but devoured him. Only three nights later, the two couples—two farmer veterans and their wives—were shot to death, and their landlord was officially visited next day by Ol' Cal Hubbard himself, presumably with congratulations.

The news, widely broadcast, produced in Colfax County among the whites—what the colored felt few ventured to guess—a wave of seismic shock. The sensation of a breach which they both denied and sought with an anguish of indecent haste to gloss over. Time after time Clem was stopped on the street and in the road by well-wishers who managed to assert with an overaggressive defensiveness that ostentatiously avoided the subject: "Thank God, Reverend, we live in a place where we're at peace with our neighbor." Why to me, Clem wondered, as if I represented the colored? "You remember when that boy was suing for his farm just a few months ago," they assured themselves to him—it had already become a suit, "didn't he win it? What I say is, thank God we live in peace and quiet here."

Clem wandered about in a daze, riven with guilt, his guilt, and with a need for penance, his penance. At school, outside on the steps, he noticed Rad McDowell in the midst of a knot of arguers, but he went on into the classroom without intervening. The class was not to be jeopardized by his avid need to take sides. At night he thrashed about in his bed, sleepless. What can I do? What shall I do? What must I do?

"But why are you assailing yourself," Nancy sought to soothe him, "instead of *them*? The ones that did it."

"It's an evasion! To exorcise the guilt we all feel by placing the blame on the perpetrators alone is only too easy."

"I don't see where that's so easy."

And perhaps that was the evasion. He was afraid to assail *them*. It was easier to indulge his own remorse.

Four days after the quadruple killings, near Eatonville a sharecropper was whipped with a gun butt on the highway at broad noon and riddled with shot. The man with the gun was released on the spot by the sheriff.

That evening Clem decided to go to Thurlow for counsel, against his mother's good advice. "Isn't it possible, dear," she cautioned him, "that this whole thing has created such universal revulsion that it will achieve more good in the end than you or I ever can? The woolhats will lose the election. There isn't a self-respecting person in the county who'd vote for Ol' Cal now and his gang. Why take the chance of muddying it up with some side issue?"

"Such as what?"

"Such as running to Thurlow first thing."

"If I don't go to him now," he said, "how can I face him next time we meet? How can I ever look him in the eye again?"

"Why can't you leave things alone?" she cried. "Why can't you leave alone what you can't help?"

He went to Thurlow's house after dark, walking, taking a back street around and entering through the back gate, treading softly through the yard to the little vine-shrouded porch in the rear. He was stopped before he set foot on the bottom step by an argument, exacerbated voices raised in ire, behind the drawn shade of what must be the kitchen window, just above his shoulder.

"So you'll send your little resolution, you'll make your protest, you'll call for an investigation! You've done your duty, you got a clean conscience. Then what? What'll happen? Can it bring them back alive? Will it bring them any justice? A resolution! You might's well tear it up before you start it because you only going to get it spit right back in the puss. Them guys are all going free!"

"You fall in here loud and wrong." It was Reeve's voice, tight with spite. "Power, you drunk and you out of line—"

"So what are you doing about it, Power?" Vivian, taunting. "What are you going to do about it?"

"I'm getting a hundred thousand of us together to make a march on the State Capitol. They may kill some of us but they can't kill all of us. Because we'll keep coming!"

"You just like to hear yourself talk." Reeve again, wearily. "If you don't want to do what can be done, why don't you just say so?"

"At least I ain't doing nothing and fooling myself it's something!"

"Then get a hundred thousand names. Or is it you too gutless to give even yours?"

"Now wait a minute, you—"

"Please," Vivian pleading, "you two agree, I know you do. Now don't start fighting!"

"This man said something I don't like, not one little bit—"

"How can you do the big things unless you do the little ones?"

"If you do the little things, you never get to the big. You won't get, period!"

"Will you put up or shut up or get out—"

The step creaked under Clem's foot. The argument ceased abruptly. Inside, a door was slammed. When Clem was admitted after a prolonged delay by Clelia, the morose housekeeper, leaning on her eternal mop, the back hall was quiet and the kitchen door was closed. Clelia escorted him into the parlor. "The Professor will be down in a minute. He was just about to retire."

"May I speak with Miss Vivian then?"

"Well, I couldn't rightly say where she's at right now."

Clem sat down on the puffed velvet seat of a frame-backed chair to await the Professor. Vivian was still back there in the kitchen, he could have sworn, with those two men, continuing the argument with her eyes. He was more than a little disappointed that she had chosen to make herself scarce. The first time he visited the house he had asked her, rather ineptly, "Did you study teaching?" "Not exactly," she had said. "I majored in English and minored in social work. That was my compromise." He had laughed, admitting, "Well I majored in philosophy and minored in agriculture." "And that was your compromise?" They had both laughed together then. If you have to live in a small town, it's always good to know there's someone you can talk to in that vein.

Vivian, Clem thought nostalgically now, for Julie? The lost Julie . . . "You should meet Julie Warren," he had told Vivian once. "You'd take to each other." "Gladly," Vivian said.

The Professor shuffled into the parlor, formally attired in a fresh white shirt. Clem rose to meet him halfway with a handshake. "I came—" he stumbled. What had he come for? To offer his condolences? "I wanted to know if there's anything I can do to help. What can I do?"

The Professor took the loveseat opposite Clem and, his hands placed on his spread knees, his great head nestling in his collar, stared fixedly before him through glasses that winked in the lamplight. Wondering, Clem hazarded a horrified guess, whether he ought to betray to me that he understands what I'm asking him. "The experts talk about the pain and grief my race must endure," he said to Thurlow, "in order to accept yours. But none of them seems to give a hang for the turmoil and torment, the shame we go through in times like this."

And was ashamed to say it. Was he seeking compassion for himself?

"We appreciate your coming." Several times Thurlow assured him of that. "We surely do appreciate it. It means a lot to us."

But he never did apprise Clem of what he ought to do. If the colored were preparing a resolution, he did not inform Clem of it, either out of tact, an unwillingness to put him on the spot with regard to his signature, or out of tactics, a conviction that it would be inadvisable for Clem to place his signature alongside theirs. For Clem's protection or for theirs, from habit or from discretion, he would not divulge that such a move was in the making, if it was.

While telling Clem nothing, Thurlow managed in his rambling roundabout manner to probe him quite thoroughly. "You didn't come here, did you," Thurlow inquired with desultory hesitancy, seeking enlightenment, "to give us leadership?" "Well, no," Clem admitted, and the old man was somehow relieved by his reply. And somehow without stating it outright, he implied with the same desultory puzzlement: "Then you asking us to give you leadership?" And with this implication he threw Clem back on his own resources. You know what to do! You didn't have to come here to find that out!

In the end Thurlow, grasping his elbow, trundled him out through the front door to the front verandah and standing in the lighted doorway detained him a moment. "Tell me something, Clem. There's something I've all my life been curious to know. Do the white folks really believe all this truck they put out about us?"

It was the first direct utterance, bald and unabashed, that he had ever received from Thurlow.

Clem was so bemused by it—the olive in the martini, spiked with the piquant heart of pimento—that he stopped halfway home under a streetlamp to enter it into his notebook. But he came away from Thurlow uneased in his need and more confused than ever. The mares' nests one steps into. What can I do? What shall I do? What must I . . .

He passed Julie's house, dark again except for the dim glow of a night lamp in the boy's back bedroom. Toward Julie he had a bad conscience and his avoidance of her—what else could it be but avoidance?—must spring from that. The fleeting glimpses and greetings of Sunday church could not compensate for his remissness. The part she had played in Purcell's row with him had hurt him. The part she had played in the court row over the Scott land had antagonized him. But did he have to be so stuffy about it? It must all have been minimized for her by her greater concern over the boy. She needed help now. And here he was chasing after lost causes that he was helpless to rescue. As in the last analysis he was also helpless toward her.

How can you help, really? Unless you can bring the dead back to life. Make the sick well.

Trudging up the weedy path to the rectory he felt that his life was a mishmash of mismanagement, false starts, misspent energies, inability to choose a direction and stick to it. What can I do? What shall I do? What must I . . .

Altogether, within a two-week period, that fecund midsummer, in diverse parts of the state for disparate reasons, having no connection with each other, eight Negroes were slain by bullet or bludgeon or both, caught by one or more white men at home or on their way to work or in the midst of an evening stroll.

During this time, at the end of July, Clem took a trip into Bay City to find out what was being done there by the ministers' association. He brought home with him a resolution, framed in the most circumspect language, calling upon the outgoing Governor, the Attorney General, the State Bureau of Investigation, and all the powers-that-be to curb the lawlessness that was wreaking such havoc with the reputation of the state in the eyes of the nation and of the world. The resolution was to be signed by whites only.

Ordinarily Clem would have taken it first to Julie. He had tried several times in the recent past, when he had a moment to spare, to reach her by telephone. But she was either out boating on the sound "with the children"—so Kissie told him, placing stress on the plural—or off to Silver Beach "with her boys" for a few days. Now, since he had not managed to drop in on her out of personal concern, how could he go to her with a public concern?

So he went to Benson Reece with it. Unfortunately Benson, when he met him, had just returned home from a little hamlet on the periphery of the county where a registrar had been fired for refusing to take colored names off his list. "Ousted not by the majority, Clem, that I'll grant you. By a coupla coots in cahoots. You don't hear a thing of it here, but Ol' Vern sure is whooping it up for Ol' Cal back there back country."

They relaxed in slat-backed chairs on Benson's back piazza, sipping juleps out of frosted silver cups prepared by Benson's sister Sarah from her latest bridge club recipe. Clem presented the resolution to Benson. Benson sighed. His rotund face was caving in this summer, shrinking about the jaws. "You were the first one," Clem reminded him, "to nudge me out of my lethargy."

"I didn't nudge you this way."

"When these shootings started coming one on top the other," Clem said, "my first impulse was to send a wire to the Governor. I could think of all the reasons in the world why I shouldn't and I didn't. There's nothing that stinks inside you like a right impulse repressed."

"One month from now," Benson said, "every one of those corpses will be gone and forgotten. But the fact that you circulated this will not be."

He folded the resolution and passed it back to Clem. "Now that organization they're investigating up Washington for giving aid to Spanish refugees or some such thing, that'll go on. And that spy case that broke yesterday, government employees giving our secrets to the Russians, that'll keep boiling. The charges. The indictment. The trial. The appeals. Did they or didn't they? Who else was in it? On and on."

"You won't sign it?" Clem demanded incredulously.

"No sir."

"They were living their lives, they had families, children . . . And nothing's to be said about it? Nothing to prevent the next time? In fact, you encourage the next time—"

"When I see a northeaster blowing up," Benson said and blew, frowning, into his cup. "Damn, Sarah! What's this horse piss? You put water in for bourbon? I batten down my hatches and drag anchor. Till it blows over. You think that's cowardly?"

"I think," Clem said sharply, "that you're in retreat when you should be pushing full steam ahead."

Benson closed his eyes, folded his hands over his solar plexus. "I am fighting, Clem, for my registrars, my polling clerks, and my ballot counters."

"Then sign it! It's to your every interest to sign."

"You do as you like and take the consequences. Let me do as I like and take the same."

Clem later regretted his sharpness. It was as near to a quarrel as he had ever come with Benson, and he never knew how deeply his pinprick of criticism affected the tender self Benson so aggressively screened behind his fusillades of barbs. He sometimes suspected that Benson's leeriness was initiated by the phrase contained in the inflammatory handbill, BLIND AND BUNGLING LEADERSHIP. With reference, as Benson must interpret it, to his person. Not in the figurative sense of such vituperatives, hurled at random in any campaign. But as an insult to his physical being, his failing eyesight, his groping with his cane.

In less than two days Clem obtained the astonishing number of one hundred and five signatures on his resolution, going neither to his class nor his church for support. Approaching first the Methodist and Presbyterian ministers, then certain businessmen of thoughtful disposition and ladies of great age and esteem, the Bird family with all its adult collaterals, Edna Telfer at the paper, fishermen suggested to him by Johnny Herrera.

And still after he mailed the resolution off, with the extra pages of signatories stapled to it, he knew no relief. *So we all think we can fix everything up with a little exercise of our fingers, do we? We've done our duty, our conscience is clear. Will it bring them back alive? Will it bring them any justice?* Nothing would have relieved him unless it was to climb the frayed rope ladder to the top of the St. Paul steeple and toll the blackened brass bell until it pealed over the whole countryside, wave after sonar wave, shattering the blue-and-green tranquillity of the air. *What shall I do? What must I do . . .*

He had scarcely disposed of the resolution when the rumors began to reach his ears. Rumors which he read as storm signals. Signs of a far-flung net descending like a noose over the county, over Benson, over Thurlow and himself and their classes, and most specifically the two boys, Rad McDowell and Reeve Scott.

He was making his round of farms with Nancy on a fair August morning; the miasmal spate of dog days to be expected at this season had not yet begun. Nancy liked to accompany him when the weather wasn't too hot. It was an escape for her from the perpetual pressures of the household. Also they were so seldom alone at home that in the car now they shared a closeness like that of a long-married couple, needing no dalliance. Nancy had a book, *The Citadel*, to read while Clem visited, and a pocketful of trinkets for the kids who came flitting about the car.

Everywhere they stopped Clem saw indications of progress. Progress of such infinitesimal scale, it was true, and at such a snail's pace that, when he thought of it, it broke his heart; but when he saw it, as he did now, he rejoiced in it. Ray Del Vecchio, whose family had moved here from nearby Ludowici abandoning rich claybanks and profitless kilns, had a bumper crop of Ruby King peppers in his truck garden. Lonnie Truelove, who had been given a portion of his father's farm to clear and cultivate, was building up his compost pile in lieu of manure. Tom Holland was putting down a cabbage seed patch for next fall. After all, these men weren't trying to beat the world. They were only trying to make a go of it. And they could. They could.

Even Richard-Gene when they finally reached him, down at the end of a sandy road and off at the end of a rutted track that seemed to leave all civilization behind, was hard at work. Clem left Nancy in the car and beat through bushes to join him in the scraggly field. Richard-Gene's big lumbering frame squatted before a ridge, bedded up high enough to surmount standing water. He was setting out strawberry plants.

"Didn't you just say a while back," Richard-Gene demanded of him bellicosely from under the arch of his armpit, "there's a million bucks in strawberries?"

Clem looked down at the close uneven rows. This late in the season, Panamandus! "Where's your dibble? This one's in too deep: see, they'll get smothered." He loosened the roots with the dibble, carefully lifted out the plant, reset and firmed it about. "And that one's in too shallow, it'll dry up. Here."

Richard-Gene thrust aside the dibble and dug in with his hands, down into the dirt where it was mellow. He set the next plant in with the crown at the surface. He continued along the slotted ridge, squatting on his heels, firming the earth with his hands under Clem's eye until he finished. The sun shone on his matted dark hair and three-day's growth of beard making a halo of the fuzz ends, gilded his torn blue shirt and grime-stained pants. Richard-Gene was ignorant and bigoted and lazy, he attended classes mainly for the money, grew corn mainly for the still he ran in the woods with his brothers, and he'd sold the fertilizer Benson had donated. Yet now it appeared that he would have strawberry runners in the fall and fruit next year if he hoed enough weeds, fertilized carefully enough not to burn the leaves, picked off the first blossoms . . .

"Next year," Clem said, "if you all make out well enough to show you're in business, maybe we can go to the conservation service for fertilizer on their cost-share plan."

Richard-Gene, taking the mention of fertilizer as a personal dig, winked salaciously up at him. "I bet that's the last handout Ol' Benson ever gives out with, hey Preach? You ain't told me yet what you think about the news that's going round."

"What news?"

"The news about Rad McDowell."

"Well, I know his wife presented him with a fine baby girl and almost died of it. I stopped by at the hospital to see her when I was down Bay City last week."

"I don't mean that. I mean, well you know Rad's my friend and all—"

At first Clem thought that Richard-Gene was only trying to retaliate for his dig through Rad, his favorite student. But he was bothered by something, a mere nothing: Richard-Gene's leap of association from Benson to Rad.

"—I think the world and all of Rad. Anybody says anything against him I'd whip his head. But you know the way Rad is? Always taking up for the niggers and all like that?"

Richard-Gene got up from his haunches and dusted off his knees. He accompanied Clem back to the car, his small eyes poking sidewise toward him, inquiring and probing, inviting agreement.

"Well, he's gone too far now. There's one thing nobody round here will stand for." He dropped his voice, with a quick side-to-side switch of his head, looking for eavesdroppers in the bush. "He's been holdin' meetin's with niggers in the dead of night. Eatin' with them too. In secret, you know?"

"Now Richard-Gene," Clem said, "you know better than that. What would they be meeting about?"

"Well, I don't know," Richard-Gene said. "Just eatin' and meetin'."

They reached the car in a tangle of chickens, children, and hound dogs. Nancy, snowy-cool in white, smiled up at them from her novel. Clem took the wheel and Richard-Gene directed him through the tricky feints of reversing the car into the grass-grown track. "Now don't forget what I done told you." He poked his head into the window, running alongside. "Some of the fellas are pretty worked up over it."

"What's the matter, Clem?" Nancy closed her book. She had stopped getting out of the car on these trips after a few initial attempts at conversation with the women. Without his presence as a medium of communication she was lost.

"Nothing," he said. "There's nothing the matter."

"There is too. Look." She propped herself up on her knees and dove down back of the seat to the accumulation on the floor of watermelon, mustard-pickle, flowers, and eggs that had been pressed upon them. "Look what one of those children brought out to me." She dangled before him a crewel-embroidered cushion cover. "Too bad we don't have anything it'll fit. Honestly—" She refolded the cover and diving down again tucked it about the bucket of eggs. "Some of these people would give you the shirt off their backs."

They passed through Fallona, an oasis of white bungalows and Georgian brick town hall surrounded by turpentine pine.

"Such a pretty town. Isn't it pretty here? So peaceful," Nancy said with piercing poignant wistfulness as if her days were spent in mortal combat. Longleaf and slash pine fled by. "So peaceful way off here in the woods away from everything. Peaceful peaceful peaceful . . . Why you stopping?"

Clem slewed dustily off the road into the yard of a little tumbledown church. He got out of the car and struck across the sun-scorched grounds to the door. He had assumed that the place was deserted until, passing it one evening a few weeks ago on his way to a Grange meeting, he had noticed the windows flickering with some sort of illumination from within and had heard the jangle of tambourines, the roll of drums, the chant and outcries of a revival.

The place looked forsaken enough now. Only the thickets of hydrangea bushes clustered about the sagging steps, popcorned over with blue blossoms, gave it an air of life.

A sign was posted on the door, nailed over a crack in the upper panel. He had first observed the flame-yellow patch of the sign a few weeks ago from the road and had almost thought that he could read the maroon letters on it. But he had been in a hurry and he wasn't sure and perhaps he wasn't prepared to recognize it then. It was gone in the rain last week. And now it was up again, clean yellow of paper and fresh of ink as if it had just been posted up there again:

THE FIRST NIGGER THAT VOTES
WILL BE THE LAST

He stood before it with a sickening sinking of his stomach. Other sections of the state, but not this close, not here! The church was within the perimeter of Fallona and Fallona was Purcell's stronghold and Ol' Cal country from long-gone—but not this far-gone.

With his penknife he slit one of the hydrangea blossoms from the bush overhanging the top step and carried it, multifloral, a stately flower dome, blue as litmus paper from the acidity of the earth out of which it sucked its nurture, back to Nancy in the car.

A new blue Chevrolet sedan had drawn up in the yard behind his car, and Nancy was sitting in her place as rigid as a rabbit about to be pounced on. Lounging against the driver's door with his arm resting on the roof was a sandy-haired, sandy-skinned, sandy-clad man with an Ol' Cal button pinned on the lapel of his shirt.

"Looking for somebody, Preacher?"

"No," Clem said and reached toward his door handle, "I was just interested in that sign back there."

He was still carrying the knife with which he had cut the flower and —as the man didn't move from his door—for the life of him, he couldn't help it, he stuck the hydrangea behind his ear, reached into his pocket for his plug of tobacco and cut off a chew. "If you don't mind, sir, I have to be going along."

"Funniest thing how it keeps blowin' off." The man's eyes shifted from Clem to the church door and back again—even his eyes were sandy. "That's a nigger prayerhouse."

"I know." Clem turned back, squinting at the faded nameplate hung over the arch of the door:

CHURCH OF THE LIVING GOD AND PILLAR OF TRUTH

"You the fella they say been runnin' around to all the farmer vets? Drummin' up the vote for Morgan?"

Clem licked the cud of tobacco, suddenly gone dry, back under his jaw. His clerical collar, wilting in the heat, constrained his throat like wet rope. "I'm not in politics."

"Ain't you a Benson Reece boy?"

"I'm not anyone's boy." He found himself speaking as enigmatically as Thurlow sometimes did. "Fact is, I'm not interested in anyone's politicking. It's out of my line. Now if you'll please just step away from my door?"

"Well, y'all ought to be if y'ain't." He thrust his hand out. "I'm Will Royall. Running for sheriff against Chalmer Coombs. Wish me luck."

Clem found his hand seized and pumped with sand-grained vigor. "That's a nice car you got there, Mr. DeLavery." The man released himself from the door. "Almost as new as mine. Mind how you bring them fellas in your class along, hear?"

Clem inserted himself into the seat and waited for the other car to back out from behind him. He could still feel the sand-grained palm grasping his palm, the clasp of the man's left hand under his elbow as he pumped with his right. Wish-me-luck. It's so easy, so easy for them to back you into a corner, pin you down. And he'd had the gall, the colossal gall to charge Benson with backsliding!

The car behind gunned up but didn't move. With a jerk of gears Clem pulled forward, then backed out at a wide angle jolting over the uneven ground into the road.

"Clem, the eggs! You'll break the eggs!"

He didn't care if he broke an axle. He threw the throttle wide open and in the rear-view mirror saw Royall hit the road behind him.

"Clement DeLavery, you spit that right out!"

His jaw grimly clenched over the tobacco, he took a few turns from side road to side road. "Is he still following us?"

"Well, he's falling back. Clem, he knew your name. He knows who you are."

"Yup. Got my number. And my license plate. But where he got that about me advocating Morgan . . . Were you scared?"

She smoothed her skirt over her knees, kneaded and massaged her fingers over her lap. "Should I have been?" She stared straight ahead, the oblique planes of her face taut, her mouth stubbornly square. "What was there to be scared of?"

Royall disappeared. Covered with sand grit, they emerged from their circuitous route into the environs of Fallona again. On one side of the road a billboard displayed Ol' Cal's gallantly reared head, image of the common man, hayseed, grassroots; and proclaimed, the whole framed in a border of star-studded bars:

SAVE OUR STATE
GET OUT AND WORK FOR ME!

On the opposite side of the road, also in red-white-and-blue but minus the inspiration of stars and bars, another billboard proclaimed:

MOVE AHEAD WITH MORGAN!

Middleton Morgan's eyes had been gouged out and a sinister beard had been charcoaled over his cheeks. Slogans quoted from his platform were slashed to tatters.

Clem had to get out of the car and get rid of his tobacco. Nancy could be even more insistent than his mother sometimes. He looked up at Ol' Cal and blew his gob into the ditch. Why couldn't he splatter that shrewd smile? Why didn't he cut that sign down from the church door? Bringing back to Nancy instead a hydrangea blossom. Which she pinned clownishly up on top of her head.

"I can't understand it," he said to her as he slid back under the wheel. "This isn't such a hot campaign. There are no burning issues. Except the Negro—Ol' Cal's promise to restore the white primary by hook or by crook. And Morgan isn't even fighting him on that . . . The majority of people don't care that much about it, I swear they don't. It's the minority. They grab you by the shirt collar and start tying you in knots . . ."

"Let's go home," Nancy said, the silly pompon atop her head nodding, a solemn panache. "I'm plumb wore out."

But Clem would not turn home yet. There was something going on here behind Richard-Gene's hints and Royall's warnings. He was too disturbed to remain in the dark about it, he had to look into it. Although he had not planned to stop today at Carl Maynard's place, he cut once more through the backroads, past stands of black-stemmed pine, close as harpstrings under the green gloom of their foliage, buckets attached to the lip of the gash hacked into every trunk. It was back here that Judge Purcell was said to have his turpentine camp, if he had such a camp. Rumormongering was such a favorite pastime of the county, there were some people who seemed to make a lifetime profession of manufacturing rumors. Rumors sprang up overnight like dragon's teeth into a living entity that had to be dealt with.

He crossed the highway, and here the green fields rolled riverward. Clem swung with relief from the dusty road into the well-kept yard of Carl Maynard's house. Carl was levelheaded, clean-cut, clear-eyed, straightforward, the best educated of his students and the most substantial. Carl would give him the lowdown.

"Do you want me to come with you?" Nancy offered.

"No, there's something I want to take up with him, it'd just fret you."

"That's what frets me."

Clem headed first for the house, a long, low rambling structure, painted white some years before. The porch was clean-swept. The rattan settle and rocker on it were worn but in good repair. Clem knocked at the door, peering through the screen into the interior, dark with shades drawn against the noonday sun. "Anybody home?" Carl, unmarried, lived with his mother and sister, ladies who had remained assiduously invisible to Clem up to now. He knocked again sharply, his knuckles stinging on the doorpost. A blush burned up over his ears when a voice came at him from the porchside, discovering him in the act of peeping in.

"You thar."

From around the corner of the porch hobbled an ancient crone, toothless, her mouth collapsed inward to a lipless incision, her black sunbonnet bobbing as she pulled herself along on her stick, her tidy black dress just clearing the ground.

"I'm Mr. DeLavery," Clem introduced himself to her. "I'm looking for Carl. Could you tell me where on the place I'd find him?"

Pale blue eyes, saucers of skim milk, scanned him upward from his scuffed jeans to his incongruous shirt and collar.

"You a preacher-man, mister?"

"Why yes. I'm Mr. DeLavery from St. Paul's Church down Arcady. I'm teaching Carl's farm-training course now. Could you tell where in the field I might find him?"

"He ain't here."

She dug her stick into the ground and pulled herself off, dismissing him. From around the corner of the barn, directly ahead of her, Carl hove into sight, pushing a wheelbarrow.

"Say Carl?"

"Say there, Rev," Carl hailed him over.

Clem soon outstripped the old lady, but she dogged his footsteps, her black coal scuttle of a bonnet all but skimming his shoulder blades all the way down to the barn. Leaning on her stick, a staff of peeled hazel, green-tinged, she stood off a short distance as he approached Carl.

Even in overalls Carl looked fresh-bathed and laundered. He had that cleanliness to him which is native gift as well as determination, his hair slicked back under his denim cap as if just combed, his lean jaw smooth as if the lather had just been swooshed off, his clothing pressed, fitting his spare figure as if tailored to it. He was slow-spoken, articulate, thoughtful—a first cousin, Clem thought, to the English yeoman. And the scrupulous care that attended Carl's every transaction was legendary. He kept dairy cattle on the farm he had inherited from his forefathers and he was planning to build up his herd. Manure was immediately raked away from the vicinity of his barn, dried out, and then deposited in the fields. In the fields he planned to grow next winter a quick temporary crop of lespedeza and what he didn't use for feed plow under.

"I got this bull," Carl explained to Clem now, "to serve my eight cows. But I don't really trust him. You take a chance with a bull you've bought. In two–three years if he turns out to be a dud, you can lose all your time, money, and labor. I don't believe in putting everything into one piece of equipment." So he was hedging the bull around by joining two–three different breeding associations, not quite trusting any of them. "Now this artificial insemination, it's sure because you have proven bulls as sires, and the milk strain through the female line has been researched. But even then, you never know."

"Looks like in time," Clem said, "you'll really have something here."

"Oh I'm not satisfied. A long way from that. In about ten years maybe I'll have about forty Holstein. And with electricity in I'll have all my milking on machine, not a human hand touching it. And a couple of tractors in the field. Reckon by then, Rev, I'll be making enough to pay income tax?"

Carl stepped back from his wheelbarrow and threw inside a lean-to shed a burlap bag of fertilizer that was lying exposed on the ground. He bought his fertilizer "to sell on consignment" so he could be classed as a dealer and save himself money. "If it wasn't," he burst out, losing his tempered manner, "for the damnation No Fence Law! How can you keep cattle when these free-rangers are allowed to run all over your land!"

"Look Carl," Clem touched his arm. If Carl got started on the No Fence Law he'd be here with him all afternoon. He drew Carl closer and caught himself with a quick switch of his head looking both ways for eavesdroppers. The old lady was still standing her short distance off, following them as they moved.

"You heard any talk going on about this September primary? That is, anything out of the ordinary?"

"Well, now." Carl removed his denim cap and scratched down over the back of his head with it. Under lowered brows, his eyes searched about the ground for a way to say it. "One thing I do know. There's somebody going around trying to start the old Klan up and get it together again. I know because I was in it once. Though by the time I was old enough to join, it wasn't much of anything. Wouldn't do it again though." He shook his head consideredly. "Nobody cares anymore about that old stuff. It's finished."

He whisked away a few flies and detaining Clem with his hand thought further. "One thing, they claim the niggers in this county will take the election if we don't stop 'em. And you know, they say Rad McDowell is right in there with them?"

"Oh?"

"Now this is just between you and me." Now, Carl's head switched to and fro with the barest perceptible motion. He put his arm around Clem's back, speaking into his ear. "I wouldn't say this to anyone else but you. These colored folks around here—one of these days they going to have their rights. Gonna have to. I can see it coming."

"Yes?"

"But the way they got Rad now fronting for them and the way he's been buying that dynamite for them and standing up in court—"

"Now Carl—"

"And the way he beat it to Bay City the other night, middle of the night, with that Reeve, making deals with Carter Sillens, tying up the nigger vote with that skunk and bringing his vice and corruption into this county— That's something no decent self-respecting citizen will stand for!"

"I happen to know," Clem said, his ear lobes throbbing, "that all Rad did was carry his wife into Bay City in Professor Thurlow's car—"

It was hopeless. Heaping confusion on confusion, Benson said it. And through this labyrinthine skein, try and thread your way out.

Carl Maynard, cautious cool Carl Maynard, spouting such nonsense. His lean, clean jaw spotting with passion.

"Another thing—" Carl Maynard took him by the elbow and drew him all the way back into the lee of the shed, lowering his voice to an almost inaudible drone. "There's talk going on about you too, Reverend. They say you one of these CIO Reds—"

"Am I dreaming?"

"I know," Carl squeezed his arm, with sympathy. "But that's what they saying. They say you out to unionize all these pickers and packers at Sunset. And the shrimp fishermen and shrimp headers too."

"That is the most insane—"

"That's what I told 'em."

"Who? Who?"

"Oh, some of the fellas. Out and around." With the friendliest of grins, back to normal, he cracked Clem across the shoulders. "Yep, they sayin' you one of these here cussed Com-myou-nists."

Clem left Carl and headed back for the car, so dizzied he thought he was going to faint like a girl. The old lady when he passed her twirled on her stick and hobbled after him. He hastened his step, having no residue of ministerial benevolence for commerce with one who might or might not be all there. The old lady hopped after him, keeping pace, panting.

"You say you a preacher?"

"Yes ma'am."

He slowed down, this was senseless, till she caught up with him.

"Well, what's that woman you got up there in your car?"

"That's my wife."

"Oh no it ain't!"

Clem's head spun, was lopped off and screwed on backward.

"Pardon me, ma'am, but that is my wife." Why did he have to respond as if his denial would be taken seriously, as if he had to prove—? "She's waiting in the car for me."

"Oh no she ain't. Shame on you, lying to me like that. That's Pansy McLain from Tall'hassee, Flor'da."

"That's my wife, ma'am." He urged the old lady on toward the car. Fact is fact. Reality is reality. "Come on with me now. I want you to meet her."

The old lady hung back, resisting his urgent nudge forward. "That is Pansy McLain and don't you tell me different! Y'ought to be ashame, carryin' her here. Now you tell her to quit botherin' my Carl. You tell her to quit sendin' him them Christmas cards!"

But he had to keep urging her on as if she were in her right mind, as if it were within his power to convince her. "She's my wife, Mrs. Maynard. Now you come and see for yourself. Come, I'll show you."

When they arrived at the car, they found Nancy asleep in the front seat. She had curled up sidewise, her head drooping, her mermaid hair falling over her cheek, her flower crushed in the nook of her shoulder, her demure peter pan collar open over her heat-flushed collarbone, her skirt rumpled over drawn-up childishly sturdy knees.

"Pansy?"

The old lady spoke intently into the window before Clem could intervene. The name issued from between her gums with a sibilant tintinnabulation. She elbowed Clem back, so bent on conducting her test her own way that he could not or would not, being so sure of the outcome, prevent her.

"Pansy McLain!"

The curved sweep of eyelashes stirred, and that smile, that truly beautiful smile that stood her so well on so many occasions, of such dearness that none could withstand it, of such fidelity that none could doubt, unfolded from her mouth to its inset corners, over the tiny frill of her nose, the slant of her cheeks and her dusky eyes.

"Pansy?"

Under the horny face hovering over her from deep inside the black sunbonnet, Nancy swiftly straightened herself out and extended her hand.

"Why how do you do," Nancy said, with her beautiful smile.

"Thar!"

The black sunbonnet withdrew from the window. A hand clawed the air.

"You see! You see! Asleep there in the middle of the day. Dead drunk in the car. Pansy McLain"—she flourished her stick at Nancy's face—"you leave Carl alone, you hear? And as for you, Preacher"—she chased Clem around to the driver's side of the car—"whoever you are, don't you ever let me catch you around here again! Git now! Git!"

Her eyes were red-rimmed milky balls, bulging out in defense of her own. Clem closed his car door on those eyes as if they were cannon balls. Another minute she'd be bringing her stick down on his head. Or bringing a musket up from under her poplin skirts, blasting them out of there.

He beat it out to the road in a cloud of dust. Her triumph was such that Clem could not be sure for some time afterward that he was himself, that he was not in fact the unknown person reflected in those milky eyes.

"But what happened?" Nancy cried. "What'd I do? Did I say something wrong?"

He kept his foot down on the gas all the way back to the highway. The innocents expelled from paradise.

"The eggs," Nancy cried. "Please, Clem, you'll break the eggs into a million pieces."

It was the watermelon, not the eggs after all, that broke. It bounced on a jounce and burst asunder, spurting pink juice all over the crewel-embroidered cushion cover in which the neighboring bucket of eggs was tucked. Clem slowed down somewhat after that, but only long enough to scoop up the blue flower and stick it back into Nancy's hair.

"So you've been holding out on me, have you?" he said. "You've been keeping something from me. There's a side to you I know nothing about. Pansy McLain. My Florida floozie."

Nancy leaned against his arm, her dress unbuttoned all the way down to her slip. "Clem," she said in a small strangulated voice, and pointed to a cowtrack in the brush off the road, "will you drive in there?"

But they had passed it before she finished saying it and he was driving too fast and was lost in a brown study.

3

It was Eustis Telfer who capped it all for Clem. In the middle of their belated lunch Eustis blew into the dining room, breathless with the by now familiar, "You heard this thing that's going the rounds?" Seating himself at the table without so much as a by-your-leave, pouring himself a glass of water from the pitcher and popping an aspirin into his mouth from the tin he always carried in his shirt pocket. "You know all the violence that's been erupting in the state these past few weeks? Some of the niggers round here, they say, are all up in arms over it. And you know they had some military training in the war? No thank you, Miss Lolly, I had my lunch. My, how pretty you look today."

Laura who had just spent the morning in Miss Mae's Beauty Salon, having her head doused in stiffening lotion, stabbed with curling pins, dehydrated under the drier and stuffed with agitating snatches of gossip, posed vivaciously in profile. "You like it this way? Of course it'll look a lot better when it's combed out. Do have some of Ida's orange layer cake, Eustis, it'll melt in your mouth."

Eustis over protest accepted a generous slab of layer cake with a glass of iced tea. In the next ten minutes he consumed three helpings of cake and a refill on his tea.

"They're all up to something," he said, "to get back at the white folks. And you know who's at the bottom of it? That boy out on the River Road, the one put Julie out of her land? Stashing dynamite on his place and he has this cracker-boy buying it for him. Stockpiling it. Against the day."

"Now where may I ask," Clem demurred, "did you pick up this tidbit?"

"Don't disparage it." Eustis bridled, mortally offended by what appeared to be a slur upon his mental attainments. "There's something to it. They're all out to keep Henry from being elected to County Commission. And for Purcell's neck. You can't deny that. They're all out to take over control, and if that day comes . . ."

He was exciting himself to the point of belief, visualizing it, with a trace of terror in his pink-lidded eyes. That hour of reckoning, that Judgment Day dreaded by every person who has ever enjoyed a position of privilege. They'll come storming into my house, smash my furniture, tear my pictures from the walls, ravish my women . . .

"I could change the subject," Clem said, "but it wouldn't change anything else. Is there anymore to this, Eustis?"

"More? What more do you want? All that damage they did to Henry's boy that day. Tried to kill him. And when Chalmer Coombs came around to stop them, they all but blew him up. Now Julie's going to have to take that child up to Hopkins for shock treatment."

"No! Oh no—" The gasp was wrung out of Nancy.

"I heard that too," Laura confirmed Eustis, "down at Miss Mae's. I was so upset—"

"But it wasn't intentional," Clem cried. "Everyone knows it wasn't."

"Coley, that was the first shot," Eustis declared, sucking cake crumbs from under his stringy pink cheeks, smacking them over with his pale pink lips. "If this kind of thing doesn't stop—"

"Eight Negroes have been murdered in cold blood in the last two weeks! Including two young women. If this kind of talk keeps up—"

"It'll be here next!" Eustis said. "If they don't mind their onions, it'll be here."

Now tardily Laura rose from the table and closed the door to the kitchen where Ida was washing the floor. "Nothing's going to happen," she said sensibly. "Nobody's about to kill any of them. Nobody even thinks about them anymore, I'm sure, than they think about us. We're all preoccupied with our own affairs as, I'm sure, they are with theirs. Isn't that right, Eustis?"

"So long as nobody stirs it up. That's the way it is and it'll stay that way. There's something about you that puzzles me, Clem." He twitched his napkin over his mouth. "It always has. Do you or do you not believe in the separation of the races?"

Laura's teaspoon clattered to the floor. She and Clem reached down simultaneously for it, their faces meeting almost upside down under the table, her eyes meeting his, her hollowed eyes which were sinking deeper under their darkening folds day by day. He took the spoon from her and placed it on the buffet among the discarded dishes.

"I think we have a right to know," Eustis said.

"You know," Clem answered him with all his mother's vivacious lightness, all Thurlow's elusive equivocation, "I've never given it that much thought. Someday when I have the time I'll study it out. But don't look for anything less than a five-hour sermon."

He began to stack glasses and plates together, terminating the visit.

"It's Augusta Varney all over again!" he said as soon as Eustis was out of the house. "This'll grow and spread till it's engulfed us all. There's a concerted effort being made to stigmatize and isolate those two men, make a target of them—"

"This is becoming an obsession with you. It's affecting your judgment . . . Where are you going?"

"There's only one person who has enough influence on Henry and the Judge to stop all this. Who knows enough of the truth to scotch these lies."

Laura's fingers raked through her brave and brittle hairdo. "But what evidence do you have that they're the ones? You're worse than Eustis!"

"Benson says—"

"If Benson says, let him take care of it. He's the politician. Clem, don't mix yourself up in this. Your class, your class is going so well now, you're doing so much with it—"

"I know, I know. We're all so separate, we're all homogenized. Nancy?"

But Nancy had fled from their clashing voices into the parlor. Not the Nancy of their rides in the country, not the square-mouthed stubborn Nancy. Not the Nancy with a flower in her hair, Pansy McLain.

"Nancy, I'm going over to Julie's."

"Yes, Nancy, go with him!"

"I—I—" She opened the cool cream-colored volume on her piano rack. Rippled over the keys. A Vivaldi, very showy, virtuoso, demanding strong fingers and a strong back.

"Please Clem, I couldn't. Not to Julie, not about that, not now . . ."

Without pausing for a preliminary telephone call he went out into the green glare of the afternoon and took the lane to Julie's house.

To be sure of purpose in this world, he thought impatiently as he left the rectory behind, one must be free of family obligations, of ambition and the lust for possession, of every desire but dedication to the service of man and God. To be a true minister of the gospel one must be a monk. Belonging to a community of men, laboring in fraternal unity under the stimulation of one another's abilities toward the achievement of a common goal. This notion had always attracted him.

His walk down the lane was entombed in a superabundance of greenery, walled by vines and shrubbery rampant with midsummer neglect, roofed by boughs so overladen with foliage and festooned with moss the sun dripped through only in scattered droplets. Going to Julie on this so distasteful mission, he remembered wistfully the eagerness with which he had bounded up the outside staircase to that bleak loft of an office over the garage where he met with Goodfellow and Thurlow. There was his preferred pastorate. He would go into Jerusalem and into that abode where in a room on the upper floor dwell Peter, James and Andrew, Philip, Thomas and Bartholomew, Matthew and the other James and James' brother Judas and Simon Zelotes. And together they would go forth to the people offering their faith and their good works. Their demonstrable good works . . .

Not this lone journey through this green jungle.

He rounded the turn of the lane and opened the gate.

The house stood resplendent in the full brilliance of the sun, crowned with the raw green of a new roof, symmetrical with green shutters on every window, not one askew, not one missing. Glistening so white it still looked wet with paint, tinged only with the reflected blur of trees at the corners. The gravel walk was now a concrete strip and the once shabby steps were paved with patterned brickwork. In the recessed doorway he pressed the pearl button under the brass nameplate —Warren now, no longer Colfax; releasing a cascade, a veritable vesper of chimes somewhere in the rear. Kissie appeared to unlock the screen, spruce in grey uniform and starched white apron, herself reconstituted with the renovations.

"Is Mrs. Warren in?" Clem inquired of her with the sepulchral solicitude one uses when there is illness in a house.

"She's out back there with the kids," Kissie waved him cheerfully on in. "Where you been keeping yourself, Reverend? We missed you."

The clean scent of shellac and wax wafted through the hallway, borne on the breeze of fans whirring in every room. Through the open archways the rooms—white shades, unblemished as the hide of a sacrificial lamb, drawn to the sill; furniture sparser and under dust covers; chandeliers shrouded in cheesecloth—the rooms, dimmed as they were, shone with a brightness that had not been theirs before. Ceilings loomed smooth-white, their handsome corbeled moldings rebuilt, at some loss of chipped cupids and acanthus leaves to be sure. In the living room over the marble fireplace, evidently sandblasted and repolished, a contemporary mirror had been installed covering the entire chimney wall. But it was the floors, the age-dulled floors now scraped to the grain, which furnished the golden gleam, casting light over all. Quartered yellow pine stippled with red shadings and on the staircase the paler slabs of oak mounting behind the white bars of the spindles . . .

In transit through the back Clem received another surprise. The

kitchen on one side all formica and stainless steel and built-in appli-
ances. And the rest: the rat's nest of pantries, laundry, backstairs, storage sheds, swept out, clean-gone. A broad doorway confronted him,
made formal by a fanlight over it and having to one side of it a standing
gun rack, out of which the barrels of rifles pointed upward like five black
fingers, reminding him through some irrelevant association of Hedda
Gabler and her pistol practice.

He stepped through the doorway to a screened terrace very much like
that behind the Purcell house, covered with a cross-beamed roof and inlaid with flagstones. Outside on the lawn two boys, one tall and one
small, were romping with a Scottie; entangled with leash and ball, barks
and laughter. To his left, on the far end of the terrace Julie was lounging in a glider, swinging it idly to and fro with her toe. Surrounded
with swatches of drapery and upholstery fabrics, she turned through the
rainbow-splashed pages of home decorating magazines. "Who is it,
Kissie?" she asked absently and then, looking up, jumped to her feet,
spilling materials and magazines to the floor.

"Clem. Darling."

In her dress of some yellow silken stuff, her sunny red hair pinned
tightly back in a psyche knot that left her forehead and cheeks bare, she
glowed with the coral tan redheads acquire, rose-flushed, a delectable
melon. Glowed and flowed toward him, arms extended. On the momentum of emotion, swept as if by a tide high on the beach, far beyond her
intention, she flung her arms around him and kissed him, melon-tender,
melon-firm, warmly on the mouth.

"Clem, I've been running away from you!"

"Julie, you look marvelous—"

"Come here with me, sit down . . . I have such compunctions toward you. All that beastly business last spring, I let you down terribly.
There, I've confessed it."

Still holding his hands, she pulled him down with her on the glider.

"Julie, I haven't stood by you through all this."

"Ssssh." Butterfly fingers flickered over his lips, sealing them.

It was like a reunion of lovers who, meeting again years after, can only
look at each other through a blur of affection that has become most
precious to them, the wounds once so blindly and bitterly inflicted
needing now neither explanation nor forgiveness.

"Have you seen the house? Isn't it wonderful? Henry did it all while
I was away and he drove up every weekend. All I've had is the finishing
touches."

"I knew it was being face-lifted, but I had no idea of the extent—"

"The experience I've been through! Do you have time now? There's no one else I can really talk to about my thoughts and feelings. And I must." Spread-fingered she touched her breast, leaning toward him. "It's all piled up so."

"There's nothing I'd want more." He glanced at the children chasing around the lawn. "I heard today that you were going to have to take him up to Hopkins."

"Oh those ghouls! Buzzards!" She threw herself back against the cushions. "The things these folks will say. First it was all so hush-hush nobody'd mention it. Now they're all calamity-criers. Oh Coley's had a bad time of it. They examined him for everything from deafness to tumors to every last virus before they even started with the functional procedure. He's a perfect physical specimen. But all this machinery coming at him, lights and head clamps, taps and tubes, electroencephalogram, injections, being strapped down on the table . . . And there I was taking him, up with such hope and down with despair, it's been perfect hell. But I was right, Clem. I was right all along. He's not feeble-minded!"

"Then what—"

"Nobody knows! Nobody knows what goes on in that little brain of his. He's all mixed up, immured in his own self-made castle. Dr. Harrington here, would you believe it, was the first one to spot it. *Childe Roland to the dark tower came . . .*"

"But he'll come out of it?"

"No one knows! We haven't had any final recommendations yet. We're going back up to Atlanta for that next week. Dr. Wolf—I really don't like the man, isn't that awful?—he just sits there like a pussycat with this photograph of his children on the desk, all so bright and fine . . . And keeps asking the most personal questions—as if my conduct in bed had anything to do with it. He hints that the prognosis for cases like this is practically hopeless. But look, look at Coley now."

The older boy, ginger-haired, ginger-quick, threw a stick and the dog pelted after it. "Sic, sic it, Nig!" And the little boy, flame-haired, flashed after the dog.

"That's Charles, Henry's cousin's boy. He was Henry's idea and a real inspiration. Look at them together, wouldn't you take them for brothers? He's done more for Coley . . . Coley's always been so afraid of other children, the sheer activity of it, they never stop to think. But this boy is old enough to handle him like a father. And dogs, he was always so afraid of dogs. But with Charles here to ease him into it . . . Clem, you've got to help me with that."

"Anything I can do, Julie, to help . . ."

"We want to take Charles up to Atlanta with us next week when we go there to get the—news." She swallowed over the news, taking it like an evil-tasting pill. "About what Coley's treatment is to be. Charles has never been to Atlanta before and Henry's promised to show him through the capitol building, all the sights, it means a lot to a boy that age. And he'll be such a help. You know that since he's been here, it's the first time I've been able to ride in the car with Henry like a wife ought to? Coley actually will play in the back seat with Charles for a while. I can sit like a human being, without being torn apart, crawled over, weighted down— Clem, if you knew, oh I've had to overcome so much, so much selfishness toward that boy."

She hid her face in her hands, burning with a febrile excitement, then raised her head, waving as if to disperse a vapor of heat.

"When Henry first brought him, he was in such a state. His father had beaten him. He was filthy dirty. And his mother that night went to the hospital with another baby. Such a mess. And next morning Rad was off distributing the other children around with relatives. So I drove straight to the hospital that very day and begged his wife to let Charles stay with us until she was on her feet again. She was pretty weak then, didn't know how long it was going to take. Anyhow I begged and I pleaded so, she finally gave in. And do you know, I didn't really want to do it! Every time I looked at that boy, all I could think of was: Why should he have so much and my child so little?

"But Henry wanted it—Henry. What would I ever have done without Henry?"

She looked up toward the ceiling, trying to conceal the tears that glimmered in her eyes. With her hair parted in the middle and pinned so severely back, her cheekbones appeared particularly naked and de-fenseless. And her mouth without lipstick, like a bruise . . .

"Well, his mother's home now and we've kept putting off sending him back with one excuse and another. Of course it can't go on. They're bound to come for him. Clem, talk to Rad! Ask him to leave Charles with us. It'd be a crime to take him away now."

Clem had listened to her with waxing consternation. He interlaced his fingers like his mother and braced them. Catching the crack of his knuckles and annoyed with the sound of it he began massaging them like Nancy, kneading from knuckle to tip.

"But Julie, it's a family matter, I don't have the right. In the first place, I doubt if Rad beat him up so—" She made a little gesture of amused indulgence—oh you wouldn't . . . "But I know the man. He'd never be brutal."

"All right, all right," she conceded amiably. "Of course I only saw Charles afterward. Weeping—in the throes of such weeping—he'd called his father nigger-lover. Not very nice, but was it such a crime? And he's named that dog Niggerboy. Not in the best of taste and ordinarily I wouldn't allow it, but as soon as he and Henry bought the dog they had him named and were teaching it to Coley. He's well behaved enough and he's very apt too, so he must have had some raising. Though he does gobble his food. With manners and the proper supervision—"

"But what about him? Does he want to stay?"

"He'd be a rank ingrate if he didn't! After all the lengths Henry and I—"

She understood her mistake immediately and halted, fingers on throat. "But what am I doing? I ought to be fixing us some drinks. Now don't refuse—I was just about to fix something for myself and the children." Jumping up, she beckoned him along after her. "Come into the kitchen with me, there are things I want to show you. Pictures we took last week while we were out boating. You know Henry bought that runabout from Lars . . ."

She held the door open waiting for him to follow her inside. Clem stood a moment at the screen that with sliding glass walls enclosed the terrace, watching the child. Under the orange tree Colfax, braceleted in a sliver of shorts, shot up and down, holding his hands out for the blue-and-white beach ball Charles was throwing to him.

"He was always so scared of a ball before," Julie said from behind. "He'd duck away."

The ball missed its aim or his hands dropped too soon. Charles rolled it to him, tipping it along.

"Don't watch him," Julie warned from behind. "If he notices you, good night!"

So sound without. So flawed within.

He went into the kitchen with Julie, treading over a blue mirror of rubber tile. Refrigerator, fans, and a vacuum cleaner in some distant part of the house hummed pleasantly. Cabinets banded the room, above and below, separated by a strip of blue Carrara glass.

"Would you recognize it?" Julie cried. "Isn't it beautiful? All bleached mahogany." She tugged with her fingertips at the flush door of a cupboard. "Though—dare I say it?—I always had a weakness for the old tongue-and-groove." With a tinkle she took glasses down and assembled them at the silver mouth of the sink. "Cokes for the kids, I guess. Coley will want his in the bottle. And for us, what? But first while I mix, you can look at our snapshots." She pulled at one drawer and another. "Everything slides open like a breeze. You've no idea what went into organizing all this. All the snap-decisions you have to make, and if you make the wrong one . . . How does anybody ever build a house? And with all his other responsibilities—I declare, Henry's a miracle."

The snapshots were nowhere in the drawers. "Must be upstairs. Come on with me, you can see what we're doing up there. If you don't mind the mess."

Upstairs they stepped over a board on the polished floor, and the floor was powdered with plaster dust. "That's what I mean, decisions. We postponed the bathroom to remodel a few rooms for the boys, and now look at this floor." Inside the bathroom door, over the porcelain and chrome of new fixtures the walls had been excavated down to the studs. "Everything's being held up by the tile man. He's supposed to be coming in from Bay City today. That alone is a major piece of logistics: getting plumber, electrician, carpenter, and tiler together in the proper order, one-two-three—"

She snapped her fingers thrice and jauntily, her yellow skirts swinging, led him into her bedroom. The paper had been stripped from the walls. Otherwise it was relatively tidy, except for the vanity cluttered with toiletries and wallpaper books. She tore a sample from the top book and held it up against the wall. "Victorian roses, what do you think? Too much? There's a flocked white silk damask that Henry favors . . . The snapshots, let me see." Drawers flew open under her hand, crammed with hastily stuffed-in articles. "All my junk. If I didn't have Henry to keep me straight—here. Here they are."

Herself and the two boys, sea-blown in a boat, Charles at the helm. "Henry took that. And here's the picnic we had on Little Uchee. I took it. Didn't come out too good, too much light. And Charles took some nice ones. Here we are down at the Bay City Country Club. Guess what, I'm taking golf lessons. With Eula—don't laugh—she's a darn good sport. And you know what else? I'm joining the Wednesday Afternoon Shakespeare Circle. And they're going to have to take Eula in with me!"

The Shakespeare Circle was composed of a very exclusive clique, about sixteen daughters—just enough for four tables—of the ladies who had originally founded it back in 1911. It was devoted to contract bridge now rather than whist (penny a point); to the concoction of superb desserts (a competition of diminishing returns, how much more superb can you get? especially when competing with the diet craze); and to the exchange of compliments that with extraordinary succinctness cut the members, kin and offspring, down to size. Up to now Julie had succeeded in cutting the whole circle down to size by declining to participate in it.

"So I've capitulated, Clem. Now I'll be hunting up darling little old

slave cabins in the woods, furnishing them with antiques and converting them into tearooms."

She smiled to herself and instead of moving back out into the hall,
now that he had viewed the snapshots, she sat down on her bed and
gazed most seductively up at him.

He had never noticed before—or was it an illusion of the moment?—
that one of her eyelids was slightly ptotic, drooping ever so slightly
lower than the other; so that one eye was open, clear and candid, the
outward eye, and the other eye under the ptotic lid was veiled, the inward eye, beguilingly wicked. The impression disappeared in a nonce.
She closed both eyes, with an inward smile.

"I dreamt last night that you'd be here today."

"Oh?"

"Sit down here by me. I told you I wanted to talk. And with all I've
said up to now I haven't even begun."

He smoothed out the brocade spread and sat down, a little stiffly, beside her. If Kissie should happen by . . . Loathing himself for his uneasiness.

"I dreamt that you were visiting me here in this room. And I was
wandering around in front of you without a stitch on. Then I went in to
take a shower. Of course I knew it was a dream then because the shower
isn't tiled yet."

She cocked her head at him. "What do you think it means?"

He brushed at the brocade, ah Julie, Julie . . . Was this just Julie
being Julie? Or was she trying to tell him something more?

"Maybe you feel I see you as you really are. Behind the act."

"It's no act, Clem."

She was suddenly serious, the sensitive twin frontal areas of her forehead—without her usual froth of bangs her forehead did look curiously
naked—bulging in concentration over ridged brows which, sparked with
sun-bleached hairs, quivered nervously. Under half-drooped lids, her
eyes wandered, searching.

"I have another dream that recurs and recurs. I'm trying to cross the
marsh and a gang of snakes comes out and forces me back before I can
reach the other side. What do you think of that? Or shall we call in Dr.
Freud?"

"Maybe you're fighting the devil."

She chuckled with that, delighted. "All those old ideas, Clem, they're
still with us in modern dress, aren't they? The sins of the fathers are
visited upon the children even unto the third and fourth generation,
aren't they? We are born with a full cargo of original sin which we
spend all our lives trying to surmount, don't we? And we marry into the

very thing we're trying hardest to escape from. All our rebellions only lead back into the destiny that was established for us at our conception by who, when, where . . . It's not only Coley that underwent all those tests up in Atlanta, Clem. It was me. I've learned a lot about myself. And I think I've gained some insights.

"I never wanted to be me, that was the first error. I never wanted to be stuck here in the sticks, that was the second. I wanted to go somewhere and do something and be somebody, oh fine and noble and great! And when Papa blasted that dream and then Henry . . . I think I must have wanted Colfax to be as he is so I could beat Henry over the head with him and through him my father and the forefathers who made him what he was. I've always blamed Henry for Coley's trouble, and it's me —me! I'm the one . . ."

"Julie, there's no need, you're abasing yourself—"

He took her hand, stroked the glinting red-gold hairs up the coral tan of her forearm. Seeing her naked, flitting about the room in a rose mist. Flamingo . . .

"But that's not all," she said and ardently pressed his hand. "That's not all. You have to understand, for your own sake, Clem, you've got to understand! Remember last winter—remember you came in with the azaleas—that luncheon I didn't want to give and I did? There was this man there, our guest of honor—you know sometimes you meet someone it's like a visitation. Jove in disguise. The angel who wrestled with Jacob."

Julie had mentioned Philip Elwell to him more than once before, always in terms to which he reacted with the mixture of skepticism and curiosity one renders to those in exalted position who are excessively extolled.

"And what he had to tell me was so simple. Stop fighting it. Stop rebelling. Accept what you are. Adjust to your circumstance . . . And ever since then I've been doing it, and the more I do it the easier it becomes. He'll be back here the end of this month. I wonder," she mused with her ravishing transition on the flutter of an eyelid from inner to outer self, "what he'll think of his creation?"

"Julie," he stroked her wrist, "I'm not sure I exactly—"

"Accept. Adjust. What else do the psychiatrists tell you? Or the priests with their will of God? Take what you have and do your utmost with it.

"I am Julie-Ann Colfax of the first family of Colfax County. Married to a man who's able, ambitious, and just a bit ruthless. Mother of a child who needs all the idealism I have it in me to give. And whatever my name, my husband and my child require, I'll comply with. Gladly.

Willingly. I don't see how, within the possibilities that I've been handed, I could fulfill myself any better than that, do you?"

She believed it and she expected him to believe it, and coming right down to it—their hands gelidly clasped in the heat—it would be hard to think of any other way in which she could better fulfill herself.

"We do have the good life here. I have everything I need and want. There isn't anywhere on earth I'd rather live than right here where I am now."

She said it as a flat statement, meaning it with all her heart, aggressively, challenging him to take exception.

"Is it life you're adjusting to, Julie," he essayed again faintly, "or is it Henry Warren?"

"What's the difference? It's the same thing." She dropped a stinging slap over the back of his hand. "Clem, stop fighting everything so. You've no idea how easy it is when you stop fighting. And just go along as you're supposed to go." She pulled him up, "Come, let me show you what we're doing for our boys."

The warren of back bedrooms had been opened up, walls knocked through and rooms joined. A pine-paneled playroom was equipped with everything a boy could wish for. The electric train Henry had bought for Colfax, now enlarged and elaborated, was mounted on a table. On another table, test tubes, vials of chemicals. On the floor a Meccano set, and the floor itself designed with games in each corner, pachisi, checkerboard. Bookcase with a globe on top and a wall map over it. Record player, albums sprawling about.

"It was all done so fast," Julie said. "We suspended everything else when Charles came. Henry called down an architect from Savannah . . . here's the room we've fixed up for him."

Clem glanced in at the maple spool bed covered with chintz spread, the student desk and lamp, baseball bat in a corner and DiMaggio at bat taped up.

What her husband required. What her child required. And how had she bridged the gap between these sometimes opposing requirements? With Charles. The son Henry hankered for, the older brother Colfax needed. In Charles the conflicts of this family were momentarily resolved. On this equilibrium, this frail reed, she was building all her hope. A boy that didn't belong to them. And even if he did, how long would he tolerate being saddled with that child? And the child, for how long would he maintain what was perhaps only a temporary remission? And back again to Charles, how long would his parents . . .

And the errand that had brought him here today, Clem wondered, Henry's campaign of vilification, where did that fit in?

"Don't ask how much all this is costing us."

"All right," he humored her, trailing after her downstairs, "how much is it costing you?"

"A fortune! Ten thousand and it'll run more before we're through. We're spending money like bees make honey."

Back in the kitchen she threw open the refrigerator and took from a carton two bottles of soft drinks for the boys. He placed them as she directed on the serving-cart. Don't say anything, his mother's voice and Nancy's chimed in his ears, leave it alone, it'll work itself out.

From under a counter Julie drew out a bar on casters and slid open the doors. "Daiquiri, screwdriver, what'll it be? With the Judge here every other night, we're ready for anything."

"You're not," Clem asked casually, "backing the Judge for election, are you?"

"Election? Heavens, no! Just socializing. Who has time to think about elections?"

"Socializing? Is that the only reason?"

"Let's just say"—from under the drooping lid her eye gleamed wickedly—"that I have a fatal attraction for middle-aged men? Will you shave some ice for me?"

He chipped the ice while she shook the daiquiris. "You do see now," she said in a low tense voice to the chinking of the ice, "how it all hinges on Charles, don't you? You will speak to Rad about it, won't you?"

"What would you have done if I hadn't happened in now?"

"Henry has something in mind."

Clem didn't ask her what.

"But it's better if we can persuade the parents, isn't it? Just ask them for next week to Atlanta. I can't do without him. After all, Rad does owe us some consideration."

Leave it alone, let it go.

He followed her, pushing the serving-cart over the threshold out to the terrace. "How's that? He owes *you*—?"

"But of course. After that trick he pulled in court. Losing my land on me. My property. When I think of what that boy Reeve's done to me, and Rad helping him—"

"But Julie, there were papers. They had the proof."

"You mean that will? Sillens wrote it up. I happen to know that Reeve and Carter Scott went into Bay City and had Sillens write it up for them."

"But the deed—"

"There never was a deed. If there ever was a record book for that year, that girl took it. Just to confuse the issue. Chil-dren," she stepped over to the screen, "here are some cold drinks."

Coley was lying under the orange tree and Charles was engrossed in teaching the dog to sit up and beg. Julie touched Clem's arm, holding him back, and stepped outside to Charles with the bottles. "You give it to Coley. Just put it in his hand, honey, there's a good boy. And when he's ready, you'll open it for him?"

She stepped back inside, kicked her pumps off and walked barefoot over to the glider, her skirt swaying, her whole body from head and shoulders to the curve of her hips and the swell of her calves settling with down-to-earth firmness on the solid ground of her heels. "Now Clem, you're not going to dispute me. After all, I was a principal in it. That girl Vivian, why I recommended her for her teaching job. And then she turns around—"

"Julie, I know the girl. You'd like her. I can't think of two people who would hit it off better than you and Vivian—"

"So she's got you charmed, has she? Then tell me, what's she doing here? What'd she come back here for? A girl like that. With her education. You can bet your bottom dollar she's after something."

Her cheeks flamed, a dusky rose, her eyes winking rapidly. "Clem, let's not quarrel. I just can't bear . . . Whenever I think of it all, I feel as if a blood vessel in my brain . . . Reeve throwing the dynamite at Coley that day. Using Rad to help him. Look, look out there what he did to my child! Look at him now. Anybody'd do a thing like that is capable of anything. And you know who's responsible?"

She stamped with her bare foot on the flagstone. "Us! We! You and I and Benson Reece and all the rest of the nice white people. Our own softheadedness. Out of our Christian kindness, our sympathy for the underdog, we elevate them into human beings like ourselves, invest them with our reactions and responses. We put the knives, the guns, and the dynamite in their hands. We'd even give them the power to rule us—"

"Julie, do you know what you're saying?"

"I know what I've suffered."

"Julie—"

His head was spinning again. In a whir faster and faster than it had this morning in Carl Maynard's yard.

"These stories that are going round—"

He could not let it go by. He couldn't let it go without some attempt to penetrate the mass of misstatements, the layer upon layer of protective scar tissue over the original wound, the premise that was simply too unpretty to be admitted.

"These rumors, they're not just the usual prattle. They're evil and dangerous—"

"Did you know that Reeve once tried to assault me?"

"No! That's impossible—"

"You *know* him. *He* wouldn't. Only *I* was there. Of course he didn't lay a finger on me," she amended punctiliously. "But he all but threw me out of that house. Well, what did you think? Who's evil-minded now?" She burst into laughter and pointed a shaming finger at his chest. "I didn't even mention it to Henry till after Coley was blasted. And I suppose you think we'd go out and lynch him for it?" She poked her forefinger hard into his chest. "That imagination of yours, Clem, ought to be kept under lock and key."

"Julie—"

"See? See there." She crept up to the screen on tiptoe. "Look—" With a butterfly flicker of her fingers she motioned him up beside her. Charles, kneeling by Colfax, was propping him up against the trunk of the tree. He uncapped the bottle and urged it toward his mouth.

"You know where St. Paul says," she turned with a brilliant smile, brimming with tears, "*Tribulation worketh patience and patience, experience and experience, hope?* It's going to be all right, Clem. Everything's going to be all right. I just know it is."

And who was to gainsay her? With such faith, that most abused of all powers, and love, the most trivialized of all panaceas, who could say that she had not found in this instance the one and only path?

"We'll go up to Atlanta. We'll show that doctor all the progress he's making," she said, tossing her hat in the ring with an artlessness that was both laughable and touching. "Him and his picture of his children on his desk."

They stood like two ultrafashionable people against the screen, sipping their daiquiris through chartreuse straws and nibbling at salted pecans. "I love you, Clem, I really do. You think I'm an awful flirt, don't you?"

"I think you're a healthy attractive young woman."

"Now you're my friend for life."

"Julie—"

He could not leave without making one more attempt to penetrate those defensive fortifications, fossae and barricades, that citadel bristling with artillery embedded in emplacements of concrete and steel.

"There's something I came here for I can't go without—"

"I knew it! It had to be for something. It couldn't just be me." With mockery, laughing, she popped pecans into her mouth. "Aren't these good? They're toasted with butter and lemon."

"Eight Negroes have been killed in this state in the past two weeks—"

"Horrible. Dreadful. I realize that. Though sometimes they can try you so. That's all I want you to realize. That they haven't got it all on their side."

"I have reason to believe that the same thing is brewing here. And there's one person in this county who can stop it. Who knows the truth. You know the truth, Julie. Much as you may hide it from yourself, you know it. Everyone else knows it too, but you're the one that has to bring it up from underground and state it out loud. Say it out loud and clear. Coley wasn't frightened by any dynamite thrown at him. He was frightened at being locked up alone there in the freezer plant office while all the noise was erupting outside."

"No." She shook her head, with the nuts halfway to her mouth. "No! You're mistaken."

"Julie, there were people around. Hattie, Lightfoot, the help—"

"No, he was out there in the field. Henry had him in his arms and shouted out, please, don't! And it went off then and he ran with him. Everybody saw that. Everybody knows . . ."

He had recently been charged with the task of informing a parishioner that her husband and fifteen-year-old son, who had left home only a half hour before to drive to Bay City for a night ball game, had been killed just the other side of the bridge in a highway smashup. And she had stood so, with the smile of hospitality still on her lips. "No, no, you're mistaken. Why I just now talked with them. I'm ironing Dick's shirt for Sunday."

"It's not true! Why do you come and tell me things that are so untrue?"

While over her protestation of disbelief already the conviction was forming that dwells as close as death does to life. While upon him the conviction descended: She didn't know! She truly didn't know. *I* am the evil-minded one.

"Julie, I'm sorry. I thought you knew. I truly did."

"These people, these people here will say anything!"

"Chalmer investigated it at the time. It was all given to him."

"But Henry, Henry wouldn't, he didn't . . . How dare you, how dare you come here, when I've been so happy, so full of ideas and plans—"

"Julie, forgive—"

Tearing herself away she ran from the terrace out into the yard. And throwing herself down on the prone form under the orange tree she covered his cheeks with kisses. "He didn't, he didn't do that to you, not again—"

But when Clem tried to help her with the child, to lift her to her feet,

she let out with that husky double-voice of hers, in which bass tones
charged over jagged shards of shrillness, an animal howl.

"Are you still here? Haven't you done enough harm!"

For the second time that day he was forced to flee.

Driven forth, expelled, he strode back through the simmering green
heat to his dusty garage. Ignoring his mother's call from the door he
flung into his car and backed out in a roar of gas fumes.

Bungler! Jackass!

Flaying himself, he rode down the River Road and veered off it into
a parting in the juniper scrub. His car crashed through, paint rasping,
to the site of the old Spanish mission. Over the low-lying overgrown
mound that might have been the ruin of a building he rocketed into the
open area, a place of trampled grasses and fallen tombstones long ago
effaced by the elements. Here he occasionally in search of refuge se-
cluded himself, to take stock and meditate.

A lone tree on the verge of the river guarded the sanctuary, a cedar
lightning-scarred, whipped into tortured shape by the winds of centuries but still lifting on its gnarled limbs fronds that arched like the
back of a cat to the sun. Across the river the marsh shimmered, a green
sea flecked with gold and russet and the purple-black of juncus, rippling
for mile after mile to the rim of the Atlantic over the horizon. Here, the
air did most nimbly and sweetly recommend itself unto the gentle
senses, commingling the breath of broom and myrtle and jessamine.

4

Clem shot to a halt over the writhing roots of the cedar, the boughs
scraping the roof of his car.

Busybody! Asshole!

He hurled open the car door, his mother's call still dinning in his ears
like the old Geechee saying: *He hark but he ain't yeddy,* he hear but he
don't heed. And the old woman's diatribe: You a preacher-man? You
call yourself a preacher? And Julie's howl.

He tried in vain to pull himself together, to isolate the factors that
had led him into so irreparable a blunder. Obviously Julie was not going to be receptive to his appeal, so why had he persisted? Obviously
his revelation had had some significance for her that he could not have
foreseen . . .

Julie, I love you. You are my love and my darling.

Spur thorns tore at his ankles. The grass was cropped and clopped over
by wandering cattle. He kicked at whitened cattle bones among the

keeling tombstones that were themselves strewn about like unburied
fossils of a yesteryear's battle, entwined in creeper, half-sunk in earth.
Under these pitted stones the Franciscan friars who had once labored
in these vanished vineyards were dissolved away, the only remnant of
their passage being perhaps a sprig of the orange tree in Julie's yard. If
indeed this was a Spanish cemetery and not, as some claimed, the locale
of a pre-Revolutionary skirmish between British and Indians or French.
And if that barrow yonder was the mission and not, as some claimed, a
fort; or, as others claimed, an old sugarhouse . . . If anything was anything . . .

My melon-sweet Julie. My love and my joy.

In divination of a catastrophe that had not yet occurred, seeking to
prevent it by anticipation, on the basis of a verbal air-current and the
interpretation he chose to place upon it, guessing, he had with no more
than his hazard of an augury to go on engendered a family crisis of such
dimensions . . .

He was jealous of her husband and he barged in there and busted
everything up.

Julie with her yearning for goodness.

Goodness or no goodness, truth or falsehood, he didn't care. Frivo-
lous. Flamingo. Julie herself. The whole Julie.

The skull of a steer nosed at his feet, its snout elongated with a terrible meekness, its eye sockets black holes of vacancy. He was not the
only one who haunted this place. Rusty beer cans rested cheek by jowl
with broken whiskey bottles. On the pillow of a headstone the pod of a
recently discarded condom. Pale sheath deflated. The procreant drive,
the surge of flight. Collapsed.

Julie and her dreams.

The discipline of continence becomes a habit. He had never, however, been one to hold with that creed in which mortification of the
flesh is the price of salvation of the spirit; in which the unity of one's
individual self is riven into a dichotomy of flesh and spirit, id and ego, a
state of warfare, wherein over the past millennium, so he saw it with the
baffled amazement one accords to the obsolete, too much agony had
been spilled, too much intelligence expended, too much of the blood
of martyrs wasted for naught.

But now without warning the unity he thought was his—of moral
judgment and physical action; of responsibility toward himself and toward others; of personal direction and the compulsion to intervene in
what-is in order to direct the course of what-will-be—foundered on the
upsurge of an emotion too volcanic to be contained. All was annihi-
lated. There was no truth nor fiction, no law nor breach of law, no

right nor wrong. All was incinerated: his unity of self, his duality of
ethic, his dialectical trinities.

Nothing mattered but a woman's face, the glint of hairs on her arm,
the fluidity of her flanks under her yellow dress. Nothing but that. And
the salt breeze that riffled from the ocean across the marshland in the
diurnal rhythm of time.

He toed up the dirt around the sallow condom, reduced now, if it
ever had been more than that, to a leer and a snigger; giving it a decent
burial. And if the guess that had goaded him into violating the tranquillity Julie had achieved happened to be valid, what had he achieved?
The threat to the two men, Rad and Reeve, and to himself as well had
been increased. And now with this burden of emotion, this unwanted
emotion proliferating what was already too complex . . .

He was immured in a castle of too many chambers. He was crushed
like the turtle beneath the elephant who bears the universe on his back.

There was no refuge for him here today. No glittering analysis to be
condensed from the ether into an inky sentence in his notebook.

Nancy was waiting for him in the driveway when he turned in. As if
with the magic crack of a whip, alley-oop, her anxiety vanished in her
light of delight on sight of him.

"Clem, where've you been? We tried calling you everywhere. There
are a couple of fellows here to see you. They came before and went
and came back. We couldn't leave them waiting outside. Mother invited them in."

His mother sat in the parlor chatting animatedly with his visitors.
She had released the shades in the three windows all the way to the
top, although she always drew them to the sash against the afternoon
sun and certainly never raised them higher than mid-level, in exact
alignment. She had pushed every window open as high as it would go,
although she always insisted that closed windows kept the heat out.
And she had parted the net curtains back over the old tie-hooks in the
frame. No hiding from the outside what was transpiring in here!

The two men, Rad and Reeve, were deep in the only comfortable
chairs in the room while she had seated herself, straight and as tall as
she could stretch, on the piano bench in full public view.

Clem looked back at Nancy as he entered and caught her tremor of a
smile. And with that passion he had only just discovered in himself,
fiery and melting, he loved her.

His mother graciously shook hands with each man; and taking Nancy
by the arm withdrew to the porch where they stationed themselves on
rockers, making a special point of calling across the street to Miss Addie
to ask after her little pup-dog who had just been wormed. And of re-

viewing with every passerby all the trouble there had been last month with a plague of chinch bugs in the lawns.

After the mumbled greeting from the two men, given awkwardly, half-rising, Clem retired to the place vacated by his mother on the piano bench. Out of respect for her carefully achieved effect of decorum and with a rush of love, flooding up in him, for that perfect love which casteth out fear.

Sternly he prepared himself to meet head-on whatever frenzy these two had brought with them. At first his mind balked at what they were saying, incapable of assimilating it. He was still lost out there in the Spanish cemetery, struggling with that urgent upsurge, carnality or a remorse so unbearable it disguised itself as carnality . . . An absorption that found its fixed star in one person, that orbited from ecstasy to misery about the flutter of an eyelid. . . .

Then as he listened he moved over to the sofa where he could sit more comfortably with legs crossed, chin in hand. And finally to a straight chair, straddling it back-to.

"So you want to buy a tractor?"

He leafed through the manual Reeve handed over to him and through the typed-up plans for purchasing and managing.

"You think that both classes between them—?"

"Well, the way we figure it," Rad who did most of the talking glanced at Reeve, "the colored class hasn't the money to buy it. Neither has our class. But if both classes would go in together on this . . . That is, the colored could throw a benefit, a concert maybe with a barbecue after, say next month, Founders Day. And we all could participate in it, sell tickets and help raise funds beforehand. Make a big thing of this, get everybody behind it. Whites on one side the picnic grove, colored on the other—a good time is had by all. I remember when the bridge down here on the highway was dedicated, there was an outdoor banquet like that. Worked out fine.

"And with the proceeds we'd have enough for the original outlay. Then from there on we'd share in the ownership of this piece of equipment, the running expenses and whatever earnings come in from customing it out. That could be the start."

"You have it all thought out pretty thoroughly, haven't you?" Clem scanned through the paragraphs under the heading, *Organization*, and the subheads. "Who got this up?"

"Some of his friends," Rad glanced at Reeve, "at his place one night. And Miss Vivian."

"You know her," Reeve put in. "If a thing ain't down on paper, it just ain't. And the Professor checked it over, added some of his ideas."

"He mentioned the possibility of a tractor to me," Clem said doubtfully, "for your class alone. But both classes, does he think that both classes—?"

"He says," Reeve said in the Professor's most roundabout manner, "that he don't know but what the time isn't ripe for something like this."

"It's more than just a notion," Clem acknowledged. "Except for one thing. Will the other boys," he addressed Rad, "back you up on it?"

"That's what we came to you for. If you'll support it and get the Advisory Board to approve of it . . . if the sanction's behind it, they'll do as the sanction does."

"I'm afraid," Clem said regretfully, "I can't help you there."

"Why not? Don't you like it?"

"Like it!"

He looked at them both, the one flushed with eagerness, a lock of hair falling over his forehead; the other coolly controlled, commenting mainly with his eyes.

"If you knew how much I like it! For so many reasons that go so far back. Are you aware of all the rumors that are running wild around the county about you two? And me?"

He repeated the gist of his morning's travels down to the last cockeyed detail. "To tell you the truth, I have a feeling that the aim of all this is to detach you two from the group each of you has around you by means of slander, by building up an atmosphere of hostility, by revival of all the timeworn tripe. And to undermine my influence so that anything I may try to do to counteract it will be canceled out."

From time to time as he talked the two men glanced at each other in an exchange of understanding, over a secret bond—Clem felt without knowing why—so solidly welded it was indissoluble.

"Richard-Gene," Rad queried incredulously, "said that about me?" And laughed. "I can handle Richard-Gene. You ever hear tell, Rev, about the time his father-in-law had him to court? Most comicalest thing . . ."

And again: "Carl Maynard? I'll fix him. You know how hot that boy is on the No Fence Law? I'll put him onto Chalmer Coombs—Chalmer is kin to his mammy—to make an issue of it in the election. Shucks, next time up we'll run Carl for election to the County Commission. Carl will be the first one I sign on."

"You think you can sign Carl Maynard up for this tractor deal? Cautious as he is? If he goes for it—"

"I'll sign every one of them," Rad said, "but Ellery Hayes, and he's more interested in that roadside store of his than he is in farming. Besides, Ellery ain't no cracker nohow. He's a Florida alligator."

"All right," Clem agreed, having grown wise in the ways of the community, "if you sign up fifteen of the twenty boys for this and present your proposition to the Advisory Board when we meet a week from this Friday night and they receive it favorably, I'll go along with it. Fair enough?"

"Son of a gun, you drive a hard bargain!"

Clem brought his typewriter down from the study and drafted a simple statement of interest in the purchase of a tractor by public subscription for the joint use of both veterans' classes, to which signatures were to be affixed. The act of signing one's name, he recalled from his circulation of the resolution, constituting an affirmation of the person. A commitment not to be underestimated for all its apparent negligibility or even ultimate inefficacy.

He passed the statement up to Rad. "And you honestly think you can put this over?"

"I'll sure as hell try. Of course I won't begin with this right on, I'll lead up to it—"

"And you can make one up for me too," Reeve said. "I could use it."

"Why?" Clem asked, startled. "Aren't you all for it?"

"Well, we are. And we aren't."

Clem stared at him. "But I thought, I assumed . . . Isn't this complicated enough?"

His tone was too sharp, belligerent and bludgeoning, enough to shut the other man up, drive his objections back down his throat. Clem recognized it and denied it to himself. Reeve's eyes pointed, measuring him for the effect of what he was about to say, and forcing himself, with an effort, he said it.

"They say there's such a thing as separate but equal, and that's a lie. There's also such a thing as together but unequal, and that's no lie."

"Yes," Clem mulled it over. "Yes."

"The fellows in my class are willing to try this out so long as it don't cost them anything. But there are two problems involved here. First off"—he counted it on his fingers—"how to get this thing. And second, how to run it so everyone'll feel he's getting his fair shake."

"Yes. Yes of course."

"So far as our part in this is concerned, there are two things to guard against. First off"—he counted it on his fingers—"that we'll all sit back. The white folks are going to have it all their way, let them do it then. Second, that we won't talk up, for fear that what we have to say will be held against us later."

"I see."

"Unless I can offer them some kind of ironclad agreement. Arrived at by both groups, spelling out the right of each and every one regard-less—"

"You mean the colored won't trust us?"

"Or you all us. If it's not down in black and white, anyone that can take advantage will."

"You think we can get the parties together to work out such an agreement?"

"We have to. Human nature being what it is."

From the sofa where he sat, hunched forward, elbows on knees, making the wicker sofa seem more rickety than ever, less by his size than by his sheer presence, Reeve lifted toward Clem, seated by the window with his typewriter on the coffee table, a look shot through with such penetrating irony, large with such a summary of experience, and warm with such fond indulgence for that chaos of existence which forever eludes the rule of law, not to mention common sense, that Clem found himself once more flooded with emotion. The emotion that had sprung forth so impetuously for Julie on the ground of the Spanish mission, that had expanded to embrace his wife and mother, expanded now again, overwhelming him with a passion that was sentimental, romantic, and as real as bread and salt and tears.

Those two men on the sofa, himself in communication with them. In communion: he had thought always that it was they who were with-holding when it was himself who withheld. Wasn't this what he had looked for from the time he climbed the wall with Joe Hata? He looked down at the crimson figure of the tractor on the manual, the lines radiating from it outward to a circumference of circled numbers, the identifying chart of parts, the legend. Wasn't this what he had been seeking in his dissatisfaction? What can I do, what shall I do, what must I . . . ?

"There's so much tied up in this," he said slowly. "If there wasn't so much involved."

"One step at a time," they assured him. "One step at a time."

"It's risky. We're sticking our necks way out. I wouldn't bet a nickel on the future of any of us."

"If the situation is what you say it is," Reeve said, "we got no choice, have we, but to take the risk?"

"The best defense," Rad offered, "is, sometimes, an attack."

"Don't say that word. Don't breathe it. Don't even think it."

They made up a time schedule covering the following week up to the decisive meeting of the white advisory board when Rad was to deliver his signatures and plan. The burden of the initial phase, the possibility of whether there were to be any succeeding phases, fell to a great extent on him. "Are you sure," Clem asked him more than once, "that you can swing it?"

"Leave it to me."

Afterward Reeve went off for his truck, parked in the little dead-end street behind the rectory, and Rad lingered with Clem on the dirt sidewalk in front. He had informed Clem earlier that he was on his way to pick up his son Charles at his cousin Henry's house. But now he lagged unaccountably, scuffing his foot on the sidewalk and chewing on a stalk he'd pulled up out of the grass that bordered the roadside.

"I want to thank you for visiting my wife at the hospital," Rad said. "That meant a lot to her. And to me, too. Now we got all the kids back —funniest thing, much as I needed Charles on the farm with me I didn't want to go fetch him till I had this tractor thing going. He sure will like that tractor."

"Mind if I walk along with you?" Clem asked.

"I was just about to ask you that."

Reeve passed them in the truck, signaling that he'd wait up ahead. "You see," Rad confided, "I wanted to go in with them by myself and they wouldn't have me. Thought the white boys would all make a goat of me and I'd have to turn against them or take off. Know what I mean?"

"I know."

"So I realized I'd have to bring some of my boys right in with me, but in such a way they can't take over. If it can be done."

"If."

They walked down the lane through the steaming tunnel greenery, Clem a half-step behind Rad, holding back. The unity of self shattered by his conversation with Julie—he like a dutiful child trying to set reality rightside up, put everything straight—had been restored to him by his conversation with Rad and Reeve; but a larger, more hurtful and less manageable self, whose boundaries he did not yet know. All along the lane, within this self become so hurtfully expansive, he struggled both to put the question to Rad and to keep his mouth shut. He had no right, no earthly right to ask of this man what might not in the end be right for any of them: Rad or Julie, Charles or Colfax.

"Funniest thing, I been putting off going to Charles," Rad confided, hurrying him on. "We had a little set-to before he left and I couldn't go crawling. Thought he'd come begging back to me like a whiptail dog. Only that wouldn't be Charles. Now I can't wait to see him."

Ahead of Clem he opened the gate to the old Colfax residence, and at the breadth and whiteness of it, the shock of whiteness, he flinched.

And disconcerted, stopped still. He coughed out an embarrassed laugh, his eyes flashing back in appeal.

"Do me a favor, Rev? Come in with me?"

"Rad—" He stayed Rad's hand on the gate. Before Julie's house he was shaken once again with a tumult of emotion. "About Charles—"

How could he ask of this man what he had to ask of him? That mobile face with the razor-scratch on the cheek where he'd shaved too scrupulously close, that curly-humored mouth, those eyes lantern-bright, that shoulder sharply raised under the faded tan shirt . . . He was asking Rad to pull his chestnuts out of the fire. Give him quietus.

"Julie's asked me," he said to Rad, his hand on the sinewy wrist, "to speak to you. They're going up to Atlanta again next week with the little fellow and they'd like to take Charles with them. Show him the sights and—well, he's been a great help to her. Done wonders, she feels, for Colfax. In all humanity, Rad, it'd be a terrible thing to take him from her right now. If you can leave him—"

Rad shook his head. "No, no, I couldn't do that."

"For just another week?"

"No—" They entered the gate together and followed the walk around to the side of the house. "I'd sure like to oblige you, Reverend, but his mother wants him home. And me, I can't spare him no more."

They passed by the dining-room window with its clinking of china and silver being laid and the kitchen window with its aroma of roasting meat toward the sound in back of laughter and splashing and a dog's rollicking yelp. At the corner of the house their progress was halted. The rose-trellis entry to the yard was blocked by a battery of lawn chairs, heaped with Roman-striped towels and terrycloth robes.

Clem started to lift the chairs out of the way but Rad touched his arm, drawing him back behind the trellis where they could watch without being seen. In the center of the yard the sprinkler whirled up rainbow jets of water through which Charles pranced, pawing the air, a mettlesome pony. The little one in high spirits again skirted the outer drops, ducked back. Charles scootched, coaxing him inward, caught him up by the waist and spun with him till they both dropped breathless, rolling on the ground, the purple satin strip of Charles' bathing trunks now on top and then Colfax's yellow satin strip and the purple again with a gold stripe down the side.

"He's always been good with the young ones."

Rad took the thick-napped, stripe-blazoned towel from the back of the webbed plastic chair and pulled it through the ring of his hand.

"He never was to Atlanta before."

He crushed a fold of the towel in his hand, his fingers biting through texture as plush as a rug. He shook out the towel, refolded it on the back of the chair and rubbed his hand over it. Then he turned on his heel and walked back toward the front of the house.

"All right," he said harshly, "all right, you tell 'em."

"Aren't you going to speak to him?" Clem plunged after Rad. The laughing shrieks of the two boys pelted from behind the house, down the corridor of the walk. "You've got to speak to him."

Rad shook away. "Speak to him—I'd blow my top! I'll beat his brains in. He's old enough now . . . I can't make his choices for him. He's old enough."

Reeve's truck was waiting in the road and Rad hiked himself up into the cab. He reached into his pocket and leaned down to Clem with a crumpled dollar bill. "Here, you give this to him. He'll need it for spending money."

"You're angry at me?"

"Ain't nothin' to do with you. He's old enough now—"

They were gone through puffs of dust down the green-vaulted road. Clem crushed the dollar bill in his fist, straightened it out and folded it.

He could go in to her now.

Julie was upstairs in her bedroom busy on the telephone. He sent a message up to her with Kissie. She sent a message back, thanking him.

The rapprochment he longed for, the self-explorative exchange which would salvage somehow the wreckage he had wrought by transforming it, however painfully, into an experience of some value, was denied him. It was too facile a fancy. More soothing to his needs than to hers.

He tried calling her on the telephone later in the afternoon, but Henry answered him. "We're busy with the tile man," Henry said, "he just got in from Bay City. Say, were you here today?"

"Well, yes," Clem admitted.

"Did you say anything to Julie to upset her?"

"Well, we may have had a difference of opinion."

"For God sake, haven't you got anymore sense than that? With what she's going through. You suppose to be our pastor! Don't you come around no more bothering her with your opinions. You stay away from her, hear? You stay away . . ."

When he hung up after Henry, it was no longer only a matter of what he felt for Julie. It was what that brief interchange on the telephone presaged for himself. Personally. Professionally.

He sought refuge again, but not in the Spanish cemetery. In the crimson tractor.

5

With his mother and Nancy, Clem drove down on Monday to St. George to inspect the tractor for himself. Odell senior, recently deceased, had either indulged the dream of a lifetime or been high-pressured by some crackerjack salesman into buying it. Out of a shack beside which the barn was a mansion, he had sent three children to college. Odell's dentist son, vacationing here, demonstrated the machine in its various capacities and Laura who had a good eye for camera angles shot a roll of film on it. She was impressed . . . such a lovely colored family. And beset all the way home with afterthoughts: but why so secretive, maybe the equipment was included with the land in the option they let out, maybe there's some sort of double-dealing. "Son, you sure you've told me everything about this? Seems to me you're kind of worried."

Late that night, when they were all slumbering out the humid exhaustion of the trip, the telephone rang. It aroused Clem like a bolt of lightning crashing through the house. In a daze he stumbled downstairs, missed a step and turned his ankle. Hobbling, fumbling through the dark—his sister Grace, another highway accident, something catastrophic—he finally grasped the instrument and lifted the receiver in the middle of a piercing ring. A click crackled in his ear. He jiggled the hook. "Number please?"

"Wrong number," he said to his mother and Nancy who were clinging to the banister at the head of the stairs.

A few minutes or hours after he had fallen asleep again, the telephone screamed out its two rings and three, summoning him back down. He lifted the receiver. Again the click. He spoke to the operator. "Look Doris, someone's been trying to get through to me."

"Oh no," Doris said, "I haven't any calls for you. Must be a mistake."

Next morning going into class he observed Rad leaning up against a brick pillar, studiously absorbed in the tractor manual. Several fellows drifted in around Rad and peeked over his shoulders. "What's that?" "Oh," Rad said casually, "a tractor. One of these new models with a whole slew of attachments."

Clem continued on inside. While he was lecturing, the manual passed from hand to hand up and down the rows of chairs. Before he left for the day he was approached by Ray DelVecchio. "Say Rev, you hear anything about the colored boys is about to buy a tractor?"

"Something of the sort."

"Rad says they're going to run a benefit for it. You think they might could deal some of us in on this? Ain't nobody needs a tractor more'n I do."

"Well, you never know till you try."

That afternoon, in preparation for the Friday night Farmer-Veterans Advisory Board meeting, he drove to Bay City for the tractor snapshots left at a photo shop to be developed. In the evening he worked out a composite of his report and Vivian's, Nancy typing up the drafts. She made stencils of the final copy, ran them through the mimeograph, mounted the pictures of the tractor in action on a blank page, stapled the whole thing together under a blue cover. By one in the morning she had removed all her clothing but her slip. "Little Nancy Etticoat in a white petticoat and a red nose. The longer she stands, the shorter she grows." With a last slam of the stapler she slumped down in her chair, a molten tallow mass. "Twelve copies. That'll do for a start, won't it?"

"Looks good," Clem said. "You think it'll convince them?"

"I don't think," she said. "I just do."

He bent over to dab at a smudge of mimeograph ink on her nose and kissed her impulsively on the mouth. Downstairs the telephone rang. Nancy's head sprang back, her eyes dusky with alarm. Who'd be calling at this time of night? Again?

Laura flew down ahead of Clem in nightgown and hairnet, forestalling him at the telephone.

"Mother please, I don't want you to disturb yourself—"

She listened at the receiver, perturbed, and passed it to him. "Old Mr. Stowe, Ada Hemmings' father. High as Lord Harry on horseback."

Old Mr. Stowe had conceived a liking for him ever since their encounter in his daughter's bathroom. Clem had had a few discussions with him afterward, salutary he hoped, concerning the causes and cure of alcoholism. Now against a cacophony of background noises, which could be ascribed only to The Fat Hog, Mr. Stowe demanded that he remove his name from the resolution.

"What resolution? You mean the one that's already gone?"

"Take it off. I don't want it there."

"Mr. Stowe, it's been in Atlanta over a week. More than one hundred people here signed it. Under the most respectable auspices."

"Take it off. I don't want my name on no dog-damn Communistic—"

Clem hung up. The telephone rang again. Mr. Stowe, plaintively apologetic. "Ada's been frettin' me so about it. She has a public job and if I lost it on her we'll all be in the street. Now will you take it off?"

Laura was awake all night over it. "You should never have let him sign," she said at breakfast. "A character like that. As if it had any worth."

"I didn't let him. He demanded to. And he was cold sober, I couldn't discriminate. If out of one hundred and five signers, only one person —or even half a dozen—I think it's pretty good."

After breakfast, he took several bound copies of his tractor prospectus under his arm and set off to lay some groundwork for Friday night's meeting. Benson, the chairman, he did not wish to see. Benson in his present mood would only squelch him. So he avoided Benson and, it seemed, Earl Goodfellow, whom he depended on as an ally, was avoiding him. He left a copy at Goodfellow's office and another at Thurlow's house. Both the old man and Vivian were absent.

In the course of riding around however he received an unexpected stimulus from an unexpected source. As he slowed down for a stop sign in front of the Baptist church, Fred Hawley knocked at his windshield and with a mysterious gesture of his head invited him to park and follow him around the side of the church to his basement office in the rear.

In the office Fred showed him plans for his new Alabama marble baptismal tank: the old one had been leaking ever since Pearl Harbor. If he accomplished nothing else in his lifetime but the installation of that tank, he'd be satisfied. Fred's campaign against the liquor interests must be running on the rocks, Clem guessed, and he was taking this opportunity to display friendship for him as fellow crusader and candidate for martyrdom.

With his hand on Clem's arm, detaining him, Fred sent his girl assistant out on some fool's errand and then with a twinkle, beaming, he lifted the latch of the cupboard where he kept back issues of his church bulletin. Ordinarily their discourse took the form of a battle of Biblical texts, shall or shall not the crooked be made straight, should or should not the servant obey his master even as the master does his Lord God. Or a debate on the virtues of total immersion, especially when coupled with total abstinence. Fred must have found the chapter and verse, Clem thought, to beat all chapters and verses. And girded himself for the fray.

From under a heap of bulletins, Fred drew out the Savannah morning paper.

"You seen this yet, Clem? You heard it? It's all over the radio. Everybody's talking about it."

He rattled the paper out, front page up, on his desk. Last night, at a prayer meeting of the Baptist church in Lurie, the church of Ol' Cal Hubbard and his family, the minister, Ray Mason Jones, had delivered a sermon denouncing Ol' Cal to his face for the murder of the two colored couples a few weeks ago and laying responsibility for the mid-summer wave of killings at his door.

"You think you High Churchers got all the spunk, huh?" Fred rubbed his hands. "Ray Mason Jones, you know who he is? Georgia boy, born and raised, went to Tech, was captain of the basketball team and a colonel in the Marines. Right to Ol' Cal's face he told him all this feudin'-fussin'-and-fightin' between the races has got to stop."

"Looks like a very handsome young man," Clem said, making his acquaintance with the photograph in the paper. "Why are you hiding him?"

"That's right." Fred with bravado flung the paper over onto his assistant's table.

Though he hadn't intended to, it was premature yet and perhaps rash, Clem showed Fred his tractor prospectus. "A couple of the boys came to me with this idea, what do you think of it?"

Fred perused it, his smooth face dwindling down into his paunchy neck. "Tell you what I'm willing to do? You all have your advisory meeting and if they all go for it there, then you come back to me, I'll think about it. How about that? And Clem—"

He squeezed Clem's arm as he escorted him to the door. "I want you to know I'm for you too. There's some feeling around here, well—" He checked himself and wrung Clem's hand in parting. "Good luck."

On the strength of his interview with Fred, Clem bought a Savannah *Morning News* and drove with it to the house of Marcus Hadley, Fred's leading parishioner and, next to Benson, the most influential member of the Veterans Advisory Board. Marcus was also a past president of the Arcady Chamber of Commerce and the loudest advocate of progress on the County Commission. Of course progress to Marcus meant improvements, and improvements meant highway and building construction, and construction meant contracts in his pocket. He was currently erecting a motel on the highway north of town, driving post holes for the Rural Electrification Administration, remodeling the Warren house and in his spare time putting finishing touches on his own new home, which was popularly supposed to have been put together of materials intended for the two public high schools. Marcus had on occasion been very helpful to the farm-training class in obtaining building supplies at cost price.

Clem located Marcus on the shady side of his house, up a ladder painting the overhang under his eaves. He descended at once with a hearty welcome. No one looking at Marcus, truculent of brow, sagacious of eye, mouth as temperate as a marsh breeze, would ever dream of associating him with the scandal over the missing parts of the schools.

"Am I glad to see you." Marcus conveyed Clem ahead of him into the house. "I was just thinking of running over to talk to you. About this Friday night meeting. Take a look around while I wash up."

Marcus was very proud of his place, genuine California ranch type, first of its kind in the county. "Though these hicks around here," Marcus said wrathfully from the lavatory, "keep calling it a bungalow." For the second time in recent days Clem was conducted on a guided tour of rooms, kitchen all steel, bathroom all tile, den pine-paneled. "A-course it's not the Colfax house, you seen the job I done with that? Or Judge Purcell's. But it's modern. The latest thing in modernity. How you like my picture window?"

Only thing now, his kids were after him to throw out his morris chair, it didn't go with the living room. "This morris chair," Marcus punched its scuffed green-plush back, "is me. It goes, I go."

He planted himself down in it in his paint-splashed white overalls in front of the picture window. Clem opened the newspaper and passed it to him.

"See this yet? Fred Hawley just called it to my attention that you Primitives are putting us High Churchers to shame."

Marcus glanced through the story. "Ray Mason Jones is the hero of Lurie. Got a nice wife, three fine children. Got plenty of the old fire and brimstone in him too. Got a real future ahead of him. Now why'd he have to go and stomp Ol' Cal for?"

Why indeed? Why does a man have to climb the Matterhorn? With piton, clawhold, kneehold, toehold, pull himself up inch by inch? Why must a man hunt the white whale, explore the frozen poles, plumb the ocean floor? When he could be sitting comfortably in his morris chair by his picture window.

"I reckon you understand what I mean, Reverend. I'm dead-set against preachers meddlin' in politics."

He allowed Clem sufficient time to meditate on it.

"Now I've voted for Ol' Cal and Ol' Vern and the progress of the common man since I was in knee-britches. And I can tell you sure as you're sitting there that if these niggers went and got themselves killed, they must've deserved it. Only one thing"—he folded the newspaper and rapped Clem over the knee with it—"Ray Mason Jones ain't wrong! All this bloodshed, it gives the state a bad name. Scares off tourists."

Marcus excused himself for a few minutes and brought back a sheaf of blueprints. "You know where the Dixie Highway crosses Lonesome Pine Ridge? Well a couple of other businessmen and myself, we snapped up a tract of public land there for a song. Putting up this streamlined air-conditioned motel. Invested a mint in it. Catch some of these tourists hell-bent for Florida. Plenty of good fishing and hunting sport and scenic beauty too right here in Georgia.

"I won't lie to you, Reverend. I am for the peaceableness of this county because, above all, it's necessary for my personal plans. Anything that's good for the people here you'll find me for because, among other things, it contributes to my profit. I wouldn't want nothing," he smiled at Clem with his astute eyes and his mouth as meek as Moses, "to happen as shouldn't, Reverend."

"I'm very pleased you feel that way about it," Clem said. "That's why I'd especially like to have your opinion on this. A couple of boys from our farm-training classes came to me with a proposal that I think could eventually build up into a farming enterprise that would help this whole area. It would increase income, improve the fine feeling we've always fostered here between the races, might even result in some favorable publicity outside."

He laid open the prospectus on the new Swedish modern cocktail table. "I might add that in thirteen counties of north Georgia similar ventures of one sort or another were initiated under TVA and are still in operation."

His heart was pounding unreasonably hard and a crazy tightness gripped his throat as Marcus took a cursory look through the pages. He's going to say it's a harebrained scheme, he'll take it apart, tear it to shreds.

But Marcus never bothered to give it that much attention. He switched the folder this way and that, then threw it down among the ashtrays, a matter of no consequence, already disposed of.

"I thought I'd talked plain to you," Marcus said and affably smiled over his dentures. "But I guess I didn't make myself plain enough. We who have worked and toiled and sweated and struggled through more days and nights than you've lived, with more of hope and heartache than you'll ever know, to make a go of this place and build it up into something that will stand match with the rest of the world, we won't allow for nobody to mess it up.

"If you're in with those two young fellows out on the River Road like they say you are, take my advice. Stay away from them. Have nothing to do with them. They been a public nuisance from way back. If you and the Professor aim to keep your classes up, best thing for you all to do is drop them two out right now."

He shuffled his blueprints together and tapped them into alignment over his knees, rolled them up and wriggled an elastic band down over them. "That's just what I was going over to see you about today. If there's to be no trouble around here, and none of us want that, I'd like

THE CAMPAIGN 887

you to make Disciplinary Action the first order of business this Friday night advisory meeting. We'll vote McDowell out of the program and send word over to the colored Advisory Board to take the hint and do the same with Reeve. Get rid of them before they cause any serious ructions. Don't wait till the house falls down."

"But we can't just drop them," Clem protested. "They're on the Veterans Administration rolls. There's no basis—"

"That's up to you, Reverend. I'm sure you can find something. You're cute enough." Marcus handed back the prospectus from the table. "If you just think this through, I'm sure you'll agree with me." He pulled himself up out of his morris chair and with his arm heavy around Clem's shoulders walked out with him. When he clasped Clem's hand he held rather than shook it, close to his rock-ribbed chest. "It's been a pleasure. Go see Benson now and talk this over with him. Tell him what I told you."

Clem did not go to see Benson. He left his car at Mayor Dakin's filling station to be greased and walked around Oglethorpe Square on a few errands while waiting. Everyone he encountered, it seemed to him, was especially solicitous today. They took his hand with a warmer grasp. They sought his opinion on the duration of the hot spell and the brown patches left in the lawns by the chinch-bug grubs and on the latest intrigue involving a conflict between the City Council and some property holders over a cattle-barrier permit. Edna Telfer rushed out of the newspaper office to invite him and his two ladies to Sunday dinner. And Mort Green at the market presented him with a mess of mullet fresh off the boat, when making up his order. Mort had a copy of the Savannah *Morning News* on his counter. "You see this?" asked Clem out of the side of his mouth, one eye on his son at the produce end of the store. "It's all over the radio. Only—" Mort choked back his words as his son rambled over to the cash register to change a ten. "Your kids have to go to school." His children were all full-grown. "They have to get along . . ."

Everywhere, a word of encouragement. Thank God for Ray Mason Jones, Clem thought to himself with a salute to his unknown colleague. Mason Jones who a hundred fifty miles away had unwittingly, with a conscience and a courage that dwarfed his, taken the heat off him by sharing it. Yet the encouragement afforded him less solace than it should have. Every word of it, every small incident rang with implicit warning.

On his way back to the filling station for his car, a housewife he had scarcely met before called him over to her porch and while chatting with him summoned a little colored boy from the drift of dust where he was playing by the roadside. "Just a minute, Smokeman," she said to the boy and left in the middle of a sentence to run into her house. "I'll be right back." She came out with a sandwich and a glass of milk for the boy. "I feed him every day," she explained, "while his mother's off to work." Her cheeks flamed up as she spoke, and quite superfluously she took her apron off and shook it out.

Calling attention to her philanthropy, Clem wondered when he left her. Or expressing identification with him? Or staging a devious act of aggression? He stopped in his tracks. Remembering a time when every small colloquy became magnified to nightmare proportions, every small reprieve merely intensified the pressure. Funneling him toward a pin-point of surrender.

Will I never outlive Augusta!

He brought the fresh mullet into the rectory kitchen, whistling cheerfully. His mother was seated at the table paring apples, which Nancy sliced into a bowl and brown-sugared while Ida prepared the pastry for pies, chop-chopping lard through flour with two silver knives.

"See this?" Clem held the Savannah paper up within his mother's range of vision. "One minister in Georgia still has whatever it took to get him through the war."

The apple parings stripped away in automatic revolutions from his mother's hands as she read. "Poor young fellow," she said. "He'll lose his church."

Nancy wiped her hands and took the paper. "I suppose he felt he had to do it?"

Ida sidled over and peeped between their heads. "Oh my," she said, "the world is gettin' wild, I'm tellin' you. Weak and wild. All this slayin', it's been slaughter. Poor mamma! Poor grandma!" She went back to her pastry, beating a silvery tattoo through clouds of flour until grease and flour blended into grains as fine as grits. She sprinkled ice water through it turning the batter with a fork, refraining from touching it with the warmth of her hand, until it adhered into a snowy ball. "You want two of these pies to send over to Mrs. Telfer?"

"He'll lose his church," Laura repeated. The apple skin flowed from her fingers in a continuous strip, while her presentiments, unvoiced, went on and on with the certainty of prophecy. He'll lose his church and his living, his house and his family and his good repute. . . . "Oh Clem, please don't bother with the fish! I'll take care of it. Just get out of here."

Clem rolled up his sleeves and unwrapped the fish at the sink. Barging in here with his newspaper, his blood and thunder, into their serenity, their affection, their working together around the scrubbed-clean wood table. Get out of here, intruder!

He washed the fish under the faucet and began cleaning them. Hack! Off with their heads. Rip! Slit from throat to anus. Swoosh! Slosh the innards out. Scrape! Scale the skin down. Rasp rasp rasp.

"Oh!" Blood was spurting from his mother's finger. "Get away—" She thrust them all back. Him too. "Get away. It's nothing, nothing—"

Leaning over the bloodied fish in the sink, she ran cold water over the sheeting blood of her finger. Wavering with nausea. Dewing over with grey sweat. Clem peeled paper off a Band-Aid and wound the gummed strip around her finger while she pushed him away, "Leave it alone! If you'd just leave things alone!"

She had grown old here this year with him.

In spite of Henry's interdict, he attempted after lunch to telephone Julie. She had not been at church Sunday, not in itself an adverse indication in view of the fluctuations of summer attendance. He had ascertained later that she had gone off with the two boys to her Cousin Tibby's at Silver Beach for a few days. All I want, he reassured himself now as the bell drubbed tonelessly in his ear, is to know how you are, and Coley. All I want is to know how everything is.

A workman answering told him that the family had left for Atlanta and was not expected back until late in the week.

Again that night his telephone rang repeatedly and clicked off as soon as he picked it up. This time he lost his temper with the operator. "Maybe it's kid stuff," she suggested. "You wouldn't believe the things that kids'll do. Calling up Mort Green to ask if he has Camels. 'Give 'em a drink,' they tell him. And there was this girl had a crush on a teacher . . . We aren't allowed of course to give out any information."

"If this doesn't stop," Clem said, "I'm complaining to the management, Doris, and if it doesn't stop then I'm complaining to the law. And anyone who has anything to do with these calls including the transmitting of them, kids or no kids, will be prosecuted."

He was bothered by no more calls that night or ever after. Although he could clearly hear from then on, on every call to and from his house, that his line was open.

6

It was Friday afternoon before Clem managed to catch up with Professor Thurlow. He was driving with Nancy through the middle of downtown traffic when Thurlow honked at him from a parking space at the curb of the green. Clem maneuvered into the vacant space next to Thurlow's Dodge, and without getting out of their cars they held their conference.

"You look over that folder I left you?" Clem asked or rather shouted for the benefit of the old codgers who were craning about curiously from the nearest park bench.

"Well," the Professor shouted back, "I put two hundred and fifty dollars down on it yesterday and I expect to get it all back. We had it trucked up to Bay City last night and it's storaged there now."

"My gosh," Clem said in a more normal voice, dismayed, "you don't lose any time, do you?"

"I'm getting too old to worry about whether or not I can make it," Thurlow's voice also dropped, whiffling out from under his yellow-tinged mustache. "I'm playing the long shots now."

"You really think this project will go through?"

"I think," Thurlow said obscurely, "that the white folks are more afraid of it than we are."

Clem did not choose to mention at this moment the movement afoot for expulsion of Rad and Reeve from their classes. "Well, tonight will tell the tale."

"If it don't happen now," Thurlow reached over to his windshield and wiped dust off the glass, clearing his view, "it'll take another ten years. And if not this way, God knows how."

Thurlow started his car and wheeling this way an inch and that way an inch, backing and filling, nudged out into the stream of traffic.

"Ten years!" Clem said to Nancy. "I can't wait that long. We're stuck with this right now."

Nancy was massaging her fingers in her lap, her hair drooping over her cheek. "I know you think I'm a scared-cat, Clem, and I am. I've always gone along with you because you're my husband. But now I'm beginning to think you're right, not just because I'm married to you but because you're right. Only I'm still scared-cat. I still can't stand the tension, all this pulling and hauling between people I know just as people . . . Look, do you see what I see?"

Marcus Hadley was coming out of the Arcady Bank, guiding Benson across the sidewalk into his red DeSoto and driving off with him.

"Poor Benson." Nancy watched after them. "He's really losing his sight, isn't he? Please—" She intercepted his hand on the gear. "Don't start off yet. Let's cross over to the Palace of Sweets and sit in a booth in back, just the two of us together. I want a strawberry ice cream soda."

Rad was late that evening. Clem lay on the sofa with his arms up behind his head, ostensibly resting, while the mantel clock of imitation black marble ticked on toward eight. His mother had tucked herself about the open lid of the secretary, writing to missionary friends abroad. At the piano Nancy was playing with plangent fingers *Les sons et les parfums tombent dans l'air du soir.* The shades were drawn and the lamps cast an amber glow over the books in the shelved niche beside the secretary, the bowl of mixed flowers on the coffee table. The notes dripped and glistened. The clock with brazen clangor pealed eight.

"Well." Laura scraped back from the desk and taking off her reading glasses delicately wiped over her eyelids. "Looks like that boy isn't going to show up."

"Thank heavens, huh?"

"Frankly yes. You've been going too far afield, Clem. Leaving your church and your religion."

"I never was closer to it."

"You can't wait for him any longer."

Clem took his briefcase, packed with the prospectus folders he had so painstakingly prepared. For what . . .

Halfway from the house to the garage he noticed the truck drawn up in the shrubbery of the dead-end street in back. He crossed the yard to it and poked his head in the cab.

"How long've you been here?"

"Well," Rad said sheepishly, "with your lights on in the house and all, and the music—"

"You get them to sign up?"

"Nineteen of them. All but Ellery Hayes. It just seemed so sort of . . . Well, I was listening to the music."

They transferred to Clem's car. The meeting was to be at Benson's house tonight instead of at school: Benson didn't care to go out nights lately anymore than he had to. "So you didn't want to interrupt the music?" Clem said to Rad as they rolled back out of the driveway. "I'll tell that to Nancy."

Rad was daunted by Benson's house, unpretentious and old-fashioned though it was. Before Clem had even rung the bell, he was aware that Rad, having left his natural self behind in the truck back of the rectory, was tightening up. His hair was slicked down and his thin features jutted out, more rawboned than ever, touchy, scrubbed to the quick. His tan sharkskin suit, a prewar relic pressed to the sharpest of creases, constricted his movements. He pried his forefinger into his shirt collar, starched stiff as a board, shoved at his protruding cuffs, tugged at the necktie that kept humping out over his lapels.

As soon as they were inside the door, Rad got off on the wrong foot by presenting his hat to Benson instead of the white-coated boy who butlered for Benson on such evenings. At sight of Rad, Benson elevated his brows three stories upward. With a grin at Clem—so you brought your prize guinea pig along—he passed the hat, a cocoa straw too rigidly new, on to the boy. But all he said was, with gleeful anticipation, "You're late. Everybody's here before you."

Before Benson could hustle them to the dining room where the others were assembled, Rad became embroiled in another difficulty, whether or not to greet the butler with whom he evidently had some previous acquaintance. "Say Baron," he saluted in passing and was discomfited by the gracious, "And how you this evening, Mr. McDowell?" with which the servant bowed him down the hall.

Through the magenta portieres Rad stalked ahead of Clem into the dining room, head high. But retracting against his surroundings, Clem felt, as a cat retracts, retreating into its own corner, into a reticence watchful and contemptuous. He was embarrassed for Rad, annoyed at Benson's attitude and worried by the flabbergasted faces of the company at the table when the butler pulled up an extra chair for Rad and seated him among them. The meeting had not yet been called to order but considerable discussion, interrupted by their entrance, had already taken place, and there could be no doubt of what that subject was.

A chandelier of leaded stained glass, fringed with glass beads, hung low over the round table. The table was covered with an ecru-embroidered linen cloth that hung almost to the floor, bordered with fringes low enough to tickle the ankles. Around the table in golden oak leather-seated chairs the members of the board were disposed. On the upper half the business and civic leaders: Benson with Marcus Hadley on his right and Ozzie Higginson of the Hardware & Feed on his left. On the lower half the professional advisers: Earl Goodfellow, the county agent, crewcut, self-consciously adjusting his black-framed glasses; Lloyd Bird, the surveyor for the timber company, relaxed as always, with head cocked as if listening to the faroff whistling of birds in the bush; and Horace Truelove, Lonnie's father, a farmer who had his gold pocketwatch out on the table as a reminder to them all of time a-passing and the miles of dark country road he had to travel before he'd reach home. In addition, D. C. Lacey, representing the school system, occupied a place between his brother-in-law Marcus and Earl.

With an affronted and incredulous stare Marcus shuffled his chair away from Lacey, forced by the butler to allow space between them for Rad. Clem took the vacant chair awaiting him, diametrically opposite Benson at the lower rim of the table.

Whatever judgment the board members had arrived at in their discussion, they certainly had not planned to render it in the presence of the accused. Benson rapped for attention, opening the meeting.

"Since we are in my house," he announced, "I hope you don't mind, Marcus"—with an obeisance toward Marcus, the only dry man present —"if we observe the custom of the house? Boy, break out the brandy."

Rad gulped down his drink as soon as it was served him. Still brooding, Clem guessed, over that business with his hat. At a signal from Benson, Rad's glass was promptly refilled by the butler. Clem watched helplessly from his seat as over the distance of the table the glass was drained again and as promptly refilled. Benson was out to strip Rad bareass, hold him up by the heels and drop him down the spout. Just once and for all, Clem groaned inwardly, to make an everlasting fool out of me. What he did not guess was that Rad had no intention of making a fool of himself in the presence of these men, not under the eyes of the Baron.

The "matter of discipline" which Marcus stubbornly raised as the first item of business was placed at Clem's suggestion down at the foot of the agenda under Good and Welfare. No one objected. It could wait. However they never descended that far. When the meeting broke up two hours later in a glow of concord and brandy, all the differences among them had been eradicated by two items not included in the agenda. The Founders Day parade. And Marcus Hadley's post holes.

They all listened with polite interest to Earl Goodfellow's opening report on plans being undertaken in coordination with the Colfax-Scott class for a cash crop of winter onions, to be grown under optimum conditions on as much acreage as each student wished to allot. As part of the plan, the class was also undertaking a study of cooperative buying and marketing methods under Federal regulation, as described—here Earl laid several publications on the table—by the Department of Agriculture. Earl's report was followed by some academic wrangling over anticipated costs and profits, with a reminder by D. C. Lacey of the uncertainties of December weather, beginning with the great frost in 1929 when it snowed up to last year when he went swimming on Christmas Day. Horace Truelove pointedly removed the chain from his watch pocket and attached it to his watch on the table.

Ozzie Higginson then proceeded to deliver a glowing account of the fertilizer distribution, over Benson's consistent jibes. His account was followed by another wrangle, a debate among conscientious, experienced, and well-informed men on the merits of organic versus the new chemical fertilizers and the relative effectiveness versus the possibly toxic effect of the new insecticides. Horace—after a heated argument with Ozzie, in which the merchant concluded that the farmer was hopelessly backward and the farmer concluded that the merchant was hopelessly mercenary—ended it all by consulting his watch. "Let's get on with this. I was up at five."

Clem passed around his blue-bound tractor prospectus. The board members were in a hurry by now to concentrate on the main point of the evening, the last item on the agenda, and finish it off. They cursorily inspected the folder with its pictures of tractor and outlines for organization and management; and like Judge Purcell with Rose Scott's will at the court hearing, they cast it aside. Clem's elaboration of the economic advantages to be derived from the purchase of such a basic piece of equipment left them singularly unimpressed. Only Earl Goodfellow, caught between the instincts implanted in him by his training and the external pressure of those present around him, rendered any serious attention.

Earl frowned, lighted his pipe and lifted his head toward Clem, all primed, Clem recognized, to undermine the whole scheme with a host of perspicacious but peripheral exceptions to it. Lloyd Bird leaned back in his chair, more remote than ever, his ear cocked to those distant birds on the wing, his dark eyes lost in a reverie perhaps of his roguish repertoire of winter's tales. Horace Truelove yawned and wound his watch, buzzing the stem steadily between thumb and forefinger.

"We all agree with you," Earl cut in as soon as Clem was through. "We all realize that the lack of equipment may be fatal. But," he said before Marcus or anyone else in the opposition could, "why this tractor? What do you want to do it this way for? Whose idea is this anyhow?"

"This one, I should think," Clem temporized, "because it happens to be immediately available and a bonanza to boot."

He looked down at Rad who was resting forward comfortably, too comfortably, over his folded elbows on the table, a smile like the tip of a possum's tail curled in the corner of his mouth, his coat shed by now and his tie loosened.

"As for who—" Clem said.

Wordlessly Rad passed up to him, creased and crumpled, the signatures he had collected under the statement of interest.

The list of names did create an impression. It was examined with curiosity and a cross fire of mutual glances. "I can't read this," Benson complained. "Will somebody please read this off to me?" The names were read aloud.

"Why that's my son Lonnie," Horace cried. "He never told me—"

"Now, how the hell did all these—"

"I would like to reserve all questions and comment," Clem resolutely shut Marcus off, "until we have our full report. I took the liberty of bringing a member of the class here tonight to tell you all how they feel about this tractor project. After all, it's their baby. Rad McDowell, will you please stand?"

Rad refreshed himself from his glass and rose, or as Clem saw it, swayed, upward to his feet.

"What we want," he blurted forth loudly, addressing Ozzie across the table, "is the biggest crowd ever in town on Founders Day. We haven't had a decent Founders Day since before the war. Now just about every family in this county has somebody that's a veteran of some war or other, and if all of them turn out I bet we could have a parade that would reach clear around the Square and up Lancaster Street and then some. White and colored. Us for us and them for them.

"But a crowd"—he fanned his hands out before Ozzie—"what I mean a crowd. Pack the Square. And afterward the colored will throw a big barbecue picnic in the grove behind Zion Church and anyone that wants to come there for eats can. Them for them. And us for us. They'll have some entertainment too, a concert—"

"You know," Ozzie said, his eyes screwed up at Rad, "I been thinking about running a big clearance sale along about that time?"

"Perfect. We'll get the two Legion posts behind this and sell tickets all over and maybe—this is Lonnie's idea—solicit contributions from storekeepers. Print up a program and all with sponsors on it—"

"Lonnie said that? My son Lonnie?"

"Lonnie has a million of 'em. What he thinks is we could have stands-like with produce exhibits? And prizes for the best. Them grounds around Zion is plenty sizable."

Earl Goodfellow drew off his black-bowed glasses and with his fingernail dug at the grit embedded between frame and lens. "You know when I first got to be county agent here," he said and scrutinized with gratification the grit disinterred on the tip of his nail, "I was always after these dirt farmers to hold some sort of exhibit. County fair. Something."

"Lonnie thinks it could be like those harvest picnics you used to have down at your place, Mr. Truelove, everybody there from miles around. And Lu, my wife, she thinks the ladies can contribute the fixings, maybe run a sale of preserves and pies."

"Get the Home Demonstration agents in on it," Earl recommended. "Mrs. Brownlee will be only too happy, and I think the colored have theirs too now, she'd pitch in."

"Let me see that list again." Benson reached over for it. "Founders Day. That falls in the second week of September, doesn't it?" This time he apparently could read the list without aid.

Clem covered his eyes to hide his laughter. Founders Day fell about five days before the primary election, and the celebration if handled with the proper delicacy could prove a boon to the incumbents in office, particularly Benson. He was laughing too at Thurlow, made sure we wouldn't snake that machine out from under him and with the price what it is he can't lose money. And at Ozzie, who was already deep in dollar leaders for his sale. And at Horace who for once was not tipping up the face of his watch.

"You mean Lonnie still remembers them times? Lord, we used to have 'em . . ."

"Anything these classes can do to improve themselves will of course reflect credit on the school system," D. C. Lacey judiciously stated and glanced past Rad at his brother-in-law for confirmation. Marcus, disoriented by the sudden shift of direction, was groping for his bearings. He wagged his head about, seeking from face to face what it was that had occurred.

Rad did not even mention the tractor until he was about to sit down. "We'll choose up our committees to map this out and they'll choose up theirs. And some from this board and some from their board will get together with some of us from both schools to steer it." He picked up the prospectus and laid it open across his chest, pointing to the photographic layout. "We need this, we want it and we're going to have it. And you'll see, it'll work out too, just like me and Reeve blew them ditches through our land."

It was a most unfortunate allusion to make just then. It was all that Marcus needed as a beacon light out of his fog. He swept the decanter that had somehow come to rest in front of him out of his way, affording himself an unimpeded view of the circle around the table.

"What is this baloney! I'm surprised at you folks. Am I the only one cold sober here? I thought we had it all agreed before this gashound fell in—"

"Now Marcus," Benson said, "don't insult my liquor. Hush up, the rest of you, I still got the chair. We agreed to handle this like gentlemen."

"Don't hush me," Marcus said. "You know what this fellow is talking us into? Race revolution! Why I know for a fact they got a cache of dynamite stashed down there—"

"Now Marcus—"

"He's frontin' for them or they frontin' for him, I don't care. That Reeve is no good. Why I must have sent down to his mammy a dozen times for him to come work for me on them two schools. And he didn't come. Was comin' along to be a pretty fair building-hand too before the war. But all these niggers, you give 'em an opportunity, they'll muff it every time. Won't be satisfied till they have it all. Then you'll see the mess they make of it. You—"

He scraped his chair about toward Rad who was still standing. "You call yourself a white man?"

"Now Marcus, not in my house—"

"And as for you, Reverend," Marcus scraped his chair back around, "I already advised you: if you want to stay in this town, don't let them pull the wool over your eyes! We all agreed here tonight—"

"For the good of the class," D. C. Lacey stated, softening it. "Once the kind of name-calling starts that's come to all our ears, there's no stopping it. It can destroy our whole GI program."

"It can end up in bloodshed," Horace said. "And none of us want that. We don't like to eliminate these two boys, but if that's what's nec- essary to preserve the peace—" He averted his head from Rad as if it were someone else entirely he was talking about. "Lonnie's getting a lot out of that class."

"If you're all quite through now?" Benson inquired. He allowed the hubbub to subside. "Now Rad, what about all this? Are you about to march into town with the niggers and blow up the post office?"

Rad waited for the Baron who was circling the table again with the decanter. Short and stocky he bent over Rad's glass and poured. As he withdrew, their eyes met and held perhaps just an instant too long.

Rad took a snitch from his glass and laughed. "I been answering to that one every day of this week. As for dynamiting them ditches, you recommended it to me, didn't you?" He shook his finger at Earl. "And you sold it to us, didn't you?" He shook his finger at Ozzie. "And you come down to look at what we done there"—he shook his finger at Ben- son—"not once but twice. And as for the rest of this malarkey from there on out, you all know what's behind it just as well as you know your own selves. Yankee money and dirty politics."

Marcus stared up at Rad with his astute grey eyes. And stared and stared. "How much they offering you for that land, Rad?"

"Fifty dollars an acre."

"I'll give you sixty," Marcus said generously, "any time you want to sell." He turned to the others, "Do you know, do you all have any idea of what's been going on around here? I just barely got in on that piece of land for my motel. Listen to this. Wait till you hear this."

He smiled loftily about, the possessor of a piece of inside information on the inside track.

"Henry Warren and the Judge are snatching up all the land they can lay hands on, Henry with his wife's capital and the Judge with his in-law's. Using Lars Finchley as their front. Lars is my lawyer and I over-heard him one day cussing them out on the phone and I put two and two together . . . They'll hold it till Sunset's ready to expand or that river project comes in, then they'll sell out to Acme. They'll make a kill-ing on it, sure they'll make a killing. But it's nothing to what Acme will make. Now I don't mind Yankee money, it's bound to come in here. But let some of it fall in our hands! Let it be something like!

"Now don't you sell that land to 'em, Rad. You fellas hang onto that place, hear me? If they want it bad enough, make 'em pay for it. Make 'em pay through the nose!"

There is nothing more intriguing to a group of men than the inside dope dispensed straight from the horse's mouth. So Lars had made up with Henry, had he? Well, that explains a lot . . .

Thus Marcus discovered what Benson had known all along and Ben-son, smiling, made book on it. It was not altogether inconceivable that Marcus might move over into his faction of the party, support his slate of candidates. And not only Marcus.

Benson sent up to his sister Sarah who always remained aloof from his stag affairs for the engineer's elevation of the river delta that had ar-rived in his mail just a few days ago. He unrolled the chart across the table.

"All right, they're after me," Benson said. "That's politics. They're after Clem, that's religion. But this, this is all of us. They'll dredge the channel along here." He traced the fine blue lines. "The river is all silted up below the bend. Rad, that's by your place. I hope your dikes are in good order? With the river high as it is this year, you could have a flash flood . . ."

It was not Benson however but Marcus who provided the climax. "Farm values, that's not half of it. Listen to this. Will you all listen to this? You know that REA contract I got digging post holes around the county? My crew started out digging by hand but the cost was running higher than the contract price so I had to rent an earth-boring drill oper-ating on a gasoline motor and hydraulic power. Why the cores brought up by that augur has showed some of the finest white building sand you ever saw. In one area gravel beds. And in another pebbles streaked like they had iron or minerals in them. I wish I'd kept a record of where they are. Other places stuff I can't rightly identify, hard-packed like lime rock or kaolin. And of course all kinds of blue and red clay. I have it all at home in jars if my kids haven't thrown it out. One sample I have smells of crude oil. Come down to my house any time, you can smell it. Just as strong.

"Yessir, there's everything here in this county. If we're not such block-heads as to give it away. It's all here to be made."

The smoke in the room thickened and drifted in a blue haze up through the many-colored dome of the chandelier. When the moment was ripe, Benson Reece contributed twenty-five dollars as first sponsor of the Founders Day Benefit.

"This is not," Clem stressed dryly as he accepted it, "a political contribution."

"If you can get Henry and Ol' Vern to back this up," Benson said equably, "you're welcome to."

Marcus Hadley, not to be outdone, matched Benson. Earl Goodfellow promised to take charge of promotion among the farmers. D. C. Lacey agreed to act with Clem as liaison with the colored advisory board. And Lloyd Bird who had not uttered a single syllable all evening proved that whatever he was listening to, it was not the birds of the air.

"All my life," Lloyd said, "I been working in and out of these woods and fields and all I ever hear is 'sometime, someday, ten years . . .' That's the whole trouble with the South. When you got a bellyache and there's medicine on the shelf you take it now, not ten years from now. These folks have got to learn to work together if they're ever to accomplish anything. They want to try this thing, I say let 'em!"

As Clem climbed back into his car with Rad, Benson hollered after him from his front steps.

"You still think, Father DeLavery, that I'll have to squeeze through the eye of a needle to get into heaven?"

"I wouldn't worry about that, son," Clem hollered back at him. "You ain't *that rich!*"

"Shame on him," Rad said. "Trying to get me juiced on that French vinegar. When I been raised on pure undistilled white lightning."

"Did you have any idea when you went in there," Clem asked him and started the car off too fast as usual with a lurch and a leap, "of what you were walking into?"

"Oh the Baron, he give me a poke when he set me in next to Marcus."

Clem adjusted his side window at an angle. The night air rushed in on him, cool and damp, laving flesh that felt pulverized with fatigue.

"How many crises like this can you go through?"

"What crisis?" Rad asked him. "Man, do you have any idea at all of what we just now talked ourselves into?"

III

THE DECISION

[August]

1

It did not take Julie long to verify Clem's version of what had happened on the day of the explosion. That afternoon after Clem left she spurred herself at last out of her benumbed state and began with determined energy to check back. On the ivory French telephone recently installed on the bedside table in her bedroom, she first called Miss Bird.

Miss Bird hedged and hesitated. "All I know is the impression I was given, I mean I gathered as nurse on the case."

"Well, Dr. Wolf has asked me for a more precise picture of what went on," Julie probed her discreetly. "I thought maybe you could supply a few missing details."

"I tell you what, Mrs. Warren, why don't you call someone at the plantation? After all, they were right there."

She then tried Lightfoot at Sunset, with a bill in hand from a decorating shop in Bay City. "For drapery repair: the ones on that big office window I should imagine. Must have been sent here to the house by mistake . . . Well if the detonation caused that much damage, why don't you have it billed to those two men who were responsible for it?"

Lightfoot switched her to Hattie. "Mr. Warren's out right now," Hattie told her, "and I'd rather not . . . I suppose damage like that from such a distance is hard to prove or he would have . . . I tell you what, why don't you call Dr. Harrington? After all he went into the office for the, ah, emergency and saw what it was like long before I did."

She hung up on Hattie with the scene dancing before her eyes. The state of the office. Colfax locked in there flinging himself against those walls, burying himself, a rubble of disintegrating particles. Across the bedroom the fan on her dresser whirred, its rimmed face pivoting to and fro in a shimmer of dissolving blades. The perforated ribbon of snapshots she had shown to Clem cascaded overside from the open dresser drawer.

Unwilling to become entangled in one of Harrington's conversational traps, she called Dr. Willingham instead. "Tom, I'm most embarrassed to put this to you but has Dr. Harrington ever mentioned to you the exact sequence of events that preceded Coley's, ah, seizure? I thought since you're our family doctor, he might have . . ."

From Willingham's response it was evident that no one had conveyed anything to him, neither she who should have, nor Harrington who had withdrawn from the case, hadn't he, after the first visits.

"I've heard some of the stories that are going around, Julie, but if you can't tell which of them from which, how can I?"

She made a few desultory inquiries about Grace who was recuperating from her operation up in Maine and would be home at the end of the month. Grace was doing very well, Tom asserted, making remarkable progress. But with these things you never know, the patient rallies, shows dramatic improvement and then when the prognosis seems most promising . . . Only time, Julie, time . . .

Shedding all her shilly-shallying, she next tackled Harrington directly. "It's very important to me, Doctor, to have the truth," she said, holding her hand over her free ear against the buzz of the fan. "Was Colfax at any time out there in the field? Or did Henry leave him alone, completely alone?"

"In the neighborhood where I grew up"—Harrington essayed lightness, in his nasal self-deprecatory drawl—"when a third party intervened in a dispute between husband and wife, he received a royal drubbing from both."

She permitted a dead silence to elapse.

"I'm sorry, Julie, that was in poor taste. Henry's been keeping me up to date on Colfax. I understood that the acuteness of his anxieties has been somewhat diminished in the past week or two."

She withdrew the telephone from her ear. Who had given him leave to address her as Julie? Who had given Henry leave to feed him information? "All I want from you, Dr. Harrington, is the circumstance."

"I don't see what benefit is to be derived," Harrington said, impersonally professional now, "from reviving all that. You may rest assured that Henry did the only thing he possibly could to protect him while trying to combat a situation that must have seemed like a riotous outbreak of some sort. He had no alternative."

"Yes he did!" she lashed out at Harrington, losing her control. "At the first sign of trouble he could have turned right around and brought Coley home and called me back from that wedding."

"And left everything? The plantation, the freezer plant—"

"The whole goddam shebang!"

With the whir of the fan roaring up like a railroad train in the back of her head, she slammed down on Harrington. They were all in it together. They had all united with Henry in a conspiracy to keep it from her, to foist upon her a concoction so full of holes . . . Henry's will, they all let themselves be used by it, all rushed in to his support, shoring up what had by now become their will too . . .

And she? She had fallen for it too, she who knew him so well. How had she come to fall . . . She rose from the bed where she had been sitting, her arm blotched with red from the imprint of the brocade spread on which she had been leaning, redder than her tan, and rubbing at her aching arm went to the dresser drawer for Elwell's letters and began to reconstruct the events of that evening, the process that had led step by step to her fall, to her so-willing suspension of disbelief.

She had come back from the wedding that evening, the wedding she never wanted any part of, and Henry had met her on the porch with a kiss and she had tripped into the house in all her frippery and there was Elwell's letter on the hall table. Recalling it, she dumped the snapshots back inside her dresser drawer in accordion folds and pawed about frantically in search of Elwell's letter as if it might offer a clue.

The packet of letters, bound prosaically with a red rubber band, was stuffed in behind a box of discarded lipstick stumps and under a pumice stone for removing hair from her legs which she never got around to using. On top, the card that had come with her pearls. Beneath it his first note in his snub-nibbed black script on the thin starchy airmail sheet, unsigned and unmistakable. It was not the letter she was looking for, but starting to read it anyway she remembered that she had left the boys outside under the hose.

Hastily she dropped the letters on her dresser and raced downstairs. The yelps of the dog mingled with shrieks of laughter. Or was it laughter? The older boy's strained to the verge of hysteria and the younger boy's rollicking not with fun but with a fiendish glee. Around the sprinkler, spinning in a blur of molten brass from which jets of water spouting upward merged in showers of silver droplets, they chased the rainbows. Around and around, Coley running dangerously closer and closer to the spokes. Before she could scream out a warning, a few days before she had barely rescued Coley from poking an inquisitive finger into the fan blades, Charles swooped in on him. Pulling Colfax up by the arms, he flew him in circles, body stiffly outspread, away out into the grass. Then holding him, the child's arms clutched about his neck and his legs clamped about his chest, Charles came jogging to her, the little black imp of a dog churning about his feet.

"You've both had enough," she said. "Better go upstairs, dress now. And Charles—" He was sleek wet, his fair eyelashes blinking off drops, his chin dripping. "I have good news for you. Your father was here and he says it's all right for you to come to Atlanta with us."

"Here? Where is he?" The wet arm she held was shivering with more than the chill. "Whyn't you call me? Whyn't he—"

"I didn't see him, I was on the phone. He left a message with Mr. DeLavery and, Kissie says, a dollar for you to spend."

She said it with a cheerfulness she couldn't endure. It was Henry's will that had brought Charles here, had imposed him on her against her every wish, and she had gone along with it for convenience sake until now she couldn't extricate herself.

"I suppose," she added, perversely perforce exercising that will of Henry's, reinforcing it with the zest of a cruel prank played upon herself as well as on the boy, "he was in too much of a hurry to stop. Your mamma must be awfully busy right now with her new baby."

She stood Coley up on a lawn chair to rub him dry and tossed a towel to Charles. Slowly Charles wiped himself off. "You sure he said I could go?" She nodded. They were holding him here with an ever-mounting accumulation of obligations to which he, poor dupe, with bewildered willingness acceded. Coley's biscuit-brown fists twirled before her eyes, revolving with the speed of spindles, weaving a web of confusion. He wants to go home, she saw it on Charles' face through the flying spindle of Coley's fists, and he wants what we can give and he can't have both and how you can deprive him of either without injury . . .

Back up in her room, she discovered that the fan had blown Elwell's letters all over the floor. Crouching on her haunches, moving on her heels and reading as she went, she gathered them together.

His first letter to her, crackling from the page:

I've taken to translating Latin verse at odd moments en route. As a kind of crossword puzzle. Immensely relaxing. But unlike cross-word puzzles not so easily disposed of. Ego demands a destination. Do you mind if I send them to you?

From the Augustan age: Horace the urbane and Catullus the roman-tic. The translations had arrived at irregular intervals, postmarked Tsinang, Mandalay, Calcutta, Basra, Cairo. With each one she had gone flying into the back parlor for her father's college texts, his Latin-English dictionary and his pony, and with the memory of what her father had taught her—strange renascence—she tried her hand at one or two. *Odi et amo . . . Lesbia mea, Lesbia illa*—Lesbia embraces a thousand lovers . . .

She searched over the floor now for the one she had read that evening in her wedding finery, as if it held the key to everything that followed thereafter. It was a particularly tender one, she remembered, one that had touched her to the heart, moved her to rapture. Squatting on her heels she inched over the floor, sifting through the scattered sheets, stopping to reread. His most recent, last week, an ode:

> *What lovely lad bedewed with perfume*
> *Now besets you, Pyrrha, in some*
> *Pleasant cavern rose-embowered,*
> *For whom do you now plait your yellow locks*
> *With unpremeditated skill?*
>
> *Alas, how often he will weep your*
> *Broken plight and fortune changed, and*
> *Wonder at the brooding tempest*
> *That breaks the restive sea with darkling winds*
> *In his young pride and innocence!*
>
> *What dupe enjoys your treasure*
> *Now who thinks your favor always*
> *Will be his alone and always*
> *In love you'll be accessible to him*
> *Unwary of the fickle breeze.*
>
> *O woe to those to whom the unknown*
> *Beckons shining! On the temple*
> *Wall a votive tablet tells how*
> *I pledged my dripping garments to the power*
> *Of him whose godhead rules the deep.*

To which she had only yesterday dashed off in reply her own translation:

> *What slicked-up kid, all barber scent,*
> *Now lays you, Pyrrha, in some nook*
> *Of hedged-in parkland, for what gent*
> *Do you shake your blond hair?*
>
> *Damn shame he'll have to break his heart*
> *On such a tart and curse his luck*
> *And wonder why the lightning dart*
> *Picked him—the woman slayer!*
>
> *What sucker's bussing this hot jane*
> *Aflame with conquest, sure he can*
> *Always date her up again—*
> *She changes men like hats . . .*

> *You burn your finger on a star*
> *For reaching far beyond your ken.*
> *Take me, I sold my stock at par,*
> *Its whims act like that cat's!*

So it had gone between her and Elwell over the past six months. Gone on even while she was closeted with Colfax through his tests in a succession of hot, faintly crummy rooms which she was always being asked to vacate; and while Elwell was plane-hopping through negotiations and upheavals. Out of a crosshatching of quotations from another language, his always grave and stately, hers always feckless, out of the Pyrrhas and Lesbias, the Glyceras and Chloes, they had constructed a retreat for themselves, a summerhouse in a back garden most propitious to the hand holdings, the soul kissings of a pseudo-romance.

She had to creep under the bed for the last sheet, that *would* be the one she was trying to locate. Just as her fingertips reached it, it drifted another quarter inch away from her on the floor in the draft from the fan which she had neglected to turn off. Slithering back with it, finally captured, she was horrified to notice up under the box spring, just skimming the top of her head, a forest of fluff, clinging in clots and festoons. Didn't Kissie ever get under here? Now that she had the new vacuum with all the suction tools . . .

Pulling out from under the petticoated ruffling she bumped the back of her head on the low bed frame. Scrubbing at the shaggy wisps caught in her collapsing hair, or the delusion of them, she sat up cross-legged on the floor and turned the page rightside up. Instantly she was transported once more to the back garden, the sylvan glade.

> *Like a fawn you flee me, Chloe, seeking*
> *Its lost mother on the trackless mountains,*
> *Vainly fearing*
> *Murmurous wind and wood.*
>
> *Whether Spring the leaflets flutters lightly*
> *Or green lizards gently stir the bramble,*
> *Tremblingly it*
> *Quivers, heart and limbs.*
>
> *Afric lion I am not, nor tiger*
> *Savage, I pursue you not for ravening—*
> *Leave your mother,*
> *O ripe for wedlock wooed!*

She had stood in the hall that evening in her bridesmaid's finery, perusing it, with her hand on her cheek just so, amused, charmed, and diverted, sheltering it from Henry's sight. From the whistle he would inevitably emit, "Oh brother!" and the shrug she would inevitably meet it with, "Oh you're worse than Cousin Tibby, you'd have me married to him and flying to the moon." From the host of implications that would then hover in the air, all phony, falsifying and vulgarizing what was innocent.

Sharing with Henry only the last few lines Elwell had appended, inviting her for a few days to the Nest at the end of August. This month now. He's coming. He's coming.

While all the time as she stood there in the hall that evening, entranced with the letter, Coley was lying upstairs comatose under the ministrations of Miss Bird.

Now, now with this letter of Elwell's in hand she could see everything that followed from that moment in the hall unfold like the snapshots in an accordion train. Miss Bird in alarm trying to soothe her by seconding Henry's, "It was that nigger." The fortuitous influence of Violet on the telephone, "Tom's flown Grace to Hopkins for surgery." Her bout with Harrington that led Henry to the brink, the very brink of revealing his own initial part in making Coley what he was.

And with that surrender, which she arrested out of compassion for him, Henry had completely won her over. From then on she believed him. Had accompanied him to court next day in proof of the extent of her belief, believing that by going to such an extreme to prove her belief in him she therefore proved him true.

From this erroneous assumption the rest had proceeded. Her crushing sense of leaving all the burden on him during the week of the freezer plant opening, when actually she needed him then in Atlanta with her. Her gratitude for his grueling weekend trips to visit her and Coley, when actually he spent half of every weekend conferring with Vail on the golf course. Her impulsive consent to the repair of the house, which she never dreamed he would carry to such lengths as a "surprise" for her, when actually it was the worst thing in the world for Colfax to have the house so metamorphosed during his absence.

She had almost fainted when she walked up the concrete pavement to the house—that white, that revolting too-white whiteness! The blinds and the roof green like some little old bungalow, when by all the rules she had ever been raised by they should have been black! "It's lovely, Henry," she had said to him, "it's perfectly beautiful." And stepping through the door into those bare rooms, dragging Coley after her. Those floors, so yellow, so shiny. That dreadful mirror over the fireplace. Coley fastening himself to her, growing not as she had hoped more calm with his return to familiar surroundings but more distraught until they reached his room, the one place Henry had had sense enough to leave alone. Henry's grand march through the house had ended here with Coley throwing a fit on the floor, screaming until they both went well nigh into tantrums themselves trying to extract the cause from him. Two hours of it before she discovered what was wrong. Lying on Coley's bed with him she saw that the highboy at the foot of the room with its friendly face of drawer-pulls and the goblin night lamp on top had been moved from one side of his closet door to the other. Afterward, she had wept against Henry's chest, "I'm sorry, darling, I'm sorry. After you've done so much." At a time when she had planned to give all her attention to Colfax, there was nothing for it but to go on with the painters and decorators and finish the job off. And in the meanwhile Henry brought home Charles.

Foisted on her. Imposed on her. Thrust upon her.

All on the basis of a revelation by Henry that, she was convinced now, he never went through with later. He never told Dr. Wolf anything. He never managed to meet with Wolf long enough to tell him, either leaving too early or arriving too late. Busy with Vail rushing through plans for expansion of the freezer plant in anticipation of Elwell's coming . . . Of the two key crises in the history of the case then, the recent one of the dynamite had been misrepresented in the record by her report of it and the original one, the imprisonment in the crib, had never been disclosed. Henry never told it. And she not wishing to humiliate him, expecting him to tell, had not told it either. Instead she had come to blame herself for all her years of blaming him.

Believing him . . .

Back, back the whir of the fan on her dresser roared like a railroad train through the past period, reversing its landscape. Over all that she had overlooked, forgiven, acquiesced to.

Mellifluously the bell in the lower hall chimed its welcome and Kissie singsonged up the stairs, "Tile man's here."

Julie, sitting cross-legged on the floor with her letter in hand, didn't stir.

Kissie banged on the door. "Tile man's here from Bay City, ma'am."

"Go away."

"Mr. Henry said you was not to miss him."

"Let him wait for Henry then."

"Says he can come in next week if you'll just order your colors."

She didn't bother to answer.

"Miss Julie, you all right in there?" Rattling at the doorknob, opening the door a notch, peeping in. "Miss Julie?"

"Go to hell."

Within a few minutes Henry came plowing into the house. She heard him horsing up the stairs with Charles. "How's m' boy?" *His* boy! And afterward, only afterward, "Where's the little fella? He been all right?" And hollering up ahead. "Say Julie, the tile-setter's downstairs. If you'll just pick your colors, we can get him . . . Come on up here, Mr. Canoletti, my wife'll be out in a minute."

He threw open the bedroom door. "Here's your skirt from the cleaner's."

With a sharp glance at her, still sitting cross-legged on the floor, he passed her by and hung her skirt in its paper sheath in the wall-long closet he'd had built-in in place of the old armoire. "You've had two weeks to decide on a color scheme. If we don't grab him now . . ." He passed her by again to the door, this time avoiding a downward glance. "Plumber, carpenter, electrician, I've got to time them with him on the button. All of them waitin' on you to pick and choose."

"Man proposes," she said with a rasp like the growl of a dog in her throat, "God disposes. You propound. We compound."

He turned at the door and came back into the room. He looked at her closely, crouched on the floor, her hair disheveled, her yellow dress smudged across her bosom, letters spilling from her lap, her hands madly brushing at her skin as if to rid it of strands of some invisible nastiness.

"My God," he advanced on her. "Julie, honey, what's happened to you, Julie?"

Hot, so hot his pants stuck in wrinkles to his legs, heat issued from his shirt in waves, he raised her gently from the floor to her feet. "Julie, look at me."

She handed him a stinging swat across the jaw. "You deceived me!"

He understood at once that she knew. She could see the anxiety dart through his eyes, not what had she been told but who had told her. Her attitude frightened him and fear made him brutal and brutality, yielding its own peculiar pang of pleasure, made him immune.

"You deceived yourself," he said, stating the simple truth. "I never deceived you as much as you deceived yourself."

"I believed you! I believed every word you told me."

"You believed what you wanted to believe! You convinced yourself and everyone else."

"You said—"

"I said, I said, I know what I said. I said what I had to say to protect you. Because you can't accept reality—"

"Mr. Warren." Canoletti calling from the bathroom. "I haven't got all day."

"I'll be right with you . . . And whatever I said, it was never half what you made out of it. *You* said. You propagated—"

"You think you can tie me up in knots—"

"Mr. Warren."

"And turn the whole thing inside out—"

"Look Julie, will you can the crap? We got to get out there. Yes, Mr. Canoletti . . ."

She didn't follow Henry at once but hung on the pearwood bedpost, grasping at its carved spiral for purchase as if she had to climb up it from a floor foundering beneath her feet. The locomotive roared through the back of her head, hurtling over the rails with a shuttling of rods and a clangor of couplings. The blood vessel was bursting in her brain. The seams of her skull were cracking apart.

"A thousand bucks!" Henry's yell of pain resounded from the bathroom. "What the hell you think I'm made of? A thousand bucks for just these walls, the stall and the floor? Sure I want ceramic. Sure I want the best."

She didn't want tile on all the walls. The half wall on three sides was to be papered.

"Julie, Jul-lee! What color? OK then, Canoletti, yella. You think yella'll go good?"

She didn't want yellow. Not with those blue fluorescent tubes he'd insisted on for lighting . . .

"Julie," he called down the hall again, appealing. "Canoletti can only do it next week if it's cash on the line."

She drifted to the bathroom. The room was in that twilight state when the old has been demolished and the new has not yet taken shape. The sunken tub, the washbowl encased in a marbled white formica cabinet known as a vanitorium and the low china-bowl toilet all rested forlornly over gaps in the floor where piping lay exposed, tarnished a grisly green about the joints. The wall of the old sewing room had been removed to allow space for the stall shower and the ceiling above, between the rooms, was crumbling. Plaster showered down with every step the two men, both of them big strapping heavy-footed men, took from one spot to another.

"Sure hope that ceiling won't cave in on me," Henry said worriedly, upward. "I wasn't counting on that."

"Well, you know these ladies," Mr. Canoletti gallantly nodded to Julie in the doorway. "They think you can go switching everything around, pulling walls out, to match some pretty picture in a magazine and it'll stand up for them."

"He wants a thousand bucks. Two hundred on deposit now," Henry explained to her, "and the balance when he's through."

"Guaranteed," Mr. Canoletti supplemented. "All my jobs are guaranteed. It may look like nothing at all to you, ma'am"—he was an expansive Nordic giant, eager to ingratiate himself—"but we have to go back to the battens and start all over. I see you have that one wall prepared already. We cover it with chicken wire and cement over that and then lay the tiles on the wet cement, measured all out and cut to fit the corners. Then there's the grouting. . . . Now this floor, mosaic, you want octagonal I suppose? What would you like for your design?"

She looked through the book of designs he proffered her, flicking through the pages without comment while Henry went to answer the bedroom telephone. Fish he could insert on the walls if she liked. Sailboats. Swans. The floor with borders or without. Greek key. Maltese crosses at geometric intervals. Fleurs-de-lis.

"The price is according to how elaborate you want it. You think I'm making money on what I charge? It's all on the books. Every Saturday I'm running to the bank to meet my payroll. My kids—I see you got children—honestly I want to send them to Scout camp for a couple of weeks, I can't do it."

Henry came back in grimly with the checkbook. "All right, two hundred now?" Unscrewing his pen and beginning to fill out the blank, he looked at her inquiring permission. It was only during the past few months that she had put her money, the residue from the sale of the plantation five years ago which she kept against all advice in a savings account instead of investing it, under his name jointly with hers. As further proof of her trust in him. As if without the surrender of her funds there could neither be absolute trust between them nor any justification for trust. Henry had not withdrawn a single cent up to now without her permission. Now she refused to signify permission.

Scowling, he drove the pen across the check, forced to hack through the tacit compact between them.

"We have four bathrooms," she said chattily to Mr. Canoletti while Henry completed his entries. "One for the maid downstairs and one for guests. One for the children up here and one for us. As soon as they're all finished we'll throw a party for everyone in town to come view our bathrooms. This will be the *pièce de résistance*. We'll serve martinis on the tank top and baptize the yellow tiles. Did you read in the paper the other day, Mr. Canoletti, where a man and his wife were electrocuted while taking a bath in an all-steel tub? I wonder if that could happen to us?"

"But this's a porcelain tub," Mr. Canoletti objected reasonably. "Which reminds me. How about your accessories? Soap tray? Grab bar? Towel racks?"

He was not a Nordic giant after all, Julie decided. His fair hair and skin had the greyness of cement dust ingrained in them. It was the Romans who built baths . . .

She continued to lean against the doorway after Canoletti left, staring into the bathroom at Henry. With arms upraised she rubbed through her disarrayed hair, fingers rotating over the back of her scalp.

"Well, what are you standing there for like a zombie?" Henry said. "We're due at the Judge's for dinner."

He was still burning over the callousness she had forced on him by her refusal to sanction the check. Against the small but critical change of climate he sensed in that transaction, all the resources of his temperament rallied.

"Now go on," he said with an edge of fond contempt. "Get yourself ready. Move."

She continued to lean in the doorway, staring at him while she rubbed over the tendons at the base of her skull.

From the towering medicine chest which precariously overlapped the glass shelf where the plumber had stored it, a mirrored affair flanked with its own set of fluorescent tubes, not yet connected, Henry took his shaving case and snapped open the hinged lid. He sniffed at the aroma of roasting meat ascending from the kitchen.

"Don't tell me you forgot. Eula called you about it just a couple of nights ago."

He lifted his gilt razor out of its groove in the blue-plush lining of the case and fitted a blade in, an English blade Vail had tipped him off to, longer lasting, cleaner cutting, always good for reference-to over cigars.

"They invited these people down from Augusta just to meet us."

With his twist of the razor stem the twin gates on top closed down over the blade, sealing it in. Nuzzling into his hands he rinsed the slippery sweat off his face. In the mirror every bristle on his padded cheeks stood out, discrete and clarified. He slapped lather on, smoothed it around the thin slab of his mouth and into the declivity, still firm, under his chin, spread it outward from the deepening flanges of his nostrils and with a soapy finger touched the two brusque hairs that sprang between his eyebrows.

"I loved you," Julie said with a lingering amazement. "I loved you for what I thought you'd become. I began to love you all over again."

"You never loved me." Spreading the skin under his eye taut between his fingers, he shaved with delicate sweeps of the blade. "You only loved your idea of what I was. From the beginning. You love what's yours. You love what's dependent on you. You love yourself for it."

He pushed past her through the door and shouted down to Kissie to feed the kids dinner when it was ready, they were going out tonight, and came back past her repeating passionately, "Not me! Never me. Yourself. Nobody else."

She stayed only long enough to watch him step from spread newspapers into the skeletal structure of the shower, temporarily covered with plastic curtains that always managed to shed a mud puddle. The All-American male. With the dingus between his legs, dingdong. How she could have lain next to him, touched, fondled . . .

With no idea of what she was to do with it she took the steel razor blade from the glass shelf where he had left it and holding it before her, wetly pinched between thumb and forefinger, stalked back into the bedroom and dropped it on her dresser top. So sharp. So shiny and so sharp. It would make a clean incision.

When Henry padded into the bedroom ten minutes later with a towel swathed about his waist, all his clothing had been removed from the closet and was heaped on the bed. Julie was starting in on the drawers with his socks and his underwear, stacking the folded pieces in toppling piles.

"Look Julie," he said appeasingly, refreshed and ready to make up, "we're not going back to where we were six months ago."

"You bet your life we're not. This is my room. I don't want you in it anymore. Ever."

Her hair was combed, she'd changed into a starched white housedress, made herself tidy; and that obstinacy which he knew so well from the past was patent in her every movement, concise and deliberate, with none of her usual flurry of indecision. Ignoring her he went to the bedside table and called Marcus Hadley.

"Marcus? Canoletti's been here. He's coming in on Wednesday. Now how about the other guys?" Seeking the perfect conjunction of carpenter, plumber, electrician. "Now you swore to me up and down—not another jam-up for Christ sake! Tell 'em there'll be a bonus in it."

Julie dropped a sock out of the bunch she was carrying and kicked it out of her path and this gesture, like her spurning of the check, struck Henry with a qualitative significance and this time with all the force of physical rejection, a shudder of revulsion.

"Now you take that stuff and put it back where it belongs," he said while waiting for Marcus to go over his schedules.

"You have used and abused me," she said, "and trampled over everything I ever cared for. You broke my father's heart, you sacrificed our child—"

"OK, Marcus. You check with them and let me know. We'll be at the Judge's from six on."

The peace of many months was over. And while trying to restore it, to return her like a flood stream gone out of control back into her proper channel by browbeating, bludgeoning, sandbagging her back in, he was in some vital part of himself glad that it was over. Glad to be free of restraints. Glad that his mastery of her was destroyed. Glad of the challenge to renewed conquest and renewed subdual that her opposition to him provided. Glad to shuck the comfort of a civilization that had become too confining for the raw and harsh uncertainty, with all its risks, of more primitive terrain. To start afresh from scratch. With scratch, bite, gouge, and stomp.

If she was spoiling for a fight, she'd get it.

"Used you?"

He laid the telephone down and fished her yellow dress up with his toe from the floor where she'd dropped it. He flung it over the back of a chair where, finding Elwell's letters on the seat, he scooped them up and threw them on the night table.

"Who used who? That's a good question. Why, you shiftless slovenly slipshod bitch, I pick up after you, wipe your nose, wipe your ass—"

Drawing her shoulders up, Julie went on cleaning out braces and belts, shoelaces, shoehorns. *Like a fawn you flee me, Chloe . . .*

"I stand you on your feet and for every step you ever take I have to boot you into it. Fix your house up before it falls down on you. Take the mess your old man left—and no matter what I've done, it doesn't hold a candle to half the stunts he pulled—and build up a decent life for you out of it. And as for Colfax, you'd never have gotten to the point of getting him a competent diagnosis if I hadn't shoved you—"

Afric lion . . . tiger savage . . .

"All these years I've worked, I produced. You never produced anything but good intentions."

His cuff links rattled out of her hand back into the drawer. Her eyes traveled uneasily toward the letters on the night table, but disdaining to get past him to get at them, she stood her ground, hanging onto the drawer for support but taking every blow with a smile of bitter scorn, superior to it, tougher than she used to be, able with her ultimate weapon to deliver blow for blow, no mean adversary.

"You were a bum on the waterfront," she said to him. "I gave you everything."

"You gave me nothing!"

He was out to pay her back for every time she'd ever made him jump the stick to win her favor, for every time she'd ever made him coax and crawl, shift and haul, just to effect the least little detail. For every time her resistance had been such as to cause him to clobber her over the head in order to set her into action.

"You ain't got nothing. You never had nothing. It was never yours to give."

He paced about with the stripe-bordered white towel sliding down over his low-slung hips, as splendid as a figure in a bas-relief with all his spoils, conquests, triumphs.

"It never belonged to you. Your great-aunt, Isabel Colfax, legitimatized that son of hers before she died. Took out adoption papers on him, must have been lost in the courthouse fire. And your daddy was her lawyer, he drew it all up for her, he knew. Then when he got himself appointed her executor, he hid it all so deep—"

"What are you saying? What are you twisting up now?"

"You're such a stickler for the truth, the whole truth and nothing but: here it is. The laugh of the century. When I was getting ready for that court hearing you put me up to, I went through his files with a fine-tooth comb—"

"Why didn't you tell me then?"

"I didn't want to burden you with it."

"But if he had such a paper, why'd he hold onto it?"

"Why do people hold onto the most damnable things as if it was some part of their immortal soul? Like love letters for instance."

"You give me that!"

Packing Elwell's letters together, he held them high in the air while she danced at his feet like a pup-dog jumping for a stick.

"Give me—" She flung herself on him, catching at his inflexible wrist.

"All these years nothing, nothing's been yours. Not even that little old cornpatch you laid claim to."

She sank back breathlessly from her assault. "That is mine. Mine from my grandfather Gil. It's morally mine."

"No it's not. Not morally, legally or historically."

"But Lars, Lars Finchley, Lars wouldn't falsify—"

"Lars was the one who turned up the Scott deed of sale when he was searching the title. Put that in your pipe and smoke it."

"Not Lars. Not Lars . . ." She put her hands to her head, her face twitching convulsively. "But the record, who took the record?"

"I'd rather not have you burdened with that either. Unless by knowing you'd like to be accessory to a felony? Now pick up my clothes and put them back where they belong."

She was clawing for the letters again and he held her off straight-armed. "You'll have 'em back after you've picked up my clothes. Not before. And while you're about it, hand me my socks and my shorts and those pinstripe slacks there and a clean shirt."

He had long since lost his towel and now dropping his arm he held her off with his massive thigh. Bearing her back on the prong of his lifted thigh, he brought the letters up forward and picked one off. "*Like a fawn you flee me, Chloe,*" he began reading aloud in a mawkish falsetto, "*Seeking its lost mother . . .*"

She retreated to her dresser and from under a snaky tangle of ties slipped out the razor blade she had taken on vague impulse from the bathroom. With it in hand she walked over to the bed and unhesitatingly, with a series of efficient jerks, slashed off all the bone buttons, front and cuff, from his best white linen jacket.

There was no sound throughout between them but her labored breathing. When she was through, leaving a stubble of threads and shredded cloth, she lifted her head and panting, with breast and belly heaving, blade in hand, said, "Now give me the letters."

He gave them to her and began to dress with clothing fumbled from the bed, his own breath diminishing in hoarse exhalations, spent.

"Julie," he said after a pause in which the very air of the room was sucked up as in one of those firestorms that follow on the saturation bombing of a city, "we've come too far for this. We been through too much."

He had regretted it from the moment he told her. Having stripped her of every other illusion, he didn't have to strip her of her property too. It was this, not his arsenal of humiliations, not the horseplay over the letters, that troubled him irremediably.

"I didn't mean to tell you all that. Forget it. You've been under pressure enough God knows. And I've had a lot on my mind."

She tweaked her red rubber band down over the letters and stowed them away under the pumice stone back of the lipstick box in her drawer.

"I had thirty-five thousand dollars in the bank three months ago," she said stonily. "Where is it?"

"Tied up," he said, hardening again.

"Whose is it?"

"Johnny Herrera's."

When he was all dressed, informal in an expensive sports shirt in lieu of jacket and tie, being too intimidated to ask her where his tie clasp was, he made one more effort.

"Come on, Julie, snap out of it. I really don't see what difference all this makes. None of it makes any difference when you add it all up. We're getting along good. Everything's going fine. Never better."

"What difference? What difference?" She clutched her head between her hands as if to keep it from flying apart. "I," she stamped it out with her foot, "I—*I* am Coley!"

Unbelievably, she did not go with him. And unbelievably, he drove off without her.

From behind her bedroom curtain she watched him leave with Charles beside him in the leather seat instead of her, gingery and bright in his whites. The railroad roared through her skull over continents of time in reverse, turning truth into fraud and fraud into truth, all that had been said that was so true and so untrue, so untrue and so true . . .

With Colfax and the Scottie underfoot, she carried Henry's clothing, bulky and heavy in her arms, down the hall to Charles' room, making a half-dozen trips in all. In a flush of candescent heat she mounted to the attic, an oven burning with the dust of the dying sun, and dragged out a folding cot. Toting it with all its mustiness of mattress in her face, she stumbled down the stairs, bumping child, stepping on dog, and deposited it in Charles' room, leaving it there, open but without sheet or cover.

2

The trip to Atlanta, which Julie had depicted to Clem as a gay holiday excursion to be conducted in a spirit of family harmony that would most favorably prepare Coley for the visit to Dr. Wolf, took on from the beginning aspects of a battle to the death.

They had planned to drive up Tuesday, spend Wednesday sightseeing between Henry's business and political appointments, and of course, necessarily, resting up for the session with Dr. Wolf on Thursday. But Julie who had taken both boys with her to Cousin Tibby's at Silver Beach over the weekend, no more willing to stay under the same roof with Henry than she was in the same room with him after their quarrel, decided to extend her stay with Tibby through Tuesday, thus delaying the trip by an essential day.

The long trip seemed to her, as she contemplated it, just another one of those impositions foisted on her not for her benefit or Coley's but for Henry's convenience. She needed neither the extra day in the city, sightseeing for Henry and Charles, yes, but for her and Coley a delusive fancy; nor the extra mileage entailed in the ride at this most uncomfortable season of the year; nor the so-called rest-up which would in fact involve a phenomenal rushing to and fro from place to place.

For the "trip to Atlanta" was itself a misnomer. A euphemism they had adopted as a protective cushion against their actual destination, adopted it to the point of literally contriving the roundabout journey in a feint as deceptive to themselves as to everyone else. Though Dr.

Wolf resided and practiced in Atlanta, where up to now Julie had consulted with him, this time they were to meet him in Darbyton, a city associated by some citizens with the Confederate Shrine located there, by others with cotton mills and by all with "going crazy." Dr. Wolf spent part of each week at the State Hospital for Mental Diseases in Darbyton, and here they were to present Colfax at ten, Thursday morning, for observation under drug therapy.

Excessive as their route now appeared to Julie, over eighty miles out of the way, she still could not bring herself in mind and body to that Thursday hour, to those grounds, to that building housing the outpatient department where Wolf was to receive them. She regarded the day at Darbyton with a reflex as powerful as if, faint with hunger, she was being ordered to consume a dishful of live angleworms.

She couldn't go without Henry then. She counted on him for support through an ordeal that meant to her leaving the last outpost of the normal for the vast limbo of the abnormal, a passage from one state of affairs to quite another which she was not prepared to undergo even temporarily, even once. *I can't bear up under it!* She foresaw that. All through her withdrawal from Henry at Tibby's, she knew it. The more she repudiated him in her review of the past few days, the more she was led back to him by the imminent prospect of the next few days. Impossible to resume living with him. Impossible to do without him.

When she telephoned Henry from Tibby's cottage to postpone the trip a day, she did not mention curtailing it. The weather was too hot, the beach was too nice, Charles was making such friends with some boys at the church camp nearby and Colfax was overcoming his fears of the water. (This despite Tibby's unhappy gurglings in the background, and despite the constant friction engendered by the aversion Tibby concealed under her doting over Colfax and his demonic responses to it.) Henry, relieved to have her back on speaking terms at least, yielded without raising the issue of his appointments in Atlanta. He had some suspicion of what she was leading up to and went to work on long distance at once to circumvent it by rescheduling his activities to late Wednesday afternoon and evening. Vail obligingly promised to have his boys tour Charles through the Capitol and show him around. Dinner reservations at the hotel where they were staying, an evening out on the town afterward. Great. Big thing for a kid.

They therefore started out early Wednesday morning, though not early enough to suit Henry, with two entirely different ideas of where they were going that day, Henry's very concrete, Julie's not yet fully crystallized, neither of them voiced and both already in conflict.

The hour of departure had been fixed by Henry at five-thirty in order to take advantage of the cool of the day. Julie lingered until six-thirty getting Coley through breakfast. Coley had decided that he was to be a kitten today and licked at his cereal with his tongue, and every effort of Henry's to hurry him was countered by Julie with the charge that it was his pressure for speed that was causing the delay. When they entered the car she maintained her separation from Henry by leaving the front seat to Charles and taking her seat in back with Coley. Consequently Coley clambered ceaselessly from back to front and back again, still a kitty, creeping on the floor, crawling over shoulders, cuddling with kisses that turned into nips and caressing with pats that turned into pinches. In addition, Henry was driving a steady seventy that at a swerve could hurl them all out of the open convertible into the road.

By inference Julie pitted the child's antics against the direction in which Henry was traveling with such break-neck momentum. "He was up all night," she claimed. "He's so overtired."

"Then why didn't you give him a pill?"

"I don't like those pills. Once you put him on barbiturates you have to break him off, then where are you? What he needs is a cool relaxed place where he can just drop off to sleep, s-s-s-sleep, sleepiness, sleepy-head, sleep. As long as he's in the car he'll just keep fighting it."

They spoke hardly hearing each other, the air through which they sped tearing the words out of their mouths and leaving them in tatters behind. Henry ignored what he assumed to be a hint and adhered to the highway that led to Atlanta.

The flatlands, scorched brown with the August heat, rose gradually to gullied hills spectacularly striated with clay in colors from blood-red to royal purple. While Charles was playing a finger game with Coley, Coley bit his wrist. Charles yelped. Henry skidded into a screeching halt.

"For Christ sake, Julie, you want to get us all killed? If you can't control him—"

He examined the scalloped arc of toothmarks on Charles' wrist. She had depended on Charles as a fulcrum through whom the antagonisms of the family could be more or less neutralized. Now the bite on his wrist, a quite vicious one too, was being annexed by Henry to weigh the balance in his favor. He lifted Coley who was howling as if *he* had been bitten back over the seat into her lap. "Keep him there."

"Daddy scold me?" Coley sobbed heartbrokenly in his language of reversion of person. "Daddy scold me?" And, his wet cheek plastered against Julie's dry cheek, he comforted her, "Don't cry? Don't cry?"

The dusty villages with their spate of store-front loungers and over-alled Negroes gave way to the flourishing fields of cotton and tobacco country, the diagonal enfilades of pecan orchards. "That's where Ol'

Cal Hubbard has his plantation." Henry pointed out to Charles a well-shrubbed gate. "Our next governor. Built himself up into a millionaire out of nothing at all. Goes back yonder for miles. And there"—he pointed to a glimmer of greenhouses—"there's another big place. Belongs to some Yankee nobody around here even knows by name."

"What do they do with it all?" Charles asked, awed.

"Come down couple of times a year, take a look around, shoot a few quail, entertain, have some prime hams flown back."

"Gee." Charles gnawed at his knuckles, unusually subdued for a while. "Cousin Henry," he asked seriously, "you not aiming to put my daddy off his land, are you?"

"Whatever give you that idea? You know I'd do anything for your daddy. If only he'd let me. How's that wrist?"

Behind them Julie turned through pictures of Alice at the Mad Hatter's tea party, which Coley had turned upside down to look at. A very happy unbirthday to you.

In the late morning they stopped at an attractively awninged roadside restaurant on the outskirts of Macon. Making good time. They'd be in Atlanta before two. Attempting to keep Colfax pacified, Henry ordered a Coke for him before the meal was served. The bottle the waitress brought to the table was perpendicular however, not bulging with the curves Colfax liked to clasp between his hands. While the waitress laid out their food, a search was instituted through the restaurant and the neighboring barbecue and hush-puppy stands for the type of bottle Coley preferred. "You know, the kind shaped like a nigger wench?" Henry made a joke of it. "He don't go for the beanpole figger." No such thing. Don't make 'em anymore. "Well, you suck this"—Henry took the straw out and pushed the bottle across the table to Coley—"or nothing at all."

Coley pushed the bottle back. Julie sprang up, her dress dripping. Henry shoved aside his plate of fried chicken and slaw, swimming now in syrupy black liquid. Before anyone could catch it the bottle hit the floor and every diner in the half-filled room was craning around at them. The waitress, tight-faced, whipped off the tablecloth while Julie sopped herself and the child with napkins.

"This is insane," she said when she sat down again. "It's absolutely loony. We ought to have our heads examined. Trying to cram everything into one day. He feels it. He resists it."

Henry stared down at the dark splotch on the undercloth over which the waitress was throwing a fresh covering. How many times had they lived through that splotch, circumscribed by it, sucked in by it like an animal trapped in a mudboil. Splotch. She never intended to go through with the trip to Atlanta, had been itching to spoil it for them from the outset, throwing roadblocks in the way of it all the way up here, and now she was breaking it up.

"We'll take the next road to Darbyton from here," she said, rallying them with determined brightness. "Put up at some overnight place. And maybe late in the afternoon visit the Confederate Shrine. Though it's not much to look at really."

Henry sent Charles to the cashier's counter for a package of cigarettes. "In just two hours," he told her, "we'll be in Atlanta. I switched all my appointments to this afternoon because of you and I can't switch them again. Vail has arranged for his boys to tour Charles around, and if you have it in you to disappoint him after all he's taken . . . We owe it to him."

"We owe—"

Charles with drooping head and slumping shoulders was wending his way back through the tables.

"I can't handle this alone, Henry," she said. "If you don't take me to Darbyton now and see me through tomorrow, you'll never have another chance to take me anywhere."

Henry took the next branch road to Darbyton and installed her and the boy in a comfortable air-cooled motor lodge. "I'll be back here first thing tomorrow," he promised her, "just like we planned to begin with. Maybe you're right, it's best for you two not to get yourselves all tired out . . ." And he drove off with Charles to Atlanta.

He called her up at nine in the evening to find out, his voice rich with well-being, how everything was going. Was Coley sleeping? Yes. The Vails were dining with him at the hotel and they'd introduced him to a couple of big wheels from the Cherokee Club and when he started describing to them the future of southeast Georgia . . . He had a date with Dan Garner for breakfast tomorrow morning, oh no it wouldn't keep him.

"I know how you feel about this, Julie, but honestly it's not all as bad as you picture it. I spoke to Wolf over the phone tonight and he told me there's no reason to be so jumpy about it. Don't worry now, I'll be there. I'm with you."

She slept badly that night, plagued by all kinds of dreams. The snakes chasing her back across the marshland. That again . . . And a smell. She dreamed that Henry had a smell to him, to his hair and skin, his breath, his saliva and semen, his testicles and anal fold, not a stench, not fetid, pungent rather, ferny like pasture grass trampled by cattle, with an insidious strain of sweetness in it, strong and penetrating, that was most offensive to her. She could smell it on her pillow where he'd rolled over toward her. And she couldn't stand it. She thought: Am I going to spend all my life in the arms of a man whose smell I can't stand? She was going to divorce him because of that smell. Then in her dream she woke up and the smell that she had thought was Henry's all through the years was her own. It was her own smell. Issuing from her organs and juices, her skin, her clothing. Clinging to her like the smell of her vomit after she'd thrown up that time in the colored women's toilet in the courthouse. Clinging to her dress, fingertips, all over.

She awoke then in the strange bed in the strange room in the darkness. No smell. Only the roar of the air conditioner.

She cupped her hands over her nose, sniffing into them. Soap. She had complained afterward to the Judge about the condition of the colored lavatory in the courthouse, and he'd had both the women's and the men's room cleaned out and converted into much-needed storage space. The colored then, coming in from all over the county to shop and transact their affairs, had no sanitary facilities whatsoever in the center of town. Sufficient concern about it had been expressed by merchants to compel the County Commission to allocate funds for an outdoor comfort station for them. Only, as the Judge reported with caustic chuckles, wherever it was to be built adjacent property holders raised such a holler it would in all likelihood never be located anywhere.

Julie thought about it now. Over and under the shuttling rods of the locomotive that roared through her head. If she'd only not objected, however objectionable . . .

If she'd only gone to Atlanta she wouldn't be alone with this now. Over and under, under and over, driving out sleep. Macbeth hath murthered sleep—sleep, sleep, the innocent sleep, sleep that knits up the raveled sleeve of care. Macbeth went mad and Lear went mad.

When she was a senior in high school, she remembered now, she'd had her tonsils out after a quinsy. The operation was bungled and went on for two hours and during it, she remembered it now distinctly, a small beam of light ascended from her chest and hovered under the high narrow ceiling of the operating room and through the roar of ether in her ears annunciated: *Vita victrix, vita triumpha.* Those very words. And when she woke up in the hospital room she was babbling the memory passages her father had assigned her to learn. And she'd said to the nurse at her bedside, "That's Shakespeare." And she had recalled the glow of light and the annunciation. And had thought: *Consciousness never dies* . . .

I shall go mad with this. I am going mad with it.

"How do you put up with it?" Henry had asked her after the spilled bottle at lunch. "What is there in you that's so willing to put up with it?" She didn't put up with it. She could have taken Coley by the shoulders and shaken him till his bones rattled. She could have pitched him through the plate-glass window.

She turned over in bed now and put her arms around the warm form huddled against her. An amorphous bundle of energies drifting with every current, the creature of every impulse? Or was there a shape to his personality if she could only discern it, a design to his behavior if she could only read it? You love what's dependent on you, Henry had accused her, you love what's yours, you love yourself. The child murmured in his sleep, nestling up against her shoulder. She kissed the top of his head, blew into the radiating whorl of his hair. All she had. The end of the line.

His hair under her fingers was no longer as soft as plush, his skin no longer as tender as silk, his legs no longer so chubbily rounded. Coarsening, hardening, growing rangier. In a few years, what . . . Is it love I have for him or sentimentality or some neurotic compulsion? I don't know. Do I really hate him and therefore have to prove how devoted I am, what a martyr, the great and glorious Julie Colfax? I don't know. Is he an intolerable burden to me? Yes. Could I abandon him? No. What remains then? Take everything else away, what remains? His need. My responsibility. Hope. Hope that through my unremitting efforts, someone else's discovery, a miracle out of the sky, we'll uncover the hidden spark and the spark will burst into light. And if it never does, if it's not there?

I'll not go mad with this. I'll not . . .

In the morning Coley was quiet and withdrawn. He ate nothing of the breakfast set before him in the lunchroom attached to the motor lodge, but devoted himself to adding up sums with toast crumbs. Julie ate little, straining to glimpse through the sun-glare on the window every car that turned in from the road. At nine-thirty when they were back in their cabin the telephone rang. Long distance from Mr. Warren.

"Julie? Look honey—"

"Goodbye," she said and hung up. A kid . . . A kid in his baseball suit playing ball with the boys.

She sat in the cushioned green vinyl chair in front of the telephone, crumpling, dissolving. I can't, I can't! When she tottered upward the back of her legs above her stockings, heat-fused to the upholstery, felt as if the skin were being flayed off. I can't, I can't! With the saving grace of anger she called the desk for a taxicab. Then she fastened on her pearls, took Coley by the hand and walked out on the ringing telephone to wait with him by the roadside for the cab. The early morning sunshine had vanished. A light rain was falling.

"State Hospital," she said to the cab driver when he arrived, with a smile as if she were ordering a vanilla ice cream cone for the child from an especially accommodating, always accommodating to her, fountain clerk. "The Out-Patient Clinic?"

She crossed the line that divides the known and the normal from the abnormal, health from disease, freedom from subjugation, outside from inside, into the green grounds; was borne up the curving driveway to the congeries of brick buildings. She paid the driver, "Thank you so much." Ascended the granite steps with Coley hugging so close to her side their legs got mixed up. Traversed the white-colonnaded portico posted WHITES ONLY, an arrow for COLORED pointing to the right base-mentward. Entered through tall black portals into the busyness of the institution, contained within ginger-tan walls, permeated with the odors of disinfectant, anesthetic and decay. An environment that once you entered it—the dread thudded through her with the jar of the heavy door behind—you might never leave again.

Dr. Wolf would see her soon. She was waved by the receptionist to one of the long benches where people sat like passengers in a railroad station waiting for their train. The misbegotten and the bedeviled. The afflicted and the downtrodden. They read newspapers, conversed, joked or simply sat, sunk in gloom. With Coley she sought out a vacant place as far as possible from the next person. She could feel sorry for them all, and she did. But she was not one of them. It was the one straw she held onto for dear life. We are not *they*.

Julie walked into Dr. Wolf's office fully prepared to divulge the missing and perhaps most crucial phases of the boy's background. You see my husband did this terrible thing to him, twice over. And what did I do about it? I kept quiet. I covered up. I told nobody. I lived with it.

But during the six weeks in which she had been intermittently interviewed by Dr. Wolf, largely for the purpose of exchange of information—she was not in therapy and he was not an analyst—they had achieved more antagonism than accord. Wolf disturbed her. She was convinced that his attempts to probe beneath her veracious version of her family life were motivated mainly by a compulsion to pull her down a peg; to put her in her place, before his desk; to force her into the position, inferior to himself, of all those troubled souls who came to him seeking succor. And she disturbed Wolf. He was convinced that her portrayal of a happy successful young couple living the best of all possible lives in the best of all possible worlds was motivated mainly by her compulsion to pull rank on him; to turn their consultation into a pink tea at which she was of course the gracious hostess; to embarrass him and then with the most charming facility in the world make him feel at home in his own office.

At one of their early meetings Julie had remarked disingenuously, "Wolf, why would anybody of that name choose to be a psychiatrist? Isn't the patient bound to see himself as Little Red Ridinghood?" Dr. Wolf had been most unprofessionally nettled and she, quick to observe, had hurriedly amended, "I'm sorry, I apologize. That was most unforgivably rude, wasn't it? Actually you seem more like a pussycat." She had fingered her pearls. (Who could be so heartless as not to forgive her?) And he had glanced over Coley's head toward the silver-mounted photograph of his children on the corner of his desk, the only adornment of a teakwood expanse uncluttered save for the cards he filled out as his clients talked.

In Julie's presence Dr. Wolf had soon found himself dropping things, he a slim trim silver-blond who had only recently resigned his commission as a major in the Army and who still bore himself with the clipped curt manner of his command, in which he had excelled at spotting malingerers and weeding out Section 8s. Fatcat? Hardly . . . He would rescue his pen from the tweeded broadloom that padded his office floor, with the blood rushing to his head from having stooped so low. She would touch her pearls and he would glance toward the photograph of his children. Both of them with their talisman. Out of rivalry or attraction—since attraction often masks a contest of egos and rivalry often armors similarities too much akin for comfort—they continually, as the phrase goes, rubbed each other the wrong way.

"But what has that got to do with it?" Julie would resist his adroit questioning. "I assure you, Doctor, that whatever problems my folks had it was over money. Not sex. On that subject they were quite enlightened for their day." "But don't you think," Wolf would persist, "that what they were to each other had something to do with making you what you are?" "You mean," she would retort, one jump ahead of him, "that Coley is what he is because of what we are? That it's our fault?" "Mrs. Warren," he said with all the sympathy he could project, "we are not here to find fault or fix blame or pass judgment. That would lead us only to a dead end. We're here to help you, to explore the chain of causation or the synthesis of causes which may have brought about this particular syndrome." And she tried, she tried very faithfully to help *him*. But on the whole she sustained the story she had told him the first time when she appeared with her husband.

"In our experience," Dr. Wolf had hinted to her again and again, "there is usually a conflictual factor in the marriage." She couldn't help him very much there. No drinking, no gambling, no extramarital affairs, no sexual apathy or impotence, no latent homosexuality, no episodes of mental disorder. "Of course there have been conflicts in our marriage," Julie admitted to him, "as there must be in everyone's." With an eye that indicated to Wolf, his too. "But mostly it's been over a difference in values. I don't know whether that's very helpful to you or not but it's been important to us. The worst of it has been over Coley and that couldn't have been very good for him, could it? But now I recognize that something is wrong and I agree with Henry that something must be done, we *are* working things out. You don't have to worry yourself about that." She was always free with such generalities, never with specific incidents. "My husband can fill you in on that sometime when he has time, I'm sure."

She was what the lawyers call an uncooperative witness and what Wolf called a constipator. Some people came to him spouting before they were even inside the door. And others held back like a tot who deliberately retains his bowels. Only there is no purgative for the unwilling spirit. All his subtle urgings had not succeeded in dislodging whatever burden lay compacted in her cerebral gut. Or, to vary the image, she reacted upon him like a woman who submits herself to a competent gynecologist for an internal examination and makes a personal issue of disrobing: no, I will not undress for you, I will not let you see my nakedness under the gown; and who even when lying upon the table, sheeted and stirruped, takes the rubber-fingered and instrumental probings as an invasion of her person, personally perpetrated by another person . . . Stubbornly by her attitude she injected into their relationship an emotional element that did not belong there, creating an awkwardness between them that was distracting and deplorable.

Yet all this, thornily present under the surface of their every meeting, was superficial.

She was not the patient, Wolf had frequently to remind himself. It was her boy who was the patient. She was an intelligent and concerned parent who had so far proved almost as unreachable as her son. Colfax had responded only to his performance tests and to these remarkably well, the mother also being quite proficient in her performance! From his fragmentary observations of them both, however, Wolf had gathered sufficient evidence to form a clinical picture.

High-strung sensitive wife, aggressive executive husband. (Masochosadistic tendencies?) Her father ill over prolonged period in the home coinciding with unemployment and financial difficulties of husband during child's first year. (Not uncommon pattern, the old question: Why do some survive and others succumb under identical circumstances? Susceptibility? Organic or functional?) And where is the husband, the abbreviated and canceled appointments whether with the wife or separate? (Obsessive success drive? Guilt? Which came first?) And the child himself. Placidity-irritability, agitation-withdrawal, anxiety-apprehension linked with discontinuity of slumber, assaultive-destructive trend. On the positive side: ability with play materials; capable of attachment to a few close individuals. Brought in on occasion of convulsions caused by dynamite cartridge thrown in his direction. (Prognosis???)

Obviously to treat the child one must also treat the parents. But where, Dr. Wolf speculated, will such treatment lead? To a voyage of self-discovery and mutual rediscovery? Or to the breakup of the marriage? Or as sometimes happens under crisis the exposure of disturbance in at least one of the parents so deep-seated that commitment follows? (In the case of such a child, with so little to hope for, the old old question: Is it worth it? For a couple getting along relatively well, of what benefit to dig, to dredge up?) Theoretically, the trouble-spot if it exists in the elders will erupt sooner or later anyhow. Theoretically, one has the chance to head it off by attacking it directly, by providing the preventive insights. Practically, most people manage to muddle through in the blind belief that the eruption will never come, that the adjustments they have made, the fictions they operate by will last their lifetime. *Après moi*, the deluge.

The night before he was to meet with the Warrens at Darbyton, Dr. Wolf working at home prepared his conclusions, offering several alternative proposals. As a physician he would of course wish them to pursue investigation no matter where it might lead. As a father he would not care to influence their decision one way or another. (And here he glanced out the glass wall at his children splashing in the illuminated swimming pool, so safe and sane, so lively and lovable, begotten of a success drive wedded with sensitivity. He bullied her, heaven help him, and she forbore and went her way and what they had together and would have yet was good. Wasn't it?) Wolf completed his card file on the case, pleased rather than otherwise that he was finished with it. As the diagnostician he had explored it as thoroughly as was possible in a short span of time. From here, Brandon Colfax Warren would have to be taken to a treatment center more specialized than any presently available in the state.

Still he was not satisfied. That woman, the boy's mother . . . He was not finished with her. He had only begun. He'd hardly scratched the surface . . .

Wolf occupied a privileged corner office in the Darbyton hospital, large and light but of a Spartan bareness compared with his modern office in the city, with faded linoleum in place of carpeting, framed board members of 1907 vintage in place of abstract paintings and on the back of the worn desk an untidy row of publications. His first patient, preceding Colfax Warren, was an impeccable young man who had been arrested for impersonating a doctor at a maternity hospital, where he had been delivering babies for six months before a forgery in his records caught up with him. Actually he had been reared in an orphanage and had quit high school in his sophomore year. The young man stretched out nonchalantly in the chair beside Wolf's desk.

"Go ahead tell me," he invited Wolf, "I'm a psychopath."

"What do you mean by that?" Wolf asked in his curtest Army major manner. "What is a psychopath?"

"Anybody that's smarter than the psychiatrist."

In place of the impeccable young man in the chair Dr. Wolf saw Julie-Ann Warren—his failure with her. She belonged by the divine right of her own assumption to the elect of the earth, those who consider themselves exempt from damage, defeat, and loss, the wholeness of whose beauty and perfection is not to be marred by the scars which lesser persons are prone to. She would never have to resort to the extreme devices by which a psychopath seeks to distinguish himself from the undifferentiated mass. She was already up there. Even the tragedy of her son was transferred into an attribute of her superiority. My God, Wolf upbraided himself, I haven't even gotten her over the first hump: the recognition that this problem isn't hers alone, that it didn't happen only to her, that it's shared with thousands, perhaps hundreds of thousands of others, no one knows how many. And with this recognition to surrender her uniqueness, to become merged with the group, to be eased by consciousness of participation in a common plight, widely distributed. And with this ease, this submergence of self in the many, she would lose something of her singularity of feeling, yes, and something of her sovereign individuality, yes . . . But oh, how the individual fights with beak and claw, with what wildly beating wings, to elude the net of definition! Against being grouped, classified, tagged with terminology, reduced to material for casework studies, punch-carded and reconstituted as *Correlations in Phenomenology among Mothers of Schizophrenics in the 2–8 Age Range*. She would not place herself on that side of the fence. She would not surrender.

Wolf was standing at the corner window when Julie entered the office with Colfax, looking through the wire-meshed window to the fenced area behind the building for female patients, an enclosure which his first daughter, long ago when he was an intern here, had dubbed "the ladies' playpen." He turned from the window toward Julie and she turned from the door toward him, each of them animated by the sincerest intention to do better, and at once, as if lying all this time in wait since the last time, all the superficial dissidence that operated between them had them in its toils again.

Wolf glanced involuntarily toward the corner of his desk where in the city the photograph of his children stood. Julie, bringing her son in with her arm around his shoulder, touched her pearls. It was all ready on the tip of her tongue: You see he took so long being born, he couldn't get out of the womb, and then when he was just over a year old my husband tied him up in his crib and for more than eighteen hours he couldn't get out of that, and then this last May he was locked in the office. He's shut up in this box and he throws himself against it and gives up and throws himself again . . .

Wolf came from the window toward her, the wolf sly in his granny-cap, the sleek pussycat waving his tail, the peeper under petticoats. Nothing would tickle him more, Julie thought, than to declare me off my rocker. Comely young matron, fine old family, a stark raving maniac.

"How nice to see you again," she said, "and how are your lovely children today?" Glancing toward the corner of his desk. "Oh, of course, they're not here. I bet you miss them. Colfax, shake hands with Dr. Wolf. We've made so much progress . . ."

Inadvertently Dr. Wolf bumped against the corner of his desk, knocking off his cards. He stooped to pick them up, the blood rushing to his head. She hastened to help him, bending down with him, and he had, rather brusquely, to fend her off. "No no no, that's all right . . ."

Years ago, after his internship here and before the war, when he was young and idealistic, Wolf had gone home to Chicago and worked for a while with juveniles in a South Side settlement house. The boys looked with a certain skeptic scorn at the professionals who sought to guide them. No matter what you say, the juvenile look said, you're where you are and I'm where I am. But if there was anyone they scorned more than the professionals, it was the wealthy liberal sponsor who furnished part of the financing. The sponsor would drop in at any hour, sometimes in tennis shorts, sometimes in white tie and tails, usually with his girl, a black-haired jewel of a girl, rosy-skinned, sparkling with the joy of youth and the excitement of the views she shared with her companion and the pride of love possessed, however temporarily. The sponsor, with the girl at his shoulder, would stop a boy in the corridor for a chat, always the boldest and most scornful of them. And the product of all the best that civilization had to offer would look into the eyes of the product of all the worst with a solicitous, sympathetic seeking as if here he might find the answer to the riddle of humanity.

Julie looked at him, Wolf thought as he rammed together his disordered cards, not with the scorn of the unfortunate for the privileged, but with the solicitous sympathetic seeking intensity of the rich sponsor on his way to somewhere else.

"Your husband telephoned a while back," he said to Julie. "He's been detained in Atlanta but he'll be down later."

"Yes, I know," Julie said lightly, consoling him. "What with his job and all this politicking here lately, he's been terribly tied up. Now Coley, come out of that corner. It's this room," accusingly, "it's like a box, he hides himself . . . But we have some good news for you. A poor relation of my husband's, a ten-year-old boy, very mature for his age, has been living with us the past few weeks and I wish you could see how Coley's taken to him. It's been simply marvelous. I'd hoped we could have him with us this morning, you'd be so impressed—"

Dr. Wolf laid out his cards on Colfax Warren in rows on his desk like a game of solitaire, each of them typed out by his secretary, headed in caps and numbered. His eye flicking over the headings, he assorted them in proper sequence. *Defect in emotional rapport:* how better could one characterize this moment? Hebephrenia: it was to laugh and to cry. *Inappropriate and disjointed speech:* blocking, symbolization, condensation, incoherence. *Distortion of affect:* what's hot is cold.

"I hope you have some good news for us too."

Tiredly Dr. Wolf took from his desk drawer Form 1-K. "I think we'll wait with my conclusion and recommendations until your husband arrives. I wish I could have some good news for you, Mrs. Warren, but I'm afraid it's a little more complex than that. As I've pointed out to you before, it this were a behavior problem, I could refer you to a good analyst. If it were neurological, we could try drugs and possibly surgery. But if it's schizophrenia, as I now believe it is, and even a specialist sometimes can't be sure, then we are confronted with the question: Is it emotional or physiological? If it's emotional, then a course of intensive psychotherapeutic work with both child and parents is indicated, and this may or may not yield some improvement. If it's physiological in origin, as some authorities are beginning to think—perhaps a hereditary factor, a missing quantity, an enzyme—then sooner or later a chemical solution may be found.

"This whole field is in its prehistory. We are at the same stage as we were with tuberculosis and the infectious diseases a half-century ago. There are all degrees and varieties of this illness and it's far more widespread than anybody guesses. And there are very few institutions of real merit working with it, that is combining research, experimentation, methods of education and care. You have ahead of you a long slow difficult process, requiring endless investigation, patience, willingness to learn, understand."

"But this drug, you asked us to bring Coley here today so this new drug could be tried on him."

"I hold out no promise for the drug. The drugs as well as the shock therapies have produced only negligible results with children. But since it's harmless and the effects will pass off fairly rapidly, I thought we might give it a try. Will you sign the release, please?"

Julie took Form 1-K from him and read it. It was a waiver of responsibility for the hospital. Wolf unscrewed his gold-topped fountain pen and passed it to her.

"But," she demurred angrily, "this means you want Coley to be used as a guinea pig! We're not the kind of people—"

"I feel it's worth a try. He may respond. It may open him up a little. We have a couple of other youngsters with him. They'll be under observation for several hours."

His voice was carefully devoid of reproof. When they attack you, you have them put under restraint and taken away. When they throw their blocks on the floor, you pick the blocks up without comment. When they make amorous advances, you don't take part. When they inject the personal into a routine that is by training, habit, and repetition impersonal, setting up such vibrations with their winces and gasps as to destroy the fiction that the rubbered finger and the internal passage are disembodied entities, detached from the person—you ignore it.

"But I don't think you understand, Doctor. This is my child! I can't let him be subjected to some trial-and-error . . ."

Although the half hour he had allotted to Julie was well-nigh terminated, Dr. Wolf very nearly succumbed to the temptation to tell her a tale handed down to him by his grandmother from the old country. The son of the quality-lady of the village, so the tale ran, had been whipped by his schoolteacher for misbehavior. The lady, in her black velvet and pearls, summoned the teacher to her home and after hearing out his complaint against her son solved the matter thus. "Next time, don't punish him. Get hold of some charity pupil and pull his pants down in the sight of my Mischa and apply the rod well. Throw such a scare into my son that he'll never misbehave again."

Tapping his cards while Julie hesitated over the release, Wolf restrained himself from telling her the story. But told her another instead.

"My grandmother had a tale she used to tell from the old country. One day a teacher met a woman weeping bitterly in the road and he asked her what the trouble was. And she said, 'See?' and held up the necklace she was wearing. 'My pearls, they're too thin! There's not enough of them to look like anything with my black velvet dress.' The teacher went a little farther on the road and met another woman weeping just as bitterly. He asked her what the trouble was and she held up the pot she was carrying. 'See? The barley in my soup, it's too thin! There's not enough of it to feed my children with.'"

It was as near to an expression of disapproval as Wolf had ever permitted himself toward anyone on the other side of his desk. It broke a long-standing rule of his. And all the while he was in it, he reprimanded himself; for he too had his dichotomies and ambivalences always at war within him. *Don't scratch beneath the surface, don't try to break through, leave her be.*

Firmly Julie signed the release, bending her head low over the paper as if she were nearsighted. The letters leapt up large on the page, wavering and clashing through a film of pellucid brightness. *I'm underestimating him. I'm not giving him his due. Throw away your cards, Dr. Wolf! Let's start all over again.*

Wolf was standing when she handed back the form, ringing for the nurse.

"Do you really think of me," Julie asked in a low voice, "as the lady with the pearls?"

"I think you have a special luster," Wolf said, softening. "A luster of specialness that's supremely important to you, perhaps indispensable—"

"You think I'm incapable of accepting reality?"

"I think you're quite capable of it. If you so choose."

With the nurse she coaxed and pried Colfax loose from his corner, dragged him with scuffing heels down to the office of Dr. Stieber who was to take charge of him. While Coley shrieked for her, Stieber whispered at her, "Go, go," and Wolf drew her away.

"I'm afraid you'll have to wait in the reception room, Mrs. Warren. I'm due in the wards now."

"Dr. Wolf." She caught at his sleeve as he turned to leave. "There's something I have to tell you. There is a missing quantity, and it's not an en—enzyme—"

"Later, I'll see you later."

"Dr. Wolf." She ran after him down the ginger-tan corridor. "Dr. Wolf, will you do me a favor? I can accept reality. I can and I want to. Everything. All of it. Take me with you on your rounds."

Dr. Wolf regarded her oddly over his shoulder, his slim trim head reared, his eyes quizzical, his thin lips drawn back over his teeth in an appraising half-smile. Wolf would never—it was another one of his unbreakable rules—take a woman whose state of mind was inaccessible to him, the mother of a patient, one of those who occupied the chair on the other side of his desk and therefore on the other side of the fence, through these wards and these rooms. To the victor belongs the spoils and to the victim—and this despite his stories and his sympathies was his predominant prejudice, which she so acutely sensed—the stigma of ineptitude.

But a rich sponsor, a member of the board, a colleague, a friend and equal from the same side of the desk . . .

"It's pretty fierce," he said. "You think you can take it?"

"I can take anything."

Correct in her pale beige dress and pearls, glowing under her velvet-banded straw hat, she smiled at him, one eye wide open, angelic, the other ever so slightly drooping, full of deviltry. In the light of what you know, Doctor, don't we all harbor the germ of insanity? You too?

"Come." He held out his arm.

Accompanied by nurse and aide they proceeded down the corridor to the first of a long series of double doors, metal-plated and covered with interlinked wiring like a coat of mail over armor. With a clanking of keys the doors were unlocked into the passageway to the women's building, and locked again behind them.

3

Due to the current critical shortage of residents Dr. Wolf conscientiously at considerable sacrifice of potential fees spent two days a week at the hospital; incidentally catching up on experience missed during his war years, with an opportunity to participate in staff work, which he particularly enjoyed, as one of the leading younger men coming up. For Julie the journey through the hospital, up and down the three and sometimes four floors, from building to building, was a thing of shreds and patches.

The interview in the admission room. A woman in her thirties thick and sallow after an operation, high up on a cot. Dr. Wolf with his cards, making entries. Wolf: "How are you feeling?" "Lousy." "Your name?" "Karen Price." "Your age?" Home address, number of children, place of employment, etc., etc. All of which Mrs. Price answered without hesitation. "What month is this?" "August." "What day of the week?" "Thursday." And then at last the key question: "Do you know where you are?" The woman raising herself on her elbow: "Darbyton State Hospital." "Do you know why you're here?" "I was about to ask you that. I had an operation, I'm sick, I don't belong here." "Who brought you here?" Silence. "Don't you know who brought you here?" She sank back from her elbow, lips compressed. "Didn't your husband bring you here?" Vehemently: "I got no husband." "Isn't Anthony Price who brought you here your husband?" "No!" "It says here that he is." "Div-vorce." "You're divorced?" "I divorce him last July. That's why he brought me here. So he don't have to pay."

"That may," Dr. Wolf remarked in an aside to Julie as they left Mrs. Price, "or may not be true."

"But all those details about her marriage, you think she was making it all up?"

"It may be so. Or may not be. With some people reality begins to change into something else the instant it's happened. And with some people it never occurred in the first place. We'll have to check this out with her husband."

"Oh."

The elderly arrayed on benches, row after row like the people outside in the reception room, passengers in a railroad station waiting for a train.

"But these are old folks," Julie protested, following on the heels of Dr. Wolf. "They don't belong here."

"There's nowhere else to place them. What to do with the aged? That's another field still in its prehistory."

"Oh."

Concourse of women, a conglomeration of age and condition noisily thronging the halls, the sporadic rain outside the windows creating a steamy and restless confinement within. Bundle on a bed. "Mrs. Roberts, aren't you going to get up today? Mrs. Roberts . . . Most beautiful girl you ever saw," Wolf explained to Julie. "Husband in oil down Venezuela, he doesn't know yet. Two wonderful children. Started with social drinking. Her family tried cures, sanitariums. We've had her back twice."

"But why here? She doesn't belong here."

"Alcoholism. Another one we don't know enough about."

"Oh."

Adolescent girl, no more than fourteen, darkly pretty, elbows on windowsill, moodily staring out. "Chronic runaway. Was picked up in a Savannah hotel room with three sailors. Her father's a superintendent of schools. They had her committed here."

"But here, how can she ever . . . She doesn't belong . . ."

"It was preferable to the public disgrace of having her sentenced to reform school. Mishandled her all the way. Now they've had her put away. Out of sight, out of mind."

"Oh."

Julie stayed close to the doctor, with whom she belonged.

In every ward they swarmed up to him with their plaints and pleas as soon as he appeared. Trailed after him as he left.

"Doctor! Doctor!"

Everywhere as the armored and mailed doors were unlocked and locked again.

"Doctor! Doctor!"

Why he's a god, Julie thought, dispensing his favors, privileges, passes, transfers.

"Doctor! Doctor!"

Ascending with changing escort of nurse and aide the locked-in flights of stairs to the more disturbed wards. The smells increasing. Disinfectant. Body odors.

"Doctor! Doctor!"

A frowsy ash-blonde scratching at her pubic hair. "Doctor, the niggers been chasin' me. Niggers are gettin' in everywhere. It's account of the niggers I had to leave the Catholic Church. Doctor, when can I go home to my kids?"

A flashing bellissima manic-depressive, gay with ribbons, sashes, trinkets. Julie almost jumped out of her skin when she touched her. "You a doctor too?" "Why no. No I'm not." "This is Mrs. Warren," Dr. Wolf introduced her gravely. "Any relation to Winnie Warren?" A popular hillbilly singer. "Why no. No I'm not." "That's OK, Dr. Warren. Did I used to dance to his band! Did I used to have me a ball!"

A cleanly mulatto woman in a hoover dress in a small dark cell. Sobbing with tears that trickled through her fingers. Dr. Wolf touched the rough brown ridges of her hair. "You'll be all right. We'll be sending you to visit your family one of these weekends. You'll be all right." "In such a mess. In such a mess."

"Doctor! Doctor!"

He prescribed to the nurse medication and alterations of regimen for individuals singled out now and then. But on the whole he passed swiftly through, silver-blond, slim and trim, curt and clipped, apotheosized.

"Doctor! Doctor!"

A sea of troubles. The multitudinous seas incarnadine, making the green one red.

"You're God to them," Julie said to Wolf. "Don't they make you feel like God?"

Wolf took it as a compliment, or so Julie thought, and tossed it off as a jest. "So long as I don't feel I'm God twenty-four hours a day, Mrs. Warren."

"Oh."

A few moments later he pointed into a white chamber so crammed with high narrow tablets of beds the nurse coming out had to edge through sidewise. "There are patients in there under restraint and rotting with bedsores simply because we don't have the personnel to attend them. We have only two nurses for this whole building at night. We don't have the funds, we don't have the staff, we don't have the equipment. That nurse there—" He nodded back over his shoulder.

"Yes I noticed her. She's very good."

"She's a patient."

"Oh."

The din and the stench mounted with the flights of stairs. Floor D was lined entirely with sheet metal. When they opened the doors the odor of urine struck them in the face like the breath of a blast furnace. Then it engulfed them, an ammoniac diffusion displacing the air. Some were frozen in bizarre postures. A black-clad exclamation point of a woman with one leg wrapped about the other, crowned with a bush of white hair. Under the command of some mysterious force not to move, not to make a sound, lest the earth lose its gravity, fly off its orbit, smash into the sun. Others wove about frenetically, arms, legs, mouths, eyes moving in ritualized order, in accordance with the gravitational cohesion of a systematized dementia: orbits of isolation colliding and whirling away. Along a dim passageway skeletal forms crouched on the floor, knees upraised out of flimsy garments, heads sagging from the neck, emaciated hands dangling. Shades from beyond the grave, yellowed grey, in dewlapped cerements of grey, deteriorating in their own offal. Under a dusty grey beam of daylight, high up—consciousness never dies?—from a tiny window set in the roof.

And still the cry.

"Doctor! Doctor!"

Blowsy, red-faced, plodding barefoot after. "Doctor, you got to get me out of here. Back on C. I'll be good, honest, I swear I'll be good."

He passed on.

Plucking at Julie. "I don't belong here, you can see I don't belong—"

"Are you all right?" Wolf said to Julie.

She was paralyzed with horror, fainting, sinking. And swimming. Swimming and sinking.

"We're going down now," he said briskly, "into a much more hopeful situation. Electrotherapy."

Down the corrugated flights of stairs. Down into the bowels of the building. "It doesn't hurt them really. We use it with certain types of schizophrenia, manic-depression, involutional melancholia. If there's no response after a few months, when we have to give up trying, that's when it hurts. Unless there's spontaneous improvement then, there's likely to be regression all the way up to Floor D. Of course it should only be used in conjunction with other forms of therapy. And sometimes that's lacking."

Patient clumps into the basement room. Without pressure from her attendant aides, plunks herself down on the vulcanized black rubber cot. Gag, a black rubber bar, thrust into mouth. "We've had very few instances of tongue-biting or dislocated jaw." Electrode discs on her temples. Band of ductile black rubber wound around her head. They hold her prone. The controls on the black box release the voltage. The needle on the white face of the metered clock above moves radially. The body jolts, heaves upward from the small of the back, rigidifies in an arc. Slumps. Aides at head and foot sling her, unconscious, buttocks pendent, over onto the recovery cot. Next.

Screaming all the way down the corridor into the therapy room, dragged, fighting, kicking, spitting. NO NO NO nonononono. Don't take me in there—it's awful, it's terrible—no-oh . . .

"It doesn't hurt," Dr. Wolf reassured Julie, "really."

NO NO NO NO

Wrenched, pushed, hurled upon the inflexible black rubber, pinned down by four men.

NO NO NO nonononono don't DON'T DO-ON'T

Electrodes fastened on the twisting disheveled head. Every bone, muscle, sinew, nerve-fiber straining to break free. The gag in the mouth expelled. Shoved back in.

Under the circle of pale, accustomed, serious, and wisecracking faces. Upward arc of the spine.

Coley. Me. Coley. Me. Coley. Me.

Slump. Deadweight.

"Purely subjective," Dr. Wolf said.

"Oh."

Julie was no longer sure whether she was with the doctor or with the patients. With those who rule or the ruled. With the outer or the inner world. Which side of the desk or which side of the fence . . .

The kitchens were manned by inmates, the dining room, sewing room, laundry, beauty parlor. Very nice. Occupational Therapy: newest of the buildings, clean, quiet, orderly, and almost empty. Looms being threaded with bright textiles, clays being sculptured, weekly newspaper being printed on a hand press, posters being splashed with color announcing the next patients' dance. Elite purview of those who had graduated into the status of the elite: soon to be released.

Here in OT they encountered a woman doctor, rumpled white coat open over her dress, hands in pockets, hair ruffled, eyes a-snap. Small and sturdy and winsome as they come. Had been scrapping with administration over sneaking her violent patients in. "They're the ones that need the occupation as much as anyone does. The more violent they are," she said emphatically to Julie, rolling back her loose cuffs, "the better I like it. There's a struggle going on there . . ."

"In direst need of social workers," Dr. Wolf said to Julie as they left OT for the men's building. "For casework follow-up and guidance to the families. So they won't land back. It's getting near lunchtime, would you like to have lunch with me afterward in the staff dining room?"

His honored guest? His respected friend? Or humoring her as he would humor a patient?

Into the men's block with a clangor of keys. "Won't take long here. I'll get to the colored later if I have time. I suppose you're wondering about the mulatto woman back in B? Has some sort of influential connection."

"That helps?"

"It always helps."

"Oh."

She should have begged off. Should have pleaded fatigue. But one must always keep up the appearance of imperviable detachment, mustn't one? She swam through the male wards in an hallucinatory fluid, thrashing as an inexpert swimmer will to stay afloat, tiring herself the more thereby. Flailing and floundering, spluttering and sinking amidst the mockers and scoffers, the moaners and groaners, fist-thumpers and head-bumpers. Napoleons? None. Hitler. Stah-leen. Amazing how they keep abreast of the times. A most interesting character, mining engineer from South Africa, knew Cecil Rhodes, syphilitic paresis. *He's* happy, not a care in the world, the best state of all. Wolf eyes slanting, grey twinkling with points of yellow malice. Fatcat splendidly waving his tail.

On the sunporch off the main ward Julie was introduced by Dr. Wolf to a young man straight out of every moonlight-and-magnolia romance ever written. A very perfect gentle knight. Tall, slender, asthenic, elegant in white silk surah ice cream suit, he courteously rose from his deck chair at the approach of the lady, offered his seat which she declined and remained standing in converse with her. "And where are you from, Mrs. Warren?" "Colfax County." "Ah the *lost gordonia.* It's never been found?" "We've looked for it. For a hundred and fifty years we've looked for it. All up and down the river and in all the swamps. But we never found it again."

Enjoying the freemasonry of their allusion, the parlance of a common upbringing—Dr. Wolf was sharply eyeing Julie, with some bafflement—they mourned that wild magnolia discovered by John Bartram, described by him in his journal and transported north by him in his saddlebags, but never seen on the banks of the Ocachee again. All had some vision of it, gorgeously white-blossomed within glassy green leaves on a slender grey tree as smooth as satin. All sought it, generations of school children, picnickers, expeditions of naturalists. All thought at some time or other they had it in their grasp. But lost. Irrevocably. Irretrievably. Forever lost.

"I'm studying the habits of starlings," the young man went on to Julie, indicating the grounds outside. "They nest in the hollow of that big tree over there." A thick tall tree dividing into wildly distorted boughs, clawing at the bulbous sky. "Looks like a chestnut, doesn't it? But I'm told it's a Japanese princess tree, the loveliest blue flowers in the spring with the oddest scent . . . The starlings sharpen their beaks on the dogwood before they pick up my crumbs. They walk on the lawn like respectable businessmen, don't they? And when they flock together, it's a regular Chamber of Commerce meeting. Then they fly off—look—don't they look like the ashes of papers blowing up from a fire?"

They watched the starlings fly off with the first drops of recurrent rain, like cinders blowing up from a fire.

"Dr. Wolf," the young man turned to him, "I've been thinking a lot about the patients. We don't do enough in the way of outings. It would make such a difference if they had something to look forward to. If we could take a half-dozen of them, say, up for lunch someday at the Cherokee Club. My brother could arrange it." Dr. Wolf agreed that it was a fine idea. "About a week from today then? I'll write to my brother." "Do that." His brown head gallantly inclined, his brown eyes pools of tragic poesy, he took Julie's hand at parting. "Until we meet again?"

Behind his back, as soon as they stepped off the sunporch Dr. Wolf winked at her. And that wink, that twinkle of amusement, regrettable and irrepressible, which placed her on his plane, beside him, above the flaws and foibles of the weak—that wink Julie would not share with him. She did not belong with Wolf anymore but with that young man back there on the deck chair.

"But it's a perfectly good idea. What's wrong with it?"

"My dear girl, do you know what the Cherokee Club is? I've never been admitted to it myself."

"But he says his brother . . . He will be out of here sometime won't he?"

Dr. Wolf shook his head.

"But he's going to get well? He looks as well as I do!"

Dr. Wolf shook his head.

"You mean it's hopeless?"

"We never say that."

"Oh."

Dr. Wolf stepped aside to speak with another doctor. "But they understand they have to have the signature of two physicians for commitment—?" Julie drifted off by herself into the men's ward. There in the middle of the floor among all the long tall legs stood a little boy. With hair like cornsilk and eyes of cornflower blue, rosy with the bloom of the petal on his skin, cherry lips with the glisten on them, touched with dew. Wearing blue shirt and jeans.

"Why son," she said, "what are you doing here? Did you get lost?"

"And what are you doing here?" he answered her. "Did you get lost?"

She smoothed his yellow hair, touched his cheeks. "Oh darling, you darling, you're just a baby. How old are you?"

"Eight. How old are you?"

"Doctor! Doctor!" It was her own voice calling.

"Oh there you are." Dr. Wolf joined her. "With Tommy. How are you today, Tommy?"

"They're not going to stick anymore needles into me, are they?"

"The needles will make you better."

"But he's a child! What's he doing among all these adults? A little child."

Dr. Wolf drew her away. "This was recognized early. His parents have taken him everywhere. To every top man in the country, every hospital and school. Tried everything available. Turned themselves and their bankbooks inside out. During the war they managed to get to England to talk with Anna Freud. They heard of a German psychiatrist who had had some success with children and they arranged a meeting with him in Switzerland—"

"And still he's ended up here?"

"When they brought him here six months ago he was eating his feces."

She turned away from Wolf and there was Tommy again, gazing trustfully up at her with his clear blue eyes. "Why is pain?"

Dr. Wolf went on to a middle-aged man in undershirt and Julie walked swiftly away toward the locked doors at the end of the ward. One must not burst into tears. One must preserve decorum at all costs, mustn't one? "Mrs. Warren, Mrs. Warren—"

As Dr. Wolf closed in behind her, the doors ahead were unbolted from the other side and from between them with a delusional clarity, fractured on the refraction of teardrops wavering on the verge, stepped Dr. Francis X. Harrington. Her hand flew to her cheek. Her mouth flew open. She tried to sidestep.

"Mrs. Warren—Julie—"

She could have shrieked. She could have run through the wards, ducking and dodging. While they closed in on her from both sides, trapping her there, locked in the box . . .

"Julie, I came up—"

With that forelock drooping over his broad forehead, and that deprecatory sneer curled in the corner of his mouth making him superior to himself. She could have knocked away the hand he thrust out.

"Julie, your husband called me early today and asked if I could come support you through this—"

I got no husband!

"So I caught the morning flight—"

The niggers are chasing me. The niggers are everywhere.

"And here I am."

Along the floor they dragged her, kicking and spitting. NOnononono . . .

But in the locomotive that roars through the back of the skull sits an engineer. In the brain there resides a monitor at the controls.

"Dr. Wolf, this is Dr. Harrington. From my home. I believe you've been in touch?"

She knew who and where she was, and not only that. With the clarity of certainty she knew what she had to do from now on and where she was going.

At twelve-twenty, less than two hours from the time Julie had first entered them, the last armored doors were locked behind her. She, Harrington, and Wolf adjourned to the staff dining room where they served themselves cafeteria-style from the counter and carried their trays to one of the black-topped tables by the wall. Julie was extraordinarily hungry. Her waves of confusion were vanquished, if not banished, by food. The grinding sick hollow inside her was stoked, if not stanched. "Worse than these roadside restaurants," she grumbled with mouth full, "I've counted only six bites of meat," and went back to the counter for a second veal en brochette, the men being too busy with shop talk to render her her usual meed of attention.

She listened to them only intermittently, never thinking that what they had to say might have some reference to herself and Colfax. Dr. Harrington out to impress Dr. Wolf in a hurry. Dr. Wolf with equanimity maintaining his position of authority. Their fancy footwork gradually losing out to their interest in the subject.

"But the drugs," Harrington inquired of Wolf, "what are you using? Benzedrine? Ephedrine sulphate? Caffeine citrate? Sodium amytal?"

"The amytal."

"But didn't the Bradley tests show that they were of little value at that age? And the shock therapies: insulin, metrazol, electroshock. Very disappointing."

"We can only try a variety of approaches. So long as they don't produce any irreversible effect. We are unfortunately dealing with something where all the discoveries are still ahead of us. Even with adults we're up a tree—"

"What about prefrontal lobotomy?"

"That was introduced only ten years ago."

"Dr. Antonio Egas Moniz of Lisbon, 1936, who will indubitably come up with a Nobel for it one of these days. Back in 1931 I was performing my prefrontals at the Mattapan Hospital. He beat me to the punch."

"Oh, you're that Harrington?"

Dr. Wolf drew back a little distastefully, the man of good repute from the man so unlucky or so foolish as to have lost his. "I had no idea . . . Now that I think of it, someone around here did mention that there was a neurosurgeon—"

"Is a man to be damned all his life for a single slip? Are these hands" —Harrington lifted them somewhat melodramatically over his ham sandwich—"these hands to be crippled?"

Harrington's brooding brow confronted Wolf's protuberant underlip, indiscreetly revealing disapproval.

Without thinking very much about it Julie rushed into the breach. She unfastened her necklace and swung it under Wolf's disdainfully distended nose. "Who's being the lady with the pearls now? And who's wearing the black velvet dress?"

"Well—" Wolf conceded, and pulled his chair back in. He was already smiling quizzically, his thin lips drawn back over his teeth, in anticipation of the story this would make. You know who I ran into at Darbyton? Remember that fellow up in Boston, some years ago, was doing the frontal-lobos?

"To get back to the point," he said to Harrington, "I'm inclined to go slow when it comes to that type of surgery. I know there's a rash of enthusiasm for it now as there always is for anything that looks promising, until its limitations and side effects show up. Frankly I'd tend to wait until we see more of the long-term results. After all, you're cutting the fibers of the brain—"

"It relieves the tension. It eliminates the emotional pressure."

"But the patient is permanently impaired."

"What is he now? At least he'll be lucid."

"It's a form of castration. The intelligence may remain the same—"

"But out in the open, remember that, out in the open—"

"But what of the driving force? You can come out with a human vegetable."

"Not if it's done right. As for driving force, who needs it? I mean that. If you go along with the Freudian structural hypothesis, you resolve your intrapsychic conflicts by sublimating them into acceptable forms—and you're Dr. Wolf. But if you can't—and how many can?—where does it leave you? Stuck with drives that may destroy you. If you're in a state that's accessible to analysis and can afford it, well and good. But if you're beyond that, if you're beyond reach, if these drives are raging inside you like tigers in a cage, then it's our first job, isn't it, to save the mind even if we have to alter the personality to do it?"

"So what do we produce? Joe Blow. Easy come, easy go. Nothing bothers him. Is that so bad? Impulsive but passionless. Careless but compliant. We have a lot of those down in our part of the country, don't we, Julie?"

"What? Oh. I thought you implied once that we were all split personalities—"

"Pardon me. I'll amend that. Lobotomized personalities. No kidding though, you get rid of the repressed rebellions, the struggles, the questionings—which most people compromise away anyhow . . ."

Amidst their general laughter, Dr. Wolf acknowledged, "I am acquainted with one such case. Brilliant boy. Acute onset in late adolescence. Ran stark naked out of his dormitory one night. Four years later his parents consented to surgery. He made a satisfactory adjustment at a lower level of achievement."

"There you are. So he won't be an Einstein. He'll conform with the crowd. Drift with the current. The good citizen. The prototype of the coming era."

Laughter again. "You missed your calling, Dr. Harrington. You'd have made quite a satirist. I suppose no one objects to amputation for gangrene—"

"This is far less serious, I assure you."

"Only it's not gangrene. And it's not a leg. We don't really know what we're doing. A four-hour operation—"

"Half-hour. I do it in half an hour. I can still do it." Harrington shook his broad hands. "I can still do it in the dark. Easier on the patient than many a tonsillectomy."

"You mean the closed technique? But you're working blind! Don't you run risk of hemorrhage?"

"None at all. Three per cent mortality. I never lost a patient. They're up next day talking with their families."

The two men became involved in a discussion of the open versus the closed operation. Harrington delighted to have his hand in again even thus vicariously, Wolf engrossed in the details. "You mean with just light anesthesia—there's practically no aftereffect in the way of shock, pain, bleeding?" Still, Wolf was not fully persuaded. "Maybe. Maybe after every other avenue has been explored first."

"By whom? How? This hospital and every other one like it is so jammed with patients you can't get to explore—"

"It's the old old question. A choice between the quick and drastic solution at some incalculable human loss, and the long hard search."

Henry arrived as they were finishing their ice cream, hurrying straight to their table. "Oh Harrington, you're here. Good." His man at the conference. "I'm sorry, Julie." Kissing her cheek. Pulling up a chair. "I dropped Charles off at the Confederate Shrine. How's Coley?"

Dr. Wolf glanced at his watch. "We'll have a report on him in about an hour."

"Terrific. I was breakfasting this morning at the Cherokee Club with Dan Garner—you know Dan? Congressman from our district. When who should blow in but Ol' Cal Hubbard—you know Cal?" Henry was bubbling with it, it was too good to keep. "Cal's had this throat ailment all through his campaign. Can't hardly speak above a whisper. 'A politician with laryngitis,' Dan says to Ol' Cal, 'is like a prostitute with a broken pelvis.' Say boy—" Henry arrested a busboy in mid-passage. "How about bringing me some of that Salisbury steak? With plenty of French fries . . ."

They assembled in Dr. Wolf's office at two o'clock. The report on Coley was none too sanguine. He had not responded verbally at all to the drug. Though he had completed four jigsaw puzzles of graduated difficulty. A little girl had bopped him over the head with a block. He was continuing under observation through the afternoon.

Dr. Wolf now delivered the conclusions and recommendations he had prepared for them last night.

"There are several courses of action open to you. You could go on keeping him at home until the next crisis—"

"Oh no," Julie said quickly—and Henry looked at her. It was what he had most feared she would insist upon. "So long as I believed that he was really normal, so long as I believed that love was enough, that I could by myself make something of him, it was all right. But now . . ."

"Or you could place him in a custodial school or institution. Where,

I am bound to point out, the tendency to further withdrawal may be fostered rather than remedied."

"No," Henry said promptly and Julie looked at him. It was what she had always feared he would insist upon. "As long as he's anywhere like that, we'd never have a minute's peace."

"Or you could in time have him committed here."

"No!" Both together.

"Don't mistake me. The state hospital for all its present shortcomings is in general the best place available for the mentally ill. We don't go in for depth analysis or delvings into the unconscious, but we do try in our interviews to track down the cause and thus a cue to the cure. We're practitioners of Adolf Meyer's psychobiology, seeing the patient as the end-product of the total forces making up his life, hereditary, environmental, physiological, and emotional. However in most states as yet, including this one, facilities for children are almost nonexistent.

"Therefore, as I suggested to Mrs. Warren earlier, it might be advisable to move close to a treatment center elsewhere. There are all too few of these. Some are extremely costly, some have residence requirements that will take time to meet and all are so booked-up for months ahead that it's almost impossible to obtain an appointment. There is one in Illinois doing some good work with children, though that was disrupted by the war. And one in California, though that's just getting started. Nevertheless such a center combining research with therapy, education, and care should be tried. You as the parents would have to agree to therapy for yourselves as well—"

"What's that?" Henry interrupted. "What you saying?"

"You as the parents would be placed under a psychiatrist, probably two, working with you separately. If not that, then a social worker."

"Are you proposing that we leave our home, my job, drop everything, put ourselves in the hands of some twerp—"

"Isn't it a cruel hoax," Dr. Harrington interrupted from his stance in the rear, "for the parents to sacrifice everything to something that will yield so little progress, if any, that it can hardly be called progress at all?"

"I have gone into that," Dr. Wolf said stiffly, "quite exhaustively with Mrs. Warren. You understand, don't you, Mrs. Warren?"

"Yes," Julie said. "I must confess I got off on the wrong foot with you, Doctor, to begin with. But I understand what's necessary now."

"Two years from now," Wolf said, "ten years, twenty maybe—"

"Maybe never," Henry said.

"No, not never. With the accumulation of experience and effort, the breakthrough will come. You have the opportunity to contribute to that."

"Tell me the truth, Doctor," Henry demanded. "The God's honest truth. If this was your child, what would you do?"

Unconsciously Dr. Wolf glanced toward the untidy stack of publications on the corner of his desk, where in his beautifully appointed office in the city the silver-mounted photograph of his children stood. For a moment, the merest moment, he imagined it, immersed himself in it with a shudder he couldn't quite conceal. His child. Forsaking the glass-walled home, the swimming pool, the flourishing practice for the torture of hopes blasted . . .

"I'm afraid," Wolf said, more to himself than to them, "I'd be tempted to try almost anything."

This sentence, charged more with emotion than thought, Julie took as confirmation of the decision she had already made, and Henry took as confirmation of the decision he had already made.

"We'll think it over, Doctor. We'll let you know."

Wolf was in a hurry to get on to his next patients, waiting overlong outside in the reception room.

"You can tell the young man on the sunporch," Julie said lightly to the doctor as Henry and Harrington supplied her with her scattered gloves and handbag, "that the starlings arrive alone at their meetings. But they always fly off together. And tell him, tell him from me, Doctor —that I—I—I'll keep looking for—for the—the *lost gordonia?*"

She choked on it. Her tears splashed, scalding. Her knees crumpled. She broke down and wept through her fingers like any other poor suffering woman on the face of the earth.

Late in the afternoon they gathered Colfax up, sleeping, and piled into the convertible. It was still raining, a slow vaporous downpour.

"God," Henry said, "it's good to get out of there. To breathe!" Deeply he inhaled the moisture-laden air, thick with grass scent and gas fumes. And again with heaving chest filling, emptying, flushing out his system. "Just to be in a place like that is enough to give you symptoms."

They picked up Charles at the Confederate Shrine, all agog with the gun collection and the battlefields under glass, and drove back to the motor lodge for dinner. Coley slept on. "He's sedated up to his ears," Julie said indignantly, but it was much easier for her to have him asleep. Despite their fatigue and the rain they decided to try to make home that night. Charles curled up in the back seat. Coley was tucked in on a pillow on the floor. Julie rode in front between Harrington and Henry.

"We spent all that money," Henry complained, "and all that time and we're right back where we started from. They don't know."

"Don't say I didn't warn you," Harrington said. "Wolf is a neuropsychiatrist, I'm a neurosurgeon. He's for medication, that's his method.

I'm for excision, that's mine. He'd tell you they never perform a prefrontal on a child, you won't find a doctor anywhere who'd do it. I'll
tell you there always has to be a first time. In my opinion, the earlier
you have it over with the more chance you have for adaptation and education through the growth years. We could make medical history with
it . . ."

The two men talked about it over the miles of glistening black road,
the jagged daggers of red and yellow light shimmering in the puddles,
through the curtains of rain whipping against the windshield, the arc
of the wipers sweeping at the pointillism of drops. They settled it between them.

"Once you make up your mind to a thing like this, the sooner the
better. I'll go up to Hopkins next week to brush up."

"First week of September then. You can make your arrangements."

"Never," Julie said. "Not without my consent you won't. You can't
do it without my consent."

"Of course with your consent." They patted her reassuringly. "Naturally with your consent."

They sat in their seats of power disposing of a child's fate, and they
no longer had power to do so. Julie was past argument with them and
past anger. She had made her mind up where she was going and what
she would do and nothing, no word or action of theirs, could prevent
it. Everyone at sometime or other in life descends into the inferno,
climbs barefoot up the stony slopes of Calvary, is buried in the pit and
sold into Egypt. She had been there and she had survived, reborn. The
mission she had yearned for in her girlhood fantasies was hers at last.
She had her purpose. She had direction. She was at peace with herself.

The next afternoon she began writing her letters for Colfax, just as
she had written once—so long ago—in search of a farm-training instructor for the veterans. To two neuropsychiatric institutes, a hospital, a
school, two foundations. Offering her services as a trainee nurse, technician, tester, teacher, play therapist, typist of case histories or assistant
to anyone in any job for which she was fitted in return for Coley's treatment. In a week the routine replies began trickling back. State residence
requirements three years. No opening for an intake interview for eight
months, and following that no opening for treatment, if accepted, for
another eighteen months. Fees of thirty-five dollars upward per day.
And from all of them, her desire to place her services at the disposal of
the institution commendable but unfeasible in view of the relationship.

Her sense of mission was fanned rather than dampened by discour-
agements. By this time Elwell's arrival was imminent and she counted
on him, as she must have counted on him in the back of her mind all

along, to transform the impossible into the possible. He would cut the red tape. He would exert his influence on her behalf. He would understand and help her.

4

At the beginning of August the road ahead, it had seemed to Henry, up to Elwell's second coming at the end of the month lay as straight as an arrow and as smooth as velvet. His home was in order and his only problem there, Colfax, would, he believed, soon be on the way to solution. At Sunset he had the job licked and his only problem there, the strip of land occupied by Rad and Reeve, would, he believed, soon be liquidated by flight or surrender. None of it achievable of course without sweat and strain, promotion and pressure, but in the long run the details disappear by the wayside, it's only the action that emerges from them that counts. By the end of the month he should be practically in the clear.

In a matter of hours, however, his bed of roses at home became a bed of thorns. With the discovery that Colfax had been locked in the office instead of his father's arms when the dynamite went off, Julie turned from a complaisant wife into a viper. The quarrel that had ensued, which Henry considered a family spat that would soon blow over, though perhaps he did go a little too far with it, blew up into a storm he couldn't control. After the session at Darbyton, which perhaps he should not have left her to face alone, though he thought at the time that having handled it she'd get over it, she began herself to behave in a manner that he could only interpret as absolutely batty. Julie was bent on leaving here. If he would come with her on her hegira to some as yet unspecified institution in some as yet unidentified locality, where she planned to dedicate herself to Coley and other children like him, then they might be able to make a life together. If not, she intended to divorce him.

As if this were not bad enough in the privacy of the house, where they now lived separately, meeting only at meals or in the back parlor for formal discussions, she carried it outside.

Henry received a telephone call one day at Sunset from D. C. Lacey, asking him to drop in after work. The school superintendent who conducted a year-round real estate business on the side kept his office at the academy open for Henry until almost six. After Henry had admired the new quarters and D.C. who was running on Benson Reece's slate for reelection had reiterated the axiom common to both political factions,

"Yessir, everything's going around here, everything's moving ahead," they settled down to the matter at hand.

"I don't know how to begin." D.C.'s benign forehead beamed pale mauve under the fluorescent light. "This is mighty embarrassing. Do you know that Julie's been here to see me?"

"Well, she's still on the Board of Education. I suppose she wants to catch up with the meetings she's missed."

"It's not about that. She wants to have her house appraised at its present value."

"Good idea. We've done all this remodeling on it, we better increase the fire insurance. Just don't tell old Arthur, I don't want my assessment raised."

"It's not that either. She's interested in selling. Wants to know about the market. Whether there are any potential customers around. How long it will take."

"Is that so?"

"You not thinking of leaving here, are you?"

"Oh no. No. Nothing like that."

"You going to build?"

"Well, I like the old house myself. I suppose she's got some bee in her bonnet from these magazines, one of these new-style plate-glass models."

"I see. I understand the house is hers? Or rather was, that is, she's been putting it over, hasn't she, in both your names?"

"Look D.C., you're not taking this seriously, are you? It's one of these women's whims. You ought to know. You come up with a buyer and she'll back down."

"Then she has the right to sell? I could call Maclay at the courthouse and find out for myself, but it'd just start a lot of loose talk over nothing."

"No she can't sell. There's some legal entanglement in the background that I don't want to go into now. Just play along with her. Don't upset her. She'll forget the whole thing in a week or so."

After D.C. parted from him, Henry stood on the school steps a while watching the evening traffic flow by. He wiped over the incipient jowls under his jaw. "Jesus Christ."

That night after dinner he dropped in on Harrington who was leaving next day as per plan for his refresher at Hopkins. "Now I don't say that Colfax will turn out a world-beater," Harrington warned him. "But he'll get along. A few hours after surgery he'll be aware of his surroundings. Next day he'll be looking at picture books and talking to you. Then there'll be a relapse in his toilet habits for a period and he may act sort of silly. But with a few months of retraining and rehabilitation . . . I have in mind an excellent sanitarium outside Savannah where the psychologist and therapists will work on him under my direction. And with the early start he's making . . ."

For Henry, wishfully, it was the advantage of the early start that was most persuasive. At the plantation, weren't seedlings transplanted from the seedbed as soon as they were a few inches high? And didn't they after their initial vigor droop for a while until they were reestablished in the new soil? And from then on shoot up, spread their root systems underground absorbing moisture and nutrients until they were fully developed? But if left too long in the seedbed, the plants could not be moved without damage to the roots that had grown, as grow they did up to a certain point even in a cramped environment.

And to alter the child, wasn't it obviously as true the earlier the better? Just as soon as he was old enough to stand the change? Wasn't he just the right age now?

Now that he was convinced that the condition could be corrected, Henry lost all patience with the boy in his present state. Every day that passed was to him a day lost. Every hour that fled by only entrenched Colfax deeper in his incapacities. The time was growing late. Since it had to be done, best it be done quickly. He walked about with the dewy expectancy of a pregnant woman. Soon. Soon.

Only he couldn't convince Julie. "You're out to ruin him," she charged. "There's no risk," he maintained. And there it rested, except that she was moving even as he was in the direction of an irreversible action.

Far more alarming than the call he had received from D. C. Lacey was one that came the following week from Lars Finchley. Also through the switchboard at Sunset. "Henry," Lars said, "Julie's just left my office. She raised a lot of questions. In fact, I'm quite upset. She's given me permission to go into it freely with you. Can I see you now?"

"Here? No."

"Then here. Will you drive right over?"

"I can't right now."

"I wish you would. I'm so distressed and distracted I can't give my attention to anything else."

Too bad. Henry himself was so distracted he couldn't give much attention to anything else for the remainder of the afternoon. But when he dropped into Lars' office late in the day, he found Lars on the contrary altogether calm and collected.

"Julie asked about the original deed to the Scott land. Since she was the claimant, I was under the impression that she must know about it.

No matter what I'd done, I figured that since Julie was in on it too it couldn't be all that bad. If misery loves company so do our misdeeds. But it turns out I had no company."

"Look, Lars, I'm not interested in your internal affairs. Is that what you were so distressed about?"

"That was the least of it. You think these things can happen, Henry, and just vanish into thin air? We survive our defeats. But they leave their imprint." Lars tapped his head, his craggy face corrugating. "The cortex. Another fissure, another wrinkle upon the tabula rasa with which we were born into the world. In the totality of life every flutter of an eyelash leaves its trace somewhere, adds up in some form."

"If you been drinking, Lars, will you please"—Henry glanced back at the slackly open drawer of the dusty old file case—"let me have some of it? So we can both philosophize over this together."

"I told her that I had seen the title but that I was no party to its disappearance. I was ashamed before her."

"Look, Lars, you've nothing to be ashamed of. You ought to hear these guys up in Atlanta, what they do twenty-four hours a day every day of the week. Only thing we have to be ashamed of, it was so puny. Too puny to boast of. We're a couple of pikers."

"Especially since it didn't succeed anyhow."

"OK, OK, don't rub it in. Proves my point. There's nothing to be ashamed of."

"Then she went on to the Herrera family. Seems she believes that all she has is theirs."

"Seems she believed the Scott land was hers. Even took me in. Are you going to fall for another one of her notions?"

"Henry, you're talking to me. Was Johnny Herrera the legitimate heir of Isabel Colfax?"

"There are no documents extant."

"Unless a copy of the adoption was filed with the state office of records in Atlanta."

"Who's going to think of looking there?"

"I am. If it's not there, we're right back where we are now. If it is, that creates a new situation. Of course if I don't choose to look, if I know what I know now and don't choose to look—"

"We're right back . . ."

"No we are not. But let's table that for the moment. Seems further that Julie drove down to Johnny Herrera's shack yesterday. But couldn't get up the courage to go in talk with him. Just parked there looking at the barbed-wire fence, the dogs, the pitch of the porch, the tin roof . . . But while she was there she noticed Johnny's son Laurie, the crippled one, hobbling around on his crutches with his kids at his heels. What she plans to do now is liquidate all her assets, and somehow the sight of Laurie gave her the idea that if she offers to share the proceeds with them they'll agree to it. They'll allow her half, she thinks, in view of her father's consolidation of Sunset and the price she obtained."

"I obtained! Look, Lars, I want you to keep this under your hat, but what that girl has gone through this summer with the kid, I don't mean to say she's cracking up or anything like that but right now she's so addled—"

"She wants to initiate divorce proceedings against you."

"On what grounds for Christ sake? After what I've stood from her!"

"That's what she wants from me. The grounds. She's willing to wait until after the elections. She doesn't want to injure you in any way. She'd like to make it as innocuous as possible."

"Innocuous! It'd be the biggest thing that's hit that courthouse!"

"And if you don't agree to it, she'll throw the book at you."

Oh, no. Henry melted downward in his chair. Not that. Not about my tying Colfax up that time . . .

"She'll charge you with misappropriation of her funds. Sue you for every penny you owe her."

She wasn't crazy after all. Smart. Smarter than he'd given her credit for.

"Naturally I told her I couldn't represent her. Since I'm being placed on retainer by Sunset."

"Now, Lars, you know I haven't got the power to do that."

"I understand that Elwell will be here in about ten days. You can swing it."

"You using this as a springboard for a stickup? Lars, I'm surprised."

"You should have come earlier. While I was still distressed. Now I've had time to think it over. From all angles."

Lars gazed through his gilt-printed second-story window, in which some of the lettering was scaling off, to the monument in Oglethorpe Square.

"Security is the supreme law of my generation. Born in one war, schooled in the depression, graduated into another war. We're all out to make it now while the making's good. A man can't live forever between two worlds, his principles and his practice. You commit yourself to one or the other and you don't look back.

"I committed myself to you that day in the courtroom, Henry. I've repeated it every time I've taken my family out on a cruise in that boat I bought on expectations—and we've had some good ones, down the inland waterway to Florida, up the coast from the Keys to Fort

Myers. Better than I can afford. I sold out for it, Henry. And now I want the payoff."

"You getting you payoff! All those land deals for me and Burnson."

"All the dirty work you and Purcell alias Burnson can cook up? You think I can be satisfied with that? I want the clean stuff. The corporation accounts. Sunset—and from that I can latch onto Southern Power and maybe a few crumbs from Pulp & Timber. That's my dish. I'm not ambitious like you, Henry. I haven't got the p. and v. in me for anything big. I just want to make it."

Henry knew how much it must have taken out of Lars to screw himself up to this point, and he knew that any promise he could make him was an empty one. Lars' ruddy head, ruddier in the light of the sun sinking behind the courthouse, tilted about at him inquiringly.

"I'll do my best for you, Lars." String him along. "You can depend on that."

"I will. There isn't another attorney in the county that Julie would go to. Her second cousin in Bay City, I gather, she doesn't have much confidence in. And naturally she's reluctant to pick someone out of the hat. So I've referred her to a classmate of mine in Savannah. He's away on vacation now but will be back the first of the month. In the meantime, I suggested to her that she better make sure that this is what she wants. If she still feels the same way after these few weeks have gone by, she can file for separation. I also suggested to her that she let the Herrera business slide until she has everything back in her hands."

"Good. Good. Just stall her along, I'll work it out." Henry made ready to leave, but Lars wasn't letting him go that quickly. Lars tilted back in his chair and crossed his arms behind his head.

"What brought all this on, Henry?"

With a heartfelt groan Henry sank back down again. "The boy. She wants to go chasing around the country looking for a cure. We been told there is no cure. Unless we try an operation. I'm all for it. She's against it. That's the whole story."

"Then she is," Lars bounced back forward, stricken, "on the verge?" His eyes crinkled with consternation. "We had the same thing with Grace, so afraid of the knife. What we've been through over that operation—"

"How is she?"

"Recovering. Not the same Grace of course. But she'll be able to take her children back, take over her house again. It wasn't just the operation, she let it go so long. She's been living on morphine."

Lars had never intended to tell this to anyone, but some impulse, an obscure resentment of his wife's attachment to her sister, a need for sympathy for himself, prompted him on. "It's been a nightmare. Violet flying back and forth. We've had all the kids. I'm telling you if it hadn't been for that boat this summer—you know we named her the *Grace W.?* You won't mention this to anyone?"

"No. No, I won't. About that other thing, Lars, I'll put it over. I sure as God will." They shook hands with the warmth of a pledge sealed, with the bond of an irrefrangible intimacy. The troubles with women . . .

When Henry reached home, he was too shaken to trust himself to enter. He leaned against the screendoor, his forehead pressed against the copper wiring, losing himself in the breathing silence of the interior. The house, complete in its regeneration now, afforded him no pleasure. On their return from Darbyton, seeing the mood Julie was in and anticipating an attempt by Rad to take Charles back, he had sent Charles off for the remainder of the month to the church camp at Silver Beach. He missed the greeting with which the boy always tumbled out to meet him, a cry of gladness that was near hysteria sometimes with relief. There was nothing there now for him in the house, neither son nor wife nor the conviviality of company. Julie and Coley rattling around the big rooms. A morgue. A graveyard.

"But why are you doing this to me?" he demanded of Julie after dinner in the back parlor, trying to contain his disturbance within the bounds of logic. "I can't believe you've that much against me. It's that Wolf, he put you up to all this!"

"I'm not against you. No one is. Why does it always have to be me or you? Us or them? Henry against the world? We have a common problem. We can work it out together. If you'd go along, it'll make all the difference, for you even more than for me."

She was working on her damned afghan again, crocheting the panels together—it was almost done. On this suffocating night, ominous with the rumbles of an approaching storm.

"You smell brown sugar? You smell brown sugar?" Colfax piping up at him from his feet.

"Why, it does smell like brown sugar." Julie glowing up at him from the peacock blue wool twirling through her fingers. Sniffing at the air. "Smell. Brown sugar."

He left Julie with Colfax in the back parlor—or rather, his pecky cypress den—to go running through the house shutting windows. The smell of brown sugar suffusing the air intensified to the sharpness of gunpowder. Canopied clouds, brown over the blackness of the night sky, pressed downward. Draperies puffed from the windows with the splatter of rain and the shock of thunder. Henry slammed down the last of the upstairs windows and rushed back down to the yard for the lawn furniture. In the back parlor Julie was covering Colfax with her body against the terrors of the storm.

Next morning Henry telephoned the director of Carillon Hills, the private hospital outside Savannah where Harrington had scheduled his operation on Colfax. He confirmed the date, the morning of September 5, and reserved a room for the boy for a period of six weeks to two months at eighty dollars per week, exclusive of special nursing care and extras. He deferred visiting the hospital personally for fear of being depressed by it or diverted from his purpose. A very attractive brochure was sent him in the mail, and he contented himself with it.

He made no effort either to conceal the brochure from Julie or to display it to her. If she happened to notice it on his desk at home, she said nothing. Whether she learned of the step he had taken or merely suspected it, she soon countered it with another one of her own. Worse than the letters of application she had sent all over the country, worse than her excursions to Lacey and Lars. She took the whole issue to Clement DeLavery and with no reservations whatsoever, nothing withheld, laid it bare before him.

Henry heard of it in the by now familiar manner. Clem telephoned him at Sunset in the middle of the afternoon, asking him to stop by at St. Paul's for a chat. Henry lost no time in getting over there.

"I thought I told you to stay away from her," he attacked at once when they seated themselves in one of the empty pews. "What she tell you?"

"Everything."

"What do you mean everything?"

"All of it."

Something like the shock of thunder through the curtains the other night struck painfully in Henry's chest. Clem then. After all the years he had staved it off, Clem was the repository. It was Clem's eyes that looked into his with a knowledge, an image and association that was not to be endured in any man anywhere that touched upon his existence. There was just this one little thing in his life, the harness of cord twisted through the bars of the ivory crib, the knots tied fast . . .

"You must have suffered a great deal over this."

Son of a bitch!

"The important thing for you both now, I should think, is to refrain from carrying your opposition to the point of no return."

I'll fix your wagon!

"Perhaps if you took some time off now to investigate all the several possibilities?"

The stained-glass tranquillity of the empty church, a setting Clem must have chosen as appropriate to the solemnity of their subject, contributed to Henry's rancor. For the reason that he considered the church his own, on his side. And that Clem was taking advantage by using it for intervention on behalf of Julie. Casting him, Henry, in the role of miscreant and penitent.

"Surely there's a rational way out of this. That'll be best for all three of you."

The sun-browned young cleric, his boyish crewcut sunlit a tawny brown, youthfully offering his solace and guidance Henry could regard only with a grimace of undisguised contempt.

"We have investigated. We have found out. There's only one possibility open. Everything else is in the realm of speculation. We have nothing to lose by it. He can't be of any less use to himself than he is right now. If his mind can be cleared before it's any further habituated—"

"But Henry, *Harrington*. It's an act of desperation."

"What do you know about Harrington? What do you know about this kind of ailment?"

"Well, not much."

"Then stay out of it! Stay out of my concerns! My wife and I'll settle this between us. Just you stay out of it."

Henry came out of the church in a towering passion, his flesh palpitant with rage. Julie had given him away to Clem. That was the end of Clem in his vicinity, his locality, the range he frequented, anywhere their paths might cross.

From then on Henry viewed Clem as the author of all his conflict with Julie. It was Clem who had started her off on this tack. Clem who had wrecked the peace of his home. And not only his home, everywhere he turned, in whatever direction, there was Clem with that long-jawed, foxy grin of his, blocking him off.

Even his continuing failure to obtain the strip of land that bisected Sunset he ascribed directly to Clem's machinations.

After the court hearing in which he had been so ignobly routed, he was advised by the Judge, "Anything that happens to either one of those boys now, Scott or McDowell, will be laid at your door. Whether you're to blame for it or not. Wait a while." And Lars had adamantly refused to resort to any further legal dodges. "We've made ourselves objects of ridicule and there's no disgrace, no disaster that's harder to recover from than ridicule. Those two characters are folk heroes enough now, took on one of the biggest powers in the county and won. Let it lie." So, busy otherwise, he had waited and bided his time. While Clement DeLavery took charge of the GI class.

All of a sudden he'd waked up to the significance for him of this new state of affairs. He had to contend now not with two isolated dirt farmers off in the backwash, one of them colored, but with two veterans attached to groups of some standing, meeting regularly, among whom they remained heroes of a sort. Moreover the colored class which he had hardly noticed heretofore and the white class which was being highly publicized were sponsored by advisory boards composed of leading citizens of both groups. Whereas a few weeks before a shotgun blast through a window, a fire in the night might have aroused a ripple of outrage, transient though momentarily embarrassing, now neither one of the boys could be touched without touching off a wave of active support for them. For this consolidation of their status Clem was as the first cause primarily responsible.

"What we need to do in this county," Judge Purcell declared at a Fourth of July conclave of top-secret political backers, "is change the climate of public opinion."

With this sentiment Henry heartily concurred. During the summer he did not come out openly in support of Ol' Vern and Ol' Cal but he did work behind the scenes. The main issue of the state campaign, restoration of the white primary, was conducive to race intimidation, division of the races, deterioration of relationships between colored and white. In Colfax County the rumor mills were set to grinding, leaflets were distributed in the rural districts and plans were made to approach Ozzie Higginson concerning a revival of his Klavern of the Klan with some cash and a cut on the nightshirts and paraphernalia as bait. The one element lacking in a local campaign singularly devoid of any local controversy other than apportionment of offices was the most essential —dramatization. Something to whip up a little excitement, heat it up, make it all come alive. This something Henry supplied.

"The way that damfool cousin of mine and that nigger friend of his up the track have been carrying on together is a shame and a scandal. And the most disgusting part of it, everybody's with them. And you know who's behind it all? That preacher-teacher so-called, DeLavery. And Reece is right behind him. There's the coalition you have to break up if you're to beat them out."

The process was verbally drawn up by which the two boys were first to be detached from their classes; then made pariahs of; and finally assailed in such a manner as to cause them to quit the county or be run out of it. In the process the forces aligned or identified with them were to be tarred with the same brush, isolated, silenced. None of the schemes involved Henry personally. All he had to do was sit back and watch developments.

Then overnight, or so it seemed to Henry, everything turned hind-side-to. The week he went up to Darbyton with Julie, Rad was to be expelled at the Friday night advisory board meeting and his expulsion was to be used as a lever against Reeve. On Saturday morning after he had returned from his trip, no such thing.

Marcus Hadley answered his discreet inquiries about what had happened the night before with a tirade concerning the check made out to the tile-setter when the contract particularly specified that all moneys were to be paid to Hadley & Co. Later in the day he tried to sound out Ozzie, with similar success. Ozzie was all taken up with a dollar sale he was to run next month.

"And you can tell them," Ozzie said covertly to him over his busy counter, "that the proposition they made me—you know? I can't go through with it."

Henry pretended not to understand. He was not supposed to have any knowledge of, let alone connection with, that aspect of activities. Will Royall of Fallona, the Judge's candidate for sheriff, was handling it.

"Tell them," Ozzie insisted on giving him the message, "I gave it my most serious consideration. Even got myself up one night in my old rig. But I'm way past that kind of thing. And my son would be against it. I have to stick to what's good for my business. After all," he threw in gratuitously, "Sunset don't buy no seed or feed from me."

"I know," Will Royall cracked when Henry reported Ozzie's defection to him. "He got all rigged out and took a look at himself in the mirror. In his hood and his robe and didn't get a hard on." The prospect of reviving the Klavern was discouraged by the apathy Will had encountered everywhere in the area. In Bay City where Mayor Sillens was playing both ends against the middle by backing a third candidate for governor, the board of aldermen under the pressure of the NAACP—the NAACP!—had that very day denied the Klan a permit to parade through downtown. "It would have been a shot in the arm for us, folks from here would have gone to take a look. Don't know where the hell we're going," Will groused glumly to Henry, obviously wondering whether he'd picked the right side after all.

It took Henry almost a week to piece together the information that Rad and Reeve—far from being expelled, assailed and on the skids by the end of this month—were in fact way ahead of the game. Christ Almighty, they'd captured Founders Day!

And behind it all, directing it all against him, was Clement DeLavery again.

As the end of the month approached and the date of Elwell's second coming, Henry was moved to rush through anyhow the dramatic device that had been planned to trigger off the climax of the campaign. Of course the receptive public atmosphere and the organizational preparation they had hoped for were lacking. And he had never wholly approved of the plan. It was too delicate yet too crude, too tricky yet too simple, too contrived yet too fallible, leaving too much to chance. Nevertheless he tipped Will off to go ahead with it.

Saturday evening Henry stayed safely at home with Julie. Dr. Harrington was back from Baltimore, brimming with fresh experiences. Between them they made a concerted effort to confute Julie's foolish fears with their acumen.

That same evening Betty, the seventeen-year-old divorcée who waited table at the café, took a ride out the River Road with her ex-husband, Barber Brookfield. Although the night was still young, they'd both had more than enough from a fifth that had been furnished them. At the twin mailboxes they turned off the road into the dirt track and at the cedar grove pulled up into the clearing. The few cars parked there ahead of them didn't bother them, they had been forewarned that there might be a houseful of niggers to be dealt with and possibly McDowell. They had also been forewarned of the dogs. Barber hopped over into the back and Betty pressed down on the horn, blowing it loud and long. "Call off your dogs," she shouted up the path when the porch door was opened. "My car's broke down or run out of gas." Barber uttered a vulgar noise from behind and Betty giggling, "Hush up," climbed out of the car to grope somewhat unsteadily up the dark path by herself. "Reeve Scott? This Reeve Scott's place? Reeve, will you come out and let me have some gas from your truck?"

Barber crept up the path behind Betty with his flash camera slung over his shoulder, poised to shoot. "Reeve," she called from the foot of the steps, "will you come on out and give me a hand?" Reeve appeared on the porch and Betty ran up the steps. When they met the flashbulb was to pop and she was to scream bloody murder. That was all.

Haplessly, after all the misfires Henry had already been through this month, this one had to misfire too. Lulabelle McDowell stepped out on the porch before Betty reached the top step and called down, "That you, Betty Brookfield? Come on in a while. Want to see my new baby?" Betty stepped inside and not only was Lulabelle there with her baby but Carl Maynard—Betty and Carl had once been very close and nothing appealed more to Betty than playing up to an old flame with lots and lots of flirtation. Also Reverend DeLavery, Miss Thurlow, Harold

Sanderlee with his guitar and Bessie Sanderlee with one of her chiffon cakes. Betty being a sociable soul joined them all in a round of ginger beer. Barber growing impatient outside knocked at the door. He was likewise invited in. Thus Betty and her ex spent all evening at a planning committee meeting of the Founders Day Barbecue Benefit and had themselves a jamboree.

All day Sunday Henry expected to hear from some quarter that the hue and cry had been raised. Hearing nothing of the kind—silence, utter silence—he threw caution to the wind and called Will in the evening. "You heard anything," he circumspectly asked Will, "about some girl around here getting lost in the woods last night and running into some nigger who made indecent overtures to her? A pass at her? Something like? Is there any truth to this?" "Well," Will answered him just as circumspectly, "ain't nothin' been developed yet." They were waiting for the pictures then. That, it seemed to Henry, was being just a little too excessively unprecipitous.

The photographs were delivered to him by Will next night at a prearranged spot on the road. Henry examined them under Will's searchlight. Lulabelle McDowell with her baby, Betty on one side of her and Reeve on the other. "What the hell is this?"

Acridly Will related to him the tale of the evening.

"Howcome they let Barber take pictures then?"

"Said he wanted to snap the baby."

"Oh boy."

At the fireplace vivaciously chatting Vivian Thurlow and towering over her, foxily grinning, who else but Clement DeLavery?

"Deerhead." Laconically Will pointed to the antlered head above them. "Said he wanted a shot of the deerhead."

"Jesus Lord," Henry groaned, "what's going on in this county! Stuff like this and nobody gives a shit."

He stowed the envelope of pictures into his glove compartment and thought no more of them for the time being. Chalmer Coombs all over! Flubbed the dub! Snafu! After switching from one side of the political fence to the other he was rewarded with the selfsame breed of bunglers. Drips! "These are no damn good to me."

"Barber wants his fifty bucks."

Henry made an appropriate rejoinder.

The net result of the intrigue by which Reeve and Rad with him were to be hounded from the county or to flee it gladly was baby pictures. The net result of his and Harrington's argument with Julie was a definite appointment made by her with the Savannah lawyer Lars had mentioned to her, his secretary squeezing in an hour for her on the first day he'd be available, September 2, next week.

When Henry came back on Monday night from his rendezvous with Will, he stomped up and down his house, shouting and banging around furniture. He knew from the start what was right! He knew what had to be done! Then why did everybody have to combine to trip him up? Why did everybody have to stop him? He knew! Julie locked herself and Colfax in her room. Henry battered at the door. Dashed downstairs to the rack of rifles resuscitated by Julie from the belongings of Isabel Colfax.

The rifles pointed black-fingered upward against the white wall at the rear of the hall. Henry pulled up one of the guns by the barrel and held it stock up as if about to smash down over the heads of all his enemies, beat them to a pulp. He put the rifle back in the rack, appalled by it, and remounted the stairs.

"Julie." He twisted at the knob of her door. "Together we make sense. Without each other we're nothing." She didn't open up.

Thus matters stood on the eve of Elwell's arrival.

Henry had only one hope left. Elwell himself. Instead of dreading the man, he was almost by now looking forward to him. Hoping as Julie did to find in him a deliverer, a *deus ex machina* dropped down from the skies who would change the tide of fortune. Once before Elwell had straightened Julie out. Once before Elwell had recognized his worth and backed him up on the job. Elwell would save the day.

5

In the past six months Elwell had traveled over eighteen countries, covering four continents; and over some part of twenty-six rivers, many of them among the longest in the world, by outrigger canoe, sampan, barge, paddlewheel, steamboat, biplane, helicopter, and DC-3. He had with him a team of twenty-odd persons: civil, electrical, mechanical and sanitary engineers; hydrographer, topographer, and geologist; agronomist, conservationist, and ecologist; economist, sociologist, and publicist; physician, nurse, three secretaries, two interpreters and a general factotum or troubleshooter. The team spent most of its time in the field, preparing background studies on the feasibility, scope and possible sites of the multiple-purpose dam systems in which Elwell was so vitally interested. It was the team's task to map out projects that would serve to drain jungles, irrigate deserts, create storage reservoirs the size of inland seas, divert the flow of watercourses by excavation through mountain barriers if necessary, supply hydroelectric power—making vast areas of the earth arable, habitable, and profitable.

"Lenin only wanted to electrify the Soviet Union," Tompy Thompson, the chief engineer, originated the joke, "Elwell wants to electrify the world." And Dr. Wade, the conservationist, the same Wade who had had the good luck to make himself known to Elwell on the Sunset inspection tour last winter, added his saving bit of skepticism, "A poseur of course. But what a poseur. Like Churchill." When such *lèse-majesté* reached Elwell's ears, he was more amused than affronted.

Elwell spent his time largely in the capital cities. It was his task to negotiate with the heads of government for a commitment of funds which, in addition to funds he was to help them obtain from his own government, would finance the proposed projects over a period of years. He was also concerned with laying the groundwork for organization of Acme investment capital around such raw material resources and products as were to be developed in the reclaimed regions. Once again he was wedding, in the long-time formula of his success, public expenditure with private gain.

Thus *The Elwell Plan* moved into its initial phase, an operation of a magnitude beyond even his original estimate of it, so far-flung in location and implication that it would take the remainder of his life to consummate it. This was to be the sole function and object of his summit years, the culminating achievement of his existence, the epic of the epoch. "All we are given," his friend Hartley Hunt had once said, "is an empty canvas. The problem, goddamit, is how to fill it." Better than you did, Hartley. Better than you.

But just as his team wrestled throughout its studies with almost insurmountable obstacles of terrain, water volume, and velocity, lack of transport and labor skills, Elwell encountered in the seats of government conditions no less difficult. Collapsing colonial empires. Crumbling feudal oligarchies. Land reform movements on the march. Guerrilla leaders fighting in the wake of their war with the Japanese for the postwar leadership of their nations. "All Asians are either corrupt or Communist," a French marshal complained to Elwell. "Of the two I prefer the former." Along the Hwang Ho, the Irrawaddy, and the Mekong, National Liberation Front Armies now become People's Front Governments were in occupation. In India, where the nationwide demand for independence from Britain brought in its train demands for freedom from endogenous class and religious domination, the valleys of the Brahmaputra, and the Ganges on the east, the Indus on the west—locales of future Pakistan—were riven by bitter internecine riots. The Middle East —here Elwell nursed a fond association with the Tigris and Euphrates of ancient Mesopotamia, the Jordan of Palestine—was a cauldron of boiling oil, swirling with Anglo-Franco-Sovio-American rivalries, rival factions striving for hegemony, revolutionary parties striving for national autonomy and Jewish-Arab hostilities thrown in for seasoning. Even in Africa, on the Nile and the Niger, the Zambezi, the Limpopo, the Congo, signs of restlessness among the natives. Everywhere a volcanic upsurge in which the outer crust was moved by the desire of nations for self-government and the inner core by the desire of the populace for possession of the soil they worked. What troubled Elwell most was the frequency with which he discovered the right people on the wrong side. Poets and professors aligned with the peasantry against Western interests. Sons of noble families, known to him from his prewar days, looked at him with the sardonic eyes of Hartley Hunt on a Paris street corner.

Still, pounds of schematic diagrams accumulated. Draft agreements were concluded. Concessions were tentatively lined up. The allocation of contracts to the American construction companies who would eventually build the dams was discussed. *The Elwell Plan* was wanted all right, though only too often on the other fellow's terms!

Elwell hurried through the last stretch of his trek, which took him from the pampas of Paraguay to the wilderness of the Canadian northwest. In the middle of it he was annoyed by a radiogram from his father-in-law, Howard Herron, requesting Thompson's immediate return for consultation over some engineering problem he was having with a pet project of his on the estate. Elwell himself flew back to the States a few weeks later.

First in New York his law firm, Cudahy & Gates; then in Washington his liaison with the State Department and the White House, Douglas Gilmore; and afterward, most important, at Heron's Nest, Howard Herron, chairman of the board of Acme Life Insurance—all said no. None of them had the authority to turn him down, no one had the temerity to reject him, but *The Elwell Plan* was out. Someday perhaps. Not now. He had not mistaken the need of the age but he had miscalculated its direction, and the proof of this was borne out not only by the trend of United States foreign policy but by the evidence of his own alarmed dispatches. There were forces on the loose in the world today that threatened alike the country's security and the company's securities; and that must be combatted wherever they manifested themselves, in whatever form.

His energies were required now, at once, without delay, for another purpose, as large in dimension and as challenging: evaluation of the Communist menace on a global scale and, concomitantly, reorganization of Acme investment policy around the industrial requirements of a long-term war perspective, cold and/or hot.

This new prospect did not appeal to Elwell as much as it should have, probably, as his wife Marion privately observed, because he did not invent it. And for other reasons as well, not the least among them the taunting ghost of Hartley Hunt. Hunt's grease-penciled last testament hung before Elwell like the disembodied grin of the Cheshire cat. Carnivore. Money-grubber in the marketplace. Whoremonger of the world. *Pimp it well, Flip.*

More than once before in his career Elwell had been forced to scrap a cherished project. He had gone on to the next thing next day just as he would eradicate one love affair with another, immersing himself in the ardor of a fresh experience. But this time he was loath to let go. He went through the motions of calling a conference of experts in various fields, military, scientific, industrial, and political, for the last day of August at Heron's Nest; but did not cancel his scheduled visit to Sunset Hill the day before. He acknowledged the necessity of what lay ahead, but clung to his choice. The months and miles that lay behind were still too much with him. Constituting for himself and his team the foundation of a great endeavor? Or the memory of a fantastic junket?

While his guests were arriving at the Nest for the three-day conference he had called, to begin next day, Elwell did what he always did when he hit a blind spot: went on location. It was a sentimental journey, this afternoon of his at Sunset. Back to the beginning, back to the place where, during his gestation of *The Elwell Plan*, he so vividly saw in the turbid brown waters of the Ocachee its embodiment and prototype.

The journey was also at this critical juncture of his destiny a search for an answer. Through some occult chemistry, whenever in a nebulous state of mind he managed to escape the pressures of the empyrean atmosphere in which he dwelt by transferring himself bodily to some ordinary environment and giving himself up to it, whether it be tenement roof, mine pit, factory or, as in this instance, plantation, his ideas would begin to condense, solidify, regroup. His way out of the fog in which he was drifting, lost, would of itself reveal itself. It was in some such mood last winter that he had first gone to Sunset. It was in this mood—not as he had originally planned it, in happy conclusion of the first episode—that he went now, nostalgic and seeking.

This time Elwell was driven directly without escort or fanfare from the airstrip to Sunset. He stepped from his car head jutting forth, heavy shouldered, spare of frame. Against his mahogany tan, his flying black brows and scowling mouth with its cruel dip, like the slit beak of an eagle, appeared both less prominent than they had with his winter skin and more integral with his physiognomy. In place of black Homburg and topcoat he wore a sola pith helmet and a pale pongee outfit hand-embroidered by eight-year-old girls in a Hong Kong loft. He had dozens of these pongees, very cool, very practical, very pukka sahib.

Henry received him, very much in command of himself. "If you'd like, Mr. Elwell, you can send your car back to town and have it pick you up there later. I got my boat anchored here, we can go by river after we're through and my wife'll meet us at the dockside."

"Splendid."

The plantation was thriving. New blacktop on the River Road continued through the gate up to the main buildings. "County's widened it all out for us," Henry said and pointed with his field glasses toward the tip of the island. "See that green spot down there? Greener than all the rest? That's reclaimed swampland. Convict gang hired out to us by the warden from the stockade. Had a lot of trouble with them, regular savages, nothing but animals. But they doing the job."

With Vail at his side, a faithful Collie dog now, endorsing him, Henry exhibited the busy processing room of the freezer plant, the refrigerant system, the chill room banked with racks. "Operating three shifts at the peak of the season, profit's surpassed all last year earnings." In the air-conditioned office he and Vail laid out their plans for plant expansion. "This freezer industry's been on the make since before the war, now watch it boom. And not just produce. Fried chicken, shrimp, gumbo—look at here." Henry unrolled an artist's sketch of a Geechee girl toting a basket on her head against a blazing sunset background. "How you like that? Sex and food. Lincoln freed the niggers, now we'll free the ladies."

Under Elwell's prodding Henry did not this time deny that he was having a problem keeping the cost of his field labor down. "I'll bring in migrants from outside if I have to. Import 'em by the truckload and then when we're through with 'em, *out!* I don't have to take anything from anybody around here. Come on with me, there's something new; you'll like this."

Henry led the way to a small white building with an adjoining greenhouse, an experimental substation of the state department of agriculture, established here on the grounds at Oliver Spenser's invitation. In the laboratory a studious middle-aged technician was testing snapbeans for disease resistance. "These are Logans." Henry motioned Elwell over to the earth-filled growing table. "Best freezing strain that's been developed. Good appearance—dark green, long pods. Bloom by September, ready to pick first of October. Cross between Stringless Black Valentine and a variety of U.S. No. 5 Refugee, that right, Prof?" He took the sponge from the technician and a multi-needled perforator. The perforator he dipped into a jar of bacterial solution. "These here plants produce about twenty-five marketable pods to every one put out by the Tendergreens we were growing here before. There . . ."

Placing the bacteria-tipped perforator over each of the primary leaves of a vigorous plant and the sponge beneath, Henry plunged down through one leaf-center after another. "We'll see now how long this'll stand up before it breaks down." He returned the instruments to the technician and gave him a friendly punch on the shoulder. "Can you imagine," he confided to Elwell, with the pathos of one who has everything at his fingertips and all performing for him, "I envy this guy? Nothing in the world on his mind but breeding the perfect blight-resistant snapbean. No, no, don't give me credit for any of this. It's all due to Spenser." He indicated Spenser supervising some pottings in the greenhouse. "It's his doing. Spenser, take a bow."

Elwell was as much impressed with the progress of the man as he was with that of the plantation. He was pleased with himself for having insisted on keeping Henry last winter over Vail's objection. Reassured of his own instinct. You select your seed, stimulate, cultivate, cross-pollinate and suddenly, magically, it's there, begotten. Henry was compacter of build than he remembered, more decisive in his movements, cohesive with the mastery of a job which he was even now outgrowing. His brush of dark hair, clipped high over his temples, tapered to a point on his forehead; his cheeks sheared down to a hard jawline; his mouth, clamped tight, bore the stamp of endurance. Yet his eyes warm brown, quick with intimacy, held one like a charm.

While Henry commandeered a jeep to take them down to the riverside dike where his boat was docked at the landing, Elwell rendered his considered judgment to Vail in parting.

"Now that you're planning to expand the plant, you'll have to expand the property. When do you begin to purchase?"

Vail glanced sharply at Henry who, poker-faced, took the wheel from the driver. Unperturbed he held open the jeep door for Elwell. "There's nothing we'd like better, Mr. Elwell," Henry said. "Only it's easier said than done. All that across the River Road belongs to the Arcady Bank and they're holding onto it. Up the road to town there's mostly these little old homeplaces belongs to colored and they're holding on too. None of it's for sale, and you know why? All account of that one neck of land that cuts through here."

He passed his field glasses to Elwell and Elwell stood up in the jeep with them, adjusting the lens. He rotated into focus the ragtag strip of wood and field. "But isn't that the same— I thought I spoke to you about it months ago!"

"It is and you did. Every property holder on this road is waiting on us to offer those two guys anywhere from twenty thousand up. They all got the idea that the potential value of what they have is ten times what it is now, and that Acme's out to grab it all away from them. A second invasion of the Yankees."

"I told you," Elwell said frostily, "that it must be eliminated. If you can't handle this one small item . . . Vail . . ."

"He's tried," Vail interposed hastily. "There isn't anyone we'd have sent down here that could have tried any harder or done any better."

"Tried is immaterial. The road to oblivion is paved with glorious efforts. And discarded strains of snapbean. Either you can put this over, Warren, or you can't."

"It's quite a story," Henry said, conveying with his intimacy of eye an enigmatic significance. "And it's not finished yet. The last chapter is still to be written. While we're on the river I'll tell you."

"I have never been especially interested in explanations. Or hypothetical endings."

"You'll be interested in this one. Good luck, Vail."

It was Henry who needed the luck, but Vail gazing after the jeep as it jolted off didn't bother to wish it. He had absolute faith in Henry's ability to overcome anything.

From the height of the dike they descended the steeply sloping slip to the landing. Elwell holding to the rail braced his bare-toed feet in thonged sandals against the crossbars to keep from sliding—always so much easier for him to climb up mountains than down. Henry, slowed up behind him, refrained from offering a helping hand. He jumped ahead of Elwell into the cockpit of his trim white runabout and with his boathook brought it athwart the landing, holding the bobbing boat steady until Elwell settled into the cushioned seat.

Looking up at the grey concrete rampart of the dike, streaked with freshly mended fissures, Henry said moodily, "Man is rock. Woman is water. And water can wear away stone. You have to keep reinforcing." He cast off, using his boathook as a pole. "River's silting up all through here. Engineers down last month say it needs dredging all the way from Arcady into the sound. Had a ten-foot tide last May, another half-foot we'd have been underwater."

Elegantly virile in his embroidery-collared pongee, Elwell lifted his head and crossed his legs, sandal dangling from his corded mahogany foot. His scowl creased one corner of his mouth lower than the other, the corner into which he generally fitted his pipestem. Henry concentrated on piloting the boat through the mudbanks into the channel. Starting up the motor, he said nothing further until they approached the brush-tangled barrow that marked the intersection of the Scott-Mc-Dowell land.

"There it is." He throttled down. "Look at it. You can't dicker with folks like that. They're like those Russians. You got to drop a bomb on 'em."

Elwell showed a flicker of interest, his head in white pith helmet turning shoreward. "Why do you say that?"

"Look at that dike of theirs. Nothing but a heap of earth, logs, and ballast rock. Other night they were up all night in a rain squall, sandbagging it. One of these days a crack'll open up. And that sluice gate, one good shove and the water'd shoot through."

"Don't underestimate the Russians," Elwell settled back, testily. "They have some tremendous hydraulic projects afoot. Down at Dnepropetrovsk, I've seen photographs of their layout plans. They can irrigate the steppes. Make Siberia the land of tomorrow. As soon as they recover from their war losses."

"Then I should think," Henry said, "that the time to hit them is now. I can tell you that from my own experience."

Elwell took his pipe out, relaxing, and packed it from his pouch. His frown softened, with that changeling light that could transform his face to a prep school boy's, mordant and mischievous. He fitted his straight-stemmed pipe into its pocket in the lower corner of his mouth and elaborately looked over both shoulders and up and down the luminescent water shrouded with boughs, a million miles from nowhere.

"I don't see any Russians."

"Then listen to this." Henry, not taking the most direct route back, steered through a slough of swampland, kneed cypress, and bulbous-trunked tupelo growing into the stream. "I believe and I always have believed, Mr. Elwell, that the only sure way to vacate that piece of land is by force. You got to go in shooting. Now I could do that. Or have someone do it for me. The only drawback there is that the knowledge of my part in it would rest with another person. Either way I could get them out of there and get away with it too, if one of them wasn't a white boy. That's the catch. Even so, I could risk it and ride out the fuss."

Elwell withdrew his pipe. "Are you asking for my permission?"

"No, Mr. Elwell, I am not. I'm just as opposed to the use of violence as you are. I could do it and get shed of them and their land would sooner or later be acquired by Sunset and the slate would be wiped clean. Including me. I'd be out of a job. Everything I've built up would go on a-building, but I'd be out of the picture. Beat it. Skiddoo."

"Precisely." Elwell took off his glasses, blew on them, accepted a tissue from the box Henry pulled out for him from the underseat locker and wiped. "I appreciate the dilemma. Continue."

"In any case, six months ago it could have been managed. But now? I wonder. I've tried every other tactic in the book. Money. The law. Pressure. Propaganda. Even a little frameup. And every time I touch them, they multiply. Those two buggers—got no more sense than to pound sand into a rathole and hardly enough for that—started off with nothing. Then they paired up against me. Last spring when their corn crop was about to be washed out, they blew ditches through their fields and when I sent the sheriff out on a charge of breach of peace, they had a houseful of colored folks waiting and they cowed him. I took Julie's claim to that nigger boy's land into court—you recall she said it was hers?—and he got the Mayor of Bay City to prove it was legally bought by the Scott family years ago and the cracker-boy stood up in court with papers to back him up on it. They carried the day and most of the court with them."

"The question of the century." Elwell puffed at his pipe, entertained. "*Whose land is it?*"

"Before I go any deeper into this, would you care to fish? Shoot?"

Henry thumbed toward tackle, nets, and bird gun in waterproof casing stowed aft. "Wild turkey, dove, quail, lots of small game around. Of course it's out of season but no one'll stop you. River's loaded with bream, stripers, cat and crappie, and down below here in the cuts and inlets there's grouper, drum, crevalle jack, channel bass. Couple of youngsters a while back hooked a fifty-pound tarpon with broke-back minnow for bait. Didn't have a gaff aboard so they landed it with a paddle."

"You may if you like. I'm more interested in the other game."

"I thought you would be. Now they're both going to school on the GI Bill, some sort of farm-training course if you please, milking the taxpayers. And both classes, all veterans, are lined up solid with them. They haven't got the capital, they haven't got the equipment to develop a hill of beans, but do you know what those two have put all the others up to now? White and colored together? Buying a tractor! Organizing a co-operative to buy a tractor."

"Here?" Elwell looked up and down the banks: the boat was throatily chugging now through marshland, reeds high overhead interspersed with wild rice, broad-leafed and as tall as corn. "Here too?"

"They're throwing a benefit for it about two weeks from now and they got almost every leading citizen in town and folks here and there all over the county helping them do it."

Henry slid open the locker again and removed from it an oilskin-wrapped packet. He handed it to Elwell. Elwell unknotted the ties, his fingers awkward with it. Henry reached over and with one hand undid them. "Trick I learned from a one-armed man."

Blue-bound folder, mimeographed, detailing the proposed purchase of the tractor. Several fliers, all mimeographed, bannered across the top, *BENEFIT BULLETIN*. A "Draft Constitution and By-Laws" commencing with a preamble that restated the four freedoms of the Atlantic Charter.

"Are you lost?" Elwell glanced up from his amused reading of the preamble to find Henry nosing through creeks that wound changelessly one into another. "Or are you looking for something?"

"You can get lost here sure enough. Old rafters on the river used to say they could hear a conversation forty miles off downstream, two miles cross-country. I thought you might like to see those two birds with your own eyes. They're usually out here fishing this time of day."

"Indeed I would. They didn't think this up all by themselves, did they?"

"You bet your boots they didn't. They got this preacher behind them, my own preacher! Got a bad background. Was mixed up with a union once and jailed for it. Told us that himself his first interview with the vestry. We didn't think anything of it at the time, it all seemed so remote. Take a look in the manila envelope. The picture with the deerhead. I'm having copies of all this made."

Elwell inched the photograph out of the manila envelope. Young man tall under the deerhead, standing in semi-profile, elbow on mantel, at ease, laughing down toward the colored girl who chatted vivaciously up at him from behind her typewriter on the table. There was something about it, in the gloss of blacks and whites and shades between, that electrified, shocked. Too frank and too free.

"Shocks the pants off me," Henry said, "every time I look at it. If there is any doubt anywhere that this is a Communistic experiment that preacher fella has everyone involved in, there's the answer. I've talked with Dan Garner about it and we've tipped off the FBI office in Bay City to investigate."

"I must admit it does look suspicious." Elwell reinserted the photograph into the envelope. "Is this your last chapter?"

"Only half of it. Right after that court hearing it became apparent to me that in order to get hold of that lousy stinking little hunk of dirt, we were going to have to turn out the whole present government of this county. Follow me?"

"Very clearly."

"I lined up on the q.t. with the opposition faction. Now I don't know what you think of Ol' Cal Hubbard, probably not much."

Elwell snorted.

"Right. But like him or not he's going to be next governor of this state. And Dan Garner will be reelected congressman from this district. He's running unopposed but he has Hubbard's commitment to appoint him senator when Wes Ross resigns in December, and he's anxious to deliver the vote from here."

"Ross is resigning? I *have* been out of touch."

"Old age has caught up with him, that's the word. And in Colfax County I am going to be chairman of the Board of County Commissioners. With my own sheriff, school superintendent, members of the grand jury, the works.

"In about three months, Mr. Elwell, that strip of land will be under condemnation proceedings. For a good cause. The colored fishermen around here have no waterfront facilities for their boats. We'll pass a bill to build it for them back there on the riverside with the Scott-McDowell properties as access to it. In about six months it'll be plain that the county hasn't the money—and it doesn't—to build that kind of facility. Then Sunset will take the property off our hands."

"Did you think all this up by yourself?"

"No," Henry said honestly. "Julie's father did. That's how he snatched Sunset Point. It's in the tradition."

"All this if you win."

"We'll win. And there are other advantages. We'll be in a position then to pick up whatever property we want at a reasonable price. As a matter of fact, there's a Yankee been speculating around here, Burnson, cornering all the good buys around. My lawyer represents him . . . and I think it would be a good idea, incidentally, for Sunset to retain this lawyer—"

"Are you in on this deal?"

Henry's hands froze to the wheel. "Mr. Elwell," he said quietly, giving him the knife, letting him have it, "you must realize that my wife sold Sunset to Acme for thirty-five thousand dollars and it's now worth about two hundred and fifty thousand. This is public knowledge. It's also well known that the taxes have not been proportionately raised. There's been some talk . . ."

"I'd be in on it," Elwell said curtly, "if I were you. Though of course I'm not you."

"If I had any intention, Mr. Elwell, of dealing myself in on anything," Henry said, "it wouldn't be for peanuts." Though it was. It was. "While I was up in Atlanta this summer I had opportunity to match myself with some of these men in the General Assembly, and I have as much on the ball as any of them. And I know what this state needs. More Sunset. More Acme. More outside money coming in to modernize and industrialize us. Ol' Cal may be a mental has-been, but he has some young heads with him now who are looking to the future. We can shelve the dead wood. Next election I'd like to run for state senate. With the right backing I could be lieutenant governor, go to Congress. Make Julie happy. She's limited here."

"First win this one."

The estuary was so divided here that whether they moved north, east, south, or even west at some points, they passed in a matter of minutes through the vegetation of fresh-water, brackish, and salt-water marsh. Through islands dense with spartina and the spartina alive with grasshoppers, the mud with nematodes, the water with algae, the bottoms with detritus which decomposing fed marine life; and upward, at the throaty throb of the boat, into the sky overhead the flight of heron, crane, spoonbill. And between islands of high sand ridges, white-duned, the nesting place of thousands of gull, royal tern, the secretive pelican. And islands luxuriant with cassina, nodding sunshades of palms, shaggy-armed oak. The many-mouthed Ocachee. Archetype and prototype.

Henry sped up Captain's Cut between Campion Hummock and Little Uchee. Around the bend in a deep slit of bay, a favorite fishing ground of theirs, he came upon the two in their inboard motor bateau: Reeve sitting astride the stern, Rad standing astride the flat bottom. Both wore only battered hats and rolled-up dungarees. They were bait-casting.

"My own blood-kin," Henry said to Elwell. "I'm raising his oldest boy. Say Rad," he called across the water, "what you catching?"

"Don't come in here with that runabout! You'll scare 'em off."

Henry forged into the bay toward Rad, churning up waves that rocked the smaller boat.

"Stand back!"

Henry cut his motor and drifted up alongside. "What you got there?"

Neither of the men replied, merely staring at Henry and his passenger. Rad reeled in, rebaited with small shrimp from his pail.

"If you worried about Charles, Rad, he's at Silver Beach Camp now. Doing fine. Y'ought to see how he's growing."

"If Charles wants for me to see him," Rad said and turning his back swung his line out, "he knows where I am."

The boats were parting and Henry reached with his boathook into the bateau bringing them smack together again.

"This Rad McDowell, Mr. Elwell, the boy I was telling you about. Rad, take your hat off to Mr. Elwell, a director of my outfit and one of the biggest men there is in this day's world."

Rad lifted his hand in an offhand salute. Elwell nodded distantly. Henry ignored Reeve, looking through him as if he were invisible. Reeve ignored them all.

"Mind if I drop a line?" Henry asked.

"It's a free country," Rad replied.

"You after something in particular down there?"

"Big old bull redfish," Rad said, more amiably, peering down into the water. "If you ain't chased it away. Must be all of eighteen pounds."

"And you expect to catch it with shrimp heads?"

"Got as good a chance as the next fella. Just you stay off my anchorage."

Henry reached back into his gear, selected a six-ounce rod, attached a reel of nine-thread line and strung it through, sorted through his tackle box of spoons, feathered jigs and plugs. "Give it a run for fifteen minutes or so, huh?" he said to Elwell. "Julie won't be meeting us till after five-thirty. Try it."

"Thank you, no. I'd much prefer to watch you."

Henry let his line out and, trolling, held the rod between his knees while he handled the boat. They circled around the bay back to the bateau again. Henry threw over an eel he'd caught. "Something for your supper." Second time around, Rad motioned him in closer.

"Hear you're getting to be a pretty big shot yourself, Cousin Henry," he said, deadpan, and reaching over into the runabout with his paddle held the two boats parallel. "In politics and all."

"I presume I can count on your support?"

"I don't know about that. But I got a slogan for you."

"Sure enough?"

"Every farmer an owner."

Henry winked at Elwell: You see what I'm up against? "Don't go away so soon." He gripped Rad's paddle. "I got a proposition for you. You all want to be on your own so much, how about selling us everything you produce that we can use? Of course it'll have to be graded out. What do you say?"

"All depends on the price you pay. We been talking about leasing us a truck next season and shipping direct to market."

Henry nudged Elwell: You see how far they've gone? "Was that your notion or DeLavery's?"

"It was mine," Reeve said without turning from his backward perch on the stern.

Henry let go the oar and fished for a while in silence. He confined himself to the vicinity of the bateau, trolling in narrowing orbits around it. Sedulously Rad and Reeve continued their casting. Suddenly all three fishermen turned startled heads toward one another and bent close to the water, listening.

"Ssssh!"

"Sh sh sh . . ."

Henry stooped overside, ear down, awed, motioning Elwell down with him. A murmur, a rustle rose eerily from the water. Spine-tingling. Scalp-crawling. Elwell pulled back. "What is it?"

"Ssssh."

"My God, there must be a whole school of drum down there," Henry whispered. The sound evaporated in the air. Ceased altogether. "They say the Indians around here used to tell a spooky story about sweet singing from underwater."

As Henry finished speaking, his boat shot forward across the bow of the bateau. "Cut your lines!" he yelled. "You got your lines fouled with mine."

"We got him! We got him!" Rad was reeling in furiously.

The fish broke water in a shimmering arc, coppery red.

"We got him!"

Henry threw anchor overboard and began reeling in as furiously. "Cut loose, cut loose, you fools!"

The runabout spun madly, banged up against the bateau all but swamping it. The two boats careened together down the current, pulled forward by their tangled lines; and, dragged by their anchors, clashed again.

For a moment, in a dizzy crisscross of movements, Elwell, jarred, saw himself being spilled into the water, being discovered clinging ignominiously to splintered boards in this company, in this unlikely spot. Or, more degrading still, submerging here, sinking, he and all the labyrinthine layers of his life, he who had only lately sailed the Yangtze Kiang and the Orinoco, who had flown through blizzards in the Himalayas and a lightning storm in the Alps, who dealt with profit curves and hydrographic profiles, government policy, and the translation of the measured syllables of Latin verse into the accented meters of English—all this, all the convolute layers of himself and all the blazing streamers, all the unlived portion yet to be of his so well-starred fortune, all to be sucked under. Ludicrously, drowned like a cub scout on his first canoe outing . . .

An able swimmer, the newscasters announced over every radio in the land, *and not far from shore* . . .

"You crazy?" Henry shouted at the bateau and dropping his rod started hauling in line hand over hand. When the line became too taut, slipping wetly away from him, he began winding it over his hand, winding till he was cheek by jowl with the plunging bateau again. Drenched figures. Astonished whites of eyes.

Whipping out his knife, Henry slashed Rad's line short, and, with the large part of it entwined in his own line, hauled away free.

Panting, his cheeks dripping with sweat, brine, or tears, he sank back into his seat and began to play the fish. When he scooped it in with his dip net, the tackle was so knotted together, a hook in the mouth and another in the palpitant gill, that it was impossible to tell who had made the first strike.

"Gamey devil." Elwell unfastened the frogs of his soaked pongee jacket.

The fish lashed about, red-streaked and fantailed, flipflopping in the net. "No more'n fifteen pounds though," Henry said. "Who'd a-thought anything that light would put up such a fight?"

The fish jumped from the bottom of the boat to the gunnels, carrying the net in which it was snarled. It jumped again and yet again, thumping, gasping, twisting, flopping, and jumping once more, its gills opening like mouths.

"I'd clobber it," Henry said, "but it'd lose that pretty red shine before we could get it to ice. Too bad I didn't bring a pail along to keep it in water."

Henry's hand, unwound from the line, was puffed white over lacerations.

The spray flew as they sped over the sound into the sunset. Coming in with the homebound shrimp boats flying pennants from their masts, nets aloft.

"Do you suppose she'll still be waiting?"

"She'll be waiting. There's no one likes more to hang around a shrimp dock than Julie does. That's where I first met her."

Homeward homeward. Curiously light and liberated, the pongee riffling over his crossed thighs, his jacket open over his sun-blackened chest, Elwell lounged among the cushions. Overcome with the sensation that had been his that first time on the road to Arcady. I have been here before. This land of islands and almost-islands.

> *Paene insularum, Sirmio, insularumque*
> *Ocella, quiscumque* . . .

Catullus home from the dust of foreign strands to his country retreat on a littoral such as this. Homeward from his own far voyagings, spartina of salt-water marsh and mangrove swamp slipping back into the past, white dunes and coral reef.

> O Sirmio, star of isles and headlands
> That infinite sea and limpid landpools
> Bear on the breast of Neptune's twofold godhead,
> Now gladly do I once more behold thee,
> Enthralled—how remote from me lie Thynia
> And the Bithynian plain—that sound I see thee.
>
> What blessing more welcome than when carefree
> The mind rests from toil, the soul forgets grief,
> When worn with wandering we return to home-gods
> And sleep on the bed we oft have longed for?
> Here's solace enough for so much travail.
> All hail, O charming islet and rejoice, joy
> Ye Lydian ripples, ring ye laughters
> That lurk in the nooks and crannies of my house!

She was waiting for them on the ramshackle pier, flame clouds bannering the sky over her and splashing beneath her in the black waters below, antique warehouses and tattered shrimp factories merging in a rosy golden haze behind her. Skirts blowing, hair blowing.

Attendant nymph, votive deity of the region—such extravagances of fancy Elwell was wont to afford himself, with indulgence for what was archaic and absurd in them, during his rare moments of respite. His words were already forming toward her across the water, contrapuntal with the duality of meaning that had run like a fugue through their letters. "Ocella. Literally little eye. Nipple. Center of the globe. I've never been quite satisfied with the translation. Can you help me?"

While Henry, unnoticed, coughed at the mucus that clogged his throat, strangling with consternation. He'd reached the man, he'd reached through to him, he was coming back in a blaze of glory. And Julie . . . Julie had outmoved him again.

Ocella, Elwell pronounced it as they slid toward her. Leaning on Henry's shoulder and grasping-clasping the hand she dipped down to him he spanned the gap from boat to pier. In delight he tipped up the chin of her little son beside her.

"What a perfectly beautiful child," Elwell said.

6

"Sounds sticky," Marion said.

"She's quite sincere about it. A perfectly charming young woman determined to throw overboard her whole life up to now and whatever future it may contain for her, her very identity, in order to assume a role of virtual anonymity, in a sphere largely inhabited by defectives of one sort or another. Chuck everything . . ."

"Are you sure she isn't a little bit disturbed herself?"

Elwell opened the champagne-curtained French door of his wife's sitting room a little wider to the outer darkness of the balcony. From one of the bungalows where the musicians Marion had invited to entertain his conference guests were housed, an oboe bleated tentatively, tuning up, over the faint lapping of water on the shore. Out in the harbor the crimson eye of a barge winked a warning to late incoming boats—it had been engaged to remove the underwater barriers his father-in-law had had installed during a submarine scare in 1942 when a tanker had blown up, or had been blown up, somewhere near here. Howard was now convinced that there was no further danger to him and his stronghold from invasion by German submarines. The channel—deep enough to accommodate at one time the Morgans' succession of *Corsairs*, the Astors' *Nourmahal*, Joe Pulitzer's *Liberty*, floating castles complete with gymnasiums and concert halls—was being cleared now of its barbed-wire defenses, some of it still mined. Though the bygone yachts were not likely to reappear on the scene, such was the continuity of Howard Herron's touch, and Elwell's too, that the barge in its sweepings of the coastal shelf would no doubt strike either Spanish gold or oil deposits.

Off to the north of the house, from a wooded area more than a mile away, the dull rumble of excavation machinery sounded the night through, product of Howard's latest scare: Soviet attack from the air. The distant rumblings, occasionally chewed to shreds by rivetings, ratchetings, and drillings—a shrillness of crickets—set Elwell's teeth on edge. At times in the past several days he had wondered if the entire course he was being propelled into were not the product of an old man's paranoid imagination. Though he knew better. The course was not Howard's alone, it was that of the nation. And the danger was not merely subjective.

On the seaborne night air the oboe lifted a sunny pastorale, its narrow aperture blown into with all the breath of his body by some shepherd, rosy-cheeked. Sweetly piercing, serenely calling, lilting over hill and dale.

"She could be absolutely daft," Elwell said, drawing back from the balcony door. "Or the sanest person I've ever met. At any rate, she disturbs me."

"Ah?"

Elwell disdained, unwontedly, the inquisitive inquiry of that *ah*, and all the passing episodes and permanent undercurrents summed up in it. His wife, stately in cascading ivory satin robe de style, cut like a man's greatcoat, was going over correspondence at her desk; not actually a desk but a Foullet table of amaranth and tulipwood, inlaid with oval marquetry panels. This table and its environs she used as her "Hartley Hunt" center of operations, her household and family center being more comfortably established elsewhere. She had been busy since Hartley's death last January with "getting up" a retrospective exhibition of his work, and the task of locating the canvases, many of them scattered and in storage, had proved unexpectedly taxing, even with expert assistance. Over her table now hung, newly discovered by one of her aides in the attic of a house they had once occupied in Greenwich, a post-impressionist nude from Hartley's earliest period. Herself as a young girl emerging with awkward grace, fine-boned, from conglomerate patches of dun, bronze, brown, and olive pigment. It was not surprising that the sitting room in its paler cast of off-whites, beiges, and buffs with glints of gilded bronze should seem to emerge from the painting, her taste in color always tending toward the brown-tinged, muted and subdued.

"And with so strong a desire to help," Elwell said, scanning the painting of his wife, just now recognizing on close approach that it was indeed she. "To do what is most right. To the point of self-renunciation."

"People who give up everything for an ideal," Marion said, signing a letter, "usually don't have very much to give up. They are simply asking to be dissuaded with something more worth their while."

"It's not always that simple."

"Isn't it? All for love, all for art, all for mankind—always adolescents who haven't lived long enough to have anything at stake. Idiots! And if they do insist on going all out," she said with unaccustomed vehemence, writing, "where do they end up? Down a blind alley. At the bottom of the rubbish heap!"

"Marion," Elwell said from behind her chair, studying the fey creature in the painting, brown-nippled, with a coltish distortion of hip, "if it had been Hartley Hunt who got off the boat with you thirty-five years ago instead of me, which of us would you have married?"

She swung about in her chair, an iron-boned figure, ravaged of face, spotted with moles and brown-shadowed indentations. "You ask me that now? After thirty-five years you ask me that? What can it possibly matter?"

"Hartley had the mills then, he had the money. I was only on the fringes, hanging on by the nails. If he had come off the boat with you that day and gone on to law school and joined up with Acme—?"

"I was very much in love with Hartley. Such a silly phrase, in love, but there it was. And so were you. Oh, I don't mean in any glib homosexual sense, the way these attachments are thrown around nowadays. But you were just mad about him too. It was his magnetism that polarized us. And he asked you to go to Paris with him. Not me."

So in a fit of pique—she would never in her unsentimental girlhood have admitted to heartbreak, or having a heart to break—she had offered Philip Elwell something more worth his while than all for love, all for art, all for mankind, and he had walked off the boat with her. At that fork in the road. And all this time since thinking himself king to her queen, he was pawn. With her loose hold Marion kept a very firm grip on necessity.

"And if it had been you Hartley asked to go to Paris with him?"

"I'd have gone. But only in order to bring him back again."

"But would he have come back?"

Her eyes, her one feature unchanged, her splendid grey eyes under the brown-smudged eyelids were amused and aloof, as if eternally watching from the royal box the races at Ascot, much diverted.

"It's no good raking over coals thirty-five years cold," she said and turned back to her papers. "I haven't thought of Hartley a dozen times a year until I got involved with these paintings of his. I don't imagine he's been much on your mind either."

"Not until recently. Recently he's rarely been off it."

"And ever since I started with his show, it's been nothing but one snag after another. We're slated now for the Whitney first of October, but if it weren't for the money-raising to restore the church at Oradour I'd never put it over. Hartley's suicide there, the sensation it created, my association with Anne Morgan restoring Rheims after the first war . . . That's been the gist of the publicity. But the paintings themselves, no one is interested, even the dealers haven't stirred up a flurry. And I had a fight with Sarah Gans over the date, she has some White Russian she's sponsoring at the Modern. Sarah has dedicated herself and her forty million dollars and every finger she has in every museum board and foundation fund to making non-objective art *the* movement of the twentieth century and herself the Lorenzo de

Medici of it. Sarah has a gift for the abstruse; she should have been a mathematician, all things human are alien to her. But I must admit she's come up with some very striking stuff. There! What do you think of that?"

Marion switched on a spotlight. On the entry wall of the sitting room a panel sprang forth illuminated, vibrant with juxtaposed geometrics, color within color laid on with brush and palette knife to a relief sculptural in effect. Elwell walked up to it. Retreated back.

"Smashing," he said. "I suppose it has some form of internal organization?"

"So has a Saristan rug. And a crystal. It's decorative. It's splashy. It hits you in the eye. And above all, it mystifies. We all immediately go into competition trying to outshine one another with our comments. Its success depends on the brilliance of the exegesis."

"Well, is it a masterpiece or a conversation piece?" Elwell, intrigued, directed the spotlight at one angle and another over the craggy surface. "Is it a good painting? Or is the painter a good promoter?"

"Your guess is as good as mine. It's a shot in the dark. I outbid Sarah for it and she could cut my throat. *Pensée Number 5*. Between the two of us we started quite a run on Numbers Six, Seven, and Eight, but this was by far the best of the lot. The color is superb, they say. And the spatial relations. And the interplay of light. Philip, you and I have not kept up. We're out of step. Personally I got lost with the cubists. I went along up to the point where the artist started expecting the eye of the beholder to put together the component parts. After that . . . Which brings us back to Hartley. Look back now at the way he did me."

Elwell stood fixed before the panel. "It does reflect the complexity of our age. After all, we can't look at a sunset anymore without also seeing it as an astronomer might. Out on the marsh today, the landscape appeared to me through the eyes of my hydrographer, a drainage pattern—my ecologist, a cycle of wildlife—my soil-man, the chemistry of mud and the diatons. How you could encompass it all artistically . . ."

"You wouldn't. You'd paint four parallel lines and a vertical. With great technical proficiency. *Marsh at Sunset*. Now to get back to Hartley. If he'd only put my breast up behind my ear there and magnified my thighs into tree trunks and transposed my eye and my navel and sliced me up, we'd have something now. At least my entrails should have been showing. As it is, it's worthless."

"Were we that wrong?" Elwell asked. "Didn't he have some spark of genius?" Asking her: *Didn't I? Didn't I have it in me to become . . . ?*

"He was stringently honest with himself. He struggled very hard with his materials. He was forever searching. That last period of his up in Biddeford during the war—*Mill End, 1944, Saco Sludge, Woman at Loom, Tex's Tavern*—mature, marvelous and utterly dated." She sighed ruefully, the lovely chimes of her voice echoing through her expiring breath. "He may be taken up again. If someone manages to keep his name alive. Sometimes I think he was the last American painter to study anatomy. There are bones under my flesh up there. Though perhaps my entrails should have been showing."

Elwell returned to *Pensée Number 5.* "Remember how we all felt then? How glorious it was? Breaking out of the old molds of convention into freedom of expression? Now the new modes have acquired their own convention. Stylized, stratified, case-hardened, tyrannical—"

"So much for that. Feel better now?" Marion switched off the spotlight. "The worst is yet to come. The crates have all been unpacked, the pictures for the exhibition have all been selected and suitably framed, the publicity is out, the critics are lined up and I've got Teddy Baldwin—you know Cissy's ex-fiancé, he's a full professor of fine arts now—to do a biography. Only through some oversight we failed to consult with the authorities at Oradour. I have just learned from them that they do not want that church reconstructed. They want to leave the ruins as they are. As a memorial to what happened there."

"But surely if you contribute enough for an exact replica of the edifice—"

"No. I've had Baldwin over there arguing with the mayor, the prefect, the sub-prefect, the parish priest, the relatives of the victims. They don't want the damn church. When Sarah gets wind of this she'll laugh her head off. We'll be the laughingstock of Fifty-seventh Street."

"But another church? A school? An orphanage?"

"It wouldn't be the same thing. That's where I am now. Incidentally, Baldwin is looking for some last message Hartley is said to have left you."

Elwell leaned over and swept her table clean, blotter pad and all off the marquetry.

"Philip!"

"Cancel it. Forget the whole thing. It was doomed to begin with."

"Philip, I can't just drop—"

"It's not so easy, is it? I've toured my river. I've mapped my dams. I've had my fun. But that's not the direction history dictates. I'm out of tune with the times. Get off the boat. Back to terra firma! But what if I should choose to go to Paris with Hartley?"

"Philip, you are upset. That girl did disturb you."

"*Ça n'importe.*"

He began meticulously to pick up her notepapers, envelopes, and releases from the floor.

"And the husband didn't mention a word of it? About the son? The marriage breaking up?"

"Nothing. It was quite a production, admirably stage-managed. My respect for him went up by leaps and bounds."

"A pretty pickle."

"She said to me later: '*If I give up that child, everything decent in me will go with him.*'"

Marion's nostrils wrinkled in humorous distaste as they generally did when she was confronted with any manifestation that smacked of overstatement. "In my candid opinion, Philip, you'd better steer clear of this. It's full of boobytraps."

"She'll be here tomorrow."

"Not with the conference, with everything else. That oboist in Myrtle Cottage is a fairly attractive girl. Perhaps you'd like . . . All right, what room?"

He handed her papers back to her, his thickened knuckles and her freckled fingers touching, their eyes unflinching, sharing between them the long train of triangular relationships that had been theirs since Hartley.

He kissed her cheek good night. "Buy *Pensée Number 1*," he advised. "You'll do well with it."

"I don't think there ever was a Number One."

Their laughter, the laughter of the long-married, erupted in chortles that dittoed back and forth as he left her room for the long corridor back to his secretaries, his preparations for tomorrow's conference, his concern with affairs of much larger consequence.

At seven in the morning Julie unpacked Colfax, Kissie, and Charles, coopted from camp for overnight, at Cousin Tibby's cottage. Hurriedly she dumped extra bedding on a cot, jiggled bureau drawers in and out looking for a bathing suit for Kissie, poked a loose reed back into the wicker chair under the window. "Now remember," she admonished Tibby, "if you have any trouble with him telephone me and I'll get back here if I have to walk the waves." Tibby who would ordinarily have bridled at the burden being imposed on her flapped in her wrapper after her in a state bordering on ecstasy. "Didn't I tell you he'd invite you there? Didn't I tell you you'd go? And to think old Mr. Herron is still alive, poor soul, can't move hand or foot they say . . . It was your mother's dream, you know. Julie, you pretty as ever." "If he can't sleep tonight put him to bed with Charles. Or Kissie, if that doesn't work. I'll try to cut it short. I'll try to be home this evening if I can."

Greyed gauze curtains fluttered in the windows with the poignant prickly scent of innumerable showers dried into them, the texture of the many dreamy girlhood summers she had spent here, listening to the creak of rockers on the porch, the purr of reminiscences. Sand drifting up through the floorboards gritted under her feet. She put three pounds of hamburger and four cartons of milk into the turret-topped refrigerator she had given Tibby when her kitchen at home was remodeled.

"Julie, it's a miracle straight from heaven. A second chance. How many of us live to have a second chance? This your big chance, Julie. Grab it, play it smart, take 'em over. The chance of a lifetime."

And with Coley's petal-soft kiss on her cheek and Tibby's outcries ringing after her—don't spoil it, don't mess it up!—she drove to the airport. The wheel steady under her hands she pressed down on the gas, pushing eighty. The goal she had to achieve today was clear to her. Nail him! Though the uncertainty of nailing anything, particularly persons, was becoming increasingly evident to her day by day. Her original conception, so clean and bold—to leave Henry, pick up Colfax and go—was dividing daily and subdividing into difficulties of how, when, and where to. Things slipped out of her grasp, slippery as seals. The job was too big for her. She needed outside help of a swift and specific order to concretize her objectives.

There was no postponing it. The interim situation at home, already too prolonged, could not continue; the exercise of routine arrangements growing more and more cumbersome, the game of maneuvers against Henry's determination more exhausting, the omnipresent tension of everything in midair more unbearable. "Any minute now," Henry had said to her this morning, "the back zipper on your dress'll get stuck and you'll holler for me and that'll be it." She needed a friend with the power, the prestige and the money—oh yes, the money!—to provide her with an immediate solution. With that feverish obsession with which the poor in desperate plight seek out the rich, she drove toward Elwell. He must because he can! And with remarkably coolheaded confidence, single of purpose, firm of aim, I can because I must!

She pulled up smartly in the airport parking lot, missing two cars by a hairsbreadth as she slid into the slot between them; locked up, top and windows up, and stepped into the lunchroom for coffee. These actions, small in themselves, moved through her with the force of a declaration of independence. She was on her way into the wide world. The movement of strangers about her in the lunchroom, the impersonality of the waitress, the acrid taste of coffee and cigarette, a note of deference when she inquired at the information window for the Herron airstrip—"You know all the time I've lived here, must be nigh on forty years, I've never been over there?"—and the wink of a friendly mechanic, undressing her with a glance from head to heel, all yielded to her a distinct and enjoyable individuality, unwed, herself, her destination that of her own will.

Out on the field a yellow and green Piper Cub, about as big as an insect, was just alighting on the airstrip. A young man in yachting cap, striped jersey, and dungarees, looking more like a Ph.D. on holiday than a pilot, jumped down to take her bags and help her up into the cockpit.

Hiking up, high-heeled, in slim dress, she lamented, "My skirt is too narrow for my aspirations."

"A punster, hey?" the pilot said with a boost from behind for which she should have swatted him one.

But when she looked around at him he was so owlishly serious, a collector of puns, that she laughed at herself quite merrily, with post-facto appreciation. "I've never flown before," she confessed. "Will you take me over Silver Beach and Arcady?"

The engine roared up. Wheels skimmed over the airstrip, and with a transition that affected her in her inexperience as qualitative, a change of condition from one state of being to another, lifted from the ground. On insect-wings they banked steeply toward a cloud, leveled off. The land spread out below, blue-pink tinged, revealed with a transparence more lucent than that on earth; moving on a grand scale at an august speed over which she hung, without sensation of motion, stationary. Silver Beach dwindled to a hyphen, and all the heart-heaviness with which she was so urgently filled for that to which she was so closely bound was diminished in size to less than a dot, in time to less than a tick of the watch on her wrist, to less than the passage of a single pulse. All that was so immense to her became so minuscule, a splatter of greens and bronzes outward to the barrier islands, reaching in a chain northward to the Carolinas and southward to Florida, on the edge of the indigo sea. Oh God, she closed her eyes, help me! Help me to be strong! Help me to see it through.

They dipped, catching a glimpse in passing of white-colonnaded, massive grey building, more seigneural manor than ante-bellum mansion, more hotel than home.

"Is Mr. Herron still active?" she asked the pilot. "Of course," she amended scrupulously, "I don't expect to see him."

"I've never seen him myself," the pilot answered her.

Through an opening in the trees, invisible a few seconds before, they glided down upon the twenty-five-hundred-foot runway. A stepping stool was rolled up and she was handed down by another young man in isinglass-visored white cap. To a territory as different from the mainland she had left only five minutes ago as a stage set is from reality, and as distant from it as another planet in another galaxy. Was Paradise ever like this?

The light was more brilliant here, the atmospheric pressure lighter upon the body, the air easier to breathe. Here all the details of living were taken care of by others, all petty cares were removed. As if she had been deprived all her life of sufficient oxygen, the sustaining element of life, Julie absorbed through senses, pores, lungs the invisible presence of money. Money in such quantity that it was taken for granted. That it was by nature *there*, to be received and expended as lavishly as need be without a second's thought. Money, like air, water, food, and sex, is a problem only when you don't have it. And when you do, it's the key to the locked door, the motor that lifts the plane, the ability to move mountains. Liberation.

Across the runway, in a grove artfully disciplined deer gamboled, pheasants paraded. Beyond the dark wood a park opened, bathed in sunlight, shimmering with the white marble of a pergola, statuary, the rainbow spray of fountains.

Up the runway, ahead of the insect Piper Cub a gigantic silver bird was discharging passengers, dignitaries of a more dazzling species than ordinary humankind. A tall woman in a high-crowned broad-brimmed hat circulated among them, welcoming. Newcomers and old-timers, grown acquainted on the plane trip if they were not already so, clustered about her.

Walking toward the closed circle Julie experienced fleetingly the moment of panic in the mental hospital when Dr. Wolf unlocked with a clangor of keys the first set of metal-plated doors.

Then the tall woman in the unfashionable hat and the shirtmaker dress, a little longer than was currently the style, advanced to meet her.

"And you are Mrs. Warren?"

She had the most beautiful speaking voice, Julie thought, that she had ever heard.

The baggage, unnoticed, was whisked off in a pickup truck. The gentlemen were dispatched in station wagons. For the ladies Mrs. Elwell had ready a horse-drawn equipage, a char-à-banc with banquettes installed as in a bus facing one another, suitable both for sightseeing and conversation. "I thought some of you might enjoy our scenic route if you're up to it at this ghastly hour. If not, one of the cars—" Oh no! They were all enchanted. What a delightful idea . . . Who would have the gall to beg off?

They jogged over a white shell road on the shoreside between date palms from which the boots were trimmed, the trunks clipped like French poodles up to the foliage. Julie had been seated by Marion Elwell, next to her. She took no part in the chitchat concerning personalities she knew naught of: what an awful time the Carrolls had had at Acapulco, how well Elva was doing now that she had married again and decided to become a champion skeet-shooter. At one point early in the ride, Mrs. Elwell's freckled hand resting on her forearm as if reserving her for future reference—the hand of a horsewoman used to controlling, assuring—tightened with the slightest of pressures.

"I want you to know, Sophie"—Mrs. Elwell leaned forward to the lady opposite—"that Mrs. Warren is very much interested in the treatment of disturbed children. She's planning to make a lifetime study of it."

Sophie, wife of the General Pat Mencken who had so distinguished himself in the OSS during the war, regarded Julie, beady-eyed. "How fascinating," she said. "When most young women your age are interested only in where they're to park their fannies at the Stork."

The other ladies entered their murmurs of polite approval. "That's what Polly Lydgate's taken up now." "No no, it's not that. Something else." "Bone disease."

That subject exhausted, they moved on to the next by a series of tangental leaps, leaving Julie behind tagged and disposed of. A minor petitioner with an ax to grind.

Julie held her peace nearly to the end of the carriage ride. They passed the famous tropical gardens, hedged with bougainvillea, where frangipani, stephanotis, and specimen orchids were grown. They waved at a couple of early-bird golfers on the nineteen-hole links laid out by a Scotsman imported for the purpose at a cost of a quarter of a million dollars a quarter of a century ago; the greensward was drained by hundreds of underground pipes pumping excess water into a sump pit concealed in a picturesque ivy-twined rice-chimney ruin, and emptied thence into the yacht basin. They rendered grave homage as they passed to a little brick museum which included among its worldwide collections a group of Imperial Venus shells gathered by Marion's brother who had died young, cases of birds he'd had stuffed, a display of Indian arrows he'd dug up that had been tipped with the stings of stingrays for arrowheads. After the tennis and badminton courts the approach to the house was marked by a great avenue of oaks.

"You've kept them!" Julie spoke up. "How wonderful. Fifty on the left. Forty-eight on the right."

"Why I've never counted them," Marion said. The ladies looking back began to count.

"And the Topel trees in there." Julie peered through the wisteria-draped boughs. "The yaupon and holly crossed by that man they brought in from the German Imperial Court to work up at Airlie. There must be some fig trees, and mulberry, and a few olive . . ."

Marion's brows arched ever so slightly. "Have you been here before, Mrs. Warren?"

"Oh, my family once owned Heron's Nest." She pronounced it Harness. "My great-grandfather's brother Horace gave it to his second son Mose," she added offhandedly, "for a wedding gift."

Seldom had anyone ever ventured to upstage Marion Elwell. The ladies peeped at Marion with startled apprehension. Sophie twitched a wisp of handkerchief out of her handbag and squeakily blew her nose. Under the shadow of her broad-brimmed hat Marion's mouth, uncoated by lipstick, puckered as if she'd bit tastefully into a pickled onion.

"Some people are born with it," she observed to Sophie apropos of nothing at all. "Like perfect pitch."

The enormous reception hall, two stories high with carved mahogany ceiling and hand-woven carpeting thick on the floor, Watteaus and Fragonards on the walls, was as busy as a railroad station with arriving and departing guests. While Marion attended to a few farewells, Sophie, who *had* been here before, shepherded the ladies into the music room and assuming the role of hostess, or tourist guide, called their attention to meubles, bibelots, and objets d'art. Not for the late Mrs. Howard Herron, who had vied with the Mesdames Stotesbury and Stuyvesant Fish, Vanderbilt and Whitney, the unpretentious bungalow hideaway of some multimillionaires of her period. She rode the crest of the New-port-Sarasota-Palm Beach tide, running the gamut in her décor of all the Louis' from XIV to XVIII, transporting not only Aubusson tapes-stries but the walls on which they were hung from the châteaux of royal mistresses. Every single thing in the music room had its history of precious materials, priceless craftsmanship and peerless pedigree. A Meis-sen group of dancers that had belonged to Elizabeth of Austria. A Sèvres clock garniture that had belonged to Victoria of England. A golden flying goat of Etrusco-Celtic origin that had belonged to Sultan Abdul Hamid II of Turkey.

There were two pianos. One of satinwood and ivory, the cabinet made by Wright & Mansfield in England and the interior by some Frenchman, a hundred and forty years old. The other of gargantuan proportions in ebony, every inch of it sculptured: the legs, the music rack, and even the soaring wing of the lid. Its keys were mother-of-pearl. The wife of a physicist who had been invited to Elwell's conference frankly gawked at it. Julie irreverently picked out chopsticks on the nacre keys, cocking her ear to the tone. She looked up, caught in the act of laughing at the piano, into the face of Marion Elwell.

They recognized each other. They were of the same stripe. Kindred spirits. Possessed of a self-assurance so egregious that they could be permitted any lapse of taste, any breach of manners, any monstrosity. Rather than admit to embarrassment by changing certain of her mother's furnishings, Marion flaunted them. Instead of getting rid of an atrocious Rosa Bonheur, she displayed it on the wall beside a Tintoretto. Not out of ignorance but immunity.

Taking Julie in arm, she led the way to breakfast. "You must all be starved. Is there anything, Mrs. Warren, that you would particularly like?"

"Hummingbirds' wings on toast," Julie said.

In spite of her laughter over the ebony piano, Julie was deeply affected by the luxury surrounding her. To be waited on hand and foot. To sip from a cup of Pompadour rose. To be shown to her bedroom where her clothing had already been unpacked, pressed, and put away. And such a bedroom . . .

Curtained French windows opened wide to a balcony overlooking the sea. A pale green brocade armchair waited invitingly by the bed. And the bed itself: the headboard wreathed with carved figures and upholstered in ecru satin; spread with lace over a gold counterpane; the whole surmounted by a canopy in back which ascended, draped and gathered, into, of all things, a small gold crown. A bed for a princess.

She wandered into her bathroom. The bathtub seemed to be carved out of a single slab of marble; and the faucets, the work of some latter-day Cellini, were, what else, gold seahorses, whose eyes sparkled with green gems exactly matched by the bath crystals.

Back in the bedroom she sat down on the cushioned gilt bench before the cream-and-green dressing table, inset with panels of painted pastoral scenes, shepherds with their shepherdesses. Her face was reflected in the mirror above, curiously framed—the ubiquitous figure of a Daphnis eternally-chasing after a Chloe eternally-luring and never quite catching up. She clasped her burning cheeks. Oh my! Oh Julie-Ann! Unlike her experience with Dr. Wolf, here she was getting off on the right foot. From the minute she hiked up into the plane she was off. She knew it without knowing how. She could feel it. Everything was turning to her hand. I'll do it. I'll get what I'm after. I'll nail it.

Shortly afterward, she was even more deeply affected in quite a different fashion. She was on her way out to the terrace with a covey of ladies when she was singled out by a secretary and led by him down an arched corridor through the ground-floor wing reserved for Elwell's offices to the River Room.

7

The River Room which had originally been conceived as temporary headquarters of *The Elwell Plan* and permanent adjunct to Elwell's new Washington office, should have been dismantled a week ago. But Elwell had not seen fit to issue the enabling orders, and its dioramas, models, color transparency panels, designed by a promising young man who had worked with Rockwell Kent on the General Motors Exhibit at the 1939 World Fair, its files of maps, profiles and preliminary exploration reports, remained as the nerve center of an operation that was perhaps already dead.

The entire wall facing the Renaissance entrance doors was covered, windows and all, by a forty-foot mural, skillfully lighted. It depicted one of those monumental structures that united in its building the creative capacities of all the major branches of engineering and in its ultimate realization all the major functions of river system planning. From landscaped slopes threaded with access roads and railroad spurs, the white span breached the waters: a complex of multiple arches and spillways descending from the height of its axis; bulkheads and over-flow sections with platform for gate maintenance; pen stocks, conduits, trash racks; to the low rectangular sluices at the base. On the left embankment above the tail race, under the lee of the dam, serviced by a towering gantry crane lay the windowed cube of the powerhouse; steel-sheathed generators on deck and transformers connected by high-tension wires to the switchyard, a forest of skeletal spires distributing the production of electric current. On the right embankment, the navigation channel was controlled above the service bay by locks that, strong enough to withstand wave action, wind, and earthquake, shone like pairs of cuff links.

Beneath the mural the floor space was dominated by a centrally placed three-dimensional table model, under glass, equipped with running water and what may well have been growing grass, furbished with strata of mud and clay, dotted with papier-mâché cities and identifiable landmarks, exhibiting in its entirety the proposed Ocachee River Project. Above it a quotation: *Each river system from its headwaters in the forest to its mouth on the coast, is a unit and should be treated as such.* —*Theodore Roosevelt.* Below it another quotation: *Water resources planning must be expanded to embrace in its scope conservation and development of natural resources, agricultural and industrial growth, and the cultural and recreational life of the region.—Franklin D. Roosevelt.*

When Julie was introduced into the River Room through the bronze doors held open for her by the escorting secretary, she unabashedly gasped.

"Mr. Elwell will be with you shortly," the secretary said, and retired with a nod toward the extremity of the displays leftward, "I believe you've met these gentlemen?"

The three gentlemen occupied with their viewing took no notice of her. Two of them she recognized from breakfast this morning, Douglas Gilmore of the State Department and General Mencken, husband of the sharp Sophie. The general, now much less formidable in civvies, inspected with pink pent-up energy. Gilmore, disciplined of frame and manner, thoughtfully contemplated. They were being shown about by a third man she vaguely recalled from Elwell's first visit to Sunset, the phlegmatic engineer.

"Every river system is unique," the engineer was making his point with an acid punctiliousness that etched itself on Julie's mind. "And what works with one cannot be applied literally to another. For instance, in the Tennessee Valley we encountered a rock foundation of calcareous shale that appeared fairly tight . . . At Diablo the Skagit was diverted by tunneling through solid granite and the riverbed at the bottom of the gorge was filled with boulders through which we drilled six-inch holes and poured grouting to anchor a wall . . ."

Julie went straight to the table model of the Ocachee Project. Curiously she touched a switch labeled *Legend*.

The table was darkened. A spotlight from an interior projector beamed toward one side. A modulated voice issued from a soundtrack, citing statistics synchronized with the moving spotlight.

Upstate, the upriver tributaries rushing down from the rocky hills were spanned in steps by a series of dams, each with reservoir for storage of water during flood periods and release of water during drought. Midstate, twenty miles north of metropolitan Ludlow, the main dam, three hundred fifty feet high and more than a mile across, carried on its summit a four-lane superhighway; from its base it backed up the river for forty miles, forming a tremendous lake surrounded with forests, parks, and beaches; and from its generators it dispatched a quarter million kilowatts of low-cost electric power. Downstate from Ludlow through Arcady to Bay City the channel was dredged to a depth of twelve feet for inland commerce by boat. In Colfax County, pumping stations and retention basins drained eighty thousand acres of waterlogged delta land.

Julie touched another button, labeled *Chronology*.

Through a cinematic device the spotlight from the interior projector bathed the scene in dingy grey, transforming it to the semi-flood conditions that pertained as often as four times a year: frothy yellow waters eroding banks, inundating crops, undermining waterfront buildings. Next moment the grey atmosphere darkened and the peak flood conditions that swept the watershed every fifteen years prevailed: the river blood-red with clay inundating farms, villages, whole sections of cities. Then the air lightened, illuminating the present with its isolated shacks, gullied bottomlands, stagnant towns. And lightened again to full sunlight, revealing the future: vessels on the river, campers on the lakeside, tractors in the fields, electricity in the houses, the wheels of industry turning.

The spotlight switched off. The Ocachee River Project resumed its original appearance as a table model.

Over the cessation of the soundtrack, the voice of the engineer down the room continued, not at all well modulated, steely with the knife-edge of its own certitudes.

"The structural types differ as much as the topography of the sites on which they are built and the functions for which they were designed. In one place the main aim may be reclamation. In another, bridging the gap between an area of heavy rainfall and an area of scarcity. Here . . ."

The three men moved toward a pole of fly maps and lost themselves within the leaves.

". . . Here we can take advantage of the excess rainfall in the west and bring it to the east where you have semi-aridity and desert by constructing an artificial river eight hundred miles long. To begin with a high barrier—here, at this lake—and through aqueducts, reservoirs, and pools service the entire territory along the way—"

"Too bad there isn't the money for it," General Mencken interrupted, crisply. "And without funds, it's a waste of time even thinking—"

"Take about thirty years, four for basic studies, four for preliminary surveys, twenty or more for construction." The engineer flipped the map over, oblivious of objection. "Other places the problem is seasonal. In Eastern China along the lower reaches of the Yangtze, Hwang Ho, and Huai there's plenty of rainfall summer and autumn, too much. Then an acute shortage—"

"You're not going to do anything in China, are you?" the general impatiently cut in.

"If we aren't, they will. The history of irrigation works in China goes back two thousand years. While we were in Tientsin I flew up into the northern provinces where they had been fighting the Japanese all through the war—"

"You mean the Communists?"

"I'm not defining their politics, that's not my field. But they've been digging ditches and canals with their bare hands. What they don't have in machinery, they make up in numbers."

"They're taking Manchuria, Thompson, and they'll take the whole country!"

"China is out," Douglas Gilmore said, and, stepping back, flipped the map over.

Keeping an ear open to developing hostilities and growing quite hotly exercised over them, Julie dallied at a discreet distance before a panel of posters. The posters were assembled and charted like a genealogical tree with head, main stem, branches, and subsidiary members hanging in lines from every box. She followed the table downward through descendants and collaterals of collateral descendants, overwhelmed by the sheer organization involved in only one such project in its several phases. Conception, Tentative Layout, Design, Execution and Operation. Divisions of Water Control and Planning, Construction, Power, Regional Studies.

The Division of Design alone spawned a host of staffs, technical and engineering, with responsibilities that included even the structural steel design of the heavy equipment. Comprehending inspection, testing and drafting services; department of contract specifications . . . Soils laboratory . . . Hydraulic laboratory . . .

She sidled over to the adjoining panel of Cost-Benefit Ratios, on which estimated costs were balanced, crimson-figured, against dollar values expected to accrue over decades.

On the other side of the Cost-Benefit panel, Thompson the engineer was insisting, "Nothing will be undertaken for its own sake. Only with the anticipation of profitable enterprise. Mr. Elwell has had that aspect looked into very thoroughly. Here on the Gold Coast, for example, the opportunity for a hydroelectric dam system that will feed power to a good part of West Africa is colossal. Not to speak of corollary benefits in opening up hundreds of thousand of acres to agriculture, inland transportation, fresh-water fisheries . . . But the main thing is bauxite. He'll get together a combine of American and British firms to tap the deposits, finance smelting and reduction plants."

"And when you have it all built up," Mencken said, "the natives will rise up and nationalize it and boot everyone out."

"Now, Pat," Gilmore demurred, "not in Africa. What I can't understand is the logic of this. Here you have people living in a primitive tribal society, static for centuries, who still use wooden hoes if anything. What they are going to do with electricity—"

"If they can rise up in Indonesia and Indochina," Mencken continued his own argument, "it can happen anywhere. It's contagious."

"They'll still need the dams," Thompson said.

"I suppose you'll go in and help them with it?"

There were no further words for a while. The great maroon-walled chamber, once a ballroom, was silent except for Mencken's clickings as he gave display after display the white-glove treatment, with Gilmore at his elbow; and parade-line review, with Gilmore at his heels.

They're pulling it all down, Julie thought with hot partisanship. Tearing it to pieces. Lighting matches to it. Herself somehow identified with it all, with the mass of material so cleverly condensed in these visual aids, which in one and the same moment daunted and diminished her, enlarged and exalted her. And identified with him, burningly with him whose it was.

She wandered among cutaways of spillway chutes: Morning Glory, Fontain; high or low according to the amount of discharge; with radial gates and without them; with tunnels and without.

Paused by the operating model of locks: gates scaled down to the decimal point from 110 by 600 feet; the water levels fed through twelve by twelve foot longitudinal culverts in each section of lock wall; the floating boom of four reinforced concrete units.

Minutely examined the hydro plant. Turbo-generators nestling like sterilizers in a hospital room, enamel-white, egg-domed. Distributor stretching like a recumbent dinosaur on the bottom floor. Access balcony to three-hundred-ton crane; access gallery to draft tube. Control tunnel; control room with solid façade of dials, key punches, gauges. And the mechanics of the installations: of governor, generator, oil system, compressed air system, rainwater and treated water systems, sewage-disposal and drainage systems, two automatic fire-protection systems.

"He's gotten hipped on this whole thing," Douglas Gilmore said, "and gone off the deep end."

Julie glared around at him. Gilmore stared past her, a trifle austerely, to the hydro plant. Thompson had disappeared.

"It's not a matter of policy," Mencken declared. "It's the toys."

"I beg your pardon?"

"The props. Put three brigadiers around a terrain bas-relief and they start deploying personnel and matériel. They disassemble and reassemble and if there's a dozen pushbuttons so much the better. It gets you after a while. You're possessed by the game."

"What would you suggest?"

"A new toy. Has Elwell ever been up at Oak Ridge?"

Pat Mencken bestriding his narrow rug like a colossus. His blue eyes snapping under reddish fringes of brows, his pink domed forehead exuding in a pink haze his gratification with the game that possessed him. A knack for knocking off thumbnail sketches of personalities that, whether they fit or not, never failed to make a direct and lasting hit.

"Some people," Mencken elaborated, "can't think without a pencil in hand. They have to write it out or sketch it out or just plain doodle. Others slide-rule it out. Or act it out." He paced around a table, acting out his cast of characters. "You have those who stick strictly to HQ and figure out the problem from data. And those who have to be in the field in order to formulate . . . There's a little bit of all this in Philip. An idea man who has to have a physical object to hang onto. He can be brought around."

Gilmore rested back against a table model, pulling at his lower lip, thoughtfully digesting.

"If you can do it, Pat, more power to you. No one is foolish enough to announce an appointment without first making sure it will be accepted. Harry hates even to offer an appointment without making sure beforehand. As it is, I hardly dare mention . . ."

Remarking Julie at last they lowered their voices and moved off to Elwell's desk at the head of the room, situated in what must have been the orchestral alcove. Mencken took Elwell's high-backed leather chair and eying Gilmore airily reached for the telephone.

"Oak Ridge . . ."

The rest was lost to Julie, spoken with head intimately turned aside into the oversize mouthpiece of the telephone.

She was both exhilarated and appalled by these intimations in her presence of affairs of state. Fiercely defensive for Elwell and deliciously pleased with the immense importance attached to him by his attackers. She stood before a panoramic color transparency, craning her neck back to take it all in. With their attendant bulldozer, concrete mixers, steam shovels, cranes, men swarmed over the scaffolding of a semi-completed structure. In a detail at the side three coveralled workers lowered the towering drum of a rotor on cables through the roof hatch of the power-house into the pipe coils of the stator below.

Exhilarated and appalled. Dizzied, dazed, demolished, groping for what had brought her here . . .

"Cheops. Chichén Itzá."

Elwell, hands in pockets, sauntered into the center of the room, whimsically looking up at the spectacular forty-foot mural of the dam. "I sometimes like to think of myself as a poet manqué. But whenever I confront this I know that here is the poetry, the art of our time. This is our creative surge. Nothing less."

"It takes my breath away," Julie said with a crystalline distinctness that carried from one end of the room to the other. "If there is such a thing as being awe-struck, I am it." She hurried to Elwell's side in a turmoil of loyalty and, yes, love, adulation. "Feel." She touched his hand. "I'm shaking. That I should trouble you with things so personal in the middle of all this . . ."

Elwell pressed her hand warmly. "Not at all. You point a moral and adorn a tale. It haunted me half the night. Do you mind if I use you as a symbol and source of morale at a time when I need it badly? Ah Pat. Douglas."

"Magnificent." In a roseate glow Mencken hastened toward them. "Up at TVA the big mistake we made was underestimating power needs. We've had to expand repeatedly to meet defense demands, particularly for the nuclear research and development plants. By the bye, I've taken the liberty of requesting some films to be flown down from Oak Ridge. We should have them late today."

"You worked this out, Philip, with the perspective of a declining defense economy," Gilmore said consolingly. "And paradoxically whatever survives of it will be on the basis of support to our defenses. It's not all lost by any means."

"Indeed?" Elwell said. "Our conference is assembling now up at Mr. Herron's board table. Julie"—he drew her arm through his—"how would you like to meet Mr. Herron?"

"Why—" She began to laugh at the stupefied expression on Mencken's face as he, phrenologist extraordinary, tried vainly to place her.

"It was your mother's heart's desire, wasn't it?"

"You remember my telling you that!" She marched with Elwell arm in arm out through the massive, minutely decorated bronze portals. "And I came down with chicken pox."

"Well, you don't have it now. You should see yourself."

"Just a minute, excuse—" She broke away and darted up the corridor to a flower-filled urn. From it she selected a single white rose, about to open. Holding the posy before her like a little girl at a tea party, with primly spread skirt she sallied back. "Shall I curtsy to him?"

They ascended miles, it seemed, of crimson-carpeted staircases to the suite where Howard Herron, paralyzed by two coronaries, unable to be moved, still was able to command corporation heads and cabinet ministers from almost any part of the globe into his presence. Even now he was referred to by certain publications as "The Great Mogul," a title they passed on to him after the decease of Pierpont Morgan. At which Herron invariably cackled: "They flatter me." He was also referred to as "The Last of the Moguls." At which he cackled: "At least a Mogul on his last legs."

Elwell regaled them with anecdotes on the way up. "Nothing gets by him." And Douglas Gilmore recalled a visit to San Simeon where he had been taken up to the Celestial Towers in Mr. Hearst's very personal private automatic elevator—an ancient church confession booth!

"Would you like," Elwell politely offered, "to take the elevator?"

"Oh no, this is fine."

"I prefer the exercise myself. Though I must say the age of conspicuous consumption represented by places like this is giving way to—indubitably no less consumption but certainly less conspicuous . . ."

"Don't tell me," Gilmore muttered back to Mencken at the next art gallery of a landing, "that there's a twin to that confession booth here!"

The passage outside Herron's suite was crowded with persons who had somehow wangled themselves this far in the hope of being admitted. There was a stampede toward Elwell which he motioned away. Inside, the anteroom was jam-packed with personages Herron must have invited for some purpose and who were now left cooling their heels. There was a flurry of secretaries toward Elwell with cables to be read, papers to be signed.

Their arrival was announced to Herron over the intercom if not precisely with a fanfare of trumpets and hautboys, then with a deference almost as resonant. At the door to the bedchamber, Mencken suddenly drew up short like a Victorian maiden about to be compromised and indulged in a short and sharp exchange with his host.

"Thompson isn't in on this, is he?"

"Why?" Elwell paused in the act of knocking at the door which was kept locked from the inside as a precaution, despite the pre-announcement of all those who were permitted to enter.

"I wouldn't feel free to express myself freely in front of him. He's a Commie."

"And I'm a lawyer. Do you have any proof of this?"

"Oh, I couldn't swear he's a dyed-in-the-wool card-carrying . . . It's his attitude. I can smell it a mile off. And it's a dead giveaway every time. We've no place for that sort, they're mentally undependable, emotionally unstable."

"Thompson is a top-ranking engineer, and as long as he is on my staff he will not be excluded."

"Not from top-secret information? In which our national security is at stake?"

"What we may gain in security, General," Elwell said patiently, "we'll surrender in quality. Heaven help our nation without the Thompsons. However, he will not be with us this morning. Our opening session is to be strictly confined to considerations of policy."

Mencken grunted, hardly mollified for having been put to such straits over a nonexistent point. Elwell knocked and they waited for the door to be unlocked, unbolted, and unchained. "You scratch his skin," Mencken warned, "and you'll find that underneath he thinks this whole plan of yours is a scheme of Uncle Sam's to impose Wall Street imperialism—"

"That it is," Elwell said as he entered the bedroom, steering Julie by the elbow. "If I could only get Wall Street and Uncle Sam to back it up!"

Across the floor, on a bed of rare acajou wood mounted on a dais and surmounted with festooned draperies of pale green silk brocade, between bedposts that had been fashioned into life-size figures of the Empress Josephine, pillowed in snowy linen, Howard Herron held his audiences. He was simultaneously giving ear now to a Philadelphia philanthropist, speaking into a cluster of telephones and issuing orders to an aide while in the background a nurse hovered over him with stethoscope and oxygen mask ready poised.

His benign head was bald as a baby's and his skin was almost as bland. There was something feminine in his appearance, possibly because of the hormones with which he was constantly being injected. His face was more like that of a very old woman than a very old man, like that of a eunuch who has never known a beard or like that portrayed in the paintings of those Popes Innocent who bore within their dulcet brows the understanding of a voluptuary.

It was only when she was quite close to the shrunken figure on the vast expanse of bed that Julie noticed the balloon. Herron was holding between his hands an inflated pale-green balloon, squeezing and manipulating it to keep up his circulation.

She was not sure whether she had meandered into the Wizard of Oz or Alice in Wonderland or the hallucination of a patient at Darbyton. To her Herron was the spitting image of the South African gold prospector in the second-floor men's ward. "*He's* happy." Dr. Wolf's chuckle throbbed in her eardrums. "Syphilitic paresis. The happiest state of all." At this moment she was not even sure that she herself had not been confined at Darbyton that day and that the experience she was living through today, the morning plane flight, the River Room and now this

—the only feature lacking was a royal rail—were not the product of a systematic delusion.

She was frightened to death. Her cheeks were as stiff as baked meringues.

"This is the young lady I mentioned to you, Howard, who wants to throw everything overboard," Elwell said.

"And you want to throw everything overboard for her? Well, I can hardly blame you." It was a flat thin falsetto that was expelled with guttural effort from somewhere deep in his chest. "Come here, you lovely child. Let me feast my eyes on you, since there is so little else that I can feast on."

Julie was borne forward by the rose in her hand. Its petals, pink-fluted on the outer rims, had unfolded in the space of her journey upstairs. Pure white now, half-blown, golden-stamened within its skirts. Drinking in the warmth and the light. With a barely perceptible languor.

"You've brought me a rose?"

Instantly at a gesture of Herron's hand all the profusion of flowers arranged in porcelain and crystal within the vicinity of his bed was whisked away. The telephones were removed. The visitors vanished. Julie's rose, immersed in a bud vase and sprinkled over, was placed on the bedside commode. Its languid petals lifted, twinkling with beads of water.

"Youth. Youth." Herron caressed the plumply glistening green balloon with his finely wrinkled hands, molded and kneaded and mauled it. "Youth never values itself. Youth always wants to kick the bucket, jump the traces."

"That's Marion's reaction."

"Always trust Marion's reaction. The older you get, the more you lose your physical command, the harder you try to hold onto what you have. You don't give an inch. You tighten your grip. You can't afford to take a loss. Will you please an old man's fancy, child, and sit with me a while?"

Julie slipped into the chair Elwell drew up for her. "I'm not all that young," she confessed.

"Closer, child, closer. Let me breathe you in."

From under his womanish eyelids, his bright agate eyes regarded her. The balloon in his hands was twisted tight about the middle—it must pop!—and released in a new shape, bulging above and below.

"You're on the threshold. At the beginning. The very beginning. I envy you that. Beginnings are so much nicer than endings."

"She wants to attach herself," Elwell reminded him, "to an institution for severely disturbed youngsters."

In this setting it sounded priggish and pretentious and not a little absurd.

"It's not just that. It's—" Julie struggled for it, watching with fascinated apprehension Herron's pinchings and pummelings of his thin-skinned balloon. "I want to get out of the kind of life I have. Where everything's *us* against *them*. Ourselves against everyone else. I want to be part of a world where I'm working together with others for something that needs to be done. No matter how long it may take or how hopeless it may seem."

"This is our problem, Howard." Elwell tipped up Julie's chin like a portrait photographer adjusting her head to its most becoming angle. "Blessed with all that God ever gave any woman. Ready to abandon every rationale of self-interest for a vision. There are these people and there is this impulse and it's more widespread than we think and it must be reckoned with. And they're not all that young. As I discovered on my recent trip."

The balloon rasped and squealed. Mencken and Gilmore, unintroduced, had joined the conferees assembling at the distant board table, situated in the embrasure of bay windows overlooking the galleried central portico and the sea; a table around which, it was said, men had on occasion gathered "more important in time of crisis than the government itself." Still, Elwell lingered with Herron mulling over the disposition of one Julie Warren; or rather, not over Julie but over the outcome of an argument in which she was an unwitting pawn, that had been going on between them without explicit statement far too long.

Elwell had no illusion that through Julie he could dissuade his father-in-law from his *idée fixe*. It was Howard's conviction that the nation was on the verge of war with the Soviet Union, and that every other available nation, every resource of manpower and material must be mobilized for the coming battle. The only question remaining open in his mind was *when*. Not that Howard desired such an eventuality. "We don't make history," he always contended, "we only take advantage of it." But once Acme's capital was committed to an investment program, the program was always protected and promoted every inch of the way. "We can't afford," Howard then contended, "to take a loss."

It was not to dissuade Howard that Elwell had brought Julie to him, for dissuasion was impossible. But to prick that complacency of his! To prick him into some awareness that there were other forces and courses! And to prick, maliciously, with that most potent instrument, Howard being Howard—a pretty girl.

"There are these people," Elwell said to Herron, smiling at Julie, "who feel that the big job now is the alleviation of misery, poverty, disease,

social oppression, the threat of war. More of them now than ever before. You have to take account of that."

"Charming." The old man never took his eyes from Julie. "Absolutely
charming. I do take account of it, Philip. I do. And so do you. At a cost,
if you will permit me to put it vulgarly, of more than two million three
hundred and sixty thousand per annum in donations, endowments—"

With a sharp report—everyone in the room jumped—the plumply
glistening green balloon burst and shriveled to little wormy shreds in
Herron's hands. With an effort that brought the sweat out in lines on
his forehead and the veins out in ribs on his temples, Herron hauled
himself over on the pillow, straining toward the cardboard box of balloons on the burled top of the commode.

"Shall I blow one up for you?" Julie forestalled him with quick sympathy, offering him the box.

Howard pored over the balloons in a dither of indecision. "Which
one?" he asked her.

Julie selected a cerise balloon and affixed it to the nozzle of a toy
pump, covered with nursery-patterned paper. Pushing the two cardboard
cylinders of the pump one inside the other, she began with face pink as
if she were blowing by mouth, with little heaves of her shoulders, huffs
and puffs of her chest, to inflate the balloon. In and out. In and out.
The cerise balloon elongated, tensile with the air pumped into it.
Longer and longer. Brows ferociously knit, she detached the elastic neck,
attenuated it, concentrating on twisting it through itself in the tightest
of knots.

Elwell touched her cheek, and she turned to his touch with a spas-
modic movement that brushed against his fingertips. Affection? Admiration? Gratitude? Of the three it was admiration that he most required
as he went reluctantly to take his place at the head of the conference
that he had so unwillingly convened.

Pat Mencken had been making hay during Elwell's absence. Entertaining the company with his ringside view of climactic events.

"And here we were at Yalta all lovey-dovey, rosy-posy, even Jimmy
Byrnes who never liked the Russians like Stalin. We ironed out our dif-
ferences. Eastern Europe. Germany. Voting procedures for the UN,
including the veto which we in the military especially insisted upon.
Schedule of Soviet entry in the war against Japan. Everything agreed on.
The high point."

Pat's voice zoomed up, overamplified by the speaker Herron had had
Julie turn on at his bed. She adjusted it down to normal.

"Ah Philip, this is an old story to you."

"Go on," Elwell said and took his seat at the board table, looking down the double file of conferees, each with white pad and ashtray before him, each with head upturned to Mencken who, colorful and expansive, reveling in his mufti freedom from restraint, gave vent with ample gesture to his experience.

Elwell knew Mencken as a first-rate behind-the-scenes manipulator who on occasion liked to play the chowderhead. But Mencken's gratuitous broadside at Thompson before entering the room perplexed him. The general was quite capable of hurling irresponsible charges around. Always however with a purpose. And what could the purpose be, unless it was to drive a wedge between engineer and employer? Get Thompson out of the picture . . .

"That was Yalta, the beginning and the end," Mencken said, relishing it. "Inside of two weeks we're negotiating German surrender terms in Italy, leaving the Russians out. They throw a fit. Meanwhile they're in Rumania, goosing the king into installing their hand-picked cabinet. We throw a fit. Then Poland! Winston had been counting on getting his own men in from the London government-in-exile, as he did in Greece in '44, dumping the partisans who were in control there. But this time the Russians steal a march on him, backing the Lublin government, no outsiders allowed. Notes fly back and forth. Raising hell, demanding free elections, our style, as soon as conditions allow. But when did they ever conduct such elections? And for that matter how many countries do? And if they had gone through with it and an anti-Soviet coalition managed by fair means or foul to win? Then what? There was one thing we all knew. The USSR was not going to stand for any revival after the war of Winston's original *cordon sanitaire*. They were not going to have their borders surrounded by a ring of hostile states. So they disposed of the sanitary belt by replacing it with a security belt, and threw away the key."

Laughter. Mencken in the heat of his image had thrown away his cigarette, and now rescued it, sticking it reminiscently in his mouth.

"I had dinner at the White House one evening along about then. Mid-March, 1945. Less than a month after Yalta. Food was lousy. Filet of sole. Eleanor was there. She called him 'Franklin' and he called her 'Darling' . . ." Mencken drew on his cigarette, dwelling with fond felicity on it. "Just the three of us. And as exasperated as Franklin was over the Polish business, he also felt that there would always be collisions of one degree or another between us and the Soviets. That it was inherent in the relationship. That the best we could do was work out each one as it arose. When I pointed out that they were morbidly suspicious and secretive and God knows what else, he argued that just because they were it devolved upon us to allay, insofar as we could without sacrificing our interests, that element in them. Too many of us, he thought, took an unholy joy in the Elizabethan sport of bear-baiting. Though we couldn't negate the existence of basic conflicts, we could negotiate. After all he'd been through four years of it. That was his position, wasn't it, Doug?"

Mencken appealed to Douglas Gilmore for authentication, not to Elwell who knew the answers as well if not better. Elwell reached for the fresh white pad before him and began to doodle over its inviting surface. Why this review by Pat now? And in so mild a tone? Allowing room even for a sigh of nostalgic sentiment? None of the usual denunciations. One of Mencken's sneak attacks? Is he baiting *me*?

Out of the corner of his eye Elwell observed Mencken shove away from the chair behind which he was standing and in the course of pacing along the side of the table begin to edge, with apparent spontaneity, closer and closer to himself.

Gilmore after the elapse of a moment's reflection concurred with Mencken. "The fact of the matter is, with the defeat of the enemy in sight each of the allies was rushing into the power vacuum as fast as he could to advance his influence as far as he could in preparation for the next phase. We too.

"Withal, Roosevelt firmly believed that amity could be maintained among us. That though this path was fraught with difficulties it must be pursued. That if the will was there and the need, solutions could, with the application of infinite patience and fortitude, be sought for. And that the search itself for methods of settlement, for cooperation, even in its failures, would lead us halfway to accomplishment.

"Just the sort of simplistic vision that attracted him. Of course all the advisers who encouraged him in it are out now."

"They're not with Harry, that's a cinch." Mencken laughed in appreciative anticipation. Shuffling and sidestepping he was nudging forward up the table in the direction of Elwell. Heads pivoting after him as he went.

"I don't think Harry ever was taken in by any such pipe dream," Mencken said. "You remember the statement he made the day after Hitler invaded them? 'If we see that Germany is winning we ought to help Russia and if Russia is winning we ought to help Germany and that way let them kill as many as possible.' I doubt if the Russians ever forgot that. Or Harry either."

Mencken had almost reached Elwell's chair when Elwell, doodling, looked sharply up at him. Mencken slid back a chair or two, awaiting his next opportunity.

"As I think of it," Mencken said, "three pictures stand out in my mind. Are you in a hurry to begin, Philip?"

"Not especially. Whenever you're through. Go on."

"*Molotov*," Mencken said with a flourish of his cigarette. "Ten days after Roosevelt's death he arrives in Washington on his way to the first UN meeting in San Francisco. Sent by Stalin as his expression of respect, a tribute. The Foreign Minister. And nobody of any rank meets him at the airport. When he's received in the White House, he's hauled up on the carpet by the new President and in language without the slightest resemblance to diplomacy told off. They could either go along with us on the Polish issue or, by implicaton, drop out of the United Nations. The Hammer didn't know what hit him. I was there. Tickled pink. All of us were. We'd had just about enough. From then on it was cat and dog. Naturally it was their interpretation that since we didn't need them to win the war in Europe any longer, we were all out now to take over what was coming to them. But they still had one ace in the hole. Japan. They were ready now to join our battle there in August.

"*Churchill*. That July. At Potsdam. In the palace of the Prussian kings. Oh he was in a foul mood. If you've ever met him, you know right away he's a tremendous egotist of course. A showman. And something of an anachronism, a relic from another age—like the whale, on a grand scale. And he came to Potsdam without a pot. He was losing the British elections. He was beginning to realize that between the USA and the USSR, England was slipping into the status of a secondary power. And it was becoming plainer to him every day that although he did not become the King's First Minister in order to preside over the liquidation of the Empire, it was cracking up nevertheless. And we, we ride into the Potsdam Conference on a tide of elation. The evening before, shortly after our arrival, we'd received the news from Alamagordo. It went off. It works. It's ours! The A-bomb.

"Even before we informed Churchill of it, he knew that the only salvation for himself—that is, for the England he embodied—lay in his own veins. The blood of the Dukes of Marlborough and of Leonard Jerome, the American banker. It was his strategy now to weld a union between British global policy and the American capacity to implement it. Just as he saw so magnificently on June 22, 1941, what he had to do, he saw it again on July 17, 1945. All his speeches since indicate it, the emphasis on our common language, our common heritage, our common responsibility.

"So we came to the Conference with the secret of the bomb. Winston came with his belligerency, the fire-eater at his fieriest, with no Roosevelt to restrain him. Heaping fuel on every antagonism between us and the Russians. And the Russians came with something too, their date, August 8, for entering the war against the Japanese. Six months before at Yalta, we and Churchill had estimated that two million men would be required to beat Japan. As we saw it then, we needed Soviet help. Now with the bomb, we neither needed nor wanted it. They couldn't get a rise out of us on this point. And again they didn't know what hit them. On August 6, we dropped the bomb on Hiroshima, having told Winnie at Potsdam but not Joe. Naturally they interpreted it as a gang-up on them. That bomb was the seed of everything that's followed since.

"There is a third picture . . . Is it getting late, Philip?"

"I'm giving you till eleven. Go on."

"*John Foster Dulles.* London. September 30. First Conference of Foreign Ministers. He went as Republican adviser to Jimmy Byrnes. Foster has, I suspect, always felt that we fought the wrong war and has always regarded Stalin, I suspect, as a reincarnation of Napoleon leading the revolutionary hordes across Europe. For ten days at the London Conference, in violation of the Potsdam agreements, the French and Chinese ministers sat in on the treaty discussions for Eastern Europe. When the Russians finding themselves consistently outvoted four to one finally objected, demanding that all the decisions made during this interim be thrown out along with the intruding ministers, Jimmy asked Foster what he should do. 'Refuse,' Foster told him. 'No compromise. No appeasement.' And with these words he pronounced the epitaph of an epoch. And the birth of the policy we adopted from then on. Foster fathered it.

"Tell me, Philip, as one corporation lawyer toward another of similar age and stature, aren't you just one little bit jealous of the role Foster is playing?"

So there it was. Mencken had crept, sneaked, and pussyfooted around three international conferences and around this table to the rear of his chair, Elwell felt, in order to administer this stab in the back. To render him before this company: Gilmore from State; Browne, the economist; Lynd of United Dynamics; Riker who had been with the Manhattan Project from the Chicago stadium to Alamagordo; several of Acme's top echelon executives: to render him before them into a personality sketch, a caricature. He was Molotov hauled up on the carpet at the White House. Churchill at Potsdam, the slipping monarch. . . . Or Foster Dulles in London, the man of destiny. Foster, that upstart! That pious preacher, that conservator of private fortunes, that sibling who competing with his more adventurous brother, in maintenance of himself as elder and dominant, was carrying his law practice into the arena of foreign affairs . . .

"You make me feel almost sorry for the Russians," Elwell said without looking up from the sketch that poured unguided from his pen onto the pad before him.

"I mean to!" Mencken barked, the mellowness of his reminiscence shed like a discarded costume. "All this eyewash every day of the week about how they're victimizing us doesn't go down with me. We give them as good as we get, and sometimes first and faster and a hell of a lot harder."

"And it's paying off," Douglas added. "There was a time not so long ago when the Red Army could have marched to the Atlantic if they'd wanted to and there was nothing really there to stop them. Now there is. There was a time when the Communist parties could have taken France and Italy at the polls. Not now. We've put our support, our money, and our arms at the disposal of those political forces that are friendly to us, and by doing so we've saved half of Europe. Through the UN we backed the Iranian complaint against the overdue presence of Soviet troops on their soil, and the troops were pulled out. We pressured them to quit Manchuria and they did. It is our objective to contain them on every front, not only along their borders but within every country that may be subject to the extension of their influence. Otherwise, by the logic of their ideology and of current conditions they would in a very few years dominate the world. And we are the only government now left with the strength to prevent it.

"This is the situation, Philip, which subsumes all other considerations. This is the all-consuming task to which we must devote everything we have for as long as we can see ahead, and longer . . ."

It was not to stab him in the back with invidious comparisons, Elwell suddenly realized, that Pat Mencken was hovering behind his chair, breathing with steamy superabundance of energy down the back of his neck, stretching from side to side. But to peek over his shoulder at the doodling! To espy some helpful clue to his character from the automatic writing. Whether it was a nubile nude overembellished with parts or abstract circles and peaks. In his style, tactically, Mencken was working on him. And Douglas tactfully. And the others quizzically following.

Wordlessly Elwell tore the sheet off the top of his pad and passed it up over his shoulder to Mencken. Mencken, trapped, had the grace to redden. The figures on the page suggested a map. Of the Euro-Afro-Asiatic land mass with its bulging subcontinents, peninsulas, isthmuses, archipelagoes. On the outer edges left and right, slivered, North and

South America. Inscribed about in an ellipse, black nibbed: *Lesbia mea
. . . Lesbia illa . . .*

"Lesbia," Elwell obscurely explained, "embraces a thousand lovers."

He received the scrawl back from Mencken who could make nothing
of it or of him. Before rising to open the formal conference Elwell tore
it to shreds and dropped it in his ashtray, dipped his lighter to it and
watched the flames dance up.

They were being fair enough to him. His choice was clear. To go along
with them or to drop out. To excise these many months of chasing rainbows up the rivers. To put behind him those years of active preparation
for a course quite contrary to that which was being taken now: Teheran,
Bretton Woods, Quebec, Dumbarton Oaks, Yalta, San Francisco. To
dissociate himself from that eclectic team of Roosevelt, Hull, Hopkins,
Stettinius, Stassen—the dead, the dying, and the displaced . . . Or, his
sentence to be pronounced in the strong and certain words of Henry
Warren: "We'll shelve the dead wood." In the laughter of his wife:
"Hopelessly outdated."

The leadership of the nation had left the boat to Paris—a leaky
freighter—and left Hartley Hunt—the long and blundering and perhaps not altogether fruitless struggle—to marry the daughter of the Old
Mogul on the familiar ground of *Realpolitik.*

The fire in his ashtray burned out, a final margin curling with the
orange rim of an ember in the nest of blackened tatters, brittle as November leaves. Outside the bay windows the sea air sparkled, its serenity
marred only by the black finger of the barge in the harbor and the distant clatter of concrete mixers crushing gravel in their collective maw.

Elwell glanced back toward Julie. She was bending with head close to
Herron toward the speaker concealed in the drapery back of the bed.
But at Elwell's glance she turned as if touched on the shoulder and
looked at him with a blithe expectancy.

Lesbia mea. Lesbia illa.

As pure of purpose as she declared? Elwell doubted it. No one is that
pure. Ambivalent Julie. His ambivalent self.

The conference, following a formula he had developed some years
ago, brought together several bodies of knowledge, having ostensibly no
connection whatsoever with Acme's financial state or its stake in financial futurities. In fact, the accrual of vast sums of money which could
not be allowed to lie idle would hardly be mentioned here at all today.
Rather, a frame of reference would be established, within which long-
term trends and short-term risks would in due time be charted. But in
spite of the orientation of the present conference, already so obvious,

and in spite of the possibility of personal obloquy, Elwell was bound to have his say.

"This is not the first time in history," he addressed the ten men, "when wartime allies have fallen out upon the cessation of hostilities. There were those in the past administration who anticipated this eventuality and sought to forestall it by developing an international machinery for the settlement of disputes and the promotion of cooperation. Perhaps they built better than they knew. Perhaps it may yet serve to temper the growth of antagonisms and ultimately to survive them.

"At the end of the war our country stood at a fork in the road. We could seek a *modus vivendi* with the Communist elements in the world, and granted the uncertainties incurred predicate our prospects on an era of peaceful construction. Or we could take the other path, a fight to the finish."

"Don't forget," Mencken interrupted, "we have the bomb."

"Don't underestimate the Russians," Elwell answered with what was by now a weary reiteration. "If we have it, they will. What do you think, Riker?"

Riker, the physicist, looked up from his pad, a doodler too, with his answer, also too often reiterated. "Five years."

"All the more reason," Mencken said reasonably, "why we should act now. When they are in the weaker position—they had twenty million casualties and their industry was practically destroyed."

"The public isn't ready for another war this soon."

"They can be made ready," Mencken said. "There's a new blowup every other day."

"On the basis of our confidential reports, some of us have reason to believe," Gilmore supplemented, "that with sufficient external pressure, the regime may collapse from within. There is privation, unrest—"

"Don't count on it," Elwell advised.

A secretary drew one of the window curtains against the intrusive dazzle of sun and sea. Elwell's water glass was refilled. It was apparent from a certain eager-beaver shine from the Acme executive group that they were speculating on his demise—Elwell's out. The corporation needed no such individualist as himself in its directorate. Under their various hands it would continue on its own momentum, self-perpetuating, an aggregate of interacting organisms. Nevertheless he was bound to deliver his opinion, dispassionately, without advocacy but with candor. As he would to a client who was unwisely pyramiding investments on none too sound a base.

"When history is written this period will be looked back upon as one of unmitigated folly. Of provocation leading to provocation, threats to threats, crisis to crisis until we are all so inextricably involved that who began it, they or we, becomes irrelevant beside the fact that all of us, we and they, have become the creatures of our own Frankenstein. It can only culminate in catastrophe. Or failing that, our raw materials, our production facilities, the labor of millions of men over millions of man-hours, our organizational and technological ability, our best brains and talent will be stockpiled until they have accumulated into a scrap pile of such cosmic waste as to benumb the imagination.

"And make no mistake about it: in the process of converting ourselves into a garrison state, geared primarily to war preparation, if not war it-self, we will not be what we were. We will not be what we might other-wise have been as a nation, as a government, as a people. I will not be the same man next year. Nor will any one of you."

Mencken sprang up, choleric or with a show of choler that was just as effective. "We cannot afford at this point, Philip, any opposition that will undermine our unity, any skepticism that will subvert our determi-nation—"

"Are you questioning my patriotism, General?" Elwell asked, and sat down. The general growled. Elwell laughed, fitted his pipe into the crook of his mouth and ppt-ptting at it dipped the flame of his lighter into the bowl.

From then on the conference proceeded amicably enough. In the province of the experts. Maps, graphs, and drawing boards were assem-bled, illustrating material quite different from that in the River Room below.

Lynd of United Dynamics treated them to a scholarly forecast of the American Century which would dominate all quarters of the globe and the Pax Americana which would ensue as a logical consequence. Elwell liked that. He agreed with it. If only it could be put into practice. "Who's being utopian now?"

The bookish economist, Browne, expounded with a pointer on the business cycle. With overexpanded production facilities and overstocked inventories we were, in spite of a backlog of consumer demand, on the verge of a downward spiral of cutbacks and general recession. But should the government subsidize private industry with adequate financing, should it enter the market as chief customer, particularly in the field of hard goods, we might well be on the verge of an expansion unparalleled in our history. Elwell liked that. He agreed with it. If only it could suc-ceed in the long run. "Who's being socialistic now?"

Riker who had left Los Alamos after the war to spend some time at Peenemünde and later at White Sands, lectured briefly on the future of nuclear weapons and delivery systems. It was fascinating, fantastic, and

not easily assimilable. Elwell sat up with a barrage of questions. Mencken nudged Gilmore. Fusion produces a thousand times the explosive
power of fission? Guided missiles that will travel into outer space? Riker
sketched out a rocket on a launching pad. "The greatest phallic symbol
of them all," Elwell commented. "Let's get back to manned bombers,"
Mencken proposed. "Phallic or anal, take your choice," Riker grinned
at Elwell. Elwell always derived inordinate gratification from his ability
to get along well with men who lived in close physical contact with their
work. "Gentlemen, gentlemen . . ."

Julie listened with Herron to the speaker for quite some time. Although she understood little of what passed, she felt somehow implicated. "Are we going to have another war?" she asked Herron once,
naïvely, and exclaimed in dismay, "But I thought you were connected
with a life insurance company!" And again, "We're losing China? But
when did we have it to lose? What I mean, I've just been through a
thing like that. Losing a piece of land that wasn't mine."

To which Herron equably replied, "Lovely child. A woman should
never be anything more than a lovely child." He asked for her hand and
she gave it to him. He clasped it under his hands crossed over his breast.
She thought after a while that he was drifting off to sleep and began
very carefully to slip her hand back out from under.

"Would you like a peach?" Herron asked without opening his eyes.

From the fruit bowl on the other side of his bed, where the nurse attended with ready instruments, Julie chose two ruddy-cheeked golden
peaches. "Will you peel one for me?" Herron requested, "please?" Julie
peeled away the furry skin, his eyes now brightly open watching the
parings strip stickily from her fingers. "Now we will eat them," the old
man said with a lick of his tongue. Together they lifted their peaches to
their mouths and bit into the juice-oozing flesh. "M-m-m-m."

When Elwell looked around again at them, they were contentedly
eating peaches.

8

By the time Julie descended from her after-lunch nap, it was known
to everyone in the house that she had spent almost two hours this morning with old Mr. Herron. It was also known by the subtle caste system
that obtains in such places, categorizing guests by the guest room assigned them, that she was staying not in the bungalows nor the pavilion
nor yet the favored suites of the main house, but in the Elwell wing itself. And what could that mean? Unless . . . ? She was a Girl with a

Gimmick. An odd gimmick, true, but an ingenious one and that's what
it takes. Obviously on the make. And getting there.

"Julie," the ladies called to her from the cardroom. "Julie, in here."
She was on a first-name basis with them all. "Julie, will you make a
fourth?" "Julie, over here—" She was appropriated by Sophie Mencken
for a rubber of contract, with tablemates who were such whizzes that
the cards were dealt out almost as soon as they popped out of the shuf-
fler and tricks were zipped through with the speed of an old Mack Sen-
nett comedy. "Well, I don't know," Julie said as she sat down next to
Sophie, "I haven't played much," and straightaway with that amazing
luck that had attended her all day picked up a run of hearts and began
raking the pennies in. While she was playing, in the flush of success, an
elderly lady of ramshackle elegance, her black toque pierced with a jeweled pin that must have passed through the center of her skull, a cigarette cocked rakishly in her mouth on the end of a holder, rouged to the
ears and mascaraed to the eyeballs, brushed by the back of her chair and
bending close over her whispered into her ear: "You are adorable." Before she could recover from that Sophie leaned over to whisper wickedly
into her other ear: "Look out. Or should I say, congratulations? Lucy
Prynne. Adirondack Steel. She's a notorious Lesbian." And before she
could recover from that or start hitting a losing streak, Marion Elwell
wended between games of gin rummy, backgammon, canasta, directly to
her. "Julie dear, I don't believe you've met everyone here yet." Taking
Julie under her wing, Marion ushered her from table to table, spending
a few hospitable moments in well-chosen words at each. "Some of them
can be very useful to you," she intimated to Julie between introductions.
"At the opportune time."

The ladies gazed after the pair with delighted speculation. One of
these days Marion Elwell is going to overplay her hand. She'll take one
chance too many . . . After all, who could forget the Southern girl,
daughter of a Kentucky stable groom, who through a series of marriages
parlayed herself into the leadership of the beau monde, the haut monde
and the ineffable title, Best Dressed Woman in the World? Or the
Baltimore debutante who cost a king his throne?

Marion pursued her stately circuit unperturbed, her serene eyes un-
clouded by doubt, her splendid manner unruffled. She never chose to
ignore Philip's occasional peccadilloes. On the contrary she took a positive pleasure in the women he was attracted to, and why not? They
were usually vivid youngsters with a great yearning to attain the heights,
on the stage, in the press . . . There was the Irish coed who crashed all
the gates into the front office to interview Philip for her college paper
and who was now a syndicated feature columnist. There was the dancer

at someone's party with her astonishing agility of limb pirouetting on one toe through an acrid haze of perspiration, who was now a prima ballerina. They might begin by falling in love with Philip but invariably they ended up devoted to her. And Philip might begin by falling in love with them but invariably he ended up more devoted than ever to her. Having retired long ago from an act no longer becoming to her, preferring always to confine herself to those activities in which she excelled, Marion permitted her husband his infidelities while preserving for herself what was far more important to her, her dignity. Philip's protegées, she considered, performed a service for him somewhat above that of a good secretary and below that of a good physician. He was a little restless right now, what with the river thing. He needed someone to rub away his disappointment, recharge his vigor. The diversion of a fresh romance. And Julie, whose crusade Marion now classified with the Irish girl's college paper, appeared to be an apt enough candidate.

Pat Mencken appeared at the cardroom door in search of Julie for a round of golf, and Marion paired her off with him. "But I'm only just learning," Julie said. "Then you can't hope for a better teacher," Marion told her. "Out with you." And completing her circuit at Sophie Mencken's table she gazed contemplatively back at the door. "Isn't she a darling? I do wish we could take her up to New York with us."

"And what would you do with her?" Sophie asked.

"Public relations. Absolutely." The upper and lower registers of Marion's beautiful speaking voice took Julie's measure. "Can't you just see her hitting up Gus Kahn for fifty thousand dollars in a worthy cause?"

"I saw her finesse," Sophie agreed sourly. "Anybody that can pull off the stunts she tried on pure fluke is a peril to the orderly processes of society."

On the golf course the general corrected Julie's stance, furnished her with tips on the selection of irons, improved her grasp on the club and standing behind her, holding her wrists, went through a series of practice shots with her. Meanwhile he pumped her concerning Philip. Julie didn't mind. She frankly enjoyed the attention she was receiving, for whatever reason. She flowered in the limelight. It made all the difference in the world to her to be elevated out of the obscurity in which she had arrived this morning to the recognition of being singled out, accepted. And also, truthfully, to be released out of the harshness of the past weeks into a semblance of normal living. Pat Mencken turned out to be not such a bad fellow at all in spite of his morning's gruffness. In fact, he was very nice. With his reddish fringe of hair, his healthy pink glow, his exuberance.

"So he translates Latin verse?"

"Don't tell him I told you, he's very good at it. I've made a few stabs myself."

"Great swing there. Don't be afraid, give it all you've got! You'll make it to Aiken yet . . . You have? Last thing I'd ever guess looking at you. Unscrambling syntax."

"Not really. It either comes to me all at once or not at all—"

"Latin verse, eh? Translates from one medium into another, hm? It figures."

On the third hole she smacked the ball with a number five iron over a hundred yards into the green. They both ran after it screaming. "It isn't! It can't be! It didn't!" But yes it did. Her ball had rolled into the hole and there it nested winking innocently up at them. They hugged each other and they pounded each other, whooping. "I'll probably never do it again, never in a lifetime!" Julie cried. "I don't believe it, I just don't." The hole-in-one called for drinks. They trekked back to the pavilion and under the striped awning Pat set her up on a table and they had a couple with the crowd. On the premise that Julie was at the end of the line of a bum marriage and at loose ends, Mencken quite seriously offered to arrange an officer's commission in the WAC for her. "Veterans Rehabilitation. It's wide open. You'll be a colonel before you know it."

Julie was still laughing over it when Douglas Gilmore invited her out for a sail around the harbor. Douglas turned out to be very nice too, rather austere and difficult to talk to at first until she recognized that under his lean and lonely visage lurked a painfully shy young lad. They took out the dinghy, a neat little cedar-straked boat with canvas sewn in bands of blue and white, and scudded before a fair wind—up mains'l! up jib! bring her about! Julie had not been out sailing since she was a high school girl, and she loved the scrambling with ropes, ducking under boom, the partnership of fitting action to action, hand-in-glove, skipper and crew. And truthfully, she loved the attraction she exercised. Elwell's interest in her had excited a like interest among his associates, pleasantly amorous but tacitly non-competitive, acknowledging his priority. She exercised another attraction of which she was unaware: Elwell's approval stamped her with the label *safe*. Making her eligible for future reference. "So you're interested in mental health," Douglas sounded her out, and wondering as Mencken had before him just what Elwell had in mind for her offered quite seriously to find her a spot in the Children's Bureau.

"Ship ahoy!"

"Port ahoy!"

They tacked in, spray flying. "Julie! Jul-lee-ee! Hurry up." A turnout was waiting on the jetty. Hands thrust out to help her jump from the bow, but she made it herself, caught the lines Douglas threw out to her and hitched them around the mooring cleats. All the recently arrived guests were on their way at this moment to the livestock stables, a visit there being practically mandatory for anyone who stayed at the Nest. Cars were lined up at the end of the jetty, adding boaters and swimmers to their passenger load. Waving and shouting everyone in like a Sunday school picnic.

"To the farm! The farm!"

"The Cow Palace!"

Julie was swept along with the tide into a station wagon and minutes later was delivered at the farm into the arms of Philip Elwell. Dark in his whites, his silver-winged head jutting forth, he plowed through to her and lifted her out by the elbows. His beaked bird's face in which flying brows and nose conjoined was smooth with the rigor of the public man, preoccupied.

"Philip! I've been dying to see you."

"Are you having a good time?"

"It's like a dream. As if I were living in a dream . . ."

People were rushing them along toward the stables. They had arrived here at a most propitious moment. Bonnie Maid, bought at auction for over fourteen thousand dollars, the highest price ever paid for a female of her line, was in heat and scheduled to be served by the prize bull, Black Sultan. "She's nervous, she's skittish, they always are the first time." "He has excellent points." With punctilious scientific detachment the Sultan's male attributes were cited and his ability to sire, theoretically, as many as one hundred and twenty calves per week. The Herron stables had been among the first in the country to experiment with artificial insemination. But a few months ago Mr. Herron had handed down a papal bull . . .

Punctiliously the head stockman, controlling the seething surge of the party toward the pens, steered them first to the main stable, indeed a Cow Palace or, more accurately, a Cow Cathedral with its campanile of a silo, its peaked slate roof, its cream stucco sides pierced with windows. The visitors trooped into an interior of unglazed red tile flooring and glazed white tile walls bearing blue-figured crests. Every stall was lighted by a window, was cleaned by troughs of water flushing through. The laboratory for the diagnosis of diseases glistened with stainless steel and glass equipment, the crests repeated in the terrazzo floor. There had been some trouble with Bang's Disease some years ago when Mr. Herron had given up the cattle for a while and they'd run wild and every one of them had to be hunted down and shot.

Elwell's hand remained under Julie's elbow with a grip that tightened now and then. Later their hands dropped and locked, merging spontaneously, swinging between them. "It's very good of you," she said, "to come out when you're so taken up."

"Not a bit." His beaked bird's face was quickening out of its disciplined tightness, coming alive. "I can't remember when I was last here."

With detached scientific curiosity everyone jostled for a front-line view around the pen. Julie found herself pressed up against the fencing, Elwell behind her, his hands on her arms.

Bonnie Maid was led through the gate. Her slant black eyes gleamed with soft intelligence. "We've had to watch her like a hawk," the stockman explained, "or she'd be mounted by and mounting every animal in sight from the dogs to the hogs." Her haunches rested lightly on mincing legs. Her tail switched friskily. Julie could have reached through the fence and petted her velvety spotted hide. The faces fringing the fence were composed, observant but contained with a scrupulous non-involvement. "You can always tell when they're built deep and blocky like that." From around a fencepost Sophie Mencken gaily waggled her fingers at Julie, and from somewhere nearby Marion Elwell's lovely cadence compared the procedure with that employed for a stallion of hers that had been put to stud.

The stable door opened, electronically raised, and from its mouth Black Sultan rushed out headlong. Bonnie Maid planted her forelegs, nervously twitching before the mature bull; then swerved and bolted. The bull hurtled past Julie with all the blunt momentum of his two thousand pounds, in a blur of bristles and sweat, tasseled genitals and flying dirt. Terrified into incredible feats of agility, the heifer feinted and dodged, plunged and reared, escaping by a narrow and narrower margin. Too late the stablehands ran shouting for the breeding crate. The Sultan leaped for the Maid's tail, and Julie about-faced toward Elwell. Taking his elbows she backed him out of the throng of onlookers.

"Reckon I'm much too country," she said fliply, puncturing the nonsense, "to get a bang out of a thing like that."

"There's no actual hurt—"

"I know," she said through an unearthly screech that burst from the pen, "it's purely subjective."

She kept walking away from the pen rubbing at her arms where Elwell had held them. "You've changed since this morning."

"You've changed too."

"No I haven't! If you could just give me a few minutes? Can't we go off somewhere by ourselves?"

"Of course. Of course, any time."

But he had one more stop to make first on his itinerary and Mencken and Riker were halting him, "Ready now? Might as well look it over while we're here." With them and their wives and a half-dozen others, piling into the leading station wagons, leaving all the lesser lights behind, Julie whirled off again.

The wooded grove north of the house, kept orderly by a small army of landscapers, gave way to thicker woods heavily overhung with wisteria and honeysuckle vines, rough with underbrush, wax myrtle, palmetto, foxgrape, and prickly pear. The sound of construction, heard as a distant thrum from the house, swelled to the distinct chattering of drills, the clangor of power shovels.

"My goodness," Julie said to Elwell, "what are you building out here, a factory?"

"I wish I knew."

The cars turned into a crushed gravel path, crawled through jungle that darkened the late afternoon to dusky green gloom. They were brought up short by a barbed-wire gate and a young man in military helmet and suntans who checked identification. "Am I cleared?" the general inquired plaintively and with laughter they passed through the gate. Arriving from the most primitive of spectacles, performed for them by the beasts of the barnyard, to the most civilized.

"Chichén Itzá," Gilmore cracked slyly.

"Touché," Elwell acknowledged.

"But what is it?" Julie asked.

In a clearing in the woods that descended like an amphitheater to an excavated depression, in the center stood a completed dome of solid concrete blocks. Around it in a wide encompassing pit men and machinery were engaged in the erection of auxiliary underground chambers and tunnels.

Tomb? Or womb?

They were met by the chief engineer, a short husky fellow who had undertaken the job a half year ago with great energy and enthusiasm and now was greyed, begrimed, and harried enough to die of it. Busily he unrolled blueprints for Elwell and Mencken's and, as an afterthought, Riker's inspection. The work had gotten off to a bad start from the beginning when a bulldozer, insufficiently shored, rolled over two laborers, crushing them to smithereens. The first wall had collapsed twice and last week a crane operator was buried under a gravel slide. And everything, every piece of material and equipment, had to be brought in from outside by boat or plane and assembled here. Still, when you took into account all the problems of sinking a foundation in this kind of soil . . .

Called away by an emergency yell on the walkie-talkie that hung around his neck, the chief turned them over to his consulting engineer, Thompson, for further guidance.

"You here?"

At the sight of the phlegmatic Thompson, Mencken drew himself up in soldierly disapproval and with no transition whatsoever from the skylarking spirits he had been indulging began curtly to dress him down. "If you're building an air-raid shelter, why did you have to plan it so far from the house? And that door down there . . ."

Thompson led them over the plank extending from solid ground to the tiny niche of a doorway in the dome. The ladies teetering and shrieking hung onto the shirts of the men in front of them. "That entrance is no good," the general badgered Thompson who had had nothing at all to do with the design of the structure—he had been summoned back from the final phase of his globe-girdling trip with Elwell for the sole purpose of ironing out the bugs resulting from the water table. "Most radiation travels in a straight line," Mencken said. "What you need to reduce the hazard is a right-angled parallel wall here. It's completely exposed, right, Riker?"

Riker, embarrassed, ducked his head.

"And the way things are developing, in a couple of years this will all be obsolete. Do you know anything about the effects of nuclear blast, heat and fallout?"

Thompson unlocked the corrugated metal door. "I'm a stranger here myself," he said. "It's all new to me. Cyclone, earthquake, tidal wave I have some answers to. But this?" He threw open the door.

The electrical system on which lighting, ventilation, cooking, and water facilities depended had, as it all too frequently did, conked out again. The ladies squirmed and squealed after their gentlemen through the narrow aperture into the darkness of the cave inside. "You'll find electric torches on the shelf to the right," Thompson instructed, and leaving them in the vestibule strode back up the plank.

"Thompson!" Elwell called after him. "Come back here."

The wind rippled and billowed through the back of Thompson's shirt.

"Whole subject needs further research," Mencken informed Elwell. "We have to put our colleges and graduate schools onto it, it's all in the pioneering stage. But I'd get rid of that guy. He's no use to you."

"You have one hell of a nerve, Pat Mencken," Elwell said, not without a tinge of admiration.

But Elwell had not once, Julie noticed with a twinge of uneasiness, spoken up during Mencken's sniping at Thompson. But then men never like to stop a fight, it's a violation of the male code. She clung close to Elwell's side, her hand tucked in under his elbow.

Marion who was familiar with the progress of the building here located and distributed several torches. "Now if we all stay together . . . I called this Father's Folly at first, but now it seems there may be something to it. He was very concerned during the last war with the increasing number of civilian casualties, Pat, and that's why he had it built so far from the house, which would be the natural target—"

"I stand corrected, ma'am."

"You see"—Marion passed her beam over the vestibule—"there is an inner and outer shell of solid blocks with an insulation of gravel, I think it is, between. He had a thorough study made covering all sorts of contingencies."

"After you, ma'am."

"There's a ramp here, no stairs."

They descended into the humid volume of the hemisphere, their torches tossing small spots of light about them. Amidst giggles of excited eeriness someone began to sneeze—Riker—against an alien dust or drift of mold pricking at membranes of eye and nose.

"Now here is the food storage center."

Marion slid a wall panel back on the side, her beam disclosing shelves upon shelves of canned foods. "During the siege of Leningrad, according to Father's figures," she said with the same cadenced detachment with which she had discoursed upon the points and pedigree of Black Sultan, "a third of the population died the first winter of hunger and cold. About a million of them. More proportionately as well as numerically than the combined fatalities of Hiroshima and Nagasaki. We have enough here to feed thirty persons for a period of a year. Over there"— her torch shone on a stainless-steel door at the end of the compartment —"we have freezer lockers for meat, fish, vegetables, and baked goods. And in one of the outer buildings, as soon as it's up, we'll have someone working on growing complete gardens of produce under artificial light. There'll be provisions made for keeping some of the livestock."

"Heavens!"

"How tremendous!"

"A regular Noah's ark . . ."

Withdrawing from the food section Marion flashed torch upward over the wood-paneled wall to a set of grilles. "The ventilation ducts. I don't know exactly how it works but the ventilating system is a self-contained unit, releasing oxygen from chemicals and reconstituting it from the feedback, circulating heated and cool air according to the temperature requirements. I doubt if it'll ever get actually cold here. But hot . . . That's presenting a phenomenal headache. I think Father's going a little overboard on it myself, but he was struck with some statistics someone leaked out to him. In Hamburg the saturation bombing brought about firestorms, whatever that is, and people were roasted alive in their shelters. Or asphyxiated. Carbon monoxide. Sixty thousand in one night. Three hundred thousand in Dresden, and that was with conventional weapons—"

"I never heard that before."

"Is that true, General?"

"Where'd he get his information?"

"I must admit that the whole matter of safety has become quite an obsession with Father. He's held death at a standstill for the last fifteen years and he's determined to hold it off—as long as he lives! Devours everything on this subject."

She slid back another panel.

"Our kitchen. You could see it all so much better with light. Where are the generators, they ought to be on again any minute—" She twisted at faucets. "The pumps must be out too. Anyhow we have three different methods of water supply. As I understand it—am I scrambling this up, Mr. Riker?—hypothetically all our waters could become contaminated."

Riker was sneezing again and wiping at rheumy eyes with the back of his hand. "Hypothetically"—he got hold of himself with a handkerchief —"the entire atmosphere could become poisoned. The earth could become uninhabitable. Its surface could be reduced to radioactive ash. Hypothetically. It is my personal belief that our development of these armaments will act as a preventive. No one will dare challenge anything we choose to do. We have a head start now and if we can keep a step ahead of any competition . . . Of course there is a calculated risk involved."

He worked with the corner of his handkerchief at his eye as if a cinder were caught under the lid. "A calculated risk in our handling of materials. We don't really know yet all the factors we're dealing with. But if you calculate that as a risk, it's very little when you stack it up against what there is to be gained."

"No risk at all," Mencken asserted. "Even the fallout from testing is minimal. You see, Philip, the requirements of our economy and our defense coincide. It all fits together. Like a poem."

Julie had been dropping back. While the ladies exclaimed over the adjuncts of kitchen and bathroom she dawdled forlornly, left behind in outer darkness, letting the clustered lights move on without her. No one missed her. "And this is our library." The splendidly serene voice rippling with an undercurrent of laughter. "At last a place for the Harvard Classics! And record collection, back to Galli-Curci and Farrar. And cans of films. The vault for Acme's papers . . ." Far and farther off, the voices receding, the lights dwindling to diamond points, the dimness descending in veils about her, the blackness in thick velvet folds, suffocating . . .

But where do I, where do I fit in? And Coley . . . ?

She tried to cut across the chamber to them in their perambulation of the outer perimeter, to rejoin her proper constellation. She stumbled over furniture, barking her shin, floundered on the soft lap of a chair. With stiff legs, cautiously scuffling over carpet and flooring she groped her way back to the wall. She slid clammy fingers over the paneling, feeling along it. Scrubbed her knuckles over her cheek, brushing frantically at the dangling thread of a cobweb or a wisp of her own hair. At a scratching on the wall above, her heart exploded into her ears. The scratching sprang down the back of her hand. She shrieked.

"Julie?"

They all hastened with lifted torches back toward her, searching. "Where are you? Julie—"

In Elwell's ray of light, a little jeweled lizard was scuttling up her forearm. "Oh . . ." She lifted it by the tail. "Just a garden lizard." And set it down in the palm of her hand. "How silly of me." Smiling up from it to Elwell warm with ashamed apology. "I must be a little on edge."

The ladies shuddered. "Ugh, the ugly thing!" "Julie, how can you? Put it down!"

She turned her hand obliquely for the lizard to crawl over the back. "I'll take it outdoors where it belongs and let it go there." In Elwell's spot of light the lizard reached the side of her thumb, its horny green head poking over, claws gripping. "Go on," she urged, "go on over, you dope. What's the matter?" Her brows knit in concern. "Is it blind?"

Just as she finished saying it, peering at the slotted eyes of the creature, they were all momentarily blinded. All at once all the lights in the room, lamps, shaded rods, and panels, went on. Normally soft and harmonious but blinding out of the darkness. The ventilators hummed. Music throbbed up, a fluid symphony of strings. Their eyes widened, grew accustomed, surveyed the territory through which they had been filtering with—they suddenly realized it—such leeriness.

"Why it's lovely."

"Beautiful!"

"Who wouldn't want to spend a month, or a year, or a lifetime—"

Sophie flung herself down on a divan, fanning herself with her hand. "Well, Marion, where's the deck of cards?"

All the furnishings here were clean-cut concise Danish modern, lavish only in the grain of teak and the texture of leathers and fabrics. Surrounded with pebbled beds of plants that leaned elephant-leafed over arcs of water.

"Just a minute"—Marion held up her hand—"there's one more thing. I haven't seen it yet myself." She stepped back to one of the panels, opened a switchboard. Abracadabra.

"Oh!"

Overhead the domed sky was blue, drifting with downy clouds.

"Father had someone down from the Hayden Planetarium—" Marion played with the buttons behind the panel. A rosy flush of sunset rimming the hemispheric horizon. Purple dusk. Stars glittering. "When it's all arranged, I believe we'll have a sequence of the seasonal night sky . . ."

They were all somewhat keyed up because of the previous darkness, impatient for the night sky to be sped on to dawn again. And blessed daylight.

"Ahhhh."

Julie pocketed her lizard. Overhead cumulus clouds scudded, massed, puffed, parted and disappeared. Through pale blue haze a rainbow shimmered. She caught Marion's eye, and they exchanged a spark of silent laughter as they had over the mother-of-pearl keys on the ebony piano this morning. Oh no! Now that's a touch too much. *Outré* is the word for it.

In the center of the company, on a zebra-striped rug between divans, Elwell struck a pose, hands in pockets, head craned back skyward, making ready to issue one of his pronouncements.

"Apparently it's all underway, already upon us, willy-nilly, whether one would or no. One can only hope that as a by-product the fringes of knowledge will be extended somewhat. Unless we're all exterminated at the switch."

"Oh Philip. You exaggerate—"

"Don't be so pessimistic!"

"There's no risk of that," Mencken asserted.

"But doesn't the secret of any calculation, General, lie precisely in the ability to take all possibilities into account, including the possibility of miscalculation?"

"Granted. Put it that way, Philip, you're talking about the nature of life itself. Isn't all life from the moment we're born, every move we make, every step forward we take, a risk . . ."

They were all in a tremendous hurry to get back to the house and a drink or two or three. "I'm pooped." When they crossed the plank outside again it was evening, the trees dripping blood-red against the flaming afterglow of sunset.

"And after it's all completed"—from the brink of the abyss Marion waved back at the submontane masonry—"the whole thing will be covered with soil and leveled off and replanted with trees. Nobody will be able to spot it from the outside. Thank you, Thompson"—she nodded gratefully to one of the khaki-clad engineers who was not Thompson and who had no more to do with it than Thompson—"for getting our electricity going for us. It was just in the nick of time."

Up in her room later Julie tried to call Cousin Tibby and check on how Colfax was doing, but all the outside lines were tied up. She had tried once more to speak with Elwell after their return from the shelter, but the excursion had taken too long and he was all tied up. "After dinner," he promised her with a warm pressure of his hand, "tonight?" "Yes . . . yes . . ." Earlier, when she was with Herron in the morning, she had tried, subtly she thought, to advance her cause with him. And he had laughed, "I'm not going to win this one for Philip. You'll have to do it all by yourself." She had taken it as a sign of encouragement. A go-ahead signal. A pat on the back and a dare.

From the sandalwood-scented closet she took a short white lace dress she had bought for one of Sukey's showers. A little Irish lace dress of gossamer-spun linen thread, not nearly as fragile as it looked. Took her white satin pumps, treed by someone—not Henry—from the rack below. Stripped for her bath and waited for the telephone to signal that her connection with Tibby was made. Waiting, she folded back the counterpane of the bed and sank back on the downy pillow under the princess crown. And slept. Five minutes? A half hour?

All day long she had been passing through a series of chambers, one after another, portals unlocking. Fleeing through a petrified forest of catatonics, frozen in their attitudes under the enchanted spell of Howard Herron. Fleeing from the cacophony, the grimaces and antics of the asylum. Through the landscape of the River Room and the obstacles of the golf course. Sailing heady with success, admired, acclaimed, on the pinnacle, toast of the party, belle of the ball, Queen of the May. Dr. Wolf, "Oh there you are." And Henry with fond contempt, burring, resonant in her ear, "Aw Julie, cut the bull."

I can't go back, she thought before opening her eyes, I can't go back to that! O God, fix it for me so I won't have to go back . . . But back where she didn't think . . .

9

The circuit to Silver Beach was busy now and it was late, too late to wait any longer, almost eight, dinner like the tour of the stables being mandatory. Julie bathed and dressed quickly. Marion Elwell tapped at her door, "May I come in?" and fastened her pearls for her around her neck. Julie bent forward to the mirror, wreathed by Daphnis and Chloe, smoothing her lipstick with her fingertip, pearls swinging forward from the scalloped neckline of the white lace. Now I really am a lady in pearls.

She consumed with great gusto quantities of dinner for which her French was inadequate. *Perles fraîches de la Volga.* "Oh caviar. Do you know we catch sturgeon on the Ocachee? Our old cook used to pickle up the roe with capers for hors d'oeuvres. And Mamma called them whore's ovaries?" She had a couple of good tales to tell about the rivermen. *Quenelles de brochet:* some sort of fish dumplings served with white wine. *Riz pilaff.* "Shrimpers fix rice while they're out shrimping something like this—*pilau.*" Roast capon with Madeira sauce and a goblet of red wine.

After dinner they were herded into the chapel to be entertained with chamber music. Julie watched the young woman oboist sturdily with distended cheeks puffing. A pastoral air, Daphnis and Chloe, Strephon and Phyllis chasing over rocky rills and green dells. *Like a fawn you flee me, Chloe* . . .

But Elwell was nowhere to be seen. Vanished again.

She went looking for him from room to room. And on a hunch down the long corridor to the River Room. She stole in through a side door. The room was in darkness except for the dusty white effulgence of a film projector focused upon the wall covered with the forty-foot mural of the dam, over which now a screen was suspended.

The displays had been pushed back and chairs were drawn up under the screen in a crescent. Shadowy heads thrown back, faces white-glistening. On the screen two men on a platform, mid-air, lifted with their arms an elongated rod into a towering concrete façade, punctured with hundreds of slots. "Our first nuclear reactor." Snarls of tanks, tubes, conveyors, cables. "Uranium hexafluoride feed plant." Gigantic white-padded robot fist reaching out from a diminutive face behind plate glass.

"Inside of fifteen years"—Riker predicting—"we will be tapping sources of energy that will exceed in the passage of seconds all that has been achieved, cumulatively compiled, since man threw the first stone."

"Private industry"—Mencken persuading—"has already taken it over under contract to the government. What we need, Philip, is someone with your backlog of experience in wedding the public and private sectors of our economy. Who can gear the flow of government funds into industry and the flow of industrial production to the government. The job you did as adviser on the War Production Board is only the beginning for a man of your organizational capacities. Think of co-ordinating under an independent agency a range of activities that includes mining and metallurgy: the location of new sources of uranium, zirconium, beryllium, tungsten, and the mills for upgrading and refining the ores. The building of reactors and turning mills for the fabrication of parts. Chemistry and health physics. Electronics, virtually in its infancy now, for the plotting of instrumentation with ultra-precision analytical and inspection processes. Research: even brain labs that will systematize methods of thinking—"

"Miss!" a GI stationed at the Renaissance doors hissed down the room at Julie. "Miss!" He tiptoed toward her on the double and took her arm. "How did you get in here? You're not supposed to . . ."

Before she could object she was out in the corridor again. Again alone, forlorn and disconsolate. An awful disquiet tugging at her heart.

She retraced her steps to the library. It was after ten on the ormolu clock over the green marble fireplace. She took the telephone into a corner nook and called Tibby.

"Up? Of course he's up, when isn't he up, he has us all up . . . Julie, guess what's happened? You'll never guess—"

"Has something happened to Coley?"

"No, not Coley, nothing happens to Coley . . . One of those convicts Henry has dredging the swamps at Sunset went berserk this afternoon, hit the deputy warden over the head with a shovel."

The outer world goes on. "But Coley, is Coley all right?"

"And he's escaped! A hardened criminal, a maniac, on the loose! I've locked both doors and all the windows. We're stifling." With an abrupt drop to practical reality. "How you makin' out?"

"If Coley is giving you any trouble—"

A group of marauders stampeded into the library, Riker's wife, young people, and among them, Douglas Gilmore, hair mussed and wild-eyed. "Julie, there you are." "Julie, join our team!" Charades . . .

She covered her ear against them. "Will you put him on, Tibby?"

The charaders put their heads together, bent on a stroke of genius. "*Cant-i-lever*. Can't I leave her? Get it?" "No, no, I've got something better . . ."

"This is me, darling. Mummy. It's Mummy."

"Mummy." The word traveled faintly over the wire. And silence.

"You still there, baby?" Breathings. "You having fun? Did brother Charles play lots of games with you today?" Silence. "Honey, can you hear me?" Nothing. "Coley, it's your mummy, I wanted to say good night to you."

"*Barcarolle!* Can't you see it? Bar." With an owlish leer Douglas flipped a lock of hair down over his brow, guzzled from an imaginary bottle. "Car." Steered crazily down the aisle. "Roll." And flung an arm around Julie's waist. "Come on, Julie, you be the roll." Rotating his hips. "It'll be a panic."

"Coley?"

"Don't be a fool, Julie. Stay there just as long as ever you can. If we're not all massacred in our beds . . . Good night!"

Coley . . .

In the great reception hall they were dancing now. Julie skirting through was spun off in a tango. Swirling, dipping, sidestepping, she only barely managed to disentangle herself at the shallow marble steps leading out to the terrace. On the terrace too, detaining arms thrust out, "Julie," from which she twisted away, running to the stairs and down to the driveway. She passed the swimming pool, translucent green with underwater lighting and the beachhouse, ablaze with lights in shower room and kitchenette, and the beach, floodlighted, where the cabañas had been folded up like the tents of the Arabs and quietly stowed away. A stray dance tune wafted after her on the breeze.

It was just one of those things, One of those craz-zee things, A trip to the moonnn . . .

Away from the precincts of the house altogether. Around a curve of shore through tall grass and dunes. She rolled off her stockings and stuffed them into her pumps. Stuck her bare feet into the sand. And looked back at the house, massive under the night sky, twinkling in all its windows, bays, and corners. An extravaganza that harbored no place, not the slightest least little bit of space, for desperation.

She walked over sand silver with moonlight and hardened into wavelets, her sliver of a white lace dress blowing about her knees. Until she reached a breakwater that leaned like an old split-rail fence from the dunes down into the water. Crossing her arms over a log post she gave herself to the movement of glistening black combers. Frothing with moonlight, swelling, retreating, rearing upward again to shatter in shards of foam.

Here Elwell found her shortly afterward.

"Julie—"

"Shshsh . . ." she signaled back at him.

"Is there anything—"

"Shshsh . . ."

He reached her side and bracing himself weightily on her shoulder peered sharply about.

"There." She pointed, whispering against his ear. "Don't make a sound."

On the beach a loggerhead turtle as antediluvian as the lizard that had run up her arm thrust club head out from under gleaming wet carapace and supporting its three hundred pounds on rubbery loose-stockinged flippers lumbered with false starts this way and that, startling at every sound, searching about, ready to retreat, upward toward the dunes; following a trail as alien as land is to sea and more than a million years old. It waded through black skeins of seaweed at high-water mark, and up into the softer sand more consonant with its familiar element. There it, she, rested after her laborious journey, surveying the terrain, searching for a sheltered hollow among the clumps of tall grass.

"Nn-nnh." Julie clapped her hand over Elwell's mouth when he started to speak. Noiselessly she climbed up on the rail and perched there, watching with face averted from him the turtle as she scraped out first a bed for her body, spraying sand like water from her swimming frontal flippers, throwing the sand back in handfuls from her hind flippers, showering herself with sand. The turtle rested again. Then, bedded down, began to bore out a deeper receptacle beneath. Resting. Excavating. Packing firm.

Propping Julie with his shoulder—he was again in his pongees, the warm breezes riffling—Elwell tentatively touched the lace filigree of her dress, her warmth of flesh glowing through. Stroked down the tender skin of her biceps into the nook of her elbow. With head averted as if none of it were happening to her, no touch, no tingle, no deeper sub-dermal stirring, she strained toward the oblate form sinking beneath the undulant strands of grass.

Minute after minute. As if his hand were detached from his person. Hovering upon the nape of her neck. Her hair. *Lesbia mea. Lesbia illa.*

"Now!" She slapped Elwell's arm and jumped down the other side of the rail. "Come on!" She raced up into the dunes over a track as heavy as the tread of a tractor. "Nothing will stop her now. She's laying."

At the rim of the crater she threw herself down prone and after a minute's hesitation Elwell stretched out beside her. Dangling over the edge, Julie reached down in and shoveled back some of the sand from under the huge turtle frame. Every four or five seconds an egg faintly plopped. Drops rolled from turtle eyes glossy with moisture. The turtle shell was barnacled with minute sea animals.

"I rode once on the back of a turtle down into the sea."

"I'd like to have seen that."

Elwell's hand rested on Julie's shoulder, strayed down the cleavage of her spine. She turned her face inquiringly and he kissed her. With an agglutinous jellied suction from which she tore her mouth back.

"You've given in!"

He responded with anger, a man of such lofty position that he considered himself above accusation—in all his experience no one ever openly criticized him. And a man under such pressures as no mere chit of a girl could possibly fathom.

"What do you know, what do you understand of what goes into things like this? How can you presume to judge!" Driven with the cruelty of a defeat, a beating, a rout that he would not admit to. "You, how long do you think you'd last coping with the dreariness and drudgery of some institution, cleaning up slops, a nonentity, ground under the heel of other people's aims? They'll eat you up alive."

"I came here because I need help. Now!"

"You came here because you wanted to come here! To try your wings. To soar."

She sprang to her feet, stared down at the piercing and implacable face. He had never meant to help her. It was all a trick. She'd been taken in.

She ran from him, ran without intention of it to the water, and once she felt the water lapping under her feet, warmly annealing, she kept running. As fast as the dragging lag of the current would let her. Dashing through waves. Plunging in deeper.

"Julie!"

Perversely at that peremptory command she struck out into the breast of the incoming tide. Buoyantly lifted she thrashed through inky blackness toward an ever-receding silver flutter of moonlight. She could hear Elwell somewhere off to the right, swimming strongly. "Julie—" And that thin echo over the wire, like a last drowning cry, "Mummy . . ."

The ocean billowed around her, endlessly. In the dark she lost her bearings, unable to tell direction ahead, behind or sidewise. The surface heaved and sloped, sloped and heaved. She turned and turned again, her dress wrapped about her thighs. Took in a mouthful of water as she tried to call. Flailing and sinking, spluttering upward, she was borne on the tide back into the shallows.

"Julie—"

She shuddered back from him violently. "I don't need you! Stay away from me!" Panting and bedraggled she pulled herself up the shore, retching up the bitter brine.

"Julie, I'm going back to the beach house for blankets and towels."
She batted away his helping arm.

"I won't be long. Stay till I get back here. Don't move."

When Elwell returned the beach was empty. He had been badly shaken up before when he lost her for a few moments in the water. Not *there* again! No sign of her anywhere. Across his path the turtle dragged herself slowly, wearily back from a ritual for which nothing in her life before prepared her, back into the vasty deep which was her atmosphere, food, and home.

Suppressing panic—not now, not an insane thing like this now!— Elwell went back up into the dunes to the nesting site where the turtle had laid her eggs, calling, "Julie. Julie."

There was no sign of the nest anywhere; the sand heaped back over the eggs by the flippers, smoothed out. In a month, six weeks, the babies would hatch out two feet down there in the dark, nothing to tell them which direction was up, down, sidewise, and they would dig to the surface and head for the sea. Inevitably. According to their nature.

"Julie! I'm up by the turtle nest."

Grimly excluding the train of scandal that forced itself on his imagination, he gathered driftwood and under a sandy declivity in the dunes built a fire. In snowy robe, cross-legged, he crouched beside it feeding chips into the flames under the bow of a skeletal bough.

She appeared from a fringe of trees not far off. Disheveled as a gypsy, glinting with laughter over something clasped between her hands, she slid down the sheltering declivity into the circle of firelight.

"What do you have now?" Elwell asked crossly. "The serpent of Eden?"

She brought it up under his nose, a small furry ball, crease-eyed. "Possum. Must have fallen out of its mother's pouch."

Her hands folded back and from its haunches the baby possum took a flying leap and scampered off. "Oh . . . Now it'll get gobbled up . . ."

"Julie, you'd better get those things off and bundle into a robe. I have a thermos of hot coffee here. And a steak if we want it. And a bottle of wine. Catch." He tossed her a robe that matched his own. "So you came back to me. Why?"

Shame-faced, she toed with finely modulated foot in the sand. "There wasn't anywhere else for me to go."

Swathed in their robes, they cooked their steak over the fire on sticks, ate from planks, interspersed the morsels, tender-rare, smoky-rich, with swallows from the bottle. And lying back on their blanket, they talked.

"This is the way it is," Elwell asserted. "It isn't any other way. The one-world idea split in two. I wouldn't say that I'm sure we'll win over them. I can't even say that a society based on private wealth is necessarily superior to one based on public ownership. All I know is, I am what I am. An American, a capitalist, and an attorney. This is mine and I will fight for what's mine as they will fight for what's theirs."

"Even to the point of—you said it—extinction?"

"To the last drop of my blood. We're locked in a deadly embrace, and neither one of us will drop our arms for fear the other won't. There's no escaping it. Nothing can escape its own inherent nature."

"But what about the rest, the rivers?"

"A mirage. We all have these mirages, Julie, as you should know. They serve to fill a gap, tide us over a vacuum."

"But the Ocachee! Everyone at home, they're all counting on it. All their hopes are pinned . . ."

"It'll have to wait."

"How long?"

"Indefinitely. Unless at some future date we want to build a plant there for the manufacture of thermonuclear materials, though more likely it'd be another river."

She sifted sand through her fingers, too sensitive by now to his sensitivities to speak out, to breathe a word of reproach. "You sweep down like a wind," she muttered rebelliously nonetheless, "and pick us up and drop us—"

"Julie. Julie, there's no choice. Oh some dams will go up, piecemeal, here and there. And I suppose I could start up some foundation for the propagation of the faith, go to some subcommittee of the UN with it. But I've never been one to wait in antechambers, hat in hand, bypassed by the period I live in. Eclipsed by others of lesser ability. Nor to devote myself in obscurity to a task out of passion for the task itself. Nor to chance everything—derision, contempt, failure—on a million-to-one shot at immortality."

He leaned up on his elbow and tossed chunks of wood into the fitful fire. No words could serve to salve the wound of a rivalry that refused to die, to give surcease to the pain of self-discovery that had been his today. He was not the man that Hartley Hunt was. He was not willing to take the risks, to make the sacrifices by which he might rise above his time.

"Tomorrow," he said over his shoulder, "I am being appointed by the President to a position that's tantamount to a cabinet post. That vests in me such powers, opens up such realms of possibilities . . . I'm pleased, excited, fascinated—"

"And tomorrow I go back to my husband?"

"Not back, Julie. Forward. You can do a great deal for him. There's no telling how far he will go. Someday you may be First Lady of this state. Which would you be, Julie? Of the elect or the damned?"

"I don't know. I don't know anymore. I don't know what I am."

"You are a host of golden daffodils. You're Chloe, Pyrrha, Lesbia." He turned toward her on the blanket.

"You mean that I'm a better actress than I am a human being."

"You're the kind of a woman who was made for love. Men will love you when you're sixty."

"The queen bee?"

"The queen bee."

"Always the queen bee." She laughed, chiding, turning over on the blanket toward him. "How can you talk of love? Love isn't important to a man like you, Philip. Only importance is."

"And to you," he said, "only men of importance."

He reached over the gap between them. "Now that we understand each other . . ."

Ever since she had left the hospital at Darbyton, it seemed to Julie now, she had been fleeing from what she experienced there, though determined to flee toward it, as if by fleeing toward it she could flee from it. She had been fleeing from everything it represented, the deprivation, the degradation, and by denying that she was fleeing—all the strenuous letters of application, the frenzied schemes—she fled. Here. To this. I don't want to struggle anymore. I don't want to be deprived anymore. I want to have what I can have while I can have it. And still denied it. No no. It isn't so, no!

They opened their robes to each other, seeking refuge. And found in their need more than they bargained for. It was his rationale he drove into her, I'm right, I'm right, you know I'm right, falling upon her, all a-tremble in her first adultery, like the bull of so many excellent points, of strong level back and rump, flesh evenly distributed, full-thighed. This is the way it is. No other way.

Her head jammed back against a log, his bony knee wedged down. The revulsion of his earlier kiss—a taint of breath as from the grave, he's old, he's old—was dispelled. And the suction of each other's breath, the medium through which the soul finds egress, of each other's saliva, of sweat to sweat, of bodily secretions, achieved a fusion out of the cleavage of heaving, sobbing, gasping, in which there was a very burst of suction, drawn from each other, with plasmic plasticity; an explosive expansion which transcended, excluded, every other earthly concern.

"O God, O God, what are we going to do?"

"Julie, we can't let this—"

"I know, I know . . ."

And having said as much, they turned again, seeking. As if in the perfect sexual union resided the escape from and the solution to all the turbulence within them.

"Am I right, Julie? Am I right? Tell me I'm right."

"Right—wrong—what does it matter . . ."

They rolled up in their blanket stiff, cramped, bitten up by sand-hoppers. Yet stinging, burst asunder, bruised and blooming in each other. They slept.

Taking her early dawn canter on her favorite gelding, Marion Elwell came upon them. Nestled together like babes in the woods. Precariously she leaned from her sidesaddle with her riding crop and with its noosed leather whip tickled the back of her husband's neck, the tip of Julie's nose.

Awake, awake.

IV

SEE WHAT TOMORROW BRING

[*August–September*]

1

At seven-fifteen on the morning of September 5, Brandon Colfax Warren lay on the operating table, his head shaved, his arms cuffed in sleeves attached to the table, his legs encased in white stockings and strapped down, his body in split-back johnny sheeted over. He was sleeping lightly under an intravenous injection of sodium pentothal. In sterilized cap, mask, gown, and gloves, scrubbed to a supernal asepsis, Dr. Francis X. Harrington, his assisting anesthetist, and two operating-room nurses took their places about the table. The child's cranium appeared oddly old, its bumps exposed down to the fringe of hair left uncut in back. His brow was sublimely smooth. His eyelids drooped, chiseled, bronze eyelashes fanning over rosy-tan cheeks. From his slightly parted mouth the breath ascended with sweet regularity. Respiration normal. Pulse normal. Blood pressure normal.

The anesthetist plunged the hypodermic of procaine, long-needled, into left and right temple. Minutes lapsed, permitting the drug to take effect. Rubber-fingered, the anesthetist inspected the eyes, no reaction, and stepped back.

Before signaling the nurse for his instruments, Harrington paused an instant, smiling to himself under his mask. The boy with scapular dangling from dirty string around his neck about to dive into the flotsam-strewn black waters of Boston Harbor, he touched the air before his forehead, breast, and shoulders. In the name of the Father, and of the Son, and of the Holy Ghost. *In spiritu sanctitatis tuae . . .*

He lightly nicked each temple in the immobilized head, marking the points of entry. Reached out, hand curved, for the electric drill the nurse held ready. Into the nicks he bored with buzzing drill, through tissue and bony shell, grinding holes the size of a dime into the interior. Bleeding slight. The electric drill was removed from his hand and the blunt shaft of the leukotome inserted. With the leukotome in his grasp he penetrated the small burr-hole on the left and manipulated the instrument with infinite delicacy side to side, up and down. The only risk that Harrington anticipated was concentrated in this action, in this region, here. That in severing the anterior thalamic fibers, no piece of the brain itself should be abscinded. Not to cut too much. Only the white matter concealed inside, not the grey. Adhering to the pattern of X-rays memorized, imprinted in his own brain. To come out of this with a passable human being, normal enough within the broad range of the normal to pass muster. Not a mess.

Into the opposite burr-hole the blunt instrument. Side to side, up and down. The connection between the thalamus, seat of emotion, and the prefrontal area of the cerebral cortex. Slit. Disjoined.

Pulse slightly up. Blood pressure slightly down. Respiration . . .

"There's no risk," Henry told Julie once again. "Harrington's got his whole professional future tied up in this. He's staking everything on it."

In lawn chairs designed with a relaxing backward tilt they sat rigidly forward, uncomfortable, on the grass outside Carillon Hills: hospital, sanitarium, convalescent home, whatever one chose to call it. A country villa with the air of an exclusive private school. Nuns flitting across the grounds in billowing habits, their starched spheroid collars topped with winged bonnets within which head and identity alike were swallowed up. Not a bad place at all. If one didn't mind the old people wandering around, at a loss.

"You'd never get another doctor who'd give it this much time and attention," Henry said. "Let his practice go to pot all this last month. Has a whole program laid out for the therapist after."

He had once asked Harrington, "What's the worst that can happen? Can he die?" And Harrington had informed him of the worst. That the boy would be relieved of his anxiety symptoms, his fears and his tensions, the distress he suffered. Too much so. "Where he was mainly a worry to himself before, all the worry will be on you. Slop through everything. That is the calculated risk, but a very minor one." "He'd be better off dead." It was a grunt more than anything else. Closing a conversation that neither of them ever reopened.

"I'm not worried one bit," he said to Julie now, gazing at the hospital door from which Harrington was to emerge. "It'll come out all right. All for the best. You'll see."

Idly Julie turned the pages of Vogue. Attenuated ladies attitudinized in tweed slubbed with silk, slung with furs, arrayed with the appropriate accent of jewelry and accessory, celebrated with captions as striking of imagery as a deathless poem.

She had never consented to this. Never. Had been dragged here, heels skidding down the basement corridor. Screaming *DON'T*. Don't don't. No it's terrible it's awful. Flung upon the rubberized table and the electrodes pressed down.

She never gave her agreement.

She had come home from Heron's Nest into the middle of a two-day furor over the Negro escaped from the convict gang. The whole town was in an uproar over it. You could open your back door and there he might be, a murderer, serving twenty years at hard labor for manslaughter. It was all over the radio and the Bay City newspapers and Henry in such a state over it, moving heaven and earth to keep Sunset's name out. The fugitive was tracked down and shot before dawn of the second day, fortunately in the next county, making it possible to hush up his attachment to Sunset from then on.

Because of Henry's harassment, she could not conveniently keep her appointment in Savannah with what she was already referring to shabbily as "the divorce lawyer." On the heels of the convict trouble came another development just as distracting in a different way. Dan Garner, expecting to be appointed to the Senate, had half-promised his congressional seat to a state senator from this district and that would leave a vacancy in the General Assembly along about next spring that Henry might well step in to from the County Commission. A shaky chain all hinging on Ol' Cal, whom she deplored but what could she do? With the election only a few weeks off and a rally in the offing, all the politicking, warmed up, poured through her house. She put herself out to be very nice to everyone.

But it wasn't only Henry. It was herself. In such a state. On so many levels.

On one level, exhilaration. Her very skin danced, springing with flushes of delight. When she saw Elwell's photograph on the front page of the Savannah paper, NAMED TO NEWLY CREATED POST. When she heard his voice on the radio. The Elwell she knew. Who had lain in her arms. Hers. Evenings when the telephone rang she ran, her heart jumping out of her skin. And then sedately. "Yes? Yes. Yes. Uhm. Mmm. Me too." Ah love, ah love.

On another level, humiliation. A sere salt-desert of humiliation. At the hands of Marion Elwell's good-humored and humorous acceptance of her. A treatment that disparaged while it indulged, made light of something that was anything but light, drained it of meaning, dehydrated it. At breakfast that morning Marion Elwell had told a little story, just such a spontaneous little reminiscence as she herself might have dredged up had she been Marion. "I've always regarded myself as one of the most emancipated women of my generation," Marion had said. "But then my mother was quite emancipated in her way for her day. I remember she was buttonholed at tea once by some reformist after her to join a society for the rescue of fallen women. And Mother told her, 'But I approve of prostitution. I consider it an altogether necessary institution. We owe these ladies of the night a debt of gratitude. What would decent women do without them!'" And being an old hand in her own right at such games, she had answered Marion with an innocence to match, "I've always admired people who make a virtue of necessity." She was not going to be put in second place, to play second fiddle to Marion Elwell! As she was now. It was unendurable.

On still another level, cleverness. Despising herself for it, exulting in it. Clever. She had met Elwell after breakfast that morning cool, at a distance, impersonal. And he as cool, distant, impersonal. Then at the moment of parting they'd moved like a shot toward each other. "Stay, stay another day, come up to Washington—" "I can't, I can't—" With that awesome bruising passion sweeping them both, she had left him wanting. That was clever. And afterward considering what she had to do, how to make the most of it now she had it; to move with it as far and fast as it would take her; not to be left behind, cast up high and dry, wreckage. No matter where this might lead her—to Elwell?—to another marriage?—she had first of all to hang onto what she had. To consolidate and advance it. Henry.

The week flew by. The date approached. She thinking all the while, knowing better: he won't go through with it. He'll postpone. There'll be no operation.

Too fatigued to think straight. Too wound up to sleep.

She didn't stop what was coming. She simply stopped resisting. And when resistance crumbles, palliatives creep in.

She ran into Clem one morning all busied up and enthusiastic with his Veterans Barbecue. Why I wrote all over the state for someone to teach that class, she reflected, and all the time he was right here. Like Frank Harrington.

She went to a homecoming tea for Grace Willingham. Not the same Grace of course, a scarecrow of her former self. But still something. Cracking macabre jokes about female spare parts and, scorning the use of a prosthetic, carrying her cigarette pack in the empty pouch of her brassiere. Violet guilelessly proclaiming over her third cocktail that Grace's illness had cured her of her hives: just goes to show when you're confronted by a real problem. And Tom Willingham on the porch later, detaining her with his private anguish. "You think you love a person. You think what you feel is love. You don't know what love is until you've been through something like this with someone." She had gone home with those words of Tom's, the words of that little stumpy-legged man, ringing in her ears. Everything changed in that family but what had to be done was done. And scarred, limping, they survived.

And there was the incident of the splinter. With camp closed and school due to open she had gone out to shop for Charles. And returned to find the household in tumult. Coley had picked up a splinter in the ball of his foot. Every time Kissie approached him with her needle, he ran screaming. Kissie chasing him all over the house. Charles trying to corner him. She begging and coaxing, making wild promises . . . They had to wait until Henry came home. Then Charles held Coley's legs down and she pinned his arms down. Kissing his wet cheeks, his splashing eyes, her soothing murmurs drowned in his shrieks. His body twisting and tossing, his knees tearing upward to kick off. "Henry, we can't, we'll bring on another convulsion." And Henry industrious with the needle, "We've got to, it's got to come out . . ." Then all of them falling back limply, streaming wet, eyes meeting in shamed misery. Do we have to go through this every time a splinter . . .

And so gradually step by step she had been brought to this, to consider the unthinkable, accept the impossible.

The nuns flitted by her over the grass, attending their charges. She had seen herself as a sort of nun, a sort of angel of mercy, a Florence Nightingale on the battlefield, an Anne Macy to a Helen Keller. The apple-cheeked woman doctor in the OT building at Darbyton, sturdily rolling up her sleeves, "The more violent they are the better I like it. There's a *struggle* going on there." She had seen herself striving over the years, even if her own child could never benefit, then for some other child . . .

"They say," she said to Henry, indicating the nuns, "that they're very dedicated." Coley was frightened by the sight of them. Had cowered into her skirts.

"It'll be all right. It'll work," Henry said, resolutely suppressing his qualms. Why should he burden her with them . . .

Dr. Harrington strode toward them with the light of victory in his eyes, hands extended.

They were permitted to see Colfax for a few minutes. A little wan on the pillow, but he recognized them right away. Just as alert. Dr. Harrington drove them out of the room, away from the hospital. "Go back in to Savannah, take in a movie, an art gallery, anything. You're no good here."

They had left Charles with a cousin of Julie's in Savannah who had boys his age. Henry took them all out to Tybee for a swim. Julie bought herself some clothes. She was meeting Elwell in Washington the week after the primary election. Tweed slubbed with silk. Alligator shoes. Dreadfully extravagant . . . Both she and Henry brought back a bagful of toys and picture books.

In the evening they saw Coley again briefly. He was sleeping. They deposited their gifts and tiptoed out into the corridor to talk with Harrington. He's looking good. Don't you think he's looking good? Ate a good supper, every scrap on his plate. You know the trouble he always makes eating.

"He'll be like this for a few days and then there'll be a relapse," Harrington warned them. "It'll take a period of retraining—"

A nun was approaching down the corridor, chanting prayers, crucifix swinging from her girdle. They parted to allow her to pass. Past the open doors of the rooms, undeviating, *O my God, I return thee thanks for all the benefits which I have received this day. Give me light to see what sins I have committed* . . .

Her floating black veils brushed by them.

Hail Mary, full of grace, the Lord is with thee: blessed art thou among women, and blessed is the fruit of thy womb, Jesus. Holy Mary, Mother of God, pray for us sinners, now and in the hour of our death . . .

They rejoiced in her wake. "Like a seedling when it's transplanted," Henry rejoiced. "Then it takes hold."

Julie took his hand and rubbed it over her cheek.

Leaving Dr. Harrington, they went back to the small tourist inn nearby where they were staying. Last evening they had been given a double room with twin beds. Tonight Henry sat in his pajamas on the edge of her bed, waiting for her to come out of the bathroom. Julie walked around the other side of the bed and tugged at the spread to turn it back, waiting for him to get up off it.

"Come back to me, Julie. Aren't you ever going to come back?"

Is there anything worse in this world than being married to a man you no longer care for? Unless it's turning your back on his needs, his tenderness?

Shortly after midnight the telephone on the dresser began to ring like a ballpeen hammer raining down blows. Half-asleep Henry stumbled toward it in the dark. Julie sat up and switched on the lamp in the bare, worn, rather tawdry little room.

"Yeah, yeah. Speaking. Yeah." His voice dropped an octave. "Yeah. When? Yeah. Yeah. Yeah, we'll be right there."

He stood for centuries gripping the ledge of the dresser, facing the mirror. Unable to turn his head. The unbelievable and the unforeseeable had occurred. Working in the small-scale area inside the skull, Harrington had grazed a major artery. Massively hemorrhaging.

"It's all over," Henry said.

Waiting for the blood-curdling shriek. The tiger claws down his back. Outside a dog was howling in short sharp rasps. Pulling against a stake to which it was tied.

"He didn't know a thing. Didn't suffer no pain. Just passed out."

The shriek. The shriek.

Dog rasping like a rusty chain. Without letup.

Julie uttered a short dry laugh. Of ironic wonder. Of discovery.

"I'm free."

Henry turned, stunned. Free for what? But surely the hysteria, the shriek must come. "Honey, we still got Charles. We still can do so much good—"

"I don't give a good goddam about Charles."

Waiting for the shriek, the delayed shriek he went toward her. "Honey, we got each other. I have you. You have—"

"I don't give a good goddam about you," she said and with business-like dispatch, matter-of-factly, reached for her clothes and began to dress for the trip to the hospital "I don't give a good goddam about anybody or anything in this world but me."

2

The plan for the Veterans Barbecue and Founders Day Benefit assumed body through a series of meetings during August.

In the initial stage, Rad warned his class: "We're going to hear a lot of stuff about this from here, there, and everywhere. Some of it from folks we look up to and some of it from our own kin. Not all of it good. We're trying something new is got to be tried, and that always does rouse up opposition. Unless we prepared for that before we start, better not start at all. Make up your mind right on, there's going to be talk. And there's only one thing you can do about that."

He paused suspensefully, a grin flicking over his thin curly whiplash of a mouth.

"Let it in one ear and out the other. In one ear and out the other."

And Reeve warned his class: "I know a lot of us would rather we did this on our own if we could. We all know each other and we know just about what to expect of each other and how to handle it. But with them, that's a horse of another color—what I mean, color. We going to run into a lot of stuff we don't like. Dirty words and cross-eyed looks and things said and done, some of it with the best of intention. They don't know. They just don't know. That's the worst of it. And that's not all. You all wondering if the white class had hit on this first, would we be in on it. We all know the answer to that."

"Damn right!"

"And if they did ask us, wouldn't we all be looking for the catch? Behind doors and under the beds . . . Now they in on it at our invitation. And you all lookin' for it to fall in their laps. They'll take over. We'll be left with the dead end of the stick. Now there's just one thing we can do about that."

He paused suspensefully, glowering around, the crease biting between his brows.

"It's up to us. We all learned from our mother's knee, 'People don't respect you anymore than you respect yourself.' It's up to us to make them see and respect our right! No matter what the price! And if we don't do that much now we got the opportunity to, I don't want to hear nothin' 'bout it later."

From both classes three-man committees were elected to draft a constitution for the cooperative association that would assume legal ownership of the tractor once it was purchased.

The committee from the colored class was composed of Reeve, John Newgate, and Hagan Power plus their instructor, Professor Thurlow. Reeve had a furious argument with Vivian over it.

"Why High Power?" he raved. "Why did they have to vote him in?"

"He's a leader. There's a certain element in the class that follows his lead."

"He's a misleader! Just looking for trouble. Will raise more sand than the alligator did when they drained the pond. Then he'll pour the sand into the gears and throw the whole works into the pond and tell you, 'I told you so.' Much as you may like him—"

"Power, stay way from my door! They elected him just to make sure those folks don't get away with a thing. Not a thing . . ."

The committee from the white class was composed of Rad, Carl Maynard, and Richard-Gene Jeems plus their instructor, Mr. DeLavery. Rad had a row with his wife over it.

"Richard-Gene! Why Richard-Gene? When they could have picked Lonnie, he's all for it—"

"What you so excited about? I just don't see no sense in getting that excited."

"He'll sit on his hands. He'll drag his feet. He'll laugh the whole thing outa town."

"They put him in just to see that no one puts anything over on them they can't swallow . . ."

The two committees were immediately confronted with the problem of where to meet. A place where they could meet together.

The white school? Impossible. Would antagonize too large a section of the white community. The colored school? Maybe. The colored would feel in control here to a degree, as hosts to the visiting whites— no, no that wouldn't do either. Why is it the only place you're free to mingle always has to be colored . . . The churches? Same problem. The courthouse? Where either group could meet separately but not together. Private homes? Not official enough. Aside from being too controversial.

All of it all the more of a problem because no one would say any of it aloud. They just shook their heads. Where?

Luckily, the joint committee from the advisory boards of both classes convened first to help establish the fund-raising drive, the community sponsorship and the parade arrangements that would precede the benefit. They met in the office of the county agent, Earl Goodfellow, and in the course of laying concrete plans, some of which would never be realized, held an excellent talk, so far as it went, on the necessity of building good will between the races. Limited though the talk was, coming as it did from six prominent local citizens at a time when Ol' Cal was riding high, it contributed much toward establishing a sense of security around the project. It was voted at this meeting to ask Mayor Dakin to head the list of sponsors.

Subsequently the two class committees met in Goodfellow's office to draft their constitution and by-laws.

They distributed themselves formally around the table, Clem and his students on one side, Thurlow and his students on the other; Goodfellow representing the county at the head; Nancy DeLavery and Vivian Thurlow at the foot, acting as secretaries pro tem. Richard-Gene was late and so was Hagan Power. In view of the distance of their farms, it was agreed to delay the opening of the meeting fifteen minutes for them.

Several awkward attempts to start a conversation foundered on Carl Maynard's aloof self-containment and John Newgate's rugged simplicity, unfeignedly wonderstruck. Finally somebody said something about the price he was getting for pole beans, and they were off. The farmer's troubles. You don't get the price for what you produce. You go to buy and you pay the price someone else puts down. You go to sell and you get the price someone else puts down. You work all season to make a crop and then you have to dump it. This started Earl Goodfellow off explaining parity to them. "Now what is that thing? I never did rightly understand it." From parity Earl went on to Federal price supports and crop insurance, if and how they could be applied to the family-size farm.

Just as the fifteen-minute delay was up, High Power stalked in, slick as usual in sports shirt and slacks. He threw himself down on a chair and looked around, suspicious and smoldering. Two minutes later Richard-Gene strolled in, sloppy as usual in T-shirt spilling over his chinos. He squatted down on a chair and looked around, suspicious and smirking.

Three hours later they queued down the outside staircase of the garage with a six-page rough draft Constitution & By-Laws. Borrowing for its statement of purpose from the Atlantic Charter; for its voting procedures from the United Nations; for its rules and regulations from the model used by both their American Legion posts.

In elated self-congratulation they lingered in the street in front of the garage. "That does it." "Hits the nail on the head." "Squares the circle." "I don't see how anyone can take exception."

All the offices of the organization were to be split on straight biracial lines: co-chairmen, co-vice chairmen, secretary from one and treasurer from the other; executive board to be composed of the officers and three from each class plus the instructors. This had been worked out in a very few minutes. It had to be done that way, if it was to be done at all. The mere fact that they were meeting here together now proved it could be.

Then they had bogged down for almost an hour over voting procedures. A routine enough matter ordinarily. The majority rules. But it was here High Power pulled the joker he had brought along out of his sleeve. "Suppose," he said, "some motion or resolution or action comes up that all the members of one group are for and all the members of the other group are dead-set against. Whoever happens to have the majority present would have it their way. The thing could be rigged. I know that my people are afraid that you all will gang up on them. And some of you all must be afraid that we'll gang up on you. We can talk from now till tomorrow morning how much we all trust each other and how much we all think of each other and how we'll all be brethren in the sweet by-and-by. But them's the facts of life. How you going to lick that one?"

That was where the United Nations had come to the rescue. The principle of unanimity. In the event of a disagreement along racial lines, any member could call for "A Vote by Groups." No action could be taken then without a majority vote of each group, polled separately.

If the action was defeated, members of both groups would work on a new proposal until a mutually acceptable formulation was achieved.

"It's only a safety valve," they all agreed on the formula they had evolved to fit their peculiar circumstance. "It may never have to be resorted to," they hoped. "It could become very cumbersome," they realized, "and slow things down sometimes to a standstill. But it's the only way we can bridge the gap of white and colored, past and future, the way things are right now. That is, assuming everyone is amenable to reason."

Now that they had their draft, they didn't want to leave each other. They wanted to stay there in front of the garage though it was almost eleven and under the stimulus of the candor they had enjoyed keep talking. Richard-Gene was plainly fascinated by Power. "Some of these days," he promised, "I'm comin' around to your place and have some of that King Kong you sellin' on the sly." "Some of these days," Power promised him back, "I'm comin' around to your place and have some of that boiled hoochypap you puttin' out back there in the woods." Newgate was poking Carl in the shirt button, "Trouble with this county, they's no funds. The big landowners run the county don't want taxes. Sunset and Pulp & Timber—" "You can say that again and then some. It all falls on the little fella . . ."

"Why don't we all," Clem suggested, "adjourn to my place for some coffee?"

"Yes," Nancy chimed in, "do come. Please?"

"It's so far past my bedtime," Newgate begged off, "it's most near my up-time. Thank you all the same." And he was gone.

"No no, it's too late," the rest told Clem and Nancy. "You all go on." Clem and Nancy reluctantly took their farewells. "My mother's been a little edgy—" "She never sleeps till we get in." And departed amidst laughter. Mothers! Till you're ninety years old . . .

"Vivian?" Professor Thurlow beckoned from his conversation with Goodfellow.

"Think I'll stay out a while longer, Grampa. One of these boys will carry me home." And Thurlow and Goodfellow drove off, one behind the other.

That left High Power, Reeve and Vivian, Rad, Carl and Richard-Gene. Where to?

They parted. "See you all." The whites taking the highway to The Fat Hog for beers. The colored taking the back streets down Shrimp Alley to The Bird-In-Hand.

At The Bird, High Power called from their booth for double Scotches all around; and nursed his while Vivian and Reeve filled up on ribs and rice.

"You satisfied?" Reeve demanded of him over the red-lacquered table.

"It's all right," High Power acknowledged. He pulled his carbon copy of the draft out of his back pocket and judiciously considered it. "So is the Ten Commandments. The Sermon on the Mount. And the Bill of Rights. Only one thing wrong with them." He punctured the air with his cigarette. "They never been put into practice." He was pleased nevertheless with the part he'd played. "How'd you like that when I told 'em to their face we don't altogether trust 'em? How'd you like that?"

"What came of that," Reeve gave him his just due, "was the best thing that happen there tonight. Those guarantees—"

But Power was already off on another tack. Reading from the draft in a rumbling bass, " 'Being mindful of the principles enunciated by our late President, Franklin Delano Roosevelt.' Enunciated, was that your word, Vivian?"

"It was Rad's idea. He got DeLavery to bring that stuff in—"

" 'Freedom of speech and expression,' " Power went on reading, " 'everywhere in the world.' That means right here. 'Freedom of worship everywhere in the world.' Think I'll sashay into St. Paul's next Sunday. 'Freedom from want, which translated into world terms means economic understanding which will secure to every nation a healthy peacetime life for its inhabitants.' I'll buy that. So long as it includes Colfax County. 'And freedom from fear, which means worldwide reduction of armaments to such a point in such a thorough fashion that no nation will be in a position to commit aggression against any neighbor, anywhere in the world.' Freedom from fear . . .

"What do you suppose would have happened if we'd all piled into DeLavery's house tonight for a cup of coffee? Tomorrow—" Power zipped his finger across his throat. "Freedom of expression. Freedom to worship. Freedom from want and fear. Only one thing wrong with it. The rulers of this country don't follow their own logic. And nobody knows that better than we do. You wait and see how things shape up."

"You were there tonight. You saw what went on," Reeve said. "If you give people the incentive—"

"Virtue is its own reward," Vivian came to Reeve's support, "but how much more so when it pays off."

"Now we come to your contribution, Reeve." Power ruffled through the pages. "The rules governing finance, use, operation, and maintenance of said tractor. Ha. The proof of the pudding. The heart of the matter. What happens when the white man wants to use the thing before you do? *Who—backs—up?*"

"It's all down there," Reeve said shortly. "At least it's down there. And if we can't start from that, I don't know where the hell we can."

He slid out of the booth and strode with his nickel out to the amber-lit spot of a dance floor and the rainbow-lit song of the piccolo. Power, gratified, poked his head out around the corner of the booth, gazing after him.

"That is a man," he said to Vivian. "That is really a *man*. One of the few real men I've ever known. If things ever change, Reeve'll change them. Not me. Oh I'll be out there on the barricades with him, but he'll be callin' the shots. You been walkin' out with him, baby?"

"More than that."

"Keepin' company?"

"Mm hm."

"You have an understanding?"

"Sort of."

"You promised to him? You go'n marry him?"

She drummed her fingers on the red-lacquered table, her garnet-polished nails staccato tapping. "I don't know. I just don't know."

"You love him?"

"What I feel about Reeve makes words like love seem paltry. It's not just love. It's something else. Bigger."

"You think you too good for him? That when you bring this plowboy around to your sorority sisters—"

"They'll say to me, 'Vivian, where can I find some more of that?'" She laughed. "Maybe it's that. Maybe I'm too attached to my nail polish. Maybe he knows too much I don't and I know too much he doesn't and the two can't jibe. Or maybe they do. Maybe."

"It's a problem. I don't say it's not a problem. You'll have a lot to overcome. But believe me, believe me when I tell you this. Take a chance. Play it. You'll never be sorry."

The narrow scoffing face with the cleft of a knife-cut in the cheek, rascal, gypsy, heartbreaker, slickster, hipster, and shill: he was entirely serious, entirely in earnest.

"Six months ago when I first came here"—Vivian sipped reflectively at the ice-watered residue of her Scotch—"I was so cynical. So hard, so tight, so salty. Now I believe, I could believe in almost anything—"

"Don't go overboard." Reeve was back. Tapping his feet to an old Count Basie record. Holding his arms out.

In the middle of the speck of a dance floor Vivian put her arms up around his neck. He put his arms down around her waist. And locked, they danced on a dime, scarcely moving.

"You still want to marry me?" she said against his chest.

Reeve drew his head back and scrutinized her, searchingly. "Ready?"

"Maybe."

"Soon?"

"Maybe."

In the prismatic spotlight of the piccolo he twirled her off, pulled her in, twirled her off with a casual flip of his wrist. To the questing seeking music. In and out. In and out.

At The Fat Hog, a roadhouse crowded with carousing couples from Bay City who would retire later to the cabins outside, pickups for the night and tourists about to be clipped, the three men crammed in around a table.

"Well?" Rad demanded over the noise while they waited for their beers, "what do you think?"

"Well, I tell you," Carl said, loosened up for once, "what have we got to lose? There'll be plenty of snags, it can get out of hand but . . . So far so good. You know I been talking to these people all my life and tonight I found out we never talked at all? It was like stepping into an ice-cold shower, needle spray. I'm all braced up."

"Tell me about this una-una-votin' thing, Rad, once again, will you?" Richard-Gene begged. "I don't get it."

"It's a simple matter of forcing us to find a common area of agreement," Rad said before he stopped himself. Richard-Gene bland as a baby. Pulling his leg.

They consumed three beers batting the pros and cons back and forth, arriving at common ground on how best to present the draft to the class.

"The fact is, we need this. The question is, are we ready for it?"

"So long as we stick to what we need first and foremost, everything else'll fall into place."

Carl being a bachelor gave a girl acquaintance across the floor the high sign. Richard-Gene being a married man did likewise. Rad rose from the table. "This is where I cut out. My old lady's waiting with an ax."

Jovially Richard-Gene clapped Rad on the shoulder, leveraged himself upward on him and leaning on him with all his weight announced, "Think I'll go out and tie a coupla niggers to a tree."

"You ain't got the guts," Rad said and left.

The constitution was ratified by the two classes separately within the week. No attempt was to be made to bring the classes together before the barbecue when, on payment, the tractor was to be delivered. Meanwhile committees and subcommittees were formed to handle various aspects of the preparations. When the occasion demanded, the committee heads of one group consulted with their opposite numbers in the other group. Vivian was in charge of program. Earl Goodfellow was in charge of produce exhibits. Under the home-demonstration agents whose aid had been enlisted, Lulabelle McDowell and Bessie Sanderlee visited the class wives, organizing food and food sales: there was even talk of setting up a permanent ladies auxiliary for each class. Carl and the Baron took care of ticket distribution. Hagan Power was in sole command of Hospitality, a synonym for security at the gate.

It flowed. It cohered. It built. And viviparous, it multiplied.

"Now I understand what the monks meant when they spoke of being God-intoxicated," Clem declared at home. He was these days Man-intoxicated. The barrier he had always felt between himself and the mass of humanity had dissolved. The communion he had sought from boyhood on—jumping the mission wall, riding third-class carriage through the deserts and mountains of the East, escaping his uncle's house to live with Gloria and Tim Hodges, quitting seminary for the war—that communion between himself and the plain rough boisterous vigor out there was taking place. That fusion . . .

And naturally of course these nights he was making love to his wife.

The night they came home from drafting the constitution they reeled into the house a little heady with it all. It had come off so well! Who would have expected . . . "I always thought that Reeve was good-looking," Nancy remarked, undressing, "but that Hagan Power—" "He's not good-looking." "No. But the *way* he looks . . ." With a dreamy smile Nancy hugged herself, shivering.

Clem had locked the door then against his mother's protestations over the cross-ventilation and had taken to bed with Nancy against her yielding closure and her closured yielding. Next morning Nancy walked in bliss as if nothing like this had ever happened to any other woman since the world began. "Hide your face," he said to her, "it's written all over. Shame on you, Pansy McLain."

He never did find out, though, the origin of Nancy's fear. She wouldn't tell him. "It's not that important anymore." Some traumatic childhood experience, some little black spider of a secret that had assumed for her monstrous proportions, that had dominated all the years of her growing up, that had frozen her into a vise of fear, that had caused them immeasurable misery through the months of their marriage and had indeed almost destroyed it—it wasn't important anymore. "Let's draw the veil on it," Nancy suggested with a hint of coquetry, "let's leave some mystery . . ." A little spider buried away in a box. That at the first touch disintegrated.

And naturally of course during these weeks his mother observed the enthusiasm on him which she found so attractive and so dangerous. Unable to call any longer on Nancy's dubious assistance to infiltrate and dissipate that enthusiasm, she became alarmed for them both. After the draft constitution was mimeographed, circulated and voted on, she insisted on seeing it. They tried to withhold it from her. "What's the matter with it? Is there something in it you want to hide from me?" No, not that, they just didn't want her bothered up. She read it.

"You've gone stark raving mad. Why, it's sheer insanity. Nothing like this is going to be tolerated around here."

"But it is being tolerated," Clem pointed out. "It's been approved. As an attempt to find some means of working together. What is this Voting by Group after all but the Voting by Orders we have in the church?"

"Don't bring the church into it!"

"For years we've maintained unity between warring factions, High and Low Church, through voting by orders, equalizing the weak with the strong. In Palestine now, you have similar proposals from some quarters for establishing a binational state, Jewish and Arab. And in India with the Hindus and Moslems. There doesn't have to be the rioting and massacre, the relocation of populations, partition. Whether it's the security council of the UN, down here in Dixie or anywhere else on earth, people either find some way of resolving differences or the frictions become accentuated into antagonisms and the antagonisms into violence."

Laura looked at her son. Why if he was to be a preacher couldn't he just preach and if he was to be a teacher couldn't he just teach! Why couldn't he stay within bounds? Stick to his own last. And his own kind . . . Nancy, poor fool, shining up at him. You'll get used to it, girl. You'll get tired and bored and pestered. And wonder how you could so lightly toss away everything of value for such nonsense . . .

And they who craved her approval more than they knew shook in their shoes at her look.

"I don't care what authority you cite," Laura said to Clem and Nancy. "I don't care what analogy you drag in from what far corner of the world. Someday, my darlings, you'll have a child and you'll warn it not to wander out into the road. And it will. And you'll see the car bearing down. Listen to me, listen to me for once. Drop this! Let it go . . ."

But of course the telephone rang just then with some new plan to be set into motion, some new obstacle to be conquered.

As August wore on and Laura grew edgier with the activities that incessantly invaded the house, Clem suggested that perhaps she ought to vacation a while up at her brother Mark's place in the mountains. She suggested in turn that as long as she could be of any help or protection to him, her duty lay here.

Her premonitions were not altogether groundless. At a bridge and canasta party one afternoon she became embroiled in a completely irrelevant argument with Ada Hemmings over the Russians. "They're here," Ada claimed over her cards. "They have their agents all over." According to Ada, in the event of war paratroopers would be landed right here in this county. Where? On those two adjoining farms out there on the River Road where they had all those explosives stashed. Niggers were being trained there as part of an underground conspiracy, meeting there every night. And a certain influential person was in charge of organizing them, using the veterans' classes as a front and subverting the whole community into a base for Moscow. "If you don't believe it, it's because you been blinded and disarmed." Laura found herself defending the Russians, of whom she knew little and cared less.

"They don't want to go to war with us, Ada. They have their whole country to build up."

"How do you know so much about it?" Ada answered her. "Have you been there?"

Laura came home sick over it. She sat in the hall with her hat on reporting to Clem and Nancy. "I declare that woman is on the verge of a nervous breakdown. She ought to see a doctor. Of course everyone knows it's just politics. But if she's saying these things, then the Judge and Henry, all of them . . ."

At last she pulled herself to her feet and with her hat still on went into the kitchen to see about dinner.

That evening she said to them pensively, "I spent more than a year in that internment camp in Luzon. The food was wretched. The sanitary and medical facilities were miserable. I saw my husband, the best, the bravest and handsomest man I ever knew waste away day by day. Still I stood up to it better, I think, than I have to this place."

"Mother . . ." Clem was profoundly moved. But he was called away soon after to attend to some minor crisis and Nancy went with him.

Despite her dire predictions, the plans for the Barbecue Benefit proceeded more or less peaceably. Occasional conflicts breaking through the superficial smoothness the two groups had achieved usually resulted on analysis in a deepened, if less complacent, understanding.

The escape of an unknown Negro on the last day of August from the work-gang at Sunset, convicted on a charge of manslaughter for an unknown crime, who bashed the deputy warden over the head for an un-known reason, created waves of nervous repercussion far and wide.

To Laura DeLavery it came almost as a relief and justification. "You think you have it all under control, don't you? You think it'll all go your way? All the disturbance over this, it'll be turned against you. This is the beginning."

Everywhere that afternoon mothers were calling their children in from the yards, shepherding them with watchful endearments inside.

That evening posses combed the vicinity of Sunset, fanning out from there. The baying of bloodhounds could be heard all over the country-side. Farmers stared out of their windows into the moonlit surround-ings, all the familiar objects suddenly alive, potent; their ears attuned to the distant barking, the quickening of the scent. Those who were white were later routed out of bed and were asked, while their out-buildings were being checked, to join in the search. Those who were colored were routed with their families out of bed and were marched outside while the searchers walked through the house from end to end turning out furniture, clothing, and bedding.

Rad McDowell was one of the first to be asked to join the search parties. He declined. "You the law. You find him."

"If he was to come here," Lulabelle asked him afterward, "would you let him go?"

"I don't know. I don't altogether know what I'd do."

"But if he was crazy and you had to shoot?"

"I don't rightly know what I'd do. But I won't track him down."

She wasn't asking only about the convict and Rad knew it. Whether he was doing the right thing, the right thing about Charles. Whether by declining to do anything to influence the boy one way or the other . . . And persuading her . . . They went to bed thinking as they did every night: Suppose he's on his way here now. And hearing the hounds: He couldn't get here tonight.

At Reeve's house long after the searchers had left the two nephews who were staying with him through picking season clinked restlessly in the brass bed they shared in the alcove. "Say Reeve," they hissed through the darkness, "what you go'n do if he falls in here?"

"I don't know," Reeve said from his couch across the room. "Reckon I'd do my best to get him away."

"Why he may be the most depraved man in the world. Just because he's colored . . ." It was their father, the policeman in Chicago, talking. "If he was white, you wouldn't do that for him."

"N-n-no. But then again, maybe . . ."

Reeve was as restless as his nephews. Keyed up with resentment, thinking in one part of his mind: Everything was going so good, everything was going so fine. Now the first low-down trifler comes up, hits a man on the head—I'm responsible, the finger's on me. Loathing himself for the thought, traitor to himself. And keyed to the faroff yelping of Chalmer's hounds, thinking in another part of himself, How many of that other class are out there: Lonnie, Ray DelVecchio, Carl? How many? There's something about a pack of white men with their guns and their dogs hunting down a black man, no matter what he's done, or hasn't done . . .

He got up shirtless, pulling the string of his pajama pants tight and went out on the porch. He peered through the black-and-silver fronded cedars. No movement out of the ordinary. No sound. He shrank at a rat-a-tat of distant shots as if punctured through the shoulder blades. Then the dogs were off again. Someone had taken aim at a shadow.

He went back into the house and skirting the brass bed pushed open the door in the wall where his mother's yellow pine dresser used to stand and entered the room he'd built. Even now at night it was lighter and brighter than the age-darkened main interior.

He walked into the center of the room and stood there as he sometimes did, breathing it in, breathing in the newness. Of refinished pine stock. Creosote and turpentine, shellac. The plasterboard was up now, nailed over the framing and the nails covered with two-inch strips of molding. The plank flooring grained like watered silk. Three double-hung windows open to the river breeze. Vivian standing here with him today: "When I'm with you, love, I'm with you. But when I'm not, I don't know, I just don't know." And he to her: "At least it's not the other way round." This room growing from day to day so visibly with things that were invisible . . .

How can you build up anything for yourself when there's so much running loose in the swamp out there!

In the morning Reeve rode with Rad to school. Talking it all over, they agreed very sensibly between them that everybody knew how Sunset was working those prisoners out there, that they were having trouble over going into snake-infested muck without boots, that sooner or later something like this was bound to happen. Then they went on their separate ways to their own classmates, to face the music.

That night it rained, rained in great black sheets that whipped against windows so hard the curtains on the inside stirred and swayed. Whites blinking out through the blurred glass said: "Them dogs won't catch him tonight." And colored turned away from their windows: Some poor mother's son, their own, themselves . . .

He was shot before dawn miles away in the next county, and with the shot the two-day furor over him died.

But in the wake of it, as if taking advantage of the effect it had created, the flame-yellow circulars reappeared, now widely distributed over town and country. An invitation to the people of Colfax County to attend a *FREE BARBECUE & POLITICAL RALLY* to be held in the Arcady City Park, to be chaired by Judge Purcell and featuring *OL' CAL HUBBARD (YOUR NEXT GOVERNOR), DAN GARNER (YOUR FAVORITE CONGRESSMAN)* and *HENRY WARREN (YOUR MAN OF THE FUTURE)* as main speakers. *Join the Crowd! Everybody But Everybody Will be Here! Free Food for All! Gifts for the Kiddies!*

Dated ten days hence. On Founders Day. Same day and hours as the Veterans Benefit.

3

The circular was brought to Professor Thurlow's house by Father Hall early on the first morning it was out. "You know that fellow over to Fallona who's running against Mr. Coombs for sheriff? Royall?" he said to the Professor. "He delivered this to me himself. Personally."

Vivian, helping Clelia in the kitchen clean up after breakfast, listened to the two old men in the dining room hemming and hawing over their coffee. "Oh oh," Clelia, swishing dishes through the sink-water, observed gloomily. "Pressure's been brought to bear. He's withdrawing his church."

"Oh no! Hush now—"

"It's all out in the open now," Father Hall declared. "The Warrens are tied up with Purcell and Purcell has tied them up with Ol' Cal. If Cal wins governor, as he no doubt will, that's bad enough. But if he wins this county, the whole slate we're supporting—Reece, Lacey, Dakin, Coombs, and the Commissioners-at-large—they'll all go under."

"Lots of white folks"—the Professor hawked, struggled with his phlegm—"don't hold with Ol' Cal or Ol' Vern either. They wouldn't touch 'em."

"Got a song to go with that?" Father Hall said tartly.

They both blew on their coffee and sucked on it a while.

"Now Miss Julie, I'd never have thought that Miss Julie—" Father Hall mourned. "I can't imagine it even yet. Her going over like that. She'll carry all the women with her."

"I wouldn't say that. We may be in for some surprises. We're making more headway than you can shake a stick at with some of these crackers."

Father Hall creaked around in his chair a while. "Well, you know," he admitted, "I never could stand a cracker. All I have to do is see one and I get mad. He has to be a pretty good cracker before I can be nice to him."

"Is that a Christian way to talk?"

"It may not be Christian but it's candid," Father Hall said. "When Miss Ada falls into my church she's tolerable. But them—I had too many a window broke. Besides," he added piously, "I never believe in working with white folks unless they all agree amongst themselves."

"Then you think we ought to wait till Judgment Day?"

"I didn't say that. But you put yourself in my position. Zion is a landmark in these parts. Folks come to me from all over to show them the plaque and the records. They see me as keeper of a trust and a tradition. Now when you and DeLavery approached me I was willing for you to hold a patriotic benefit for the whole community there, provided the community would back it up. I was more than willing for my wife to write her brother Malcolm to come down sing for us. I always feel a concert contributes to harmony. But now with this rival barbecue and rally in the city park, everybody'll be going there."

"If you can be admitted there, you doing a lot better than I can."

"All right, all right about that. But with all that razzle-dazzle down there running simultaneously, you know what comes before Judgment Day, don't you? I'm not about to have no Armageddon on my church ground."

"You mean we should call it off then?"

"I didn't say that."

"You forgetting it's my down payment on that tractor? I signed a promissory note on it and had it conveyed to Bay City, all for the sake of these children. If you pullin' the rug out from under—"

"I didn't say that. What I mean, maybe it'd be wiser to put it off a little. Maybe the Benefit would do better held separate places. Maybe it would have been better to begin with to buy two smaller tractors instead of the one big one. Of course they'd never let us have ours till they had theirs first, but if we helped them to it then maybe they might help us."

Vivian couldn't stand it a minute longer. Ignoring Clelia's glum satisfaction, she switched off her apron and followed the two old gentlemen from the dining room to the porch.

"I have some news for you too, Father," she said, "before you go. All the tickets are distributed. Mr. Reece paid for the printing."

"Yes, yes I know."

"And the posters are ready. With your brother-in-law's name prominently featured. Mr. Hadley and Mr. Higginson dug into their jeans for that. In fact, I think Mr. Higginson has his poster already up in the window of his store."

"Then why haven't I got mine yet?"

"It'll get to you. It'll get to you. And if you can keep a secret under your hat, Mr. DeLavery has written this whole thing up for a friend of his on the Mission Board in New York. And he has faith that it will bring in a sizable contribution."

"Money talks." Father Hall's thin face crinkled indulgently. "You don't have to sell me, sweetheart. I'm sold. You don't have to tell me. I'm told. But a lot of people are going to be all shook up. I mean our own people. First that convict shooting. Now this. And if they come bothering me, that we ought to step aside that day . . . You can't blame them. They have to live here. You don't."

They watched him walk off, a desiccated leaf skittering before a light breeze.

"This world will never be free," Professor George Turner Thurlow pronounced, "until the last preacher is strung up by the guts of the last politician."

Vivian had a full morning ahead of her.

At the post office, going in she encountered Clem on his way out. "I want to see you," they whispered hurriedly at each other in passing.

"My house," Clem suggested.

"I have an appointment at the hairdresser," Vivian said, "and a couple of other things—"

"Drop by this noon then?"

Everyone was rubbering around at them, easing over, ears out. They had grown rash and reckless with too close a familiarity.

Vivian took her place in line before the general delivery window, preparing for the little ceremonial of exchange that always took place between the postmistress and herself. Mrs. Lawton had lately stopped giving her space in her grandfather's box, too full up; and all the other boxes were at present taken, no vacancies. She inched toward Mrs. Lawton between a starched slow-moving matron in front of her and a bulging impatient businessman behind, the usual tension accumulating.

"How are you, Mrs. Lawton? Anything for me today?"

"Oh hello, Vivian. There sure enough is." The pieces were extruded from the cage one by one. *Life. Afro-American. Negro Digest.* A long envelope from the U. S. Government stamped OFFICIAL BUSINESS. Then her personal letters. A picture postcard from Japan. Pale pink stationery, deckle-edged, from St. Louis. Altogether too much mail.

In the refuge of her grandfather's sedan, Vivian adjusted herself under the wheel and under the peepings-in of passersby opened her mail.

First the long envelope from the Civil Service Commission forwarded from several old addresses. A P-4 job in the New York office at the Treasury Department, paying eighteen hundred a year. Now it had to come. *Now . . .*

The pink letter from her mother in St. Louis, from whom she heard about once every two years, exclusive of Christmas. Her mother had raised her, sending her down here summers, put her through college and then had moved on, married again, to raise another family. Working all the time. *Somebody to rub you, that's love . . . Don't marry anyone unless it's someone can do something for you . . .* Only no one ever did for Mamma.

Vivian unfolded the pink notepaper. In the shop where she worked, her mother wrote, there was this fellow who had a nephew with connections. "And if you have enough of your practice teaching in by now for a certificate, he can get you fixed up in the school system here just like that. How about it, honey? You must be so fed up by now . . ."

The picture postcard from Japan said simply: "*Come on out here, the moon is fine. Elsie.*"

Vivian looked up from a mountain-girt bay, delicately colored, to the sandy street straggling off from the post office between shaggy palmettos. Elsie had left her husband in Virginia and her baby with her mother and enlisted in the WAC. "Too much of a mental burden," Elsie had tabbed off her husband. And, "Ten busted romances are better than one bust marriage." Come on out here . . .

Come on out here. It was a regular siren song this morning. Come on out . . .

At the hair parlor in the front room of Augusta Varney's bungalow, Vivian lay back in the reclining chair, warm water gushing over her scalp, Helene's firm fingers massaging, thumbs rotating, the clean pine-tar aroma of shampoo and lotions invigorating, the purr of gossip soothing, "Well, you know, she's the Spanish type . . ."

Come on out here. Come . . .

Helene toweled the excess moisture out of her hair. Circled the hand drier around, blowing air about in clean warm swirls.

Reeve . . . Reeve . . .

"How are the tickets going, Helene?"

"Good. Only I just now heard—didn't I just now hear from someone? —the whole thing's canceled."

Vivian sat straight up out of Helene's lotion-patting fingers, twisted around in her plastic bib. "Where'd you hear that? No such thing! Why, I just met Mr. DeLavery—"

Helene twirled her tongs up red-hot from their cradle of blue gas flame. "I wouldn't count too much on him if I was you. After the way he did Mamma. Publicly. Right here in this house."

"But they compelled him—"

"That's what I mean. He means well. He tries hard. But never mind that. You go ahead. Depend on him. And if he lets you down, you don't have to stay here to be ridiculed. You can always pack up and go."

The same attitude, adamantine, met her wherever she went throughout the morning. Her reassurances concerning the Benefit were taken with a grain of skepticism. Nothing's keeping you here. You can always take off.

She climbed the narrow dark stairway to Mabel Dawson's office over the barbershop. Mabel had spent twenty years on and off the job of county home demonstration agent according to what was left for colored from the public budget. She was a well-organized, easy-mannered woman, always in the same style blue dress with white piqué collar. She liked her work and she knew her people.

Over Mabel's desk on one side hung a framed newspaper clipping: a dim yellow picture of the first canning demonstration she ever conducted, in the picnic grove back of Father Hall's church, with two zinc tubs and two joints of stovepipe; the farm women who came there that day had put up over five hundred quarts of fruits and vegetables. Over the other side of her desk hung a recent photograph, similarly framed, showing the women gathered this summer to do their canning in the efficiently equipped home economics classroom of the new Colfax-Scott school. Directly over her desk, between the two pictures, the bulletin board on which she tacked up assignments for the Benefit was graced with a publicity still of Malcolm Gregory, Father Hall's brother-in-law, the most popular baritone of the southeast church circuit and quite a glamour boy. On the shelves beside her desk homemade aprons, jars of jelly and other donations she had collected for the sale booths were stored. The shelves were filling up. But Mabel, framed by all this behind her desk, was not in any easygoing mood today.

"Where you been so long?" she attacked Vivian as soon as she appeared. "Of course I got the sisters straightened out," she belligerently answered a question re a fuss that had cropped up in the food committee. "They're willing to do the cooking but they can't go batting around the country to pick up the stuff, who's paying their gasoline?

And how much collards and how much coleslaw? How many people you expecting to this thing, Vivian, do you know?"

"About three–four hundred," Vivian said. "If everything goes as it should. And if it doesn't rain."

Mabel threw the flame-yellow handbill on her desk. "You see this yet?"

"Mm-hm. Gets around fast."

They eyed each other over it. "I suppose they're expecting us to bow out now, out of respect," Mabel said. "And I suppose if we don't, we'll have a flop on our hands."

"Dis de employment?"

A woman wandered into the office, a sagging lump of a woman with a rag around her head and her children dragging at her skirts, her legs encased in tan cotton stockings that wrinkled down over her ankles into broken-heeled carpet slippers.

"Next door, ma'am. You in the wrong office."

The woman stood fixed in the doorway, trapped in her own immense immobility. She raised a slow finger pointing to the glossy print of Malcolm Gregory on the bulletin board. "Who that?"

Mabel explained to her in detail who Malcolm Gregory was and why he was coming and what all the jelly jars and aprons were doing on her shelves and how they were planning to use the money from the Benefit.

"Anything you have to contribute," Mabel said briskly, "we can show or sell? Quilting, needlework, preserves, or pastries?"

The woman wandered out with her passel of children, but in another minute she was back fishing in her cracked black satchel of a handbag.

"Ain't got nothin' I can give y'all," she said, "but will a penny help?"

Mabel pulled a pad toward her, made out a receipt in the name of the Fund Committee and presented it to the woman in exchange for the penny.

"All right," she turned pugnaciously back to Vivian, "you can laugh."

"I'm not laughing."

"But that penny means more than all the dollars of those merchants downtown. You see what I mean, if this flops? It'll be such a setback. Better if we'd never tried it."

Vivian opened her handbag and took out her copy of the constitution. "We've had our ups and downs with this, Mabel, ever since it began. But whenever we're down, I take this out. Those boys did this. It's here. It's alive. It can't be repealed." She handled it tenderly, like a baby. "We can't let it be killed."

"It's just a scrap of paper," Mabel said. "Unless we succeed. Of course you don't have to face it. You can always jump the first bus."

"But I can't! I have my school contract."

"Nobody'll stop you. They'd rather any time you quit than kick you out."

"But why is everyone so sure that I'll—"

"Until you settle down here as a permanent resident, Vivian, there isn't anyone going to think you serious."

At chorus rehearsal in the church Vivian struck up with her baton before the ranked boys and girls the medley of patriotic airs that was to open the program. And the choral accompaniment for Malcolm Gregory's concert arias. And *I want to be ready I want to be ready I want to be ready to walk in Jerusalem just like John . . .*

Joyously, joyously, they lifted every voice and sang till earth and heaven rang. Over the stony road they trod.

They trooped down from the dais vibrant, glowing, exuberant with the pride of life, brown and brilliant with a spark, a fire that was not to be quenched.

"They'll sound a lot better when this place is filled up," Rebecca Hall rising from the piano called across the nave to Vivian. With the note of reserve in her voice, the corrosive grain of skepticism. "If everybody comes that says they will."

"Oh, they'll come," she called back. "They'll come. Next time, boys and girls, your white shirts and blouses, black pants and skirts."

She walked out of the church with Rebecca and spontaneously without consulting each other they surveyed the grounds. Church and picnic grove were surrounded all the way around by a high wire fence overrun with morning glory vines, wild rose climbers, and shrubbery. The only entry lay through the gate in front.

"Father isn't feeling so good today," Rebecca told her, a pursy prissy spinster with an expression of perpetual disapproval about her mouth. "Shame on it, his ulcer's acting up." She coughed off a dry grating laugh. "I've lived through so many times with him before. He's my daddy and he don't show it, but things cut him up so inside . . . This may be a big promotion for some people, a chance for self-expression, a stage. If it goes over, they're the heroes. If not, goodbye and gone. For the rest of us who have to foot the bill, it's nothing but worry, pain, and trouble. Are you sure, girl, it's worth it? I'm not."

"I think we've moved ahead from where we were before."

"Where ahead? I don't see anything moved ahead."

Rebecca had a music pupil waiting on the other side of town. Vivian gave her a lift as far as Clem's house. "You don't mind if I drop you off here?" she said to Rebecca. She drew up behind a new Plymouth parked in front of the rectory—visitors?—and dismounted anyway. "Mr. De-

Lavery asked me to stop by at noon and it's past that now." Rebecca lingered by the car and before her prussic-acid smile Vivian sailed up the path and up the steps to the front porch and rang the front-door bell. Thereby violating the tacit protectiveness every respectable colored person practices toward well-disposed whites. Exposing him before callers in his home, before neighbors in the street. In broad daylight. Enjoying it. Enjoying her skirmish with Rebecca, enjoying in anticipation the contretemps with Clem. Let him welcome her in. Let him wince underneath if it bothered him any. Let him writhe, let him know what it is to smile and hide behind it. Being such fine familiar friends. It was a breach of discipline and she didn't care. It was more important to put on a show for Rebecca. Girl, you should have seen her sashay in there. Onward and upward.

Behind the black crossbar of the tall narrow screendoor the house door was open. In the long hallway all the white cross-paneled doors were shut like sealed faces. She rang once more, imperiously.

The nearest of the doors opened and Mrs. DeLavery slipped out and pulled it carefully to behind her. She approached with a startled frown. "Oh it's you," she said with relief and opened up, "thank goodness. Come right in."

"If Mr. DeLavery's not here—"

"Right this way."

She drew Vivian to the door at the foot of the hall, opened it into the dining room, ran across the dining room and opened the door to the butler's pantry that led into the kitchen. She pulled up a chair in the dining room between the doors and plumped Vivian down on it. "Now you stay right here."

"If you having company—"

"And if anyone else shows up, front or back, you go immediately and turn whoever it is away. You understand that? *Let no one in.* Not my son or his wife. No one!"

With a pat at her lace collar and at her feathery curls, Mrs. DeLavery hurried back down the hall to the parlor. "You see, gentlemen, I *am* busy . . ." And closed the parlor door behind her.

Vivian sat alert to the slightest stir at front door or back. Now what have I walked into? Everything, everything's inflating so . . . We're terrorized and we run all the risks. They're terrified and they risk nothing.

Down the hall Mrs. DeLavery issued from the parlor with two nicelooking, nicely tailored young men. "I'm sure, Mr. Rogan, you'll find there's some mistake." She herded them deftly toward the door, away from any chance view of the dining room. "Yes, I'll tell my son you were here. You needn't make the trip again. He'll see you at your office in Bay City. Thank you." Vivian recognized the phrase, the sound, the strangulation stifled under the light bright words. "Thank you for coming."

She returned down the hall with such rapidity Vivian didn't have time to stand up. "You . . . What have you done to my son?"

"Ma'am?"

"You're the one. They just now showed me the picture. In some house with him."

"What picture? I'm in no picture—oh." She remembered. The girl that fell into Reeve's house that night half-drunk. And her boy friend with the camera. Taking the shot of the deerhead. So friendly. So friendly and so natural they overcame all suspicion. "Oh . . ."

"You're ruining him. I don't know what you expect to gain out of this but you've taken a fine young man, such a wonderful career ahead of him . . . And without a thought in the world you break him. For nothing. For nothing that'll ever come to pass."

"Mrs. DeLavery," Vivian rose, "I'd better be going."

"No—" The woman blocked her path, her face and neck grey and straining out of the lace collar. "Not before we've had a good talk."

Gripping her arm, Mrs. DeLavery steered her into the kitchen. "We'll have a cup of tea." At the sink she filled a kettle from the faucet splattering water all over it, and set it down sizzling on the gas flame to boil. "You're an intelligent girl." She dabbed over the grey moisture of her face with her handkerchief. "I don't know why you ever came back to a town like this. With your Eastern airs and education and high-flying ideas. There's nothing for you here. Nowhere you can go. No opportunity for advancement. No future. If you can't get away, if it's matter of money, I'll help. If it's a job you need, I have friends of some influence, I'll write to them—"

Vivian looked around the muddy brown walls of the kitchen, the bib aprons hanging from a hook on back of the door, the dishes stacked on the drainboard, a palmetto bug flitting about.

"Mrs. DeLavery, I have my roots here. Attachments. Obligations."

"Then leave my son alone!"

"It's not me. We're all in this together."

"Then tell your people to get away from him! Get off his back! You've no idea of the harm you all have done him, the damage you're causing. It's been such a shock to me. I've had such a shock—"

She poured the scalding water from the kettle into her teapot, spilling it, and set the pot down to brew, a tall white pot with a mountain scene etched on the side. With a napkin folded around the handle she poured two cups, composing herself in the act, the naked distortion of her features disappearing under a winsome vivacity, haunted and haunting.

"Part of a presentation set to my husband and myself for service in the field. You think I don't understand, Vivian, I do." She reached over the corner of the table in a gesture, two women having tea together, the older counseling the younger. "I sympathize with your cause. I defend you all every chance I have in and out of season. When there was all the panic this week over the prisoner who escaped, I spoke up for him. Vivian, it's not too late to save him."

"But he was shot. They shot him."

"Shot? Oh, please—*Clem*. Help me save him! Tell him that you all have decided that the time isn't right . . . Oh dear, what am I thinking of?" She bustled about the refrigerator bringing out cream and lemon. "Which? I like it plain myself . . . He'll be here any minute now. Tell him that. The time is not right . . . It's really evaporated milk."

Vivian sipped her tea, the singing of the young people resounding in her ears. The letters whispering in her handbag. *Come come*. And the constitution whispering in there with the letters. *Reeve Reeve*. The woman's face floating in a steamy vapor over her teacup. Old grey-nose white woman.

"The time is not right. And that's the truth of it." Mrs. DeLavery rose at the sound of the car outside. "There they are now. Dear?" She called from the back door. "This way. Guess who's here to see you? We're having some tea and such a nice chat."

"Vivian!" Clem came in with Nancy. "Sorry I'm late, we were down at the *Courier*. Edna's running her lead story on the Benefit this week. Come on, what are we doing here in the kitchen in the gloom?" He moved them, teapot and cups into the dining room. "We'll have some tea ourselves. Nan, more cups out, and some of Ida's cake . . . Well, now it can be told. Remember I let you in on my secret, Viv, writing to the Mission Board? I was hoping maybe fifty dollars? This morning in my mail there was a check. From funds contributed by an anonymous donor. Two—hundred—dollars!"

"That why you asked me to stop here?"

"You wrote to the Mission Board!" his mother cried. "You roped them into this?"

"Now, Mother . . . Edna had the check photographed up to go with her story. What did you have in mind, Vivian? You look worried."

"I think you all ought to know before you go any further," Mrs. DeLavery stated, "that there were two men here a half hour ago from the Federal Bureau of Investigation. They inquired about a roommate they say you once had, Clem, who was mixed up in some sort of student organization. Carl Anderson."

"I don't know any Carl Anderson." Clem cut himself a fat chunk of cake. "Never heard of him."

"But it wasn't Carl Anderson they asked all the questions about. It was *you*."

"What'd they want to know? What right do they have to come barging in—"

"Every right. That job you have teaching those boys on the GI Bill makes you a Federal employee."

"Of all the silly asinine . . ." Clem laid his fork down. "Getting you wrought up over nothing, some mixup."

"It's not nothing! Before they left they showed me a picture they had —to make sure it was the right person they said—of you and Vivian in someone's house here. At some sort of meeting. It was a shock."

Clem looked at Vivian and she at him with that night in their eyes, that room, the persons present. "Agh! The deerhead. And the baby— I don't think that boy would go to the FBI. That's impossible."

"Now Vivian and I have had a very fine discussion about this Benefit, Clem. You won't repeat anything that's passed here today, will you, Vivian? You understand that it would destroy Clem. We're taking you into our confidence. Entrusting ourselves to you . . . We all know that a lot of plans have been made and a lot of work has gone into this, but it's not too late for us, very quietly of course, just to let it slide . . ."

"Mother, what on earth are you talking about! Just because a couple of men . . . there's no reason . . . Vivian, you're not thinking of dropping—"

"I wanted to see you this morning," Vivian said, "because of the circular about the other barbecue. Have you heard about it?"

"Oh that. Who hasn't? I found one in my car. They'll probably get a crowd but I doubt if it'll cut into us too much. In the first place Ol' Cal isn't going to spend any time here."

"Ol' Cal!" Mrs. DeLavery cried. "Ol' Cal is coming *here*?"

"Not for more than five minutes if at all. This county isn't important to him, it's only important to his local camp followers."

"Then I wish," Vivian said, "that you'd reassure Father Hall. Buck him up a little. Someone is pressuring him, we suspect, maybe Mrs. Hemmings, to change his mind about the premises."

"Then you *can* stop it now! Thank God."

"Of course I'll talk with him," Clem said. "Scheduling a rally like that this late in the campaign, last minute . . . Let's just go on as if there were nothing of the kind. How's the chorus doing?"

"You should have heard them today."

"And the food?"

"Mabel has it straightened out. I'm afraid Nancy and I will have to do more of the chauffeuring. If that's all right with you, Nancy?"

"Any time. Just call."

"Stopit stopit stopit!" The grey fists crashed down on the table. Till the dishes danced. "Stopit stopit stopit . . ."

"Mother—"

At Clem's approach she flung herself down on the dingy threadbare carpet and rolled on her back in an orgy of self-abandon, a horrifying spectacle, kicking, her skirt sprawled over grey-veined thighs, white-gartered from undergarments dull with repeated washings.

"Iwonthaveit Iwonthaveit I wonthaveit I wonthaveit . . ."

Nancy ran for the telephone, called the doctor. Vivian ran to the kitchen and brought soaking-wet cloths and knelt applying them. Clem lifted the distraught head trying to force liquor from a glass between the foaming lips.

"Itsnotnothing itsnotnothing itsnotnothing . . ."

Outside, back in the car, Vivian looked at the tall narrow house, apparently so solid and so stable, that had been occupied by a succession of pastors of too brief duration.

She started up the car fast, out of there, away. From the terrible racking broken sobbing. Away. To the River Road. To Reeve.

A crowd had assembled at Reeve's place ahead of her. Her grandfather sat with Father Hall up on the porch, quietly wrangling. In back where Reeve was working on the house preparing it for painting, several newly arrived white boys had joined in with High Power and Sanderlee, bringing copies of the handbill. Reeve was reading one now over a sheet of sandpaper.

"That old skunk!" Lonnie Truelove yelled. "First thing we try to do something for ourselves that old skunk has to come in, break it up."

"They throw a barbecue, that's their right," Carl Maynard argued. "We throw a barbecue, that's our right. That old Purcell, he's had my vote and my family vote—"

"We'll outlive Purcell," Reeve said and gave Carl back his circular. "You can send his wife an onion to put it on his grave. There's one thing I know. We made up our mind where we going, we put one foot ahead of the other we may get there. But if we don't, we won't. You put a seed in the ground and it comes up flowers and where the flower was it fruits. You take larva, it'll change skin six times before it turns out a caterpillar and then the caterpillar spins itself a cocoon and change itself again into something it never was before, a butterfly.

You see a crayfish when it sheds its shell it sheds everything, stomach lining, eyes, grows out all new. I don't know about you guys but these last few weeks I been thinking about that fruit, those wings, new stomach lining, new eyes."

He began to scuff with his sandpaper at a stubborn roughness in the siding. "This house right now. Looks like a dog with the mange. Couple more days it'll be all stained, paint trim around the windows."

"That a house?" High Power solemnly inquired. "I thought it was a piece of furniture."

They all fell to criticizing. "You left out a dent there. And this scratch here . . ."

Then they all whooped off in their cars down the track to Rad for his opinion.

Vivian perched on a sawhorse watching Reeve. The house was badly weathered so half his job lay in the preparation. He had pulled out all the rotting boards and replaced them, had boiled up buckets of sudsy water and scrubbed off every last speck of surface dirt. Then he'd scraped down and puttied in. Now he was sanding it smooth before staining.

There were so many things this house needed more than it did outside appearance. But sometimes what's necessary must take precedence over what's needed. This was his flag and his trumpet and his rallying cry.

He moved lithely in his coveralls, supple back flexing, brown hand reaching. Lean and hard. From the balls of his feet, muscled calves, narrow hips, small-buttocked, taut waist, straining shoulders, arching throat, arm uplifted, reaching beyond the ability of all the gathered height of his body to attain, from the tips of his fingers reaching it. With a frowning concentration that she could see through the back of his head. The crease biting deep between the bars of his brows. The dark eyes, gold-flecked, measuring distance, obstacles, opponents, worth. The disciplined planes of his cheeks. The flaring nostrils. The mouth robust, warm, and firm.

She sculptured him out, every feature, tactile to his textures. The crisp black hair that capped his head. Skin as smooth as vellum, as smooth as polished stone. Branching collarbone, single brusque line of hair between his ribs and in his armpits, flat abdomen and rough black crop of hair out of which the male member sprung grape-brown, silken-sheathed. Anatomized him. Competent to purpose, wary, proud, with no waste motion, directed to the object. Clamping his teeth on fear. Nursing incertitudes in silence. His hurts in loneliness.

The sandpaper rasped.

From her distance on the sawhorse she bent over him with the words of the old old language. You want some? And was plied with the old old answers. Is it good is it good? And tossed under him, fretting with the old old plaint. You worry me you worry me. Till the sweet hot spunk. Sculpture anatomy language dissolving in the wine-dark sea.

D' butter fum d' duck.

The sandpaper rasped releasing flurries of wood dust. A jay squawked in the treetops.

She thought, Don't be a fool. She said, "Reeve, I'm ready."

With the alert turn of his head, she thought, This is a mistake. She said, "My mother was a good woman but the wrong one for my father. My father was a good man but the wrong one for her. He killed himself, shot himself through the temple in a little room where cockroaches were hanging from the light chain. Because what he wanted of this world he couldn't have. And what he could have he didn't want. There's a little bit of all that in both of us, Reeve. It won't be easy."

He came toward her, his dark eyes no longer searching, judging, appraising. Knowing. "We'll have great children."

She thought, Any port in a storm. She said, "You're home to me."

He kissed the top of her head, the tip of her ear, her mouth. "What happened?"

"Hold me tight."

Embracing, peppered with sawdust. Married not on a bed but a sheet of sandpaper.

"Something happened?"

"All the awfulness," she said, "the pity and the wonder of life." . . .

They were married five days later in a fine church wedding with all the fixings, in the presence of family and friends. Mabel Dawson and Carter Scott attending them. Hagan Power's two little stepdaughters in Sunday frocks and bonnets strewing flowers. Rebecca Hall playing the Wedding March from *Lohengrin*. Father Hall united them. Malcolm Gregory come down early for his concert later in the week singing *I Love You Truly* and *Oh, Promise Me*.

A few of the older women who always managed to attend every ceremonial arrived late, having hastened here from the St. Paul cemetery. Wiping their eyes over the Warren child they had just seen lowered in lawn-draped ivory casket into his grave, they recalled Rose Scott and Sukey Purcell last spring. Isn't it funny, isn't it strange, how a funeral and a wedding will cross?

From the sidelines they examined the bride's waistline with particular interest. My, this was sudden . . .

4

The morning of the Benefit Rad rose before sunup and went at once to the window. In the moonlight a low-lying mist on the fields shimmered like the mirage of a lake. "It's all right," he called back to Lulabelle. "It's going to be all right. Not a cloud in the sky."

The bed clanked as she stood up out of it. She stepped over to the hamper where the baby was sleeping. By her movements, the suggestion of a sag in her step, the whisper of a sigh on her breath, Rad could tell the mood she was in. Still pining.

She came up beside him at the window in the old Sunday shirt of his that she'd taken to wearing for a nightgown. Her breasts were swollen hard underneath and every so often milk gushed out soaking through the cloth, the cloth over her breast drying later in stiff yellow splotches. She plucked at the irritant splotches, holding them away from her nipples. Pining, Rad thought without looking at her. Last thing at night and first in the morning. Pining for Charles.

"It'll be a pretty day," she said. "Turned a mite cooler too."

The ground mist was breaking up in shreds that caught like silver cobwebs in the inky growth.

"I'll bring up some fish for breakfast," he said. "Must be a mess of them down there in the trap."

"River sure is high for this time of year."

What she didn't say was what he knew was on her mind. Hankering. Grieving. Rad, I want my boy! It was a forbidden subject, a territory that he by his attitude had so interdicted she didn't dare infringe upon it. They'd been all through it. From the time he came back from the Warren house without him. It's up to him. It's his choice to make. I won't have him look us in the eye years from now and think we deprived him of his chance. And she being newly home from the hospital, wrapped up in the baby, having confidence at last in him, her husband, that he knew what he was doing had submitted without protest. "He'll come back," he told her, "he'll come back on his own. Every time I ever run from home I always did." But Charles didn't come. And still he didn't go after him. So one day after they had heard that he was at the church camp, she packed the children into the truck and drove to Silver Beach for him. The campers were all in the messhall eating and she sat outside in the truck listening to the babble of voices, the clatter of silver, and then when they started trooping out she put her foot down on the gas and tore out of there. She loved all her children according to what they were, but that boy, that boy was the jewel of her eyes. She didn't mention Charles anymore. There was the tractor. She thought—Rad knew what she thought—that once the barbecue was over, once they had the tractor here, something to show, everything rolling, that he would go back to the Warren house for him. Invite him to Sunday dinner. "It's up to you." How could anyone expect of a ten-year-old boy—it's up to you? You old enough now, it's up to you?

Day slipping after day, Rad felt now with the full bitterness of her reproach upon him, in a compound of pride and postponement. Until now it was too late. You can't go up to a house of mourning and say, "Now you don't need him no more. Give us our son back." But he had believed every night, every morning that Charles would come back of himself. He still believed that. He'll be back.

Lulabelle brushed against him peering out the screen, her hair hanging in braids to her shoulders, her face screwed to a point. Seeking in the ripple of a shadow, in the dawning light.

"It don't seem right! After all the work we done for this day, he won't be—"

Rad jerked angrily back for his pants on the back of a chair. Don't start in, don't start in now!

"I better get going. There's so much . . ."

The baby let out a cry and Lulabelle ran from the window with a fine spray flying through the thin shirt over her breast. "There there"— she took the baby up in the crook of her arm, frantically unbuttoning— "you hongry now, you hongry?" Guiding the nipple with her forefinger into the groping lips, between the sharp cartilaginous gums. "Take it, take it." And when the grip of the gums was satisfactorily established, the tugging upon the swollen-hard compacted sphere begun, she yelped in agony, "You biting me, you little devil, ooooo." As the rush within was released, she scooped up with her finger a creamy drop that had spurted out beforehand and tasted it on her tongue.

"What you lookin' at, man?" she demanded of Rad. And with self-complacency she announced as she always did, petting the back of the little round fuzzy head so voraciously fastened upon her, "I got that much milk."

Rad closed the door behind him and tiptoed through the parlor where the young ones were sleeping. In the kitchen he had to search for the kettle to set it on to heat. The table was covered with buckets, the dry sink, the stove. Every available vessel, the laundry steamer, the baby's bath pan, was filled with potatoes. In every public function there always has to be some to-be-expected unexpected last-minute crisis. This time it was the potato salad. Lonnie Truelove's wife who had accepted responsibility for the ladies making it had come down yesterday with chills and fever and her sister-in-law had been called away and her neighbor down the road had misunderstood or had been misinformed . . . Last night Lonnie and a hastily organized brigade of young ones had dumped the potatoes here on the porch, bushels of them. Then had lit out. "I ain't feelin' so good myself." All evening long the kids were scrubbing and Lulabelle was boiling up and he, when he came home from helping set up the picnic grounds, was skinning those goddam spuds. The salad wasn't half-finished yet. There were the greens to be picked and chopped, the hard-boiled eggs to be cut through, the boiled dressing . . .

Peculiar that Lonnie's wife would fall sick just now. And Lonnie, his strongest support in the class . . .

On the riverside Rad prodded with a long pole along the foot of the dike for the catfish trap he'd let down a few days before. The water was high, higher than he ever remembered it this season, slapping against the banks, pressing. He pulled up the trap, a cylindrical drum of meshed wires. Whiskered bullheads flopped about inside in disoriented search for an outlet. Caught swimming in through the open end of the conical interior and down through the small end into the hole. From which there was no turning back. No getting out of it. Fool fish.

He strung the bullheads up on a stick and slung the stick over his shoulder. With the sun up now, swimming out from behind scarlet-and-gold clouds like the king of glory, Rad trudged back along the old rice canal, turbid and silty inside the closed sluice gate. Tomorrow they'd have the tractor and the use of a dragline.

Bacon was sizzling in the spider. Coffee was bubbling in the pot. The kids were all up chopping celery and green onions for the potato salad. Lulabelle took the fish from him to clean and he retired into the nearest free corner with a cup of coffee keeping one eye on the stove and the other on the kids. Then Vivian came knocking at the door with a pailful of eggs.

"So you did it," Vivian said, spying the buckets of potatoes.

"Of course I did it," Lulabelle retorted. "Did you think I wouldn't? Come on in."

"Well, I kept boiling up these eggs and boiling them, all the time wondering if I wasn't wasting my time. Where'll I put them?"

"Yonder." Lulabelle floured up a slice of fish and tossed it in with the bacon. "Had your breakfast?"

"I could stand another cup of coffee. Then I have to run."

The kids began on the small speckled hard-boiled eggs, rapping them against the edge of the table. "Lord but these guinea eggs got shells like rock. You need a hammer."

The two women stood with their coffee cups, eggs banging all around them. Rad reached past them to fork over the fish on the stove.

"Happy?" Lulabelle asked.

"You're married. You tell me," Vivian said. "How long does this last?"

"It goes away," Lulabelle said. "But something else takes its place. You so knit together. And it comes back sometimes, goes away and comes back. You got one thing ahead of you though. When they put your first-born into your arms."

Womantalk.

"Move, move," Rad grunted at the kids. He flipped the fish over onto a plate. "Time's a-flying. We'll never get to the parade."

Ruby stubbornly lagged, picking at the fractured shell of her egg and dropping bits of it under the bench. "Hurry on up," Wyatt urged her, the uncertainty of his control over the younger children shrill in his voice. "We'll be late for the parade." Ruby stuck her tongue out at him. "You ain't my boss. Charles is." She squeezed the egg with shell still clinging to it into the potato salad. Wyatt exasperated leaned over and walloped her. The two women jumped.

Now what!

Donnybrook.

"Charles! I want Charles! Charles! Charles!"

From deep in her hamper, the baby, Ella-Rose, looked up with wide dark eyes as if she could see and understand everything.

"Oh, how I wish this day was over with!"

Finally the pots of potatoes were all stowed in the truck and a sheet draped over them to keep the sun and the flies off. The young ones, scrubbed and dressed, were packed in with the potatoes. Lulabelle sat up in the cab with the baby in her arms, a bundle of diapers in the blanketed basket at her feet, two pies beside her and on the ledge back of her head her plants for the horticulture exhibit. Up to the last the potato salad plagued them. At the icehouse back of the bank they unpacked it all again to be refrigerated until the picnic hour. Too many tales around of mass food poisonings.

Rad left them in crowded Oglethorpe Square looking for a favorable spot at the curbside, and went on to the American Legion Hall where the ranks were assembling. Khaki-capped, blue-capped with a sprinkling of navy whites, they were marshaled in formation behind their color bearers. The marching band warmed up with a few tentative measures, a dull thud of drum beats surmounted by glittering brasses blaring into the sun.

The bunting-draped reviewing stand mounted on the courthouse steps was occupied by a host of local dignitaries including Mayor Dakin and his wife, members of the County Commission and their ladies, Benson Reece, D. C. Lacey, Ada Hemmings who had somehow inserted herself, and Eustis and Jessie Telfer who had also wangled themselves in. While they glanced impatiently toward the Legion Hall waiting for the parade to begin, Ada held forth. Ada was given to bursting out with hysterical utterances ever since she lost her secretaryship of the Historical Society a few months ago in a dispute over the missing deed book; but no one minded that. Ada could always be counted on to furnish an otherwise tedious moment with something interesting, food for later talk.

She had been against farming the Founders Day parade out to the Legion to begin with, she declared. She had fought it up and down the Historical Society, but there was no one there to take the responsibility. And the UDC chapter—the United Daughters of the Confederacy, extinct for the past five years due to a factional rift in the leadership—none of those who used to be in it would take any action. And the Order of the Cherokee Rose, with all due respect to the gentlemen who belonged, they just didn't seem to give a damn for the past anymore. She'd gone to everyone, she'd done her best but the suspension during the war had killed it. This was nothing like the Founders Day celebrations she remembered.

"Remember, remember how it always was? Such a show. So colorful. The Highlanders in their bonnets and tartans and kilts, their sporrans all fringed up like anything swinging from their belts. And the Indians in their blankets and breechclouts. Painted up with war paint. Whooping and prancing."

"Yes yes," Mrs. Dakin agreed with her, "wasn't it a sight!"

"I was always there in the first float," Jessie piped up, seconding Ada for once. "Wearing crinolines and pantalettes—I couldn't let the bodice out any more if I tried. And all the colored mammies in kerchiefs and aprons. And Harold Wylly, I remember we got him all tricked out one year in ruffled shirt and knee-breeches and he wasn't dark enough, we had to cork him up."

"And the year that float—you recall it, Benson, the bank had a float fitted out like one of those schooners that used to clear the port with I don't know how many thousand feet of timber—"

"And the rafters, we had them too, in their raggedy shirts, singing—"

"It was such a procession. It moved so slow. Stately. All horse-drawn."

"The buggies. Every family in a buggy. We had a wagon and I'd be up there with my father and we had our yardboy in a box back of us. How he loved to flick that whip . . ."

"It's not historical," Ada cried. "All the history's gone out of it. There's no history to this."

The martial strains in the distance quickened, plucked at those ordinarily forgotten responses, latent as if in cold storage, that a parade never fails to excite. Of anticipation. Suspense. A breathlessness. Are they coming? You see them? No, they're just falling in. Don't you see them? Not yet. Not yet.

Below the reviewing stand and all the way around the Square the crowd spilled over the curbs clapping and cheering, whooping and whistling, hoo-hooing and waving, getting under one another's feet in a scramble for balloons, frosted custards, and coolie hats hawked by the vendors. You see them? They started yet? Where are they?

The tread of innumerable feet in unison. The soaring of trumpets.

"Here they come!"

Patrolmen for the day, white-bandoleered, spread arms pressing the crowd back from the road. A contingent of state highway police whizzed by on motorcycles. Chalmer Coombs and his deputies rolled behind them, waving flags from the windows of their coupés. Then in lone splendor as always a single open car appeared, chauffeured, carrying in the rear O. Z. Higginson, Sr., born the day the War between the States was ended, garbed in his father's Confederate uniform or a reasonable facsimile thereof. A second car conveyed the Spanish-American War veterans, lifting their hats to all and sundry. Followed by the Grand Marshal, Lloyd Bird, the ruminant raconteur transformed into the very model of a martinet. Hup hup hup.

Under their standards, five abreast, troops in the tin helmets, Sam Brownes, and puttees of World War I swept into the Square, accompanied by coveys of cavorting small boys and dogs. Preceding the band, the drum majorette caparisoned in baby-blue satin looped with gilt braid, shako, abbreviated uniform, and high-stepping boots, twirled her baton in incredible feats of jugglery, leaping and pirouetting to catch it in the air, powdered legs flashing.

"Who's that girl?" Marcus Hadley up in the reviewing stand jabbed D. C. Lacey in the back with a hard forefinger.

"Let me see, she's a junior, Isabel Herrera, Johnny's granddaughter."

"You don't mean Isabel Colfax's—uh—hm—"

"Well, that's one direct descendant anyhow," Ada Hemmings conceded, "of an original settler."

Boomp-pa boompa-pa bup-pa-bup.

Bass drums and snare drums rattled in street beat. The columns of

World War II in campaign caps and olive drabs, stockinged sailors, a line of WACs and WAVES, several women in Legion caps and capes who had been at some time or other in some place or other affiliated with an auxiliary.

"What the hell is that?" Marcus again, with his finger in Lacey's back.

From the street adjacent to the courthouse the colored troops joined the parade. First a car conveying two Spanish-American War veterans. Then a group of high schoolers in black cocked hats, white shirts, and black pants—counterpart of a similar group in the white parade, the Marion swamp raiders.

D. C. Lacey passed his hand over his eyes. Last week the principal of the Colfax-Scott school and one of the teachers had dropped in to discuss the salary situation and in the course of his hedgings they had made off with a batch of new textbooks and all the extra cocked hats around.

"They say it's all in the history books," he explained weakly to Marcus. "In the Revolution or the War of 1812 or something, some Haitian volunteers landed somewhere near here to help us against the British."

Marcus turned from D.C. who was plainly getting too old for the job to Mayor Dakin. "What history books? What kinda history they teaching over there in that school?"

"You know more history than I do," the mayor, a politician with a flair for steering clear of controversy, answered him. "I been kicked out of some of the best colleges in the country. Georgia Tech. Georgia State. Only history I'm interested in"—he stuck his hand out with a gimme motion—"is makin' the shekels. Only," he concluded plaintively, "that don't seem to do me no good because I ain't makin' any."

The colored band was preceded also by a drum majorette, an eight-year-old girl in rose satin, spinning her stick skyward, turning handsprings.

"Who is she?" "Isn't she a doll?" "Look, look at that, would you . . ." And the band.

"I don't care, there's something about a colored band when they turn out, all spic and span, spit and polish. When the beat is right and the brass is high . . ."

With a ruffle of drums the troops wheeled to a halt before the reviewing stand, closing ranks, marking time; colored on one side, white on the other; all the grades, shoulder patches, insignia, ribbons of so many different associations, places, experiences merging in the bright September morning under the shadow of the towering bronze monument in the green.

"Never had them all together like this before."

"Goes to show how many this county has contributed to the service. And they're not all here. Not by a long shot."

"It really makes you stop to think. Don't it make you stop to think?"

The two bands blew into their instruments from the bellows of their lungs with cheeks, lips, teeth, and tongue moulded to the embouchure of tuba, trumpet and trombone, piccolo, flute and clarinet. *The Stars and Stripes Forever.* Hurrah for the Red, White, and Blue. *Da da dada-DAHdahdahDAHdah* . . . Uniting paraders and crowd in a surge of triumphant emotion, the most jaded among them feeling an alien prickle up the nose, a stinging under the eyelids; all personal identity not so much obliterated as conjoined with every other. Benson Reece, before whose clouded vision everything blended in a blur of prismatic hues, took off his glasses and inspected them as if they were playing him false. He leaned over to whisper in Mayor Dakin's ear. Dakin shook his head laughing, unable to hear him, and replied in the vein of a politician whose diplomacy is his prize asset. "Looks like we out-Independenced Independence Day and Out-Armisticed Armistice Day. And as for Founders Day, well I reckon," he said with uncommon sweetness, "we all Founders here."

As the marchers right-faced and turned down the east side of the Square heading for their dispersal point, an interruption occurred, totally unplanned for, at least by the committees in charge of the parade. From Lancaster Street, leading from the residential section, a motorcade roared in with blowing horns. Attaching itself to the tail of the white marchers and cutting off the colored in the rear, it assumed unto itself all the fanfare and the credit of the vanguard before it. Judge Purcell's Lincoln, Dan Garner taking bows from the back of the open Chrysler loaned by Read Motor Sales, Henry Warren's tan convertible, Hill Caslon's two Buicks, the Finchleys' Chevrolet and a whole string of others, trucks, jalopies, and buckboard wagon. Tooting, ringing bells, whirling noisemakers, streamered with stars and bars, bannered and postered with slogans, plastered with stickers. *Ol' Cal for Governor! Back Ol' Cal! Crackers for Ol' Cal! Save Our State! Grow with Garner! Win with Warren! Vote Right, Vote White! Barbecue & Rally City Park Today Come One Come All* . . .

At the sight of the motorcade the crowd, beginning to break up, swarmed together again. Lulabelle was herding the children past the bank to the icehouse alley where the truck was parked when Wyatt tugged at her skirt, Timmy jumped up and down and Ruby shrieked. "Charles! Charles! Mamma, there's Charles!"

There he was passing her by, in the front seat of the convertible between the woman in black and the man in the Stetson hat, between the two of them just as their son used to be, dressed in a grey suit with a black band on his sleeve. Leaving her children, holding the baby on her shoulder, Lulabelle ran after the car. Through barricades of arms and legs, families hurrying to meet with their uniformed men, teenagers shoving in around the drum majorette.

"Charles! Charles!"

The horns, the hubbub, the ear-splitting male whistles rending the air drowned out her shouts. Hoarse and panting she fell back, pain stabbing her side, pinpoints piercing her eyes. The baby, jarred, squalled on her shoulder. The crowd swirled about her. Thronging into Ozzie Higginson's dollar sale. Entering parked cars to take the highway to Zion or to the city park off the same highway according to previous plan or inclination of the moment or the intention of whatever group one happened to be with. While she stood on the sidewalk with mouth open, tears streaming down her cheeks.

She met Rad at the truck in the icehouse yard. "Everything OK?"

"So far so good," he said grimly. "They sure pulled a fast one."

"Something wrong?"

"No, nothing's wrong. Go on, get in there."

He didn't ask was there anything wrong with her. Riding, she rediapered the baby and nursed her to sleep.

"Damn Richard-Gene." Rad leaned intently over his wheel pushing up the highway, ramming through the knot of traffic at the branch-off to the city park. "When he's with me, he's one thing. When he's with his brothers, he's another. Never can tell what he's up to."

"Something's wrong," she insisted. "Something's on your mind."

"Nothing, nothing, nothing." He drove bumpily off the highway into the field outside the fenced grounds of the church that had been assigned as a parking area. He surveyed the cars already there ahead of them, drawn up hood to hood against the fencing. "Not bad. Not bad at all. Ol' Cal won't be there nohow. Holed up at home with that throat ailment he's been suffering from. Can't speak above a whisper. It's all over the radio." He helped her down from the truck with baby and basket. "Now go on. Would I let you go in there with these young ones if there was anything wrong? Got your tickets? You all go on into the church, grab yourselves some good seats. I'll follow."

But when they came around with him to the entrance gate of the church they descried the first sign of trouble. On the other side of the road four cars were lined up in the grass, loaded to the gills with Chalmer Coombs and his deputies, all of them armed to the teeth and ready for anything.

Inside the gate High Power and Carter Scott presided over the recep-

tion table. "Tickets? Tickets please?" Along both sides of the path up
to the church young men stood casually about in fairly close formation,
most of them in their parade uniforms.

"Go on," Rad urged Lulabelle toward the church steps. "Ain't nothin'
to worry about. There's Mrs. Dakin now. You stick with her. I'll just be
a minute."

He waited until she vanished inside, the baby in the basket over her
arm and the children at her heels. Then he jostled through the crowd
seeking Reeve, and was waylaid every step of the way. In spite of the
disruption of the motorcade, much of the temper of the parade had
carried over here. Groups of uniformed men, white and colored attracted to each other by recognition of familiar emblems and devices,
kept hauling him into their midst. "Say, would you look at that fruit
salad—" "You remember Bill Hill? He was with the 101st—" "Me, I
fought the war in the ATC, Gander, pulling guard, man, was it cold—"
"Go on, you never saw overseas. You sold Post Toasties in the PX . . ."

He discovered Reeve at the side door of the church, breaking through
a path for Vivian and the chorus. Drawing Reeve aside, he gestured with
his head toward the road. "What goes?"

"Chalmer? He sent for Carter—you know he always talks to Carter—
to offer us protection. And Cart told him no, we don't need no protection from him and his deps. Seems like Chalmer's dead sure there's
bound to be a disturbance here. At the first sign of any such thing he's
coming in with his men, ring down the curtain, send everyone home."

Rad glanced back toward the road . . . Chalmer had been under a
heavy barrage of criticism lately from his opponent for sheriff. The
charge: laxity. Laxity toward whom or what requiring no further eluci-
dation.

"Well, I just now heard something from Richard-Gene," he spoke into
Reeve's ear. "I don't know how much reliance to put on it. He's been
staying away from meetings altogether, steering clear of this whole
thing. Now he tells me in the middle of the parade that he had a run-in
with his brothers this morning about it all and they're coming down
here to break it up. He may just be talking off the top of his head. But
then again, he may not be. On the other hand, if there's payoff involved—"

"Richard-Gene just now went in there. He's in the front pew on the
white side, took the seat we had reserved for the mayor and his wife."

"Great."

Reeve waved Vivian on into the church, blew a kiss and accompanied Rad down to the Hospitality Committee. High Power listened
with one ear while continuing to attend to the table with Carter. "Tick-

ets? Show your tickets please? Yeah, yeah," he said to Rad. "Good deal.
I dig you. Thanks for the tip. Go on in."

"But don't you want . . . shouldn't I get together some of my contingent?"

Power's eyes never left the crowd pouring past, identifying, sizing
up. "Inside please, inside," Carter hurried them on. "Program's due to
begin. Go on in, Rad. Enjoy yourself."

"But look—" He was being prodded toward the door as he had
prodded Lulabelle.

"The thing we have to avoid above all," Reeve said to him, "is trading
blows. That's the number-one thing. No blows."

With a hand on Rad's shoulder he propelled him into the vestibule
and went back to join the Hospitality Committee at the gate.

The church was strictly segregated. Colored entered through the left
of the double doors, the whites through the right. The pews on the left
of the nave were assigned to colored, those on the right to white. The
overflow was sent up the single dusty stairway to the galleries under the
eaves where again company was parted, left and right, according to
race. By the press of sheer numbers however, and as a consequence
of the natural mobility of people, here and there lines broke down
and such a commingling took place in certain congested areas that the
ushers gave up trying to maintain the division and devoted themselves
mainly to conducting guests of honor to their appropriate pews.
And even here distinctions went awry.

Mayor Dakin finding that Richard-Gene Jeems had preempted the
place to which he was shown in front retired rather than share the pew
with him to the second row, preserving his wife from contact with such
riffraff. Only to be joined in the second row a moment later by a cracker-
gal with a baby in a basket and a string of young ones. Father Hall
beckoned the mayor up to the dais from which he was to deliver a welcoming address to the crowd, leaving Mrs. Dakin in the pew with Lulabelle McDowell, a perfect stranger insofar as Mrs. Dakin was concerned.
"My, did you ever see such a crush?" she complained to Lulabelle.
"Would you believe it I don't know a soul here today?" She twisted
about, her soft blue eyes flitting from face to face. "None of the better
class of people. If it wasn't for my husband speaking in the public interest, and Benson . . . Only Benson had the sense to leave his sister
home I see." With aggrieved soughs and sighs she besought Lulabelle's
sympathy. "Only other time in my life I ever was in a colored church
was right here last May. When Julie-Ann Colfax's old mammy passed
on, and then it was so different. It was all so different . . . I wonder

where Mrs. DeLavery . . . I thought at least Laura DeLavery, and Nancy . . . Where are the DeLaverys?"

The absence of the DeLaverys was causing a flurry of delay in the opening. Father Hall sent his wife back twice to the house to telephone them, and the operator rang until she was tired. There was no answer. Father Hall found a half-dozen different matters to attend to before ascending the pulpit, suffering with the loss of Clem, his brother in the cloth and chief prop, an attack of anxiety as acute as Mrs. Dakin's over the scarcity of the better white people.

The chorus assembled behind Father Hall. His daughter Rebecca took her seat at the piano. In the sacristy his brother-in-law, Malcolm Gregory, impatiently consulted his wristwatch—colored people's time! If the concert didn't begin promptly at eleven, the audience would be so hungry before it was finished . . . Father Hall adjusted the white tie over his cassock, raised his arms for attention, bowed his head.

Rad waited in the vestibule through the invocation, then made his way forward to Lulabelle. Avoiding the anxious inquiry in her eyes, he craned about estimating the composition of the crowd. About two-thirds colored. One-third white. Carl Maynard under the gallery. And Lonnie, blessed if it wasn't Lonnie.

"Where's the Rev?" Lulabelle whispered at him.

"The Rev? Clem?" He scanned the rows behind him. "Well, he's got to be here. He must be here somewhere."

Throughout the mayor's address, tactfully brief and adorned with a few fetching phrases, Rad squirmed about. His head jerked around at every sound from the door that might indicate a commotion outside. Vivian stepped out on the dais and took her place before the chorus, her figure unbelievably slight against the stepped arrangement of boys and girls in their linear white of shirt and blouse, black of pants and skirt.

"This group of numbers," she announced in a thin reedy voice Rad scarcely recognized, "is dedicated to the men of our armed services who fought so gallantly in the defense of our country. Will the audience please rise?" She turned and lifted her wand.

"My country 'tis of thee, Sweet land of liberty . . ."

With perfect timing, in concert with the singing voices, The Terrible Jeems Brothers escorted by kin and boon companions, about a dozen in all, swaggered up the road from their cars to the churchyard gate. Not drunk—it was too early in the day yet—but they were feeling no pain. Sniggering, nudging one another, they winked at Chalmer and his deputies as they passed them. With giggles of bravado that lilted upward to a soprano edge of nervousness they shoved, frisky and fettlesome, through the gate.

"Tickets? Tickets please? Gentlemen, show your tickets?"

"Now you let us in here, nigger-boy—"

About fifty colored men moved in around the table, forming a closed circle about them.

"Why, Mr. Jeems," Carter welcomed the oldest and beefiest, the leader of the sortie, "you looking for your brother? He's right in there with the other boys from his class. I'll be glad to show you to him. Do you have your tickets yet? Seventy-five cents for adults. Twenty-five for children."

The closed circle of colored men about the table thickened. A few of them carried baseball bats, loosely as if interrupted by curiosity in the midst of their batting practice. Several of them held hammers, apparently from the booths that had been temporarily knocked together along the side of the church. One was soothing a German shepherd dog, checking him with the frayed rope tied to his collar.

Momentarily disconcerted, the invading party consulted among themselves, collected the money in small change for tickets and flung it on the table, a few coins rolling to the ground. "Pick it up."

"Right this way, Mr. Jeems." Carter with his hand under the elbow of the oldest brother hurried him through the circle ahead of the others, leaving them behind.

As the eleven men moved up the path, the circle of more than fifty men parted and moved with them alongside.

"Now what is this? Just what the hell—"

From the open door of the church the music rolled outward.

> "From the halls of Montezuma
> To the shores of Tripoli
> We fight our country's battles
> In the air, on land and sea.
> First to fight for right and freedom
> And to keep our honor clean
> We are proud to claim the title
> Of United States Marine."

The youngest Jeems brother who had been a commando turned mild small eyes about at Reeve, Richard-Gene's eyes, with the same expression of good-natured bafflement from which pugnacity was always ready to spring like a knifeblade.

"Hush, hush," people brandished down at them from the church doorway, admonishing silence. Some of the standees were holding hats over their hearts. An old man was actually drawn up rigid in salute.

The depth of the basses lifted skyward the sweet young bravura of the girls.

> *"Here's health to you and to our Corps*
> *Which we are proud to serve—*
> *In many a strife we've fought for life*
> *And never lost our nerve . . ."*

Singled out, infiltrated, separated, lost to one another, the Jeems party was scattered to diverse points in the church, squired by the ushers into the proximity of the most respected whites present.

Hot on the heels of their disappearance Chalmer arrived at the gate with his deputies. "What's going on here? You having some kind of fuss?"

"Not a bit," Carter said. "Everything's just fine, Mr. Coombs. Isn't that right?" he said to High Power.

"There's going to be trouble in there. I saw who went in." Chalmer started forth and his deputies after him with their hands on the holsters dangling back-hip.

"If you'd care to go in for the program, Sheriff," High Power invited, detaining him, "we'll be proud to have you. Only you'll have to leave your firearms outside."

"What?"

"Sssssh," the standees brandished from the steps.

"This is a place of worship," Carter explained. "And with all those women and little children in there . . . If you don't mind." Carter extended his hand among the deputies. "You too, Sheriff. That's the rule. No arms and no bottles."

Chalmer looked into the courteous sympathetic eyes where no hint of anything but helpfulness could be discerned, looked at the extended hand where rested, in his belief, the united voting power of the colored community. He looked about the grounds which seemed to him to be teeming with soldiers, running children, and women toting picnic baskets. Listened to the uproar of applause, stamping feet and whistlings that erupted from the interior of the church. And felt that somehow somewhere in some nightmare he had been through this before.

"Unbuckle," Chalmer snapped at his men, spurning Carter's hand. "Stash 'em in my car. And Tom, you stay with it. Don't you let no one near there, hear?"

In the church Malcolm Gregory was being introduced to the audience, a singer frequently referred to by the gossip columns of the colored press, and not without some justification, as "Dixie's dark Gable." He had that charm, that magnetism, that old black magic. He sang lieder, chansons, and canzonets in native tongue.

Programs rustled up. Attention surged stageward. Reeve threaded

his way down to Rad. "You seen DeLavery yet?" he whispered into Rad's
ear. "We sent down to his house and there's no one there."

"Neither hide nor hair. Wasn't he suppose to deliver the invocation?"
Their eyes turned, searching the audience. Full house. Too full.

"The benediction," Reeve said. "We're counting on that benediction."

Mein glaubiges herz . . .

5

The morning of the Veterans Benefit Laura DeLavery rose early after a
sleepless night, dragged a chair into her closet, climbed on it and took
her luggage down from the shelf, the luggage with which the Mission
Board had equipped her on her return during the war from the internment camp. Cheap luggage of the type most easily obtainable at the
time, of a plasticized canvas with leather corners, already scuffed and
a little dingy as well as horribly dusty. Into it she packed her meager
belongings, including the mended porcelain teapot broken upon her
arrival here. When Clem and Nancy came downstairs for breakfast later,
they found her standing in the hall dressed for departure, her handbag
under her arm, her gloves on and her best hat—the same white-veiled
hat she had worn on the day of his ordination when he had blessed her
first among his congregation.

She was leaving at once, she announced to their astonishment and
dismay. She had given them time enough to make their choice. To drop
this lunacy in which they were engaged. Or she would not stay here to
see them bring the roof down about their heads. And they had consistently shrugged her off. "Mother, you're overtired." "Mother, I can't
—it's impossible." Very well then. Her alternative was at hand.

Clem himself believed she was suffering a post-reaction from that
never precisely described year in the prison camp in the Philippines,
the never quite revealed circumstance of his father's death. From the
shattering shock of that moment when the Japanese general had not
simply and civilly knuckled under to them.

"Look, Mother," Clem tried once again now to reason with her.
"You're having a very understandable attack of jitters. Tonight it'll be
all over. Nothing's going to happen that shouldn't."

"Can you take an oath on that?"

She was not to be dissuaded from her course unless they were to be
dissuaded from theirs. She was going to visit with his sister Grace a while
—she never said "my daughter"; Grace with a thirteen-month-old child

and another on the way, in a two-room apartment. From there she would
make her plans.

"But why not Uncle Mark? You'll be so much more comfortable,"
Clem suggested, thereby crassly conceding her departure.

"How can I face Mark? After what you're doing to yourself. He's
never really gotten over the way you betrayed him that time. And now
me . . ."

They could drive her to the Bay City railroad station where there was
a train due at eight-thirty. Or she would walk out of the house now, bag
and baggage, to the bus stop in the public square.

They drove her to Bay City, Clem dressed for the Benefit in the clerical garb she had bought him, riding the car Mark had presented him as a
symbol of renewed faith in him, carrying in the inside pocket of his
tunic Mark's latest missive to him, handwritten on the stationery of
Butler Mills in answer no doubt to some hint dropped by his mother.
A sermonette, characteristically Mark.

> It is one of the unfortunate features of the human race that they
> are jealous of others in every walk of life if they think others have
> more than they do. They are principally inspired by envy of the
> more gifted and the more successful, and they will find every reason
> and excuse why they do not have as much or more than others do.
> They try to pull you down in all manner of ways. Few of us if we
> possess anything will retain it long unless we have innate ability
> to do so.
>
> This envy business is the cause of nearly all our troubles both as
> individuals and as a nation.
>
> The love of Jesus Christ is the only thing I know that will save
> this world from its sin and selfishness, and that comes from God
> and not men. Men can be loved or led by love to do constructive
> things, but seldom can it be accomplished—as you may well re-
> member—through force and threats of force. We must not place
> ourselves as judges over others, as no such authority is given us for-
> tunately.
>
> P.S. Please do not answer this since I do not care to argue and I
> love you.

The drive to Bay City was as unpleasant as Laura could make it, with
none of the honeyed circumlocutions, the playful tenderness, the winsome vivacity in which her criticism was customarily couched. Stark
naked, flagellant, her accusations sprang upon Clem with a demonic
fury. The Truth! The Truth!

They had come here in such hope for him and now it was all crumbling to dust. He had taken a town of good and gentle people and

turned them all against each other. Instead of arousing the best in them he had provoked the worst, incited the evil that lay dormant in their natures. Out of some esoteric neuroticism that she could never fathom he used the Christian ministry as a denunciatory weapon, and with a deviltry that had been his since he was a child wielded it upon his own kind, waging a suicidal war to destroy what he came of.

"You say we don't love. What kind of love is it that you can give with such facility to everyone but to those to whom you owe it most? What kind of a pastor is it that deserts his post? That leaves the nearest and dearest of his flock in her hour of need. Julie . . ."

From the time she had learned of the death of Colfax Warren she had held Clem responsible for it. If he had paid some mind to what was going on in his own parish instead of running all over the land-scape, if he had seen Julie long enough to talk with her, he could have prevented that operation. The child would be alive today.

Clem attempted at first to reply to her with all his stock replies. He believed in the Church Militant. He believed that it was his function to awaken the conscience, not to lull it with such soporifics as provide a preprandial digestive for an overheavy Sunday dinner. He looked upon his class as an enlargement of his ministry and his parish. Far from neg-lecting his church duties, he was doing more—everyone agreed . . .

"Why wouldn't they agree! Instead of giving you a raise next year, they have you now at a bargain. The more you do for nothing, the less they value you for it. And they will treat you in the end as people always treat bargains. Cheap is cheap."

Poor Nancy, cringing, attempted to intervene. "Mother, he loves you. We both love you."

"Love? What is love?" The Truth! The Truth! "At your age love is nothing but self-gratification. Thrills and throbs. And whoever hap-pens to be cause or object of it can be purely accidental, even immate-rial. You don't love the other person for what he is but for what you feel. What do you know of what love is? The ability to live for someone outside the self. To embrace him even when you have to grit your teeth. To pour everything you have into him and lose . . . All right, all right, when you're confronted with the doom you've brought on those sorry creatures you think you're helping, you'll find out in what stead your love and theirs will stand you."

In a stuffy passenger coach in which the air-conditioning had failed, Clem found his mother a seat. He stowed her luggage up on the rack and supplied her with a *Collier's* he had bought in the station. His lips descending to her cheek, the soft dun cheek sunken upon the bone, moved. Mother, you're not going! Her large dark eyes lifted toward him. You're not letting me go! Her head in the pretty white-veiled hat arched back.

"And one shall say unto him, What are these wounds in thine hands? Then he shall answer, Those with which I was wounded in the house of my friends."

The train diminished to a distant dot. The parallel of tracks joined on the horizon. Yesterday's late news jigged jaggedly over the sleepers. Clem opened his hands, unmarked by the stigmata of crucifixion or the blood of murder committed.

"Come," Nancy urged him. "Maybe it's best this way. We'll write to her tomorrow when it's all behind us. And we'll say as we would to a child who's waked up in the dark, after we've put the light on, 'See, there's nothing there.' Or like that story you tell of the man who's been bowed to the ground so long he won't raise his head, 'Look, that's the sun up there.'"

They ate breakfast at the fountain in the railroad station, eggs on toast, yolks coagulated, whites dried to a crisp on the underside, cold and coated with grease. Clem rested his forehead on his hand, shielding his eyes from the clerk's view. With the clash of couplings outside, the roar of a through-express, he was back in Butlerville again that night after his mother had visited him in the rooming house, when he leaned over the fence rail by the tracks under the railroad embankment. Our lives have a pattern if we could only discern it. If we could only see the forest for the trees, fly up above ourselves in some sort of psychic airplane and look down upon the configuration. Must I being killed kill over and over?

Am I sorry, Nancy wondered with that honesty that had lately come upon her for the most intolerable of self-admissions. She swallowed the soggy toast down the stricture of her throat. Or glad, relieved, unburdened. Mistress now in my own house. Only to discover that his eternal debate with her meant more to him than anything I can offer . . .

After coffee and the lavatory and a session in the public phone booth, Clem returned to Nancy briskly determined. "Let's go. We'll clean this up now once and for all."

He had just made the appointment for which his mother had pleaded all week long and which he, too busy, had brushed aside. With the office of the Federal Bureau of Investigation. From the station he drove through the morning-jammed thoroughfares to the post office building a few blocks away.

"But we'll be late for the parade," Nancy protested. "We'll never make it."

"It won't take more than a half hour at most. There's nothing much to discuss, really. I should have told you this before but Miss Bird hauled me under a tree yesterday to let me know in strictest secrecy that two men had been at the *Courier* talking with Edna Telfer about me. On the basis of a civil-service job I'm supposed to have applied for or some such thing, Edna, it seems, informed them that I was a very fine young fellow who had done more for the county in the past eight months than anyone else had in two hundred years. But after Edna, Birdie gathered, they went on to Ada Hemmings. I can only hope that Ada furnished them with a full account of the time I washed her dishes for her."

"But your job . . . I can't see what your objection . . ."

"Except that Edna was told not to tell anyone. And except for the fact that I haven't applied for civil service. I'm a teacher appointed by the state department of educaton, paid out of VA funds."

The post office, brick Italian Gothic, extended a full block. They ascended the granite steps, passed through one of the stone-piered round-arched doorways into the lobby, looked up the floor and room number on the white-lettered black index at the far end and mounted a flight of metal-stripped steps, narrow and iron-railed.

Mr. Rogan received them with a cordial handshake, a man of youthful maturity whose keen and kindly manner invited confidence. He introduced them to his assistant, Mr. O'Meara, a six-footer like Clem but with the shoulders of a football player. Nancy was tendered a chair.

"This way, Mr. DeLavery," Rogan motioned him toward a glass-partitioned cubicle.

"Anything we have to say," Clem stated amiably to the pair, "can be said in the presence of my wife. Nancy?"

Her knees quaking, Nancy preceded the men into the cubicle. Her eyes flew to the photographs and sketches, side and full view, of most wanted fugitives from justice who, squint-eyed and jowled, beetled above her on the cream wall. Her ears throbbed with the percussive tap of typewriters adjoining the cubicle, the tick of teletype, the buzz of intercepting telephones. A regional police conference in preparation. A fingerprint query.

Rogan took his seat behind the desk. O'Meara quickly closed the door behind himself and drew up a chair between Clem and Nancy.

"I dropped in to make an inquiry," Clem explained, armored in the dignity of his uniform, the cloth. "It's come to my attention that you've been seeking information about me. On what basis do you conduct such activities?"

Rogan stretched, folded his hands behind his head with an informality that was most attractive and laughed. "We are empowered to ask the questions, sir, not you. As an investigatory body."

"But where's the crime? There's no crime to be investigated."

"Cigarette? Mrs. DeLavery? We may investigate the possibility of a crime."

"Before it's taken place? Without evidence of any threat to anyone? What crime?"

In the ensuing silence Nancy picked up her chair and brought it around Mr. O'Meara to Clem's side where, sitting down, she could like his mother tug at his coat, step on his toe. Rogan clasped his knee and rocked back reflectively, his eye dropping, Nancy thought, in a convivial wink at her. O'Meara, decorous and disciplined, containing his movements within the periphery of his height and bulk, eyed Clem from under his thick eyelashes. O'Meara and Rogan resembled each other in their crewcuts, grey flannels and superlative grooming, the barbershop manicure of their nails, the soft-toned black polish of their shoes. Decency shone from both of them. Otherwise they were quite dissimilar of appearance and temperament.

"Feel free to present your position frankly, Mr. DeLavery," Rogan said. "We always welcome the other man's point of view."

"Unfortunately we don't have all morning," Clem said. "But I would like to point out to you if I may—" He leaned toward one and then the other, appealing in his emphasis. "You have no idea of the havoc you can wreak, the disturbance and alarm and yes, the tragedy, you can cause by the mere exercise of looking into the affairs of a private citizen, guilty of nothing—"

"Yes, that is a possible side effect," Rogan owned. "But we have a job to do and what other people may make of it is, I'm afraid, beyond our control. It's just a small item, we assure you, that was raised in relation to you. And most circumspectly too."

The matter of the civil-service application was quickly cleared up. A misunderstanding. It was, rather, that one Carl Anderson of Atlanta had used the name of the Reverend Clement DeLavery as a reference on his application.

"I don't know any Carl Anderson," Clem said promptly and rose to take his leave. "Now that we have that straight, it should close—"

"One more detail while you're here. O'Meara, will you bring in the file?"

From the battery of cabinets outside in the aisle O'Meara delivered a thick folder that reminded Clem of military dossiers he had once observed in passing on the desk of an intelligence officer. How had they come to collect background on him—and so much of it—from where . . .

He sank back down in his chair, his mouth clamping dangerously. Nancy's hand stole to his sleeve, a touch of warning, staying him. Rogan flipped through the folder extracting items which he did not attempt to shield from sight. The blue-bound tractor prospectus. A schedule of committee meetings. The cooperative contract.

Where from? Earl Goodfellow? In all good faith? Or an agent, someone paid to report?

From the house of my friends?

"That," Clem said to Rogan, "is a model contract and charter for cooperative associations, sent us by the Department of Agriculture."

"Yes, of course. One moment. Here." With a disarming smile Rogan unfolded the constitution. "A most interesting document. I'd like to know more about it." His finger traveled down the margin. "This clause for instance. Concerning the election of officers."

"Oh." Clem's grimness vanished. He broke into a grin. "You mean 'Equal Representation.' I'm glad you noticed that."

"Yes. It piqued my curiosity. What's it derived from?"

"Well . . ." Clem, revived, plunged eagerly into an exposition that had by now become theory with him. "When you have two groups as you have here, one with a long history of domination over the other, representation must be divided equally from the top down in order to overcome the inequities inherent in the situation. This way each group feels that it is being represented by its own spokesmen in the governing body and neither group feels that it is being arbitrarily ruled by the other."

"This was your concept?"

"No. I think it came from the men themselves."

"Who?"

"I don't recall. It just seemed logical to everyone, fair is fair. Biracial representation suggests to me of course the council of orders in the church—"

"And the Soviet Council of Nationalities?"

"There!" Clem said. "That's the idea. We have certain analogies here to conditions in a multinational or binational state. It isn't sufficient by itself to guarantee—"

"This." Rogan's forefinger traveled over to the next page. "The veto. That thing the Soviets are always pulling in the UN."

"The veto?" Clem was puzzled for a moment. "Oh. You mean the 'Principle of Unanimity.' I was just about to mention that. One of the colored veterans raised the objection that even with equal representation in our officership we could run into massive disagreement on racial lines. Well, you can't draw people together by pulling them by the hair.

Any more than you can win a woman's love"—he smiled at Nancy—"by acting as if you're already married, even when you are. Here the method evolved by the church for resolving similar conflicts occurred to me, that is voting by orders. Also, the method used by Congress when two committees are working on the same bill and must arrive at a unified text in order to move it forward. And certainly the prime example of the UN Security Council."

"What did you say the name of this colored veteran was?"

"Well—" Clem collected himself with difficulty from the pleasure of sharing the fine points with someone from the larger world, outside the small confines of Colfax County. Nancy's foot pressed against his. "I'd prefer not to refer to any one individual. We all knocked this out together. It's not the millennium by any means. An intermediate step, not the final solution. In some areas of conflict, it may bog us down in hopeless deadlock. In others it may promote tremendous progress."

"Am I correct in assuming," Rogan asked sympathetically, "that you believe in race equality as the final solution?"

"I believe that all men are born equal in the sight of God and before the law. And that we are all, every one of us," Clem nodded about inclusively, "different from one another."

"But you are extremely preoccupied with the Negro?"

"No more so than with the white. When I think of all the many ways in which whites are prevented from pursuing a normal relationship with colored, we're not free. Our freedom is curtailed. But when I think that on the basis of what our two classes have accomplished so far, right now in Arcady, at this very moment, men with so much potential for violence between them are getting together—in celebration—for the purpose of their common improvement."

Clem lifted his hands. There you are.

"Well, Nancy, we must run now. Mr. Rogan. Mr. O'Meara—"

"We understand that at some of these meetings," Rogan said, "your members are addressed as 'comrades.'"

Again Clem sat back. "A meeting was held by my class," he admitted gravely, "to ratify the constitution. In the American Legion Hall. They were addressed by the adjutant as 'comrades.'"

"Forgive me if I seem to entertain a few reservations, Mr. DeLavery. Are we taking too much of your time? Perhaps we'd better postpone—"

Nancy reared up from her chair. "We're due—"

"No, no," Clem said. "If it won't take too long, let's have this out now. I don't want anything hanging over us."

"Good. You're very right. We'll make it as brief as we can. In our experience unhappily—as Mr. O'Meara who is our expert on the subject can testify—noble experiments are seldom as pure and holy as they seem."

Mr. O'Meara who had not ventured a syllable up to now bowed with the merest inclination of his head. Younger than Rogan, he had the air of one who has been scrubbed, brushed, and drilled from childhood in respect for his elders, teachers, reverend fathers, all symbols of authority. Insubordination was not in him. He had made his way up through law school at the top tenth of his class by a combination of ability, initiative, and respect for people in a position to aid him.

"In our opinion," Rogan resumed, "there may be more to this apparently innocuous project than meets the eye. We received a complaint not long ago of certain manifestations indicative of Communist influence—"

"Complaint by whom?"

"I can't tell you that. A responsible party. Are you sure, Mr. DeLavery, that you are not being manipulated and directed in all this, without your knowledge, by some person or persons with connections of which you are unaware?"

Clem was giving his attention to the well-bred Mr. O'Meara, his eye attracted by the one discordant note in his otherwise irreproachable dress. A gold ring on his middle right finger, almost as thick—it impressed Clem, exaggeratedly—as a brass knuckle, with an intaglio upon it capable of inflicting quite a nasty bruise.

"Is there any possibility, Mr. DeLavery," Rogan reiterated, "that you are acting under Communist influence?"

"Suppose I were for the sake of argument," Clem answered him. Nancy suppressing a groan restrained her hand from springing to her throat in consternation. She knew that tone, that raillery, that readiness for the fray. "Is there anything wrong with what we're doing?" Clem asked Rogan. "Is any law being broken? What's the specific charge?"

"I don't think you understand the seriousness of the plight our country is in," O'Meara spoke up at last. "We're menaced by a deadly foe from without and by subversion from within. I should think, sir, since you are a member of the clergy and your aims and ours have so much in common that, if you have nothing to hide, you would regard it as your loyal and patriotic duty to cooperate with us. Instead of evading . . ."

"Now wait a minute," Clem said, "I don't follow—" And Nancy's heart sank. His mother is right, he has to raise issues, he enjoys it, he glories in it, he likes to plow in. "How does the relationship of policeman and priest enter into this? I don't see the connection. Not at all. Between

the country's external defenses, its internal security and what we're up
to in Colfax County. Just tell me what the specific offense is."

"You think it's far-fetched?" O'Meara demanded with dreadful disbelief.

"Now, now," Rogan the older and more broadly experienced inter-
ceded upon the younger man's zeal. "This may all very well be a purely
local rumpus up to the local authorities to handle. But if there is a link,
however tenuous . . . You say, DeLavery, that you never met Carl
Anderson?"

"Not to my knowledge."

"To the best of your recollection then, Albert Johnson?"

Clem sat up slowly in his chair and stared at the material disgorged
by Rogan from his file. Albert Johnson: the pseudonym of his youthful
folly.

They had everything there in that dossier, accumulated from how
long back? They had the goods on him. The strike paper with the picture of seventeen-year-old Clement Butler DeLavery over the name Albert Johnson. The record of his ten-day incarceration in Fulton Towers.
The dismissal of the Atlanta judge warning him of a capital sentence for
insurrection. A list of his cellmates. One Carl Anderson by his rightful
name. One Timothy Hodges . . .

With every item Rogan read aloud he struck another nail in Clem's
coffin.

"You knew Tim's sister, Gloria?"

"Yes, she was active on the welfare committee of the union." He had
nothing to lose, Clem decided, by admitting the full truth, withholding
nothing. He had committed no wrong.

"Gloria Hodges," Rogan informed him casually, "is now an attorney
in California."

"Gloria a lawyer?"

"A so-called labor lawyer. Married to a Spiggot."

"A what?"

"Some sort of Spic, Mex, Greaser—you know." Rogan watched him
closely for a reaction. "Are you in touch with her?"

"Gloria a lawyer? My Lord, she was just a little old—"

Clem clapped his hands over his eyes. A rag, a bone and a hank of hair.
Crooked smile, crooked teeth. Kidding the pants off him. Ferociously
at war with all the folderol of the intellectual . . .

Rogan passed a news photo over the desk to him. A tailored young
woman in repartee with reporters. Poised . . .

"I'd never in this world recognize her."

"She went to night high school before the war. And to college while she was working in an aircraft plant in L.A. She's associated now with practically every Communist cause in the book."

Clem was less startled by this disclosure than he should have been. That Gloria might be a Communist, a Communist sympathizer, fellow traveler, fronter—this he could well imagine. ("Your Uncle Mark's a murderer, say he's a murderer, say it!" "There are some things, Clem, that you will never understand. Only the working class of people—") That she might be a drudge by now, a drab in the streets, a barfly, yes, yes that too he could imagine in the grief of human waste. But a lawyer! It was beyond his ability to assimilate.

"You mean she argues cases? Oh, brother . . ."

"If you'd care to have Mrs. DeLavery absent herself?"

"What for?" He looked into Nancy's wide scared eyes with a twinkle of reassurance. Don't you see, she glared back at him, you're making them madder by the minute?

"You don't deny that you and Miss Hodges were quite intimate at that time? In fact, you occupied adjoining rooms."

"As incredible as it may seem"—Clem most reluctantly returned the news photo to Mr. Rogan—"what may be adducible from the proximity of our rooms is in whole and in part erroneous. I was as intimate with her brother, you might as easily infer homosexual . . . A lawyer! Oh Lord . . ."

"That union she introduced you in to was Communist-led."

"A number of unions were at that time, I understand. And so were some of the hunger marches and the unemployed councils. Not for the sake of a foreign power but for the need that was there. However, I personally never led a union, a hunger march, or an unemployed council. Or even joined one."

"Why not?"

"Because I couldn't make the leap! I was always torn two ways."

"Aren't you the least bit conscious of the implications of your attitude?" O'Meara prodded him. "When anyone else would register shock, revulsion or at least shame for having been such a simpleton—"

Try as he would Clem could summon up neither shock nor shame, only a strain of nostalgia, a rush of excitement that was with him to this day.

"I wouldn't have missed it for anything," he told Rogan and O'Meara. "Oh, I've pulled my share of boners, some of them stupid, most of them silly. But with more skepticism and independence of mind than anyone would give us credit for now we went searching for some comprehension of our social and historic environment. For some means to solve the paradox of overproduction and underconsumption, of want amidst plenty. The battles of street, factory, coffee klatsch, the war—that, that too—we went into with a dedication of spirit, a willingness to sacrifice, a conviction of man's capacity for greatness that, simple or not, mistaken or not, I can't bring myself to renounce. We gave the best, the best of ourselves."

"You were being used by cynical, wily, and relentless forces for their own opportunistic objectives."

"A dirty trick." Rogan sighed. "A dirty joke. Poor lad." With a spark of affection he placed the seventeen-year-old Clement DeLavery back in the folder. "Well, enough of this battle of clichés . . ."

They moved in on Clem then. They let him have it.

"You knew Stephan Galt?"

"Oh yes! I was very much attached to Steve and his family. Last I heard he was at Los Alamos."

"You knew him at the time he was fired from the university? You signed a petition for him, participated in student demonstrations—"

"Indeed I did! Our entire faculty was under attack. Steve had refused to sign a loyalty oath imposed by Cal Hubbard who was Gov—" He was startled by a jab in the ankle from Nancy. "Steve was never political. I was trying to convert him from atheism and he was trying to convert me—"

"An atheist? I see." Rogan browsed deeper into the folder. "You were friend and roommate of Joseph Turner at seminary?"

"You have the record there."

"You won't deny that Turner was political? We have a list from the League against War and Fascism, the North American Committee to Aid Spanish Democracy, the Scottsboro Boys . . ."

Joe—Joe Turner and his organizations! On the membership or mailing list of every organization from America First to YPSL, and if there had been one beginning with Z he would have been on that too. You'd have to know Joe.

"We have resolutions he circulated, some signed by you. Meetings you attended with him. A party one night at which you sang Red songs . . ."

All of it. All of it. From where? For how long? Who told them?

The splendid songs that night—the splendor of internationality—Bandiera Rossa, Freiheit, Los Cuatros Generales. Madrid, your tears of sorrow. One Christmas holy evening . . . Just like a tree that's standing by the waters . . . And the pretty girl he danced with, she peddling her pamphlets, he peddling his own original theory of church and state. "What are you," she said up at him, her mouth close enough to kiss, "some kinda nut or something?"

"Did Joe Turner take you to the party at 113 West Sutton on the night of—"

"Joe never was a Communist," Clem asserted. Harboring his own years of private resentment against Joe. The anti-fascist who never went to war. The conscientious objector who never went to jail. The champion of Negro rights who ran the church camp at Silver Beach. Who always managed to escape the consequences of his own thinking. As Joe must harbor resentments against him.

"Turner," he said, "is a pacifist."

"Did you say a pacifist?"

Clem bit back his tongue, clenched his jaws. No more. They had it all. Had pried with their fingers through half-forgotten events that were uniquely his possession, his life. Had invaded the chamber of his thoughts. Whether by the efficiency of their operation, omniscient, omnipotent, omnivorous. Or by shrewd guesswork, patching together just such bits and scraps as he had inadvertently dropped concerning others. And how inadvertently? Thinking to protect himself thereby or to knife his erstwhile friends—friends or betrayers?—out of some irresistible instinct, man's infinite capacity for meanness?

In how many files. And cross-files . . .

Rogan looking up from his file, with soft compassion: "It forms a pattern, doesn't it?"

O'Meara with his drubbing blows, close to the body: "It's hard to believe that a man of your intelligence can be as naïve as you claim to be. Unless you're a lot more clever than, as you say, we give you credit for. Do you still maintain that this organization you've formed in Colfax County, bringing together around yourself a number of young veterans in a manner contrary to local custom is entirely your creation, free from any outside influence, direction or affiliation?"

"Free from outside, yes. My own creation, no. Others—" He checked himself.

Rogan rapped out the *Courier's* reproduction of the check he had received from his friend on the Mission Board as a contribution to the project. And with it a signed story on the project published by his friend in the bulletin of the church's League for Social Action.

"This League is well known," O'Meara commented, "to be shot through with left-wingers. I could name you a dozen."

"You're way out in left field," Rogan said. "And how far out it's up to us to determine. I'll give you another opportunity to answer this. Is it possible that from Butlerville on, at the instigation of the Hodges, brother and sister, you were passed along, unbeknownst to yourself, from contact to contact up to the present date?"

They had put him on the bus to Athens. With a chew of tobacco. Go on go on . . .

"Aren't you a victim of the machinations of people you blindly trusted? If you'll come clean with us . . ."

Clem made one more effort to communicate to them with all the sincerity at his command how he came to be as he was. "I grew up in the '20s when national boundaries seemed to be fading into the past, when to be called a citizen of the world was for a man of intelligence the highest praise. I passed my youth in the '30s when to be concerned and to act according to one's conviction was for the man of conscience the highest achievement. I came to maturity in the '40s when our nation was allied with Britain, France, Russia, China, and the partisan forces in every occupied land, and when to fight for any or all of these on whatever front he happened to be was for the soldier the highest patriotism. You'd have to condemn a whole generation . . ."

They made one more effort to communicate to Clem with all the sincerity at their command why they must be as they were. "Our country is threatened on every front by Soviet expansionism. It is our responsibility to track down their espionage agents—and they are here, as you must know from the daily headlines. And to locate and identify those groups and individuals who at the instant war is declared are prepared to go underground, take to the hills, form a fifth column for purposes of propaganda, sabotage, military aggression against the democracy that spawned them . . ."

The effort at communication failed both ways.

They didn't speak the same language. The boy who had jumped the mission wall, who had defied the paternal image, the stern father with his chastening rod. The protestant, the rebel, the petitioner for redress of grievances that were sometimes not even his own . . . And these men to whom obedience was second nature and the norm of nature. For whom it was impossible to understand why he could not accept their statement that a condition was so because they, embodying his government, said it was so.

They had not read the same history books. "This investigation is trespassing upon territory," Clem insisted, "that is specifically forbidden by the First Amendment." "Are you familiar," they said to Clem, "with the Smith Act of 1940?" He quoted Thomas Jefferson. They quoted J. Edgar Hoover.

They could not agree on geography. "In Soviet Russia," O'Meara declared, "you wouldn't last two minutes." "But I'm not there," Clem said, "I'm here."

Or the year they were living in. "What war?" Clem demanded. "After

Hiroshima how can there be another?" "Any hour," they told him, "any time. The advent of war, Mr. DeLavery, does not depend on your consent." "Then America's strongest defense is to remain what it always was. If we discard our liberties in the name of defense . . ." "We are dealing today with a situation in which every branch of our government, executive, judicial, and legislative, every walk of life has been infected with the ideas of these vermin. Our only defense is a good pesticide." To them he represented a breed that under the circumstance of changing times was as dead as the dodo. And to him, they represented . . .

As the discussion waxed more abstract, Nancy shrinking within braced her deepset shoulders, squared her chin. Hiroshima, now he was off on that one again! Antagonizing. Polemicizing. Anything for a polemic! She could have killed him with her bare hands then and there.

Once again, for a third time Clem was offered an opportunity to admit the error of his ways, to denounce his experience as delusive and himself as its dupe, to exorcise the devil of which he was possessed. To repent, to pray forgiveness, to prove himself by adding to their files the name of every questionable character he had ever encountered in every questionable place that he had ever been.

He could leave here a cleared man. Or he could leave here under a cloud. To be hanged until he was dead on the gibbet of his past. And all his associates now and henceforth with him. And everything he touched . . .

Clem declined the opportunity to clear himself.

"Have you ever belonged to an organization that advocates or conspires to advocate the overthrow of the United States Government by force and violence?"

Clem did not reply.

"Are you now or have you ever been a member of the Communist Party USA or a Communist-front organization?"

Clem did not reply.

"Mr. DeLavery, your silence leaves us no choice but to draw our own conclusions. What are you? What side are you on?"

The old student gibe. A metaphysical materialist!

It was Nancy who lost her temper, leaped to her feet and bursting out of her habitual timidity attacked. "How dare you! How dare you impugn my husband, a man who's worked day and night, every breathing moment, for the succor and benefit—"

"Mrs. DeLavery, you are not involved. Unless you support your husband in his views?"

Clem reeled out of the cubicle in a daze. Surrounded by accusing faces. The walls had ears. A microphone behind every gangster mug. A recorder in every drawer. The gorgeous brunette typist with earphones over her curls. There once was a man named Rippers who got all tangled up in his zippers . . .

Stripped and whipped. Assaulted in his person. Ravished.

In the shelter of his car he leaned toward Nancy, her features square-cut, smoldering, and kissed her cheek.

"I don't care what you've done," she cried. "Because I know what you are!"

He sprang back to the wheel and with a clash of gears and squeal of tires swung out too fast into the stream of traffic. He could have strangled her with his bare hands.

"BUT I HAVEN'T DONE ANYTHING!"

To father, uncle, judge, mother, wife. All I did was go out to see what was there and got lost . . . I went down to pick up a woman in the ditch . . .

"Clem, please, you nearly sideswiped . . . Why didn't you answer them? Why didn't you tell them?"

"With what they have, heaven alone knows what from heaven alone knows who? They'd have me up for perjury. I should never have set foot in there. I should never have opened my trap."

"Clem, slow down . . ."

"Because I didn't have to! It's none of their business. I love my country as Cordelia loved her father Lear. No more and no less. I have never done anything against the interest of this country and as a citizen of it I don't have to beat my breast, My country right or wrong!"

"Clem, please . . ."

Out on the highway he calmed down. "Nancy, reach into my pocket and take out my notebook. Read the first line in it."

She reached into his pocket, dipped up with his notebook his plug of tobacco. She passed the tobacco to him. He bit off a chew. She opened the notebook to the first page, to the first grandiose line entered with a flourish in the gift that had been Gloria Hodges' substitute for scraps torn from the margins of newspapers.

I am a child of the age.

"What does it mean?" Nancy asked.

The road ahead slid behind them, trees, telephone lines, lone houses.

"I should never have let her go! I should never have let her go like that. She's right. I sacrificed her and her peace of mind . . ."

It was late. They had been in that office, Nancy reckoned, for over an hour and a half. The parade must be over. The concert program should be beginning, if it began. Unless no one showed up. All the un-lesses . . .

She turned the looseleaf to the last blank page, dated it with jogging pen and wrote.

We are innocents abroad.

The long wail of a police siren pursued them. The arm of the law waved them over to the roadside.

"Where's the funeral?"

. . . The concert was in full progress when they squeezed in through the vestibule and slipped in among the standees in the back of the church. The packed pews were hushed, heads raptly lifted over the indolent sway of palmleaf fans.

Lungi del caro bene . . .

The tone that issued from the rounded lips of Malcolm Gregory flew forth like a dove, a little palpitant dove that he'd conjured up out of his hands. O love. O sorrow. O longing of lovers parted . . .

The bold eyes sweeping the audience came to rest, it seemed to Nancy, on her. Reached down into her palpitant heart and drew it forth. Urged it to wing. O love. O sorrow. When two that love are parted . . .

Beside her Clem slouched against the wall, hands in pockets, head sunk in gloom. "Someone here now," he muttered between his teeth, "is reporting back everything."

Applause. Storming. Tumultuous.

Look, she touched Clem's sleeve. Look, it's all we worked and hoped for. Look, the sun's up there.

Someone found them and led them forward to the reserved front pew where they took their seats next to the usurping Richard-Gene and his brother. "You late," the Jeems brothers chided them.

Du bist wie eine blume . . . The chorus joining in, tender and clear, a spring bubbling.

They closed with the spirituals. Shadrach. I want to be ready. I'm drinking from a fountain that never runs dry.

Sing it!

Sing it!

Sing for Jesus!

Clap your hands! Pat your feet!

The sorrow songs from those young throats, the praying songs spoke with neither prayer nor sorrow. Glory. Jubilee.

"Lift every voice and sing"

The colored rose and the whites perforce with them to one of the loveliest of anthems.

"Till earth and heaven ring . . ."

The chorus pelted down from the dais, an irrepressible stream.

Clem's benediction sounded to Nancy thin, dry, and a little hollow. "Love is stronger than hate. Love is the conqueror of fear . . ."

They spilled out of the back exit of the church into the picnic grounds, the colored out of one side of the doorway, the whites out of the other.

"That was some sweet preaching!"

"That was some sweet singing!"

The colored flowed off to their portion of the grove and the whites to theirs, the dividing line marked by the barbecue pit in the clearing far back, where several men were roasting on spits chicken, fresh ham, side meat, ribs.

Nancy descending the steps was overtaken by Mrs. Dakin. They waited on the white side of the divide for their husbands who had been detained in conversation with Father Hall at the altar. "And to think"—Mrs. Dakin clutched Nancy's arm—"that the first real cultural thing we've had around here has been gotten together by these poor darkies."

As soon as Clem appeared, Mrs. Dakin was up the steps catching at him. "You know I've always felt guilty about what my folks has done to the Nigra?" she confided to him. "As my father used to say—he'd say it when we were off by ourselves and nobody'd hear him—we've all done some bad things here in Colfax County and someday our chicks are coming home to roost."

They waited together at the foot of the steps for the mayor. "But you know," Mrs. Dakin amended herself out of some oblique train of thought, "they never had any kind of civilization? Even back in Africa where they all were indigenous."

It was the sort of monologue that Clem was always bringing home to be set forth at table, tangily, for family delectation. And to be debated with his mother as evidence—of what?

But Clem did not savor Mrs. Dakin now. She was leaving in a moment with the mayor for the other barbecue where they must also put in an appearance, giving tactfully equal time to both and committing themselves to neither.

Mayor Dakin tripped down the steps toward them, still engaged in conversation with Father Hall, his hand on Father's shoulder. At the foot they parted.

"You're not eating here, are you?" the mayor asked Clem and Nancy. "Benson's left for home, be back here later."

"Just a minute," Nancy murmured, "excuse me," and detaching herself from the group darted in the wake of Father Hall across the divide.

"No, no, I don't need you," she waved Clem back to the Dakins, "I want to congratulate Mr. Gregory on his singing."

When she turned around Father Hall had been hauled off into another conversation and too shy to interfere she went on by herself to the colored picnic tables. Fighting shyness every step of the way, feeling on her back all the astonished faces behind her, seeing before her all the equally astonished faces here. "Can I help you, ma'am?" "You looking for somebody, ma'am?"

"Mr. Gregory."

She was shown to the table where Malcolm Gregory sat with a coterie of admirers, joshing over the joints of chicken they were being served on paper plates. "Go on, go on pick it up," he urged the giggling girls. "You can't suck bones with a fork." And helping himself to a ladle of vegetables. "I don't like onions. If you stood them up and danced them on the table I wouldn't like onions. Yes?" He twisted about toward Nancy who stood behind him flexing her fingers. Setting down his paper napkin, he rose.

"Oh don't, don't stand," she pleaded. "Please don't interrupt your meal. I just wanted to tell you how much I enjoyed your singing. The Handel and the Secchi, the Schumann, I've seldom heard such musicianship. And the spirituals, especially the spirituals—"

"I sing the songs of my people," Malcolm Gregory said coolly, "but not to cater or kowtow."

She flushed, her hands interlacing before her as in prayer. She had come here the intruder, and he was condescending, or thought she was condescending. "What I mean, I felt as if you were singing straight at me."

"You did?" He was a flirt again, the old black magic dancing out at her. "I suppose there is a certain sympathetic response that sets certain persons off in an audience. If I could make everyone feel like that—"

Still she hovered, unable to take the chair someone proffered her and unable to tear herself away. "You see, my husband's done so much—and everyone's so afraid—there's so much misunderstanding, even in one's own family—"

"And there doesn't have to be?"

"That's what I meant. Thank you."

She fled back to Clem. People were clapping his shoulder, shaking his hand, urging him to sit down and eat.

"Maybe if I quit teaching," he said to Nancy as he walked with her, "then this whole thing will blow over. No one will bother—"

She kept stepping back with him out of the way, "Beg pardon—oh hello . . . Quit? Leave all these folks high and dry?"

"Nancy, there's going to be a hassle. And I know how you hate a hassle. I can't put you through the wringer—"

"Oh that?" She looked up into his granite face. "You still worried about that?" She linked her arm through his. "Where'll we sit?"

The divide she had just crossed was no more. Men drifting as if by gravitational attraction toward the barbecue pit, kids scurrying with soda pop, shrimp fishermen who spent all week cooped up in the same boat visiting back and forth at each other's tables, Portuguese who were as the saying went "white by day and colored by night" further confusing the scene.

Nancy sauntered with Clem toward the McDowell table. "May we eat with you?" Lulabelle in a fluster sent Rad off for more plates. "Aren't you proud," Nancy said to her, "aren't you proud of your husband? That he had a hand in starting all this?"

Before the end of the meal Clem was himself again, in movement. Listening to half a hundred queries, checking and dispatching, setting in motion the final details of the afternoon's activities.

6

The parade in the morning and the scent of competition in the air had brought out a good part of the local white population at the city park, three-quarters of a mile cross-country from Zion and two miles around by the road. It was a festive crowd as well, happily consuming hot dogs and hush puppies, pepper-sauced bar-b-q on a bun and shrimp crusted with cornmeal batter and fried to a curl, coleslaw out of paper cups and blackeye peas; washing it all down with Doc Pepper and beer from the barrel. Families sprawled under sycamore trees humming along with the band that played in the octagonal green bandstand and calling after tots who had wandered off to the music and lost themselves in the musky mystery of the shrub-enclosed latticework foundation of the stand. Over all hung an amusement-park suffusion of spun sugar, popcorn, re-used shortening, sweet, sharp, and rank.

The crowd attending the Veterans Benefit had gone to it over a suppressed twitch of apprehension. The crowd came here to the political rally nurturing a spark of anticipation. While the one held in check its vague fear of "some kind of trouble," the other was on the lookout, equally vague, for some kind of excitement.

The general spirit in the park was somewhat dampened at the outset by the news of Ol' Cal's illness, a well-kept secret up to now. Not so much because it deprived them of the leading candidate's presence as because it robbed them, those for him and those against him and those uncommitted alike, of the show. Ol' Cal always put on a good show. Their disappointment was only slightly appeased by the arrival of Representative Dan Garner and his wife. Garner was running unopposed for his own seat. No fun in that. Their craving for entertainment was only to a degree assuaged by the appearance of Judge Purcell on a buckboard wagon, coatless, displaying a decent pair of black galluses, hardly a substitute for Ol' Cal's celebrated crimson. It was the first time Judge Purcell had imported his woolhat-style campaign from back country to the county seat; but otherwise his attempt to capture party domination from Benson Reece was an old story, repeated every few years for the last two decades. The only really novel element here today, promising a modicum of drama, evoking a tickle of titillation, a twinkle of speculation, was incorporated in the person of Henry Warren.

No one doubted that having declared himself for County Commission, Henry was in. His aim in running for office, however, the coup for which he was given credit of swinging Dan Garner into Ol' Cal's camp, his open support now for Purcell endowing him with respectability, were all ascribed by popular opinion to his effort to "get those two fellas down the River Road outa his back-hair." Every time he caught hold of them, they ducked out from under. Every time he had them beat, they beat him out. Right up to this nigger fish fry of theirs over the way. In which they had mobilized Benson Reece, the ministers and the merchants, the Legion posts and a chunk of Purcell's woolhat support. Now that it had not been stopped as might have been expected, nor had it flopped according to the gleeful reports of emissaries traveling back and forth, what was Henry going to do about it? He wasn't just going to let it pass by, was he?

Picnickers who rushed up to Henry to pump his hand, who jumped up and waved at him every time he sallied by with the Judge and the Congressman, retired to their blankets in the grass tucking grins under their chins. Waiting in passive recumbency to learn what he was up to. Nothing like a fine old-fashioned feud to add spice to sport.

"When you look at a man," the Judge instructed Henry as they circulated through the park, "you tally his kin." Henry who had been circulating through the county during the past few weeks under the Judge's tutelage was amazed as always by the number of people the Judge knew by name and how much he knew about them. He was just as amazed at the number he knew himself and knew very well within a few minutes by falling in with the Judge's palaver. "Yo' boy's in the service? Where's he at? Why shoot, I can get the Red Cross to see to it." "Jackson, don't I

SEE WHAT TOMORROW BRING

know you from somewhere? Shucks I was born on Liveright Road right around the bend." "Yeah, I remember your dad. He's a good old boy. You met Congressman Garner yet? Dan, I want you to come over here and meet an old friend of mine. His daddy's having some trouble with his pension money."

Between encounters the Judge resumed his instruction. "Individuals are interested in only one thing, how much you can do for them in the way of favors. But a crowd, you always have to move a crowd. You always have to win them beyond the point where it's no skin off their backs which set of crooks get in. That's how they look at it, don't they, Dan? Which set of crooks gets in. Not principles, not issues, not all the hard work you do. You have to rouse 'em out of their natural inertia. Look at 'em now. Eating our eats, drinking our drinks, all for us. And half of 'em won't even bother to haul hiney to the polls next Tuesday primary. If we want to win the county, Henry, we got to win this town today. I've tried all I can. Now it's up to you."

As important to them as personal victory was the ability to deliver the vote to Hubbard's column, the White Supremacy ticket. Dan Garner's senatorship, Purcell's fond dreams of the Federal bench, Henry's political future depended on it. It was only for this reason that Dan had consented to come today, here to the least and most unlikely section of his district, one commonly conceded to be in Reece's—and Middleton Morgan's—pocket.

"How does it look?" Garner asked the Judge.

"We-ell I teh y'—" The Judge, whose frostiness had thawed to folksiness in the heat of his summer's campaign, cast a canny eye upon the crowd, of a composition unusual for him. He had gained a reputation in the past for being able to tell within a fraction of a percentage just how much his slate would lose by. But now in addition to the stalwarts Will Royall had carted in from Fallona and the standbys from the rural precincts, he counted the ladies. A garland of them arranged in lawn chairs about the periphery of the umbrella-table, thoughtfully provided by Eula, where Julie with the able assistance of May Garner held court. In black, the tragedy of her recent loss upon her, Julie—darling wonderful Julie, perfectly marvelous how she's bearing up—exercised more of an attraction than ever upon her followers. If she came out of seclusion today, there must be a mighty powerful reason for it. Swayed by this thought, the ladies had turned out in numbers "to be with her," gathering about her with a sustenance that would be substantiated, the Judge hoped, in the ballot box.

He also counted the Finchleys, Hill Caslon, the younger businessmen drawn by Henry and the interests he represented. The Eustis Telfers who would never before have associated themselves socially, let alone politically, with anyone under Ol' Cal's banner, but who were now distinctly dissatisfied with "the way things are going round here." And the housewives . . .

"Hard to say for sure," the Judge said cautiously to Garner, and began to tally if off on his fingers.

"We got seven precincts to Benson's five, but he's got the population. And twenty-two percent of the vote right off the bat against us. What I mean, let's call a spade a spade, every nigger that can vote will. We can take sixty percent of the white vote, a landslide anywhere else, and still lose the election. That's just it! If we could get hold here just once, get the polls under our boys . . . As 'tis, we need seventy-one percent vote for us."

An impossible figure. Beyond the wildest reach of the imagination.

"But with the admixture," the Judge ventured cautiously, "that we have here today . . ."

"It's building," Henry said confidently. "All the agitation in the state this summer, the broadsides around the county, everything we could and couldn't put through, it's all cumulative. And that scare over the prisoner who escaped turn of the month, don't underestimate it, it had its effect. Now if we can bring this to a head today, slambang, zowie," he smacked his fist, "raise this mob off their butt-ends . . ."

The Judge and the Congressman, both shorter than Henry by a head, exchanged glances. Garner inserted a thick finger under his stiff collar, cleared his throat, hesitated. Purcell adjusted the bows of his glasses more comfortably over his ears: he was wearing a bone-conductor now as a hearing-aid concealed in the heavy tortoiseshell frame, and he liked it very much though he missed the pinch of austerity conferred on him by his pince-nez.

"We hate to bother you, Henry, at a time like this," Garner said in suitably sepulchral tone, "but would you consider—"

"Do you think, Henry," the Judge blurted it out all at once, "that you could speak today? You know, at the end? Dan would precede you."

They were making him the patsy, Henry perceived, passing the onus of the outcome on to him. If they took Colfax County they would all share in the honors. But if they lost, the failure would be his, blamed on his windup speech. And most sympathetically too. Poor soul, he wasn't up to it.

But he was not averse to their urging either. It had been agreed beforehand in view of the burial of his son only five days ago that he was not to be asked to speak. Yet it suited his plans, his plans required it. To step into Ol' Cal's place.

Only Julie. Henry looked toward her at the table, introducing some housewife to May Garner, the consummate hostess. If he could have counted on Julie's predictable reactions, scorn, anathema, excoriation, he would have agreed now to speak and hoped to batter her down on it later. But with Julie this last week, he was always lunging his shoulder through a door that wasn't there, falling through space . . .

"They'll vote," Garner said sententiously, "for the side they think will win. Not in Washington, Henry. Not in Atlanta. But here. In this neck of the woods."

"Well—" Henry demurred, stalling. "Hey there . . . Say . . ." A ring of men observing them in conference was closing in around. "I know it's selfish to allow something that affects me so personally to jeopardize—"

"Now Henry, if you don't feel you can . . . It's just we think you could deliver the Sunday punch."

"Well, it don't seem right," Henry yielded them the point, "that the common cause should suffer. I'll have to consult my wife first. I have to respect her feelings."

"Certainly, certainly. Of course. Go ahead."

"Splendid woman. Truly splendid. Holding up remarkably. A real guiding star."

"Yes," Henry said, looking toward Julie at the table. "She is that." My guide star. My nemesis.

The trio so intriguing to the crowd—Purcell obligingly snapping a gallus now and then; Garner in planter's hat, starched whites and string tie; Henry in the sober charcoal appropriate both to his mourning and his managerial position—broke up. The Judge beckoned to Will Royall who, all one sandy tan, with a lope to his gait as if already packing the sheriff's pistol on his back-hip crossed a tongue of lawn to him, saluting from his poplin hat as he went the picnickers right and left. Will took his stance by the Judge, raking the scene before him with his eyes, addressing it from under his breath, giving the Judge the benefit of his replies without once turning his head to him.

"Henry's on," the Judge informed him. "You still got the placards we ordered for him?"

"Yuh yuh yuh."

"And the helicopter's all set?"

"Yuh yuh yuh."

"You got to keep this moving, Will, right up to the speaking. You got to keep heating it up. Don't let a minute drag tail."

"Yuh yuh." He made a ring of thumb and forefinger. In the bag.

"Warren's delivering the main address." "Garner's introducing *him*."

"Give 'em hell, Henry!" It was all over the crowd before Henry ever reached Julie.

Henry pursued a roundabout route to Julie, seeking Charles. He never spoke to Julie now if he could help it without Charles between them, never sat down at table with her without Charles there as buffer. The moment he was alone with her panic overtook him; everything flew apart like a swarm of birds uncaged.

"You seen my boy?" he inquired as he went down the paths of the park. "He's around here somewhere." And was sidetracked. By Ike Lucas who had lost his liquor license and wanted it back in his wife's name and no two fees either. By Bix Lyon, the Ford dealer, who wanted his niece on the county payroll in a position to extend his influence. By Hill Caslon and a bunch of shrimpers wanting to talk riparian improvements.

You walk like a king holding forth promises.

And nod like a king with the sword dangling from above by a thread.

Here and there through the crowd he spotted certain rough-and-tumble characters. Leroy Jeems, the Marine commando or so he claimed, a bully and a braggart. Russ Dobie who rustled stray cattle on the side under cover of running his trucking business. They had come back from Zion not with reports of riot and mayhem, but chawing a bone. "They got a real sure enough barbecue pit back there. Sheet-metal lined. Fire's been going two days." Like Chalmer Coombs, like Betty Brookfield and her ex, they went, disappeared, were sucked in. Met up with kin, socialized around and returned without shame or chagrin. To send others over for more of the same. "Just two bits a chop."

Throwing the gauntlet to him. "Give 'em hell, Henry!"

A woman on the grass held up toward him a tomato that could only have been grown by Willie Bean, a colored farmer who annually won first prize with his beefsteaks at the Bay City Fair. Now Willie must be exhibiting them at that goddam fish fry.

"Big as your head," the woman winked up at him provocatively over her crimson orb. "They sure are going strong over yonder."

"Let 'em," Henry said, "and God bless 'em. If that was all there was to it!"

"Why what do you mean, Mr. Henry?"

"Stick around. You'll find out."

"What you go'n do, Henry? You got somethin' in mind, Henry? Give 'em hell . . ."

Henry shook away from them. Suck-asses! Waiting on him . . . They'd find out. They'd go there do it themselves. Tear the tables up out of the ground and beat them into pikestaffs. Pull down the produce booths, turn the tomatoes into missiles. Send them squashing.

They'd do it themselves! With their own hands . . .

"Charles? Say Charles? Anybody seen Charles?"

He circumvented blankets, blundered behind bushes upon teen-agers making love and children making water. He was always looking for Charles. To speak to him, take him into conversation, show him off, have him close. To touch him. To know he was there. All this past week, every night since Colfax died he would tiptoe at least once into Charles' room just as Julie used to tiptoe to Coley first month after he was born, I can't hear him breathe! From the foot of Charles' bed he would listen—a boy sleeps so deep, not a sound out of him—and would reach for the long low mound under the coverlet, not a stir out of him. Suppose he falls sick back here and we don't hear him. Suppose something happens: a pain in his side, polio, a car in the road, drowning. *Suppose he's taken too.* To have to live all your life with that suppose . . .

Henry caught the ball thrown at him on the fly.

Charles was stretched out on the ground with Junior Telfer not far from the bandstand, the portable radio between them tuned up to the ball game, gloves, balls, and bats strewn about. Henry pitched the ball back and it smacked into Charles' hand, idly upraised. "Say Junior," Henry said and caught straight-armed a fast one from Charles, "who you think is going to win? The Graybars or the Bearcats?"

"Colored folks is," Junior averred somnolently, listening to the ball game. "They going to have to do something to get on. Why you know all these houses that are burning down, they all colored folks's."

"Why you say that? Who's burning 'em?"

"They got no fireplugs," Charles answered for Junior.

The hard stinging smack of the ball in his palm. Even the kids. Even the kids . . .

"If they're burning down," Henry said and tried a slow curve, "it must be themselves that's bringing it on. Come on, Charles."

"Where?"

When I say come on, you come! Only you couldn't talk to Charles like that. He was beginning to understand some of Rad's difficulties with the boy. But where Rad muffed, he wouldn't.

"Come on over with me to Julie. We're having a family powwow."

Charles turned back to the radio and turned up the volume.

"Charles!" He tempered his tone. "It's something very important. I want you in on it."

The spine stiffened under the white shirt. The ginger head burrowed down into the elbow. Junior Telfer, clumsy with embarrassment, twiddled at the dial and switched the wrong way, up to a blast.

"Charles!"

"I'm not going."

"Why not?"

No answer.

"Charles, you coming?"

"No!"

When you answer me, you say yessir! Only you couldn't tell Charles. Couldn't order him. Couldn't force him. And he couldn't have it out with him, not in the sight of all these people. And he couldn't back down, not before Junior Telfer.

"Why not? Tell me why not?"

No answer.

Henry bent and yanked him up by the arm. For a moment the clear hazel eyes met his, fierce with fear, glowering with tears.

"Have I said or done anything? Has—" Henry swallowed. "Has Julie?"

Charles was amenable neither to pleas nor reason. He was not going to go with him to Julie. He just wouldn't, with no explanation, no words to define it. Henry had to resort with a glance at radio, ball, bat, to the one last appeal. "Do it for me. This one time. All the things I do for you, do this for me?"

With his arm around the boy's shoulder he walked down the winding path that led to the table. "I know you don't like all these ladies and all making over you . . . Say hello, son, to the gentleman? Yeah, this m' boy . . ."

After a while Charles sidled over closer to him. "I can go home to my folks now, can't I? You and Miss Julie, you don't need me no more?"

Oh for God's sake! Not that. Not now.

"Charles, listen to me—"

"Ain't they never go'n come for me? Don't they want me no more?"

"Listen to me good—" He fondled the boy's back, finding the pointy shoulder blades. Angel wings. "I'm getting to be a pretty big man around here. I may be a pretty big man in this state someday. And you the only thing Julie and I got left. We need you, we need you now more'n we ever did. You understand?"

Scuffling. Mumbling.

"What's that?"

"Reckon."

"With us behind you there's no limit to where you can go, what you can be. You realize that?"

"Reckon."

He nudged Charles before him through the ladies wreathed about the table. They were interrupted in their path by a woman who rushed up to Julie, seized her hand and wrung it.

"Mrs. Warren, I heard about your loss. I know what you goin' through."

"So good of you." Julie placed her hand on the homely freckled arm. "How kind. We did everything we could . . . But God wanted him. God must have wanted him. He's with God now."

They waited while Julie asked after the woman's name and family, introduced her to May Garner, provided her with a cold drink. "One of the compensating things about a thing like this, if anything can compensate, you find out how kind people are. How much they care. I want to thank you. Thank you from my heart."

She was simple, genuine, touching to tears in a performance Henry had already witnessed dozens of times, perhaps no less sincere for the repetition. Even when, a moment after, she turned to May Garner with a smooth swift readjustment of self, relaxing against the webbed back of the chair, legs sleekly crossed. "Why do they come? They must get something out of it."

"Now Julie, you mustn't—" May Garner for all her white hair and worldliness couldn't quite cope with this refusal to accept the balm of convention.

"Not that I blame them at all. It's a sort of play, a vicarious experience, an opportunity to expend emotion at someone else's expense. Yes, Henry?"

She was luminous with the shimmer of sorrow on her, the sparkle in her eyes of one who has seen and endured too much. At the same time she was brilliant with the assurance of a woman who knows she is loved, who has discovered her powers and the skill to use them, who has left behind the cramping confines of her immediate surroundings and stepped into the limitless expanse of the great world. They spot it on her, Henry thought, they sniff it out—the money, the prestige and the glamour, the connections—and they're on her, hanging to her skirts, breathing with her breath, dipping their fingers, catching a sip.

With her hat off, fanning it before her, her throat rising superbly out of her clean-cut black dress, she lifted her head upward toward him, shining smooth, not a hair escaping, not a wisp, not a curl, from the deftly wound chignon in back. Over her chair Cousin Tibby hovered, already chaperone and companion, whispering to intimates as if to set them at ease, "It was a blessing . . ."

"Could I see you for just a minute?" Henry asked of his wife. Drawing

Charles along he adjourned with Julie to the privacy of a nearby tree. "They want me to speak—you know, as the finale?"

He waited, bracing himself for her barrage of objections. Waiting as he had been waiting for days, he knew now what he was waiting for. The shriek. The maternal shriek that had not erupted either in the dingy tourist room outside Savannah or at the graveside.

"Oh." Her mouth puckered. "So they stuck you with that hot potato. Well, I'm sure, dear, you'll handle it very well. Just play hard to get."

"What was that all about?" Junior Telfer asked Charles when he dropped back down beside him.

"I don't know. He's making the main speech."

"Well what'd he want you for?"

"Beats me." Charles plucked moodily at a patch of browned grass. "How's the game? Hey!" The bat cracked like a shot over the air. All the shadows fell away, all the broodings and perplexities with the roaring upsurge of that distant crowd to the soaring ball.

An airplane flew over the park leaving a trail of white smoke. *WIN WITH WARREN.* "Say, that's your old man." Junior jabbed Charles in the ribs and they both jumped up, heads craning back.

On the trail of the plane a helicopter circled overhead, the whole crowd standing, straining expectantly. The band struck up *Dixie.* The helicopter buzzed over the treetops releasing a flock of balloons, flame-yellow and maroon. *SAVE OUR STATE.* In the stampede for the balloons a child was nearly trampled, a woman fainted and had to be given first aid, fenders were scratched and crumpled in a traffic snarl on the road outside the park. But the balloons bubbled everywhere on a rising tide of excitement. Junior and Charles shinnied up trees and crawled precariously out on branches to free those ensnared in the leaves.

Paper caps, armbands, and buttons blossomed. *VOTE WHITE VOTE RIGHT.* And penny crackerjack boxes were distributed. *CRACKERS FOR OL' CAL.* The band played *Ta-ra-ra-bom-der-e.*

Capped, banded, and buttoned, stuffing themselves with crackerjacks, the two boys romped along with the crowd to the softball field. Here they played darts, pitching at a grinning-mouthed Sambo. Knock 'em dead, boys! Right between the teeth!

Then the field was cleared for Will Royall. For an exhibition of trick shooting that put an itch in the trigger-finger of every person present who had ever handled a gun, male and female, old and young. Will shot from the hip, he shot backward from between his legs, he shot from a position flat on his back on the ground. He shot blindfold, knocking a can off a stump. He sighted two revolvers at once and split the bullets on the cutting-blade of an ax.

"Who will hold this hat for me?"

Will wheeled about with a Texas sombrero pitched atop the barrel of his shotgun.

"Anybody here will hold this hat?"

Henry stepped forward and held the hat aloft. Will aimed, working up a maximum of suspense, an anguish of gasps and whistles. His shot pierced the crown.

"Now, who's gonna wear this hat for me?"

Henry clapped the hat down on his own head.

"Wow!" Junior clutched at Charles. "Wow!"

"Wow!" Charles' breath expired with a silent scream from his open mouth.

The peak of the hat was perforated.

"Will, you're slippin'," Henry said, removing the sombrero and examining it. "That one singed my hair."

The inflammatory handbills broke out like a fire set by arson, all over the place. The boys in the thick of it passed them around, Charles inventing his own slogans. "You voting for my pal?" he asked as he handed out handbills. "Vote for Ol' Cal! You for me? Elect Henry!"

The loudspeaker summoned the crowd from the ball field and from all parts of the park to the bunting-draped platform that had been erected not far from the bandstand. "The speaking! The speaking's about to begin!"

Ladies and guests filled the few rows of benches that faced the platform. All the others either brought over their own folding chairs or sat under the trees blanketing the ground all the way back to the road. Charles and Junior scrambled themselves a front position at the feet of the ladies in the first row. The band played *For He's a Jolly Good Fellow*. Half-listening to the speeches on the platform above him, Charles half-read through the assortment of handbills still gathered in his hand, half-understanding.

The Judge, a gallus-puller and knee-springer, whooped it up for the White Man, denounced the Wall Street interests and their stooges in Atlanta, the bankers and the lawyers, the blue blood and the blue chips, extolled the rule of the rural counties and paid tribute of course to the White Lady. Annamary, his niece, was openly perishing with laughter over his oratorical antics. "Still dishing out the old magnolia tea," Julie, the obvious object of his encomiums, commented to May Garner. Eula, unperturbed, started the applause at all the appropriate pauses. "Are *We* going to give a *ONE HUNDRED PERCENT*

WHITE MAN'S VOTE in this county against that muddlin' moderate Middlin' Morgan"—"Boo boo-oo!" —"and all his middlin' muddlin' meddlin' backers *ALL THE WAY DOWN THE LINE?*" By their cheers he had it. Even though Lars Finchley after an argument with his wife who insisted on staying through to the end left the park and went back to his office for a bout with the bottle in his bottom file drawer.

The Congressman, a lapel-clutcher and arm-waver, went to work on the Communist menace which he had observed firsthand on his recent European tour. A conspiracy that had spread so far and wide that its international network might reach into one's hometown, one's neighborhood, one's church, one's family. Over an enthralled hush—this was beginning to hit pretty close—he listed the earmarks by which such traitors and their liberal flunkeys might be identified. Particularly those who concealed themselves behind the Nigra, exploiting his credulity in order to advance their own cause. To his grief and horror he had learned upon his arrival here today that a movement of highly suspect origin was in operation in this county and that its chief target and victim, whom they all knew, whom he was honored to call to this platform, would, he believed, if sufficiently urged, despite his understandable reluctance at this time, report to them his personal experience.

The accolade that greeted Henry could not have gone off better. A flock of placards reared up in back and were seized by youths in the sidelines who snake-danced down to the platform with them. *WE WANT WARREN.* Everywhere the chant went up to the stomping of feet. *WE WANT WARREN.* The drums in the bandstand rattled up a storm. *SPEECH! SPEECH! SPEECH!*

For several long minutes in the vicinity of the platform Henry continued an earnest colloquy with Mayor Dakin. In the spirit of non-partisanship Dakin had acted as official welcomer here just as he had earlier at Zion. He had dismounted from the platform afterward, and was complacently enjoying the success of a Founders Day that featured two such well-attended events when during Garner's speech Henry buttonholed him. "How's it going over there? Hear it's a regular coon convention. All their candidates on hand?" "Why, it's nothing political," the mayor protested. "Of course Benson's judging some of the contests this afternoon, but other than that, wouldn't nobody go electioneering. Lots of white folks there too." That should have shut off Henry's baiting, but it didn't. "If I was in authority, I wouldn't allow no mob like that together. Soon or late somebody's bound to brush up against somebody and you gonna have such a riot." "Not at all," the mayor said serenely. "Nothing like that. Why, when I left there this noon they were all mingling, just as friendly." "Mingling? Did you say *mingling?*"

"*WE WANT WARREN!*"

"Give 'em hell, Henry!"

"Say Dakin," someone shouted, "you comin' out for Warren?"

Henry was lifted to the platform on the arms of his cohorts and Dakin with him. Garner received them both with open arms. Above them swayed the campaign portraits of Ol' Cal. Pennants fluttered like licks of flame from the wire on which they were hung. Drums boom-boomed with the rhythmic intonation of a camp meeting, in one of those revivals when people wrought up to a pitch of frenzy roll on the floor squawking like chickens and barking like dogs.

Garner conducted Henry to the microphone at the center of the platform. Henry held his arms up for silence and when he had finally achieved it bowed past the microphone and spoke over the edge of the platform with an intimate urgency audible enough to be reiterated all the way back to the last outfringes under the trees.

"Julie? Charles? Will y'all come up here with me?"

Julie deep in conversation with May Garner over some absolutely exquisite pure silk yardage May had brought back from Lyons and intended to have made up into draperies either did not hear Henry at first or didn't understand. She was hoisted to her feet and helped by Eula to the platform as if she were crippled. Charles took an inconspicuous seat at the end of the platform. His face usually so lively was smooth as an eggshell, vacant to the point of stupor. Squatting on the ground beside him with the portable radio, Junior Telfer softly played hillbilly music under his ear.

As Henry began speaking, the picture began traveling around the audience. An enlarged photo—there were perhaps six copies, no more, just enough to whet curiosity. And stimulate a quickly communicable thrill of shock.

People always said afterward that Judge Purcell spoke from habit, Dan Garner spoke from the head but Henry Warren spoke from his heart. They all remembered afterward how deep Henry spoke from his heart.

Taking his cue from the shrewdness of the Judge's hodgepodge—not anti-black but pro-white, not pro-Cal but anti-Morgan—and from Garner's dignity of delivery, Henry launched forth with a quietness that disappointed the appetite for brimstone but allayed a temper equally strong here, that of skepticism and detachment. He praised the beautiful recreation park in which they were come together today—actually a product of the WPA—as his own favorite type of project. Referred to

schools, white and colored, born of the dreams, devotion and energy
his wife had poured into them. Promised to institute as soon as he was
elected to office a program of riparian improvements which would even
include docking facilities on the river for colored folks and a swim hole
for their kids.

"But of all this, no matter. I'm here today not as a candidate but as
a witness. For God knows I couldn't come here today for any other
reason. I prayed this morning, I prayed on my knees: What shall I do?
And the answer came to me as it did to the prophets of old. Go! Go
and tell the people. Go and warn them that what has happened to you
can happen to any one of them. You've heard of enemies overseas.
You've heard of treason infiltrating our nation's capital. You've even
heard that it may be right here, here in this state, in this county,
threatening you, me, and all of us."

He repeated familiar charges with a new twist. That the dynamite
blast directed at him, at the progress he had brought into the county,
at Sunset, had claimed its first martyr in his son. The high explosives
were being stockpiled to this day at those two farms on the Sunset land.
That the two veterans' classes at the schools were not classes in farm
training but in Marxist ideology.

He named names. "You all know I tried to get justice for my boy.
The murder of my boy because that's what it ultimately was. You all
know I didn't get it. You know what I got instead. I went to Chalmer
Coombs—he turned me out of his office. I went to Benson Reece—he
was too blind to see it. I turned to my pastor, Clement DeLavery—a
man more interested in following the dictates of Stalin than in the care
of the souls under his guidance . . ."

He took them into his confidence. "And why? What'd it all start
from? A colored boy whose family my wife thought the world on. Ain't
no one has done more for colored folks than Julie here. That's why he
had to get at her first. As a dry-run for what's coming next. War on the
white folks! A Red-inspired race war! You all know it. Each one in your
own heart, you know it. To take away from you what's yours. You
know that.

"But that nigger-boy by himself would never have been able to do
anything. Worse than the nigger who turns against his benefactor is the
white man who backs him up in it. My own kin, a man I've loved and
treated all my life as a brother. When his boy, his son here, saw what
he was up to and said to his face what he was, he whipped him. You
should have seen the condition he was in when he came to me. This boy
here. Charles, stand up."

Charles pulled himself waveringly half-up from his chair and dropped back.

"This boy has displayed more courage than all of us put together. I swear to you all here and now, I take a pledge before the Lord God Almighty, so long as there is a God and a law, that I'm raising this boy for my own son. I won't turn him back. Because a man who'd rather pick up for niggers than look after his family ain't fit to be a father, ain't fit to be loose among decent people, ain't got no right . . ."

Most of what Henry said now was being filtered through a miasma of indignation and disgust. The picture moving as if by suction from hand to hand showed a cracker-gal, Lulabelle McDowell, seated with her back to a table, head coquettishly cocked, eyes blissfully downcast, a bemused smile upon her lips. Over her stood a big black buck nigger, Reeve Scott, smiling down on her with the same expression of bemusement; his arm behind her shoulder with hand ostensibly resting on the table, about—it couldn't be plainer—to hug her round and play. A woman like that . . . A woman that would do like that is lower than a whore. She's beneath a dog's notice.

The picture eventually fell into Junior Telfer's inquisitive fingers. He naturally took it back with him to the portable he was guarding and passed it up to Charles.

"They've taken this whole town in," Henry intoned into the microphone. "They've taken half the county. They say it's a plan to buy a tractor. I say it's a plan to mix the races! And if you don't believe me, ask Mayor Dakin—stand up, Mayor—what he saw there at that church today with his own eyes. They say it's a benefit they're holding. I say it's a disgraceful shame and a scandal and debauchery of all we hold sacred!"

He lifted them out of the ordinary. He invested their inchoate day-to-day existence with the shape and sweep of history. He played upon their deepest fears: the Red and the Black, Race Mixture and Race War being correlative. Unless they acted the day of reckoning was upon them. When the pleasant intimacy of their own society would be rent asunder. When the cherished sense of tribal privilege would be wrested from them. When the tables would be turned, the master become servant in his own house and the servant become master, the fair-cheeked daughter become bearer of the dark seed and the fair-haired son become the shunted-aside, the jostled-back. The rule of the ignorant, the irresponsible, the violent: Who would not fight to the death to prevent that?

"The day has come, the hour has struck when this evil must be rooted from out our bosom!"

Amidst the plaudits accorded him for his declamation—"I never knew you had it in you!"—and the congratulations for his humanitarian-ism—"Wonderful what you're doing for that boy, simply wonderful!" —Henry did not miss Charles at first. Families were drifting off home-ward. Small groups that had gathered—"Something ought to be done!" —were shifting about at a loss. Waiting for the next move . . . from the other fellow. Even Will Royall with his shooting-irons.

Before Henry's eyes the impact of all his efforts was losing cohesion, momentum. Someone had to kick them in the pants. Lead them by the nose.

"Come on." Henry rounded up the Judge, the Mayor, and the Congressman. "Let's go see what's cooking over there, huh? Just give it a look-see and blow. For our own information. Where's Charles?"

Junior said, pointing with the portable down the path to the exit, that Charles had taken off thataway. Ada Hemmings who swooped down on them pushing her divorced daughter's fifteen-month-old daughter in a gocart confirmed Junior, pointing with her parasol. Yes she had seen him skin out of the park and hit the road. Hastily Henry packed Julie and the Garners into his car. Carrying herself like an avenging angel, Ada plumped down among them with squirming toddler, bottle bag, diaper bag, collapsible gocart, and parasol. "Why I wouldn't miss this for a farm!"

Judge Purcell's Lincoln followed them from the park. A stream of cars fell in behind the Judge, the remainder of the crowd galvanized at last into action. Now and then at the side roads a car turned off, conveying families away from the direction of possible trouble. Other cars attracted by the general excitement joined in.

"Maybe you better let us off," Dan Garner suggested nervously to Henry. "May and I are dog-tired. I have this dinner tonight in Bay City and two more speeches."

"We won't go in," Henry assured him. "Just stop as we pass by. You'll have something to talk about. Judge wouldn't risk a scratch on that ebony finish of his, would he?"

"I can't wait to see their faces," Ada cried. Her handsome head tossed and curveted, fluffy hair flying from the pins. "I bet they all just pick up and turn tail? I bet they all just pee their pants?"

"Ada!" Julie remonstrated, looking around at her. Ada's excitability, always excessive, had been surpassing its usual extremes for several weeks now.

Henry concentrated on the side of the road, keeping an eye out for a spruce young figure, clean-combed and nicely dressed. He turned from the cut-off into the highway and doubled back toward Zion. Halfway there he discerned far up ahead a boy trotting along the sandy shoulder.

"Look, isn't that him? I thought so. Making a beeline . . ." Slowed by a blockage in the highway traffic he had caught up with, he pressed his horn. "Say Charles! Charles, come back here!"

At the shout the boy trotted faster. As the car, now in a crawling line, gained on him, he turned a dirt-streaked face back at it. His shirt-tail was hanging out. His pants were rolled up to his calves and his shoes were slung over his shoulders. A long scratch on his cheek had bled and dried in rusty smears: he must have cut cross-country at least part of the way.

Henry leaned across Julie and opened the door. "Now Charles, get in here. Get back in here!"

Charles dodged away, crossed the road through cars halted by some obstacle up ahead, dove into the Johnson grass on the opposite side and fled through it toward Zion.

"There, that's gratitude for you," Ada said with satisfaction. "Doing you just like his daddy. The more you do for others—" Her words died away in the taut silence around her. Henry nosed along, nudging at the jolting jalopy in front of him.

"What's the hold-up?" the Judge shouted from behind. "Must be an accident."

"Probably some Model T," Henry muttered. "Run out of gas and all creation's out to help 'em." He smacked down on his horn, the cars behind echoing him.

"I hope," Dan said worriedly, "there's not going to be anything rash. Because if there is—"

"Maybe," Julie suggested as if just waking up to what was brewing, "we better turn back and drive home. I'll fix some drinks."

The cars ahead of them, released, moved on at a snail's pace. As they neared the church it became apparent what the obstacle was. By one of those mischances that had bedeviled Henry from the day he first engaged Reeve Scott and Rad McDowell—a mischance of fate or timing or failure to take all factors into account—a trailer truck was extended over three-fourths of the road. From the back of it the tractor was being unloaded at the church gate under the supervision of Professor Thurlow. Bright red, fresh as new, with all its attachments and appurtenances. Chalmer Coombs waving a red flag, only the less red by the dinginess of weather and wear, was directing a trickle of traffic past, first from one direction and then from the other.

Henry rammed his convertible in as near to the gate as he could get and jumped out. The massive patience he had maintained through this day, this week, the months before, heaved ominously up within him. Pressure gripped the back of his head in a tightening vise. His ears whirred, the inside of his skull rang: that damfool stunt with the shot through the sombrero, the speech that had boiled up in him like a steam turbine . . .

"Get that thing out of the way!" He kicked at the double-wheeled truck.

"Say Henry." DeLavery, assisting Thurlow, absently glanced around at him. "How you doin'?"

"Let me get through here!"

"All cars parked outside, sir," one of the colored soldiers politely said. "Here, sir, let me show you." About to lead him out around into the backfield.

The barbed-wire fence that girded the Zion grounds, overgrown with thorny climbers, vines and shrubbery, was girded in turn by a mass of cars that belonged to those inside, their roofs shimmering dully in the afternoon heat. Henry, balked by the tractor, caught glimpses past it through the gate of a vista that nothing the mayor let drop had prepared him for.

"My Lord," Ada gasped as she wheeled the gocart up beside him, "they're dancing in there!"

"Good God"—the Judge pussyfooted up with Dan Garner, peering in at the jam of onlookers waiting for the tractor to roll in—"there goes my seventy-one per cent! Put the cracker and the colored together and you can kiss the South goodbye. Come on, Dan, I'll ride you and May—"

"Now wait a minute," Henry snatched at them. "Not so fast! You not giving up . . ."

They turned on him an odd look, the look of the old pro who has seen them rise up fast and fall even faster. They'd thought they had a comer here. This time they really thought they had a comer.

"Of course not." The Judge gamely patted Henry's shoulder. He still had his judgeship, guaranteed by the vote of the other two counties in his circuit. Dan still had his seat in Congress. As for the rest, they'd fight for their commitments on top where it counted, though not quite with all the ammunition they had hoped for. "I hate to leave you now, Henry, but it's getting late for Dan and I promised to take him in to Bay City. That was a bang-up job you did today, Henry. The rally, your speech— we never had anything better. I know you'll do your best to finish what you started. Good luck."

Dan Garner warmly clasped Henry's hand. "Fine appeal you made, Henry, one of the finest I ever heard. It's enterprising young men like you who hold the future of this great state . . . It's up to you."

The Judge delicately eased his Lincoln out, calling for a readjustment of cars in the rear. Several of them swung out in an arc after him back down the highway to home and town.

Will Royall, however, drove his car straight up to Chalmer's red flag, drawing with him a motor contingent of Fallonians, a digression that could only result in a crucial diversion of forces.

"What the hell is going on with you, Chalmer?" Will shook his fist in the face of his opponent, taking full advantage of the opportunity to make a grandstand play. "Creating a traffic hazard. Clear this damn contraption out of here!"

"Move on, move on," Chalmer hollered, "you blockin' the road! I'm sheriff here. What you carryin' there, Will, an arsenal? Move on, move on you all, anybody don't move is under arrest."

Will and his Fallonians, unable to turn back, were routed down around the Four Corners to the Fallona Road.

The remains of the crowd who had followed Henry here debouched from their cars and flocked about him.

"I'm going in there to get Charles," he shouted back at Julie.

Ada led the way, squeezing with her gocart through the cranny between tractor and gate, zooming past Carter Scott and Hagan Power, plunging through the company inside.

"Come on." She charged past conversational coteries, haranguing them. "Come on you nigger-fucking cock-sucking bitches! Come on! Come on you mother-fucking buggers . . ."

One of Ada's nervous breakdowns, so long impending, so often dreaded, so firmly contained within nightly mutterings over household drudgery after her day in court, was upon her now in all its peculiar efflorescence.

But even Ada's invective did not achieve the effect it should have. Under Henry's nose an old colored woman patted the arm of her companion. "Why I know her. Just a minute." And the colored woman proceeded full sail into Ada's path. "Why Mrs. Hemmings, I ain't seen you in I don't know how long. That your little grandchild?" Peeping in under the brim of bonnet. "My. She's cute. Kitchy-koo, look at oo. Chk chkchk."

The distorting grimace disappeared from Ada's face as if wiped off, replaced by a simper of gracious gratification. She preened over the child, primping her bonnet, fanning out her skirts.

While Ada chatted with the colored woman, redoing her long coil of hair with stabs of her hairpins, the other women in Henry's train strayed off, lured by the call of friends and the announcement over the loudspeaker of winning exhibits. They scattered among the booths, temporarily hammered together of weathered board, to inspect peach jam and muscadine jellies, pickle jars packed with green cubes of watermelon rind, flowerets of cauliflower, corn relish speckled with pimento peppers, pig's feet loose on the bone, pink frills of shrimp, shad roe, calves' ears. They disappeared under lines of quilting, crewel-embroidered hand towels, aprons, potholders, all priced irresistibly low. They were dragooned by proud parents into viewing the 4-H hobby show. They were besieged with raffle tickets for a turkey donated by Mort Green's market; a radio donated by the Hardware & Feed; a popcorn bedspread crocheted by Carl Maynard's mother, bordered all around with fringe that thick. They were swept off in the stampede to the cake sale when Bessie Sanderlee's three-layer New Orleans spice cake, frosted with swirls of lemon-flavored white coconut icing, was unveiled from its wrapping of wax paper to be auctioned off to the highest bidder.

Most of them annexed their men—husband, son, and brother—and hauled them off with them.

"Rad McDowell!"

Henry barged through the line of booths alongside the church, accompanied by Hill Caslon and Eustis Telfer, with a motley crew at their tail of filling-station loungers, teen-agers on a lark, ancient bench-warmers from the green in Oglethorpe Square.

"Anybody seen Rad McDowell? Where's he at?"

Everybody had just seen Rad and nobody knew just where. Henry elbowed on in a dazzle of astonishment. "Why this is the worst thing I've ever seen. I never thought to see anything like this." All he could see as far as his eye could reach was mixing-mingling-and-mongrelizing. Everywhere he saw the selfsame people he had addressed from the platform, the same white-billed cap shadowing the burnt-brick cheek, the same cotton print flouncing over tanned legs. All in with the niggers.

No booths came tumbling down, no jars smashing, no lines crashing. No tomatoes. All it would take to start it was one finger raised. No one raised it. They didn't. And he couldn't.

It was like a swelling tide inundating his own ranks, engulfing them.

"Please mister"—kids dark and light raced up to his men and stopped them—"will you open my pop bottle for me?"

A bespectacled brownskin woman accosted Hill Caslon, beseeching, "You seen Miz Teague? You know Mr. Teague works on your boats? Miz Teague has my handbag with her and all my money." And a second woman intervened with the first, a tall broomstick of a woman dragging a string of scrawny youngsters after her, "Where d' picnic ground, ma'am?" And a third woman intercepted with a tray of benne candy. "Try it. It's good. I cooks up my milk and sugar till it hairs . . ." And

Hill Caslon with his hand in his pocket on the pistol he always carried there.

"The McDowells," Henry demanded about hoarsely, "I'm looking for Rad McDowell."

Stumbling through dewlaps of potato sacks strewn on the ground from the ladies' potato sack race, he searched through rubicund faces still blowsy with strands of helpless hilarity.

"Play ball!"

A ball whizzed past Henry's ear and a high schooler flew over his feet. "Out of the way!" Marcus Hadley umpiring the game gestured frantically at him. If the game wasn't mixed, for all Henry could make of it it might just as well have been.

"Look at that shortstop." Henry poked Eustis. "If he's Portuguee, I'm an Indian. Why don't somebody stand up and yell to high heaven—"

"Mr. Warren! I didn't know you were here." Father Hall hurried up, all sweetness and light. "Why didn't someone tell me? And Mr. Telfer. Let me show you around. Minds me of the time—remember?—when the bridge was dedicated . . ."

"I'm looking for McDowell."

Father Hall waved vaguely all the way back to the gate. "Went out there I think, some time ago, with one of his boys. I been intending to call you, Mr. Telfer. There's a Telfer in my parish records, oh an early date. Any time you'd like to see it, I'll be glad to . . ."

Henry lost a half-dozen men back at the ball game and Telfer of course with Father Hall.

Rejecting the contradictory information he had received from various sources—the McDowell family hadn't left, that alone was certain— Henry circled the barbecue pit from one side to the other. A ring of stamping and clapping youngsters surrounded one of the tables in the picnic grove. Up on bench and table a combo of band players had formed around a guitarist. Black fingers plucked at steel string, caressing neck and belly, head lowered to catch external vibration, internal resonance, a man making love. "Pick that box!" Lips pursed buzzed into the mouthpiece of the trombone, and from the glistening bell, the calyx, issued the plaint of yearning, mellow and strident, of a man who yearns for love. "Blow that horn!" Bare hands slapped a drum, a syncopation of staccato beats, easy, breezy, a rain of blows as light as summer rain, oh love oh love oh careless love. "Hit that skin!" Dancers caught one another by the hand, pulled in, let loose, twirled, lifted by the waist, soaring.

One girl at the edge of the ring, flinging her head to the beat, lifting her bosom, jigging her hips, was unmistakably white. So young, so fresh and so pearly a mist shimmered out of her. From a table on the other side of the barbecue pit a bleat cut in. Members of the white band sitting on table top with their assortment of instruments, the tenor sax responding to the rasping wail of the trombone. Oh yes? Nono. Oh no? Yesyes. Da dada tata ta? Unh unh. Uh huh? Idontcare Idontcare Idontcare.

"Why that's my niece!" One of the old gaffers behind Henry ejaculated. "Fridella? Come on out of there, Fridella. Fridella?"

The misty maiden tossed a smile over her shoulder and undulating snapped her fingers with the click of castanets. Sway like the breeze, man . . .

"It all goes to prove," Hill Caslon who had caught up again with Henry observed, "that as my father always said, when you have two races dwelling this close together you have to have laws to keep them apart. Where's Will Royall now with his trick shooting?"

"Where are you?" Henry snapped. "You got a gun on you."

"If nothing's happened up to now," Caslon said equably, taking no offense, "it's not going to. In a mob there always has to be the few that do the job. The rest just cheer them on. And people such as you and me, Henry, look away or better still stay away. I can't afford to be publicly involved anymore than you can."

"I'm not leavin' till I find my boy. I'm gettin' him outa here."

With his dwindling escort, the more impatient as their number decreased, Henry went seeking from group to group. "Rad McDowell. Anybody here can tell me where Rad is?" Straining after every bright head in the distance. Every flash of white shirt.

Charles? Charles?

7

Outside the church grounds, in the truck cab under a pinoak's plunging branches, Lulabelle was nursing her baby. Why is it they always want to nurse the more the minute you get into a strange situation? Hang on till you could die. Draining, draining till if there's no milk left there must be blood. Get off, goldarn you, get off! Let go-o . . . She shooed flies and gnats away. At last, inserting her finger in the pursed posy of a mouth, she found it loosening, releasing, falling away, sated to laxness. The eyelids closed, pale mauve, flower petals. And the eyelashes, the longest eyelashes, pure gold. And rosy cheeks, the reddest rose . . .

She held the baby belly-to on her diapered shoulder and patted her back waiting for the bubble of air to come up. Up, goldarn you, up! Never had a baby to take so long . . .

"There's someone here"—Rad poked his head in through the truck window—"that wants to see you."

"Hush, goldarn you! I just now gotten her lulled."

But there was something in the timbre of Rad's voice, in the light of his eyes, in the hush of the children outside that caused her to turn, fumbling at the buttons of her blouse. Now of all times to bring someone . . .

Rad opened the truck door and Charles climbed up in beside her.

"Mamma?"

"Oh," she said. "Ohhh." Her eyes flew over his face, scratched, his hair, mussed, his shirt, torn. "What have they done to you? What did they done!"

"Nothing, ain't nothing . . . That the new baby?"

Her head cocked coquettishly to one side, her eyes downcast, a bemused smile on her lips, she folded back a corner of the blanket offering him a view of rounded cheek.

"They say only the children of the rich is pretty. But we think she is the prettiest thing."

"Let me hold her?"

She passed over the baby, quickly thrusting diaper underside onto his shoulder. "She'll spit up all over."

"Remember Ruby?" Charles humped the baby up over his shoulder, thumping at the small of her back. "She was a hellion. P-foo, all the diapers I changed . . . What she called?"

"Ella-Rose."

"Mamma?"

"Son?"

"Mamma?"

"My firstborn one. My prince. My shining glory."

Her fingers touching over the scratch on his face, he kissed the rough palm of her hand.

"I said he'd come back, didn't I? I said it—"

"Hush!"

Baby in basket, they threaded back through the parked cars along the fenceside to the gate. "Say Rad," people called to them from all around, "Henry's in there looking for you. He's been looking all over."

"Let him look," Rad said. Joyous with the boy and himself, he steered him to the tractor at the gate. "Wait till you see this outfit, I bet there's nothing at Sunset . . . Well never mind that. I want you to meet the smartest crop man in all south Georgia." With his hand on Charles' back, he moved him toward Professor Thurlow.

Reeve and Vivian were trimming up the tractor for its grand entrance. Slinging streamers around it, sticking flags into every interstice that would hold one, they were both intensely conscious of Julie sitting in the tan convertible no more than a few feet away, watching them.

"In Europe," Vivian said to Reeve flinging him a ribbon, "in these old peasant countries, when they have a pageant through the streets they decorate a bull, throw garlands of flowers around his neck, festoon him with ribbons, hang brushes in his ears and bells on his tail." Talking, talking against the poised sophistication of the woman in the car. "Goes back to pagan times I guess. Glorifying the male."

"The things," Reeve said, "the things you tell me. Tell me more."

"Old grey-nose white woman," Vivian muttered. "What she lookin' at?"

Several times Julie resisted the impulse to rise from her seat in the car and gawk boldly over the fence to see what was going on in there, find out what was taking Henry so long. But to learn was to become implicated. Or as bad, be compelled to make the decision not to become implicated. Don't find out.

She sat back with the enforced detachment of a lovely lady bored to tears. Her life stretched ahead of her, a long corridor with doors on both sides locked and sealed. Undeterred by the cries locked behind those doors, the cries of memory and imagination, she walked her course. Next week after the election, her reunion in Washington with Elwell. She would be the guest of the Garners at their Georgetown house, let him call for her there. Of her levels of feeling toward Elwell—the tremulously expectant, the mortified and vengeful, the clever—it was cleverness that surpassed them all in the end, that lay uppermost now. She was not leaving Henry for a man who'd only be frightened off by it if she did. She would hold on to Henry, building him up as fast as she could, as long as she had to, until and unless she had someone—if not Elwell, then someone else—better in hand. The monthly meetings of the County Commission would take little of Henry's time. He could commute to Adelbert Smith College late afternoons, not much of a college but nearby, and with what knowledge he had already acquired and a few courses he'd have a degree by next June. It could be worked out. Perhaps a generous contribution . . . And the state senate, with Acme support behind him. And after that . . . Until and unless Elwell, or someone . . .

"Julie?" Clem came up to the car, interrupting the flow of her plans.

Wiping grease off his hands. "How are you, Julie?" Worlds hanging balance in his tone. "How've you been?"

"Don't you worry about me." She was caught off guard by a discordant catch in her throat. "I'll make out." She laughed lightly over the rasp in her throat. "I dreamt about you last night."

"Again?"

"The same dream. You were visiting me. And I wandered around naked in front of you. Then I went in to take a shower. And when I came out I said, 'Are you really a mental specialist?'"

"Julie—" He passed his grease-streaked hand over his eyes. "Julie, I feel I've failed you. Somewhere I failed."

"Afraid to interpret that one, aren't you? It's only because you see me as I am, isn't it? You see right through me." She laughed with all her old wry warmth, a sprite of mischief peeping up at him from under the brim of her hat. Then she composed herself gravely, with all her old warmth of concern. "In the same dream I dreamt that you were poor and starving and I was wondering how I could help you?"

He stood with hands helplessly clasping and unclasping over the car door. But of course it wasn't just to find out how she was that he had come over here. It never was just that. He looked worriedly back over his shoulder.

"I hate to say this to you now, Julie, but Henry went in there a while back with a pack I didn't like the looks of . . ."

"Oh Clem." She sank back and tapped a cigarette out of her case and while he fumbled with a paper matchbook lighted it from the red glow of the car lighter. "You're always in such a stew." With bright brittle derision. "Don't you realize that Henry will never do anything that'll put him on the spot? He went looking for Charles."

"Charles is out there in the parking lot with his family."

"Then send tell him."

"No," Clem said with a sharpness that implied, she thought, a cutting rebuke. "I'm having no more to do with that."

"Well, don't look at me! I did my best."

Someone called Clem away. Julie stared through the windshield, angry, watching his retreating back, the black shirt with sleeves rolled up over the elbows, the narrow head inclined toward the caller, one of the men working on the tractor. Better to feel furious than tragic.

She contemplated the tractor, amused at the figures swarming about it. Like flies around a shrimp-pile in August. Peasants in some pagan ceremony decking the sacrificial bull, dancing through the streets with him. Only this was no bull. Blazing red, a monster of iron parts and motor power.

Not so long ago she would have been in the midst of all this, consulted, sought after, the focal point through which the goodwill of the community flowed from one race to the other. Now she sat outside and above it, excluded, ignored, displaced by a machine. When Reeve passed by her for the third time without a word, toting rolls of streamer paper from the trunk of the Professor's car, she called to him. Idly to fill the void left by Clem or capriciously to satisfy a craving to be cruel she arrested him in his journey back to the tractor with a peremptory challenge he could not pretend he didn't hear.

"You're not going to walk by me, Reeve, and not speak?"

"Ma'am?"

"Come over here where I can talk to you." Everyone was craning around, staring. She enjoyed his discomfiture. "Over here to the car."

With his hands wreathed in rolls of crepe paper, yellow and white and blue, he approached the car, dark and pulsating, wicked-eyed, the crease biting between his brows.

"How you, Mrs. Warren?" he said politely. "I was most sorry to hear about you loss."

"Don't put on," she said, driven by the capricious need to make herself felt, to penetrate below the superficial surface of his responses if she had to pinch and squeeze and twist his arm to do it. "You don't have to put on with me. There's something I want to know that perhaps you can tell me. Something has happened here in the last few months . . . Reeve, what's happening to us? Where's all the good feeling there used to be? All the little kindnesses and decencies? The respect?"

Reeve looked longingly back over his shoulder to the tractor. To High Power grinning: What she want, a hunk a ass? To Vivian frowning: Old grey-nose white woman, what she want? He could only think that she had chosen this moment, the high moment of his accomplishment, his wife won, his friends won, the tractor and the organization of it won, to try before all of them, in the face of his victory, to humiliate him, pull him back down where he belonged—under her foot. Draining him of the serenity of all his hard-earned powers, dragging him down into the slough, into the undertow of all the gone-years. You can't break out of the way it's been and still is. You can't get free.

"Reeve, answer me! Where has it all gone? Ever since I can remember, when I'd wake up in the morning, all day long, any time, you could hear colored folks singing in the kitchens, out the yards, in the street. You could always here colored folks singing. I never hear them singing anymore. All this division among us today, all this dissension you're sowing: Where's it all going to end?"

His eyes glowed on her with a look: Didn't he know he could be lynched for a look like that? If Henry should come out now, Julie thought, and catch that look, no jury would convict . . .

"Something's been lost out of our lives," she said to him, returning look for look. "A quality of feeling, the kind of selfless devotion your mother gave me. I said it at her funeral and I say it again and I'll always say it. There was something we had then." She shook her head at him, filled with an inexpressible grief for that inexpressible thing that had been taken from her like a dead child torn out of its grieving mother's arms.

"Oh, I've made my mistakes, I admit that. For whatever harm I caused you I'm sorry, and I apologize." All the cruelty had gone out of her. She was making her amends and it cost her more effort than she would ever have believed. She was pleading with him.

"But it wasn't all bad, was it? There were good things to it too, weren't there? Tell me the truth now. The truth. The way it really was."

Did she know what she was asking for, so innocently sitting there in the car in front of all this crowd? A sock in the jaw, a kick in the slats, to be assaulted and beaten and left for dead was nothing, Reeve thought, to this. What she wanted out of him was what he above all need not give her. The one brutality he most mustn't. An honest answer.

"You want it straight?" he said with brutal relief, laying it down, committing himself body and soul.

"Yes. You showed me things, Reeve, remember, when I was a little girl, baby birds blown out of their nest in a storm—"

"My mother never loved you more than she did herself," he said. There it was, on the line. "She didn't work for you. She worked for us."

He started away and she called him back, the peremptory note back in her voice. "Reeve, I'm not through yet." And with a thinly quivering, wistful smile she asked, "Do you hate me?"

Reeve gazed again longingly back at the tractor. Carl Maynard and the Baron were hanging the banners of the Marion Carter and Charles Young posts on either side. Vivian was beckoning with her fingers for the crepe paper to be spiraled around, birthday style. Thurlow was up on the seat about to start, Rad's boy braced between his knees holding the wheel with him.

Hate? He turned back to Julie. Lila-Lee's milk—after her. His father crawling under the house with him to share his shame. The plow his mother harnessed to her back after the mule was taken. All the years of invidious comparison. White is right and black is evil. That crept through his own race like an infection. Get white, get right or get out. The second-rate. The back seat. The door shut.

That radiant creature with everything on her side, the world at her command, badgering him with questions. Like an imperious old woman after a misspent life. The last duchess. Her cigarette shaking as she inserted it in her mouth. He was crushing the crepe paper roll in his hand. All the years of cussing the Colfax.

"I can only answer that," he said enigmatically, and what it cost him to admit it he would never have believed, "like my mamma would. Anybody you know about you can't hate."

He went back to the tractor and with Vivian quickly looped the last of the trimming around. High Power nudging him, "What'd she want, a hunk a ass?" And Vivian grumbling, "Old grey-nose white woman, what'd she want?"

What she want?

"Feels we're destroying her," Reeve said. He slapped the flank of the tractor—*ban*, done!—and signaled at Thurlow. "Mash 'er down!"

"Destroying her! With her husband in there just champing to wreck and rampage?"

"Start 'er up! Clear the way! Clear the way in there!"

The tractor, bandoleered and banderoled, roared through the gate, pawing up the ground, exhaling smoke from its stack, old Thurlow waving his yellowed panama, young Charles, the gingery one, squirming precariously about for a glimpse of the motor under the hood. The crowd parted like the waters, like the fresh field turning; surged alongside cavorting and clamoring; and closed in the wake of its clattering attachments. It rolled between the booths to the open area in back of the church where on a podium of assembled benches the charter of the Colfax County Veterans Cooperative Association was to be presented to the elected officers of the two classes.

No two accounts of what occurred next ever exactly concurred.

Henry ran into the path of the tractor shouting and gesturing at Charles to come down. Thurlow couldn't swerve because of the press of the crowd and he couldn't brake to a halt soon enough. Henry was pulled back. He then tried to lunge up onto the step-plate for the boy. He was again pulled back.

Benson Reece broke through to him. "Now Henry, don't cause a disturbance."

"Disturbance? What the hell you think you got here? Now let him go peaceable. I'm taking him peaceable—"

Lulabelle broke through. "Now you keep off from my boy! Look at the condition he's in. Look how you done him."

And Rad saying with an awful dispassion, "He don't want you no more? Can't you see he don't want you no more?"

Everybody was beginning to grin by this time. A derisive devilish grin.

Making a monkey out of Henry at the hands of his poor-trash cousin.

Henry rushed at Rad. Someone biffed Rad from behind with a rabbit punch in the back of the neck, sending him flying toward Henry. Somehow Rad sidestepped, avoiding an exchange of blows. And Henry's fist connected with Benson Reece. With the upturned sardonic smile. Dentures caving. Glasses slithering. He pummeled to the ground a man old enough to be his father.

"For Christ sake, Henry!"

He was pulled back once again. Hill Caslon reappeared with Eustis, fending off Clem and the speakers who came thrusting in belatedly from the podium.

Eustis and Hill hustled Henry down to the gate and outside to his car, opened the door and shoved him in.

"Now Henry"—they slammed the door on him and held it fast as he tried to plunge out—"go home and take a nice cold shower. Julie, take him home. Fix him a good stiff shot of whiskey and draw him a nice warm bath."

"But what on earth . . . You didn't get into a *fist fight?*"

"Worse than that," they answered for Henry. "He hit Benson." The two of them were grinning, a sneaking snicker of a grin that escaped sidewise. "Busted him right in the kisser. Broke his false teeth. Must have stepped on his glasses." Their grins were not for Benson in the dust, but at Henry upright. "We'll go back see how Benson is. Get him away from here now, Julie. Yeah, we'll let you know . . ."

Julie drove Henry home, a nervously responsive grin twitching at her lips as the full implication of Telfer and Caslon's attitude impressed itself upon her. "So they beat you! Those two boys out on the River Road beat you out. They've won. Hands down. You're through."

Then the full meaning of the disaster as it affected herself began to sink in. "You mean you won't win that election next Tuesday? It's all been for nothing? All we been through? Nothing will come of it?"

Home was worse. They rattled through the big empty rooms without the cushioning of Charles between them, with nothing to insulate their abrasive consciousness of one another. Charles was gone and in every room Coley danced, in the sunbeams fluttering through the window curtains, in the patina of the oil portraits, in the twinkle of silver and polished wood. The source of all the conflict in their marriage had also been its bond, binding them together even now in a compact of recrimination, self-justification and complicity.

Henry fixed their drinks on the portable bar in the kitchen—he was the one to fix them, bourbon on the rocks for himself, with soda for Julie. *I wanted him dead, I must have intended it from the first.* Sitting

on the sofa in the living room like a guest in her own house, Julie swiz-
zled her drink about, the fizz exploding wetly against her fingers. *I gave
him over into the hands of a quack, a maniac. Between us we killed him
. . .* The sacrificial lamb to a future that was not to be.

At such a time as this husband and wife should be able to creep into
each other's arms, weeping for the torment in which they have entrapped themselves. All is not lost. All is not lost.

"I think," Julie said, "I'll have another one."

With her fresh drink, stirring it reflectively, she went to the telephone
in the hall and called long distance, person to person. While she waited
for her call to be put through, Henry went upstairs for his shower.

He undressed in Charles' room, which he had been using since his
banishment from his own room, even during the past week when Julie
with surprising acquiescence, more indifferent than affectionate, had
readmitted him to bed. Charles' belongings were scattered all over the
room. A baseball cap lay on the pillow where it had been tossed, still
holding within its crown the shape of his head. His sneakers still stood
by the bed where they had been dropped, askew, tongues dangling,
strings straggling. Henry slid back the closet door and shuttled through
the clothes for his robe. A pair of boy's chinos fell with a bump of the
hanger to the floor. Henry fished them up, went through the bulging
pockets. Bicycle key. Foreign coins. Occupation money, he must have
been holding onto it all these weeks. A clot of tissues, stuck together
with dried mucus, the living fluid . . .

In the playroom that connected Charles' room with Coley's, the
blocks that should have been gathered up and given away still lay where
they'd been left, in the form of a city the boys had constructed together.

The fine spray of the shower, tattoo-needling, aroused him from his
torpor. The shower head and the fixtures not paid for yet, the plumber
unpaid, the debts he owed Marcus on the house. And the debts for the
rally, the hot dogs and hamburger, the beer and the ice. Eight hundred dollars he'd taken from the Sunset account when spot cash was
needed. Counting on deals he had his eye on after the election to make
it up. As soon as the news of this day's fiasco got around, they'd all be
on him.

Drying himself, he scrubbed at his skin with the towel as if he could
rub it all off. With the robe hanging loose over his shoulders he wandered down the hall toward Julie's bedroom. How could it be? How
could it have come to pass? All botched. All gone. All in a single minute.

Julie's connection had been completed. It was not usual for her to
telephone Elwell. Usually the calls originated from him. Over the banister Henry could hear the intonation of an exchange, familiar to him

almost nightly now, intimate, provocative, articulating more than was pronounced; every syllable sending forth wave upon wave of an insinuation that beat wave upon crimson wave through his blood. An insinuation which he accepted nevertheless stolidly as he might accept a bribe in an envelope, persuaded by his own conviction that he had no idea what it was. He had gambled that Elwell would send her back to him. And she'd been sent back with her value increased a thousandfold.

"Mm-mm? Mmmmh . . . Well, don't lose any sleep over it."

A chortle of husky laughter.

"It's so important to him. And he's such a dud at it."

Henry recoiled from the banister, staggered into the bedroom as if struck through the head, the heart, the gut, and the groin. He had no way of knowing what she was alluding to or whom, and no way of confronting her with it. At the frail root of the pride most precious to a man she struck. At the very axis of his being. With a single slash.

On her dresser Julie—careless carefree Julie—had left her last letter, another piece of poetry. *Catullus 72*. The first four lines in Elwell's thick black script, the last three in her elegant scrawl.

> My mistress says she would not dream
> Of loving anyone but me
> Not though Jove himself desire her,
> Swearing thus fidelity.
>
> But on the wind and fleeting stream
> A woman's vows should written be
> When implored by her admirer.

Henry read and reread it, every syllable sending its wave on crimson wave of intimation through him. Julie came into the room in her lacy black silk slip, carrying dress, brassiere and girdle, stockings and pumps, having shed while she was speaking on the telephone all that was sticky and restrictive on her. With scarcely a glance she passed him by, threw her scrunched-up garments into a corner, threw a fresh white eyelet-embroidered wrapper over her shoulders and left for the bathroom to shower herself. She in her filmy floating wrapper flitting past, he in his bold-striped robe impotently, reduced to a jelly, watching.

She was dumping him. Produce or be dumped.

He pulled open her dresser drawer and scraped through the tangle of sanitary belt, loose tampons and discarded lipsticks until he located the other letters, elastic-banded, under the pumice stone. The bedside telephone rang and he crossed the floor to answer it, taking the packet with him.

"Mr. Warren?"

"Yes ma'am."

"You not go'n let them get away with this, are you, Mr. Warren?"

"Who is this?"

Bang the telephone. He clicked the bar.

"Number please?"

"Doris? Who just called me, Doris?"

"I'm not allowed to give out that information."

"This Mr. Warren, Doris. Who was it?"

"I didn't notice, Mr. Warren."

"Next time, notice."

Everyone loves a winner. Everbody leaves a loser.

The telephone was no sooner back in its cradle than it rang again.

"Henry?" Will Royall.

"Where in damnation were you? Where'd you disappear to?"

"Chalmer confiscated my guns. I couldn't leave them guns . . . Look Henry, some of us been talking. That church—"

"Don't you touch that church!"

"Well some of us thought . . . A little lesson—"

"Leave that church alone! I know this town. They'd burn it down to-night and take up a collection for it tomorrow. We don't need no collection for no nigger church."

"But it'd sure throw a scare—"

Bang the telephone, this time Henry banged it.

If they were going to do something about that church, why in God's name did they have to call him about it! The telephone rang again. Doris. "Do you want to know what that was, Mr. Warren?"

Bang their heads together!

Replacing the telephone, Henry stared at the wallpaper over the bed, a white-flocked paper with the design and sheen of damask. He scanned it for the almost invisible junctures back to the corner where it had first been hung. The telephone rang once more.

"Son of a bitch, Henry, I been trying to get you for most an hour. Your phone's been tied up—"

"You found out how Benson is, Hill?"

"Shook up some. But I guess he figures the way things stand he got the best of it."

"Well, I hope you conveyed to him how sorry I am. That cousin of mine, he's had it in for me since the day he was born. So when he plowed in, naturally I prepared to defend myself and when Benson stepped between . . . Poor old soul, he means well but his faculties aren't what they were. His sight's gone—"

"Sure Henry, sure."

"Now you and Eustis weren't there, you didn't see it. It was all so confused. Anything you can do to correct any misimpression, you'll do me a favor. It was pure accidental."

"Sure enough. Sure enough will."

"Tell Benson I'll pay for any damage."

"Already done that. Boy, that fuss sure cleared the field. Folks picked up with their kids—and scoot! Had hardly anyone left for the ceremony. Out, gone, vamoose! Half hour later you could have swept through with a broom. Nothing there but the litter."

Thoughtfully Henry replaced the telephone. Hmmm.

During the conversation Julie had trailed back in, all soft and dewy in her wrapper, little damp curls clinging about her brow. She took up her knitting bag from her vanity bench and retreated with it to her satin-tufted Dolly Madison chair, a gift from the Judge. Arranging herself prettily under the high rose-carved oval frame she shook the peacock-blue afghan out over her lap. All the panels joined now, all the twining flowerets and loveknots on it. Only the scalloped border, begun on one side, remaining to be crocheted all the way around.

She drew her thread out. "If you're hungry, I'm not, there's chicken in the refrigerator."

"What you messing with that thing for? Rose is dead. Laura DeLavery took off this morning, they say, without a word of goodbye to anyone. Who you go'n give it to now?"

"I think—" Julie bit her lip against a bubble of escaping laughter. "I'll give it—" She bent over her work with shaking shoulders, rocking with mirth. "I'll give—give—" Then she spluttered out with it, laughing so hard she moaned. "I'll give it to Marion Elwell."

"You'll leave it around till it falls to a frazzle. You'll lock it up in a trunk somewhere and forget about it. The moths'll have it."

"I'll have it done tonight." Her steel hook glittered in and out. Her fingers flew, flinging over the yarn. On and on. "I'm going up to Virginia this weekend. Some sort of house party. Don't know just when I'll be back."

"Not before the election! How'll it look? If you don't show up with me to cast the first ballot—"

"What for?"

"Julie, what's come over you? What's got into you?"

"If there's one thing I learned from you, Henry, it's never to wear a millstone around my neck. I made a fool of myself today in front of a black boy who was so wrapped up in that damn contraption of theirs he wouldn't give me the time of day. Made a regular sentimental sap of myself. Trying to hold on to something I once believed in. The milk of human kindness. To help, not to hurt. You were right. You were right all along. There's no such thing. There never was. There's only maneuvering. A mad scramble between the ins and the outs, the haves and the have-nots. If there's any rationality to human behavior, which I seriously doubt, that's it.

"Well, I'm a have and I'm going to have whatever there is to be had. I'm in and I'm going as far in as I can get. I've become exactly what you always wanted me to be, Henry. And no cheap tricks with that pack of letters in your hand will bail you out. It was all written in the first century."

"If I was Philip Elwell I wouldn't care to have it read aloud in a courtroom."

She slid the afghan several inches up over her lap. "Topside now—I happen to know that you've been pretty chummy with Annamary. Some girl saw you one night parked out on a back road with her and she told her mother and her mother mentioned it to her cousin who lives down here. And at my party for Sukey everyone saw it, Annamary was giving you the glad-eye and you were giving her plenty. And that first week I was up in Atlanta with Coley, when you were entertaining at that party for the freezer-plant opening? She was here all that night, wasn't she? I don't think that that'll sound very well either in Judge Purcell's courtroom."

"But that was the night of the gale! She stayed after to see to things and the wind went up to seventy miles an hour, the tide was up ten feet, wires were down, there was a washout on the road . . . There never was anything between me and Annamary!"

"Prove it."

Henry pitched the letters back at the dresser. Clambered into his work clothes. Stormed downstairs. Stopped in the hall to make a telephone call.

"Marcus? You know that wallpaper up in the master bedroom? That we waited so long and paid so much for? It's on crooked! The first panel's just a mite off kilter. Over the bed it's listing. Back of the vanity it's keeling over. And by the time it gets around to the dresser it's going down like the *Titanic*. You don't get a penny out of me, not one penny, till that's taken care of."

In the kitchen he fell ravenously on the cold roast chicken, tearing it haunch from haunch with a crackle of bones. He jabbed the beer-can opener into a couple of cans and drained them as he stood. This was his kitchen. Those were his cupboards. That was his wife upstairs. It was his town and his county and his boy out there.

"Julie," he shouted up from the foot of the stairs, "I'm going out to Sunset. Couple of accounts I have to straighten out."

She must have closed her door. Sitting in her high-backed satin chair, the lamplight shining on her bent head, the spread in all its peacock splendor flowing over her knees. Some well-heeled old fossil? Some careerist riding the crest? Some starry-eyed young socialite? Or himself, her husband, on the rise, forever waiting for that delayed shriek of grief and accusation?

Sand rattled up under his fenders. Spatters from the newly tarred surface of the River Road sprayed over the waxed body of the car like pellets of buckshot. Henry drove without lights into the driveway of the upper section of Sunset, to the equipment sheds. From the first move he made with those boys it had gone wrong. No matter how he prosecuted it, they were always in the right and he was always in the wrong. Yet he had known from the start how it had to be done. No acting through others. No hiding behind the law. No kid gloves. On his own. Alone. In the dark.

At the last shed, an outpost plastered with warning signs, he loaded two cases from inventory, likewise labeled with warning signs, into his car. He drove to the riverside and unloaded his cases, eased them down the crossbars of the inclined slip to his boat. When he poled the boat downriver, the water still as a pool scarcely rippled. He moored beside the bateau at their dock. When he stepped out on the makeshift dock, his weight on the wood was enough to slop water up over it.

Time and again boating past here he had noticed how high the river was. Sediment was piling up on the opposite shore along the marshland due to the skew in the bend of the river above Sunset. A series of cloudbursts during the summer had washed more than the usual burden of soil into waters which, slowed down here, stagnant, could no longer sustain it in suspension but deposited it on the bottom. The engineers surveying the lower river in July had shown him with their gauges and hydrographs how the Ocachee was shifting its bed all through this locality. The flow of the stream no longer fitted the channel. Diverted it pressed against the timbered sluice gate, the earthwork dikes, backed up into the ditching inside. One good push—he had often thought that. One good push.

Their slip, a flimsy structure, wobbled underfoot as he ascended. From the summit he surveyed the fields, blackly silhouetted in the moonlight, the sweet potato crop, the late corn, the early fall planting. Luck was with him. Up the rice canal the tractor was parked on the spoil-pile slope, ready for bulldoze or dragline job in the morning. Directly below the dike the magazine the men had built to storage their dynamite stood like a privy gone astray, isolated on a knoll of uncultivated meadow.

There was an autumnal clarity and crispness to the air which he associated with going-back-to-school. Through the cool clarity of the air the sun warmth conserved from the day rose out of the earth with a smoky sultry richness, with the malty mellowness of harvests ripening. On a sweet-gum tree the leaves stirred as if the process by which their verdure would soon be permeated with scarlet had a sound to it, audible to the attuned ear. Almost the seasonal orbit of the planet could be felt, mobile through the grass beneath him.

In less than an hour Henry docked his boat back at Sunset and drove down the River Road past the twin mailboxes to the lower section. He parked in front of the packing shed, waved to the nightwatchman on his rounds and entering his office switched on all the lights. He sat at his desk staring at the round face of the watch on his wrist, following the circuit of the second hand. His fuses were electrically timed, but there was always the possibility that they would go off too soon or not at all. At the first blast the nightwatchman rushed in. "Them two guys crazy out there?" Henry reached for the telephone and called Chalmer Coombs.

Behind him, on the two farms everything went off like clockwork. At the first blast, that of the magazine, the two men, Rad and Reeve, ran from their houses down the track to find out what was happening. What Henry didn't and couldn't know was that Professor Thurlow had been trying out the tractor throughout the early evening. He was to train four officially designated operators from the two classes in the next few weeks, whose labor was to be repaid in kind or cash as it was employed by the members. Thurlow had left the tractor beside the canal and was walking back toward the house, in no hurry since Vivian had driven off with his Dodge to a teachers' meeting at school. As he neared the cornfield he decided on an impulse to go back and take another look at the tractor. He never reached it.

At the second explosion, that of the two cases half-buried in the embankment on either side of the sluice gate, the Ocachee poured through the shattered timbers into the already brimming ditches, overflowed the slopes. The adjacent diking crumbled under the concussion and breached by the waters crumbled the more. Within minutes the arbitrary willful wayward river, too long pent up here, moved in. The ground was wiped out from under the tractor. Crops were submerged; livestock was swept away, outbuildings, undermined, smashed up against each other. What Henry did not and could not have reckoned on was the magnitude and velocity with which the flood would culminate in a wall of water, rolling forward in a broad flat crest from four to six feet deep where the land dipped.

He could not have guessed that part of his own crop, on the Sunset side of the paddock fencing, would be lost. And certainly he never dreamed that the children would dash out on the porch after their father, that the mother glancing down almost casually would discover the water mounting the steps. That seizing up Ruby and Timmy, pushing Wyatt ahead of her, she would run to the persimmon trees over the well and that Charles would run back into the house for the baby.

It was a mercy, everyone said later, that Henry was close by. He phoned Chalmer Coombs just as soon as he heard the first blast, not knowing what those boys were up to now, and summoned him to the scene. During the night he rounded up his own crews and dispatched them to his pumping stations and out over the two farms. He personally directed the rescue, wading waist-deep through muck, working like a demon without rest or respite.

It was a horrible thing to happen, a stinking slimy sight next day. The houses caked with dirt, contaminated, uninhabitable. Furniture and clothing despoiled. Reeve's house, the new room with plasterboard walls a soggy ruin, with books, pictures, records . . . Rad's house, the tottering porch blotched with broken plants and in the kitchen the remains of two hundred and fifty-three jars of home-canned fruits and vegetables. Carcasses of chickens floating about the yards. The sow that had just farrowed with her litter. Uprooted peach trees.

Shifts of fifty men slaved around the clock for three days to put the dikes back in order against repeated inundations. On the third day they brought the tractor up from the bottom of the rice canal. Besmeared and rusted. A hunk of junk.

Dreadful.

And yet not unexpected. Something like this, almost everyone agreed, was bound to happen. Those two boys went too far. They brought it on themselves. It was an accepted fact, proven now, that they had been stashing dynamite out there all over the lot. Some people believed that they were careless with the dynamite. Had left it lying about. Had let it build up under conditions too dry or too wet into spontaneous combustion. Or had perhaps that night dropped a cigarette in the vicinity. It was also believed by some people that intoxicated by their defeat of Henry that afternoon and inflamed by the tenets of a foreign creed, they had planted the dynamite that night as an assault on Sunset and it backfired. Even many of those who attended the Veterans Benefit came to assume that one or all of these interpretations was indisputable truth.

For the disaster was ineluctably interfused in everyone's mind with the Benefit.

Among the whites who had made merry there, who had had such a good time, the reaction had set in at the moment Henry hit Benson. The self-consciousness set in from the moment they left the Zion grounds and the guilt set in from the moment the first echoes of the explosion reached them. The guilt and the necessity of repudiation. They had violated the community mores and looking back on that afternoon they could not understand—as if they had participated in an orgy, a blood bath—what possessed them. It went too far. It got out of hand. It was someone's fault.

The feeling among the colored lay on the other side of the same coin. It was great while it lasted. But like those who tempt the gods by daring too much, they knew in their bones that retaliation, swift and implacable must fall. Someone was bound to get it.

It did neither Reeve nor Rad any good to deny the presence of large quantities of dynamite on their property. All they had in that magazine, they claimed, was fifteen pounds left from their last ditching. No one believed them. Of course they'd say that. It did them no good to point out certain anomalies in the event, to suggest that someone else might be behind it. Who would go to such fantastic lengths? And even if someone had—this too was thought—he must have been justified.

It did Clem no good to protest that the form the Benefit took could not have been planned beforehand, that it was completely spontaneous and that once it was underway it could not have been controlled. He was chiefly to blame. It was his responsibility to see that those attending toed the line, and if they didn't to send them packing. The chief blame for the aftermath was also placed at Clem's door. He had encouraged those boys in their relationship, had indoctrinated them with his ideas and put them up to whatever they were up to. If anyone lit the fuse in that dynamite, morally it was he.

This view was confirmed by his summary dismissal from his teaching post a few days later without explanation.

At an emergency vestry meeting on the eve of the election, Benson Reece requested the resignation of Clement DeLavery from the pastorate of St. Paul's and St. Augustine's "for the good of the congregation, the church, and the country." The request was unanimously ratified and forwarded to Bishop Lorimer by wire within the hour.

The results of the election were curiously mixed. Ol' Cal carried the state and lost Colfax County by a slender margin. Judge Purcell failed by the same slender margin to unseat Benson Reece from his chairman-

ship of the Democratic County Committee. Henry Warren was elected
to the Commission by a comfortable majority which in relation to the
Judge's loss strengthened his political position considerably: he ran
well ahead of his ticket. Will Royall, to widespread alarm among the
colored, replaced Chalmer Coombs as sheriff.

For Henry his triumph was a hollow one. All that he had done to
earn it, and it had still gone awry. Nothing was settled by it. The two,
Rad McDowell and Reeve Scott, had escaped with their lives. They had
returned to their farms. Their land was still there, the stumbling block
yet to be removed. The victims, drowned by the flood waters that night,
had been instead others. The leading colored citizen of the county,
George Turner Thurlow. The infant Ella-Rose McDowell. And the
boy Charles.